WEST END

WEST END

A Novel

Laura Van Wormer

DOUBLEDAY

NEW YORK   LONDON   TORONTO   SYDNEY   AUCKLAND

This book is a novel and the story and events that
appear therein are entirely fictional. Any resemblance
of the fictional characters to a real person is
unintentional and coincidental. Certain real people are
mentioned in the book for the purposes of enhancing
and adding reality to the story, but obviously the
fictionalized events involving either fictional characters
or real persons did not occur.

Published by Doubleday,
a division of Bantam Doubleday Dell Publishing
Group, Inc.
666 Fifth Avenue, New York, New York 10103

DOUBLEDAY and the portrayal of an anchor
with a dolphin are trademarks of Doubleday,
a division of Bantam Doubleday Dell Publishing
Group, Inc.

Library of Congress Cataloging-in-Publication Data

Van Wormer, Laura, 1955–
  West End : a novel / Laura Van Wormer. — 1st ed.
    p. cm.
  I. Title.
PS3572.A42285W4   1989
813'.54—dc20   89-32676
                                                         CIP

ISBN 0-385-24468-1
Copyright © 1989 by Laura Van Wormer
All Rights Reserved
Printed in the United States of America
September 1989
First Edition
DH

FOR
Loretta Barrett
AND
Nancy Evans

with heartfelt thanks to
Dianna Whitley,
Shaye Areheart, Paul Aron, David Burr, Patricia Elliott,
Nell Hanson, Lindy Hess, Sara Maxwell and Betty Prashker
for everything,
1983–84 especially.

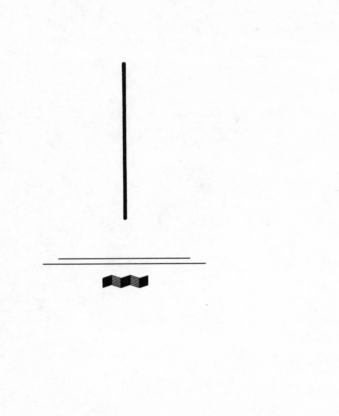

1

Alexandra Waring

Alexandra Waring was just one of those women America decided to fall in love with.

In January of 1988, in Washington, D.C., Alexandra and a film crew from The Network received clearance to tape an interview on the back steps of the Capitol. To go through the hassle of obtaining permission to tape there—instead of at the usual Elmsite around front or down by the iron horse—was yet another extra effort made by her producer, Will Rafferty, to make Alexandra's reports look just that much better than anyone else's.

It was hard enough for any correspondent to get air time on the evening news, but nearly impossible for one who had alienated The Network's anchorman, Clark Smith—which is exactly what Alexandra had done the previous summer when she refused to let him steal an exclusive from her. And so, as the Washington *Post* noted, even though Alexandra had been hired as a special congressional correspondent for the evening news, presumably to make use of the contacts that came from being the daughter of an influential former congressman, "Ms. Waring has evidently been stricken from Smith's 'A Correspondent' list and added to his 'S' list—'S' as in SEND TO SIBERIA—because her reports are rarely to be seen after nine o'clock in the morning."

Still, Alexandra had managed to develop a national following through her work for the morning news group and through the "Washington Report" segments she did for The Network's radio division every drive-time evening. But most important, in terms of her stature and exposure, was her ability to crack the evening news—despite Clark Smith—every five weeks or so with a scoop. And this, the interview she was now working on, would hopefully produce such a scoop.

The wind was very high in Washington this day and was wreaking havoc on camera with Alexandra's hair. (It was rather wildly gorgeous to begin with, Alexandra's dark hair was, and Will Rafferty smiled, knowing how fan mail always surged into The Network whenever the wind messed up Alexandra's hair, even if just a little.)

Holding her hair back off her face with one hand and extending the microphone with the other, Alexandra was talking with Congressman Alvin Maurier. The congressman was going on and on—talking in one long sentence, it seemed—when suddenly he stopped, appearing to be slightly mesmerized by Alexandra's extraordinary blue-gray eyes.

"Do you or don't you believe the Pentagon's report is truthful?" Alexandra took the moment to ask.

"Uhhh," the congressman said, snapping out of wherever it was he had just been, "at this time I can only say that I believe the allegations merit a thorough investigation."

"If now you're calling for a full investigation," Alexandra said, taking a breath, "what else are we to assume, Congressman, then you don't believe the Pentagon's report is entirely truthful about what's been happening on those Army transport planes flying out of Panama?"

He hesitated and then smiled a little, looking as though he might reach out and tweak Alexandra's nose. "Okay," he said, nodding once. "I think the Pentagon can tell us more about these allegations concerning cocaine trafficking by Army personnel."

Something caught Alexandra's eye and she turned suddenly, squinting down the stairs at something off camera. Following her gaze, the congressman took a step down to see better, saying, "What the heck is he . . . ?"

"Careful," Alexandra said, taking his arm and pulling him back.

On the videotape a man could be heard shouting something in the distance and then there was a shot. There were screams and the camera reeled, showing the Capitol dome and the sky. There was another shot and the camera swept dizzily down the stairs. The scene came into focus: a uniformed cop and a plainclothesman were wrestling a man in an orange poncho down to the ground.

"Waring's hit!" someone yelled in the background. "He shot Waring!"

The camera flew back up the stairs to Alexandra and the congressman. Alexandra seemed distracted; she was just standing there, frowning, still holding the microphone, staring down at a small hole in the shoulder of her raincoat. When she raised her head to look at the congressman, a spurt of blood spilled down her chest.

"Oh Jesus God, oh Jesus God," the congressman said, lunging to help hold her up.

Alexandra looked down at her shoulder, inhaled sharply and looked away, the color in her face draining to white. She brought her free hand up to cover her wound and, closing her eyes, slowly sank to the stairs, the congressman sinking with her, holding her as best he could.

"Are we rolling? Are we rolling?" a correspondent from a rival network screamed at his cameraman as they came dashing up the stairs.

Alexandra's eyes flew open. "No way," she said, struggling to turn toward her own camera. She winced slightly and then tried to smile. "This is Alexandra Waring reporting from the Capitol Building in Washington," she said. And then she fainted.

All afternoon The Network showed Alexandra getting shot and that evening Clark Smith's newscast came in first in the ratings for the first time in three years. ("Sure beats the Persian Gulf," the director said in the New York control room.) Audience response was so tremendous to the footage, in fact, that The Network ran part of it as a news break throughout prime time as a promo for a half-hour special they threw together for eleven-thirty, "The Shooting of an American Newswoman." ("Hey," a researcher in The Network newsroom said, looking at his computer screen, "we're in luck—Waring's good copy.")

WARING, ALEXANDRA BONNER. Broadcast journalist; b. Lawrence, Kansas, October 30, 1957; daughter of Paul Allen and Elizabeth Lynn (Bonner). B.A., Stanford Univ., 1980, Phi Beta Kappa. Station reporter, KCLI-Radio, San Francisco, 1976–77; sta. researcher, newswriter, reporter, KFFK-TV, San Francisco, 1977–81; sta. reporter, weekend anchor, KSCT-TV, Kansas City, 1981–86; sta. anchor, WWKK-TV, New York City, 1986–87; Capitol Hill correspondent, The Network, 1987—

Western Women in Communications Award, 1983; Emmy Award (Midwest), Taylor-Bainbridge Award for Documentary, 1984; Communicator of the Year (Midwest), 1984; Women in Broadcasting Award (Midwest), 1985; Handerville Award, Investigative Reporting, 1985; American Farmer's Award for Excellence in Reporting, 1985; Kansas Women's Caucus Award for Individual Achievement, 1985; Emmy Award (N.Y.C.), 1986; New York City Press Club Citation, Best Newcomer, 1986; Independent Allied Press Award, 1986; Press Corps America Citation for Feature Reporting, 1987.

As the evening progressed, so did the other half of the story, in the person of the assailant, Rudolph Gadulaher. Mr. Gadulaher, it seemed, had become quite taken with the lovely network correspondent and, to bolster his courage to ask her out on a date, had taken a pistol and some Quaaludes with him on his quest. After following Ms. Waring and her camera crew to the Capitol, Mr. Gadulaher had taken the Quaaludes and then after about an hour it just seemed to him that the best way to get Ms. Waring's attention would be to shoot her. And so he shot her. Mr. Gadulaher told authorities he had purchased the handgun for self-protection. He said he lived in a dangerous neighborhood.

But the first American newswoman to be shot on television was the big story, and The Network was by no means the only news organization on it. As *Newsweek* reported in its next issue, when her stretcher was unloaded from the ambulance at Capitol Hill Hospital, "more media cables were swarming around Waring's unconscious body than snakes around St. Patrick."

And with the coverage came the crowds. Hundreds of people gathered outside the hospital to publicly wish Alexandra well. The police arrived, setting up barricades for crowd control and roping off special areas to accommodate the press. Network officials scurried in and out, truckloads of flowers began arriving and miles of electrical cables crisscrossed the parking lot. By the time the floodlights came on at four forty-five, the main entrance of Capitol Hill Hospital had taken on an uncanny resemblance to a Hollywood premiere.

After X rays and stabilization, Alexandra was rushed onto the operating table, where a team of orthopedic surgeons removed two bullet fragments that had lodged in her lower left collarbone. The news that Alexandra was going to be absolutely fine did not get confirmed for hours ("No REPORTERS!" Head Nurse Badaglia was seen and heard screaming down the hall on TV—live), and so the press continued to stand vigil outside.

The first personal friend of Alexandra's arrived around five o'clock in an airport station wagon. After honking frantically to get through the mess of cars, flower trucks and microwave media vans, the station wagon pulled up to the entrance and let out a good-looking though obviously distressed man with blondish-brown hair. The lights for the TV cameras came blazing on and some photographers' flashes went off in the man's face and he ran straight into the reporter from the *Inquiring Eye.* "Hey!" the reporter said, grabbing the man by the tie. "Didn't you used to be married to Julie Stantree? Aren't you . . . ?" He let go of the tie to snap his fingers twice.

"Please," the man said, great brown eyes pleading, "let me see her first. I swear I'll come back out and talk to you." He turned to the policemen. *"Please,"* he said again, "I'm Gordon Strenn. I'm Alexandra's—"

"This way, Mr. Strenn," a plainclothes cop said to him.

["Gordon Strenn arrives at Capitol Hill Hospital from New York Tuesday night," read the photo caption in the next issue of the *Inquiring Eye.* "Strenn, 35, producer of TV's 1987 movie, *This Side of Paradise,* enjoys another kind of paradise as Alexandra's longtime on-again, off-again boyfriend. The ex-husband of glamorous TV star Julie Stantree is hoping to make the equally glamorous TV journalist Wife No. 2."]

At seven-fifteen a dark blue limo pulled up under the lights of the hospital and a very tall, dark-haired man and a very beautiful blond woman got out. The lights glared and flashes flashed and one of the reporters yelled, "Michael, Michael Cochran!" and another called, "Hey, Cassy! Cassy, hi, over here!" and then all the TV people were closing in on the couple, pleading for assistance to get inside, or get info.

"We'll do our best," the man promised, pushing people aside, pulling the woman along behind him.

["TV News Producer Michael Cochran arrives with beautiful wife, Cassy," the caption read in the *Inquiring Eye*. "While Alexandra and Michael were both at WWKK in New York, rumors linked them at play while Cassy was at work at rival station WST."]

At ten a black stretch limousine swept under the lights of Capitol Hill Hospital, out of which stepped another very tall, dark-haired but graying man in his late sixties or so. "Congressman Waring," one reporter yelled out as the former congressman helped his wife out of the car, "will your daughter getting shot alter your view on gun control?"

"Mrs. Waring," another voice rang out, "how do you feel?"

"Will you take Alexandra back to Kansas?" someone else asked.

["Alexandra's parents arrive from Kansas," the *Inquiring Eye* caption said. "While Mrs. Waring sat at her daughter's bedside, the nine-term former congressman drew cheers from the crowd by calling for a health care reform bill at an impromptu press conference."]

At midnight Alexandra's attending physician, Dr. Kenneth Ranhanjian, told The Network he didn't give a damn about their ratings and went outside to officially announce that Alexandra Waring was going to be absolutely fine and everybody had to go home now so the patients of Capitol Hill Hospital could get some sleep.

The following evening Alexandra was sitting up in bed, giving an exclusive interview to Clark Smith in New York via satellite. She was looking remarkably well for a woman who had undergone shooting, shock and surgery within the last thirty hours. She was subdued, yes, but whatever energy she lacked was made up for by the radiance of her eyes against the dark blue-gray satin dressing gown she wore.

What viewers did not see was that the dressing gown was actually cut in several places and then tucked and pinned everywhere to cover the intricate workings of tape, plaster, gauze and slings that covered her wound and lashed her arm in place up over her chest. They did not see the makeup kit on the windowsill. They did not see Will Rafferty standing to the side of the camera, listening into his headset; Gordon Strenn and Michael Cochran standing guard at the door; Nurse Badaglia, frowning, standing between Gordon and Michael with her arms folded; Cassy Cochran crouching at the end of the bed, holding the arch of Alexandra's foot in her hand as if to anchor her to the bed; nor did they see the young man standing by the window, aiming a microwave antenna at the TV van down in the parking lot.

Viewers did see Alexandra and hear her say she was fine and hoping to be released in a few days, and they heard her say how, from the bottom of her heart, she wished to thank everyone for their cards and flowers and, most of all, for their prayers—and they saw her wink at them, saying that evidently they had worked.

Viewers did not hear Cassy Cochran whisper, "She's fading"; they did not hear or see Will cup his hand around the mouthpiece to talk into his headset; and they did not see Nurse Badaglia move toward the bed. All they knew was that Clark suddenly said good-bye to her and Alexandra was gone. Had they been able to continue watching, viewers would have seen Alexandra's eyes starting to flutter and Cassy Cochran and Nurse Badaglia reaching her at the same time on opposite sides of the bed.

"Darn it, I told you," Nurse Badaglia said, pulling Alexandra's face toward her with one hand and pushing the button to lower the bed with the other. "Hold the back of her head, Mrs. Cochran—that's it."

"Is she all right?" Gordon whispered from behind the nurse.

"Of course she is," Nurse Badaglia said. "Aren't you, Lois Lane? Hmmm? Still with us?" Under her breath, "I don't know how she lasted this long without a painkiller."

"Needed a clear head," Alexandra murmured, eyes closed.

The following morning, at headquarters in New York City, the chairman of The Network was throwing a fit. "Why can't she be featured every night?" he demanded, swatting the glass out of the hand of the president of the news division. (The glass went flying, spilling Alka-Seltzer all over the place and landing with a soft thump on the plush carpet.)

"Because Clark won't work with her."

The chairman looked at him. "Clark? *Clark?* That nutcase? What the hell does he know?"

"His contract gives him control over the evening news—we can't afford to buy out his contract—we don't have a replacement for him even if we could," the president said, reciting the familiar facts while pressing the top of his stomach.

"And the guy shoots Alexandra!" the chairman yelled, shaking his fist at the heavens.

"The chairman is upset," the executive vice-president of News said the following day, starting the meeting with the vice-presidents of the news division.

"The chairman is bullshit," the president of The Network News said, offering a more accurate picture of the situation. "He wants Waring reporting every weeknight and he wants her to anchor the summer showcase in documentary."

"The chairman's in her pants," the vice-president of public affairs whispered to the man seated next to him, "that's what Clark told me."

"Consider the source," the vice-president of news coverage whispered back. "If Clark could hold its head, he'd fuck a snake."

"What's that?" the president said. "What are you two whispering about down there?"

"I was saying I think our problem is with Clark and not with Alexandra," the vice-president of news coverage said.

"What Clark says goes and he says N-O *no* on Waring," said Clark Smith's former college roommate who was now executive producer of the evening news. "As a matter of fact, he thinks she should be terminated altogether."

"Leave it to him to want to kill her for being shot," the executive vice-president said, rolling his eyes.

The president looked to the vice-president of administration. "What year of Cluck Head Clark's contract are we in, anyway?"

"Four."

"So we're up to . . . ?"

"Four million three hundred thousand dollars," the vice-president of administration said. "It will cost us thirty-one million to break it at this point."

"Waring's current salary is two hundred thousand," the executive vice-president said. He picked up a copy of the report that had been circulated to everyone around the table. "Everybody read this?" The men murmured yesses.

It was the latest MARKET, AUDIENCE AND RATINGS RESEARCH report The Network always swore it did not use in connection with the news division.

In our test groups [the report that was not supposed to exist said] the reporter maintaining the highest consistent ranking is Alexandra Waring. As shown on the following charts, Waring leads *all* of the correspondents in three crucial areas: *likability, believability* and *clarity.*

VERY STRONG RATINGS POTENTIAL

"Her age is a problem," the president said. "She's only—what? Thirty?"

"Exactly!" the executive producer of evening news said. "No experience, no credibility—"

"She's got plenty of experience and plenty of credibility—but not national," the executive vice-president said.

"Except what she's done for us this past year," the vice-president of news coverage said.

"Which has been very good," the president said.

"Which has been excellent," the executive vice-president said.

"And she did get that national press corps citation," the vice-president of public affairs thought to mention.

"That still doesn't give her years of network experience!" the executive producer of the evening news insisted, pounding the table. "I don't know how you can even mention that—that *girl's* name in the same breath with Clark Smith!"

"Oh, cram Clark Smith," the executive vice-president said. "Look, it's no secret—we all know our vastly experienced anchorman vastly sucks as an anchorman, the evening news is in the cellar and Waring's the first thing we've had in three years that the public has been even remotely interested in."

The room fell silent as everyone thought about this.

"Are you aware," a voice finally said from way down at the other end of the table, "that Waring's contract expires at the end of the month?"

"Who is that?" the president whispered behind his hand to his executive vice-president.

"Burnem, legal department," the executive vice-president whispered back. And then, in his normal speaking voice, he said, "Yeah, we know, Burnem."

"And that Waring has expressed no interest in renewing it?" Burnem continued.

"Yeah, we knew that, Burnem," the executive vice-president said impatiently. "But that was before."

"No, sir," Burnem said, "that was this morning."

Word got around fast that Alexandra Waring was playing hard to get. In a company where security was someone in the lobby demanding to see an I.D., employees at The Network were at first only amused at the idea that the same lovely young woman who had always made it a point to say "please" and "thank you" to everyone was now, they said, holding management by certain members of their anatomies without the slightest apology. But then, as the days went by and there was no word of a contract renewal, employees began to wonder if the rumors management had issued were true, that Alexandra was making outrageous demands.

However, even if this were so, there was a good deal of evidence piling up to indicate that maybe an outrageous contract could be in order. So many flowers had been sent to Alexandra by fans that, by the time The Network finished redistributing them, they had brightened the rooms of every hospital, health clinic and nursing home over a forty-mile radius. And then there was the *Inquiring Eye*'s fascination with Alexandra—three issues in a row now—a tabloid honor usually reserved only for those with TV shows in the Nielsen top twenty.

And then there was her mail. The get-well cards, letters and mailgrams addressed to Alexandra at the hospital were at first rerouted to the Washington Bureau, but then the mail already flooding directly in there—in combination with the mail being trucked down from headquarters in New York—started choking the corridors and then spilling down the fire stairs, and so finally a moving van had to be brought in to haul the whole "Dear Alexandra" Operation to a warehouse in Virginia.

"One hundred sixteen thousand five hundred ninety-two and counting," the assistant to the president of the news division reported to his boss.

The president, covering the mouthpiece of the phone with his hand, made a sound implying that he might die right there on the spot.

"Want the breakdown, get-well cards to letters?" the assistant asked him, glancing down at the clipboard in his hand. "Religious theme? Humor? Obscene suggestion? They're feeding the demos into the computer as they go."

The president waved his assistant away, took a swig of Maalox out of the bottle sitting on his desk, uncovered the phone and said, "Sorry, John, someone just came in with a bulletin on the Persian Gulf. Where were we?"

"You were saying, six hundred fifty thousand, coanchor weekend news, four documentaries a year," John Mohrbacher, Alexandra's agent, said, "and I was telling you how sorry I am that you don't seem to be able to hear me—for the last time, Alexandra doesn't want to stay at The Network."

"Well, where the hell does she *think* she's going to work if she doesn't work here?" the president demanded.

"I'm not at liberty to discuss it," Mohrbacher said. "And nor do I have to. You have no option on her." He sighed then. "Look, my client has done her best to leave gracefully. She warned you six months ago, damn near died for you, put your news in first place and gave Clark an exclusive interview, what more do you want?"

"She's still under contract to us."

"For two more weeks."

"She's not leaving!" the president screamed.

"Oh, she's leaving!" Mohrbacher screamed back.

Silence.

John Mohrbacher cleared his throat and said, quietly, "You keep calling me and I keep telling you all I can tell you—Alexandra is not renewing her contract with you, Alexandra is not interested in negotiating with you, Alexandra only wishes to thank you for the year's experience you have given her. Do you hear me? Alexandra's not coming back. She told you that six months ago after Clark blocked her from the evening news, she is telling you again now."

The president slammed his elbow on his desk and then clutched it, wincing like mad. Then he turned his chair and knocked the Maalox over with the same elbow. "Stop jerking me around, Mohrbacher," he growled, yanking open a drawer, searching for something to stop the expanding puddle of pink all over his desk.

"I am not jerking you around, I am telling you the truth," John Mohrbacher said, sounding tired.

"No one's going to do better than our offer, you know that," the president said, trying the set of drawers on the other side of the desk. "Fuck!" he yelled as the pink stuff dripped down onto his crotch.

"Look," Mohrbacher said, "don't waste your time. It's over. We warned you six months ago and you did absolutely nothing."

The president—standing now, situation Maalox hopeless—was staring out his office window, thinking. Suddenly he regripped the phone, bent over slightly and hissed, "Seven hundred fifty thousand and that's as high as I go."

As negotiations allegedly continued, speculation on Alexandra Waring ran high through the television news industry as a whole. Most of her peers thought she was doing what many of themselves had done in recent years—simply following her agent's instructions and holding out for more money. And who could blame her if that was what she was doing? Any network that was dumb enough to pay four million three to Cluck Head Clark Smith deserved to start a Million Dollar Correspondents Club, didn't they?

Another industry theory was that Alexandra didn't want to work in network news at all anymore and was vying to return to the small pond of local news as the biggest fish of them all. And as word spread about how many visits one of the local news biggies in the number one market—New York City—was making to Georgetown to see Alexandra in her recuperation—Cassy Cochran, general station manager of WST—the theory started to gain currency. And then when the *Times* business section reported rumors that WST might become a superstation in 1989, distributed nationally through a cooperative cable system, about sixty percent of the industry then believed Alexandra was about to move to WST as an anchor.

"So are you discussing plans for Alexandra's work at WST?" a reporter asked Cassy Cochran one Friday afternoon as she stepped out of a chauffeured car in front of Alexandra's condominium.

"Am I what?" Cassy asked, laughing, brushing back a strand of hair from her forehead. She was very photogenic, Cassy Cochran, a beauty, still, in her forties, with blue eyes that still outdazzled the lines around them. Though she very much dressed the part of sophisticated New

Yorker, she wore her genuinely blond hair up, casually, in a way vaguely reminiscent of the early seventies. It suited her.

The reporter followed Cassy back around to the end of the car where the driver was standing. "Alexandra's coming to work for you, isn't she? At WST in New York?" he persisted, watching as the driver opened the trunk.

"Take those two first, Gil," Cassy said to the driver, "and tell Gordon they need to go straight into the freezer."

"Those two" were stacks of square white cartons tied up in string. They looked as though they might contain frozen dinners or something. Also in the trunk were five grocery bags, a basket of flowers, some video cassettes and two large bags from Saks Fifth Avenue.

"Would you like some grapes?" Cassy asked the reporter, breaking off a small bunch from the top of one bag. "Here," she said, pushing them into his hand, "and I've got some oatmeal cookies here somewhere too. You must get hungry out here."

"Uh," the reporter said.

"I'd invite you in," Cassy said, looking at him back over her shoulder, "but we promised the doctors no visitors until next week. The excitement," she added, straightening up and slipping some cookies in the reporter's coat pocket. "This kind of injury can cause permanent nerve damage in her arm and so we have to take every precaution. Oh, here," she added, "take a V8. Sorry I don't have any straws."

"So she *is* coming to work for you," the reporter said.

"I wish she was," Cassy said, smiling. "But I'm afraid I'm here only as a friend. I just flew down today to do the shopping," she said, reaching for the flowers and video cassettes. "And check in with the nurse—check the patient's aesthetic environment and entertainment, too. Give me your card," she said then, juggling the video cassettes to hold her hand out to him. "I'll see what I can do about Alexandra talking to you next week."

The reporter dutifully chronicled this exchange in his paper, along with the small scoop that, according to the videotapes he saw, Alexandra's idea of entertainment was "World War II with Walter Cronkite."

A small percentage of the industry, a bit on the negative side as both a general rule and favorite pastime, was convinced that Waring was looking to bump a certain prominent network newswoman out of her job. As soon as the network of the newswoman in question denied the story, this of course then became a very popular theory. In fact, a reporter caught Alexandra's mother coming out of the Nelson-Atkins Museum of Art in Kansas City to ask her about it.

"Does Alexandra want to follow in her footsteps?" Mrs. Waring said, repeating the reporter's euphemistic way of asking if Alexandra was after that prominent newswoman's job. Mrs. Waring shook her head slightly. "I'm afraid Alexandra would sooner freeze in a snowstorm than follow in anyone's footsteps. She's been that way since she was a little girl."

"So—" the reporter started to say.

"So if I were you," Mrs. Waring said, taking hold of the reporter's arm and speaking confidentially (the First Lady of the Farm Belt—as Mrs. Waring had been called in her Washington days—was very comfortable around the press), "I wouldn't waste much time looking at the beaten track—I'd be looking at the wide-open spaces."

The gossip network in TV news was the fastest news and information service in the world. Linking every major newsroom in the country, the A-wire (as it was called) was utterly without fact checking and was considered by many to be the only fun thing left in the industry. Six bulletins were issued, one right after the other, and were so hot as to threaten to melt the A-wire altogether. The bulletins were:

1) Alexandra Waring was sailing with Ted Turner in the Gulf of Mexico.
2) Alexandra Waring was circling Central Park in a limo with Don Hewitt.
3) Alexandra Waring was strolling East 52nd Street with Steve Friedman.
4) Alexandra Waring was eating Cuban-Chinese food in Harlem with Roone Arledge.
5) Alexandra Waring was landing at an East River helipad with Barry Diller.
6) Alexandra Waring was marrying Geraldo Rivera.

So everyone was very disappointed when Bitsy Bourner announced in her column that Alexandra hadn't even set foot outside her home since she got out of the hospital. "She can't move very well," Gordon

Strenn was quoted as saying. "Not until she gets the cast off. It goes over her shoulder and then down across her chest."

When asked how Alexandra's spirits were, Strenn told Bitsy to imagine a tiger in a straitjacket. "She can't even bathe by herself, which drives her crazy," he added. Bitsy then reported to her readers that when she asked Gordon who it was that helped Alexandra to bathe, "he would only smile like the gentleman he is." And then when she asked him where, for heaven's sakes, it was that Alexandra was going, he said, "There are a few people Alexandra would like to tell first, in person, before making an announcement."

"Well, there you have it, folks," Bitsy then wrote to her readers, "Alexandra is definitely going *somewhere.*"

On Friday, February 26, the chairman of The Network was standing in his office, looking at a sheet of paper with the handwritten notations:

Our Last Offer [it said]
—$7,500,000 Package
  —$1,500,000 a year over 5 years.
  —Bonus scale (see back)
—Anchor weekend evening news.
—One feature biweekly on evening news.
—Second substitute for Clark Smith.
—Four documentaries a year.

"Nice work if you can get it," one of the chairman's secretaries said, reading over his shoulder. "I bet everyone's going to start getting shot at around contract time now. You watch."

The chairman grunted, stuffing the paper in the pocket of his jacket. "I'll get the price down," he said, rubbing his eyes. "She's a reasonable girl." He lowered his hands and sighed. "Those knuckleheads downstairs—christ, we pay *them* enough." He looked at his secretary. "Are you old enough to remember "Give Me Some Stout-hearted Men"? The song?"

His secretary was twenty-two, so it was possible that not even her mother was old enough to remember it. The chairman proceeded to mumble one or two lines—about stalwart men who would fight for the right—and his secretary smiled very pleasantly until the phone buzzed and she had to answer it. She listened, nodded and hung up. "She's here."

The chairman looked across the expanse of his office to the grandfather clock. As he did so, it struck the half hour. He smiled. "Go get her," he said.

When Alexandra was shown in the chairman walked around his desk and held out both of his hands in greeting.

"Hello," she said, smiling warmly, extending her right hand to him. (She could only extend the one hand since her left arm was in a sling —a sling made of an Hermès scarf, but a sling all the same.)

"Hello, my dear," the chairman said, taking her hand in both of his. After a long moment he released it and gestured to a chair. "Please."

"Thank you." She sat down, crossing her leg at the knee.

"I trust you are well enough to be flying up here today," he said, settling down in the chair opposite her.

"Oh, I'm much better, thank you. Certainly well enough to see you. It was very important to me that I did."

She was wearing a simple navy-blue dress and he thought she had never looked more ravishing. "You should get shot more often, my dear," he said. "It agrees with you."

Her eyes, as always, were brilliantly beautiful, and her wide mouth, as always, was full of subtle promises. Her posture was so very good (he had always liked that about her—Alexandra's tendency to appear much taller than she was, a trick he himself had learned at an early age) and her movements were graceful, unobtrusive. There was the energy, too, that was ever present with her, a kind of drive one could sense coursing just beneath the surface.

He liked the sling best though. Wounded, she seemed possible.

She leaned forward slightly in her chair, eyes looking earnest. "I wanted to explain to you personally why I'm leaving."

The chairman looked at her. This was going to be a little tougher than he had expected. He raised his hand to signal that she was not to continue. He patted his breast pocket, then extracted a pair of reading glasses and put them on. "About this figure of seven million," he began, retrieving his notes from his pocket, "I must say I'm a little surprised at you, Alexandra. I pegged you as a journalist, not a movie star."

Her face fell. "They haven't told you anything, have they?" she said. She closed her eyes, shook her head slightly and reopened them. "It's not the money."

"You listen to me, little miss," the chairman said, pointing a finger at her. "I've got men almost twice your age out there working for me and do you know what they make over five years? Do you?"

Alexandra didn't say anything but the chairman could have sworn he heard her say, "Thirty-one million dollars?"

"I think it's a disgrace for a young girl like you to use Clark Smith as an excuse to cause such trouble," he said.

"Please," Alexandra said, leaning forward in her chair, wincing and then retreating back, bringing a hand up to her shoulder. "Please listen to me."

The chairman waited.

"If I wanted to work within the traditional structure of network news," she said, "there's no question that this is where I'd want to work. No network is bigger, no one has as many resources, and certainly no one has as much power as this one does." She paused, running her tongue lightly over her lower lip (and then waiting for the chairman's eyes to come back up from her mouth). "But that's the problem, that's why I have to leave. The Network is simply too big, too complex and too powerful to let me do the things I want to do."

Despite himself, the chairman smiled. He loved it when adjectives like "big" and "complex" and "powerful" were used in connection with his network.

"So it's the structure I'm leaving," she said, "not the people here. Not you, certainly. You've been very kind ever since I—"

"Damnation," the chairman suddenly said, mouth dropping open.

She looked a little startled.

"Don't tell me you were serious the whole time," he said. "Don't tell me you're really leaving."

Alexandra, looking a little confused, nodded.

"Oh, shit, I don't believe this," the chairman said, getting out of his chair. "I'm going to kill that knucklehead, I swear. Tells me he's been working on this negotiation for weeks," he continued, crumpling up the notes and throwing them on the floor. "And now he's got me wasting time on you as well," he muttered, moving around his desk.

Alexandra stood up.

"Traitor," the chairman said, not looking at her.

Alexandra did not move.

"I don't care what we did or didn't do—I don't want to talk about it!" he said, slamming his hands down on the edge of the desk. "Do you hear me? I don't want to talk about it!" He sighed, letting his head droop, and reached around behind him, groping for his chair. He found it and sat down heavily, plunking his hands down in front of him and staring at his gold pen and pencil set. After a full minute, his face slightly less red, he looked up at her, said, "Well?" and made little motions with his hand to indicate that Alexandra was now to shoo.

"I'll never forget your kindnesses," Alexandra said quietly. And then she turned around and walked to the door.

As she opened it the chairman said, "So where are you going, anyway?"

Still holding the door, she turned. "With Jackson Darenbrook."

"Darenbrook!" the chairman yelled, bouncing in his seat. "Jackson Darenbrook! What the hell are you going to do with that yahoo?"

"Build my own network," Alexandra said.

2

Jackson Darenbrook

"Uh-oh," Jackson Darenbrook said.

He was sitting in the back of his limousine, reading the papers in front of the Plaza Hotel in New York, waiting to take Alexandra to her first day of work.

"ALEXANDRA WARING TO LAUNCH DBS NEWS" the headline of the article said, but that was not the source of the "uh-oh." Nor was the wonderful head shot of Alexandra or the first part of the article, which pretty much ran along the lines of their press release: Alexandra's departure from The Network, Darenbrook Communications' venture into broadcast television with DBS—the Darenbrook Broadcasting System, Alexandra's work history . . . ("What New Yorker can forget Miss Waring's short tenure here in local news? While anchoring the nightly news for WWKK, she won the hearts of critics by changing their format emphasis from soft news to hard and combining their six and eleven o'clock newscasts into an hour during prime time. But it was with her gorgeously hypnotic eyes and affinity for the medium that Miss Waring won the hearts of viewers and succeeded in almost tripling the news ratings for WWKK.")

And then the "uh-oh." The article quoted "one of the most prominent figures at The Network who wished to remain unidentified." The figure, Jackson had no doubt, was Alexandra's old nemesis, Clark Smith. "Frankly, we're just glad she's gone. Her being such an intimate friend of the chairman's was a problem. We don't go for that kind of thing here—but apparently Darenbrook does. She is a fairly good-looking girl after all."

And then Jackson winced, reading on to find that the newspaper had asked Regina Baxter—a network correspondent known for her bitchiness—what she thought about thirty-year-old Alexandra being paid what was rumored to be well over a million dollars a year. "I think," she said, "someone should tell Jackson Darenbrook that what goes for a million dollars in Hilleanderville, Georgia, can be bought for about two hundred dollars a night in New York."

Jackson threw the newspaper down on the floor of the car.

Jackasses. Jealous, petty, neurotic, self-serving jackasses.

He should know, he had been reviewing the work and reputations of television newspeople for months now in his search for *her*—she who would become the symbol of DBS News, she who would gamble her career on what many said was the foolhardy venture of the decade.

Another broadcast TV network? With ABC, CBS, NBC, PBS and Fox broadcasting already? With CNN and the other cable networks, other cable franchises, superstations, pay movie channels and the video cassette market steadily draining viewers from broadcast programming? Was Jackson Darenbrook now as crazy as the rest of his family, the loony-tune Darenbrooks of Hilleanderville, owners of the Darenbrook Communications media empire?

Oh. Just a part-time broadcast TV network. So Jackson was just part-time crazy, was that it?

"Good grief, Mr. Darenbrook," the lady at the Media News Associates had said to him back in May of 1987, when he began his search. The lady had been Ms. Dee Rendelhoffer, the account executive assigned to help him in his—as the file said—"secret search for unspecified anchorwoman for unspecified television newscast probably airing in the fall of 1989."

(Media News Associates spent a great deal of money sending people to motel rooms around the country to make videotapes of local newspeople. As a result, someone looking for talent could come to them and say, "I need an anchorman of Yugoslavian descent," or, "We're looking for a Greek movie reviewer, preferably female," and MNA could provide tapes of every Yugoslavian anchorman and every Greek female movie reviewer who had been on the air in America in the last year.)

In any event, Ms. Rendelhoffer had read a piece of paper that Jackson had given to her and was evidently surprised by it. Lowering it to her desk, she smiled and said, "You realize, of course, that this list is extremely ambitious."

"*Am*bitious," Jackson repeated, smiling too. (His drawl tended to pull a little farther south with any hint of resistance in the air.) "You told me to write down ten people I was looking for."

"I asked you to write down ten *qualities* you were looking for, Mr. Darenbrook," Ms. Rendelhoffer said. She glanced down at the list. "Surely you can't expect to hire Diane Sawyer."

"She's from Kentucky," Jackson said, bringing his knee up to hold in his hands, "and people from Kentucky tend to do noble things. Take Abraham Lincoln."

Ms. Rendelhoffer blinked.

"You know, the President," Jackson said.

"Yes, I know Abraham Lincoln," Ms. Rendelhoffer assured him.

"Well now," Jackson said, smiling.

"I don't mean I know him-know him," Ms. Rendelhoffer hastened to say. Mr. Darenbrook was grinning at her now, blue eyes twinkling.

Jackson Darenbrook, at forty-seven, was a man with considerable attractions. He was very tall, about six foot three. But though he had a full head of brown and gray hair, wonderful cornflower-blue eyes and terrific white teeth, like most staggeringly wealthy men, he was only said to be very handsome when clearly he was not. He was charming and rather dashing, though, and as the very fit, athletic type he was, even if he had grown up to be a clerk in a shoe store, rare would be the woman who didn't note his body with a slight inner smile. But he was not a clerk in a shoe store; he was the chairman of Darenbrook Communications, the private conglomerate made famous by its newspapers, and Jackson Darenbrook was said to be personally worth something in the vicinity of one hundred million dollars.

But more important, at least to Ms. Rendelhoffer, was the fact that Jackson Darenbrook had been a widower for seven years, which in her eyes did something toward redeeming his dreadful reputation as a ladies' man. (He was always in one of the tabloid newspapers. "VIVA LA COCONUTS," the caption beneath the photo would begin. "Media tycoon Jackson Darenbrook looks like he has his hands full with Elissa Zamborina, shortly after she was crowned Miss Coconut by the World Coconut Growers Association last week in Honolulu.")

"About Diane Sawyer," Jackson said.

"Yes," Miss Rendelhoffer said.

"Now, imagine if she had been born and raised in New York instead of Kentucky," Jackson said. "You know she'd never have turned out the way she did, not in a million years. She's really *American* and that's what I'm looking for."

"What?" Miss Rendelhoffer said.

"I want a real *American*," Jackson repeated.

"I beg your pardon," Ms. Rendelhoffer said, sitting up straighter, "but I was born and raised in New York and I certainly consider myself a real American." (She was rapidly coming to the conclusion that maybe she should have been dreading this account instead of looking forward to it with such gleeful anticipation.)

"Oh, I'm sure you are, don't get me wrong," Jackson said. "It's just that the rest of the country probably wouldn't think so."

Ms. Rendelhoffer's mouth fell open.

"This is New York," Jackson said, gesturing to Miss Rendelhoffer's window. "It's like Los Angeles, like Chicago, or Philly. Most Americans only imagine what these huge cities are like, and some dream all their lives about what living in one of them would be like. But whether they fear or dream about the big cities, they *all* like nothing better than when one of their own takes on a big city—competes with the best in the world—and *wins."*

Ms. Rendelhoffer swallowed. "Wins?"

"Wins," Jackson said, nodding. "And that's what I'm after, a winner that people can identify with, cheer on her success. But she's got to have that whatever it is that makes big-city people like her too," Jackson added, leaning forward. "I want even the worst Miss Fabersham to say, 'Why look, Estelle, that anchorwoman from Kentucky is even more sophisticated than we are.' " He smiled again and sat back in his chair.

"I see," Miss Rendelhoffer finally said. Her eyes went back down to the list and she read, "Linda Ellerbee."

"Now see, if we can get somebody with even half her charisma and writing ability—" Jackson began.

"This is in addition to being from Kentucky?" Ms. Rendelhoffer asked him.

"Texas," Jackson said, looking at Ms. Rendelhoffer as if something was seriously wrong with her mind. "Linda Ellerbee is from the great state of Texas."

"Texas," Miss Rendelhoffer said, noting this on her list.

"As coincidence would have it," Jackson said, "I was born in Texas myself. At the airport, Love Field in Dallas. Company plane crash-landed and sent Mama into early labor. The doctor who delivered me was on his way home to Jacksboro and so Mama named me Jackson Andrew instead of Andrew Jackson." When Ms. Rendelhoffer only looked at him, he added, "Mama was from South Carolina."

"I see," Ms. Rendelhoffer said slowly, eyes returning to the list. "Mary Alice Williams," she read.

"Oh, wow," Jackson said, "now see, there you have more of that whatever it is. She's super smart, sophisticated and savvier than hell, but still reports every story as if she just can't get over how fascinating the world is. I can't leave the room when that gal's on. I just think, *Well, Mary Alice, you're right—this* is *the most interesting thing I've seen all day."*

Ms. Rendelhoffer was blinking rapidly. "And you credit this to . . . ?"

"Minnesota," he said. "St. Paul is by no means a small city, but it sure doesn't crank 'em out jaded and cynical by the age of six like you-know-where." He winked.

"Minnesota," Ms. Rendelhoffer repeated, making a notation on the list, wondering if she appeared to have been jaded and cynical since the tender age of six. "Okay, next is Judy Woodruff." She looked up. "I assume we are to now discuss the merits of Georgia."

"She's from Oklahoma," Jackson said. "You're thinking of her Governor Carter years."

"Oklahoma." Ms. Rendelhoffer wrote this down.

"But Deborah Norville's from Georgia and she's on the list," Jackson said, "so which do we want to talk about?"

"Let's start with Woodruff," Ms. Rendelhoffer suggested.

"But wait," Jackson said, snapping his fingers, "I almost forgot. Write down Sylvia Chase, will you? She's out in San Francisco now— but she's from Minnesota too."

"Okay," Ms. Rendelhoffer said, writing this down.

"And I've got Jane Pauley there, right?" he said.

"Yes," she said. "And she's . . . ?"

"Indiana," he said.

"Indiana," she repeated, nodding, writing.

"Indiana, right," Jackson said, leaning forward to watch.

"Now what is this?" Ms. Rendelhoffer suddenly said, sitting back and frowning at the list. "You've got written down, all in one entry, Brinkley-Brokaw-Cronkite-Gumbel-Moyers."

"North Carolina, South Dakota, Missouri, Louisiana, Oklahoma," Jackson said. "I'm just trying to draw you a map. See, if we just draw a line connecting all of these states, then we'd have the area outlined that we should be looking in."

"Wait a minute, Mr. Darenbrook," Ms. Rendelhoffer pleaded, covering her face. "I've never worked this way before," she said from behind her hands, "I need a second to think about this."

"Sure thing," Jackson said, sitting back in his chair again and folding his hands.

After a moment Ms. Rendelhoffer lowered her hands. "Perhaps,

Mr. Darenbrook," she said quietly, pushing the list to the side and folding her hands, too, "in twenty words or less, you could just tell me what it is you are looking for."

"Twenty words or less," he repeated.

She nodded.

He looked at the ceiling for a moment and then leaned forward, folding his arms and resting them on her desk. "I want an anchorwoman," he said, "from somewhere out *there,* who can survive life *here,* so she can be loved *every*where, *al*ways." And then he winked. "That was twenty words, Ms. Rendelhoffer."

MNA sent him no less than one hundred and twenty-six tapes to watch, but it was one of his own employees—Gordon Strenn, the producer in charge of their first miniseries—who led him to Alexandra. "Watch her reel and you'll know if you want to meet her. Meet with her and you'll know in a second if she's what you want." And so Jackson had watched her reel and he had wanted to meet her and, when he did, he knew in an instant he had found the star of DBS News. The young woman simply had it. Creeping crickets, Alexandra Waring *was* it.

As she walked across the lobby of the Ritz-Carlton in Washington, D.C., that September afternoon, Jackson's heart had quickened in recognition of that elusive quality called class, that glorious all-American kind of class that wrapped confidence in humility, energy in grace and good spirit in good manners.

And she had been born and raised in Kansas.

She looked different than she did on TV though. She was thinner in real life, which didn't surprise Jackson, since TV cameras added about fifteen pounds on him too—or anyone. But he was a little surprised at how Alexandra "traded up" on camera, being one for whom the camera's slight distortion came as a gift, bestowing her with a kind of soft, low-glowing beauty on screen that she did not possess on her own. Oh, Waring was a head-turner all right, but she was more striking than beautiful off camera, more angular than soft. *(Well,* he reconsidered, glancing down at the rest of her, *soft enough in the right places.)*

"Mr. Darenbrook," Alexandra had said that day, extending her hand and raising her face to look up at him.

When she turned those eyes on him he stopped breathing for a second. Geez Louise but this girl had eyes.

Alexandra's smile expanded, giving what seemed like even greater intensity to her eyes.

To die for, he thought, taking her hand and shaking it vigorously. "And *Cosmopolitan* says I've got a nice set of baby blues."

"They're really not very blue," she said.

He stopped shaking her hand and simply held it, leaning to peer into her eyes. She was right. They were more gray than blue; the blue in her dress was performing this trick electric. "I'd like very much," he said, resuming the enthusiastic shaking of her hand, "to write a letter of thanks to your mother and father anyway. 'Dear Mr. and Mrs. Waring, thank you for giving your daughter the most beautiful eyes to be found north of the Mason-Dixon line.'"

A slight furrow appeared across her forehead, which was a reaction either to what Jackson had just said or to the fact that he would not let go of her hand—it wasn't clear which.

"My grammar school sweetheart, Mary Flo Potter, has the most beautiful eyes in the world," he explained, now simply squeezing Alexandra's hand. "She owns a gas station and weighs three hundred pounds but still has the most beautiful eyes in the world and most times I'm back in Hilleanderville I drive thirty miles out of my way just to see them."

Alexandra's smile was still holding, but the furrow in her forehead had deepened.

"Damn, but Strenn's a lucky guy," Jackson heard himself say next.

Her mouth parted slightly in surprise. Then she averted her eyes and laughed a little, stepping back a moment to slide her hand out of his. Then she stepped forward again and looked him squarely in the eye. "Is it really any of your business if he's lucky or not—where I'm concerned?"

"Oh, hey, listen, Alexandra," Jackson said quickly, "I'm sorry—I don't know who that was that just said that. I don't know what I'm saying—which is exactly what Mary Flo's eyes did to me in grammar school. I don't want to offend you—all I want to do, Ms. Waring, is prove to you that I'm worthy of your trust and loyalty.

"Lunch?" he said in the next breath, offering his arm. By now his drawl was practically dragging in the front veranda. He knew he was acting like a jerk, but he couldn't help it, and he wasn't sure if he wanted to help it since this was the first time in years he had found himself in danger of becoming tongue-tied. Novelty was novelty.

He held his arm a little higher. "Won't you let me build you a network? Please?"

He would never forget how Alexandra laughed at that moment. It was a wonderfully warm, gentle laugh, and instantly she had relaxed, slinging her arm through his and walking on with him to the Jockey Club.

He wasn't the least bit surprised at how scary-bright Alexandra turned out to be and how easily she grasped the principle of the DBS television network. "Part-time programming for independent stations around the country," she said, helping Jackson to get it straight. And her eyes grew bright as Jackson tried to explain how DBS News would work. "We'll use each station's local newsroom as a bureau desk," she said, helping him again. "We'll do headlines on international news, and focus on a domestic news hour. We'll use local news reporters but frame the coverage within a national outlook from our headquarters in New York."

Jackson then sent Dr. Kessler (Darenbrook Communications' resident scientist, who, with his assistant scientists, had designed the technology behind the Darenbrook Broadcasting System) down to Washington one Saturday to have lunch with Alexandra and answer any questions she had about how the DBS News system would work. According to Dr. Kessler, Alexandra possessed a rather extraordinary knowledge of satellite communications technology.

"How extraordinary?" Jackson asked him.

"Vell," Dr. Kessler said over the phone from Washington, "eef I vere to compare her to Mr. Peterson"—Mr. Peterson was Langley Peterson, the president of DBS—"he knows nothink compared to vat dis girl knows." After Jackson laughed, Dr. Kessler added, "She vants to know our transmeeting and receiving capabilities to and from fife geographic points around the vorld—includink Moscow! Now vat kind of questions are dese for a domestic news operation?"

Jackson grinned. "The same we've been asking you, Herr Mad Doctor. She's trying to figure out if we have the capacity to go global."

"Vell, vat shall I tell her?" Dr. Kessler said.

"Everything she wants to know," Jackson said. And then, "So what do you think of her? Think you and the Nerd Brigade could work with her?"

Dr. Kessler chuckled. "Vell," he said, "eef she can get me on top of a horse, she vill probably get me to vork vith her."

"On top of a horse?" Jackson said. Dr. Kessler was about sixty-one, five foot three and close to a hundred seventy pounds. "Where the heck are you?"

"Virginia, I tink. Ve vere talkink about horses and I vas saying how as a boy I had always vished to ride, but vith the vor—the next ting I know, I am here and Miss Varing is vaiting outside vith a horse."

The week after that (with Dr. Kessler safely back in New York and able to stand with his legs together), Jackson had a lengthy breakfast at dawn with Alexandra in Washington, during which she proceeded to draw a flow chart for Jackson to illustrate her point about how, if he were willing to restructure the chain of command of his proposed news division, DBS News could be in operation by the fall of 1988 instead of 1989.

"This is a very interesting plan," Jackson said to her. "And I see that it all rests on one thing."

Alexandra only smiled, pencil poised over the legal pad she had been sketching on.

"It all rests on you," Jackson said.

"Yes, it does," Alexandra said.

And so, by the end of November, on the strength of a handshake, Darenbrook Communications had proceeded on a crash schedule at their new broadcast center in New York to ready themselves for the arrival of their anchorwoman—who would be free to sign on in early 1988, just as soon as her contract with The Network expired. As Jackson would say—laughing and shaking his head—leave it to Alexandra to become a national heroine in the meantime.

The history of the corporation Alexandra was coming to work for was inseparable from the history of the Darenbrook family. The start of the empire had begun in 1926 when Jackson's father, Elrod Bunkhauser Darenbrook (alias "Big El"), won, at age eighteen, a newspaper in a New Orleans poker game. While running his paper, Big El met and married the widow Biddens of Richmond, Virginia (Lillian), which added two more newspapers to his holdings. Big El also acquired a son in 1929, forever nicknamed Little El.

During a wild party on a cruise ship returning from Europe, Lillian fell overboard and drowned. Big El then married (while on a bender, or so people said) a hat-check girl from a New York nightclub named Gigi. Big El took Gigi home to New Orleans, where in 1933 she produced twins, Norbert and Noreen. But when Big El's debts began to curtail their lavish living style, Gigi ran away with his brother in 1935.

When his divorce from Gigi was final, Big El then married the thirty-eight-year-old Miss Madeline Magee of Hilleanderville, Georgia, an heiress whose two newspapers he mortgaged to keep possession of his three, thus expanding the family holdings to a total of five. At Madeline's insistence, he relocated the Darenbrooks to Hilleanderville, in the Magee family homestead, a three-story, ten-bedroom mansion on Mendolyn Street. Madeline gave birth to a son, John James, in 1936, but then died while giving birth to a daughter, Cordelia Louise, in 1938—an event which sent Big El on a bender for darn close to a year and made him darn near lose all the newspapers.

Big El was married the fourth and final time in 1939 to his secretary, Alice May Gaines, a marriage that was to establish the family fortunes and offer a period of grace in the turbulent upbringing of the Darenbrook children. Alice May continued to work for her husband and, after giving birth to Beauregard in 1940, opened the company's first day-care center at their Atlanta offices. Almost immediately she conceived her next, Jackson Andrew, whose crash-landing delivery occurred in 1941. And then, when Big El went overseas in 1942 with *Stars and Stripes,* Alice May took over the Darenbrook newspapers.

While America was at war, Alice May replenished the managerial ranks of their newspapers with women and instituted child-care facilities at all of them. At the end of the war the Darenbrooks bought twenty weekly papers around the country and then reassigned their wartime trained women to run them. Child-care facilities remained a permanent part of company policy.

Big El moved them into printing plants and Alice May launched new weekly after new weekly, following the boom expansion of suburban communities on the East and West coasts. In 1951, Alice May delivered the unexpected delight of a beautiful daughter, Belinda Cecile, and so another Darenbrook baby made the tour of the company offices.

By 1954 the heir apparent was young John James, who worked with his parents to buy three more city papers and run them from red to black. But nothing would better secure the family's fortunes than the Darenbrook employee policy that Alice May, Big El and John James devised and instituted. Job sharing, benefits banking, profit sharing, child care . . . these were the words that would keep unions out and the Darenbrook presses rolling better, faster and strike-free for decades. In 1955, when they launched a textbook company, the corporation was renamed Darenbrook Communications, which by that time included eight city papers, three hundred and two weeklies, and seven printing plants.

Alice May was killed in an automobile accident outside Chicago in 1956 and Big El went to pieces, drinking so heavily that young John James had to take over as chairman of the company. The Mendolyn Street house in Hilleanderville became steeped in depression. Big El took over the sun room and sat there, day after day, drinking, roused out of his brooding only when baby Belinda came tripping in, which, given Big El's state, the nanny did not often allow. Cordelia got pregnant at Bible college and had to marry Kirby "Kitty" Paine—a preacher man with big ideas on how to spend Darenbrook money. The twins stole thousands of dollars of securities from Big El and ran off to Europe. Little El became horrendously overweight. Beau fell in with gamblers at college. Jackson, however, was an indefatigable good-natured teenager and, with Cordelia and John James acting as surrogate parents, seemed to weather those years well: he had very high grades, was a football, basketball and track star, and worked every weekend at their local paper, the Atlanta *Parader.*

A year after Jackson graduated from Duke, in 1963, John James was kidnapped. The Darenbrook family paid the million dollars ransom, only to find that the kidnappers had killed him the first day they got him.

And so Jackson Darenbrook, at twenty-three, became the chairman of the board of Darenbrook Communications, and a new board of directors was formed, whose membership would remain unaltered for the next twenty-five years: Big El (with his drinking problems); Little El (with his eating problems); Norbert and Noreen (with their compulsive spending problems); Cordelia Louise (with her greedy husband problem); Beau (with his gambling problems); and Belinda (with her later sanity problems). It was a collection of interesting temperaments, to say the least.

For the next seven years Jackson managed to keep the empire intact as he had received it. When he married the lovely Barbara Bennett in 1967, Jackson moved himself and corporate headquarters to his wife's native Richmond, Virginia. They had a daughter, Lydia, in 1970 and a son, Kevin, in 1972, and it was shortly after that that the Darenbrook empire started to expand. Four more city papers were bought and turned around; two national magazines were launched; the textbook operations were doubled; and four new printing plants were built. And then, in 1980, a whole new endeavor into computers was announced: the Darenbrook Library, the largest electronic research information system in the world.

In 1981 death struck the Darenbrook family again when Jackson's wife was killed in a freak accident at their country club. Jackson disappeared from public view until 1983, at which time he reemerged as a run-around playboy eccentric the public scarcely recognized. And it was this new free-wheeling and -dealing tycoon who battled the board and won, and proceeded to launch a new communications satellite called TELENET DBS and, in 1986, broke ground on the Upper West Side of Manhattan for a new corporate headquarters complex that would include a major television studio facility.

The door of Jackson's limousine suddenly swung open and there stood Alexandra, radiant, in the driveway of the Plaza, wrapped in a full-length navy-blue cape against the cold. Her hair was dark and lovely, and her eyes were dazzling. Even the snow on the ground seemed to be working to her advantage. "Good morning," she said, smiling in at Jackson.

The Plaza doorman, in full-dress uniform, who was holding the door, peered in as well. "Good morning, Mr. Darenbrook—again!" (Jackson was staying at the Plaza too.)

"Good morning," Jackson said, scooting over to make room for Alexandra. He watched her as she slid in. "You're certainly very beautiful this morning."

"Thank you," she said. She turned to look out at the doorman. "And thank you."

He tipped his hat and closed the door.

"How's the shoulder?"

"Okay, thanks," she said, rearranging her cape around her with one hand, her other arm hidden underneath the cape, presumably in its sling. Then she nodded to the paper on the floor and laughed. "I see you've seen what my charming friends Clark and Regina have to say about me."

"I oughta sue the jackasses," Jackson said.

Alexandra turned to him. "We ought to succeed," she said, "that's what we ought to do. That would be the greatest punishment we could inflict."

For a moment they just sat there, looking at each other, smiling like the conspirators they were.

"I hope you're going to be happy in your new home," Jackson finally said.

"New home," Alexandra murmured, turning to look out her window, "I like that."

They went out the Plaza driveway, turned down Fifth Avenue, and then turned right on 57th Street. They went all the way west, passing the CBS News facilities, and turned right on Eleventh Avenue, heading north. They passed car dealerships, gas stations and parking lots; they passed the ABC radio studios; and as enormous apartment complexes loomed up around them, they stopped, at 67th Street, to make a left turn. The traffic parted and as they turned in, the guard in the guardhouse waved them through.

They drove in on an elevated driveway that suddenly veered sharply to the right, in behind a massive apartment building, and then veered sharply left again, to head straight out to the Darenbrook Communications complex—which looked, from here, like a group of some sort of pale gray warehouses, with not a window in sight. There were several ramps exiting the elevated driveway, but they drove straight out, the limousine swinging around to stop right behind the tremendous concrete wall of the center building. Jackson and Alexandra got out and he led her around the corner of the building, her heels and his boots sounding gritty over the salted concrete.

The buildings were not warehouses at all. What they had just walked around was the center building of three, and the complex was shaped like a U, facing away from the access road. And on this side of the buildings, inside the U, there was nothing but glass. Three stories of sparkling glass surrounding a beautiful square.

They were standing in front of a small wrought-iron gate, between two of the buildings, looking in. There were trees and shrubs and, outlined under the snow, flower beds. The walkways were swept clean of snow and so were the wood benches. There were iron lampposts along the walkways too, looking as though they were still supposed to use gas.

At the far end of the square was a thick line of fir trees. They could hear cars passing behind it on the West Side Highway, but they could not see them. All they could see over the tops of the trees was the blue-gray beauty of the Hudson River and the cold gray clouds of the winter sky.

Jackson made a little whistling sound through his teeth. "It's very pretty, isn't it?"

"Yes," Alexandra said.

And then Jackson squatted down to brush a little snow off the brass plate on the gate with his hand.

WEST END

it said.

3
―――

Gordon Strenn

He smiled.

Sitting next to the plate-glass wall of his third-floor office in Daren-brook III, Gordon was watching Jackson and Alexandra down in the square. Jackson was in front of her, walking backward down the path, gesturing wildly as he talked. Alexandra was laughing, shaking her head, and then Jackson was laughing too, saying something, arms outstretched to the sky. A big gust of wind blew in off the Hudson at that moment and Alexandra's cape billowed up behind her as she shielded her face from the snow with her one arm. Jackson jogged over to her and with both hands pulled her hood up over her head. Hands on her hood still, he stood in front of her a moment longer, and then he moved to the side, touching her back, and guided her across the square into Darenbrook II.

"Ground control calling Gordon," his assistant, Betty, said from the door, "come in, please."

Gordon turned around, swiveling his chair.

"I thought you'd like to know that Princess All-Light-and-Love has arrived," Betty said, taking a step in. (Betty said Alexandra always sounded too nice on the phone to be for real.) "Emma in reception says she's already got the place in an uproar. Everybody's trying to get a look at her."

"I just saw her crossing the square," Gordon said. "With Jackson."

"Well if I were you," Betty said, coming in a little further, "I'd finish those figures for Langley before we lose the boccie set."

Jackson had given Gordon a boccie set with the idea that he and Betty, as the first and only inhabitants of the third floor of the television building, Darenbrook III, could get to know other Darenbrook employees at West End by inviting them over to play. And it was fun, setting up the pins at one end of the eerily vacant floor and then rolling balls down the seventy-five yards of carpeted hallway in an attempt to hit them. But Betty really loved playing because she found she did not have to aim at all but could simply hurl it as hard as she could and the ball would ricochet off the office walls all the way down and then smash the pins on the diagonal.

At any rate, Langley Peterson, the president of DBS—who was not known for playing games—had recently sent his white-haired secretary, Adele, over with part of the miniseries budget for Gordon to revise. When Adele did not come back, Langley had come over from Darenbrook I to find her and find her he did—playing boccie in the hall with Betty and Gordon and a guy visiting from the newspaper division over in Darenbrook II.

"Right, Langley's numbers," Gordon said, listlessly pushing some of the papers around on his desk.

"Pardon me for saying so, boss," Betty said, putting one hand on her hip, "but we either better get cracking around here or let Culver City handle this stuff. Winslow's agent's screaming at me every forty-five minutes and I can't get the contracts out until Langley gets the revised numbers."

"I know," Gordon said.

And he did. He was way behind on everything. The three weeks he had spent down in Washington after Alexandra was shot certainly had not helped things. And still, if his mind wasn't on Alexandra's injuries, it was on her coming to DBS, or if it wasn't about their living arrangements in New York, it was on how long it would be before they were married, and if his mind wasn't on any of these things, then he was probably thinking about how not to think about Alexandra so he could get his work done.

"I'm not a piece of furniture, you know," Betty said. "If you'd tell me what Langley wants, exactly, maybe I can help you out."

She was right. She probably could.

Four years ago, when Gordon was finalizing the budget for *This Side of Paradise* for public television, Betty Tellerman had arrived in his office as a temporary statistical typist. Like many aspiring actresses in Manhattan, Betty had been making ends meet as a temp because it kept her schedule flexible for auditions. But then Betty the temp kept catching errors in the figures being called in from L.A., and she and Gordon had gotten to talking—about how she had kept books for her father's shop in Valley Stream, Long Island, and about how Gordon as a boy from Locust Valley, Long Island, had watched his father do the books for his mother's company. ("Cannondale Clothing?" Betty had shrieked. "Your mother's a Cannondale? Even the *name* sounds like money.")

Gordon had ended up offering Betty an office job with him, which she declined. He liked her a lot and was sorry she had. As the director who later gave Betty an audition at Gordon's request said, "She's got as much chance as an actress as I do as a racehorse."

About five months ago Betty had called Gordon up to ask him if he had any work for her to do. It seemed she was in very bad straits with some institutions named American Express, Mastercard, Visa, Diners Club and Bloomingdale's, and while she wished to continue pursuing an acting career, she thought she had better work a steady job for a while to stay out of debtor's prison. ("Truth is," she had sighed over the phone, "I'm addicted to a special kind of actor—the kind that's only confused about his sexuality until he makes some money.") Gordon told her about producing *Love Across the Atlantic* as a miniseries for DBS, about the home base for the project being in New York, about his need for an executive assistant for the duration of it and how, if she took the job, she had to stay in it for one year—no ifs, ands or acting parts.

"Agreed," she had said. "Only . . ."

"Only what?"

"I better tell you that I changed my name since the last time I saw you."

"So? What did you change it to?"

"Uh," Betty said, "Cannondale."

And so Gordon Cannondale Strenn's executive assistant was named Elizabeth Cannondale, but the two were not related except by temp agency. Ms. Tellerman's dark brown hair was gone too; Ms. Cannondale had light brown hair—streaked with blond—was seriously into aerobics and was very attractive in an L.A. kind of way. But what was important was how very bright, fast and personable Betty was— simply amazing at dealing with difficult people—and what a godsend it was for Gordon to have someone who had a head for numbers and was a closet perfectionist.

"Look at that," Betty murmured, looking past Gordon to the square.

There were four—five—now six people scurrying across the square toward Darenbrook II, clutching themselves in the cold.

"They're stalking her, for crying out loud," Betty said. She shook her head. "What is it about her, anyway?"

"Fame," Gordon said, turning back to his desk.

"I mean," Betty said, putting her hand on her hip, "what is it about her that gets guys like you and Jackson so gaga?"

"Jackson?" Gordon said.

"You know what I mean," Betty said, looking at him. "Why guys like you always go for those WASP-y types."

"Alexandra is not a type," Gordon said.

"Yeah, right," Betty said, "but we know all about your taste in women, don't we? I'm sorry," she added a second later, holding her hand up. "Really, I'm sorry. I didn't mean that."

"You could quit while you're ahead," Gordon suggested.

"It's just that I saw your ex-wife on Johnny Carson last night," Betty explained.

Gordon only looked at her.

"She looked terrible," Betty offered.

Gordon still only looked at her.

Betty sighed. "Yeah, all right." She looked outside again. Two more people were hurrying across the square. "I'll give her this," she said, "this is the first sign of life around here we've seen since we moved in."

It was true. In the six months they had been here, they had never seen anyone in the square except Jackson and the children from the day-care center.

"Alexandra has that effect on people," Gordon said.

Gordon's best friend and roommate at prep school in Pennsylvania had been David Waring, the son of the big-shot congressman from Kansas. That first year, as freshmen, when Gordon was fourteen, he accepted an invitation to spend Thanksgiving at the Waring farm, and, as their plane made its descent into Kansas City International Airport, he was given his first protocol lesson.

"This side, east of the Missouri River, is *their* Kansas City," David told him, pointing out the window. "The other side, west of the Missouri, is *our* Kansas City. Don't confuse the two or Mom and Dad will be lecturing you all weekend."

"Well, how am I supposed to—"

"They've got the people and the problems," David said, "and *we've* got the solutions. That's all you have to remember, okay?"

Mrs. Waring and nine-year-old Alexandra had been waiting at the airport gate for them. Alexandra was only about four foot ten at that time, and almost all of it eyes. When Gordon looked down to say hello to her, she thrust a camera in his face and blinded him with the flash. "Hi, Davy," he then heard her say. One eye closed, Gordon could vaguely make out Alexandra hugging her brother.

"That's not a very polite way to greet poor Gordon," Mrs. Waring said, laughing, shaking his hand. "Hello, Gordon, welcome."

"So what is he?" Alexandra asked her brother, letting her camera hang from the strap around her neck and pulling a pad and pencil out of her coat pocket. "Five-six, five-seven?"

"Lexy keeps files on people," David explained.

"But don't feel bad, Gordon," Mrs. Waring said, taking his arm and leading him away, "she even keeps one on her mother."

"Five-seven and growing," David told his sister.

"Identifiable scars, birthmarks?" Alexandra asked Gordon, scooting up to walk alongside him.

It was a three-hour drive to the Waring farm, the cityscape quickly falling behind and the horizon opening up to miles and miles and miles of what seemed to Gordon to be nothing but cold gray nothingness. The wind, however, was something, hitting the side of the Ford station wagon and moving it a foot sideways this way, and then—boofff—a foot sideways the other way, a phenomenon that no one but Gordon seemed to be aware of.

They turned off the highway and drove for several miles through gently rolling fields, with an occasional house popping up on the roadside. Then they slowed to turn into a large wooden gate, painted pale gray, which had a big old mailbox next to it that said, simply, WARING FARM. David, who had been growing more excited by the minute, started pointing in one direction and then another, saying, "We've got fifteen hundred acres of wheat, a thousand of corn . . ." and reeling off livestock inventories and grazing-feed patterns. Then, hanging over the front seat, he started cross-examining his mother about some horse.

Alexandra, who had been very quiet thus far, sitting up front, now turned around and raised one eye up over the seat to look at Gordon. "You grow potatoes in Long Island," she said matter-of-factly.

"Um, yeah," Gordon said. "Some people do."

Alexandra looked over at her mother and, satisfied she wasn't paying any attention to her, looked back at Gordon and narrowed her eyes. "We don't have potatoes here because we don't like them."

"I heard that, Lexy," Mrs. Waring said, interrupting David. She looked at Gordon in the rear-view mirror and smiled. "Of course we like potatoes."

Alexandra's expression was one of high skepticism. She shrugged a "Who cares?" and turned back around in her seat.

"Brat," David said, giving his sister a little punch in the shoulder. When he did not get a response, he did it again. "Brat."

Alexandra's head whipped around. "Why don't you just go back East and grow potatoes—with *him?*" she added, jerking her head in Gordon's direction.

As the main house came into view, Mrs. Waring told Gordon its history. It had begun as a one-room cabin with a porch and cellar in 1805. In 1811, David's great-great-great-great-grandfather added three rooms and then, in 1839, David's great-great-great-grandfather had added another four, making it—if nothing else—surely the longest house in Kansas at the time. After the Civil War, in 1874, David's great-great-grandfather started work on the second floor, which actually didn't get finished until 1902, when David's great-grandfather had thought to change the front of the house from facing east to south, and added yet a couple more rooms and a tremendous veranda to this cabin–turned–farmhouse–turned–mansion of stone, pale gray clapboard and gray-weathered shingle. And so, Mrs. Waring finished, the original one-room cabin was part of the kitchen today, and the original front porch was that little porch Gordon could see jutting out from the side of the house toward the driveway.

Before going inside this Kansas landmark (or so said the plaque), Mrs. Waring pulled Gordon aside on the historic porch to apologize for Alexandra's behavior in the car, explaining that she was still upset about David going away to school. Though Gordon was an only child, after spending only a little time with the Warings, even he began to sense that Alexandra might have more to be upset about than just David being away.

Tall, dark, powerful Congressman Waring hadn't been home since September. Tall, dark Paul Waring, Jr.—with his wife Ann—was home visiting from Harvard Law School for the first time since June.

Tall, dark and lovely Elizabeth—with her "very serious beau," Alan—
was visiting home from Vassar. Tall, dark and wild Linc was home
visiting—with his girlfriend, Zu-Zu, who was also the lead singer in his
rock band—from the University of Colorado. And according to the
happily plastered old geezer—who claimed to be Congressman Waring's father (and must have been since everybody was calling him
Granddad)—Mrs. Waring herself spent at least every other week in
Washington with her husband, leaving Alexandra on the farm in the
care of Grandmother Waring, a very tall, correct old lady who Gordon
couldn't believe was married to the crocked old geezer—but was.

What a circus the household had been. Gordon had never had a
holiday like it. There were all these *people,* everywhere. And they were
all very friendly and nice to him, except Alexandra, who really was the
strangest kid. When they sat down to the big Thanksgiving dinner—
with a couple of farm workers and neighbors joining them at a series of
tables that extended the dining-room table all the way out through the
living room—Alexandra had sat across from him, taking copious notes
on his every move with unswerving concentration.

David, sitting next to her, looked over her shoulder and read, "Likes
turnips."

"Uh-oh!" Elizabeth said, sitting next to Gordon.

"I've heard of some weird preferences, man . . ." Linc said.

"What's that? Turnips?" Congressman Waring said from the end of
the table. "Wouldn't be a bit surprised to see that information turn up
when you apply for a passport, Gordon."

"Put the pad away, Alexandra," Mrs. Waring said.

Alexandra, eyes down, slipped the pad and pencil under her chair
and dropped them to the floor.

"You shouldn't let her bring it to the table in the first place, Liz,"
Grandmother Waring said. "I don't allow it."

Mrs. Waring exchanged looks with Congressman Waring.

"I think our Lexy's falling in love," Paul, Jr., said, earning the laughter of most everyone at the table—and a look from Alexandra that was
surely meant to wither his heart.

Granddad Waring, quiet until now, banged his fist on the table,
making everybody jump. "Leave her alone," he said, "all of you."

"Tom," Grandmother Waring said sharply.

"It's okay, Granddad," Alexandra said quickly, leaning forward to look up the table at him. "I don't mind. Honest." She smiled to prove it.

"That's my girl," Granddad Waring said, giving her a wink. "Show 'em what you're made of."

And then dinner and the lively chitchat resumed.

Gordon stepped out of the elevator onto Sub Level 2, the television floor, careful not to trip over the rolls of carpeting.

Six months ago this floor had been nothing but one colossal concrete bunker, the size of four hockey rinks, with a huge square section in the center that rose straight up through the floor above. That center section was where the television studio was now, and the vast space around it was now a catacomb of interlocking rooms and hallways to service it and the in-studio programs of the DBS television network. This floor, Sub Level 2, was the actual West End Broadcasting Center and, like the rest of the Darenbrook media empire, had been made possible by the technology developed in the Darenbrook electronic research and development labs, now located on the floor above, on Sub Level 1.

Gordon walked down the hallway and was immediately confronted with a choice. Should he go straight ahead? Or go left? Or right? It was a tricky decision, considering all he had to go by was blank white plasterboard and white soundproofing ceiling squares. He went straight ahead and then had to choose, left or right, and so he took a right and ran into a team of electricians up on ladders. "Excuse me," Gordon said, "you haven't seen Alexandra Waring by chance, have you?"

"You bet," one electrician said, stepping down his ladder so as to come down out of the ceiling. He looked down at Gordon. "She signed an autograph for the kids. She's around in the studio—but careful of the walls as you go. They're painting this morning."

"Thanks," Gordon said, walking on, forgetting that he didn't know *where* around the studio was. So he just kept asking painters and carpenters and carpet layers until he reached a set of double gray steel doors with a large red light over them. He pushed them open and looked inside. Nope. Wrong one. This had to be Studio B, the smaller studio that backed up to the big one, Studio A. He continued down the narrow corridor, this part with linoleum floors, until he found another set of huge steel doors. He went inside.

Wow. Studio A was really getting to be something now. Its incredible expanse made it feel a little like walking into the Metropolitan Opera House or something, though it certainly did not look anything like it. Workers were everywhere, scaffolding too, and so were hanging wires and cables and half-installed studio lights. Two sides of the studio, along the ground level, were glass. Behind the glass Gordon could see hundreds of boxes and unopened packing cases. And then, up above, on the next level, there were windows all the way around the studio, belonging to offices and labs on Sub Level 1. Gordon smiled. There had to be a hundred people peering down into the studio from up there—watching Alexandra, of course. She was standing with Jackson and another man, nodding, looking at some blueprints.

Suddenly Alexandra's head came up, as if she had heard something, and she turned around. She saw Gordon and smiled. "Come see," she said.

Following his graduation from UCLA in 1973, Gordon worked in the television group of Universal Studios until his big break came, when Richard Bernetto built a studio outside of San Francisco and offered him a job as a producer in charge of in-studio production on miniseries.

The work was fabulous, the money terrific, beautiful women were plentiful and the sex was great and the last thing in the world Gordon felt like doing in the fall of '76 was honoring David's request that he call bratty little Alexandra at her Stanford dorm to see how the freshman from Kansas was doing. But he did call and he made a date to take her to dinner, which he subsequently had to cancel. (Well, he didn't *have* to, but when it came to choosing between a gorgeous redhead who was the ex-mistress of—never mind—and David's kid sister, Gordon felt he had no choice.) He never got around to rescheduling it.

One morning in March there was an accident at the studio. A prop arm fell on one of the actors, cracking his skull, and he had to be rushed to the hospital. In the ensuing chaos at the studio, a secretary from the front office told Gordon that his mother was on the phone. Gordon took the call.

"After breaking the heart of your best friend's little sister," the voice said, "the least you can do is let her turn on the tape recorder and ask you a few questions about the accident."

"Alexandra?" Gordon said.

"KCLI-Radio—how about it, Gordon? I'd love to tell my big brother how wonderful you are."

"What kind of questions?" Gordon said.

"Let me just turn on the tape recorder—there, tape's rolling, Gordon Strenn, producer, Bernetto Studios, March 7, 1977 three-fifteen Pacific Time." Her voice changed then, dropping a half register. "How is Mr. Kirkson?"

Alexandra called Gordon again a few nights later, this time at home. Gordon had just finished having an orgasm—on top, of all people, of the redhead again—when the answering machine came on. "Hi, it's Alexandra Waring. This afternoon I got hired in the newsroom at KFFK-TV and I think it was my scoop with you for CLI that did it." Pause. "I'd like to thank you by inviting you out to dinner, but I suspect the best way to thank you would be to leave you alone. Whatever, Gordon, I did want to thank you. I'm thrilled to get the job."

He called her back.

When Gordon reached the Palo Alto restaurant near campus on the night he had agreed to meet her for dinner, he wondered if he would recognize Alexandra after all these years. Standing there, scrutinizing the patrons, he tried to imagine what a nineteen-year-old who worked in a television newsroom would look like. He looked for pads and pencils in the hands of dark-haired women.

"Hello, Gordon," a voice said close to his ear.

He started, turning to find that Alexandra was standing almost eye to eye with him. He backed away a half step, glancing down to see that she was wearing heels, but seeing too that she still had to be around five-eight to his five-ten. He also noticed that many other features of Ms. Waring's physique had changed over the years as well. By the time his eyes came back to hers, all he could think to say was, "Look at you."

She smiled, eyes sparkling, and kissed him on the cheek. "And does your file ever need updating," she said.

He had a wonderful dinner with Alexandra, super college coed. She was so very attractive and so very smart and so very . . . well, sexy or something. . . . Yes, sexy. Even at nineteen that low voice in combination with those extraordinary blue-gray eyes made her a very seductive dinner partner—though, when excited, every once in a while one of her *k*'s could kick all the way back to Kansas and one of her *a*'s could probably flatten out a road through the Continental Divide to get there. But, *k*'s and *a*'s aside, Gordon had a hell of a time trying to remember that this was David's kid sister—who wasn't even old enough to order a drink.

Something happened when the salads arrived. Gordon picked up his fork and was just about to spear some avocado when he happened to glance across the table at Alexandra. She was looking at him and something connected between them and, whatever it was, it shot straight down into Gordon's groin and something similar must have happened on that side of the table too because Alexandra blushed, dropped her eyes to her salad, brought them back up again and then, with a half laugh, said, "I don't know what just happened, but I'm not sure I can eat."

He laughed and sipped his wine, not knowing what to say.

"Um," she then said, face still blazing, "maybe you should tell me about your work."

Curious suggestion, he thought, but then when he started answering her questions about his work at the studio he realized that whatever had been in the air was now gone and Alexandra was eating just fine.

He felt very self-conscious outside the restaurant after dinner. By this time, part of him wanted in the worst way to take her back to his apartment in the city to see . . . Well, to see. But the bigger part of him said, *This is David's sister,* and he knew David would have liked him to simply take her home, so he offered to drive her to the dorm and—after laughing, explaining that it was all of five blocks away—she accepted.

They sat outside, in his car, talking, for hours. Rather, Gordon did. It grew later and later; the traffic of young women returning to the dorm slowed until only the security guard could be seen loitering around the entrance. Gordon talked on.

He talked about being an only child. He talked about driving into Manhattan every Saturday as a child with his father, to the headquarters of Cannondale Clothing. About how he would play with typewriters and adding machines and climb the desks and counter tops and drop Dixie cups of water out of the men's bathroom window and watch them fall twelve floors to 40th Street while his father smoked cigarette after cigarette, poring over the numbers of his wife's company. About how, in the afternoon, they would drive to Greenwich Village to have a late lunch with Kay and how Kay would stand in her doorway and throw her arms out, crying, "My two men!" as if they were conquering heroes. And, after lunch, how Gordon would watch TV in the living room and play with the toy soldiers Kay kept for him while Kay and his father "talked" behind the closed doors of her bedroom.

He talked about how, when they got home, his mother always asked him, "Did you have a nice time, dear?" and how he would always be standing in the doorway of her bedroom and how she would always be lying on her daybed, in a dressing grown, looking beautiful, saintly, remote, and how he always said, "Uh-huh," and Mother always said, "Yes, Mother," and he always said, "Yes, Mother, I did," and then she always said, "That's a good boy," and dismissed him.

He talked about the day Cannondale Clothing collapsed and how the doors of all one hundred fourteen stores closed for the last time. About how the lawyers and accountants had been all over the house that day and how even Mother had risen for the occasion, sweeping tragically from one room to the next, weeping, asking if they couldn't at least keep the Manhattan store open, the original store, the store on Fifth Avenue, and how they told her no, they couldn't, not if they were to keep her personal estate out of the reach of the bankruptcy courts.

It was near three in the morning when Gordon stopped talking, and he did so because his stomach hurt so much. He had forgotten that he never talked about his family. So then he just sat there, looking straight ahead at the empty street, and Alexandra, sitting next to him, did the same. Finally, after several minutes, Alexandra cleared her throat and said, very quietly, "Gordon?"

He swallowed and turned to see her profile against the streetlight. He looked at her forehead, eye, nose, mouth, jaw, moving his eyes back up to rest on her mouth. He swallowed again. Alexandra was a pretty wonderful-looking girl, he decided. "Yes?" he said.

She sighed slightly and turned toward him, resting the side of her face against the headrest. She paused and then said, "Does it matter that I'm David's sister?"

He started to speak, stopped, and then started again. "Matter how?"

"Well—don't you even want to kiss me?" she whispered.

"Oh, God," he sighed, grasping the steering wheel and banging his forehead on it.

"Gordon," Alexandra said, laughing.

He let his head rest there a moment. "She wants to know if I want to kiss her," he said to the car. He sat up suddenly and said, "Come here," although he was already on his way over. He slid one arm around her, held her chin in his hand and he did indeed kiss her.

He couldn't have stopped things after that even if he had wanted to. The kiss was complicated from the start and he knew, even then, he was falling into something that would not be easily climbed back out of. And if by some miracle he could miss Alexandra's message in the way she kissed him back, in the way she kissed his ear and neck, or in the way she murmured encouragement as he ran his hands over her blouse, then she made sure he understood by asking him to please take her somewhere.

He took her back to his apartment and found that she was not a virgin. He didn't know why, but he had thought he would be the first. But then he might as well have been since almost everything he did to Alexandra—or maybe how he did it—certainly seemed to be a first for her. And judging from the responses of her body and the quiet, involuntary sounds she made, a lot of it was an exquisite first. And he envied her. Hers was a kind of unabashed wonder and awe at what they were doing; and her gratitude, as he led her through things, felt wonderful.

They continued to see each other, week after week, and Alexandra took up their relationship—at least the sexual part—with the same concentrated effort she applied to everything that interested her. "Alexandra," he said one night, laughing, "I'm not a lab science course.

What's with all these questions?" She propped herself up on one elbow and said, "But *does* it change each time for you? It does for me. I never quite know which kind of feeling it's going to be—but it seems as though it's close to the same for you each time, whichever way we do it."

Summertime rolled around and, after a brief visit to Kansas, they drove back to San Francisco in the navy-blue MG Alexandra inherited from David. Alexandra moved in full time with Gordon and worked full time at KFFK. It was a wonderful summer, one of exploration and excitement, the last summer that Alexandra would ever have anything that resembled free time.

Theoretically speaking, they lived together for the next three and a half years, though they lived very different lives that only occasionally crossed and most often in bed, though sometimes that wasn't possible either. By the end of her sophomore year Alexandra had gone from unpaid intern at KFFK to gainfully employed researcher/writer, and by her senior year was a full-fledged newswriter for their weekend news as well. She still carried a full load of classes and her schedule left her so exhausted some nights that someone from KFFK would call Gordon to ask his opinion as to whether they should wake Alexandra up or let her sleep where she had crashed in the lounge off the newsroom. As for Gordon, he too was working very hard, only now he spent much of his time shuttling back and forth from L.A. and on-location production sites, and it wouldn't be until the end of Alexandra's senior year that he would be faithful to her.

Alexandra underwent some dramatic changes in those years. When she first moved in with him, a lot of his male colleagues had raised their eyebrows at his choosing such a young girl nobody. But by the time she hit twenty-two, when KFFK put her on the air once a week for a segment called "San Francisco Under 30," the only question his colleagues ever had concerning Alexandra was whether or not Gordon would let them know if they ever broke up.

Alexandra graduated, was promoted to senior writer of the KFFK weekend news, continued to do "Under 30," and Gordon proposed to her. She said she thought maybe yes, eventually. In November, Gordon was offered a tremendous job in L.A. and Alexandra started looking for work there. She was offered a promising position at one of the network-owned and -operated stations and then, out of the blue, KSCT in Kansas City made a pitch to the congressman's daughter. And so twenty-three-year-old Alexandra had a decision to make: she could move to Los Angeles with Gordon and be a rookie consumer affairs reporter in the number two market of America, or she could move to Kansas City without Gordon and be an investigative reporter in the number twenty-eight market of America.

And so Alexandra went home to Kansas.

"How's that?" Gordon asked her, straightening up. He had just moved the huge oak table that Alexandra had chosen to use in her office in lieu of a desk.

"Great. Thanks," Alexandra said, running her hand over its surface. "But I'm still meeting the real estate broker tonight."

Despite the fact that Gordon owned a large place on Gramercy Park (that he had inherited from his maternal grandparents), Alexandra insisted she needed an apartment on the West Side somewhere, somewhere closer to work.

"Excuse me, sir," a woman wearing green overalls said to Gordon, wheeling a plant past him. (Alexandra had selected so many plants and trees for her office that Plant Heaven had sent a professional gardener and her assistant over to "put them to bed" for her.)

"Yeah, sure," Gordon said, stepping aside. He walked around the table to Alexandra. "Come over after you get through tonight," he said, meaning that she should spend the night with him in Gramercy Park.

"You come over," she said, meaning that he should spend the night with her in the Plaza Hotel.

"With Darenbrook down the hall, great," Gordon said, rolling his eyes. "Probably be listening at the door."

"He won't even know," Alexandra said.

"I don't care if he knows," Gordon said. "I just don't feel like having him next door."

"He's not next door," Alexandra said.

"Hi ya, Miss Waring," a man in a white denim jump suit said at the door. It was Clancy Stevens, from maintenance. "I've got the TV stuff you wanted and a couple of lugs to install it for ya."

"Great," Alexandra said, "bring it in. I'd love to have it working before tomorrow."

And so, while Alexandra made Gordon move furniture around and the gardeners were plunking, potting and pruning plants, three men with hammers and electric drills installed a giant TV screen and a four-cartridge video recorder into the wall.

And then Jackson popped in. "Need anything?" he called from the door to Alexandra.

"I've got everything—and everybody," she added, laughing, gesturing to all the activity.

"Lookin' like Tarzan land in here," Jackson said, prompting the gardener to scowl at him from behind a ficus tree. "Hey," he said, turning his attention to Gordon, "what are you, the Welcome Wagon?" And then he was gone.

"Now what was that supposed to mean?" Gordon said.

Alexandra walked over to examine one of the trees. "The apartment I'm seeing tonight has a living room and master bedroom overlooking Central Park," she said to him, holding some leaves in her hand. "It's on Central Park West."

"Yippee," Gordon said without a trace of enthusiasm.

"With plenty of room for two," she added, glancing at him.

"One of us already has room enough for four," he said. "I was thinking maybe you'd like to come over and see it again."

Alexandra had taken a pinch of soil out of the pot and was rubbing it between her fingers. "What kind of fertilizer are you using on these?" she said in a louder voice.

"Kato," the gardener said.

"What number?" Alexandra said.

"Six," she said.

"That's what I thought," Alexandra said, putting the soil back.

The gardener glanced at her assistant and then back to Alexandra. "Something wrong?"

"Hmmm?" Alexandra said, turning. "Oh, no, I think you're doing a wonderful job. I just wanted to know what we were using so that when the summer light starts in here I'll want to cut back two grades."

"Hey," Clancy said loudly, swinging in through the doorway, "before

I forget—the wife wants to know how the shoulder's doin'. It mending okay?"

Alexandra turned and smiled. "Tell her it's mending great, thanks."

Gordon fell in love with Julie Stantree while he was working on a TV series called *Highland Street* and Julie was starring in a sitcom that was filmed in the studio next door. He asked her to marry him, twice, and shortly after her series was canceled she said yes. They were married, moved into a large rental in Beverly Hills and, eleven months later, had a baby, Christopher. Julie was thirty-five, Gordon was thirty-one, and the year was 1984, the same year David Waring and his wife came to visit and told him—while Julie was in the back of the house, putting Christopher down for his nap—that Alexandra was getting married in the fall.

"Huh," Gordon said.

"Name's Tyler Mandell," David said. "He's a big architect-builder in Kansas City. I think he's too old for Lexy—he's thirty-eight and sort of a buffoon, if you ask me."

"But no one's asking you," David's wife said. To Gordon, "He's very handsome and everyone says he's going into politics."

David looked at Gordon. "I don't know, I still wish you guys could have—"

"David!" his wife said, clearly horrified at what she imagined her husband was about to say.

Three months later David called Gordon and told him that Alexandra had suddenly called off the wedding, offering no explanation except that she wasn't ready.

"Huh," Gordon said.

"Mom and Dad are going nuts," David said. "They're convinced Mandell did something—you know, has a mistress or something—but Lexy won't tell them anything."

"What do you think?" Gordon said.

Crackle, crackle went the long-distance line.

"I think," David finally said, speaking slowly, "that Lexy might have done something. She's got that look these days."

"Which?"

"The sphinx."

Gordon knew that look. It was the same look Alexandra had had between the time she made up her mind to take the KSCT job and when she told him.

"Someone else?" Gordon said.

"I don't know. But there's something," David said. He hesitated and then asked, "You don't know anything about it, do you?"

"Jesus, David," Gordon said.

"Sorry. I just didn't know who else it could be."

Two months later, in October of 1984, Julie left Gordon for Émile Ruvais, a French film director some twenty-two years her senior. Ruvais was considered to be the national treasure of France and, since he was also one of the most powerful men in the movie industry, irreproachable in all matters as well, including his part in the battle for custody over Christopher, to say nothing of the Stantree-Strenn divorce. Caught completely by surprise, Gordon had to change lawyers four times over the course of the court battle to find someone who could take on Ruvais's legion of attorneys, but by then it was too late. He was divorced against his will; he lost custody of his son; and he had over three hundred thousand dollars in legal bills—which that son of a bitch Ruvais then offered to pay. Gordon did not take him up on his offer.

Badly shaken, drinking a bit too much, crying some and sleeping around a lot, Gordon moved to New York in 1985 to start work on *This Side of Paradise* for public television. He flew to Paris once a month to visit Christopher and getting used to that, in combination with his work, helped to steady him. By the time Alexandra arrived in New York to anchor the news at WWKK in 1986, Gordon had settled into a meaningless but stable relationship with a twenty-year-old model.

Alexandra was no more the same young woman he had known than he was the same young man she had known. To begin with, there didn't seem to be anything very young about either one of them anymore. And while Alexandra was as beautiful and dynamic as ever—more so, actually—there was something closed off about her now, and after a few weeks of friendly chats and showing her around New York,

Gordon put his finger on something else that was different: Alexandra no longer trusted him.

As always, if he didn't pick up on the message indirectly, then Alexandra practically spelled it out for him. No, she didn't say, "Gordon, I don't trust you." What happened was, they went out to dinner one night with Alexandra's boss, Michael Cochran, and his wife, Cassy. It was really an awful dinner, with Michael getting very drunk in the restaurant and slobbering all over Alexandra while they all tried to pretend it wasn't happening. When they finally got the Cochrans out of the restaurant and into a cab, Alexandra wanted to walk for a while and so they did, up Fifth Avenue and then across 59th Street, along the south wall of Central Park.

That was the night he told her the whole long, horrible story of Julie and Christopher. Alexandra held his hand, her head bowed, as they walked, and she was genuinely moved by what he told her. But she was not moved enough to tell him, in return, why she had called off her wedding in Kansas City.

Truth was, Gordon had been hoping that she would say, "Because David came back from Los Angeles and told me he thought you loved me." Or, "David told me your marriage couldn't last." Or, "Hearing about you made me realize that I couldn't marry a man I didn't love." But no, Alexandra didn't say any of those things.

By this time they had crossed the street and were walking back east, along the string of hotels facing the park. They were passing the Berkshire House when he asked her why she had called off the wedding and Alexandra stopped, there under the light, and looked at him. Her eyes were steady, but her face had flushed scarlet. Then she said, quietly, "I don't want to lie to you."

"I don't want you to lie to me either," he said.

"Then drop it, Gordie, please," she said, taking his hand and walking on.

And he let it drop, though when he made love to her that night it was on his mind, which perhaps had something to do with why he made love to her in the first place. Neither one of them was ready to get reinvolved; he knew it the moment after he came inside her when, instead of feeling close to her, he felt like slamming her up against the wall and demanding to know if she was happy that she had ruined his life by leaving him. But he didn't do that, and it was Alexandra on her own initiative who sat on the edge of the bed and cried, apologizing for what she said she didn't even know, but that she did know she couldn't do this, not with him, not now.

And so he let her go. Because he couldn't do it either, not with her, not yet.

But, with summer, Alexandra's popularity exploded in New York and Gordon would stare at her face on the side of buses in midtown traffic at lunchtime and wonder at how screwed up he must be to let her go so easily. And then he would be so filled with adrenalin and excitement he would think, *Who cares? Just go see her—now!* and he would dash over to WWKK, demanding to see her, and she always saw him, no matter how busy she was, and he would just sort of sit in the corner, watching her—in the newsroom, in the editing room—for five minutes or so. And then as he was leaving, Alexandra would smile, gently, as if to say, "I know. I need to know you still exist too."

And then, late at night, when she got home from the studio, they would talk on the phone just long enough for Gordon to make sure that she was not about to run away and marry someone else. Once that was ascertained, he felt okay again, and so he would climb into his bed with his model.

It all changed after Alexandra joined The Network. They were talking one night, as they had started doing as soon as she moved to Washington, and suddenly Alexandra had started to cry, saying that she thought she was going to die of loneliness, and that he was the last person she should drag back into her life but knew that that was what she was about to try and do. Gordon said she couldn't drag him back into her life unless he wanted to be dragged back in—what did she have in mind? She said she was so confused about everything that she didn't even know. He asked her how much the fact that she lived in Washington and he lived in New York had to do with it, the safety in knowing they couldn't be together full time anyway. She said she didn't know and then she broke down again, saying that she was the last person in the world he should get involved with, that if they tried to resurrect their relationship again it might only wreck everything between them.

But it didn't.

GORDON STRENN

He flew down to Washington and made love to her that very night. And as he did, she said, over and over again, "This is it. This is what I need—I need you, Gordon," and he was so very, very glad she said it, because that night he knew how much he needed her, too.

"All-Light-and-Love on five," Betty said over the intercom.

"*Prin*cess All-Light-and-Love to you," Gordon said. "One day and you're overly familiar already." Gordon pushed a button. "Hi."

"How does someone find Langley?" Alexandra asked him. There was a horrendous banging noise in the background and so she had to shout.

Gordon stood up, turned toward his window and shouted, "Did you try his office?"

"His secretary said he was on his way down half an hour ago."

"Where are you?" The banging noise on her end was getting louder.

"In what I hope's going to be the newsroom—if we can get any work done around here," she shouted. "Where the heck could he have disappeared to? If you can believe it, until we get an executive producer, there isn't anyone who can sign for anything except Langley."

"Sign for what?" Gordon shouted.

"Wire service machines. They won't hook them up until someone signs the authorization sheet."

"You can sign it," Gordon shouted.

"What?" she said. And then she laughed. "Oh, that's right—I can, can't I? But do I want to?" she added a second later. "Oh! Never mind, here comes Langley now. I'll talk to you later."

"Alexandra—"

"What?" she shouted. Now there was a sawing noise too.

"I'll go with you tonight," he shouted.

"To look at the apartment? Really?"

"Yep. And guess what else?"

"What?"

"I love you. Maybe even enough to stay at the Plaza."

There was a pause on the other end of the line and then a laugh. "You're not shouting this through the halls, are you?"

Gordon turned around. Sure enough, there was Betty, leaning

against the doorway, arms folded, and standing next to her was Jackson. Betty looked at Jackson and shrugged. "Must be talking to his mother," she said. "They're very close, you know."

"I see," Jackson said. And then he looked at Gordon and smiled. "Better tell your mama you're going to England, boy," he said. "And better tell her that you're leaving tonight."

4

Langley Peterson

Langley Peterson wondered if Gordon had any idea that it was because of his girlfriend, Alexandra, that he was being sent to England tonight. Probably not.

"And so," Langley concluded, learning forward on his desk to wrap up the briefing, "you tell Hargrave's people anything and everything you're going to need over there. I want you to take your secretary with you, because I'm going to want itemized notes on the meetings. So take Betty and then send her back to me with the notes no later than Friday afternoon."

Gordon nodded once.

"She's smart," Langley added, adjusting his glasses. "I think she should be doing more than teaching Adele how to bowl."

Gordon smiled, nodding again.

"So that's it. When you shake hands with the Brits, we're on our way," he finished.

"Sounds good," Gordon said.

It should sound good, Langley knew, because it was good. With the Writers Guild strike looking as though it might last through the summer, they had been trying to figure out a way to keep their schedule on *Love Across the Atlantic,* and moving the whole production out of the United States seemed to be the answer. And so, since almost half of the exteriors had been planned to be shot on location in England anyway, Jackson had called on his friend Lord Gregory Hargrave, and

Hargrave had extended an invitation to DBS to consolidate production on the miniseries at his studios in London.

The part Langley neglected to tell Gordon, however, was that Lord Hargrave was now a silent partner in the miniseries. So silent, in fact, that no one—*especially* the board of directors of Darenbrook Communications—knew about it. Because, if the board found out, then they would figure out that, after they had voted down Jackson's motion to double the budget of DBS News and launch it a year early in order to sign Alexandra, Jackson had *not* proceeded to fund it out of his own pocket as he said he would but had, in fact, "borrowed" the money from the miniseries—money that was now being made up by Lord Hargrave in the form of studio facilities, crews and accommodations.

Because, if the board found *that* out, then it would only be a matter of time before they also found out that the reason Jackson was not funding the first year of DBS News himself was because he had recently paid a bank consortium some sixty million dollars to make good on his brother Beau's stock market option losses in the October crash. And if the board found *that* out, then they would also find out that Beau had used *Field Day,* the Darenbrook magazine of which he was publisher, as illegal collateral on his margin accounts.

And if the board found *that* out, not only could they vote Beau off the board but they could send him to jail, particularly since company bylaws dictated that, in such a case, Beau's interest in Darenbrook Communications would then revert back to the company for nothing, and his voting stock would be divided among the remaining members of the board.

Sigh. It was never boring working for the Darenbrook family.

But Langley hated dealing this way with Gordon Strenn. Gordon was a very straightforward, diligent kind of guy and had upgraded the *Love Across the Atlantic* project from an A rating to AAA by, among other things, his coup of signing Vanessa Winslow in the lead. He deserved to know the score. But Langley knew he wouldn't and shouldn't tell Gordon anything because, if something were to go wrong and the board caught on, then Gordon would be best left out of it. Some of the Darenbrooks could be pretty nasty.

Although each board member had an equal financial interest in the company, they did not share equal voting stock. Big El, who controlled twenty-five percent of it, would, thankfully, almost always vote to reinvest a percentage of the profits back into the company for research and development, though he was apt to disagree with Jackson on how to divide it among divisions. He was, for example, the one to put the brakes on DBS News, refusing to allocate any more funds to broadcasting or to alter the financial timetable already agreed upon.

Cordelia, who ran the Mendolyn Street house in Hilleanderville where her father still lived, usually cast her eight and a quarter voting shares the same way Big El did. (Or Big El cast his vote in the same way Cordelia did, nobody was quite sure anymore.)

Little El and the twins, Norbert and Noreen—who held eight and a quarter shares each—voted for anything that put cash in their pockets and voted to sell anything that didn't.

The two remaining members of the board, Beau and Belinda, represented Jackson's power base. As the three flesh and blood children of Alice May Darenbrook, each had inherited a third of Alice May's voting shares, boosting their holdings past that of their half siblings to twelve percent. Jackson also enjoyed an extra five percent as chairman. And so, with seventeen percent of his own holdings and the twenty-four percent of ever loyal Beau's and Belinda's, Jackson had forty-one percent of the vote at his disposal.

However, these days, Beau and Belinda constantly ran the risk of being voted off the board, Beau with his gambling and Belinda with her . . .

Belinda. The beautiful, fair-haired Darenbrook baby, now thirty-seven, whose increasing episodes of insane behavior had the twins and Little El cheering her on to flip out completely. Because, if their baby sister could be proved incapable of managing her own affairs, then company bylaws dictated that Belinda's voting shares had to revert back to the board for redistribution.

And so one could say there was a delicate balance of power within Darenbrook Communications.

Since Langley was always the president of whatever new company they launched until it got on its feet, he was quite accustomed to playing "funny money" within the corporation with Jackson to properly finance projects that had been underfunded by the board. However, launching DBS News a year early with money rerouted from the miniseries—well, this made him very nervous. Although next year they would have the board-approved funds for DBS News to rechannel through the miniseries to repay Lord Hargrave, even if DBS News achieved all of its goals, since Jackson had already doubled the News budget, they'd still have the second half of the first-year DBS News costs to somehow make up.

Sitting here, in his office, Langley decided that he should absolutely keep Gordon Strenn clear of this mess.

Langley's intercom buzzed then, startling him. "Excuse me," he said to Gordon, picking up the phone. "Yes?"

"A Jim Malbern calling from Group K Productions in Tucson," Adele said. "He says it's very important."

"I'll take it," Langley said, pushing a button. "Hello, Jim, what can I do for you?"

"You can send Jessica back here, that's what you can do," he said.

Jim Malbern was evidently referring to Jessica Wright, the young talk show hostess whose contract they had recently bought out from Group K Productions for DBS.

"I don't have her to send," Langley said. "She isn't expected until April 1."

Pause and then, "She isn't there?"

"Adele," Langley called. She appeared at the door. "Have we seen or heard from Jessica Wright?"

She shook her head. "No."

"No," Langley said into the phone.

"Oh," Malbern said. "Sorry for yelling—bye."

Click.

Blinking rapidly, Langley hung up the phone.

"The Terror of Tucson," Gordon said, citing Jessica Wright's nickname as stated on a recent DBS press release.

"The hints grow stronger, yes," Langley murmured, standing up. He checked his watch. "You better get going."

"Right," Gordon said, jumping up.

Langley came around his desk and, putting a hand on Gordon's shoulder, walked him to the door. "You have a child overseas, don't you?" he asked.

Gordon laughed. "I didn't find him in a magazine ad."

"Pardon?"

"Never mind," Gordon said, stopping at the door and turning around. "But, yes—I have a son," he added, nodding. "Christopher. He lives in Paris. With his mother."

"So you'll be able to see more of him this year," Langley said.

"Plan to," Gordon said, smiling. Then he gave Langley the thumbs-up sign. "I'll call you tomorrow."

"Great," Langley said.

When Gordon turned the corner, Langley sighed slightly, dug his hands into his pockets and leaned against the doorway. He couldn't help wondering what Gordon would think if he knew the extraordinary lengths to which Jackson had gone to bring Alexandra to DBS. He wondered, too, if Gordon would notice that what Jackson had opted for as the best solution to the writers' strike was the one that put the most miles between Gordon and Alexandra, and for the longest period of time.

In the beginning, months before Alexandra had been shot, Langley had been all for hiring her and moving DBS News up a year. He approved of Jackson's committing DBS to a crash schedule of preparations on the strength of a handshake, and he enthusiastically began negotiations with Alexandra's agent, John Mohrbacher. Although Alexandra was so young and, at this point, still but a mere reporter (who had trouble getting on the air at that), the outside consultants Langley had employed had come back to him with audience reaction scores to Alexandra that were, they said, truly remarkable.

Furthermore, aside from the jealousies that came with the profession, Alexandra's reputation among her colleagues was excellent. The consensus was that she was fiercely bright, fast, reliable and fair. She was known as an extremely hard worker and an excellent writer. In fact the only real criticism they heard about her was that sometimes she operated out of a sense of entitlement so strong that employees who didn't even work in her department were often found to be working on something for her. And happily so. To Jackson and Langley, this drawback in a reporter sounded like a terrific plus in an anchor.

Mohrbacher told Langley that Alexandra had turned down five hundred and fifty thousand a year as a local anchor for WWKK to join The Network as a correspondent for two hundred thousand. The credential and national exposure had been worth it to her, Mohrbacher explained, but he wanted Langley to keep in mind that she could command six-fifty, easy, if she went back into major-market local news.

They came to a preliminary agreement that Alexandra's salary would be five hundred thousand the first year, escalating to a million in three, plus bonuses tied to gross revenues for DBS News. Fine. But then they got into the extent of Alexandra's power within DBS News and the pleasant road of negotiation took a turn down what Langley later saw as Nightmare Alley. Mohrbacher made the most extraordinary demands—"She needs approval over the executive in charge of the news division"—and Langley said forget it and then Mohrbacher said, okay, forget it, and then Jackson started yelling that he wanted the contract settled and so then Mohrbacher started in again on Alexandra's demands and Langley stood his ground . . .

When by December they had not even reached a tentative agreement on the issues Mohrbacher claimed Alexandra would never back down on, Jackson flew down to Washington to straighten it out with her himself. And by the time he returned to West End, Langley had been near apoplexy.

"Now what's the matter?" Jackson had said, looking through his mail. "We wanted it settled. It's settled."

Langley was so angry, for a moment he couldn't speak. He took off his glasses, wiped his forehead with his shirt sleeve and put his glasses back on. "That girl does not have a good effect on you," he finally managed to say.

"Alexandra's a pleasure to deal with," Jackson said. "She's a professional."

"I'll say," Langley said.

Jackson looked up from his mail.

"Yesterday her salary was five hundred thousand," Langley said, "today it's over a million." He tossed a sheaf of papers on Jackson's desk.

Jackson frowned. "What's that?"

"Mohrbacher faxed them to me," Langley said. "They're what he claims are her notes from your meeting." He paused to collect himself, but his voice started to climb anyway. "They're the thirty-eight contract clause revisions she says you approved."

"Well, Alexandra is a complicated kind of gal," Jackson said diplomatically.

"You're handing a thirty-year-old nobody the news division!" Langley cried, slamming his hands down on Jackson's desk. "Hire and fire approvals, co-copyright ownership on specials—and then there's this lunacy about her own syndication arm overseas—"

"I want her to be happy here," Jackson said. "If it doesn't work for her, it's not going to work for us."

"Happy? Happy!" Langley fell backward into a chair, holding his head in hands. "We're ruined, we're ruined before we even start," he moaned.

Jackson reached down next to his chair and came up with a tin of Cheddar cheese popcorn. "You worry too much," he said, prying off the lid. "No faith—no faith at all, Lang, that's your problem."

Langley dropped his hands and stared at him for a long moment. And then he said, quietly, "She's miserable at The Network, everybody knows that. She doesn't want local news—she wants us, Jack. We can make her, no one else will and she knows it. All we have to do is wait and she'll back down." He sat forward in his chair. "Listen to me, Jack. There's no *reason* to give Alexandra Waring all this. None."

Jackson, chewing, looked at him. "No reason," he had finally said, swallowing, "except that I said I'd give it to her." Pause. "So give it to her."

Langley walked across his office to reach the connecting door to Jackson's office. They had had side-by-side offices for seventeen years, first in Richmond and now here at West End. They were on the second floor of Darenbrook I, looking straight out over the square, west, toward the river. It was dark outside now and, below, the old-fashioned lamps were on, casting a gentle light over the square. The waters of the Hudson were black, beautiful, reflecting the lights of New Jersey from across the way.

Langley knocked on the door. No answer. He knocked again and stuck his head in. "Sorry, Mr. Peterson," Claire said. She was one of

Jackson's three assistants and was poking her head around the door leading to the outer office. "He's left for the day."

Langley looked at his watch. It was only five-fifty. When he was in town, Jack usually hung around as long as he did, until seven-thirty or so. "Where'd he go?"

"Do you know where he went?" Claire asked someone in the room behind her. Mumble, mumble. She turned back to Langley. "Randy says he thinks he went apartment hunting with Ms. Waring."

"Thanks," Langley said, closing the door. He turned around and jammed his hands into his pockets, jingling change, thinking. And then he said, "Adele!"

She appeared at the door. Adele had been his secretary for twenty years and Langley had yet to determine how old she was. She might have been sixty, but then, with her energy and dexterity, she might have been fifty and prematurely gray. Or maybe she was seventy— who knew? When the issue came up in personnel several years ago, Jackson declared that the statute of limitations had run out—if Adele had gone fifteen years without telling Darenbrook Communications how old she was, then she never had to.

"Adele," Langley said, "I want you to get Cassy Cochran on the phone. Use every number we have for her, but find her, please. It's extremely important."

Cassy Cochran. The one major source of agreement between himself and Alexandra Waring—that they absolutely had to hire her away from WST to run DBS News. As the general manager credited for making WST the number one independent television station in America, no one had the clout with the indie—independent station—managers across the country that she did. And guess who desperately needed someone to recruit affiliate newsrooms? As one who had come up through the producing ranks of the newsroom, no one had more sympathies with the needs and temperaments of that group than she whom they called Mother Confessor. And guess who desperately needed a mother confessor for the news group? And as the executive responsible for budgets that both the station and its management could live with, few had ever been so well respected by both sides. And guess who desperately needed an executive who understood how to make a news operation compatible with the bottom line?

Alexandra was convinced they could get her. According to her, Cassy had been bored in her job for years, longed to be near the newsroom again and for the first time in years was in a position to risk a move.

Langley had been talking with Cassy for weeks now, at first stunned and then delighted as he realized that he liked and admired her as much as Alexandra did. But Cassy was taking a very long time with all this and didn't seem much closer to taking the job or turning it down than she had been weeks ago.

"Zero in on her age," had been Alexandra's latest suggestion. "Tell her—" She had paused, thinking for a minute. Then she had slowly leaned forward, a smile starting to emerge. "Tell her," she said, "that forty-three is the perfect age to revolutionize television."

Then they had both laughed (because Langley was forty-three too), and then they had both frowned—looking at each other—as if they were sharing the same thought: that there was no way in hell the two of them were going to revolutionize anything until they got Cassy or someone to act as a go-between for them. Langley didn't know anything about TV news; Alexandra didn't know anything about business at Darenbrook Communications; they didn't know how the hell to deal with each other.

Adele located Cassy Cochran on her first try. She was in her office down the street at WST. "Mrs. Cochran on 1!" Adele called.

Langley walked over to his desk and snatched up the phone. "Cassy," he said.

"Langley," she said, not missing a beat.

"This is what is called a pressure tactic," he said.

"I see," she said.

"Are you coming with us, yes or no?"

She laughed.

He smiled. He imagined exactly how she looked as she laughed. Cassy Cochran was an extraordinarily beautiful woman. It had come as somewhat of a shock to him when he first met her; he had never known a woman like her to make a career off camera. ("She was always frightened by what happened to women who traded on their looks, I think," Alexandra had said.)

"Listen, Langley," Cassy said, "you're the one who's been hiding Jackson Darenbrook from me—yes or no?"

He hesitated and then thought, *What the hell.* "Yes. Alexandra and I thought he might be a little—unconventional for your tastes." And then he quickly added, "But now we want you to meet with him. Look, Cassy," he said, raising one leg to sit on the edge of his desk, "truth is, if you don't come to DBS, I'm going to have to drown Alexandra. She signed for a million dollars' worth of equipment today and hired fourteen people who I haven't the slightest idea what they do."

She laughed, softly. "I know. She told me."

"She did?" Langley said.

"I think her strategy is to make me do the job whether I take it or not," Cassy said.

"Wait a minute," Langley said, standing up. "Do you mean to tell me that you actually know something about these fourteen people?"

"I suggested nine of them," Cassy said.

Someone was tapping Langley on the shoulder. He turned; it was Adele.

"I'm sorry," she whispered, pointing to the blinking light on the phone. "But it's about Mrs. Peterson—"

Langley's stomach turned over. He recognized Adele's expression. Something had happened again. Something bad.

"Cassy," he said, "excuse me. Hold on and Adele will set up a time to meet with Jackson. I'm sorry, but I've got to go—I'll talk to you tomorrow." He pressed Hold. "Set up a meeting for Mrs. Cochran with Jack. See if you can do it for tomorrow."

Adele retreated from the office and, after looking back at him once more, closed the door behind her.

Langley sighed, held the bridge of his nose for a second and then pushed the button down on the line. "This is Langley Peterson," he said.

"Mr. Peterson, my name's Robbie Jones and I work in the building of a friend of your wife's, Mrs. Bell."

"Yes," Langley said, swallowing.

"Well, sir," he said, "the Bells are away and um, well, your wife told me to call you—"

"Where is she? Is my wife there?" Langley said.

"She's in a room off the lobby—um, the doorman is with her—"

"Where's the chauffeur?" Langley said. "Isn't the chauffeur with her?"

"No, Mr. Peterson. There didn't seem to be anyone with your wife when she, um, arrived. And she's kind of worked up, excited—you know." He took a breath. "We didn't think she should be on the streets —alone, I mean—and, um, she gave us your number."

"You did the right thing," Langley said quickly. "Where are you?"

"Nine eighty-six Fifth."

"I'll be right there. Tell her I'll be right there. And—and thanks," he said. He hung up the phone and sat there a moment. And then he called, "Adele!" He grabbed his briefcase and started stuffing papers into it. When Adele's head popped in, he said, "Tell them to bring my car around—and fast." He finished packing stuff in, closed the brief-case, slipped on his jacket and walked quickly out of his office.

He had to hurry. His wife was in trouble.

His wife, Belinda Darenbrook Peterson.

5

Cassy Cochran

"You're supposed to feel frightened," Cassy Cochran's therapist said. "That's how human beings feel when they consider changing jobs after fifteen years."

"But I don't know why," Cassy said. "It's not as if it were some kind of fly-by-night outfit. And this is what I've wanted—for *years* I've wanted to do something in news again." She paused, staring down at the carpet for a moment, and then raised her eyes. "And I honestly think it can work—that *I* can make it work. Michael thinks so too—he thinks I'm crazy for hemming and hawing like this."

"But Michael doesn't know everything that is involved," the thera-pist said quietly. "And Michael has always had you to fall back on— he's always been able to depend on you at your job at WST. And right now it doesn't seem wise for you to depend . . ." The therapist waved her hand, indicating that she need not remind Cassy of the uncertainty in that area of her life.

"If I take this job, I couldn't depend on anything. I mean, my contract, but . . ." Cassy said quietly. "Well, no, that's not true," she reconsidered. "Actually, it all comes down to Alexandra, doesn't it?" She paused, looking to the window, biting her lower lip slightly, thinking. "I find it so strange that the thought of working with her only gives me the most incredible sense of relief." She looked at the doctor. "It makes me feel as though I have somewhere to go. Somewhere other than where I feel like I've been stuck for so long." She pressed her forehead with one hand, closing her eyes. "I so hate feeling as though everyone is moving ahead in their life but me. I hate that feeling of being stuck, of being left behind." She lowered her hand and opened her eyes. "Poor old Cassy," she said with a sigh, "that's what I hear in my head every time one of these bright young things comes and goes at ST."

"But it's not true," the therapist said. "And you know that, don't you?" She paused and then asked, "How do you think Alexandra views you?" She smiled. "Is hers a mission of mercy, do you suppose, to rescue you from being stuck?"

"She's certainly not going to last long in this business if it is," Cassy said, laughing. She shook her head and recrossed her legs, smiling still. "No, I see what you're getting at. No, I don't think she thinks of me as being stuck." Her smile expanded. "At the moment she thinks I'm willfully withholding a valuable contribution to her career."

The doctor nodded. "Not once, not once in all these weeks have you said anything about being scared you can't do the job."

Cassy shrugged. "That's not one of my fears."

The doctor smiled.

Cassy checked her watch. "I better get going." She got up. "I really appreciate your making time to see me this morning."

"I think it's wonderful, Cassy," the doctor said, standing up and walking her to the door. "Whatever you decide to do—I think it's wonderful that you're willing to contemplate making a change."

"I guess," she said.

"Good luck," the doctor said.

"Thanks. I'll let you know what happens." Cassy closed the office door behind her, walked through the waiting room and out to the lobby. When her son Henry was still in private school in the city, Cassy used to come to this very same posh East 74th Street building for board meetings at the apartment of the longtime school board president, Beatrice Barenberg. Every time Cassy came and went to her therapist's office, she'd wonder if today was the day she'd run into Beatrice. ("Oh, my dear," she imagined Beatrice saying, "simply marvelous idea, getting your head examined. Should have done it years ago.")

Cassy walked over to Madison Avenue and looked for a cab.

After seeing a therapist for eighteen months, she couldn't help wondering what her life might have been like had she gone sooner. After years and years of feeling so terribly alone with her problems with Michael, the difference that being able to talk to another person about them made—honestly, for a change—was quite incredible to Cassy. It was as if the walls of a prison had fallen, one by one, until there were only horizons of choice—which at times actually seemed more terrifying to Cassy than the days she had been so used to, the days when she had felt as though she had no choice at all.

The most painful part of the process so far had been the awareness that the problems in her marriage were not all Michael's. In fact, more and more Cassy saw that whatever had been "wrong" with Michael— his drinking, his flagrant infidelity—there had been something "wrong" in her that responded to what was wrong in him—denial of how bad his drinking was, denial of his affairs, her inability to leave the marriage—that had enabled the horrendous situation to continue for years.

Well, Michael had not had a drink in a year and half, and his infidelity was no longer flagrant—he only had one girlfriend, out on the West Coast. And while Cassy had faced up to the girlfriend's existence over a year ago, she still couldn't bring herself to end the marriage. After twenty-two years—ten of which had been an absolute nightmare— now that Michael was healthier than he had ever been in his life, *now* she was supposed to give up on them? After all the time she had put in? After throwing away her thirties, she should start over again at forty-three?

Oh, they had had their moments, of course. Like the day Henry had been accepted at Yale, where Henry had been dying to go but where they had worried he would not get in. But Henry had been accepted and had run off with his girlfriend to celebrate, leaving his parents home alone, smiling at each other, marveling over the fact that they— despite all their problems—had produced this wonderful young man who Yale thought was pretty wonderful too. Yale University. Henry. Their baby. And that night the two of them had dragged out home movies they had not looked at in at least ten years and set up the old screen in the living room and sat on the couch, roaring with laughter, watching themselves with baby Henry in Chicago. Oh, remember? The skating rink? Remember those little double runners? And look at you! And there's Joe from the newsroom, remember him? Oh, and what's-her-name. And there's—

That night was one of the few times it had worked sexually between them.

But that was almost a year ago, she thought, flagging down a cab. *Of course he has to have a girlfriend—who can have sex five times a year?* The cab pulled over to the side and, as Cassy opened the door, she noticed a man in a suit standing behind her, smiling. Apparently he had been trying to get a cab too. He held the door for her as she got in. *If you only knew,* she thought, *I'd have sex with you in a second before I'd sleep with my husband these days.* "Thank you," she said.

"My pleasure," he said with a slight bow, closing the door.

Maybe you do know, she thought, giving the man a brief parting smile. "West End Avenue and 67th Street, please," she told the driver. "It's that new complex—"

"West End," the driver said. "It's called West End."

"Right," Cassy said.

They turned west and headed into Central Park.

The driver looked at Cassy in the rear-view mirror. "They're not gonna let us through the gate unless they know who you are, ya know."

Cassy smiled. "You mean to tell me you don't know who I am?"

The driver frowned, glancing furiously back and forth between the road and the mirror. "You a game show hostess or something?" he finally said. "I mean, did ya used to be?"

Ooo-ouch. I asked for that one, she thought, wincing. "No," she said.

"I was just pulling your leg." She took a breath and let it out slowly, looking at the trees, wishing that she could see buds on them. But no, it was still winter. "Actually, I'm going on a job interview."

"Huh," the driver said. Into the rear-view mirror, "Whaddaya do?"

"I'm in television," she said.

"But not game shows," the driver said.

"Right," Cassy said.

"So what kinda TV?"

She hesitated and then thought, *Why not? See how it feels after all these years.* "News. I'm in television news."

"Oh, yeah?" the driver said. "I shoulda known. That was the next thing I was gonna ask ya—what city you're from. Ya like being an anchorwoman?" he asked, looking in the rearview mirror.

She smiled, broadly. "No, I'm on the production side. Off camera."

"Huh," the driver said. "Maybe you oughta look into being an anchorwoman. You look the part. That Alexandra Waring's doin' all right for herself. She's at West End, ya know."

"So I've heard," Cassy said.

"Yeah, well, I had her in the cab once—back when she was workin' at, uh . . ."

"WWKK," Cassy said.

"Yeah. She used to do the news there. So I picked her up once, it was like five in the morning and she was goin' to work." He frowned, shaking his head. "She had newspapers all over the back of the cab—I mean, like I said to her, 'So what are you doin' back there? Wrapping fish or somethin'?' "

Cassy laughed. "And so what did she say?"

"So she said she was readin' the papers. And I said, 'You hafta read six papers at the same time?' And she sorta laughed—and then she put 'em all away and talked to me. She was real nice. I liked her and so I started watchin' her. She grew up on a farm, ya know. She's not a New Yorker or nothin'. So where are you from?"

"Iowa, originally."

"Man, ain't nobody round here who's from New York anymore, ya know? Closest we get to a New Yorker these days is Yoko Ono. She lives over there, ya know," he said as they came out of Central Park.

They continued across town to West End Avenue and turned south. As they neared 67th Street, the driver put on his signal.

The entrance to West End wasn't very impressive. In fact it was extraordinarily plain. There was one lane going in and one lane coming out, and a large, square concrete guardhouse in the middle. Lowered across each lane was an orange and white striped gate. There wasn't even a sign to indicate what this Checkpoint Charlie was for—which, Cassy thought a second later, for security reasons, was probably just as well.

"So what's your name?" the driver said. "I'll announce you with style, whaddaya say?" She told him and he rolled down his window to talk to the guard. "Catherine Cochran is expected," he said, winking to Cassy in the mirror.

"Oh, Mrs. Cochran?" the guard said immediately, bending to look in through the cabby's window.

"Yes?" she said.

"They want you to come in downstairs." To the cab driver, he pointed, "Follow the driveway, and when you get just past the apartment building, on your right will be a ramp. Turn down that ramp and it will take you down around to the back entrance of the studio. I'll call ahead and there'll be someone there to meet you."

"Thank you," Cassy said.

"Sounds like they want somethin' from ya pretty bad," the driver said, driving on after the gate rose. "The last fare I took here hadda walk in."

They drove along, rising higher and higher, turned sharply to the right behind an enormous apartment building, and then right there was the ramp the guard had told them about. They turned onto it and snaked around, easing downward, and then straightened out underneath the upper driveway, leading them into a large carport.

A security guard waved them on to what appeared to be the entrance. When the cab stopped, another guard was right there to open Cassy's door. "Mrs. Cochran," he said, standing there.

"Yes—hello," she said. "Let me just pay for the cab." She fumbled in her purse, found a ten. She handed it over the seat to the driver and was about to say, "Take seven-fifty out of that," but then drew her hand back, saying, "Thanks for the nice ride. It's just what I needed."

"Thanks," the cabby said. He turned around to get a better look at her. "Just remember, they want somethin' bad from ya, so play it cagey —that's my advice."

"Thanks," she said, getting out.

The double glass doors leading into the building slid open and a young man, thirty-two or so, with curly brown hair came dashing out. He was in blue jeans and a tweed jacket. "Cassy?" he asked, holding out his hand. "Hi, remember me? I'm Will Rafferty, Alexandra's field producer."

"Of course I do, Will, how are you?" Cassy said, shaking his hand. "And you're not her field producer anymore. You're the affiliates producer for the DBS television network."

"Yeah, right, that's what they tell me," he said. "I've only been here an hour and so I'm not used to my new exalted status. So anyway," he continued, with a little shake of his head, "I'm supposed to take you up to Darenbrook's office—" He looked over his shoulder. "Only I'm not sure I know where it is." He looked back at Cassy. "The real reason I'm here is that Alexandra told me to ask you who would be the better affiliate in New Orleans, KRQ or KLV? We have to make up our minds today and she wants your opinion."

Cassy laughed to herself, shaking her head. "I'd take KLV," she said, turning as the doors opened again behind Will.

"Cassy, hello," Langley Peterson said, walking out.

Cassy's cab driver honked twice and they all looked. He was waving bye-bye. Cassy gave him a wave back and he pulled away. When Cassy turned back to Langley, Alexandra was now coming out the doors.

"Hi!" Alexandra said, rushing past Langley to give Cassy a one-armed hug, carefully executed around her sling. "Hi," she said again, backing away a step, holding Cassy's elbow in her free hand. "I can't believe you're here," she added, eyes sparkling. She took Cassy's hand and turned to Langley and Will. "Doesn't it seem like she's always been working with us? Doesn't she just *belong* here?"

They heard the screech of tires and everyone looked to see that Cassy's cab had done a U-turn and was now coming back toward them. The guard leaped in front of Alexandra, spreading his arms out. "Watch it, watch it, Miss Waring!" he said, pushing her back.

But the driver was just excited. He stopped the cab, jumped out and over the roof of the cab yelled, "Hey, Alexandra!" He looked at Cassy. "Tell her I gave her a ride." To the guard, "She knows me," he said, pointing to Cassy. "I just wanted to say hi to Alexandra."

Leave it to Alexandra to actually remember the driver after two years. She went over and signed an autograph for him while he told her about their previous encounter. After she handed him the autograph, she shook his hand and said, "So how's your son's knee? Didn't you tell me that he was going to have to have surgery after football season was over?"

The cab driver's face could have lit up Times Square. He gave the guard a triumphant look and announced, "My son's knee is fine. The surgery was a complete success. He's playin' ball now for the University of Bridgeport."

By this time someone else had joined them outside, a black man about forty-five whom Will introduced to Cassy as Hex Hamilton.

"My mother was a witch," Hex explained in a deep, rolling West Indian accent. Judging from the way he was smiling, she had no idea whether or not he was serious. He turned to Langley. "Am I allowed to ask Cassy how many editing bays she thinks we need?" He turned back to Cassy. "Alexandra and I know we need at least six, but we are, as they say, suffering temporary technical difficulties with the management."

Langley cleared his throat and stuck his hand into his pants pocket. "The management is suffering, period," he told Cassy.

"She even *looks* like she runs the place," Alexandra announced, walking back over. She gestured to Cassy with her free hand. "Look at that pose, Hex—I think we ought to work a shot of Cassy into the open montage for 'News America Tonight.' "

"Maybe she should anchor 'News America Tonight,' " Langley suggested under his breath.

The doors opened yet again and out came a very young woman, no more than about twenty-three, who actually looked a little like a washed-out version of Alexandra. "Oh, hi," she said, "here you are."

"This is Kate Benedict, my assistant," Alexandra said. "Kate, this is Cassy Cochran."

"Thank God," Kate exclaimed, shaking Cassy's hand in a very businesslike manner. "Can you sign Alexandra's expense account stuff?"

she asked, holding up papers in her other hand. Then she noticed Langley. "Oops," she said, shrinking.

"Don't let me stop you," Langley said. "Charge it to WST."

"That's what he says about everything," Kate told Cassy. "Alexandra won't sign anything either. I really think you better work here."

"And how," Hex said.

"Seconded," Will said. "All those in favor of Cassy—"

"Wait a minute, wait a minute!" Cassy said, holding up her hands and backing away slightly. "This isn't fair, you guys—"

The doors slid open again and a figure very familiar to Cassy emerged. It was tall, lanky Kyle McFarland, the same Kyle McFarland who had been a news intern with her at WST back in 1973, the same Kyle McFarland who had been producing a network morning show, the same Kyle McFarland she had urged Alexandra to try and get as senior producer of "DBS News America Tonight." And here he was.

"Hi, Cass," Kyle said, simply giving her a little wave and dropping his hand, as though they hadn't missed a day of work together in fifteen years.

Cassy suddenly had the strongest urge to cry. There was something about what was happening that was making her feel terribly happy.

"Come on," Langley then said quietly, touching her arm. "I'll take you up to Jackson's. We won't hound you anymore."

"No, we won't," Alexandra promised.

Hex started to laugh and Kate shhhed him.

Langley led Cassy inside, the group trailing behind them, whispering and elbowing each other like unruly schoolchildren. "Ignore them," was Langley's advice as they walked through a reception area.

The receptionist looked up from whatever she was doing and smiled. "Hi, Mrs. Cochran," she said.

Cassy did a double take and the group behind her started to laugh. She looked at Langley.

"This way," Langley said, "we'll just swing through the studio on the way."

"Excuse me," an electrician said, trying to get by them with a large coil of wire. His eyes skipped over Cassy and then came back again. "Oh, hi, Mrs. Cochran," he said.

"Uh, hi," Cassy said, turning to look at Langley.

"Don't look at me," he said, "I'm not that manipulative," prompting the crew behind them to start laughing again. As Cassy looked back at Alexandra, he took her arm. "This way."

They wound around the corridors and then walked through Studio B, tremendous Studio A, through the newsroom, through Engineering A, Engineering B, the satellite room, and then back into the corridors, walking past editing, audio, graphics, film, winding back around to end up at the elevators. And every single person they came in contact with —from the head of technology, Dr. Kessler, to the carpet layers—took one look at Cassy, smiled and said, "Hi, Mrs. Cochran."

Langley and Cassy left Alexandra, Kate, Hex, Kyle and Will on Sub Level 2 and took the elevator up to the second floor of Darenbrook I. Langley pointed out his office as they passed by it and then they turned into the outer reception area of Jackson Darenbrook's office. His three assistants—Ethel, a black woman of about fifty; Randy, a balding man of about thirty; and Claire, a redhead of about twenty-five —were on their feet in a minute, all hailing, "Hello, Mrs. Cochran!"

"Please go right on in," Ethel said in a wonderful Southern drawl, showing them the door. "Mr. Darenbrook has so been looking forward to meeting you."

"Here she is, Jack," Langley announced, holding the door open for Cassy.

Jackson Darenbrook stood up behind his desk. He was a big man, nice-looking, Cassy thought. He reminded her a little of Michael, except where Michael's hair was so dark Jackson's was brown with a great deal of gray running through it, and where Michael was handsome, Jackson Darenbrook was only, well, pleasant-looking. He had wonderful blue eyes, though.

He was staring at her, his head cocked to the side. Then he looked down at his desk, back up at her, down at his desk again and picked up something that turned out to be—when he held it up for her to see— an 8 × 10 glossy of Cassy someone had blown up from her WST PR photo. "Which one of you has been retouched?" he asked her.

"Jack!" Langley said.

"Jaaack," Jackson mimicked, coming around his desk. "That was a compliment, jerk head. I meant that Alexandra's right." He held his hand out to Cassy. "She said Mrs. Cochran was even more beautiful in real life than she is in that photograph."

"Thank you," she said, shaking his hand. His handshake was dry, firm, nice.

"Go away, Lang," Jackson said, still looking at Cassy.

"Wait, Jack," Langley said, "I want a word with you."

Jackson gestured to his office. "Please make yourself at home. I'll be back in a moment." He stepped outside with Langley.

Cassy turned around. The office was enormous. One part of it was a work area, with a tremendous leather-topped oak desk, a couple of chairs, and over along one wall two computer terminals, a drafting table, and an elongated table with stacks of newspapers on it. Across the room was what looked almost like a den, with an oriental rug thrown over the wall-to-wall carpeting, easy chairs, a coffee table, magazine racks, a bar, and a large TV screen built into the wall. In the corner there was a huge oak wardrobe. There were also several trees here and back in the work area, accentuating how high the ceilings were.

And then, in front of the solid glass wall to Cassy's right, there was a cluster of two small sofas and two chairs around a low, round glass table. Cassy headed to this area and sat down in one of the chairs, facing the glass wall. It felt as though she were sitting in the front row of a wonderful movie about the Hudson River and the magnificent skies of west Manhattan. Her next thought was how desperately she needed to get out of the city if she thought the view was so pretty that it looked fake to her.

Jackson Darenbrook came back in and closed the door. "Langley told me not to make a big deal about how beautiful you are," he cheerfully reported, walking over. "I told him, 'No problem. Alexandra says she's very brainy and very controlling and so we'll talk about her brains and controlling nature.'" He sat down heavily on one of the sofas and smoothed his tie.

After people's descriptions of him, Cassy was surprised at how conservatively Jackson was dressed. Langley had described him as sort of an overeager Little Leaguer; Michael had said he was kind of a whacked-out Tom Sawyer; and Alexandra had said that he was prone to swaggering, as if he had watched too many Errol Flynn swashbuckling movies as a boy. But this man in the gray pin-striped suit—to Cassy, at any rate—seemed more like a jovial banker.

He smiled at her. "I will be in such trouble with Alexandra and Lang if I mess this up."

"I don't think you will," Cassy said. "But I'd play down the part about my controlling nature." She laughed. "Though it's quite true, I must admit."

"Great," Jackson said, slapping his thighs, "that's what we need. So, let's get right to it. Do you have any kids?"

"One, a son," she said. "He's eighteen."

"Oh," Jackson said, "then he's a little old for day care. Though," he reconsidered, "my daughter, Lydia, she's nineteen and definitely needs a baby-sitter. She just cracked up some lifeguard's Corvette in Fort Lauderdale yesterday." He sighed. "She's supposed to be at school." He waved his hand in the air as if to clear it. "Anyway, that's always my first pitch, day care. It gives people a good idea where our head's at in terms of employees—that we care about their overall well-being, and that we consider ourselves extended family here."

"That's very impressive," Cassy said.

"Hmmm," he agreed, dropping his eyes to the table. "My mother started the program during World War II. Anyway, I'll, uh—" He raised his eyes again. "I'll take you down later. It's right below us, the day-care center. It's a nice place to visit when things are grown-up and horrible around here, if you know what I mean."

She laughed. "I know exactly what you mean."

"Um," he said, "what else? We have a company restaurant. It's more like a cafeteria, but you can go any time between eight and four and get a bite to eat, see employees from other parts of the company. The food's real good, if I say so myself. It's right through there," he said, pointing to a door on the far side of his office.

Cassy looked at him.

"I get restless," he said, shrugging. "And I like to see the people who work for us."

"That's great," she said.

"When you guys get on the air, we're gonna do something about getting in there for something to eat late at night," he continued. "Alexandra wanted a kitchen downstairs, but the fire marshals say we can't do it. I'm getting you a couple refrigerators for your offices and the newsroom, though. What's the matter?" he asked her.

"Oh, nothing," she said, smiling. "I think it's great how thoughtful you are." Her actual thought was, *The chairman of Darenbrook Communications has nothing better to do than buy refrigerators?*

"Look, let's just get to it," he said, leaning forward to rest his elbows on his thighs and clasp his hands. "We really, really, really want you to join us here at DBS. Alexandra's crazy about you, that new guy—Kyle —he wants you and, more importantly, Langley wants you. So let me ask you, has Langley made an offer that you could see fit to accept?"

"Yes," she said.

He cinched up one side of his mouth and sat back against the sofa to look at her. "Creeping crickets, you sure don't say much, do you?"

She smiled. "Not while I'm trying to figure out what I'm really getting myself into."

His eyes traveled down to her mouth briefly and then, eyes darting away, he sat forward again, rubbing his eyes for a moment. He dropped his hands and looked at her. "Are we going to be able to talk to each other—honestly, I mean?"

"If you're honest with me, I'll certainly do my best to be honest with you," she said.

His eyebrows went up. "Whatever happened to that good old-fashioned 'yes' you were using a while back?"

"Okay—yes," she said.

He laughed. "Okay," he said, clapping his hands together, "let's see if it works. So tell me, Mrs. Cochran, what's the scoop on Alexandra and Strenn? Do you think they'll get married or what?"

"Yes," she said.

"Oh, you've gotta be kidding," he said, waving her away as if she herself was nonsense. "Forget the 'yes'—let's go back to where, if I'm honest, then you'll be—"

"Then why don't you ask Alexandra?" she asked him.

"We gave her a contract clause that says she can marry a DBS employee if she wants," Jackson said, ignoring Cassy's question. "We don't allow it in the same company division, normally. I let her have it so we could get her—but she's not really gonna marry that guy, is she? I mean, he's an all-right guy and everything—but, like my daddy says, a stick in the mud is a fine thing if you're on a raft, but if you're not on a raft who needs one?"

Cassy looked at him. "Are we still being honest?"

"Please, ma'am," he said, raising one knee up to hold in hands, "I'd appreciate it."

Cassy paused and then said, "I think Alexandra will marry him and I think Alexandra could not find a better husband. I completely approve of it. In fact, over and above her personal well-being, I think it's much better for Alexandra's image if she's married—certainly as opposed to her living with him. A nine o'clock newscast has some very conservative viewers to attract."

"Whaaa?" Jackson finally said, evidently finding this unbelievable. "You can't be serious. *Strenn?* You think Alexandra should marry Strenn?"

"Yes, I do," Cassy said, feeling her face getting warm.

"So much for your opinion," he said, sounding annoyed.

"As glamorous as it might seem," Cassy said sharply, "being the husband of an anchorwoman is not particularly easy, and not particularly fun a lot of the time, Mr. Darenbrook. It can be very lonely and very trying, and it certainly makes demands on a husband that few human beings under any circumstances would be willing to consider. So take the five percent high of being married to a celebrity and add the ninety-five percent of loneliness and worry and anger and jealousy that can come with any expectations of having a 'normal' wife, if there is such a thing—and *if* you do that, Mr. Darenbrook, really look at what such a marriage takes, then you'll see what an unusual man it requires to make a go of it. And that's Gordon. Besides," she added, feeling surprisingly angry at this point, "he's a very wonderful person."

"Are you finished, Mrs. Cochran?" he said. He was angry too.

"Yes," she said.

"Good," he said, slapping the sofa and standing up. "Then if you want this job we have to agree here and now that you and I will never discuss the topic of Alexandra and Strenn again. Agreed?"

"Fine," she said, quickly standing up too.

"Fine!" he repeated. He was frowning at her, a little red in the face. And then, still in a half shout, he said, "So do you want the goddam job or not?"

"Yes," she said.

He looked at her. "What?" he said, the wind leaving his sails.

"Yes," she repeated, starting to smile.

"You're kidding," he said.

She shook her head. "No, I'm not."

"Huh," he said. "Huh," he repeated, sticking his hands in his pockets, looking at her for a long moment. Then he smiled and said, quietly, "You're very protective of Alexandra—I like that. Because she's going to need a lot of support—and guidance. Lang doesn't know what he's doing. I mean, he does about the numbers, but Alexandra needs someone who can run with her but who can also slow her down."

Cassy nodded. "Exactly."

"I'm not a fool," he told her. "She's absolutely first rate, all the way, absolutely all-star material, but she's still real"—he winced—"young."

Cassy nodded again.

He leaned close to whisper, "I also think Langley needs someone to explain some of the affiliate stuff to him. We've got this guy Deeter Page recruiting—who could sell manure to pigs, mind you—but I'd appreciate it if you could look into it. Give Langley your opinion on some of these deals."

Cassy nodded. "We've already discussed it. He asked me himself."

"Great," Jackson said, nodding, smiling, looking at her. After a moment he stuck out his hand again. "Welcome to the DBS television network, Mrs. Cochran."

She took his hand. "Thank you. It's good to be here."

"Yea team!" he cried then, nearly yanking her off her feet, pulling her over to the door. He threw it open, calling, "Make way for the president of DBS News!" and Ethel and Randy and Claire all stood up at their desks and cheered.

It was at that moment that Cassy had a twinge of conscience. There was a slight complication involved in her coming to DBS that she had failed to mention, a complication, however, that apparently—after thorough discussions with the other party involved—existed only in her own head, and maybe—just a little bit—in her own heart.

The complication was that before Michael stopped drinking, Cassy had had an affair with someone who was now working at DBS.

Cassy had had an affair with Alexandra Waring.

6

Jackson's Contemplation of Alexandra Grows More Serious

The day Cassy Cochran accepted the job as president of DBS News was the day the walls of West End began to hum. Not since Jackson had announced the revitalization of the printing plant in Cahill, Tennessee (instead of closing it), had he seen such high spirits in a Darenbrook facility. It was the excitement that came with the expectation of something wonderful about to happen, and the excitement was contagious, passing from one employee to another, and it all started with Alexandra.

The hiring of Cassy Cochran seemed to give Alexandra the confirmation she needed. She was supremely confident about the endeavor now, everybody could plainly see that, as she dashed about West End, welcoming new DBS News employees and dragging them around with her; running in and out of the newsroom twenty times a day (and night), popping into the engineering and satellite rooms for ad hoc tutoring by Dr. Kessler's people; running in and out of everywhere—film, audio, editing, graphics, Studio A, the control room—checking on everything's progress; and with her every smile, her every "This is wonderful—you've done a wonderful job!" spirits rose higher and smiles grew wider and everywhere in the complex hearts started to beat a little faster.

They were all falling for her, Jackson knew, the whole darn complex was. Falling for Alexandra, this whirlwind of grace and glamor operating out of Darenbrook III. For many of the employees at West End, she was, after all, the first celebrity they had ever worked around besides Jackson himself. And although this small-scale demonstration of Alexandra's star quality pleased Jackson, he couldn't help but feel a little twinge when he walked the halls with her and employees would say, "Oh, hi, Mr. Darenbrook," while smiling like dopey dill-docks, eyes never even leaving Alexandra to look at him.

But how could anyone be indifferent to such an extraordinary young woman as Alexandra? She was so talented and fantastic-looking, and was so happy, it was impossible not to feel the same way around her. Add her energy and brains and power and celebrity and million-and-a-half-dollar salary, and who stood a chance? But people genuinely seemed to *like* her, because Alexandra was . . . well, she was kind. Yes. She was warm and kind. And when she paid attention to someone, that someone felt as though they were the most important person in the world—and that someone could be the custodian sweeping up in the newsroom as easily as it could be Jackson himself.

When Cordelia came down with the flu and Belinda said she didn't feel up to it, Alexandra agreed to fly down with Jackson and fill in as mistress of ceremonies at the annual Darenbrook Communications retirement dinner in Richmond. As the Richmond *Daily Sun* wrote in its coverage of the event (an issue of the paper Jackson went to extraordinary lengths to keep from Cordelia):

> Alexandra Waring stood in as the first lady of Darenbrook Communications and handed each retiree his or her gift as they left the dais. Herbert Maclavitch, retiring after 45 years on the printing shop floor, said, "I felt very honored. There hasn't been a classier lady up there since Barbara Darenbrook or Alice May herself."

Jackson did not dwell on that comparison, though it had not escaped his notice that night either. That Alexandra, like his late wife, Barbara, seemed made for company-family celebrations like these. These people and the years of their hard work meant something to Alexandra; she had a kind of appreciation and sincerity that was heartfelt and everybody knew it. Behind the glitz and glamor, this was a young woman who had been brought up to respect hard, honest work.

Yes, Barbara had had that too. And in these parts, Barbara's home stomping ground of Richmond, she had become something of a legend. And so a comparison to her was not something to be taken lightly.

Jackson had first met Barbara in 1966, when he was twenty-five, while revamping the Richmond *Daily Sun* (as an excuse, really, to get out of Hilleanderville). He met her on the elevator, helping her with this huge portfolio (with which she had whacked the operator in the face on her way in), and she told him she had just arrived home from Smith College and was on her way to interview for an art director's job. By the time they got off the elevator Barbara Bennett *was* the art director.

Barbara had a wonderful body, a glorious smile and the gift of laughter and was the most horrible art director anyone—including herself—had ever seen. "I really think you should fire me," she told Jackson after a week. "Another couple of days and I'm afraid I'm really going to do all these nice people in." So he fired her and the next year married her.

His family at first disliked her, mainly because Little El and the twins didn't like anybody, and Daddy and Cordelia and Belinda and Beau were upset that Barbara refused to marry Jackson until he swore they would never live in Hilleanderville. And so Jackson moved corporate headquarters to Richmond, he and Barbara built a house outside the city, and an airstrip as well, and many mornings Barbara flew Jackson to work in any one of seven Southern states. After Beau and his boyfriend, Tiger, moved to Southern California; and Belinda came up to school in Virginia and married Langley Peterson; and Cordelia and Daddy realized they saw more of Jackie Andy and Barbara than anybody else in the family, those four came to love Barbara very, very much—especially after Lydia and Kevin, were born.

Barbara was more than wife; Barbara had indeed been Jackson's partner in every facet of his life. She was extremely good at straightening out Jackson's thinking and helping him to focus on what he was doing instead of getting distracted all the time. And she listened so well, and she had a knack for managing things well—straightening out complicated problems—and she believed in her husband a hundred percent. And then some. Because she was apt to push him, too, just as she was apt to kick him in the pants when she thought he was being a jerk. They fought and they made up—which was the best part since the Darenbrook marriage possessed the peculiar phenomenon of their sex life seeming only to grow more complete with each passing year of their marriage.

Lydia had been eleven and Kevin had been nine "that" summer of

1981. They were both on the swim team at the country club and so Barbara and Jackson had been recruited to participate in the Parents' Funny Dive Contest at the club's end-of-season Labor Day festivities.

It had been one hundred and two degrees that day, at one o'clock, and all of the kids had been gathered around the deep end of the L-shaped Olympic-size pool, pouring bathing caps of water over themselves to cool off in the sun. Jackson had opened the competition in round one with a belly flop of perfect execution and had received a score of 14 from the judges out of a possible 30. Barbara had gone next —she was infinitely more gymnastically inclined than her husband— and had executed a front flip with a can-opener ending that sent water shooting into the crowd. She had received a 27. ("I bet if I looked like that in a bathing suit," Jackson had yelled at the three male lifeguards who were the judges, "I bet I'd get a 27 too.")

By round four, Barbara was leading all of the parents by a disgraceful 31 points. In this last round of diving, each parent had to involve a large inner tube in their dive somehow. Jackson tried to dive through the thing but missed it entirely, and the wake of his dive sent the inner tube drifting out. Instead of waiting for someone to bring the inner tube back into place, Barbara leaped onto the board, concentrated for a moment, and then took a running start, bounded off the end of the board, and sailed way up and then out—arching through the air, stretching, reaching—and then breaking suddenly to swoop down— swish—through the inner tube, feet together, toes pointed, barely a splash behind her. The crowd went crazy.

But Barbara did not come shooting back up out of the water like she always did. Instead, her body was listless under the water, ever so slowly drifting up toward the surface. Jackson and one of the lifeguards dove in at the same time and within seconds had brought Barbara up to the side of the pool and were lifting her to the hands waiting there. She was gently lowered onto the cement and Hugh Wilson, a doctor, was right there, leaning over her. Jackson pulled himself out of the pool and, with water still flooding down from him, he saw Hugh look back at him over his shoulder.

"Jack, I'm sorry," he said, holding his arm out for him to stay back, "there's nothing we can do."

She was dead.

JACKSON'S CONTEMPLATION OF ALEXANDRA GROWS SERIOUS

Barbara was dead. Just like that. Gone.

Jackson had pushed Hugh out of the way and was trying to give Barbara mouth-to-mouth and everyone was screaming and Hugh was saying to him, "It's her neck, Jack, it's broken, she's dead, she's gone, you can't—" and he heard him but he couldn't give up. *Oh, God, Barbara, oh, God, Barbara, you can't do this, honey, you can't die, oh, God, Barbara, honey, you have to wake up now, you have to sit up and wave to the kids so they know it's okay, that you're okay, but you gotta do it now, honey, please, honey, oh, God, oh God, You can't do this to her— come back, honey, oh, God help her to come back because the kids— because the kids* . . . and he had started to sob, curling up next to her, clinging to her shoulder, screaming in his head, *Barbara, Barbara, Barbara, please, come back.* . . .

Just one of those freak pool accidents, he was told. She had gone out too far, to where the pool bottom started climbing toward the swimming lanes. She thought she had deeper water, had let her arms fall back as she streaked down through the water. Cracked her head on the bottom, snapping her neck. Her death was instant, painless. Perhaps better this way, Jack. Would have been paralyzed for sure. Brain damage. You know. And you know how Barbara was.

Yeah. He knew how Barbara was.

He buried his wife in Richmond, of course. And every day for three weeks after the funeral he went to the cemetery and stared at the first two lines on the headstone:

Barbara Hale Bennett Darenbrook
1943–1981

and he would wonder what was going on, when this awful dream would stop. He didn't understand what had happened, why the whole world had suddenly stopped. He didn't know why everyone was so sad and why the dog was acting funny and the kids were having nightmares and why . . . why . . .

One night, when everything was beginning to sink in, Jackson slumped over the kitchen table, sobbing, asking Barbara over and over again what he was supposed to do. And then it was very strange, because it was about two in the morning and the phone rang. And it was Laurie, Barbara's sister, who said she had awakened suddenly and had been scared that something had happened—was Jackson all right?

Laurie and her husband, Hal, came over that night and Jackson had sat there, sobbing so uncontrollably that the children woke up and were frightened, and so Hal took them over to his house. And then Langley and Belinda were there with Laurie, and still he was sobbing, holding his face in his hands, telling them he couldn't stand being in this house, that he couldn't—he couldn't bear looking at the kids. He didn't know what to say to them, he didn't know how to make it better, how to make all the pain go away for them, because they missed their mother and they wanted their mother but she was gone forever. And then he fell into Belinda's lap, begging her to tell him how to make the pain go away—she knew, didn't she? Didn't she remember when Mama died, how awful it was? Couldn't she tell him what he was supposed to do?

"I want to die too," he cried as his sister rocked him, holding his head against her, crying too, "I want to go with her. I want to take her to see Mama so she has someone to talk to. Belinda, help me, help me—oh, God, let me die so I can go with her. I don't want her to be alone."

He had gone home to the Mendolyn Street house in Hilleanderville. He moved into his old bedroom he had as a kid, up on the third floor, next to Beau's old room, and stayed there for almost a year with Cordelia watching over him—making him get up, exercise, eat, go down to the Atlanta *Parader* and do some work—while Laurie and Hal took care of Lydia and Kevin, and Langley took care of Darenbrook Communications. Jackson never went back to the house in Richmond. He sold it and, as it turned out, Lydia and Kevin never lived with him again—not that Jackson ever bought another house, or even an apartment, for them to live with him in.

Jackson could not even pretend he wanted to try a home life again. He just couldn't. And so Laurie and Hal raised his children. As for him, his only hope, he thought, was noise. Distraction. Color. Lights. Action, travel, noise—oh, God, more than any-

thing, he needed noise to drown out the echo of yesterday's satis-
factions, of yesterday's contentments. *Anything* to get rid of that
horrible ache, that longing, those dreams of Barbara coming back.

And so Jackson had taken to women. Women in the sense that
one might view a painkilling drug, which did not actually get rid
of the pain but could prevent the body from registering it. And he
bought a new company jet and used it at the slightest excuse,
flying to business meetings, flying to pro football games, flying to
go out on dates, or flying to play shortstop on one of the newspaper's softball teams. He was always on the move, always with a
different woman, and somehow, between the women and the
constant travel, life became bearable to him again—very different, hardly full, but bearable.

Moving the corporate headquarters seemed like a great idea to
Jackson then, a great way to stir up a little excitement, and building a TV network was even better. What could have more noise,
distraction, color, lights, action and new women than New York
City and television?

Enter Alexandra.

Alexandra Waring was the first woman in six and a half years
who genuinely interested him personally in ways other than lust.
He had to be careful, though, both for himself and for her. She
was young and supposedly attached to Gordon Strenn, and Jackson had no desire to scare her at this early date into rejecting
either him or Strenn outright. He wished only to get closer to her,
to know her well, to let her know him well, and if she was really
all that he thought she was, *then* he would move to take her away
from Strenn. And if he chose to do that, he would do so to marry
her.

Why not? Thirty wasn't so young. Forty-seven wasn't so . . .

But Strenn was a pain in the ass and Strenn was back from
England. Jackson had been over seeing Alexandra's new apartment on Central Park West—with her assistant, Kate, so it wasn't
as if they had been alone or anything—when Strenn walked in.
They had been standing just inside the doorway of the bedroom
and Jackson—eyes on the queen-size bed—had been a million

miles in pleasant fantasy when Strenn came up behind him and said, "Hi, Jackson."

He definitely jumped. "Hey," he said, recovering and turning to shake his hand, "how are you doing, movie man? How's the Queen?"

"Great. And Lord Hargrave is too," Gordon said, shaking his hand. Then he walked over to Alexandra, murmured a "Hi," and kissed her on the temple. It was a perfectly rendered, polite reminder that Jackson was but a visitor on private property.

And then—now how the heck the *Inquiring Eye* found out that he had visited Alexandra's apartment Jackson had no idea, but the next thing he knew, Langley was flying into his office to announce that his visit had flung him and Alexandra onto the front page. "ALEXANDRA'S HOMEWORK" the headline read over a picture of Jackson climbing into his limo. (The picture was at least eight months old.) Next to it was a picture of Alexandra looking wistfully across the page at him—rather, it looked as though she were looking at his rear end.

"And did they say that Alexandra's assistant, Kate, and Strenn were there too?" Jackson had said, flinging the stupid thing back at Langley.

"No," Langley said.

"What are you looking at me like that for?" he demanded.

"If you'd stop following her around, Jack," Langley said, "the stories would stop. If you don't, they're only going to get worse."

"You mean, stop the stories before they're true?"

"I just want you to remember that this concerns not one key employee but two. And I don't have to remind you that the miniseries—"

"What are you telling me, Lang?"

"Nothing," Langley said, walking to the door. "Do whatever you want. You always do." He turned around. "It's just not very smart. Not with Darenbrook employees. No matter what she says."

Langley was such a jerk sometimes. Who could not like Alexandra, except Langley? Mr. Paranoia. Langley seemed to think that Alexandra was out to take over the company. And if there was anyone out to overthrow the company, it was Langley's pal, Cassy Cochran. Even from WST, where she was still wrapping things up in her old job, Cassy Cochran was either crash-training Langley or negotiating with affiliate stations herself, because all of a sudden there were all these contracts flying through Jackson's office and they were signing affiliates for the news group right and left. They were up to thirty-nine already and no one except Cassy Cochran seemed to know a whole lot about them. Or at least Langley *said* she knew a lot about them.

But what annoyed Jackson about Mrs. Cochran was that she wasn't even here yet, and he was already hitting heads with her over Alexandra. And this lady named Chi Chi or Cha Cha or something—Mrs. Cochran's assistant, for Pete's sake—felt free to tell *him,* Jackson Darenbrook, what he could and could not do, according to Her Highness, La Presidenta in absentia, still over at WST.

"I'm sorry," Chi Chi or Cha Cha or whatever her name was said, blocking the doorway of Cassy Cochran's office one afternoon, "but Alexandra's reviewing some paperwork for Mrs. Cochran and Mrs. Cochran said that I was not to let any calls or people through until she's finished."

"What?" Jackson said. And then he smiled, drawing himself up to his full six-three height. "Now, ma'am, I don't think you know who I am."

"Yes, I do, Mr. Darenbrook, because Mrs. Cochran warned me that you'd do exactly what you're doing," she said, offering a very cheerful smile but not wavering a bit. She was not very tall, this Chi Chi or Cha Cha or whatever her name was, but she did look pretty feisty.

"Well, now, ma'am," Jackson said, "just what is it you think I'm doing?"

"Trying to b.s. your way past me, just like Mrs. Cochran said you would—so you might as well forget it," she said.

She was right, because even when he did get past her (and no, he didn't push her—not exactly) he found that the door was locked. And even with all the noise—"That's it! I warned you," Chi Chi or Cha Cha said, grabbing the phone off her desk, "I'm calling Mrs. Cochran"—Alexandra didn't, as Jackson thought she would, open the door to see what was going on (although everyone else on the floor did).

"Cassy Cochran's holding on 5," Ethel told him when he returned to his office.

Uh-oh, he thought, but decided that offense would be the best defense and picked up the phone. "So who declared war around here? Some lady who says she works for you nearly punched me out."

"Her name is Chi Chi Santiago," Cassy said.

"Yeah, well, Chi Chi needs to be tied up. She's a mean one."

"Hardly," Cassy said. "She was only doing what I asked her to do."

"Well what the hell's going on in your office that the chairman of Darenbrook Communications can't know about?"

"Nothing," she said. "Alexandra just needs a quiet place to work for an hour or two and I told her that if she used my office I would see to it that no one disturbed her. That's all."

"Well, I wouldn't disturb her."

"No, I'm sure you wouldn't," she said, her voice turning surprisingly gentle. "But a promise is a promise and I promised there would be no exceptions—that she would have complete quiet. Please understand—Alexandra's under an enormous strain and there are some things she has to work on by herself, and I don't want her to feel as though she has to leave West End to work on them. I'd like her to know she can always find a quiet spot there. And right now, until I get over there, my office is it. Do you understand? It's very important that she feels completely safe there—that she can be alone for a little while if she needs to be."

Yeah, well, Jackson did understand, but he sure didn't like Mrs. Cochran's idea that "no exceptions" applied to him too. He started to tell Alexandra that, later, when he finally found her down in the newsroom, but quickly stopped himself. Because if there was one thing he had learned about Alexandra, messing around with her work was not the way to her heart, and it was becoming clear to him that she thought the world of her pain-in-the-ass executive producer.

So instead Jackson said, "Smart lady, that Cassy Cochran. I should have thought of finding you a peaceful place myself."

And then Alexandra smiled and Jackson, for the umpteenth time, thought she had eyes to die for.

7

The Ball Starts Rolling

On the second Monday of April, Darenbrook Communications invited several members of the print media over for an informal breakfast at West End as a kind of warm-up for the official DBS News press conference scheduled for later in May. And so ten journalists came over and ate breakfast in the Darenbrook cafeteria with the new DBS public relations director, Derek Deltz; Darenbrook Communications Chairman Jackson Darenbrook; DBS President Langley Peterson; President and Executive Producer, DBS News, Catherine Cochran; Vice-President and Senior Producer, DBS News, Kyle McFarland; and —on her first day of liberation from her sling—Managing Editor and Anchorwoman, DBS News, Alexandra Waring.

Jackson briefly reviewed the Darenbrook Communications sixty-year history of news gathering and communications in America and how the September debut of DBS News would follow family tradition; Langley outlined the technology that made DBS News possible; Cassy explained how their emphasis would be on domestic news, and profiled the kind of affiliate newsrooms they were recruiting; Kyle talked about how a production team, under Will Rafferty, was already on the road, traveling from affiliate to affiliate, demonstrating the DBS News style as depicted in the *DBS News Practices and Standards* workbook—

"The what?" someone asked.

"DBS News Practices and Standards," Kyle said. "Our bible of how we do things, from A to Z, Advertisers-Offering-Freebies-to-Reporters to Zone-Codes-of-Coverage."

—and Alexandra cited a few examples of prize-winning local indie reporters whose work would go national with DBS; said her shoulder was fine, thank you, and that, no, they hadn't finalized the format yet for the hour-long newscast, "DBS News America Tonight with Alexandra Waring," but they could expect at least four stories a night to be covered in greater depth than they were used to seeing on commercial broadcast television.

"What's the overhead on an operation like this?" asked a reporter from one of the big financial papers.

"Not too bad," Cassy said. "While most news networks have to carry the salaries and overhead of their bureau desks, at DBS we only pay the salaries and overhead of our operation here at West End—plus our transmission costs. I can't give you the exact figures," she said, glancing at Jackson, "since we are part of a private corporation—"

"Not fair," someone said.

"But I will tell you that DBS News will operate on roughly twenty percent of the budget of CBS News, and so, since you all know that CBS was up to around three hundred million last year"—she paused, smiling as everyone started to laugh—"I am confident that some of you may be able to work out the difficult math on that. Uh . . ." She waited for everyone to quiet down again. "One of the nice things about being able to operate in a sophisticated way on a fraction of a traditional network budget is that, going in, we know that we can survive—perhaps even flourish—on a fraction of the traditional network audience. And that, as you know, can bode well for things like more in-depth domestic story coverage—which just happens to be what we hope will be our specialty."

"So how does it work? With the affiliates?" a reporter asked.

"Although we don't pay their overhead," Cassy continued, "our affiliate newsrooms do act as our bureau desks—meaning whatever news coverage they have is at our disposal. So, for example, if there was—God forbid—an airplane crash here in New York, we'd have all of WST's local coverage to choose from to use in our national news. Or use a WST local reporter as a live national correspondent for DBS."

"WST has signed as the New York affiliate then?" someone asked.

"Yesterday," Cassy said, smiling.

"DBS will act as a kind of clearinghouse," Langley interjected. "Each affiliate will transmit to West End their stories and film of the day, which DBS is then free to use that day or any other day in the future."

"What do the affiliates get?" another reporter asked.

"Right now, we're offering the one news hour," Cassy said, "and part of the package is a certain allotment of ad time within it for them to sell locally. They keep a hundred percent of that ad money, of course, while we retain a certain allotment of time to sell to national advertisers."

"The affiliate newsrooms also get access to any coverage we have on hand from other affiliates," Alexandra said. "That's what Langley meant when he described DBS News as a kind of clearinghouse. So, for example, in Phoenix, our affiliate KZA might see on the daily DBS roster that we have in a report from our L.A. affiliate concerning the Colorado River that we're not using on the network newscast. Since the Colorado is a big concern in Phoenix, they can call for the report, we'll transmit it to them and, if it's appropriate for them, they are free to use it in their local newscast."

"We'll also be offering affiliates a film library," Cassy said, "so that if an affiliate in Florida, for example, wanted to do a documentary on water use in their state and wanted to use the Colorado River as an example of how other states have approached the subject, they could get file footage of the Colorado River from us."

"From the reports filed from other affiliates," a reporter said.

"Or just raw footage we've stored," Cassy said. She glanced at Langley and then leaned forward to say in a loud whisper, "Don't tell anyone, but DBS News has almost fifty million dollars' worth of electronic storage at its disposal here at West End."

"What do the reporters get out of this arrangement?" someone said.

"Well, first, there's the exposure," Alexandra said.

"No," Cassy said, "first there's the bonus money they receive."

"No," Alexandra insisted, giving Cassy a playful elbow in the side, "first there's the exposure. Some television reporters have to fight very hard for exposure." Everybody laughed, knowing of Alexandra's problems about getting on the air at her old network.

"And there are the bonus systems being worked out," Cassy said, "based on how a story is used, nationally, or in how many individual local markets. It's very complicated—"

"But we have an Accounta-5 TR-587 System—on line," Langley said, as if anyone could possibly know what he was talking about.

Everybody looked back to Cassy.

"As you know," she said, "the United States of America is a tremendous geographic area and, to reach the entire population, one has to broadcast from roughly two hundred stations. As you might not know, there are almost as many variations in union and nonunion working agreements at TV stations across the country. And it is only because of our access to the most sophisticated accounting hardware and software systems in the world that we're able to tailor-make every single one of our affiliate agreements and work out individual bonus agreements with reporters and technical crews."

"Yeah, but can your computers sign a tax return?" someone cracked, making everyone laugh.

"Let me tell you," Cassy finally said, still laughing, "I wouldn't put it past them. And the science editors of your papers are going to be invited to meet with Dr. Kessler—the gentleman who's responsible for all of the technological wonders at Darenbrook Communications— who will explain the extraordinary transmission and receiving capacities of our satellite, and the impact it may have on broadcasting as we know it."

She smiled. "Questions."

Jackson closed the door to the cafeteria and whirled around to face Cassy and Langley in his office. "You!" he said, pointing at Cassy. "I have half a mind to rip up your contract right now."

Cassy and Langley exchanged looks.

"How dare you upstage Alexandra!" Jackson said.

"What?" Langley said.

"Who the hell do you think you are?" Jackson demanded of her.

"Wait a minute, Jack," Langley said.

"You wait a minute!" Jackson said. "I'm not building this goddam division to glorify your blond bombshell here, Lang." He stormed over to his desk, muttering, "This is Alexandra's show and I don't care if we have to write her cue cards or stay up all night with her, I want

Alexandra to know everything there is to know so she can explain it to the press."

"*I* don't even understand all of it yet," Langley said, "because Cassy here hasn't finished inventing it yet! And what do you mean, let Alexandra explain it? Who's going to believe anything that your little girlfriend has to say about Darenbrook Communications at this point?"

"Langley!" This was from Cassy, who until now had just been standing there, listening, looking only mildly fed up. "For heaven sakes," she whispered, nodding toward the door to the cafeteria, "don't even kid around like that. If anybody heard that coming out of your mouth . . ." She glanced over at Jackson. "We have enough problems trying to clean up Alexandra's reputation as it is."

"Oh, *nice,* Mrs. Cochran, really nice," Jackson said, yanking his chair out from behind his desk and banging it into the wall.

"Well, you do seem to have your strategies a little confused," she said in her normal voice, resting her hand on her hip. "It's not very helpful for our anchorwoman's name to be dragged through every muck-and-mire rag in the country because the chairman apparently has nothing better to do than follow her around day and night."

"Look!" Jackson said, sitting down and slamming his desk. "Your job is to run DBS News, so go run it! Stop grandstanding in front of the press, that's all I'm saying. There's one star and you ain't it, Mrs. Cochran. Langley—ya hear me? When we put Alexandra out onstage, I'm holding you responsible to keep Blondie here back in the wings where she belongs."

"And you better—" Cassy cut herself off, touching the bridge of her nose, murmuring, "Why am I getting caught up in this?" and then lowering her hand. "Look," she said, quietly, to Jackson, waiting for him to look at her before continuing. "You're simply going to have to believe that I know a little bit more about this than you do. You're also going to have to—"

"I don't have to do anything," Jackson told her.

Cassy stared at him for a long moment. He stared back. Finally she said, "Remind me—we both want DBS News and Alexandra to succeed, right?"

He didn't answer. He was glaring at her now.

"And you hired me to make DBS News and Alexandra succeed, right?"

"Right!" Langley said.

"So why won't you let me?" Cassy said to Jackson.

"Lady, you're asking for it," Jackson said.

"Jack—" Langley started.

"No, Langley, wait," Cassy said, holding a hand up to silence him. To Jackson, "I mean it. I want to know why you won't let me do my job. Since the day I agreed to come here I have had nothing but run-ins with you. And what I want to know is, *why do I keep running into you?* Why is the chairman of Darenbrook Communications constantly underfoot? Why is he playing with the typewriters in the newsroom? Why is he in our anchorwoman's dressing room, watching them tile her shower? Why is he giving the tabloids a heyday of speculation? *What are you doing?*" she demanded, bringing both her hands down on his desk with a bang. "Damn it!" she said then, pushing off the desk. "This is her *life* you're messing with. Everything that young woman has is riding on this endeavor. And you seem to like Alexandra—that's what I don't understand—how you won't even think twice before putting her career in peril by interfering with every person and process that can help her succeed."

She flew over to the outer-office door and threw it open. "Could someone please call my office and have Chi Chi bring up this morning's clippings on Alexandra? Right now? Thank you." She slammed the door and then walked over to stand by the window, folding her arms. "We might as well go through the whole thing," she said. "We've got to settle this now." She looked over at Jackson. "Or I might as well leave. Today."

"Cassy, there's no reason to start talking of that," Langley said quietly, pushing his glasses farther up his nose. He turned to Jackson. "Is there, Jack?" When Jackson didn't say anything (he was staring down at his desk), Langley added, "I think there's been just a little misunderstanding about territory."

Cassy covered her face with one hand and laughed. It did not sound like very happy laughter.

Langley shoved his hand in his pocket and started jingling the change in it, nervously looking back and forth between the two. Jackson was still staring down at his desk and Cassy was staring out at the square.

There was a knock on the door to the cafeteria and then Alexandra peeked in. "Hi," she said, "may we come in?" Kyle was behind her.

Immediately Jackson's face changed. "Sure, come on in."

Alexandra came in, held the door for Kyle and closed it. Then she turned around and, with a huge smile, ran over to throw her arms around Cassy. "They bought it!" she said in a whisper, laughing. She released Cassy and turned to Langley and Jackson and in her normal voice said, "Not only do they think the network can work, but two almost said they thought we might know what we're doing." She turned back to Cassy, touching her arm. "Thank God you're here, that's all I can say. They never would have believed any of it from any of us." She turned to Jackson. "Isn't she the best?"

Alexandra was still carrying on about how wonderfully the breakfast had gone when Chi Chi arrived with the folder. "The legal department is copying the one from *Spy Glass,*" Chi Chi told Cassy at the door.

"Oh, that," Alexandra said, groaning and plunking herself down onto one of the sofas. "Did you see that one, Kyle?"

"Yes," he said.

"Have a seat, Kyle," Jackson said, getting up from behind his desk. "All of you," he added, gesturing to the seats around the glass table, where Alexandra was. "Come on, Lang, sit." He patted Langley on the shoulder and looked over at Cassy.

"Look through these," she murmured, handing him the folder and moving over to sit in one of the chairs.

And so they sat around the glass table and Jackson started reading through the folder. The Regina Baxter quote—the one that appeared on Alexandra's first day of work at DBS, the one implying that Alexandra was some kind of million-dollar call girl of Jackson's—had become the standard reference used by the tabloids to establish credibility for "Alexandra" stories. There were several clippings from papers that had run a wire service photo of Jackson and Alexandra at the company retirement dinner in Richmond, and one tabloid ran the following caption underneath it:

Alexandra Waring out on the town with billionaire boyfriend-boss Jackson Darenbrook. Even newswoman Regina Baxter, who prefers to steer clear of controversy, felt compelled to speak out against the woman she sees giving all women in TV news a bad name.

Jackson glanced over at Cassy. She met his eye and lofted her eyebrows, as much as to say, "Happy?"

Another ran the caption, "Jackson Darenbrook with Alexandra Waring, the video vixen Regina Baxter says is overpaid by $999,800 a night."

Jackson closed his eyes for a moment and then went on.

A blind item was circled in Roz Gladden's syndicated column:

My oh my but does a certain farm girl seem to drag a lot of dirt around with her. First we heard whispers about her old boss, now we're hearing about million-dollar moans with the new. So someone explain it to me—what's with the boyfriend? Is he deaf and blind, or just out of town too much? Or is this the one about the farmer's daughter I missed?

"I bet he's reading Roz Gladden's column," Alexandra was saying to Kyle.

Jackson looked up. "This is disgusting."

"Bitsy Bourner's column is quite nice," Alexandra said, recrossing her legs and smoothing her skirt. "Read that."

He did.

Jealousy, readers, that's all it is, pure and simple. I talked with one NBC news official who said, "Even if she were Walter Cronkite, people would be jealous. The point is, a major corporation has pledged its faith in one individual, and people can't believe a very pretty 30-year-old woman has earned it on professional merit alone." Well, readers, here's one that does. Go get 'em, Alexandra! That's what I say.

"Don't read any more," Alexandra suggested, leaning over to take the folder away from him.

"I'd like him to read them," Cassy said.

"And I want to know what we're doing about it," Jackson said to Cassy.

"Well," Langley said, "Derek"—referring to their PR director—"has a ringer he can bring in from the West Coast. A guy who's got something on everybody at these rags so they'll leave her alone."

"Oh, no!" Alexandra and Kyle said simultaneously, trying to wave this suggestion away.

"But this is very nasty stuff," Cassy said to Jackson, "and they're only warming up." She looked sideways at Alexandra. "I don't know why, but they seem to think they can sell a lot of papers dragging our poor friend here through the mud."

"Well, they're right," Kyle said. "Because Alexandra's very hot stuff."

"Thank you, Mr. McFarland," Alexandra said. "I think you're pretty hot stuff too."

He grinned and looked back at Cassy. "And so I think we should consider moving up the debut of 'News America Tonight' from Labor Day to Memorial Day and cash in on the publicity."

"What?" Langley and Jackson said together, turning to look at Cassy.

"Interesting idea," she murmured, reaching for the phone on the table.

"It struck both me and Alexandra when Derek said what a pity it was that all this publicity was going to waste," Kyle said. "And yesterday Dr. Kessler's tests with the affiliates went off without a hitch."

"How many?" Langley asked Cassy.

"They ran them with forty-one, I think—wasn't it, Kyle?" Cassy said, punching four numbers into the phone.

"Yep."

"I'd prefer to go on the air with everything nailed down," Alexandra said, "but I think Kyle's right. If we could go on the air soon—while I'm still all over the newsstands and the networks are going into reruns . . ."

"But everything has to be nailed down," Cassy said, covering the phone with her hand and speaking over it. And then she shrugged. "So we just have to hammer away night and day to get it done in time, I guess." She spoke into the phone. "Yes, hi, Rookie." Evidently she was talking to Rookie Haskell, the director of advertising sales. "I want you to call around and see what the reaction would be if 'DBS News

America Tonight' debuted on Memorial Day—right, Memorial Day. Yes. *This* Memorial Day, Rookie."

"May 30," Kyle said.

"May 30," Cassy said. "And we'd run straight through the summer, the only original prime-time programming around." She smiled. "Well, what's the point of being an alternative network if we can't do whatever we want?" she said, winking at Kyle. "Yes," she said, now looking at Alexandra. "Sure. Tell them Alexandra is an absolute knockout with a suntan." She laughed. "Okay." She lowered the phone slightly. "He wants to know if he could bring a couple of sponsors to meet you."

"Sure," Alexandra said.

"How can we—" Jackson started to say.

"Shhh," Langley said, eyes on Cassy.

"And make sure to tell them," Cassy said into the phone, "that if the writers' strike continues, then 'News America Tonight' could well be the only original prime-time programming around to watch in the fall."

"Yeah!" Jackson said, pounding a fist on Langley's knee.

"Ow," Langley said.

"Wait a minute!" Cassy suddenly said, bouncing in her seat. "Wait a minute, everybody."

"What?" Kyle said.

Cassy looked at Langley, snapping her fingers twice. "What about Jessica Wright? What's happening with her show?"

"Uh," Langley said, "she's—uh—well, I mean, she's missing at the moment—"

"You still haven't found her?" Jackson asked him.

"But when is her show scheduled? What are you doing with her?" Cassy asked Langley.

"Um," Langley said, "we're not sure. She threw a fit over Bertie Flotsheim as her executive producer and so now she doesn't have one."

"What are you thinking of?" Alexandra asked Cassy.

"Rookie?" Cassy said into the phone.

"Here," Jackson said, leaning forward and turning the speakerphone on. "Hey, Rook, can ya hear me?"

"Hi, Jackson," Rookie said.

"Okay, guys, listen up," Cassy said, putting the phone down on the table. "What do you think about selling 'News America Tonight' and 'The Jessica Wright Show' together? Back to back? As a package? Two hours of original prime-time programming against reruns for at least three months? We could head into the fall with a good audience, news and entertainment, nine to eleven. And if the strike lasts—who knows? We might clean up this fall."

"I like it," Rookie said. "I think advertisers'll like it too. Jessica's a real strong drawing card out there."

"What's the matter, Alexandra?" Cassy said.

"I'm all for trying to get on the air by Memorial Day," she said slowly. "But about 'The Jessica Wright Show' . . ." She shook her head. "I just don't know. Her style is so—so . . ." She smiled a little, looking for the right words. "I guess I'm wondering if we attract the same audience."

"You'll be the lead-in for her," Cassy said. "DBS can't put anyone named the Terror of Tucson on during family hour." The latter was said to Langley.

"No, of course not," Langley said.

"So you'll just bring a new audience to her," Cassy said.

"Okay," Alexandra said, shrugging, "if it'll get us on the air by Memorial Day."

"I'd pair up with her if I were you, Alexandra," Rookie said over the speaker. "Out West, the demos say Jessica Wright's the biggest thing to hit eighteen-to-thirty-fours since the Honda CVCC."

"You know what?" Jackson suddenly said. Everybody looked at him, and he looked at Cassy. "I think you're very smart, Mrs. Cochran."

Cassy blinked several times. "Thank you," she said.

"You're welcome," Jackson said. He turned to Langley. "And I think what we gotta do, Lang, is send out a search party and find Jessica and then," he said, turning to Cassy, "I think Mrs. Cochran should talk to the affiliates and see what they think, and she should also sit in on a production meeting about Jessica's show—if she doesn't mind, that is."

"I'd be delighted to," Cassy said.

"Then," Jackson said, turning to the speakerphone, "I think Rookie should tell us what he can fetch for the ladies of DBS, and then," he said, turning to Alexandra, "I think we hussle to get 'DBS News America Tonight' on the air by Memorial Day—right?"

"Right!" Alexandra said, leaping to her feet and heading for the door.

"Great!" Kyle said, right behind her.

"I don't know how we'll get it all done in time," Cassy said, standing up, "but we will. I promise you."

Within a minute, Langley and Jackson were left sitting there, alone.

"Hello?" Rookie said over the speakerphone.

"Slowpoke," Jackson said, leaning over to hang up on him.

8

Alexandra, Cassy, Stolen Money, Weddings and His Wife: Langley Tries to Stay on Top of Things

For the life of him, Langley Peterson couldn't understand why nobody else seemed to notice—or care—that their anchorwoman was the most manipulative creature since Mata Hari.

Boy was she good.

When Alexandra walked into a room at West End, people came alive. Heads snapped to attention; people sat or stood a little straighter; women checked their hair; men touched at their ties or, in the absence of one (which was more often the case in the news group), ran their hands once over their shaven or unshaven chins; and most everyone would smile—except the shy ones, whose faces would freeze a little, color spreading through their cheeks.

Alexandra's eyes would sweep the room quickly, assessing the situation, much like one who has joined a chess game in progress, and invariably—and Langley had seen her do it so many times he knew he was not imagining it—by the time she left she would have gotten what she wanted, though few would have realized that she had arrived with any premeditated motive. She was so damn good at it and carried so many possible mixed motives at any given moment that Langley still couldn't anticipate the direction from which she would make her approach—or sometimes even figure out where the approach was leading until it was too late.

Yesterday had been a perfect example. It had been raining heavily all morning—the skies dark outside, the pools of water gathering in the square below—and everybody who could had stayed at West End to eat lunch in the cafeteria. The cafeteria was a very pleasant place. It had a vaulted ceiling that rose up through the third floor of Darenbrook I to the skylights in the roof; the walls were pale yellow with all kinds of jazzy, cheerful art prints hanging in all colors of frames; the fourth wall, overlooking the square, was all glass; the floor was covered with a muted, brick-colored tile; and all the tables and chairs were made of wood. More than one person, on such dark rainy days, would say they didn't know why, but eating in there reminded them of eating dinner in the kitchen as a child.

In any event, Jack was in L.A. on magazine business, and Cassy invited Langley to lunch with three new players at DBS News: Senior News Editor Dan Shelstein, a balding man of about fifty-five; Satellite News Producer Kelly Harris, an energetic redhead in her late thirties; and Studio Unit Manager Bozzy Gould, a compact guy about forty or so, built like a marine—with a haircut like one, too—but with a beautiful, smoke-colored complexion.

They were sitting there, lingering over coffee and tea, accustomed to the din and chatter from having so many Darenbrook Communications employees around them, when a sudden hush fell over the room. Dan Shelstein noticed it first, cocking his head and looking around to see what was happening. It was the same kind of hush that falls when people in a restaurant become aware of someone coughing but aren't sure if the person is in trouble choking or not. Only no one was coughing or choking; it was just Alexandra making one of her entrances. And yesterday—when they had been running some official-looking (but utterly fake) studio tests so that one of Rookie's important sponsors could oooh and ahhh over Alexandra—she had been looking particularly stunning.

"Now that's what I want to be when I grow up," Kelly said, watching Alexandra, "devastating in black."

Yes, she was, Langley had to admit. She was in a very simple, sleek little black dress with a high neck and long sleeves. The dress hit her right above her knee, curved up over her hips, and fitted well over her bust and across her shoulders. Her hair—quite nearly black itself—was pulled straight back, secured with a large black bow, and except for some large silver earrings and one thin silver bracelet, she was otherwise unadorned. Eyes blazing blue against the black, she smiled and nodded to several people as she wound her way through the tables toward them, taking almost every eye in the place with her. Dan and Bozzy were scrambling to their feet; Langley was much slower, but he did offer her his seat.

"No, thanks," she said, touching his arm. "Please sit, I just wanted to see what fruit they have up here."

Warning, the alarm in Langley's head said, *she's going to ask for fresh fruit deliveries to the newsroom.*

Everyone sat down again and Alexandra stood there, her hand resting on Langley's shoulder. (He resented her doing that for a number of reasons. One, he didn't like being touched. Two, it felt like a dare. And, three, he didn't like the others at the table to assume, as he knew they were, that Alexandra had an easy familiarity with him, the president of DBS.)

Alexandra looked at Bozzy. "Things went rather well this morning, don't you think?"

Warning, the alarm in Langley's head said, *she's going to bring up expanding the area for the news sets in the studio again.*

"Yeah, I thought so," Bozzy said, looking over at Cassy. "It's a good crew—and Kyle's great."

Alexandra looked at Dan. "And I have to tell you, Dan, I scarcely recognized the newsroom last night. Chaos is turning to organized chaos. Kyle might live to talk about this experience, thanks to you."

Warning, the alarm in Langley's head said, *she's going to press for that extra news editor again.*

Cassy smiled and said, "Kelly—"

"Oh, and you," Alexandra said, turning to smile at Kelly, "Dr. Kessler is absolutely wild about you."

No, she's angling toward "borrowing" another technician from someone else's payroll.

To Cassy, Alexandra said, "Did you know that he would like to run a test with BINS, thanks to Kelly?"

Uh-oh, sounds expensive. And Cassy's got that poker face again. That's trouble—they're in this together. Whatever it is, she wants it too but doesn't want to pay for it.

"What's Bins?" Langley said.

"British International News Service," Cassy said. "It's an overseas stringer operation."

Aha! Langley thought.

"Actually, it's part of Lord Hargrave's group," Alexandra said, taking her hand away from Langley's shoulder. To Dan, "Langley is going to have the miniseries group working out of the Hargrave studios in London—"

"Yes, I do seem to detect the air of coincidence," Langley said, turning to look up at Alexandra. This was unbelievable. They hadn't even built the domestic network and Alexandra was already pushing for international tests? And he didn't have the slightest doubt that somehow Gordon's trip to London had something to do with this. "Expanding internationally, are you?" he asked her. He pointed a finger at her. "Just let me know when I should transfer Gordon's salary to your budget."

Alexandra's eyes went to Cassy.

"It's just a test, Langley," Cassy said. "Langley—"

He stopped staring at Alexandra to look at her.

"It's nothing but a test," Cassy said. "And we're just looking into it—but the Moscow summit *is* going to be over Memorial Day weekend, and it would seem a little funny if on our very first broadcast we didn't have a live report from what could be one of the biggest events in American history."

"We certainly have the capacity to tie in with BINS or somebody," Kelly said.

"Tell Langley what you told me this morning," Alexandra said.

"What? Oh, just that I'm amazed at what you've got here," Kelly said to him. "You have the best setup I've ever seen. I told Alexandra that someone really thought through the whole electronics division." She paused, smiling a little. "Alexandra said you engineered the whole thing. Getting Dr. Kessler and all."

Well, the next thing Langley knew, by the time Alexandra left the cafeteria (without even looking at the fruit, mind you), he had been

WEST END

talked into approving a satellite test with BINS—and promising that he'd get the test costs charged to the R & D department of Darenbrook Electronic Retrieval Systems, Inc.

Well, at least Alexandra was an equal-opportunity manipulator, he'd give her that. She used everybody. In fact she played all of them off one another in such complicated ways that sometimes it took awhile to track it all back to her. Even the idea of moving the debut of DBS News up to Memorial Day to cash in on all the publicity about her had had a whole other agenda attached to it, and Langley later realized that Kyle's "sudden" idea had actually been a very carefully orchestrated plot by Guess Who and her executive and senior producers to get Langley's and Jackson's wholehearted approval behind the effort. (That was another infuriating thing about Alexandra. She knew Jack well enough now to know that he couldn't resist any dramatic idea like this—Go on the air three months early!—particularly if he thought he had helped to brainstorm it.)

But that wasn't the end of the plot, because right now, this very second, Cassy was sitting in his office, unveiling the other agenda that had been attached to it—the hidden one. Now that their revised schedule to meet the Memorial Day debut was set in motion, now that Rookie Haskell had signed sponsors for the summer months—in other words, now that it was too late to back out of launching "DBS News America Tonight with Alexandra Waring" early—Cassy said, since they would be generating income three months ahead of budget, Alexandra wanted to know if it was okay if she hired three full-time DBS field correspondents with the extra money.

"What extra money?" Langley yelled.

"Early money, then," Cassy said calmly, sitting there with an open notebook in her lap, looking at him over a pair of half glasses on her nose. "We'll be three months ahead of budget and, Langley, I have to tell you, I agree with Alexandra and Kyle, I'm sure we can make up the difference before the end of the year."

"We are *not* going to be ahead of budget because we're going to have our operational expenses three months early too," he said. "And how the heck are you going to make up the money before the end of the year, may I ask?"

"We're going to use the correspondents to work on some specials," Cassy said.

"And over what network are you proposing to air these specials?" Langley asked. "Come on, Cass, I hate to sound like Jack on this one— but you *are* running the news division, *not* the network." She smiled slightly and inwardly Langley groaned. He did not feel like getting into the issue of how—at the moment—hers was the only division that had any programming to put on the network. Nor did he feel like being reminded that she was directly or indirectly responsible for over fifty percent of the indies who had signed with them as DBS affiliates. He shook his head, pushing his glasses higher on his nose. "Cassy, I'm sorry, but no," he said. "I can't let you overrun with any more immediate expenditures right now."

How he hated to say this to her! Forget Mata Hari downstairs—he trusted Cassy and, if circumstances were different, he'd think nothing of giving her more slack, trusting that she would—as she had said she could—still come out on budget by the end of the year.

(But what choice did he have? What else could he say—"Hey, Cass, guess what? Know that paycheck you and the others get? The money that paid for those cameras? The editing consoles, pencils, electricity? Yeah? Well, it's stolen. All of it. Yeah. Jack and I stole it from the miniseries and if we're not careful Old Hardhead in London's going to walk off with the whole project. How much? Oh, we're only short about forty-three million right now. So now do you understand why I have to say no? That every additional dollar you get out of me is going to force me to steal more money from another division?")

"I'm sorry, Cassy," he said, "but I'm afraid we just can't do it right now."

"Langley," Cassy said, slipping her glasses off and lowering them to her lap, "listen to me."

Langley sighed, taking off his own glasses to rub his eyes. This was not going to be good. As beautiful and as gracious as he found Cassy to be, he had quickly learned to recognize when she was about to deliver some sort of discreet (and surely distressing) ultimatum from a certain young anchorwoman they all knew.

"If you check Alexandra's contract," Cassy said, "you'll find a clause pertaining to the gross advertising revenues from her newscasts—"

"No," Langley moaned, slumping over his desk.

He knew what Cassy was about to say and it was moments like this that made him want to tell Jack to either give him back the electronics group or go screw himself, he was leaving Darenbrook Communications. This was it—the limit. The absolute limit. Never had Langley had to deal with such convoluted, screwball financing on a new division as this. Never had he been associated with such a convoluted mess masquerading as a new venture. But then Langley had never had to move sixty and seventy and maybe eighty million dollars' worth of the company around like some kind of weird Knock-Hockey game, all because Jackson had fallen for some girl with pretty eyes!

But Langley had to remind himself (while slumped over his desk, eyes closed, not caring what Cassy thought) how much he needed a television network for the IMS, the Interactive Media System that had been (and still was) his pet project in the electronics division. IMS was an extraordinary system of programs that combined computers, video, graphics and sound on optical discs in such a way as to allow a user to command the computer to follow the path of his own curiosity and imagination. "Show me what this video of men walking on the moon would look like if each astronaut weighed five thousand pounds more. . . . Let me see a close-up of what their footprints would look like. . . . Tell me how many songs there are that have the word 'moon' in them. . . . Show me the music for 'Moon River.' . . . List for me all the different recordings of 'Moon River.' . . . Play me 'Moon River' as sung by Andy Williams and show me the astronauts landing on the moon in 1969 at the same time."

While other companies were concentrating on the institutional uses of such technology, Langley wanted to pursue the commercial outlet, envisioning the day they could offer an Interactive Media special over commercial television. While Dr. Kessler had no doubts that such a program would be possible within five years, the endeavor was enormously expensive and Jackson had made it clear to Langley that, if he wanted to pursue this avenue, then he had to *build* the avenue—starting with a profitable commercial television network.

Only Jack hadn't told him he was going to make such a mess out of the whole operation! Jack hadn't told him he was going to make some changes in Langley's very methodical five-year plan for DBS—changes like moving up the news division a year and doubling its budget, pushing sports back eight months, robbing the miniseries blind, hiring a talk show hostess who was lost or dead in Mexico somewhere, canceling the game show and putting the whole soap opera idea on ice . . . Oh, yes, one could say that Jackson had made a few changes that had altered the stability of Langley's venture a bit.

And now that Langley had told Cassy no, he would not approve the funds for Alexandra to hire three field correspondents, he realized that Alexandra could do it anyway. Because Alexandra's contract guaranteed that for any "additional" news programming she did—meaning anything that hadn't been set in the budget—a percentage of the gross ad revenues from that additional programming automatically became discretionary production funds for her to allocate as she wished. And since Alexandra's contract said she went on the air in September, that meant all her newscasts for June, July and August fell into that classification of "additional" news programming and, hence, Ms. Waring did indeed have "extra" money in her production budget to spend as she wished.

Ho hum, just another lovely day at Darenbrook Communications.

Langley sat up. "I know, I know," he said to Cassy, holding a hand up. "Thank you for reminding me about Alexandra's contract." He let his hand fall on his desk with a thump. "So why bother asking me? She'll do whatever she wants anyway."

"*We* are asking you," Cassy said, sounding a trifle annoyed, "because we are all working on the same side, Langley. And not only that—we all work for you."

Langley shrugged, not feeling like getting into an argument with Cassy about whether Alexandra really worked for or with anybody.

"Langley," Cassy said, waiting for him to look at her. "I know you well enough to know that something's wrong." She paused, frowning slightly and touching at her earring. She lowered her hand to her lap and sighed. "I don't know what could be wrong with the financing of this network already, but I'm trusting that you'll tell me if there is something seriously wrong, so that I can have a fighting chance to do something about it on my end—for my group, for our people."

He wasn't sure what to say.

She looked at him for a long moment and then sighed again. "Look," she said, standing up, "I can get Alexandra to back down on this one. I'm going to suggest she hang on to those discretionary funds for a while, until we're more sure of the direction we'll be moving in this year. But, Langley—listen to me—I can't say I'll be able to do this again. I've got enough of my own stuff to work out with Alexandra on the format of the newscast, and I just can't waste my influence with her by trying to screen I-don't-know-what from you."

Langley got up too. "We're a bit short on cash, that's all. And I need you to stick to your budget as best you can for the time being." He paused. "That's it. That's all." He walked around his desk, taking her eyes with him. Glancing at her, "What?"

Still she only looked at him.

"What?" he repeated.

Cassy looked first one way and then the other, then back at Langley, drawing a hand up to her hip. "Langley, who do you think you're talking to? I've seen your budget for DBS. I've seen the production allocations on that budget—" She threw her arms out then. "How in Sam Hill could you be short on cash? You've got more padding in that budget than the Flight Deck in Bellevue."

"Forget I said anything, Cassy," he said, taking her arm. "Come on, I'll walk you back to your office. I've got to—"

She wasn't going anywhere. "Forget you said anything?"

He sighed, shaking his head. "Cassy, look," he said, sticking one hand in his pants pocket and gesturing with the other. "You know better than this. You know this is a private corporation, and that the numbers you see are not always . . . Well, you know. We have many different parts of the company to balance out, and sometimes our cash flow slows in one area when it's in the best interest of our tax situation to do so."

She looked as though she believed him, but then said, "Wait a minute," held a hand up and took a step back from him. "I just want to know one thing—can you or can you not meet the expenses of the DBS News budget that you and I worked out together—staff, salaries, equipment, transmission costs—everything as we set it down?"

"Yes, of course I can," Langley said.

"You swear?" she said.

He held up his hand and smiled. "I swear."

She lowered her hand. "And if we need just a little more money, here and there, money I know we can make up by the end of the year? Is that going to be impossible?"

"Not impossible," he said, reaching for her arm. "Come on, I've got to see Gordon. He's been trying to see me all day."

Langley walked over to Darenbrook III with Cassy, dropped her off on the second floor and took the stairs up to the third. He turned into the hallway just in time to see Gordon's secretary standing in front of several onlookers, winding up to hurl the boccie ball.

"Very graceful, Miss Cannondale," Langley said.

Betty looked back over her shoulder, offered a weak smile, and then, slowly, straightened up, dropped the ball, hung her head and sighed. "Red-handed," she said.

Langley looked at the small crowd. They were various members of the production team who had come in from L.A. and who would be moving on to London. "Hi," Langley said. "Everybody settling in okay?"

They murmured yesses, nervously disbanding.

"Gordon in his office?" he asked Betty.

"He's on the phone, but just go on in. He really wants to see you."

Gordon was not on the phone. He was standing in front of the glass —feet apart, hands in suit pockets—staring down at the square. Langley knocked on the door and he whirled around. "Langley, hi," he said, walking around his desk. "Have a seat."

As Langley pulled up one of the two leather chairs on this side of the desk, Gordon went over and closed the door.

"Sorry it took me so long—it's been one of those days," Langley said.

"You didn't have to come over," Gordon said, taking the other chair near Langley, "but I'm glad you did."

"Me too. I don't see enough of you." Langley always said that to Gordon these days—as if it could make up for how Jackson had utterly cut him dead. "So what can I do for you?"

"Uh, it's personal this time, actually," Gordon said.

"Oh?"

"Yeah," Gordon said, drawing an ankle up to rest on the knee of his other leg. "I, uh—I wanted to talk to you about Alexandra." His eyes met Langley's as he said her name.

"Yes," Langley said, ready for anything—he hoped.

"What I wanted to ask you—" Gordon started. And then he stopped. "No, wait." He brought his leg down and leaned forward in his chair. "I was hoping for a straight answer from you." He looked away for a moment and then back at Langley again. "Confidentially, off the record."

Langley smiled and nodded for him to continue.

Gordon hesitated for a moment and then said, "What's going to happen around here if Alexandra and I get married?"

"Oh," Langley said, surprised. "Gosh, that's great."

"Well, wait a minute," Gordon cautioned him, "it's not written in stone. As a matter of fact, it's not really written anywhere yet. But it's definitely in the wind," he added, smiling.

"Good," Langley said.

"Yeah, right, you say good, but what about Jackson? What's going to happen with him?"

"Nothing—that I know of," Langley said.

"It's not going to hurt Alexandra's career here then," Gordon said seriously, straightening up. "It won't affect the company's support of her."

"Wouldn't matter if she married the man on the moon," Langley said. "Not with her contract guarantees."

"I meant about Jackson," Gordon said.

Langley shifted in his seat. "You haven't been reading some papers that we all know would be better off left unread, have you?"

Gordon shrugged, running a hand through his hair.

"Gordon—" Langley shook his head. "Don't worry about it."

"That's what Cassy said."

"So you've talked to her about it."

Gordon nodded. "She's all for it—well, she always has been. And now with Alexandra being the anchor for DBS—well, Cassy's too polite to say it, but even I know maybe it's not such a hot idea for Alexandra and me to be openly living together. She'd prefer, I think, that, if we're thinking of getting married, we go ahead and do it."

"This came up, you know," Langley said, "in our negotiations with Alexandra. We told her that she was of course free to do whatever she wanted in her personal life—but that we didn't want her to publicly acknowledge that she was living with you. See, it's Jack's older sister we worry about, Cordelia—"

"The religious one."

"Well," Langley said, chuckling to himself, "in a manner of speaking —but Cordelia is very sensitive to issues like this." He sighed. "And Cordelia does carry a great deal of weight with the board and could cause a lot a trouble if she thought the symbol of DBS News was— well, living in sin, as she would say."

"Yeah, right," Gordon said, thinking. "Um," he said a moment later, looking up, "so as far as you're concerned—about our getting married . . ."

"You've got my wholehearted approval," Langley told him. "When are you thinking of?"

"I'm not sure," Gordon said. "This winter, spring maybe."

Langley nodded, started to say something, but hesitated.

"I knew it," Gordon said.

"What?"

"That you'd ask me to keep it quiet for a while," Gordon said. "Around Jackson—right?"

"Uh," Langley said, "right. If you don't mind." This was no time to get Jack furious at DBS News.

"That was Cassy's advice too," Gordon said. "And I'm going to take it. Okay," he added, slapping the arms of his chair and standing up, "time for phase two."

"Which is?" Langley said, standing up also.

"Asking her to marry me," Gordon said, adding, with a smile and a wink, "for the thirty-ninth time."

This last comment of Gordon's disturbed Langley a bit, and as he walked back to Darenbrook I he hoped that Gordon had good reason to believe that after thirty-nine times Alexandra would now say yes. Worrying about Jackson was one thing, but Langley had no desire to worry about Alexandra angling to become the new Mrs. Darenbrook.

"Mrs. Peterson called," Adele said as he came back into his office. "She's at the house in Palm Beach."

"Thanks," Langley said, thinking, *Thank God she's back on an even keel.* Whenever Belinda was feeling very well, she usually liked to go to one of their houses—in Palm Beach, Aspen or just out in Greenwich—and call Langley four or five times a day to tell him some little thing that she had just done or witnessed. But when Belinda was not feeling very well, she headed back to Manhattan, to their apartment, where she rarely called Langley, but where other people usually did—to tell him that Belinda had "gone off."

There was no other way really to describe it. Belinda, who, at thirty-seven, to all appearances was quite normal, could suddenly "go off." Sometimes it came out as rage, and she would start verbally abusing people, throwing things, threatening to hurt herself; and other times she seemed merely disoriented, drunk almost (though Belinda did not drink), and wandered around—like she had recently, stumbling into the Bells' building—as though she were some kind of street person.

And then there were these manic episodes, when she wouldn't sleep, would chatter her head off, and then suddenly she'd go into this incredible drive to—what felt like her desire to—fuck Langley to death. More, more, it wasn't enough—it was a kind of frantic and fierce grabbing and grappling, desperate and harsh and not at all loving like the old Belinda had been, *his* old Belinda, the highly passionate Belinda of the early years of their marriage.

And then, just as suddenly, Belinda would feel fine again and flee Manhattan, and call Langley, sounding happy and relaxed.

Belinda had been tested for manic depression so many times that every time someone suggested it to Langley he could cite them chapter and verse why, in as thorough medicalese as they cared to hear, Belinda's problem was not manic depression. She had a borderline personality which she was working on in therapy; she had creative tendencies that caused periods of high motivation and periods of depression; Belinda had suffered enormous emotional damage as a child which was only now coming to the surface—these were the things Langley had been told, over and over. Belinda was not crazy, the doctors insisted.

Try telling that to her brothers and sisters though, who had watched Belinda suddenly "go off" during a board meeting in the living room of the Petersons' Fifth Avenue apartment not long ago.

"I—simply—must—do—this!" Belinda had panted, yanking on a

pair of fourteen-foot drapes until the rods came crashing down on top of Cordelia and Beau. And then she ran down the back hall, tearing off her clothes, screaming at the top of her lungs that Langley had to make love to her then and there or she was divorcing him because everybody knew she only married him to get out of that horrible school Cordelia put her in anyway and if he didn't come right now she would just jump out the window . . .

"Oh, she's not crazy," Norbert had snickered to Noreen, sitting next to her on the Victorian sofa.

"Wee-oh," Little El had said, slapping his thigh in merriment, "man the butterfly nets!"

Langley tried the number of the Palm Beach house and the phone rang and rang and rang. He hung up and tried again. This time, on the sixth ring, a woman answered who said (in a form of English that seemed to be missing a few things here and there) that his wife was down the road playing tennis ("pleh tet-tetnus, yah?"). Langley said he would call back later and hung up.

He sat there a moment, looking out at the Hudson River, thinking about, if he had his choice, would he be in Florida playing tennis in the sunshine, or be sitting here, trying to deal with this mess? Hmmm. Maybe it was because the sun came out at that moment that he chose this mess. Chose here. West End. He didn't know why, really. But he did know that for New York City—or anywhere—the wind-whipped blue-gray river out there today was a very beautiful sight.

His door suddenly flew open and a young woman with a large leather bag over her shoulder came striding in. She came to a stop in the middle of his office and just stood there, looking at him—cowboy boots apart, skirt colorful, long auburn hair blown everywhere. She was wearing a silk blouse with billowed sleeves and Langley could plainly see that she was not wearing a bra but that she certainly had breasts. His eyes came up to see that her expression was one of half scowl or half amusement—it wasn't clear which—but he found it an interesting face to look at while he pondered the question, since the young woman had a rather sensational mouth and large, flashing green eyes, and an all-in-all look about her suggesting a rather enticing accident just waiting to happen.

Looking at him, she said, "I don't believe it," and dropped her bag on the floor with a clunk. "You look just like Dennis the Menace's father."

Jessica Wright, Langley presumed, was going to be a lot to handle.

9

Cassy Uses Alexandra's Hideaway

After her conversation with Langley about the DBS News budget, Cassy went back to her office, returned what seemed like a hundred phone calls, and then, when she went outside to give Chi Chi a letter, was handed another call list requiring what looked to be a hundred more. Feeling tired suddenly, she sighed, slipped off her reading glasses and held the back of her hand against her forehead.

"You haven't eaten, have you?" Chi Chi asked her. Chi Chi had worked with Cassy at WST for three years and so she was fairly good at noticing when Cassy forgot to eat, which, when she didn't have a luncheon date, was often.

Cassy lowered her hand and smiled. "Aha," she said. "So my eyes aren't crossing on their own then."

"Here," Chi Chi said, swiveling around in her chair and reaching to open a small refrigerator. Outside each of the offices on this floor there was a large, open outer-office area and in Chi Chi's there was room for her desk, a desk for a typist, a kind of counter/worktable, file cabinets, bookshelves, and, here, a refrigerator. She reached inside and brought out a carton of yogurt. She closed the door and turned around to hand it to Cassy. "Can you handle blueberry?"

"Mmm, yes, thank you," Cassy said, taking it.

"And here," Chi Chi said, finding a plastic spoon in her desk drawer and handing it to her, and then—after searching a bit—a napkin too. During the latter exercise, two of the phone lines lit up and Chi Chi held a finger up to Cassy, signaling for her to wait. So Cassy waited while Chi Chi scribbled something—talking first on one line and then on the other, only to have the first one light up again. "Why don't you go down to the hideaway for a few minutes and eat in peace?" she suggested, putting the new call on hold.

"If only I could," Cassy murmured, tapping the spoon on the yogurt. "But I've too much to do."

Chi Chi was standing now, holding the phone between her chin and her shoulder, looking past Cassy to something down the hall. Then she snatched the yogurt and spoon out of Cassy's hands, motioned to her to be quiet, put the yogurt and spoon in a large manila envelope and handed it back to her, calling, "She can't talk to you right now, Kyle, she's got a meeting to go to."

Kyle was coming down the hall. "But, Cassy, we need to go over these—"

"She can't," Chi Chi said, thunking the phone down on her desk and pushing Cassy past him and down the hall. "Not for twenty minutes. She's got a meeting."

"Cassy, Alexandra wants to know—" Kate Benedict said, coming out of Alexandra's office.

"Can't talk now—back in twenty minutes," Chi Chi said, continuing to push Cassy down the hall. She walked Cassy all the way down the hall, stuck her in the elevator, pushed Sub Level 1 for her, stepped out and waved bye-bye. "Nineteen and a half minutes," she said as the door closed.

Cassy got out on Sub Level 1. This floor was cool and still, always. The halls had wall-to-wall carpeting and were almost always empty and quiet. The people who were inside the labs and offices were almost always quiet too. The people who worked on this floor also tended to be geniuses as well, scientists and programmers and educators and creative consultants working on computer boards and circuitries and screens. The most outgoing of Dr. Kessler's electronics and computer group were working with them downstairs at DBS News, and since none of the Nerd Brigade (whose unfortunate nickname from Jackson had stuck) said much beyond utterances of instructions and notations of fact, it did not come as a surprise that the group on Sub Level 1 had chosen to remain aloof from them—opting instead to observe safely from above.

Cassy walked through the short, interconnected hallways (it was positively eerie how quiet it was when right underneath, on Sub Level

2, it was like Grand Central Station at least sixteen hours a day) and made her way around to a long corridor of offices. She stopped at the last door, which was closed, knocked softly, waited and then peeked inside. Empty. Thank heavens. She went inside and closed the door behind her but did not turn on the light.

This was one of the offices that looked out over Studio A and so there was plenty of light to see by, but not enough for someone down in the studio or the newsroom or the conference room to look up and see her, which was the point of this exercise—to have ten minutes to think, to eat something, to gear up for what would inevitably be a long evening.

No wonder Alexandra liked this as a hideaway when things got too crazy, Cassy thought, taking her yogurt out of the manila envelope; it was wonderful up here. She could see almost the whole news area of the studio; about a third of the newsroom, which was glassed in off the studio; and about a third of the conference room next to the newsroom, which was glassed in off the studio as well. Cassy loved the setup downstairs because, with the satellite room right behind the newsroom, it made her feel as though all the news in the world was right there in front of them—and all they had to do was figure out how best to explain it and then send Alexandra out into the studio to do exactly that.

And there she was—Cassy watched her while eating her yogurt—down in the conference room. Alexandra was sitting with Dan, the news editor, at the long table. She was leaning on her elbow, resting her head in one hand while flipping through pages on a clipboard with the other. She stopped at a page, pointed at something and then tapped it twice. Dan was shaking his head, no, and then Alexandra was sitting up straight, saying something, flipping back several pages to point at something else. She looked at Dan, who shook his head again —more strongly—no. Alexandra then—if Cassy saw it right—offered to arm-wrestle with him, and they were both laughing. And then Alexandra said something again and—Cassy laughed out loud—Dan *really* shook his head, no. And he won the point, Cassy could tell, because Alexandra pushed the clipboard over to him and then he proceeded to flip pages and point things out to her.

Good, she thought, *he can stand up to her.*

CASSY USES ALEXANDRA'S HIDEAWAY

They had to be careful with Alexandra. Kyle was fine with her—he told her exactly what he thought and felt very comfortable arguing with her about how they should or should not do things—but the others had a tendency to let Alexandra make decisions that were really theirs to make. It wasn't that Alexandra didn't trust people in their jobs, it was more that she was testing them all, finding the give and the take and the extent of power that her word carried—which anyone in her position would do before setting sail with a new crew on a new ship. But while it was important that Alexandra be in on every aspect of the construction of her newscast, it was perhaps even more important that she not feel as though absolutely everything depended on her.

Alexandra needed to know that there was a very real system of checks and balances in this news operation that applied to her too, even though that ridiculous contract Darenbrook had given her literally gave her power over everything—including the hiring and firing of Cassy herself. And so, while it was tricky, it was essential that Cassy and some of the others provide some limitations and structure for Alexandra to work within, because otherwise—with her temperament —she ran the very real risk of burning herself out by trying to do everything and be everything to everybody.

Hurry up and get married, Alexandra, please, Cassy thought, watching her down there. *This Darenbrook nonsense has got to stop. You don't have the emotional energy to spare to baby-sit him.*

At moments like these, when Cassy wished she could manage Alexandra's personal life, it always hit her like some sort of startling revelation to remember that she had once made love with Alexandra herself. Cassy would sit there—stunned, really—her mind saying, *Really? Really? Then why can't I remember?* and then something would flicker and she would feel a surge of adrenalin with the scene that invariably came to mind.

Oh, yes, I do remember. . . . Very well I remember.

It was a very peculiar sensation for a forty-three-year-old woman who had been married for twenty-two years to think that she had ever done anything as dramatic as that. Alexandra was the *only* really dramatic thing she had ever done, basically because Michael had always provided more than enough drama for the entire family. And ironically, had it not been for her affair with Alexandra, Cassy never would have had the strength to take a stand with Michael—the stand that had helped him to finally stop drinking.

It had started in friendship. Alexandra had been right there for Michael after he had been fired from WWKK, and then she had been right there for Cassy when Michael ran out on her and was drinking himself to death and tearing the family apart in the process. Alexandra had understood Michael and Cassy and even their son Henry, too, and Cassy had been able to talk to her in a way she had never talked to anyone. And Alexandra hadn't known anyone in New York and had been working so hard at WWKK, and so Cassy had felt comfortable holding up her end of the friendship by understanding Alexandra's own woes and headaches at WWKK. And so, despite the difference in their ages, the friendship had seemed meant to be—

Despite the fact that Cassy had known from the beginning that Alexandra was attracted to her. Alexandra had once even gone so far as to confess that she was, but then they had talked it through and the matter had been dismissed.

Only Cassy had not forgotten about it. Not for a second. Looking back on it, although she had not been fully conscious of it at the time, Cassy realized that she had not only played on Alexandra's attraction to her but had encouraged it from the start. And who would have blamed her? To be so emotionally battered and confused and lonely as she had been, and to have such a lovely, warm and wonderful young person as Alexandra so near? The one person Cassy knew who would never hurt her? The one person she knew who would never threaten her family, and who would never demand commitment, since to do so would only threaten the most important thing in Alexandra's own life —her work? And too (and it had been no small thing), Alexandra was the first person who had ever seemed to care more about being close to the Cassy on the inside than about making passes at the Cassy on the outside—at the face, the body, the package that had only prompted passes with empty mutterings of love at Cassy all of her life.

She had been the one to ask Alexandra to make love to her. And Alexandra had. And it had been wonderful. And that part, learning to feel again, to feel lovable again, Cassy had never regretted—would never regret.

No.

It ended as soon as Michael agreed to go into a rehab, and while Michael often saw Alexandra after that, Cassy did not, not until August of 1987. In the meantime, however, faithfully, the women had written to each other once a week, long, newsy letters that did much to put them on a new footing—a stronger footing, actually, because it became very clear that theirs could, and would, be a most wonderful friendship.

And it was. As soon as Gordon reentered Alexandra's life, Cassy had too, and she and Alexandra had been very close ever since. And now they were colleagues as well, and Cassy was extremely grateful for how everything had worked out.

Only, Cassy thought to herself, sighing, pressing the bridge of her nose and closing her eyes, *my whole home life has collapsed.* Michael was interviewing for a job in Los Angeles and Cassy had told him she wanted him to leave by the end of the month regardless of whether he got it or not—pretty strong hints on both sides that, although neither could utter the word "divorce", the marriage was truly over. But this was not the first time this year Michael was supposed to have left, and so Cassy thought she would spare herself the embarrassment of telling people until he actually did. But with this new endeavor at DBS for her to pour her all into, and with Michael's twenty-nine-year-old in L.A. to pour his all into, Cassy thought it might really happen this time. And she hoped it would. Even Henry said he thought his parents would be better off apart (before they strangled each other—that was the part Henry always tactfully left out).

But Cassy smiled then, looking down at the studio, thinking how lucky she was to have DBS to help her get through, to help her start over in her life. However—and Cassy's smile faded somewhat—sometimes she couldn't help it, but she felt a twinge or two around Alexandra, of jealousy, and of feeling more than a little over the hill. Alexandra was so young and had so much ahead of her. And about Gordon—ah! Now why couldn't *she* have fallen for someone like Gordon way back at Northwestern? A man's man kind of man, but without all the hooting and hollering and rock and roll insanity of the man she had chosen for herself?

And if this worked out at DBS, after Alexandra had been married a little while, Alexandra could have a baby. The one thing about being an anchor that Alexandra did not like—being tied to a desk—was the very thing that would enable her to have a child and be around to raise it. And then, with the child-care facilities in Darenbrook I, Alexandra could just bring the baby in with her—

Stop it! Cassy told herself.

She had to stop herself because she had a very bad habit of wanting to try and make Alexandra Waring live Cassy Cochran's life over again, but make it come out the way it was supposed to. Alexandra hadn't had a neurotic mother who screamed at her night and day that her beauty was a curse and that if she ever used it instead of her brain she'd be dead by forty—and so Alexandra just went out in front of the cameras, a place Cassy had looked at longingly but had refused to go, certain that the camera would become to her what the mirror had become to the witch in *Snow White*—or worse, what it had become to her mother. Alexandra had not gotten married right out of school because she was too scared to be alone and too uptight to live with a man without being married to him. Alexandra had not had a baby because she needed something, someone she could trust to love her. Alexandra had not—

There was a quiet knock on the door and then it opened. It was Chi Chi. "Sorry," she whispered, "but Langley just called. He says Jessica Wright's turned up and he thinks she's brought something important."

Cassy was on her feet in an instant and instantly she felt better. Because this was the arena in which she had always known how to live, where she had always been able to think clearly, make decisions and effortlessly move to carry them out. This was work. This was where she had always been okay.

10

Jessica Wright

Until that fateful St. Patrick's Day night in 1981, Jessica Wright had figured that her life would proceed like a lot of Eastern girls' lives did who fled their upbringings to schools like the University of Arizona: she'd have a suntan for four straight years, return home with a bachelor's degree, jazz up her résumé, polish up her suburban savoir faire, let her mother buy her some interview outfits, let her father buy her a commuter ticket and land an entry-level job somewhere "with it," like Condé Nast, Random House or CBS.

She'd marry some boring banker type (the kind that tended to be wildly attracted to Eastern girls who fled their upbringings to schools like the University of Arizona), because she would need a nice place to live in Manhattan and somewhere near the ocean to go to on summer weekends, and unless there was going to be some sort of untimely death in the family, *somebody* was going to have to support her tennis, skiing, traveling and clothes habit if she were to take such a low-paying job in the interest of remaining interesting and interested.

Or, she had thought, she might be able to only live with the boring banker until she found someone she *really* wanted to marry (the kind that tended not to be wildly attracted to Eastern girls who fled their upbringings to schools like the University of Arizona because they themselves had fled their upbringings to schools like the University of Colorado, and who wanted to be interesting and interested too, and therefore needed a boring banker type of their own or, better yet, some young thing who *had* had an untimely death in the family).

Well, after all this serious contemplation, Jessica never even got out of Tucson.

On that fateful St. Patrick's Day evening in 1981, Jessica—the twenty-one-year-old junior majoring in journalism that she had been— was in the Blue Flamingo Bar near campus, dancing a jig in her green kilt for the benefit of a photographer from the *Daily Wildcat,* when a fellow she knew from one of her classes, Denny Ladler, came in. Denny had come to pick up the host of "Our Town Tucson," a public affairs TV talk show Denny worked on, but was told that the host had already been picked up by the Tucson police, busted by a narc for snorting cocaine and Mexican heroin in the men's room.

Thinking fast, Denny pulled Jessica off the dance floor ("Listen, you're the best bullshitter I know,") and asked her if she could come with him—right now—and be the substitute host on "Our Town Tucson." Jessica said sure she could. (Jessica thought she could do anything that night, which was very often the case when she was in the Blue Flamingo Bar.)

"Okay, everybody," Jessica said to the camera that night on "Our Town Tucson," then delivering the line for which she would later become famous: "No snoozing out there while I'm on the air!" And then she flung her hand across the small stage at the man sitting in the other deck chair. "Our guest tonight is Mr. Pipo Remodoza, the city superintendent who wishes to tell us all about the Wet Garbage/Dry Trash project."

"Thank you, hello," Mr. Remodoza said enthusiastically, smiling and nodding into the wrong camera.

Jessica actually played the interview pretty straight—until Mr. Remodoza started droning on and on about how viewers could tell the difference between wet garbage and dry trash. "If it looks damp . . ." he was saying.

"Pipo Remodoza," Jessica said, interrupting him. "Why does that name sound so familiar to me? Did you used to know President Nixon?"

"I don't think so," Mr. Remodoza said.

"Oh," Jessica said, recrossing her legs and hiking her kilt (prompting a whistle from somebody, which the microphone picked up). After she finished winking (at whoever that somebody was), she turned back to her guest and asked, "So where are you really from, anyway?"

"From?" Mr. Remodoza said.

"From," Jessica repeated. *"¿Donde estaban?"*

Mr. Remodoza shook his head.

"Where-are-you-from?" Jessica said a little impatiently, hitting the arm of her chair with her fist.

Mr. Remodoza's eyes widened a little in alarm. "I'm from Queens, I'm originally from Queens," he said quickly.

"How originally?"

"Jessica!" Denny hissed, which her mike picked up.

"What?" Mr. Remodoza said, leaning over to look at Denny under the camera.

"I mean, Mr. Remodoza," Jessica said, now sounding very nice indeed, "how long have you lived here in Tucson?"

"Almost two years," he said, settling back in his chair.

"Oh, I see, another longtime resident," Jessica said, leaning back in her chair (making the entire crew strain in the opposite direction, holding their breath as she teetered on the brink of disaster, one chair leg right on the edge of the stage). "I'm from Essex Fells, New Jersey, myself," she added, thumping her chair back down (and prompting a collective sigh of relief). "So what did you do in good old Queens?"

Before Mr. Remodoza had a chance to answer, Jessica leaned forward to stick her hand in front of his face and said to the camera, "For viewers who don't know, Queens is the borough of New York City where Forest Hills is—the place where the U. S. Open used to be held and still should be held today but isn't." She lowered her hand and said to Mr. Remodoza, "The racket where the Open is now is beyond belief."

"Ha-ha, that's very funny," Mr. Remodoza said.

"What is?"

"The racket—"

"Oh, right," Jessica said, smiling, "if you're from Queens, then you must know all about rackets. So what was yours?"

"Excuse me?"

"Job," Jessica said. "Did you have a job there? In Queens?"

"Yes," Mr. Remodoza said. "I was a government official."

"Golly," Jessica said, snapping her fingers, "now how did I know you were going to say that? So does anyone know you moved to Arizona, or do they just forward your paychecks?"

"What?"

"Jessica!" Denny was heard to hiss again.

"Oh, all right!" she yelled at Denny. "But don't you think it's a little weird that a Queens government official was appointed a city superintendent in Tucson? I do."

She was a hit from the beginning. Because of the havoc the mountains and desert around Tucson played on broadcast signals, the city had been wired for cable for years and so even UHF Channel 62 that "Our Town Tucson" was on came into most homes clear as a bell. All over town, in bars and college dorms in particular, groups of people turned to "Our Town Tucson" at eleven o'clock to see Jessica interview everyone from a doctor about sexually transmitted diseases to some lady who collected cacti that she saw faces in. ("See, if you look at it this way, you can see—" "Curly of the Three Stooges!" "No, dear, this is Senator Joe McCarthy.")

In six months Group K Productions offered to take her commercial, and Jessica gleefully quit school, took Denny as her producer and jumped from Channel 62 to 6 with "The Jessica Wright Show." She didn't then—nor would she ever—have a set format for the show, choosing instead to let each topic or guest lineup dictate it. Some nights the shows were oddly affecting, like the night Jessica had on three people over seventy whose brilliant careers—as an actress, a teacher and an attorney—had been utterly destroyed by scandal when they were young. Some nights Jessica was straight-faced outrageous, like the night she interviewed the dorm mothers of the all-women university halls about what constituted ladylike behavior. Some nights they had music, featuring local bands. Sometimes they had studio audiences and sometimes they had closed sets. There were serious shows—like the teenage gang show (when Jessica got knocked right out of her chair as a fight broke out)—and there were some very risqué shows, like the time Jessica interviewed four truckers (with bags over their heads) about their best truck-stop sex experiences on Route 10.

Group K offered a syndication package on "The Jessica Wright Show" and, as the scope of her guests and subject matter expanded, so did her markets. In the hustle and bustle Jessica acquired a husband, Gary, a marriage which did not add much stability to her already tumultuous and chaotic life as *the* talk show hostess in ascension, particularly when Gary was fired from his advertising job and he announced he would be her full-time business manager. By 1985 she was seen in twenty-one markets and, after David Bowie did a show with her that fall, L.A. and New York publicists began to call. Her demographics were fabulous—capturing that elusive eighteen-to-thirty-four market but good—and her fame in the region continued to spread and, as it did, even the critics started to like her. As the Albuquerque *Times* wrote:

> Miss Wright's greatest appeal lies in her ability to change her personality at the drop of a hat. She readily admits that she does and explains, "It's my job to give each guest whatever he or she needs to open up. Maybe my bookers have an agenda in mind with each guest, but I don't. I merely want to get at whatever it is that makes that guest special, that makes them stand out from our neighbors. And if one stands out because she raised more for the March of Dimes than anyone else and the other blasted her husband through the head with his shotgun, I can hardly behave the same way with both. Some need a strong personality to react to, while others need for me to stay quiet and out of their way. And, you know, some people need kindness and"—Miss Wright laughs a low, wicked laugh—"some need a little drama onstage to reveal themselves."

Jessica's personal life, at this point, had taken a very bad turn for the worse, but, ironically, the more suicidal she felt off the air, the more her on-air work seemed to improve. The Tulsa *Sentinel* called her show, "The best chronicle of our times," and the Dallas *Telegram* wrote:

> Ms. Wright embodies the confusion of an entire generation that learned its morality from television. Why is it, Ms. Wright is apt to wonder, that families are "so weird" instead of like the Andersons on "Father Knows Best"? Why is it we see thugs gracing the society pages instead of being put away by Elliot Ness? Why do real people seem so ridiculous to us and people putting on an act seem so real? Or, as Ms. Wright so appropriately wailed to a panel of social psychologists the other night, "Somebody, *please,* just tell me why we are all so lonely in America?"

But then the problems and insanity of her life began to creep onto the show with her. Her mood swings sometimes shocked even herself;

her behavior off screen had been shocking to herself for over a year; and Jessica sobbed, alone, when the San Diego *Star* wrote:

> What will Jessica be like tonight? Will she be the gentle young woman of sympathetic murmurings or the guffawing Minnie Pearl of Country Western TV? The straitlaced Eastern dilettante or the screaming fish-wife who seems to be appearing with increasing frequency of late? Well, regardless of whatever difficulties the twenty-five-year-old may have in controlling herself these days, there is one question burning brightly in the heart of every red-blooded American male who was watching the other night: *When will Jessica wear that dress again?*

The dress in question was one Jessica had borrowed from a waitress in the El Pueblo restaurant next door fifteen minutes before air time one night. Jessica had spent the day with some man in Sabino Canyon and, although her head had been quite messed up, she hadn't been so out of it as not to know that she shouldn't show up at the studio in a torn halter top, clay-stained shorts, hiking boots and anti-snakebite socks. The dress had fit very well everywhere except in the bust, where Jessica's considerable endowment had stretched and strained the whole upper part of the dress into rather indecent proportions.

But Jessica went on, running and running, cracking clever remarks anywhere, everywhere—on the show, to the bank teller, to the ceiling, she just couldn't turn it off—and she razzled and dazzled and grew more outrageous on her show, pushing her ratings higher, promising herself that if she didn't feel better soon she would simply kill herself. And she nearly did one night—the night her husband Gary slapped her across the face so hard at a party at Denny's that she fell backward off the patio stairs, cracking her head on the cement by the pool—only Denny broke down the bathroom door and stopped her from hacking her wrists (oh, God, a safety razor—wouldn't you know that was what he would have?).

The following dawn, sitting on a rock at Gate's Pass, watching the sun come up, Jessica decided she had had enough. She could die now, at twenty-six, or she could try to make some changes in her life.

And so she made some changes.

She quit cocaine, threw out her pot; she quit Gary and threw him out too (*and* his cocaine *and* his pot *and* his pills), went into therapy and felt quite a bit better.

The show would never be as manic as it had been up to that point, but then it did get more understandable again. Her eighteen-to-thirty-four audience remained loyal, but she started to pick up—of all things —senior citizens too. (Sun City, a retirement community, gave her an award as "Outstanding Young Person on Television.") She was able, at long last, to take the show on the road once in a while and it was on such a trip last year, to L.A., just after she and Denny had been talking about how much they needed a change, that they met Jackson Darenbrook. DBS seemed to them both to be the exact kind of change and challenge they needed and negotiations had begun.

And so here she was, Jessica Wright, finally out of Tucson, here at DBS in New York—three and a half weeks late but, as she kept trying to explain to the president of DBS (who looked exactly like Mr. Mitchell, Dennis the Menace's father), she was late because she had a chance to get an exclusive interview. But Langley—or Mr. Mitchell or whatever his name was—wasn't buying it. He was angry because he thought Jessica had disappeared to protest Bertie Flotsheim being hired as her executive producer and was only showing up now because she had heard they'd bought out Flotsheim's contract.

Well, it was true, Jessica *had* thrown a fit when she heard DBS had hired Flotsheim. She had never even met the man but would hate him forever anyway. Flotsheim had once worked at a station in Los Angeles and Jessica had seen a copy of the memorandum he wrote to his station manager about why they shouldn't take "The Jessica Wright Show." It had said, in its entirety, "Big tits, but so's her mouth—I'd pass."

Jessica had already signed her DBS contract at that point and had no say over her executive producer, but she told her agent to tell Jackson that, much as she loved him, she'd go to hell before she'd ever work with Bertie Flotsheim. And when her agent reported back that there was nothing they could do, that Flotsheim's contract had been signed, well—okay, *yes,* that part was true, she *had* decided to go down to Palumboca, Mexico, to give everyone a little to think about. But that wasn't why she had stayed down there and it wasn't why she was so late arriving.

"Okay," Langley sighed, "start from the beginning."

So she did.

Jessica explained how she had driven down to a fishing village, Palumboca, in Mexico, to cool off for a few days, and how early one morning she accidentally backed her car into the Gulf of Mexico, and then how, down at the police station, she got into a terrible argument with the police because they started taking her car apart—literally, bolt by bolt, piece by piece—looking for drugs, and how, by screaming in Spanish, "You stupid fucking shitheads, I haven't done drugs in two years!" she landed in jail.

"You've been in *jail* all this time?" he asked her, horrified.

"Oh, not jail-jail," she explained. "It was more like a motel, really. Actually, it *was* a motel. It was built in the fifties when they thought they were going to get legalized gambling and—" She cleared the air with her hand. "Never mind. Anyway, it wasn't so bad—I just had to write checks all day and send out for beer and pizza, but then the mayor's wife came over to play backgammon and invited me to stay in their pool house—'cause the police chief is the mayor's brother—and so I went and that's when I found Richard Barnes."

"Richard Barnes—the writer?" Langley said.

Yes, Jessica meant Richard Barnes, the novelist who had won the Pulitzer Prize in the sixties, went through five wives in seven years and then disappeared from public life and from whom no one had heard since 1978. And Jessica had found him. He lived in a converted fishing hut by the beach in Palumboca and came over to garden with the mayor's wife twice a week.

Barnes took a great liking to Jessica and came over daily to drink tequila and play Ping-Pong, and every day Jessica would urge him to do an interview with her. At first he said he would never do another interview as long as he lived, but a few days later said that if he ever did decide to do an interview he'd do it with her. And then he started talking about how, if he ever did do an interview, he supposed he could set the record straight on all those stories people had written about him in their memoirs. ("Liars, all of 'em," he growled, "writers.")

"And so," Jessica said, concluding her tale, "I stayed as long as it took to convince him to do an interview with me. And he did. And I have it right here," she said, patting her leather bag. "Four hours."

Langley started making phone calls while Jessica sat there in his office, periodically running both of her hands back through her hair, making her gold bracelets jangle and Langley look at her. Then he would look away—while talking into the phone—and then he would try to sneak another look at her (she knew what he was looking at), but Jessica would catch him at it and wink at him and so finally he turned his chair away from her.

"Jessica baby!" Jackson cried, flinging open the door from his office. "I just got in from the West Coast and here you are!"

"Hi, Jackie," she said, standing up to receive a hug.

And then in through the other door came a great-looking blond lady, about forty or so.

"Oh, no," Jackson groaned, releasing Jessica. "She's *my* friend," he said to the lady. "Go away."

"Jessica's brought an interview with Richard Barnes," Langley said to the lady, hanging up the phone and standing up. "I was hoping you might help us decide what to do with it since she no longer has an executive producer."

"Hello, Jessica," the blonde said to her, taking her hand. "I'm Cassy Cochran. Richard Barnes—how on earth did you find him? Where is he? How long is the interview? It's on videotape, right?"

"Cassy's the president of DBS News, as well as the executive producer for 'News America Tonight,'" Langley explained.

"News, huh?" Jessica said, turning to look at her again. "I did bring my producer with me—Denny."

"Then let's go find Denny," Cassy said, "and let me find our producer, Kyle, and then we'll run some of the tape, see what you've got and start talking about what we should do with it."

Jessica looked at Jackson. "But you're not on the air yet, are you?"

"Not yet, sweetiest pie," Jackson said, giving her hair a playful tug. "But soon."

"Maybe sooner than we know," Cassy said. To Langley, "If it's good enough, we might have a special on our hands."

"It's good enough," Jessica said without hesitation.

"Then let's go," Cassy said, taking Jessica's arm.

"Wait a minute—hold on, Mrs. Cochran," Jackson said, taking Cassy's hand off Jessica's arm and holding her by the wrist. "Jessica here's a real nice girl and I'm gonna be real upset with you if you let the dogs drag her under the house."

"If the what drag me where?" Jessica said.

"Just ignore him," Cassy said, yanking her arm away from Jackson and reaching for the leather bag. "The tapes are in here, right?"

"Creeping catfish, Jessica honey," Jackson said, snatching the bag out of Cassy's hand and handing it back to Jessica, "you're gonna have to do a lot better than this if you're going to hold on to your special."

"Will you stop it?" Cassy said, giving Jackson a shove, making him laugh.

"Cassy you can trust," Langley said to Jessica. "It's Alexandra you have to watch out for."

"Oh, stop it, you two," Cassy said, taking Jessica's arm and pulling her to the door. "Come on, let's go find your Denny. Langley, I'll call you as soon as we know what we've got." And then, once they were out the door, she called back, "And then both of you might want to come down."

As they made their way down to Sub Level 2, Cassy told Jessica that, when it came to her show, she thought it would be best if Jessica didn't pay too much attention to anything Jackson said. She also told her that Langley Peterson tended to view matters in financial terms as opposed to content and aesthetics, so until Jessica got herself an executive producer Denny should talk to Langley for her, or, if need be, Cassy would. Then she started in on how wonderful Alexandra Waring was, how talented she was, how much Jessica would like her . . .

It always amazed Jessica how otherwise very smart people were very dumb when it came to talking to one TV personality about how great another one was. Why Cassy thought she wanted to hear about how wonderful Alexandra Waring was, was beyond her—particularly on the unspoken premise that, as an anchorwoman, Alexandra's work was much more important than her own. To Jessica, Cassy might as well have said, "You'll be delighted to know that Alexandra's not the kind to mind stooping so low as to associate with the likes of you."

Yeah, well, if Alexandra Waring was so high and mighty, then why, Jessica wanted to know, had she chosen TV? Didn't journalists go into TV for the same two reasons that all performers—actors, announcers, puppeteers—did, for money and exposure? And did Cassy think the insecurity and ego of an Alexandra Waring were really so different from that of a Jessica Wright? Yeah, right! Try telling Alexandra Waring how absolutely wonderful Jessica Wright was and watch *her* eyes. And at least Jessica talked *to* people on the air—what could one make of someone who only talked *at* people?

When they got downstairs they found that Denny was already with the senior producer of DBS News, Kyle McFarland. Kyle was a nice guy and sort of good-looking (not much hair though), and said that Jessica was right, she did hear a trace of an English accent. He had gone to school in England for six years as a boy. Then Jessica noticed Kyle's wedding ring and her pleasantries eased to a stop, and she handed the tapes to Denny.

Denny wore a wedding ring too, only his spouse was a man—an innovation one wouldn't suspect until one was invited to his home for dinner. Bill (Denny's other half) was a geologist and, while it was a tremendously esteemed profession in the Southwest, it was unclear how well Bill would do in New York City. So this move had not been an easy decision for the couple to make and Jessica prayed it would work out, because Jessica didn't know what she would do without the man who not only had given her a career but who had made it possible for her to live to survive her life in general.

While Kyle and Denny went off together, Cassy gave her a whirlwind tour of the floor. It was something—engineering, the satellite room, graphics lab, audio lab, editing bays, the control room, the newsroom, the news conference room—and by the time Jessica walked into Studio A itself she could feel her heart starting to pound because—oh, yeah—she could feel it in the air, feel that *it* was soon to happen. The red light would soon be going on for DBS.

But while there were carpenters and electricians and workers hammering and snipping and banging in and around Studio A, except for the lighting grid (with no lights attached), there was no one and nothing in Studio B next door. "This is why everyone was so anxious for you to arrive," Cassy said. "You've got to figure out what kind of set you want and the seating arrangement for your studio audience. See," she said, pointing to the gray burlap-covered wall, "this wall retracts to open on to Studio A. Your permanent set will be right on the other side of this wall. And so the audience will be in risers, or whatever you want, over here. And they'll enter and exit the complex from there too." She was pointing to the far wall of Studio B, where there were three sets of double doors.

Cassy turned to her. "You really need to let them hire an executive producer for you—like yesterday, Jessica."

Jessica nodded. "Why can't Denny be it?"

"He's already turned it down," Cassy said.

"He did? When?"

"While you were away," Cassy said. "Langley offered it to him, but he said he loved the floor too much." She smiled. "He also said he despised budgets and so Langley quickly retracted the offer."

Jessica looked at her. "For someone who runs the news, you sure seem to know a lot about my show."

Cassy laughed. "Well, that's why I'm in news, Jessica," she said, taking her arm to move on, "I need to know everything."

Jessica liked her. And Jessica was impressed by the tour. Compared with the facilities here, the Group K studios looked like a high school audiovisual club.

They saw the greenroom (the room—which in this case was going to be blue—where studio guests waited to go on), makeup, and a series of dressing rooms, the second of which Cassy stopped in front of. JESSICA WRIGHT, the sign said. When Jessica's eyes traveled to the first door, the one that said, ALEXANDRA WARING, Cassy smiled and said, "First come, first served, that's all." They went inside Jessica's. It was a large, empty, oblong room with an attached bathroom and shower. Cassy explained that Jessica had to tell DBS what she wanted in there —painted? wallpaper? furniture?—and answered Jessica's next question with a gentle no, she couldn't show her the inside of Alexandra's because, well, it was Alexandra's.

They wound around the hallways to reach a screening room, which was actually more like a tiny theater. Denny was in there with Kyle; Jessica met some guy named Dan and a good-looking black guy named Hex ("My mother was a witch"???). And then, when Jessica and Cassy took seats, Herself came rushing in.

There she is, Jessica thought, *Queen of the Daisy Chain.*

"I'm sorry I couldn't get here sooner," Alexandra said to Cassy, "but Rookie trapped me with these dog food sponsors." She laughed, showing marvelous teeth, and leaned over Cassy to offer her hand to Jessica. "Oh, Jessica, it is such a pleasure. I've seen some tapes of your show—your work is so good, and so are you."

"Thank you," Jessica said, thinking how she hated, *hated,* HATED this, shaking the cool hand of this very together, very attractive Miss Perfect. *I've spent my entire life avoiding people like you!* she screamed in her head, looking at those incredible blue-gray eyes. *Ever get a B, Alexandra? No, I bet you didn't. And got all the boys, didn't you? Oh, fuck you! Stop with the smile, already!*

Kyle dimmed the lights slightly and started the tape; the screen in the wall came alive and the sound of Jessica's voice filled the room. "Good morning good morning good morning good morning," her voice said in singsong, as some unidentifiable blur came into focus as an extremely tan Jessica smiling into the camera.

"Denny and Jessica indexed the parts they think best," Kyle said loudly. "So I'm going to skip ahead."

"Have we made a dupe yet?" Alexandra asked from across the aisle.

Jessica leaned forward in her seat to look at Alexandra. "It doesn't belong to you yet," she said sweetly, prompting everyone to laugh.

They were barely ten minutes into the material before Cassy was on the phone in the back of the room; Denny, Kyle and Hex were talking cutaways or something; and Alexandra was sitting next to Jessica, firing questions at her about where Barnes was, how she had gotten to him, were there any limitations she had agreed to, had he signed a release, and on and on. Within the hour Jackson and Langley and some PR guy named Derek were in the screening room too, and everybody was talking a Jessica Wright interview special produced by DBS News that would air just as soon as they could work it out with the affiliates—which Cassy said could be very soon.

"But I don't work for DBS News," Jessica said to everybody over the sound of the tape.

"And DBS News doesn't work for you either," Alexandra said, "but we'd still like to see your special get on the air—so we'll do you a favor and DBS a favor and ourselves a favor and produce it for you."

"Now hold on," Langley said, turning around in his seat to look at Alexandra.

"Hold on what?" Cassy said from the back of the room, covering the phone she had been talking into. "If we're going to produce it, it's going to be called 'A Jessica Wright Interview Special—Produced by DBS News.' "

"And Alexandra will do the opening with Jessica," Kyle said.

"She can't do this, Jack," Langley sputtered. "If we make it a DBS News production, Alexandra's going to siphon money out of the ad revenues again with that damn contract clause."

"Wow," Jessica said, turning to Alexandra, "I'm impressed. Who's your agent?"

"I'll do it for my union minimum," Alexandra called to Langley. "I'll waive everything else."

While Cassy and Langley started shouting back and forth about who would pay the overhead, Jessica nudged Alexandra. "So what kind of opening would we do?"

Alexandra looked at her. "Oh, just a little live interview in the studio, to introduce you and set up the background."

"Ugh—live?" Jessica said. In recent years Jessica had insisted on taping her show ahead of time. Her nerves just couldn't take the pressure of live.

Alexandra looked surprised. And then she recovered, smiled and said, "Don't worry, I'll lead you through it."

Langley was yelling now, and then Cassy was yelling back; Jessica looked around, swallowed and then looked back at Alexandra. "I really hate live," she whispered. "I mean, I really really hate it."

"Then we'll figure out something else," Alexandra whispered back. "Don't worry. I promise you, I won't push for anything you don't feel comfortable with."

"Did you hear that?" Derek cried from the front row, pointing to the screen. "That crack about Capote is dynamite—you gotta keep that in. And the part about Hellman too. If I can use them in a release, we'll get pickup in all the papers."

"Take it or leave it, Langley," Cassy called from the back of the room. "Let DBS News produce the special or we're out of here."

"I don't have any objections," Jessica called.

Kyle said something to Denny and he said something to Langley and Langley started yelling at Cassy, who started yelling at Jackson, who started yelling back at her.

JESSICA WRIGHT

"Money never brings out the best in people—ever notice?" Alexandra whispered to Jessica. "Come on—let's get out of here until they're finished."

It sounded like a great idea to Jessica and so they excused themselves and fled to Darenbrook III. While Alexandra filled her in a little on the good points of DBS (i.e., the facilities) and the bad points (i.e., trying to get Langley to approve anything), she showed Jessica where she thought Jessica's and Denny's offices were on the first floor, and then they took the stairs up to the second floor.

Alexandra's office was filled with green plants and trees. In front of the wall of glass there was a huge oak table with one chair pulled up to the middle of it and four wooden folding chairs stacked against the wall near it. There was a couch along one wall and a coffee table, and two chairs facing it. There was a whole load of electronic stuff built into the wall near the door; there were a couple bookcases filled with books; there were a few prints on one wall; and then, of course, there were all of these plants and trees, so many that it smelled a little like a greenhouse.

Alexandra asked what Jessica would like to drink, and after she said white wine, Alexandra's assistant, Kate, was dispatched to look for some in Jackson's office. Kate came back with a bottle and a crystal wineglass. Alexandra chose to drink grapefruit juice. *(Silly me,* Jessica thought, sitting in one of the chairs, *for supposing that Alexandra would be so wild and crazy as to have a glass of white wine at six forty-five at night.)*

They had a pretty nice time, though. Alexandra kicked off her shoes and sat cross-legged on the couch with a pillow in her lap, and while Jessica sipped her wine, she listened to Alexandra explain her mixed reaction to DBS trying to sell them—"DBS News America Tonight" and "The Jessica Wright Show"—together. When Alexandra kept asking Jessica if she understood, that her doubts had nothing to do with the quality of Jessica's show, but had to do with the different audiences of the programs, Jessica burst out laughing and poured herself another glass of wine.

"What is it?" Alexandra said.

"Whoever said *I* wanted *news* as a lead-in?" Jessica said, settling back into her chair with her refilled glass. "Listen, Alexandra, no offense, but the only reason why I'm going along with this is because, at least for the first week or so, everybody's gonna be tuning in to see Brenda Starr who got shot, or Miss VaVaVaVoom who's fooling around with Jackson."

Alexandra's mouth parted in astonishment and Jessica thought maybe she had gone too far.

But then Alexandra smiled and her eyes started to twinkle. "And I suppose the next thing you're going to do is remind me that I'm the older woman at DBS."

"You said it, not me, Alexandra Eyes," Jessica said, smiling into her glass. But Jessica inwardly cringed, knowing that it was no longer possible to ignore the physical toll the past seven years had taken on her. Her face belonged to someone thirty-five, at least. Had it been the sun? The two years of cocaine? The parties? Gary? The show? The stress and pace of her life? Her own insanity? God only knew, but as proud of her success at twenty-eight as she was, it was ludicrous to think she looked younger than Alexandra Eyes here. *Oh, brother, just look at her over there. Miss Perfect.*

"I love your cowboy boots," Alexandra said.

"They're cowgirl boots," Jessica said.

Alexandra smiled. "Yes, of course."

"Hey, that reminds me," Jessica said, "I know a great friend of yours and I'm supposed to send you a big Denver hello."

Alexandra only looked at her.

"Lisa Connors," Jessica said.

"Lisa," Alexandra repeated, nodding slightly.

Blond, lovely and some sort of a painter, Lisa Connors was the daughter of one of the richest and most corrupt land barons in the West. *(Is that it?* Jessica wondered, surprised at Alexandra's minimal response. *Alexandra doesn't want to be associated with the daughter of a crook?)*

"How do you know her?" Alexandra said, turning to put the couch pillow back.

"She just waltzed into the studio one night, telling me how she simply *had* to meet me and express her admiration," Jessica said, laughing a little at the memory, because they had all been so taken back by the kind of swirling glamor with which Lisa had made her entrance into the studio. Security hadn't even stopped her. Security would have *given* her the studio had she paused ten seconds.

"And?" Alexandra said, patting the pillow in place.

"And she lassoed me into coming to Denver for some luncheon for the Western Foundation of Communication something-or-other," Jessica said.

"For the Communicative Arts," Alexandra said quietly, now reaching to the floor for her shoes.

Jessica hesitated and then said, "Do you not like her or something?"

"Oh, I like her," Alexandra said, sliding her legs off the couch and leaning over to put her shoes back on. "I haven't seen her in a long while, that's all." She sat up, face flushed from bending over.

What the heck was going on? When Lisa heard about Jessica going to DBS, she had carried on so about what a great friend of hers Alexandra was and how Jessica had to deliver a special hello for her. And Lisa was not the type to make up stuff like that.

As if Alexandra had heard her thoughts, she said, "Lisa lived in Kansas City for a little while. And she was a bit lost in her life, I think. We became friendly—and I do very much like her, Jessica—but . . . Well, do you know how people who are a little lost in their lives tend to —to . . . ?" She was looking for the right word.

"Cling?" Jessica offered.

"Exactly," Alexandra said, nodding. "And I don't mean it as a criticism, it was just that it made me feel a little uncomfortable."

Clingy? Lisa Connors? Living in Kansas City? This was all news to Jessica.

"She's not like that now," Jessica said. "As a matter of fact, I always thought she was the opposite. Very carefree."

Alexandra smiled, but there was still something in her expression— in her eyes—that was not quite right and Jessica couldn't figure it out. Lisa Connors . . . Lisa Connors . . . What could it be about Lisa Connors that so bothered Alexandra Eyes here?

"Listen, Jessica, I wish I could talk some more," Alexandra said, looking at her watch, "but I really have to get back downstairs or I'll be here all night."

"Oh, sure," Jessica said, starting to get up but then stopping. "Um— Alexandra? Would you mind if I stayed and made a few phone calls?"

"Please do," Alexandra said, standing up and gesturing to the big oak table. She walked over to the door. "I'll tell Kate not to disturb you."

"Thanks," Jessica said, standing up. "Oh, and could you tell Denny I'll be down in a few minutes?"

"Sure," she said, "I'll see you in a bit." And then she disappeared out the door.

Jessica stood there a minute, watching the door. When she was satisfied that Alexandra was really gone, she smiled to herself, scooped up the wine bottle and walked over to the table. She sat down in the chair, poured herself another glass of wine, put the bottle down, pulled the phone closer and picked up the receiver.

Goody. She'd call Lisa Connors.

11

What Happened That Night
Part I: Jackson Gives Alexandra a Ride Home

Damn, but he hated waiting. What was it? Almost nine? Cassy, Langley, Jessica, Denny, Dan, Hex—they had all left over an hour ago, exhausted after arguing over how to handle Jessica's interview with Richard Barnes.

Hands deep in his pockets, Jackson walked across the newsroom to the AP machine to pretend to read the wire stories that were printing out.

"It's just filler material," the kid on duty said. (Jackson swore that half his employees couldn't be out of school yet, they looked so young.)

"Could be I've been in news a little longer than you," Jackson growled at him.

The kid—whose name was actually Jimmy Hallerton—looked through the glass wall at Alexandra (who was sitting at the conference table with Kyle and a reporter from their new Cleveland affiliate) and then looked back at Jackson. "She should be through soon."

Jackson shrugged, moving on to the Reuters machine. There were a few other people puttering around the newsroom and now all of them were looking at him. Geez Louise, they were *always* looking at him—as if he might suddenly shoot out all the clocks—London, pow! Moscow, pow! Peking, pow! Tokyo, pow!—and start in on the monitors—CNN, pow! CBS, pow! NBC, pow! ABC, pow! What were they all doing, anyway?

He walked over to one desk and looked over a young woman's shoulder at her computer monitor. "What are you doing?"

"Um," she said nervously, stopping typing, "I'm writing a follow-up story on the Aloha Airlines accident—the one where the fuselage ripped off—"

"I know, I know," Jackson said, "I only read forty-seven newspapers a day." Then he looked at her, sighed, and then smiled, patting her on the back. "Don't mind me—what is it? Shelley, right?"

Her face lit up. "Right."

"So tell me, Shelley, what sources are you writing from?"

"Uh," she said, pulling some papers over, "the wire services, the Darenbrook Access"—she was referring to the electronic current event library, fed with stories from Darenbrook papers—"and then reports filed from a stringer out of Honolulu. The L.A. affiliate got someone out there, but late," she added. "Still, I just checked in with him, the film is good and I'm writing a two-minute voice-over for Alexandra."

"And this is for—what? Practice?" Jackson asked her.

She nodded, looking over at a guy across the newsroom. "And I'm being timed, Mr. Darenbrook, so if you'll excuse me . . ."

"Oh, sorry! Gosh, really, I'm sorry," he said, backing away. "Hey, you," he called to the guy, "take a minute off her time."

The guy shook his head.

"What do you mean, no?"

The guy shook his head again. "Bosses always want to talk to you while you're on deadline. Goes with the territory."

"Mr. Darenbrook?" Jimmy said.

"Would you stop calling me that?" Jackson said, turning around. "Creeping crickets, how old do you think I am, anyway?"

"It's a term of respect—Jackson," Jimmy said.

"You," Jackson said, catching Shelley looking at him again. "Back to your story—pronto, let's go, move it."

"Jackson," Jimmy Hallerton said again. "Cassy told me to call her if Alexandra wasn't out of here by nine. She'd probably appreciate it if you could get her out of here."

"Mrs. Cochran would appreciate it if I got Alexandra out of here." He rolled his eyes. "Where have you been?"

"But she asked us to keep an eye on her. She was here until two last night."

Jackson nodded, looking at her. Alexandra was sitting at attention, arms resting on the conference table, nodding, listening intently to the reporter who was sitting across from her. She did look a little pale, tired. "I don't think Mrs. Cochran would appreciate anything I did, so let's just not mention me and the fact I was here at all, okay?"

"Okay," Jimmy said, twiddling a pencil. "But she does appreciate you."

"Yeah, right," Jackson muttered, eyes still on Alexandra.

"She does," Jimmy protested.

"I can imagine," Jackson said.

"She always says, if you were any different from the way you are, that none of us would be getting this chance." When Jackson turned to look at him, Jimmy shrugged. "I'm only telling you what she tells us."

"What else does she tell you? And don't start laying it on, kid," Jackson warned him, pointing a finger at him, " 'cause I don't have anything to do with your salaries down here."

"Yeah, I know," Jimmy said. "She says you're a vanishing breed." His eyebrows went up. "More?"

"More," Jackson said.

"We're supposed to take a good look at you to remember that it's people who build the great institutions and it's the corporations they leave behind that tear them apart. So we're all supposed to hope you'll live for an awful long time."

"She said that?"

"Oh, yeah. And then she's always telling us that we can either make DBS stand for something you'll be glad you put your name on, or we can all go back to our old jobs and wait to be promoted in fifty-nine years into jobs none of us want." The phone on his desk rang. "Excuse me," he said, snapping it up. "Newsroom—"

Huh, so what Langley claimed was true, Mrs. Cochran did speak well of him to her people. Well, good, she should, it was his company. But it was interesting that he heard from the outside what she said about him too. He had taken Dexter Halloway, the chairman of Rogers, Dale—the parent company of WST—up to Boston for a Red Sox game recently as his guest. Dexter was still ticked off that Jackson had taken Mrs. Cochran away from them but admitted that, since they had backed away from taking WST national as a super station over cable, they didn't have the opportunity to offer her.

Jackson had been fascinated by how proud Dexter was of Mrs. Cochran and how he tried to take credit for making her a station manager before there were women station managers. (Jackson knew Dexter had about as much to do directly with WST as President Reagan did with the Kalamazoo town meeting.) And, like Langley, he spoke so glowingly of her as a person that, like he did with Langley sometimes, Jackson had to wonder if old Dexter wasn't a bit in love with her.

They had talked quite a bit about Mrs. Cochran over the afternoon and by the time Jackson returned to West End he felt he better understood this woman who yelled at him every time he went near Alexandra and chastised him constantly about interfering, but who also, according to Dexter, told industry people that he was an extraordinarily creative businessman whom she tremendously admired for his spirit and willingness to take risks.

As a matter of fact, in the course of the PR for DBS News, Mrs. Cochran seemed as determined to build Jackson's reputation as she was Alexandra's. In an article appearing last week in the Chicago *Sun-Times,* she was quoted as saying:

> Our immediate goal is a one-hour newscast, concentrating on breaking news within America, as witnessed and reported by local newsrooms around the country. As a network, DBS is responsible for providing a national overview to these stories, linking them into a clear, cohesive and compelling chronicle of the day. At DBS, you see, we have no doubts whatsoever about the role national network news plays in our country.

As the chairman of Darenbrook Communications, Jackson Darenbrook, has often pointed out, imagine what would have happened to the civil rights movement had there been only local news.

It was her way, he began to realize, of bolstering Alexandra's credibility among her industry peers. With all of this innuendo about the two of them in the tabloids, about his reputation as a playboy, someone, somewhere needed to remind people of his own professional background in communications and point out that he had to spend a lot of time with Alexandra because he was so intimately involved with the development of DBS News (although Mrs. Cochran, in reality, tried to keep him out of the day-to-day operations). She also (or was it Langley? well, somebody) was stirring up a lot of interest in the DBS technological system as well, because Jackson was getting all kinds of friendly inquiries from outside about the possibilities of "renting" the Darenbrook transmission facilities.

Well, the technological system behind DBS was impressive, but then Darenbrook Electronics had never been a problem because Darenbrook Electronics had always made money. It was DBS News that was a problem because it would not make money for at least (and at best) four or five years and there was this matter of being almost forty-seven million short within DBS at the moment, and Jackson didn't have the heart yet to upset poor old Lang further by telling him what had happened out in L.A. About how Little El had been out there, hounding and threatening Beau at the *Field Day* offices, grilling him about his debts and rumors of a pending lien against the magazines. Jackson had been able to chase Little El out of town, but Little El had called Cordelia and Cordelia had tracked Jackson down, getting him on the Gulfstream phone during his flight back East this morning.

"Jackie, money isn't the point," Cordelia had said (which, with Cordelia's angry Last Stand of the South inflection, was more like, *"Jaaa*-ckie, *mun*-nee *i*zent tha *po*-went").

"What is your point, Cordelia?"

"I know our brother Beau is in a most grievous financial situation and it has been ascertained that you are intervening for him and may be using our magazines to do it."

"Why, Cordie Lou," Jackson had said, "what kind of story are you telling?" (When Cordelia was angry with him, Jackson tended to revert to the same strategy of denial that worked when he was a boy.)

"You listen to me, Jackson Andrew Darenbrook."

(Uh-oh, Jackson had thought, *here it comes.)*

"You and I both know that you are no stranger to the playing of the shell game and that I have looked the other way on certain projects of which Little El, Norbert and Noreen would not approve, but which I knew were necessary to maintain the well-being of the company. But you listen to me, little brother—"

(When Cordelia got on her high horse like this, Jackson often imagined her sitting on their old gray mare, Bunky-belle, with a mobile phone in one hand and the torch from the Statue of Liberty in the other.)

(Sigh. What he would give for a ride in the field with old Bunky-belle today. *Bunky-belle, darlin', how are ya up there in horse heaven, anyway?)*

"I will not stand for you jeopardizing any part of Darenbrook Communications to finance Beau's gambling. And don't bother trying to deny it! Good golly, any fool could have read that piece in the *Wall Street Journal* last week to know what he must have lost in the crash. Or how many Beauregard Darenbrooks do you suppose there are? Or do you think that down here in Hilleanderville Daddy and I need an arrow-plane and skywriter to get the message?"

"I have not used the magazines in any way to bail Beau out," Jackson said. (It was true. He was using his own money. And the miniseries bailed out DBS News and Old Hardhead bailed out the miniseries and Jackson was sure Langley would straighten the whole thing out no later than next summer.)

"I'm sorry, Jackie Andy, I am truly sorry, but I do not believe you," Cordelia said. "I know that DBS News has you tied up for at least seventy million—Daddy's got the figures right here on the kitchen table—and I happen to know that even if you robbed your poor misguided children you still couldn't be intervening for Beau on your own. You've done well, Jackie, but not that well. And Norbert says that you lost quite a bit of money on the market yourself last fall."

(Uh-oh. Cordie's on the wrong train, but she's on the right track.)

"I think, Cordelia," Jackson had said quietly, "maybe you and I ought to get together soon and go over everything, so I can put your mind to rest."

"Oh, I'm going to put my mind to rest all right," she snapped. "Because I'm going to send a team of auditors up there to get to the bottom of this. I'd sooner see Beau in jail before I allow Darenbrook Communications to finance his gambling sprees. It's got to stop, Jackie! This family has been paying his debts since he was thirteen years old and bet that nasty Elmo Puddleton a dollar he couldn't knock the twins off the porch swing."

"Cordie, come on—"

"Come on nothing! And while I've got your ear, Mr. Big Shot— these stories about you and that, that—anchorgirl. The town is carrying on so—I cannot even wheel our father down the street without someone making a remark. 'Why, that randy boy of yours, Mistuh Darenbrook, how he's carryin' on with that girl half his age.' "

At this point Jackson had clapped the phone into the side of the plane and held it there, yelling, "I'm losing the signal, Cordie, I'll have to call you tonight."

"Jackson," Alexandra said, coming in through the conference-room door.

"Hi," Jackson said, looking at his watch. "My car should just be arriving. I stopped down to see if you wanted a ride." (Okay, so his car had been waiting outside for one hour and fifty-two minutes, which was also how long he had been waiting to ask her if she'd like a ride.)

"Thanks, but it's out of your way," she said. "I'll just call—"

"It's not out of my way," he said quickly. "I'm heading uptown."

She covered her mouth to yawn. "Excuse me," she murmured, dropping her hand. "Well, if you're going that way, great. I have a friend visiting and I'm running very late."

He almost asked who the friend was. (Somehow Alexandra didn't seem the type to have friends who visited. Of course she must have friends, but still, it seemed strange to think of her ever seeing anyone from the outside world.)

He walked her up to her office on Darenbrook III to get her things, and then they went down to the carport where his limousine was waiting. As they pulled out of the West End driveway, heading north on West End Avenue, Jackson thought about how funny it was, but how the passing New York City streetlights and shadows had the same flattering effect on Alexandra that the television camera did. Her eyes were no longer a little tired-looking; she no longer seemed a trifle too thin. No. No, she didn't. She looked gorgeous.

She was talking away about Jessica's interview and he let himself think about other things—about her, actually—while he nodded and uh-huhed politely.

"She leads a rather fast life, doesn't she?" Alexandra asked him. After a moment, "Jackson?"

"What?" he said, sighing a little, trying to figure out why his heart was pounding. Oh, he knew why. Yeah, he did.

He would do it. Try it. See what happened.

"I said, Jessica leads a rather fast life."

"I guess," he said, shrugging. "Looks it, doesn't she?" He hoped he sounded indifferent enough to convince her that Jessica held no appeal for him. (Although she had before he had met Alexandra—but in a very different kind of way.)

Alexandra shifted in her seat slightly, making the leather creak. "She's married, isn't she?"

"She's been trying to get divorced for a long time," Jackson said. "He's bad news, from what I hear."

"Oh," Alexandra said, turning to the window.

He slid over a little closer and Alexandra lowered her window, prompting a blast of cool air to hit their faces. He laughed to himself, backing off, not at all sure whether she had been aware of his maneuver or not, but finding it funny either way.

She slid the window back up and turned to him. "Jackson, have you ever met Cassy's husband?"

"Ugh. Thank you, no. One Cochran's enough, thank you," he said.

She laughed. "You should someday. You'd like him, I think." She paused, smiling, her eyes glittering in the passing lights. "It's funny, but you remind me a little of him."

"Oh, hell, no—don't tell me that," he groaned. "Somebody else told me that the other day. And I said, 'Oh, so she must holler at him all the time.'" He laughed. "And the guy said, 'Yeah, as a matter of fact, she does.'"

"Not anymore," Alexandra said, turning to look out her window.

"They used to argue a lot, but not now." And very quietly, so that he almost could not hear her, she added, "They're one of the lucky ones —they've been able to turn their marriage around."

The driver had turned east on 84th Street and was now turning south on Central Park West to drop Alexandra under the awning of the Roehampton. "Oh, we're here," she said then, reaching for her purse and carryall bag.

The doorman opened the door and Jackson reached over Alexandra, said, "In a minute," and pulled the door closed again. Sitting back up straight, he smiled at her. And then he took her face into his hands and kissed her. In a moment he felt her hand come up to his chest and gently push him away.

Her eyes, in the light, that close, were not something he was likely to forget.

She closed them. And then, swallowing, she opened them. "I can't lead you on, Jackson," she whispered.

He pushed her hand away, saying, "Good, then I'll lead you on," and he kissed her again.

She pushed him away again, but this time abruptly. "Do you think I'm a fool?" she whispered. "Don't you think I would if I could?" She shook her head and then, suddenly, her shoulders slumped. She looked at him. And then she pulled herself up to look him squarely in the eye. "I can't do it, Jackson." And then, very softly, "You must believe me—I'm not someone who would be good for you. I know."

He decided to laugh to break the tension. But then, noting her expression—she was not the least bit amused—he immediately stopped, sighed, and hung his head. Literally, he hung his head. And well he should, he thought, because with the exception of Barbara— whom he had at least fired first—he had never made a pass at a Darenbrook employee before. (But this was not really why he was hanging his head. He was hanging his head because he knew if Alexandra did not think he felt badly about what had just happened, then she'd probably never be alone with him again, and if that happened, how would he get a chance to try again?)

Apparently he hung his head in the right way, for Alexandra leaned toward him, murmured, *"Ad astra per aspera,"* kissed him on the cheek and climbed out of the car, closing the door behind her.

He slid the window down. *"Ad* what?"

She turned around under the awning, wind blowing her hair. *"Ad astra per aspera,"* she repeated. "To the stars through difficulties."

"The Bible?" Jackson said.

"State motto of Kansas," Alexandra said. She smiled. "Good night, Jackson."

12

What Happened That Night
Part II: Alexandra Returns Lisa Connors' Call

Her breath was returning to normal. "Mmmmmm," she said, kissing his ear, arms still wrapped around him.

Gordon smiled into her hair. "Love you," he whispered.

"I love you too," Alexandra murmured, kissing his ear again.

He lifted his head, kissed her on the nose and withdrew from her, sliding his right arm under her neck as he rolled onto his side, leaving his left arm across her chest. He sighed, content, curling one leg up over hers. He made another sighing sound, this time deep in his throat, and then another—he swallowed—and then he was silent, starting to drift . . . drift into sleep.

Alexandra lay there, eyes wide open, looking at the ceiling. The drapes of the windows overlooking Central Park were open and the gentle stream of citylight flowing upward from the street cast faint shadows of the windowpanes over part of the ceiling, while the candle burning on the nightstand flickered light over the rest.

Blink. Blink. Blink.

After a few minutes she turned her head and kissed Gordon's temple, and then tried to slip away.

"No," he murmured, clinging.

"Go to sleep," she whispered, lifting his arm and sliding away. Naked, she sat on the edge of the bed, brought her hands up to push back her hair, and then she stretched, hard, reaching for the ceiling, and then she relaxed, letting her arms fall. She turned to look back at

Gordon. He was reaching about on the bed for her, blindly. Giving up, he rolled over onto his stomach, embracing the pillows. She crawled back and pulled the covers up over him.

She got up from the bed and went into the bathroom, closing the door softly behind her. There was the sound of bath water being drawn, and then of bathing. In a few minutes she came back out, tying the sash of a gray silk dressing gown around her. She stepped on something—ow—and reached down. An earring. She put it on the dresser, walked over to the night table, blew out the candle and went out.

At the doorway to the living room she flicked on the wall switch. A Waterford lamp on the end table next to the couch came on, illuminating a very large and very unfinished living room. Alexandra stood there, running her hands through her hair several times, looking at it. There was off-white carpeting on the floor and, on the near side of the room, a chintz-covered couch, two matching chairs, two end tables and a mahogany coffee table. That was it—except sheets of plastic over part of the floor and carpeting, unopened moving cartons, pictures leaning against the wall, bolts of fabric lying across one of the chairs, a stepladder, and various other odds and ends—odds and ends like her purse and carryall bag on the floor near the foyer, her shoes about a foot farther in from there; Gordon's shirt lying across the coffee table and, next to it, his watch and her necklace and bracelets; three couch pillows strewn across the floor; his pants—with the belt still through the belt loops—scrunched down into the foot of the couch; and her dress draped over the far end table.

She smiled.

She went over to pick up her dress and went out to hang it up in the hall closet. Coming back, she rummaged through the pillows to retrieve her stockings and underwear. She picked up Gordon's pants from the couch, shook them out and hung them over the back of a chair. And then, while fitting the cushions back into the couch, she found her slip, another earring, his boxer shorts and his wallet.

When she finished straightening up, she went—robe trailing behind her—down the hall to the kitchen. She flicked on the lights. It was a fairly large kitchen, the walls were painted a pale yellow, the wood cabinetry was oak, and there was an oak table and four chairs, next to which, on the wall, was a telephone with three different lines. The kitchen was pristine except for the table, upon which were four stacks of magazines, a Rolodex, six or seven pads of paper and a coffee mug full of pens and pencils.

Alexandra picked up the phone, punched in a number and then held the phone between her chin and her shoulder while she picked up a remote control from the table and zapped on the small TV set that was sitting on the counter. "Hi," she said into the phone, "2980." She zapped through TV stations with her left hand while feeling for—and finding—the refrigerator door with her right and opening it. "Who?" she said, stopping the station at CNN and slipping the remote control into the pocket of her robe. "Oh, no, I know who that is," she said, leaning to look inside the refrigerator. "No, he's the guy who's supposed to finish the front hall floor before the year 2000."

She took out a container of cottage cheese and a bottle of Perrier and set them on the table, closing the refrigerator door with her foot. "Oh, that's the tiler." She went about getting a spoon, a napkin and a glass, settling into a chair at the table, eyes back on the TV. "Look, do me a favor and hold these messages for tomorrow. The housekeeper's coming at nine and I'd sooner she deal with it. What?" She was smiling, taking the lid off the cottage cheese. She got up to get a bowl, came back, sat down, laughing, and started spooning cottage cheese into it. "You got it," she said. "Uh-uh, no way. I've had it. I told Mrs. Roberts that if it isn't done by the end of the month, then I'm throwing every stick of furniture, every rug, every curtain rod—every person who rings the bell—out the window and be done with it." She ate a spoonful of cottage cheese. Swallowing, "Yes. Save them for Mrs. Roberts. Thank you."

She put another spoonful of cottage cheese in her mouth, dropped the spoon, slid over a pad and snatched a pen out of the cup. "Did she leave a number?" she asked. She scribbled something. "Uh-huh." She put the pen down. "What, more? Who else?" She got in another bit of cottage cheese before dropping her spoon again to write something down. "Okay, okay." She looked up at the clock—12:07—sighed, "No, all right, thank you. Thanks a lot. And you'll hold those messages for tomorrow? Great. Good night."

She pressed the disconnector in the phone and released it, heard the dial tone, pressed it again, released it again and then, after hesitating a moment, she turned around and hung up the phone. She took the remote control out of her pocket and turned up the volume of the TV, poured herself some Perrier and ate her cottage cheese. A little while later she ate some fresh fruit salad as well. She cleaned up everything, retaining her glass of Perrier, and looked at the clock again. 12:32. She went back over to the table, sat down and, after a moment, zapped the TV off and reached for the phone.

"Connors-Johnson residence," a woman said.

"Hello, this is Alexandra Waring calling. I had a message to—"

"Yes, yes, Ms. Waring, if you'd only hold the line. Mrs. Johnson told me to get her when you called. Hold on, please."

Alexandra sat there, mouth set, eyes on the table.

"Oh, this is wonderful," a woman's voice cried on the other end. "All I have to do is send Jessica to New York and you call me back the same day."

"It would have been nice if you warned me a friend of yours was coming to DBS," Alexandra said.

"Oh, Alexandra, don't be cross with me—ask me how I am. Say to me, 'Oh, Lisa, how are you? I've so missed you!' " She laughed.

"What have you been drinking?" Alexandra said, a faint smile emerging.

"You called during champagne," she said. "Oh, Alexandra, remember? Every time I have it, I always think of you. Why don't you just fly out tonight?"

"Lisa, please," Alexandra said, pressing her hand against the bridge of her nose, "I cannot take this today. Please. I really can't."

"All right, all right, all right," Lisa said cheerfully. "So tell me, don't you just love Jessica? She's a complete and utter mess, but I find her absolutely charming and irresistible anyway, don't you?"

Alexandra dropped her hand to the table. "That's what I'd like to know, Lisa—just *how* charming and irresistible was she, exactly?"

This sent Lisa into gales of laughter.

"Lisa—"

Her laughter was sounding very far away now, as if she might have dropped the phone to hold her sides. "Oh, my, oh, my," she finally gasped into the phone. "You didn't think—"

"I didn't know what to think!" Alexandra said. "When she said, 'A friend of yours wants me to give you a big Denver hello,' I nearly had a heart attack."

Lisa's laughter was sounding very far away again.

"Lisa!"

Coming back to the phone, "Oh, my dear," Lisa said, struggling to regain her breath, "I've got tears streaming down my face and I've got guests in the next room."

Alexandra sighed, smiling despite herself. "Oh, Lisa, what am I going to do with you?"

She looked up and saw Gordon standing in the doorway, in his robe, rubbing his eye, smiling. "Hi," he whispered, coming in and walking over to the refrigerator.

"Oh, my," Lisa was saying, sniffing once, "my makeup's everywhere. They'll think I got a phone call saying someone died. Speaking of which," she said with a laugh, "how are all of your boyfriends, Alexandra? What's all this about you and Jackson Darenbrook, and how is your fair-haired boy taking it?"

"As a matter of fact," Alexandra said, "he's right here. Gordon," she said to him, "Lisa Connors wants to know how you are."

"Terrific," he said, closing the door without taking anything out. He looked at her and mouthed, "Who is Lisa Connors?"

"Gordon wants to know how you are," Alexandra said into the phone.

"Tell him I'm fine, thank you."

"She's fine, thank you," she told him, winking.

"Alexandra?" Lisa said.

Gordon pulled a chair next to her and sat down.

"Yes?"

"I wanted to tell you about Jessica calling me tonight," Lisa said.

"Tonight?" Alexandra said, putting a hand to stop Gordon's on her thigh. "I only met her tonight."

"I know, that's what she said. And she told me how much she liked you, but then she started asking me all these questions about why I had been living in Kansas City, and I wondered what you had told her."

"I didn't tell her anything," Alexandra said. "What did you tell her?" She raised one finger in the air, asking Gordon to wait a minute.

"That I was working on my painting," she said.

"Which you were," Alexandra said.

"Yes, but she kept asking me about it. And about you. And then she wanted to know if my father knew your father—or something. It was very strange and so then I asked her, straight out, why did she want to know. And she said that, after meeting you, she just couldn't imagine us being good friends. What was it she said? That you didn't seem the type to be 'collected' at my parties, which I suppose is some sort of a compliment to you."

"And what did you say?"

"I said you and I had met at parties in Kansas City, that that's how we got to know each other. We were traveling the same circuit."

"Why is she asking, I wonder?" Alexandra murmured. "Lisa, are you sure—"

Gordon had leaned over and was now kissing Alexandra's breast through her robe.

"Wait—wait a second, Lisa," Alexandra said, covering the phone. "I'm sorry, Gordie, I just—could you—I just need to hear what Lisa has to say and then I'll be right in. Honest." She kissed him lightly on the mouth. "Go on. I'll be right there. Five minutes, tops."

He lifted one eyebrow. "Promise?"

She nodded.

He kissed her again and left.

"Okay," she said into the phone, "I'm back. Listen, Lisa." She paused, biting her lip, thinking. "Does she know—I mean, does anyone out there know? About you? Or"—she hesitated—"anything?"

"Certainly nothing connected with you." She laughed. "The only ones who knew about you were the plants and they all died."

Alexandra winced slightly. After a moment, "But just tell me, Lisa, truthfully—could someone have told her something about you?"

"Well, somebody could have told her anything, but I'd be highly indignant if anybody dared to either say it or believe it after everything I've gone through with Matt."

Alexandra was holding her face in her hand. "I'm sorry, I just—"

"No, Alexandra," Lisa said, sounding rather stern, "get it out of your head. I didn't tell Jessica anything, no one I know told her anything, and really, honestly, if you came out here and saw my life these days, you'd see that there's nothing to tell. So that's not it."

"Right," Alexandra said quietly.

"The reason why I called is because, well, you know how elusive you can be about yourself, Alexandra, and the Jessicas of the world take that as an invitation to snoop around. So I wanted to tell you to relax and not be so uptight around her."

"Is that what she said?"

"No, but I definitely got that feeling. That she was puzzled by whatever you told her."

"I didn't tell her much of anything."

"Exactly. And that's my point."

Alexandra sighed. "I hear you. Thank you."

"You're welcome."

"It's just that I feel so vulnerable these days," Alexandra said quietly. "There's so much at stake—not just for me, but for a whole lot of people. And sometimes I worry if somehow, someone—"

"I know, Alexandra," Lisa said softly. "Because I know *you*, remember? And I hope you know that I would never—ever—do anything to hurt you." She sighed. "I know you think of me as the one loose cannon on the deck of your life—"

"I don't."

"Oh, but you do, Alexandra. And I know you can't help it, but someday I'd like to know that you think of me first as your dear friend —and only second as the loose cannon." She paused. "Even you need friends who really know you, Oh fearless one."

"You are my friend," Alexandra said.

"Then don't worry about one little mistake you made when you were young and foolish." She laughed. "Besides, everybody knows you were crazy in those days—you were going to marry that horrible buffoon, weren't you? What was his name, Turkey?"

Alexandra had to laugh. "Tyler."

"Egad, how could I ever forget? He was enough to drive anyone into temporary insanity."

Alexandra paused and then said, quietly, "I wasn't crazy, Lisa."

"No?"

"No."

"Well, thanks," Lisa said.

Silence.

"Okay, so go on," Lisa said, "get on with being the paragon of virtue or whatever it is that anchorladies are supposed to be, and don't worry about a thing."

Alexandra smiled. "Okay," she said.

13

What Happened That Night
Part III: Gordon and Alexandra Try to Resolve an Issue

Gordon was lying flat on his back on the bed, staring up at the ceiling when she came in. He heard her moving around at the side of the bed; there was the sound of a match being struck and then he saw the flicker of light. Alexandra was relighting the candle. He smiled.

Great. She wasn't too tired then.

The good part about not seeing her for four or five nights running was that, when he did, Alexandra was usually as wound up as he was. And if there was a good side to working out of London for the next several months, it was the new sense of urgency in their relationship, for time together, a circumstance that might have worked against other couples, but for them had always increased their desire for one another. And tonight, when Alexandra was an hour and a half late getting home, instead of yelling at her—as he had intended to do when he stalked out to the living room to confront her—he had simply fallen in love with her all over again. That's how strong it came on when it happened between them.

Whenever he got angry with Alexandra—like tonight, with each minute she was late making it build—he had to turn Alexandra into a *thing* in his mind so he could stay angry at her, and so then when he saw her—as he had tonight—the thing he was mad at suddenly changed back into her—and how could he be mad at her when all he felt was happy and relieved to see her? To see that it *was* Alexandra, *his* Alexandra that he had been waiting for—that she was indeed real and not a memory to grieve over or to be angry at, but that she was, yes, once again a flesh-and-blood part of his life.

Part of him, he knew, still half expected her to leave him.

Alexandra had stood there in the doorway to the foyer, smiling a little sheepishly because she was so late. "Hi," she had said, putting her purse and bag down.

"Hi," he said, watching her slip off her shoes.

"Listen," she said then, walking over to him and sliding her arms around his neck, "do you think you could possibly make love to me right this second? Could you?" And then she smiled, her boy-what-a-fool-you'd-be-to-pass-this-one-up smile, and added, after kissing him once, "I'll apologize for being late later. This is no apology, what I'm about to do with you now."

They hadn't even made it out of the living room.

Gordon felt the bed move and then there she was, smiling down at him. "Hi," she said.

"Hi," he said. "Everything okay?"

"Everything's fine," she said, lowering herself down on top of him. She took his face in both of her hands and kissed him. And then she really kissed him, sinking down into his mouth in the way that always made him a little crazy.

Yep. It was making him a little crazy and he felt himself starting to swell against her. She moved slightly, pressing her hips down tighter against him, and she continued working on his mouth, making a low sound of satisfaction in her own.

After a while she pulled back, kissing his lips twice and then raising her head to look at him. Her mouth was wet; her eyes were glistening too. "Oh, Gordon," she sighed, quietly, stroking his hair with one hand, "what am I going to do with you?"

"Marry me," he said.

She blinked.

"You will marry me," he said softly. "You have to because I love you more than anything in the world."

She lowered her head to his shoulder, pressing her face into the side of his neck.

He stroked her back for a while. "Alexandra?"

He heard her swallow.

"I need you, darling. And you need me. I know you do."

He felt something trickle down his neck.

He hugged her tight, whispering, "Don't cry. It's nothing to be sad about. And I don't mean to pressure you—I know how hard it is for you to make a commitment like this—"

"Oh, Gordie," she said, starting to cry.

"Darling, no," he whispered, kissing her shoulder, "there's nothing to cry about."

"I just don't know what I'm doing," she said. "I don't know what I'm doing to you."

"It's time for us to get married, Alexandra. That's all. And you're scared, and you have every right to be. But, darling—"

"But I have so little to give you," she whispered, sniffing.

"Alexandra—Alexandra darling, look at me," he said, lifting her from his shoulder.

She sniffed again, wiping her eyes. "It's true though, Gordon. I don't have enough to give. You think I do—now—but later . . ."

"Do you want to marry me?"

"I—"

"I don't mean yes or no, will you marry me," he said, giving her a little shake. "I mean, if you didn't think so much, if you weren't so damned analytical about everything—if you were just you, Alexandra, an imperfect being in an imperfect world, would you *want* to marry me?"

She looked as though she might start crying again. "Gordie," she said, her voice rising, "you're the only man I ever really wanted to marry. I've always *wanted* to marry you, but that doesn't mean that it would work." And then she buried her face in his neck again and he held her.

He sighed, stroking her back again. "It couldn't work before, you're right. But things are different now, you and I are very different. We know what we want, we've learned what we don't want. And I want you, Alexandra. I want you to be my wife."

"I know," she said.

"I want everyone to know there's only one woman in my life, one woman I love, and that's you." He laughed a little. "And I want all of those jerks who're always tripping all over you to know that there's only one man in your life—and that it's me."

Her hand was in his hair, absently playing with it. "Is it the papers?" she said. "The stuff about Jackson? Is that bothering you?"

"No," he said, lying. "What's bothering me is the way we have to live. And since you've rejected that white elephant of mine on Gramercy Park, I decided I might as well sell it and move in here with you —only I can't unless we get married."

"Oh, you could," she said quickly. "We can figure out a way."

"Cassy says no."

"Oh—Cassy," Alexandra said, sounding sarcastic.

"What do you mean, 'Oh, Cassy'? She's right. It's not good for your career. And Langley says Cordelia—"

Alexandra sat up like a shot. *"Langley?* You've been talking to *Langley* about me?"

Uh-oh. Gordon did not dare even breathe. Alexandra rarely lost her temper, but when she did it was like a flash fire burning on air.

"How dare the two of them say anything about what I should or should not do in my personal life! How dare they! And don't you start in on me about what's good for my career, Gordon. Not like that. I absolutely will not stand for it. Cassy—Langley—" she sputtered, grabbing a pillow. "Damn it," she said, hurling it across the room. "This is supposed to be the United States of America, not some—not some—not some occupied country. Damn it!" she said again, slamming her hand on the bed. "What are they going to do to me? Drag me off the air and put me in TV concentration camp if I don't get married?"

"Lex, Lex," he whispered, sitting up too, careful not to touch her. She was under too much pressure as it was, and she was overtired. He shouldn't have tried to back her into a corner.

She was leaning over, holding her face in her hands.

"I made a mistake," he said, "I'm sorry. It's just that I want to marry you so much." He sighed. "It's just that I've been looking for some way to convince you to say yes."

"It's okay," she said, still leaning over. And then she sighed, dropped her hands, and slowly sat up. "It's not you I'm angry with," she whispered, touching his cheek. She smiled, faintly. "I'm not really angry with Cassy or Langley either, at least not as angry as I feel with myself." She paused, looking at him, eyes sad. "But I have to be careful, Gordon," she whispered. "I can't just go ahead and marry you because I want to, not when I think it might not be good for you."

"Or good for you," he said.

"Oh, Gordie," she said, sounding close to tears again. "How could you not be good for me?" she asked him, swallowing. Her eyes started to fill. "You are the kindest, brightest, sexiest man I've ever met in my life. How could I not want to marry you—unless I was scared that I would fail you?"

"You won't fail me, Alexandra," he said.

She looked down, reached for his hand, and brought it back to hold in her lap between both of hers. "When you married Julie, you wanted a home life—"

"But that was—"

"No, let me finish," she said, raising her face to look at him. "I can't help feeling that what you really want is a wife-wife, Gordon. Someone to make a home for you and for her, and for your children. A home like the kind you always told me you wanted when you were little. And I'm just not there, Gordon. There are other things I can change, other things I can close the door on, but I can't change my work life. And I can't promise that I ever will."

"I have a child already," he said. "Poor Christopher, I don't see enough of him as it is. As for a wife-wife, I'm not even home for twenty-five weeks of the year. Who would put up with *my* schedule?"

"Thousands," Alexandra said with a sad smile, "thousands of women would put up with your schedule, to be with you."

"But not the one I've been in love with for ten years?"

"Oh, Gordon," she sighed, falling on her back and looking to the ceiling. "What are we going to do?"

Her robe had fallen open and he saw her left breast, the scar from the shooting not too far above it. It was a little distracting. "Um," he said, "we'll move ahead."

"And it's been a long time since we lived together," she said. "I'm even worse than I used to be, you know. Some nights I come home and think I'll just scream if I have to talk to one more person."

"Think you're telling me anything I don't know?" he said, smiling, reaching to touch the underside of her breast with his forefinger.

She sucked in her breath. "Tickles," she said.

"How about this? How does this feel?" he said, sliding his hand up to hold her breast. After a minute, "Well?"

She made a little sighing sound, of pleasure. "I think I would like to continue considering the question for a little while," she said, closing her eyes.

He moved closer to her, pulling her robe apart over her chest. He touched both of her breasts gently, exploring, and then he took them both into his hands, massaging them, feeling the nipples tighten against his palms. He leaned over and kissed her scar. It was a nasty-looking thing, still, but against the loveliness of her everything else, he had come to rather like it.

"Mmmmmm," she said deep down in her throat. And then she whispered, "Gordon?" and opened her eyes to look at him.

"Yes?" He was not going to last long in this conversation. The combination of her breasts and the sense of pending surrender in the air was getting to him.

"Is this enough for you?" she whispered, closing her eyes again. "Inside, do I give you enough? Or is there something missing, something you think our getting married will fill?"

As much as he might otherwise wish to pursue the question (which, now that he had his mouth—open—on her left breast, he had frankly forgotten already), he was more concerned about how much time he needed to give her before . . . He didn't know what it was tonight, but he was terribly excited already. He released her breast from his mouth, touching the nipple with his fingers, trying to remember what she had just asked him. No go—he couldn't remember. He kissed her breast. "I'm moving in whether we get married or not," he said. He kissed her breast again and then paused, bringing his whole mouth down on it again. God, this was the greatest. His hips were straining to find something to press up against, but he was in the wrong position.

"So we don't get married," he said, pulling his mouth away from her breast. "I want you, I only want you. I'll take you any way I can get you." And then he climbed up to kiss her, pulling the rest of her robe open with his hands as he did so. He stopped kissing her to get his own robe off, threw it behind him and then he came down to kiss her again, pressing himself hard up against her thigh. "Oh, Lex," he murmured, kissing her neck and feeling her breast again, and starting to move against her.

She murmured something he didn't hear.

He started sliding downward, his mouth dragging down her neck to her shoulder, to her scar, down to her breasts, pausing there for a while again—at first one and then the other—and then moving on, sliding downward, over her stomach, down to her hips.

He slid his body down, kicking the covers off the end of the bed, pulling her one leg down under him and then over. He maneuvered over a bit, centering himself, holding her thighs in his hands, and gently pushed them farther apart. Then he lowered his hands, coming down to rest on either side of her, and with his thumbs parted her and then eased her a little wider. He heard her let out a breath and sharply take in another, and hold it. He looked up. Her head was thrown back so he couldn't see her.

He brought his eyes back down, smiled, and sank his mouth into her, feeling her thighs seize up around him. He started moving his mouth, slowly, listening to her sounds as he did, and with every movement of his mouth and with her every accompanying sound he felt himself grinding into the bed.

He was not going to last long.

Apparently she was not either, because she groaned and then suddenly sat up, reaching down to him and pulling him up, murmuring in a rush, "No, Gordon—I don't want to come like that—I want to be with you, I want to come under you." And as he crawled up to her, she reached down, murmuring, "Let me touch you, please," and he felt her hand slide around him, touching him, holding him, and she whispered, "Oh, Gordon, you are so . . . " and he lowered himself down on her, trapping her hand between them as an effective hint. She quickly brought him to her, into the slick warmth.

"I love you," he said, pushing himself into her all the way, just the way he loved it, and she loved it, thinking how it had never changed, how splendid that plunge was when she was as ready as he.

She groaned, softly.

He pulled back, slowly, and then plunged back in all the way.

She groaned, louder, drawing a breath. "Yes," she whispered as he pulled back, slowly. He did it again, pushing hard into her, but he pulled back quickly too, this time, and then plunged in all the way again, pulled again, plunged again, pulled again, plunged again, letting himself fall into it, knowing it was not going to be long for him, but not for her either, because after briefly urging him on, her hands were now still and the fluid movement that had been with him was already starting to falter, her body jerking slightly, tightening against him as he kept at it, pulling back, plunging in, pulling back, plunging in, harder maybe, maybe harder, at her, in her, feeling her body starting to climb.

"Oh, Gordon—Gordon," she said, taking a quick breath and holding it, her body rising higher. She arched, her arms locked around him, her body straining as he kept at it, pulling back, plunging in, pulling back, plunging in, and then he heard her start to whimper and then he could feel her coming, feel her spasms around him, and he felt himself starting to go, but not yet, but then, as her body started easing back down to the bed, she whispered, "Come, darling, come inside me," and he did, right then, as he had for years, every time she said it, and he heard himself grunting with it and he came, at last, he was coming, feeling everything flooding out of him, every—last—thing—out, yes, everything out of him now, everything, warmly, yes, inside of her.

Yes. Delivered.

Shew. He relaxed, letting his face fall next to hers.

"You are the absolute best," she whispered, turning to kiss the side of his head.

"I want to make love to you forever," he whispered back.

They lay there, the air cooling around them. He felt the perspiration on the small of his back starting to evaporate. And then he felt everything that had been his, together with hers, seeping warmly down between them. He shifted, slowly pulling out of her, and then resettled, holding her tightly, nestling himself in against her thigh, wet.

They lay there.

"I'm cold," she said. "Aren't you?"

"I can't move," he said, watching her profile in the candlelight.

"Well," she said to the ceiling, her mouth stretching into a smile, "somebody's going to have to go down and get the covers."

He smiled too. "Yes, one of us will."

"Yes, I suppose so," she said, turning her head to look at him.

They looked at each other, smiling, blinking.

"So what will you give me if I get them?" he finally asked her.

"Dangerous question," she said, laughing softly.

"Why?"

"Ask me again," she said, touching his mouth with her forefinger.

"Okay. What will you give me if I get the covers?"

"Me," she said, kissing him gently on the mouth. "If you get the covers, Gordon, I'll marry you."

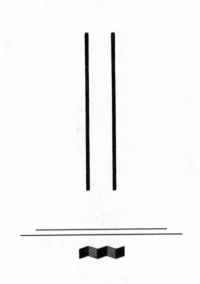

14

Langley's in for a Number of Surprises

On Friday morning, two days after Jessica Wright had arrived at West End, Alexandra started acting up with the one person Langley had trusted could control her—Cassy. It wasn't an outright fight that Alexandra picked with Cassy, but it was some sort of public declaration of independence, and it certainly came as a surprise to all.

Langley and the department supervisors of DBS News had all gathered in the large conference room on the third floor of Darenbrook III for one of Cassy's production meetings. The conference room was very light and airy—with skylights above and fresh flowers, always, on the table—and, with fruit and yogurt and danish and coffee brought up from the cafeteria on carts, they had all come to enjoy these morning meetings as sort of a big family breakfast, over which they discussed their production progress.

Cassy usually opened the meeting by briefly running down the agenda, listing the segments or aspects of "DBS News America Tonight" they would be discussing. But this morning she barely got through her opening remarks before Alexandra started in on a number of objections she had about the format of the newscast—a format which everyone knew she had formerly agreed to.

At first, sitting there, Langley thought maybe Alexandra just woke up on the wrong side of the bed (finally—human, at last), because there was an emotional note in her voice that he had not heard before. (Usually, if Alexandra was upset, she had to tell people she was upset because she never sounded upset—she always sounded like an anchor who thought her microphone might still be on.) Then he thought maybe she was coming down with the flu or something, because she didn't look so hot. And then he began to wonder if Alexandra wasn't jealous of Jessica Wright in some way, if this wasn't some kind of tantrum Alexandra was throwing to refocus DBS' attention on her, because, yes, however quietly and politely she was conducting it, Alexandra *was* throwing some kind of tantrum.

Could she be jealous of all the attention that Cassy was giving Jessica's special? There had to be a connection, Langley thought, because the day before yesterday Alexandra and Cassy had been as thick as thieves and now Alexandra was fighting her and the only thing that had happened in the meantime was Jessica's arrival.

But then, listening more carefully to Alexandra, after a while Langley began to wonder if maybe Alexandra was right about some of her objections to the format. Maybe her style should be more formal on the air, maybe they should cut the business editor's segment by a minute, cut the Friday entertainment segment altogether, throw out the weather, expand the science and technology and do the zillion other things she was talking about.

But then he had to remember all that Cassy had told him. So, was Cassy right? Did Alexandra need to loosen up a little, show more of her personality on air, interact with the correspondents in the same spirit of camaraderie that she shared with them off camera? Should they increase the on-air time of the backup anchor, did they need one soft feature each half hour and was Gary Plains, the weatherman, really so vital when it came to attracting an audience?

Alexandra, with her new argumentative nature (which had dropped half the mouths in the meeting thus far), summarized her complaints with "It's too informal, too chitchatty, we've got too many distractions from the news. We've got too many personalities doing too many things and the philosophy behind it is all wrong. Everything's getting way off track and I want it back on track."

Cassy, eyes down on her notes, waited a moment to make sure Alexandra was finished. And then, taking a deep breath, she looked at Alexandra—over the top of her reading glasses—for a very long moment. And then she took her glasses off, gently laid them down on the table, and said, addressing the room, "I want everyone back here Monday morning at nine. We'll have a new agenda worked up for discussion."

Meeting dismissed, Alexandra was the first to get up and leave the room. The others, looking at one another in stunned silence, began to file out. Cassy remained seated at the conference table, as did Langley and Kyle.

"Do you need me?" Chi Chi asked Cassy. She had been taking notes at the meeting.

"No—no, thanks, Chi Chi, you run along—I'll be down shortly." Cassy waited for her to leave and then she turned to Kyle. "So what do you think?"

"What do I think?" Kyle said, eyes widening slightly. "I think, if looks could kill, you just got murdered, Cass."

"I know." Cassy looked around to make sure the door was closed. When she turned back to them she was laughing. "Phew," she said, collapsing back into her chair and fanning air across her face with her hand. "My husband used to tell me she could get a little intense in meetings." She dropped her hand and looked at Kyle. "Wow, the temperature went up around twenty-five degrees in here, didn't it?"

"No," Kyle said, laughing, "it was more like all the oxygen got sucked out of the room."

"That's it—you got it," Cassy said.

They didn't seem very upset, but Langley felt pretty unsettled by Alexandra's performance. "Why is she so mad at you?" he asked Cassy.

"She's not mad at me in particular, I don't think," Cassy said, sitting forward and resting her arms on the table. "It's just that I'm the safest person to take a swing at." She smiled, gently, and not for the first time Langley thought about how funny it was that the same Cassy who expected people to drive themselves until they dropped in their harnesses also had a side to her—a side less frequently seen, but being seen now—that made one only long to lay one's head in her lap and be comforted. "And I'm not sure Alexandra is mad," she said. "I think she's just getting a little scared. I think we're *all* getting a little scared," she added. "It's perfectly natural at this point—are we taking our best shot, will the newscast work, do we have the right format?"

"And do we?" Langley said quickly.

Cassy and Kyle both looked at him, looked at each other and burst out laughing.

"I can see people around here have a lot of trust in our judgment," Cassy said, brushing a strand of hair off her forehead. She dropped her hand and looked at Langley, trying to keep a straight face. "That is what you hired Kyle and me for, isn't it, Langley? To combine our thirty-five years of television experience to destroy Alexandra's career and bankrupt the network?"

Late that Friday afternoon Cassy came up to his office for a closed-door, one-on-one about Alexandra's complaints regarding the format of the newscast. Cassy said that, while she had no intention of making "NAT" into Happy Talk News, or a new entry in the burgeoning field of Scratch 'n' Sniff (the frantic and manic format—for which the industry had cocaine to thank, Cassy said, "Or someone spending too many hours getting atomized on the main floor of Bloomingdale's"), she had no intention of letting Alexandra turn to the old Sermon on the Mount routine either.

The format was their biggest challenge, Langley knew, because their problem was not so much how to get anyone to tune in to "DBS News America Tonight" once, but how to get viewers to tune *back* in, night after night. According to market research, they could count on an audience the week of May 30 because, their surveys showed, people wanted to see how Alexandra was doing since the last time they saw her—when she was shot on TV and rerun hundreds of times.

(Research said 46% of all Americans had heard of Alexandra Waring and of that group, 87% said they knew she had been shot on TV, 58% said they knew she had been a reporter, 16% said they knew she was a celebrity of some kind, 3% said they knew she had been an anchorwoman, less than 1/2% said she was Jackson Darenbrook's girl-friend, and 12% said they were "Undecided."

("Undecided about what?" Langley had asked the research guy. "Who she is," he had answered. "We thought 'Undecided' sounded better than 'Specifically Identified Incorrectly.'" "Well," Cassy had said, "who do they think she is?" "Um," the guy had said, looking through his sheets, "let's see—fashion designer, won a gold medal in an equestrian event in the last Olympics, used to be on 'All My Children,' Richard Burton's third wife, Rosalynn Carter's press secretary, played the sister-in-law on 'My Three Sons,' wrote a nasty book about her mother, husband is running for President—" "Enough!" Cassy had said.)

The trick, Cassy said, was to find a format that made the most of Alexandra *and* their affiliate correspondents. Cassy said if Alexandra started playing formal networkese, the accents and regional style of their affiliate reporters would appear strange and amateurish. Alexandra had to display more of her personality, more of that camaraderie with the local reporters to make a bridge for viewers, to get them over that cultural abyss created by traditional network news—that abyss from where viewers expected reporters to come with no accent, no apparent home or regional ties.

The success of "DBS News America Tonight," Cassy had sworn from the beginning, would ride on how well they developed a news hour about America that was *honest,* that—even in its reporters— illustrated some fundamental truths about the diversity that made up America and that generated in viewers some long-term fascination with exploring it with Alexandra, as well as keeping abreast of its current events.

Cassy said she knew Alexandra believed that too but was reacting to the enormous pressure for her to prove herself and was falling into the trap of thinking that the Sermon on the Mount routine had something to do with serious journalism besides making everything appear serious —which, in their case, might end up making everybody else on the newscast look ridiculous.

And past that point, Cassy said, an hour was too long for the Sermon on the Mount format and they needed complimentary energy in the studio with Alexandra, contrasts. And even though Alexandra probably could pull off an hour of heavy-duty anchoring by herself, God help them if Alexandra ever got sick because the whole newscast would fall apart without her. So no, Cassy had no intention of letting Alexandra go through with this format.

However, Cassy also had no intention of fighting with her at this point, not when Cassy could see that Alexandra was struggling to feel more in control of her fate—a sign that her confidence was wavering. What Alexandra needed now was unequivocal support, Cassy told Langley, not opposition, not to be told she was wrong; she needed to feel that everyone was with her, do or die; and so Cassy was going to let her have her way for a few days, with the certainty that Alexandra herself would change her mind about the format when she started thinking more and reacting less.

"Which brings me to what I think set her off in the first place and for which I should commend you on your powers of observation," Cassy said, sighing a little, looking more than a little tired. "You were right—Alexandra *is* mad at me. And she's mad at you too."

"Me? Why?"

Cassy leaned forward to plunk her elbow down on Langley's desk and rub her forehead with her hand. Then she laughed to herself, brushed her hair back off her forehead and settled her chin in her hand, looking at him. "Langley," she said, squinting a little, "did you tell Gordon that Cordelia Paine would shut down DBS News if Alexandra lived with him without marrying him?"

"What? I never said any such thing," Langley sputtered, trying to remember exactly what he had said.

"That Alexandra's career would suffer if she didn't get married?"

"Me?" Langley said. "Gordon told me *you* told him that."

"I did tell him it would be better for Alexandra's career if she were married," Cassy admitted, pushing off of the desk and sitting upright, hands in her lap. "Well, anyway . . ." She looked at him, lofting one eyebrow, starting to smile. "Whatever we did say, it apparently worked since she's going to marry him—sometime within the year."

"Thank God," Langley said. "At least we won't have to worry about that."

"Yes, well," Cassy said, "we still have your frisky friend Mr. Darenbrook to contend with. I don't think he's going to take the news very well."

"Then we don't tell him yet," Langley said.

"Well, when do we?" Cassy said.

Langley shrugged. "When we publicly announce it—when we have to, I guess. The important thing is, we know where Alexandra stands."

On Monday morning the production meeting reassembled back in the third-floor conference room, people looking a little apprehensive. At 8:59:45 (or thereabouts), Alexandra swept in, saying cheerful good mornings as was her former habit, but eyes still blazing the message that she was not to be messed with. Cassy did not mess with her. Cassy—if Langley's eyes did not deceive him about the flicker in Alexandra's expression—surprised Alexandra by handing out a three-page memorandum that summarized the format changes Alexandra had proposed on Friday.

"This Friday, at four o'clock," Cassy announced, "we are having a full-run dress rehearsal of 'DBS News America Tonight.' Graphics, film, music, the set, the works—whatever we've got thus far, let's put it together and see what it looks like. We're going with the format that incorporates all of these changes." She smiled, looking over at Alexandra. "From here on in, we need to see, hear and feel everything through the studio and on tape—to react, to discuss, to modify, to accept or reject. Agreed?"

It was just what the doctor ordered. Everyone's eyes lit up at the idea of a full-scale production. Mock or not, right format or wrong, it was to put on a newscast that all had come to do at West End, and for many it had been months since they had a "normal" day's work of news gathering—Alexandra most of all. After the meeting was over, she bounded over to Cassy, whispered something in her ear and then bounded out, Kyle on her heels.

Cassy saw that Langley had been watching; she smiled and came over to him. "I am a tolerant, fair and splendid creature," she said, winking, "or so I have just been told."

It was a good thing that the news group morale had been boosted, because the following morning, on Tuesday, Cassy had to hold another meeting—with Langley, Jessica Wright, Denny Ladler, Alexandra, Kyle, Rookie Haskell and Deeter Page, the executive in charge of the affiliate relations—to announce that, despite everything they had gone through, despite all their excitement about Jessica's interview with the prize-winning novelist Richard Barnes, the affiliates did not want it as a special. (As Cassy had told Langley earlier, the station manager of their Philadelphia affiliate had said, "You expect me to pull 'First One Wins' for an interview with this guy? Forget it! The only Pulitzer our audience cares about is the one with the trumpet.")

And so, Cassy explained the situation, only nine of their sixty-one affiliate stations would agree to carry the special. Her fervent recommendation, as a result, was that, since it was the first programming

DBS was offering, they shelve it until "The Jessica Wright Show" was established, and then simply run it in lieu of her regular studio program.

After her announcement the conference room was very quiet. Jessica, down at the end of the table near Denny, looked devastated. She mumbled something about she couldn't believe the interview wasn't good enough to fly on its own, which prompted Alexandra to lean forward over the table to look at her. "Jessica?"

Looking miserable, Jessica brought her eyes up from the table.

"The interview is absolutely first rate," Alexandra said gently. "It's Barnes that's the problem—he's been out of the public eye for decades, he's missed a generation and," she sighed, "sad fact is, people don't read like they used to—or they can't read, period."

Jessica shrugged and looked back at the table. (In the few short days she had been at West End, it was readily apparent to all that their talk show hostess had two basic off-camera moods: euphoria and depression.)

Suddenly Alexandra said, "Sell it to me, Jessica."

Jessica raised her head to look at her.

"They don't know what to do with it," Alexandra said, nodding in Langley's direction, "but I do. Sell me the interview and you'll never regret it. I know how to get it on the air. I know how to find an audience for it."

"What?" Langley said, turning to Cassy. "What is she talking about? Sell it to her?"

"I'm saying I'd like to buy Jessica's interview," Alexandra said.

"Forget it!" Langley said.

"Why?" Alexandra said. "What are you going to do with it?"

"What?" Langley nearly shrieked.

"You mean sell it to DBS News?" Cassy said.

"DBS News or me, it makes no difference," Alexandra said.

"You really want to buy it?" Jessica said, starting to brighten.

"Forget it!" Langley said, banging the table. "And it's not hers to sell —Jessica was on DBS time down there."

Denny leaned over and was whispering furiously into Jessica's ear.

"Well, you *are* DBS," Alexandra said to Langley, "so tell Jessica how you're going to use that interview effectively or promise her that you'll let DBS News buy it. It would be foolish to waste such a good piece of work."

"What!" Langley said again.

"What's your idea, Alexandra?" Cassy said quietly.

"I'm not saying a word until Langley promises he'll sell it to us," Alexandra said. She looked at him. "We'll pay a fair royalty."

"Royalty?" Langley said, looking to Cassy again.

"Oh, come on, Mr. Mitchell," Jessica said from the end of the table, suddenly looking and sounding more enthusiastic about life. "Denny and I think we oughta take a flier and let Alexandra Eyes have it."

"Mr. Mitchell?" Cassy said.

"Oh, don't ask!" Langley said.

"She thinks he looks like Dennis the Menace's father," Kyle whispered to Cassy, starting to crack up.

"Cassy will do the deal and so you know we won't cheat you," Alexandra said to Langley.

Langley looked at Kyle, who now had his face buried in his arms on the table in an effort to stop laughing. Langley's frown deepened and he looked back at Cassy. "What kind of deal?"

"I don't know, but it sounds like fun," Cassy said, smiling. "And I don't know about you, but I could use some."

"Say yes, Langley," Alexandra said. "Please. Trust me."

"Trust *you?*" Langley said.

"Come *on,* Mr. Mitchell," Jessica said. "I'm dying to know what Alexandra Eyes wants to do with it, aren't you?"

Langley looked at how happy Jessica looked and sighed, dropping his hands on the table. "Oh, all right," he said. "We'll sell the interview to DBS News. Now what, Alexandra, is it you propose to do with it?"

"Syndicate it domestically," she said.

"You can't, you're part of a network," Langley said. "Networks can't syndicate entertainment programming."

"The FCC's definition of a network," Alexandra said, "calls for fifteen hours of programming a week to twenty-five or more stations. We have sixty-one stations, but even when 'NAT' and Jessica's show go on the air, we're still only going to have ten, maybe twelve hours. So, we're not a network yet and we can sell domestic syndication." She turned to look at Jessica. "So we'll sell it station by station—to whoever wants it—one of our affiliates, another network's affiliate—market by market. Or we might decide to do a deal with PBS—they'd love this and it would be a wonderful validation of your work."

"Ya-hoo!" Jessica said, holding on to the table with one hand and reeling back in her chair as though she were riding a bucking bronco. "Me on PBS—back into the family will!"

The following morning, on Wednesday, Langley and Jackson flew down to Palm Beach on the Gulfstream jet to see Belinda and make good on their promise to attend a dinner party of hers. Belinda didn't often demand Langley's presence at her social engagements, but she did insist on the first and last dinners of any given season, and this would be her last before closing the Palm Beach house, taking a holiday in Europe and then opening the house in Connecticut for the summer. As for Jackson, he would usually go to anything Langley agreed to go to.

And so, while sitting across from each other on opposite sides of the cabin, Langley told Jackson about Alexandra's sudden objections to the "NAT" format and about how Cassy had chosen to handle it, and then about the stunt Alexandra had pulled to buy Jessica's interview with Richard Barnes.

"Well, good," was Jackson's response, "it's about time Alexandra declared a little independence. Your Mrs. Cochran's been riding roughshod over her long enough—"

"Cassy's been doing what?" Langley said. "Are you kidding, Jack? Cassy's been bending over backward to accommodate Alexandra's ego while trying to make her succeed."

"She's been riding Alexandra's back," Jackson said, "and she's been riding over everybody else—including you. Sorry, Lang, but your Mrs. Cochran's overmanaging the place and you know it."

"She's not overmanaging—"

"If she's not overmanaging, then why does Alexandra feel compelled to fight her?" Jackson said. "Alexandra's her biggest fan."

"Well, she's no fan of mine," Langley said.

"Because she knows you're no fan of hers," Jackson said. "So she's doing what she thinks is best, Lang, and from the sound of it, Alexandra does know better about what to do with Jessica's interview, so let her have it."

"Forget I ever said anything," Langley sighed, giving up. Talking to Jackson about Alexandra was hopeless. No matter what she did, according to Jackson, it was right.

When they got to the house, Belinda was in one of her cool, calm and collected states (i.e., "Please don't bother me while I'm trying to get things ready, Langley. Honey, don't, I'm sorry, I'm just too tense to be touched right now and you know what Dr. Balakudian says") and she instructed Jackson to take Langley outside and run him around the tennis court.

Playing tennis with Jackson was something else. Every time he mishit the ball he stopped the game to retrieve the offending ball and slam it a country mile over the fence. His game was really off today and so they had to raid Belinda's tennis ball cannon for enough balls to finish two sets, by which time the neighbors had called Belinda to inquire why their afternoon tea was being pummeled by tennis balls.

They went down to mess around at the marina for a while, looking at boats, where Langley talked Jackson out of inviting a girl he picked up to Belinda's party. And then they went back home, where Belinda had just arrived from the hairdresser, looking wonderful but sounding a little spacey. "You boys are so sweet to come to my party," she whispered, kissing each of them on the cheek in the front hall. "And I do so appreciate it." And then she floated up the stairs, leaving them there.

"She all right?" Jackson asked Langley.

"Yeah, I think so," Langley said, shrugging, digging his hands into his tennis short pockets. "She's been doing better lately."

"Langley," Belinda called from upstairs. "Langley darling, come here, will you?"

Jackson punched him playfully in the shoulder. "Go on, Langley darling. I'm gonna go for a swim."

Langley went upstairs to their bedroom and found Belinda in her dressing room off it, sitting at her dresser, looking at herself in the mirror. "Langley darling," she said, reaching behind for him, "come look." And he stood there, behind Belinda, looking at her face with her in the mirror. "Am I still beautiful?" she asked him, smoothing the skin around her eyes with her fingers.

"Very," he said, meaning it in the physical sense, but not meaning it totally. Not too many years ago, Belinda's eyes—so like Jackson's, that same cornflower blue—had been the source of a very real beauty, with their spirit, their energy, their spark. But now . . . now Belinda's eyes seemed deadened somehow, dull. Even the whites of her eyes seemed vaguely gray now, translucent. And as he stood here, it was as if Belinda saw her own eyes through his, because she leaned closer to the mirror to look at them, but then screwed them shut—as if she could not bear the sight—and let her head fall forward.

Langley slid his hands around her shoulders, massaging them gently. "Why can't I have a baby, Langley?" she whispered.

"Oh, Belinda," he sighed, bending over to hold her. She had been saying the same thing for over sixteen years now. And he didn't know why, and the doctors didn't know why, and, as it had turned out in recent years, it was probably for the best, considering her state of mind.

"Careful of my hair," she said, her voice sounding altogether different. And then suddenly she pushed him away, stood up and walked briskly back into the bedroom. "I know you have things to do, so why don't you go and do them."

Oh, boy. She was having one of her mood swings.

"I'd like to be alone, please," she said, turning to look at him.

"Okay," he said, walking out. "I'll be out back."

"No, Langley, wait," she called as he was going down the stairs. "Come back, Langley. I don't want you to leave me."

And so Langley went back into the bedroom.

"Let's make love, honey," she said, slamming the door behind him and dropping to her knees, unfastening his shorts.

"Belinda—" Langley said. Oh, christ, he never knew what to do when this started. He knew what he usually did—and that was to simply go along with it—but despite any immediate pleasure, he always felt lousy afterward for some reason. Belinda knew how to make quick work out of him and was well on her way already and so he stepped out of his shorts and took her over to the bed and they started to make love, only for Belinda to suddenly change her mind again, pushing him off her, saying, "I can't do this, Langley, I told you. My nerves can't take it and Dr. Balakudian says you shouldn't force me."

And then she got up and went into the bathroom, leaving Langley, naked and with an erection, lying on his back, about to scream in frustration. He calmed himself down, promising himself—as he had with increasing frequency over the last five years—that he would get himself a mistress so as to spare himself this insanity that appeared to be getting contagious. And so he got up, put on his robe and went down the hall to take a shower in another bathroom.

So there he was, taking a shower—yes, a cold one—when Belinda came into the bathroom, naked, opened the shower stall, grabbed his arm and pulled him out. "Come on, Langley," she said, opening the bathroom door, "I want to make love with you, honey."

"Belinda," he said, standing there, feeling like an idiot, the shower still running behind him.

"Well, come on!" she said, skipping out into the hall.

"Honey, shhh," he said, grabbing a towel. "Jackson—"

"Good idea. I'll tell Jackie you won't make love to me and then—" Oh, great—she was yelling this down the hall.

Langley dashed down the hall, grabbed her arm at the top of the stairs—it took three tries (he couldn't see so well without his glasses) —pulled her into their bedroom, closed the door, locked it, threw his towel off and said, "Okay, Belinda, let's do it."

"Yeah!" she cried, delighted, jumping onto the bed and then jumping up and down on it.

"Jesus, Belinda, what is with you?" he whispered, going over.

"I'm happy, Langley! I'm having fun, darling!" And then she jumped up again and landed, booof, in a sitting position, holding her arms out to him. And so they actually did make love this time, and Belinda carried on outrageously—leaving no doubt in Langley's mind that the entire household, the entire *neighborhood* could hear her. (But this was infinitely better than having her threaten to kill herself, which from experience he knew would have been the next stage had he asked her to lower her voice a little.)

Sitting at the dinner table that night, gazing down at Belinda at the other end of the table, noticing how pretty she looked, how happy she seemed, talking and laughing with her friends, Langley for the one hundredth time wondered if it wasn't *him* that drove Belinda crazy. She seemed absolutely fine now.

The rest of the evening was uneventful. They danced outside on the terrace—Belinda loved to dance—and people had a very nice, relaxing time, or so they said. The party did not break up until after two. Belinda was so tired, suddenly, she barely made it to bed before falling asleep—so soundly, in fact, that Langley actually sat down on the edge of the bed and watched her a moment to make sure she was breathing okay. She was.

When Langley came downstairs the next morning Belinda was outside having coffee with Jackson. Rather, Jackson was sitting in a lawn chair, reading a paper and sipping coffee, and Belinda was sitting on the ground, in her robe, hugging her knees, leaning back against Jackson's leg, eyes closed to the morning sun.

She looked every bit the five-year-old she had been when she first started sitting with Jackson this way. They had a photograph of it somewhere.

"Langley," Belinda said, opening her eyes, "Jackie thinks that instead of going to Europe I should pay Daddy and Cordelia a visit."

Langley leaned over and kissed her on the forehead. "You want me to go with you? For a couple days?"

"No," she said, shaking her head. And then she got up, brushed off her robe, looked at him and said, "I want you to go back to New York."

Langley looked at her.

"I do, Langley. I want you to go back to New York," she said. "Excuse me." And she went back into the house.

Flying back to New York, Langley was playing around with some DBS News numbers when he looked up and found Jackson staring at him. "What's the matter, Jack?"

Jackson tossed the newspaper in his hand into the seat next to him. "The DBS financing is really a mess, isn't it?"

"Yep," Langley said.

"What if I told you I decided to clean it up? Myself?"

Langley laughed.

"I'm serious, Lang," Jackson said. He paused and then added, "Cordie's petitioning the board to audit us."

Langley's stomach quietly dropped a couple thousand feet. Right now there was no way DBS could pass a corporate audit, no matter how many sets of books he had.

"So what I've decided to do," Jackson said, "is to ask Cordelia to postpone the audit until July, and then when it comes time, I'll come clean with the board. About everything. I've decided to tell them the truth about what I've done and why—and I'm going to leave you out of it."

"You?" Langley finally said. "The truth? To the board?"

"Yeah, why not?" Jackson said, sitting back. "They can either let their money ride and make money down the road, or they can take an immediate fifty-million-dollar loss." He smiled. "Which do you think they'll choose?"

He had a point. Little El and the twins would never write off that kind of money. No, Jack was right, they would give him some time to turn things around and get them a return on their money. "But what about Beau?" Langley said. "You got into this mess to protect him."

"Beau and I have a whole other agenda with the board. It's got nothing to do with you and I'd just as soon you stayed out of it."

"Fine with me," Langley said, meaning it, though doubting this would be the case. "And what about Old Hardhead? What are they going to do when they find out—"

"They can buy him out if they want," Jackson said. "But I have a feeling they won't. Actually, they might vote to sell him the whole miniseries."

Well, that's one way of getting rid of Gordon Strenn, Langley thought. *Only you don't know that he's already got Alexandra, that they're engaged.*

"But the one thing I do worry about, Lang, is that we've got to make the numbers on DBS News look like something. I don't want the board to get any bright ideas about shutting it down."

"I hate to be a party pooper," Langley said, "but after starting-up costs, doubling the budget and cost overruns, we'll be lucky to see the black in five or six years as it is. And that's assuming it gets off the ground."

Jackson suddenly threw himself forward, holding his face in his hands, murmuring, "I know, I know." After a long minute he sighed, throwing his hands down. "I'm as sick of this as you are, you know. I'm tired of playing funny money between companies."

This was something new. Jack usually didn't care about anything except getting his own way.

"So here's my idea," Jackson continued. "Let's make Mrs. Cochran

Jessica's executive producer as well as Alexandra's and consolidate production of both programs under her. Give her some more money and a title like 'President of News and Information' or something."

Langley instantly knew it was a good idea. Unlike the news, "The Jessica Wright Show" had virtually no overhead. Her staff was small, the only on-air talent salaries she had were her own, the show was very simple to produce, and yet Jessica was the easiest show to sell to sponsors. Her show was virtually a cash cow and, by merging her production budget with DBS News, she would do nothing but eat debt for them.

"But Alexandra will never go for it," Langley said. "She'll never share Cassy."

"You leave Alexandra to me," Jackson said.

Langley rolled his eyes.

"As for Mrs. Cochran," Jackson said, "if you trust her so much, why don't you tell her the truth and blame it all on me? If you tell her the fate of DBS News rests on her shoulders, she'll take over Jessica's show so fast it'll make your head spin. Besides, we haven't given her enough to do. I told you, she's overmanaging."

Langley threw his hands up in the air. "Oh, right, Jack, we haven't given Cassy enough to do. We're only making her build half the stupid network by herself. She's still bringing in more affiliates than Deeter is, you know."

"I know," Jackson said.

"And what about Alexandra's contract? We can't do any of this until—"

"I told you," Jackson said, "leave Alexandra to me. I'll handle it."

"I love how you say that," Langley said. "I wish you could have heard her last—"

"Alexandra won't be your problem for much longer," Jackson said.

"What?" Langley said.

"Five months, tops," Jackson said. "Just until I get things straightened out with the board."

"Why?" Langley said. "What happens to her then?"

"What happens to you, you mean," Jackson said, smiling. "I'm going to give you Darenbrook Electronics back. I've been thinking about it, and I don't think it's fair to stick you with DBS, not with everything you've done for me already and not"—he paused, sighing slightly—"on top of everything with Belinda."

Langley was stunned. To run Darenbrook Electronics again was exactly what he wanted, but Jackson had said he couldn't have it until he had the television network running smoothly and profitably, not for years down the road. "But what about DBS?" Langley asked him. "Who'll run it?"

"Well, who do you think?" Jackson said.

"You?"

"What? Lang, I swear, you are losin' it fast, boy," Jackson said. "Mrs. Cochran will run it. End of the summer we'll make her president of DBS and let her overmanage things to her heart's content. Heck, if we're makin' her build the network, we might as well give it to her, don't you think?"

Langley nodded, murmuring that it sounded like a good plan. But to himself he wondered why, after resenting being stuck with DBS for all these months, he suddenly felt upset at the prospect of having to leave it.

15

Alexandra and the Marilyn Monroe of TV News

At seven-thirty on Friday morning, dressed in navy-blue sweats and white running shoes, Alexandra said good morning to the doorman and walked out of The Roehampton onto Central Park West. Crossing over to the park at 85th Street, she pulled her hair back into a pony tail, secured it with a coated rubber band and, when she reached the footpath leading in, lowered her arms to break into a slow jog.

It was an overcast spring morning, neither warm nor cold, and the trees and shrubs over the rises and dales were still brown-black from winter, green just beginning to shoot. The grass was still trampled-looking, brownish, with occasional bursts of new green, and brown leaves from the fall had settled in the thickets—the thickets where the birds had also settled this morning, chirping.

Alexandra jogged along the path for a while, crossed West Drive, and veered off through the trees, over a hilltop, and then went down, coming through a baseball field into the north end of the Great Lawn. She turned south and headed straight down the Lawn: joggers and bicyclers were out around the ring; dogs were being run and walked everywhere; young men were kicking a soccer ball around; a man and a boy were trying to get a kite in the air; a golden retriever was playing Frisbee-catch with its mistress; and three guys—two with Villanova T-shirts and one with Boston College—were throwing football passes.

Alexandra paused at one point, running in place, slowly turning, viewing the acres and acres of Lawn surrounding her and the acres and acres of trees that surrounded the Lawn and the acres and acres of residential architecture that surrounded the trees and the acres and acres of teaming cosmopolitan city that surrounded the residential architecture and too, finally, the endless acres of sky that surrounded them all. Alexandra smiled at all of it. And then, facing south again, she continued down the Lawn, picking up her pace.

She headed southwest, passing the Delacorte Theater, jogging around Belvedere Lake, slowing a little past the Castle and then heading south again, crossing Transverse Road, cutting through some trees and catching the path down the west side of the lake. She passed Strawberry Fields, crossed the 72nd Street road and picked up her pace again across the bowling greens and Sheep Meadow. She crossed West Drive, ran down along the south side of Tavern on the Green and exited the park at 66th Street and Central Park West.

Her jogging turned more playful from here on in, a kind of romp-dodge-skip affair as she zigzagged through people and neatly traversed standstill cars, making her way west on 66th Street, crossing Central Park West and passing ABC News. A stage door swung open and out popped the head of a security guard. "Hi ya, Alexandra," he said, "how's it going over there?" "Great, thanks," she said, stopping to jog in place, wiping her forehead with the sleeve of her sweatshirt. "So what's the word?" "Three," he said, grinning, "Jennings, Walters, Koppel. Glad you won't be going up against any of them." Alexandra laughed. "Me too. Take care."

ALEXANDRA AND THE MARILYN MONROE OF TV NEWS

She cut down Broadway for a block, heading west on 65th, passed by Lincoln Center, crossed Amsterdam, and crossed the four lanes of West End Avenue to reach the guardhouse outside the parking lot of the ABC radio studios. "Hi, John," she called, jogging in place. "Hey— Alexandra," the guard said, "how ya doing, girl?" "Terrific," she said. "So tell me, what's the word around here?" "Talk radio, baby," John said. "Right-wing city. Things are gettin' so hot over here, they're thinking about moving us out of the neighborhood." He rolled his eyes and she laughed, jogging on.

Alexandra continued north a block and a half and turned into the West End gate. "Good morning," the guard in the guardhouse said. "Good morning, George," she said, stopping to jog in place again. "So what's the word?" He winked. "Things are going so well, they say they might expand the DBS News staff by a third," he said. Alexandra laughed, eyes sparkling, and wiped some perspiration off her forehead with the back of her hand. "Gosh," she said, "things sound so good I think I might just want to work here." "That's what the guy from the *Post* said yesterday when I told him that," George said.

She jogged up the driveway and then down the ramp to the carport, saying good morning to everyone she passed, slowed to a walk to enter the building—good morning, good morning, good morning—and went straight to her dressing room. Closing the door, she did a number of stretching exercises, her breath gradually slowing. She stripped off her damp clothing, took a shower and washed her hair, blew it dry, covered herself with moisturizer, put on some deodorant, selected a skirt and blouse from the wardrobe, got dressed—stockings, bracelets, earrings—and then sat down in front of the mirror circled in lights to put on a little makeup.

Humming, she practically skipped down the hall to the newsroom— good morning, good morning, good morning—took twenty minutes to find out what was doing, and then went up to the second floor of Darenbrook III. Good morning, good morning, good morning; she stopped outside Cassy's office to pour herself a cup of coffee, pulled a yogurt and a bag of mixed nuts and raisins out of the refrigerator, and took them into her office with her.

She turned on the lights, walked over to the couch and sat down, picking up the remote control from the coffee table and turning on the

TV in the wall. She pushed a series of buttons, activating the VCR decks as well, and there was a series of whirls and clicks as they rewound their cassettes.

Click. Click. Click. A tape locked in and Alexandra turned up the sound as a station promo ended and a close-up of a dazzling young anchorwoman appeared. "In the news this morning, a threatened air strike in the Persian Gulf; President Reagan cuts his vacation short—"

"Morning, Alexandra," Kate said, poking her head inside the door.

"Good morning," she said, saluting her with her spoon.

"I got the—oh, brother," Kate said, disappearing when the phone starting ringing, "who the heck is calling this early?"

Alexandra looked back at the TV. ". . . takeovers on Wall Street," the woman was saying. "I'm Deborah Norville and this is 'NBC News at Sunrise.' " The screen filled with a colorful computer art graphic of the Statue of Liberty as the John Williams score that was the NBC News theme came on. Alexandra settled back against the couch, eating her yogurt, fast-forwarding the tape in places and then freeze-framing the tape when Kate came back in. "Are we set with the food for the crew tonight?"

"All set," Kate said, looking at the clipboard in her hand, making some kind of notation. "Five-thirty in Studio B."

"And you cleared it with Cassy's office?"

"Yep," Kate said, still writing. "Beer, wine, Perrier and Coke, okay?"

"Fine," Alexandra said. "And did Kelly drop off a manual for me? For the—"

"I've got it outside."

"And what about the interview schedule from Derek?"

"We got it yesterday," Kate said. "It's all written in on your schedule."

"When's the first one, do you remember?"

"Um, Tuesday, I think. *USA Today.*"

"Did we find an office for Mr. Graham?"

"I think so. On the first floor. I asked Denny Ladler since there's no one else to ask and he said fine so I guess it is."

"He's coming in today, isn't he?"

"I think so. I left a message for him, but I haven't heard back. Oh,"

Kate said, flipping through the pages of her clipboard, "before I forget, Will says he thinks your idea of a tour is brilliant."

Alexandra laughed. "Is that a quote?"

"Yep. He's at WCO in Chicago today and says he's going to start accumulating evidence to support your case immediately."

"Great."

Kate looked up. "What idea of a tour is this?"

"Only a half-formed one at the moment," Alexandra said. "Did you get those slides from Phil?"

"Yep. I gave them to Kyle."

"And how about the Copeland tracks from—"

"They're downstairs."

"And did you get the—" Alexandra stopped herself and smiled, shaking her head. She leaned forward to put the empty yogurt container on the coffee table and sat back again. "Kate?"

She looked up from whatever she was writing.

"Sit down," Alexandra said gently.

"What?"

"Sit down," Alexandra repeated, while she herself stood up. She gestured to a chair. "Please, sit down," she said, walking out of the office.

Kate just stood there, looking around, appearing a little confused.

Alexandra came back with a mug in her hand. "Come on, sit," she said, pushing Kate down into the chair and handing her the cup. "I'd at least like to know that I gave you a cup of coffee and asked you how you were before I worked you to death."

Kate stared at her as Alexandra walked back over to the couch and sat down again.

"So how are you?" Alexandra asked her.

Kate looked rather startled. "Um, I'm fine," she said, resting the mug on the clipboard.

Alexandra looked at her, expression hopeful. When Kate didn't say anything more, she smiled, gently, and said, "Would you ever tell me if you weren't?"

Kate lowered her eyes, smiling, shy. "Yes, I think so."

Alexandra nodded, smiling still. "Good." She looked at her watch. "Why don't you spend the next twenty minutes with me, drinking your coffee and seeing how people opened this morning." Without waiting for an answer she picked up the remote control and resumed the tape.

After a minute or two, while Alexandra was fast-forwarding through commercials, Kate said, "Isn't this the newscast Connie Chung launched?"

"Uh-huh," Alexandra said, switching the remote control to her left hand and eating nuts with her right, eyes on the screen.

"Wasn't it originally offered to Jessica Savitch?" Kate said.

"Uh-huh," Alexandra said, eyes on the screen.

After a moment, "What do you think of her?"

Alexandra glanced over. "Of Savitch?"

"Of Connie Chung."

"I think she's fabulous," Alexandra said, swallowing and fiddling with the remote control. "Now let's see how CBS led off this morning," she said, pushing a series of buttons—the screen flickered—and then the opening graphic of "CBS Morning News" came on, followed by an establishing shot of Faith Daniels and Charles Osgood on the set.

"Alexandra?"

"Yes?" Her eyes were on the screen.

"What did you think of Jessica Savitch?"

Eyes still on the screen. "I take it you've been reading the galleys they sent me of that book."

"Yes."

Alexandra freeze-framed the tape and turned to look at Kate. "What did you think?"

"I think I'm shocked," Kate said.

"About what?" Alexandra said.

Kate looked around the room and then shrugged. "Everything." When Alexandra didn't say anything, Kate said, "Well, weren't you shocked?"

Alexandra reached for her cup of coffee, sat back against the couch and took a sip. Lowering the cup to her lap, "Shocked about the extent of her addictions and for how many years they had been going on? Yes. About her mental and physical deterioration being so horrible that people who didn't even work with her were planning an intervention because management was just sitting back, trying to figure out the easiest way to demote her? Yes, I was shocked then and I'm shocked now." She paused, finishing her coffee, and lowered the cup again. "As for her behavior, no, I'm not shocked at all—not by any of it. It's pretty much textbook behavior for anyone with that kind of chemical history."

"They're calling her the Marilyn Monroe of TV news," Kate said.

"Oh, right," Alexandra said, irritated, leaning forward to bang her coffee cup down on the coffee table, "and Anna Karenina's the Marilyn Monroe of Victorian literature. Honestly." She sat back against the couch, recrossing her legs.

"Kate, please," she added a moment later, "can't at least you and I focus on what's *right* with the women in TV news for a change? I mean, let's just deviate wildly from the norm and at least pretend that what's *really* important is that Connie Chung is making a major contribution at NBC in the healthiest way imaginable—that now Deborah Norville is coming up to bat in her own extremely healthy way, that Jane Pauley is still and always completely wonderful and that Andrea Mitchell is as brilliant as ever and that Maria Shriver is finding her way and that maybe NBC and every network and every*one* has learned a lot from Jessica Savitch. God!" she added with a violent shake of her head. "The Marilyn Monroe of TV news. I can't even talk about it," she said, pushing the remote control. "We're watching the news, Kate."

And they did—for about fifteen seconds, before Alexandra pointed to the screen and said, "Look, Kate. Look at CBS, look at Faith Daniels up there—how long do you think it will take people to get past the Marilyn Monroe of TV news to see all that's really right—Faith, Leslie Stahl, Diane Sawyer, Susan Spencer? The system stinks and everybody knows it, but you have to look at the individuals and see what each woman is doing, because each is different and is going about it a little differently—and every accomplishment every woman makes in this industry changes the system a little for the better." She stopped suddenly and cocked her head. "How old are you? Twenty—?"

"Three."

"Twenty-three. So you weren't even born yet when Marlene Sanders filled in as an anchor in 1964," Alexandra said, adding under her breath, "not that anyone seems to remember that. Course they do remember calling ABC All Broads and Canadians, in honor of her and Peter Jennings." Alexandra was frowning. But then she smiled. "But you were eleven when Barbara Walters coanchored at ABC—you must remember that."

Kate nodded, smiling. "My mother took pictures of the TV set that first night."

"Of course she did," Alexandra said. "It was a very big night. And if television's supposed to mirror our society, imagine how your mother must have felt after all those years of seeing that she didn't exist." And then she shook her head. "And God bless wonderful Barbara Walters. Not just for achieving all that she did and does—but for going *on*. For holding her head up and just doing her job, pushing on when any less a human being would have been destroyed by the kind of unbelievable"—she searched for a word, finally deciding on, *"crap* she had to go through about that newscast."

"She's done very well," Kate said. "Everybody loves her."

"Oh, but now we've got the Marilyn Monroe of TV news to obsess about," Alexandra said. She threw her hands up. "Who cares that Barbara Walters and Marlene Sanders and people like Linda Ellerbee, Leslie Stahl, Judy Woodruff—that these women raised children *too,* on top of everything else? Who cares that regenerating life results in life and that destroying life results in death and that one is infinitely harder than the other?" She pointed to the TV screen. "Faith has a child—but what are brains and energy and regeneration compared to the slow self-destruction of the Marilyn Monroe of TV news?"

"Well, I think—" Kate started to say.

"The Marilyn Monroe of TV news!" Alexandra cried, slapping the couch. "This is all we have to talk about? Mary Alice Williams is a knock-out—she built the New York bureau for CNN, runs it, anchors over two hours of news a day, is the *only* woman, *still,* to sit in a network anchor booth at the political conventions—but do we talk about her? Forget it—not when we have the Marilyn Monroe of TV news. I mean—are brains and talent and drive and a sense of purpose and ethics and well-being so completely passé? After everything that Diane Sawyer has achieved, am I really somehow supposed to believe that her most noteworthy accomplishment has been a photo session in *Vanity Fair?* I mean, what *is* this?"

She stopped herself, touching her forehead. "I'm sorry, Kate. I didn't mean to get started on this." She dropped her hand, sighing and shaking her head. "It's just that when I see how hard the world makes it for them—the women who are so very much what America wants as role models, then sometimes I have to wonder what's going to happen to me. These women *are* what America respects, they *are* what society rewards—but still the search goes on, the probe continues. And so now they finally get the goods on one woman in network news. They found an exception to the rule."

Kate's mouth had parted in astonishment, but Alexandra's eyes had fallen to the coffee table and so she did not notice.

"See," Alexandra said, "none of my peers—none of those in the national spotlight—have had the kind of confusion I've had in my life." She paused, laughing to herself. "You *would* have to take drugs to think you could climb this high and still be free to . . ."

She paused again, biting her lip. "And if you're confused about how well you can fulfill the fundamental expectations the public has for you as the role model it says it wants, then God knows that's no time to be climbing onto a higher pedestal for greater public scrutiny—is it?" She smiled to herself, still staring down at the table, adding, "Funny how I never seem to remember until someone shouts at me that I need to look at my peers and change myself before it's too late."

"But, Alexandra," Kate sputtered, "you're so wonderful. Everyone loves you, thinks you're the best. And I've never seen you confused about anything!"

Alexandra looked up and seemed to snap back from wherever she had been. She smiled at Kate. "Thank you." And then she cleared the air with her hand. "Enough from me." Then she leaned forward slightly. "You never told me how you are."

"I'm fine," Kate said. "And I love listening to you talk."

Alexandra smiled. "Well then, listen to this—I mean it when I say I hope you'll tell me if you're ever not all right. Or if you are, and just feel like talking about something. Or just feel like talking, period. We can talk about something other than"—she blinked twice—"what we gotta-gotta-gotta do—once in a while, anyway."

Kate looked down at her clipboard and said, "I really love working for you."

"With me," Alexandra corrected her, picking up the remote control, zapping off the TV console and then scooping up the garbage from the table. "Now," she said, standing up, "what do I *gotta* do with you before I can go downstairs?"

"Uhhh," Kate said, standing up, "I've got some messages and invitations and stuff I need your answer on."

They walked outside together to Kate's desk, where she handed a spiral notebook to Alexandra. Alexandra sat her down in the chair, put the notebook down on the desk in front of her and read over Kate's shoulder, stopping to tell her what to do in response to each entry.

"See if we can set up an interview for him with Cassy.

"Make sure we keep this phone number safe somewhere.

"I'd like to send them some flowers.

"This should go on Herbie's card on the Rolodex. He's living with her now—so if we ever need to find him at night. Oh, and you better give Kyle that number too.

"Tell her we'd love to see it.

"Please send my regrets.

"You better call them back and warn them that Langley's got the feds riding with the Darenbrook trucks, so unless some Network executives want to go to prison for stealing my fan mail, they better have that warehouse open Tuesday morning.

"I'm already going to that with Jackson—so thank him and tell him no.

"Please send my regrets.

"Please tell them over my dead body." Laughter.

"Hmmm. Call Betty and see if Gordon will be in town that week. If he is, accept. If not, regrets.

"Tell them I can't do any outside things until next March, but I'd be happy to after that.

"I'll call her back this afternoon."

And then she squinted, leaning closer. "What's this? Michael Cochran's address in L.A.?" She looked at Kate. "I don't understand."

Kate shrugged. "Neither did I, but he sounded like you knew all about it."

Alexandra frowned. "That he was moving to L.A.?"

Kate nodded.

"No, no, I certainly did not," Alexandra murmured, turning to look at Cassy's office next door. Chi Chi was sitting outside, typing something.

"Do you want me to ask Chi Chi about it?" Kate whispered.

"No," Alexandra said, turning back toward Kate. "No," she repeated, absently resting her hand on her shoulder, pausing to think a moment. Then she looked at Kate. "I don't think we should say anything to anybody until Cassy says something about it herself. Okay?"

"Okay," Kate said, nodding.

"In the meantime," Alexandra said quietly, patting her back, "be sure to make a new card for him on the Rolodex, okay?"

16

Jessica at Work

When Jessica's limousine rolled into the West End carport at ten-thirty on Friday morning, she caught sight of an interesting-looking guy climbing out of a cab. "Honk the horn," she told her driver as the guy walked toward the doors leading into West End.

"What?" the driver said, turning around. "What for?"

"Honk the horn!" she yelled at him.

So the driver honked the horn (which, for a Lincoln, sounded not terribly unlike the *Queen Mary* coming to port) as he brought the car to a stop. The guy stopped also and turned around as the guard opened Jessica's door. She got out, very happily aware that the guy was not only watching her but was a lot better-looking than she had thought. "What a crazy driver," Jessica declared. "All of a sudden he starts honking the horn. Must be some kind of Detroit religious ritual."

"*Eye*-yie-yie," the driver was saying as Jessica slammed the door closed behind her. She turned and beamed at the security guard, and then up at the guy.

Great, the guy was checking her out.

He met her eyes. "You're Jessica Wright," he said, walking over and holding out his hand. "Hi, I'm Gordon Strenn—I'm producing the miniseries. I think we were supposed to meet earlier this week, but I had to go out to L.A."

"Nice to meet you, Gordon," Jessica said, taking his hand. "I've heard an awful lot of nice things about you," she added, though she didn't remember anyone at West End ever mentioning him.

"Well, I've *seen* an awful lot of nice things about you," he said, shaking her hand. "I've watched a couple of your shows. You're terrific —and we're all very glad you're here."

His handshake was nice, but his brown eyes were nicest of all. He wasn't very tall, though. With the heels she had on today, she was almost as tall as he was. Nice eyes, though. Nice face, though. Nice light brown hair, though. Nice hand, too. She released his hand, bringing both of hers up to run them back through her hair (the purpose of which was really meant to part her shawl). It worked. (God bless Grandmother Hollingstown. She had been an absolute bitch, but she *had* gotten these breasts from somewhere and passed them on so that some of her granddaughters could enjoy an occasional shortcut to becoming compelling personalities without scarcely having to be persons at all.)

While he was looking at her chest, she looked at his hand to see that there wasn't any wedding band. Of course, that could just mean he didn't wear one. But this was New York, where men almost always wore their wedding bands to the office (though, after five, some Manhattanites wore their wedding bands in the loose change in their pockets; some commuters wore their wedding bands on the same hook in their key cases as the keys to their cars or the front doors of their houses; and some out-of-towners wore their wedding bands on wads of tissue in their shaving kits).

But it had been Jessica's experience that TV producers could be a tricky lot. The producer she had gone out with last night, for example, had not been wearing a wedding band either when he introduced himself to her at Café des Artistes last week at lunch, and had he not gotten so drunk last night she never would have known he was married.

("Are you married?" she had asked him point-blank over drinks. "No," he had said. "Are you sure you're not married?" she had asked him, sipping a glass of champagne during the intermission of the play they had seen. "I'm sure," he had said. "Are you really not married?" she had asked him over dinner. "No, I'm not married," he had said. "You sure seem married to me," she had said, sitting on the couch in the hotel suite owned by the company the producer worked for. "How's that?" he had said. "Because—of *that*," she said, nodding at the erection that had been in plain view more than once that night. "I'm not that much of a turn-on—not unless you think you're doing something wrong." "You are a very strange girl," he had said, bringing out a bottle of brandy. [*Brandy,* oh boy, after starting in on brandy, who cared about anything?]

(After a rather dreadful and disappointing grappling on the bed and after several more brandies, *that* was when he had said, with his head resting between her breasts, "I am married," and had started to cry. And then Jessica had started to cry. And then she had poured the rest of her brandy in his ear, threw him off of her, got dressed, went home to the Plaza, drew a bath and fell asleep until the bath water grew quite frigid, at which time she put on her huge terry-cloth robe, dragged herself into her bedroom, collapsed on the bed, awakened at nine-ten with a splitting headache and funny stomach and decided that she really needed to get her divorce finalized and find a nice man, a nice, *single* straight guy, if there was such a thing in New York, and she had to find him very soon, and so she had gotten dressed in her Sort-of-Katharine-Hepburn-as-the-Countess-disguised-as-the-gypsy-in-*The-Little-Minister* outfit, complete with shawl and gold hoop earrings, and here she was, hoping against hope that this very nice guy here in the carport could be . . .)

And then it clicked. Click, click, whirl, whirl, even hung over this mind couldn't stop. *Gordon Strenn.* "Excuse me if I'm being too personal—and stop me if I am," Jessica said, "but weren't you once married to Julie Stantree?"

"Yes," Gordon said, nodding, stepping back and gesturing to the doors. "I'll walk you to your office, if that's where you're going."

"Thank you," she said, smiling. Jessica started in—the double doors slid open—and then she stopped dead and cried, "Oh, no!"

"What's the matter?" he asked her.

She whirled around. "You're not that boyfriend of Alexandra's, are you? Oh, damn," she said, turning around, "of course you are."

He laughed, touching her back, guiding her inside, saying under his breath into her ear, "We don't talk about that around here."

"Oh," she said, "so Jackie does have a thing for her." *Oops.* Hit a nerve on that one, she could see. "I mean," she added, "in terms of publicity for the show."

"Newscast," Gordon said, steering her past reception, waving to the receptionist. "Don't ever let Lexy hear you call it a show, that's my advice."

Lexy? Jessica thought. Lexy sounded like the name of a Yorkshire terrier. Hmmm. She didn't think there could be many people in the world who called Alexandra Lexy. Certainly Lisa Connors didn't—she usually called her *darling Alexandra.*

Well, darling Alexandra the Yorkshire terrier or whatever was a strange one, all right. Even though Jessica begrudgingly had to admit that she really *liked* Alexandra Eyes, Queen of the Daisy Chain, she didn't have to pretend she could get a handle on her. Professionally—oh, yes, Jessica could see what she was in that regard. She was one of those burning overachievers who had taken the seat in the front row of the classroom instead of the back, who had opted for good health and vitality and good clean *pep,* instead of good highs and danger and cynical, depresso-head wit. Alexandra was the A student who showed up; Jessica was the A student who showed up only for exams and got B's, or forged doctors' notes from the infirmary to get an I for Incomplete so she could finish the required work later, which of course she never got around to because there was so much else to do because the floodwaters were always rising around Jessica and it was only when the water started spilling over the sandbags that she ever did anything anyway and so present emergencies always superseded any demands as subtle as the completion of course assignments.

Anyway . . .

There was something about old Alexandra Eyes that was not quite in step with that bright-eyed Goody Two-shoes in the front row. First of all, Jessica knew that Alexandra liked *her* (it was not that she knew it but she could *feel* it, which to Jessica made her know it was real) and since most all Goody Two-shoes were generally alarmed by Jessica in real life, she knew Alexandra had to be pretty savvy. And she was friends with Lisa Connors, for Pete's sake, which meant that Alexandra had a side of her that understood the—the what? What did one call it? Artistic temperament? ("Artistic temperament my foot!" Jessica had once heard her mother say to her father. "A spiteful little brat without an ounce of gratitude in her is more like it. We should have given her to the maid when we had the chance.")

That whole story of Lisa living in Kansas City for a year was the weirdest thing. Jessica was dying to know what Lisa had really been up to there (to imagine Lisa quietly painting in Kansas City was like trying to imagine Sarah Bernhardt doing puppet shows in Parisian parks) and Jessica wondered if Alexandra hadn't somehow bailed her out of trouble. It sort of sounded like that. Like maybe Lisa had run away from someone or something, had fled to the unlikely place of Kansas City for a while and met Alexandra, who helped get her life back on track again. Because *that* sounded like Alexandra Eyes. She was one of *those,* for sure, Jessica had spotted right away, one of those who liked being in control of relationships. And helping people when they were down was a sure way of gaining the upper hand with them, of maintaining control over the terms of the relationship, just as Alexandra's help on Jessica's special was surely an attempt to win Jessica over as an ally she could control. And Jessica didn't blame her for doing it. It was very smart. She would do the same thing in Alexandra's place because, regardless of how different their programs were, it was no secret that DBS was selling them together because "The Jessica Wright Show" had the pull.

But then, in a kinder moment, Jessica would think that maybe Alexandra was simply a very nice person who genuinely liked her. But that thought didn't last very long because then Jessica would see all the advantages for Alexandra if she won her over. And then, what was it that Langley had said the other day? That if she liked walking into spiderwebs, then she would positively adore knowing Alexandra? And then Jessica would think about how crazy Lisa was about Alexandra, so then Jessica would think that Alexandra liked crazy people because she herself was so sane and serious and controlled, but then Jessica would remember how Alexandra had practically denied knowing Lisa and then Jessica would think, *Aha!, a woman whose heart grows fond only when it serves her immediate interests. Lisa is not here, cannot help with DBS, so Lisa no longer exists. Jessica is here, Jessica can help her at DBS, so Jessica is a friend worth cultivating.*

Hmmm . . . Now what would old Alexandra Eyes do if Gordon here found that she, Jessica, was worth cultivating as an ally of his own? A very personal ally? How would she feel about Jessica then? How would Jessica feel about *Alexandra* then? How about now? How did she feel about Alexandra at this very moment, as she watched Gordon looking around the mess that was supposed to be her office? He had already invited her to his office to watch the DBS News rehearsal on the closed-circuit TV at four—so that could be a sign. Of course, he could just be being nice and introducing her to other employees in West End he himself liked. But then, how many men had she known who had invited her to anything simply to be nice?

Hmmm . . . At the moment, watching Gordon, Jessica did not frankly give a hoot about Alexandra, and she suspected that maybe he —Gordon, probably the only good catch left in all of New York City— was not thinking too much about Alexandra either.

"Gordon," she said, taking off her shawl and throwing it over a moving box that had been shipped from her old office in Tucson. She turned to him, whirling a little (this skirt was made for whirling, dancing barefoot down the woodland paths in the moonlight). "I wonder if you might have a late lunch with me. Answer some of the questions I have about—about this place." She smiled.

He hesitated. (Damn it, she knew he had been going to say yes.) "I'm sorry," he said, "I can't today. I've got a lot of stuff to clear up upstairs. I'm sorry," he said again (convincing Jessica further that he had almost said yes), "really, I'd like to, but I can't." He looked a little nervous, edging toward the door. "I really should get upstairs now."

"Yes, of course," Jessica said, turning away, hoping to sound quite chilly.

"But you'll come up at four, right?" he added from the door.

Jessica, with her back still to him, smiled. "Maybe," she said, deliberately not turning around.

Silence.

"I wish you would," he said then.

Jessica's smile expanded. "Well, my life isn't really my own these days. So . . ."

"Oh," he said. A moment later, "Well, I do hope you'll come up."

She bent over to open a box, back still to him (rather, backside to him). *Aha,* she thought. He liked women who played hard to get. She should have known. Jessica got rid of her smile, stood up and turned around to look at him. "I'll try," she said softly. She continued to look at him, until he got nervous again and started backpedaling.

"Um," he said, averting his eyes, "I think Alexandra would welcome your opinion about what you think. About the, uh, newscast, you know."

Jessica nodded and turned back to the box. "I'll try my best," she said. "It's just that I'm supposed to be madly in love and he may want me to leave early." She frowned to herself, thinking how hard and cynical that had sounded instead of provocative.

"But maybe," he said, "you'll do what you would like to do and we'll see you later."

Victory! It had been exactly the right thing to say to him.

The next business at hand wasn't nearly as exciting. She had to try and act like a sane person so she wouldn't scare away the poor thing Denny wanted to hire as her secretary. Actually, Alicia Washington, a young black woman who was just graduating from NYU, appeared to be quite energetic and with it. Jessica only thought of her as a poor thing because she knew from experience that her secretaries usually left her employ crying and sobbing about how guilty they felt about leaving her, but how they were physically ill and on the verge of a nervous breakdown. And, to be truthful, even though it could be a rather emotionally demanding job, Jessica would still make them feel as guilty as possible for abandoning her in her hour of need.

("But, Jessie," Denny would sigh, *"every* hour is your hour of need, that's what the problem is. You can't make them feel responsible for the fate of your entire life, which you always do." "Well then, get a marine or something, someone who can take it!" she had once snapped at him. And Denny had, only the former Air Force administrative assistant did more than give Jessica her preparation materials one night and when the next day he reminded her of their passionate rendez-vous in one of the studio storage lockers after the Group K post-production party [which Jessica had been quite sure she must have dreamed, because not even in blackout, she had thought, could she have ever, ever . . . oh, God, with him who was nicknamed Bucky because he could eat an apple through a venetian blind?], Jessica herself had suggested he find another job, which she subsequently found for him herself.)

But, actually, even if Alicia Washington temporarily lost her looks, health and confidence on this job like the rest of them, then she would no doubt also make out like a bandit down the road like the rest of them too. Jessica was still sending her nine former secretaries checks at Christmas (guilt money? perhaps), and every other day, it seemed, she was helping them get some great new job. She rarely saw any of them again, however, not after she saw how radiantly happy and healthy they all looked after leaving her.

In any event, Alicia seemed very fast and strong in spirit and Jessica tried not to get her hopes up. But who knew? Maybe Denny was right —maybe kids who grew up in New York City were made of tougher emotional stuff than elsewhere.

Jessica took Alicia into a meeting with her to discuss the booking of guests with her brand-new bookers. These new bookers (hired away from other talk shows taped in town) told her that, for her first show, Jessica could choose from topic discussions on Sexless Marriages, Sex Addicts, Porn Addicts or Spouses Who Are Secretly Transsexuals, to which Jessica responded by suggesting they combine all four and call it "Fucked Out of Their Minds." (Alicia laughed—good sign.)

And then Jessica asked if they couldn't *please* do something a little more upbeat, maybe something about healthy sex for a change, something that would make a lot of people remember that first night that "The Jessica Wright Show" went national because afterward they had made love for the first time, or they conceived their child, or because that was the night they had had the best sex ever. ("What do you think?" Jessica asked Alicia. "I think it would be fun to get aroused," Alicia said without batting an eye, stunning the bookers and making Denny's and Jessica's faces light up. This kid was a natural.) And so they closed the meeting with the bookers promising to try and find some people somewhere who had healthy sex lives.

Then Jessica took Alicia with her downstairs to the studio workshop where they were working on a set for her, a living room (although, as Jessica explained, the only people who had living rooms like this tended to be Colorforms and talk show hosts), and Jessica watched Alicia carefully, her hopes rising higher and higher. Alicia was enthralled by everything; her eyes were growing bright, her shyness was dissolving in curiosity; and her questions were smart, fun. Oh, how wonderful it would be to have someone she could have some fun with! (How tired Jessica was of seeing that look of fear her secretaries always got by the second week.)

And it was a *great* job for the right person—Jessica told Alicia, meaning it—great experience, a real leg up to meet people in the industry, to figure out what Alicia wanted to do. And being her secretary did not really have much to do with secretarial tasks. The task was more like organizing Jessica's life, a task—Jessica admitted, sighing—that was so horrendous that she herself absolutely refused to be stuck with it.

Saints be praised, Alicia burst out laughing.

Saints be glorified forever and ever and ever, Alicia Washington actually took the job. And so Jessica took her out that afternoon for a celebratory lunch.

17

Gordon and Jessica Watch the Rehearsal

What was with him, anyway? Anybody could see that Jessica Wright was trouble.

And not only had he let her openly flirt with him, but he had invited her up to watch the news rehearsal in his office.

Gordon sighed, looking at his watch. "Three forty-six," he said.

Betty got up from the couch and padded across his office in her stocking feet to get the remote control from on top of the television set. She turned on the set and changed stations. "Maybe she got lost," she said.

Now why he had invited Jessica was beyond him. Rather, he knew why he had invited her and wondered at how foolish he was to do anything but stay as far away from her as possible. He had learned his lesson the hard way with women like her, hadn't he? A number of times? And though Jessica Wright was not an actress, all the signs of the hazards of the profession were there. And while she might look easy and be easy and feel great for a night, the price tag afterward, he bet, would be something else—whether it was an answering machine full of progressively more hysterical calls, or out of the blue, months later, the sudden ringing of his doorbell at four in the morning and then the banging on the door with the cry, "Let me in! I know you're in there!"

It wasn't that he thought Jessica Wright might be some kind of lunatic. She wasn't. Gordon was sure of that because Alexandra said Jessica was a very bright, quick and talented person, and Alexandra tended to be more critical than kind about women her age. But just the fact that he instantly felt a silent sexual rapport with Jessica, that he felt a silent rapport *period* with her, hinted to him that Jessica Wright was one of "those"—those women who could inspire the illusion of instant intimacy, of making him feel as though he had known her for years. And *that's* when his alarm bells should go off, that's when it should be booming over the loudspeakers in his head, "Chameleon loose! Chameleon loose! What you see has nothing to do with what you'll get, REMEMBER, REMEMBER, REMEMBER."

Of course, it was Jessica Wright's job to make people instantly like her, to feel comfortable with her. And she was very highly paid for her ability to seduce people into a trusting rapport within minutes on camera. But it was not supposed to be real and lasting, the rapport, it was supposed to be temporary, a bridge to get viewers across the abyss of the television medium to something that felt like personal, firsthand experience. And there was absolutely nothing wrong with being talented this way, just as there was absolutely nothing wrong with being a talented actress—so long as women like her stopped performing in their own lives!

Gordon could spot the syndrome right away, and within moments of meeting her he had known that Jessica Wright was one of those women who could not willfully turn it off. She had come on to him as methodically as she would come on to any audience from which she was seeking approval. She had even changed scripts, hadn't she? Changed her whole performance when her material wasn't going over right with him? When he did not give her the response she wanted?

(He hoped for her sake that she was still aware that she *was* performing, because the fate of women who crossed that line of distinction tended not to be good. Death, insanity or hospitalization seemed to be the way it went for them, at least in Hollywood.)

Oh, yeah, Jessica the talk show hostess, the performer—and she'd be fabulous in bed no doubt. But then, after she seduced him into thinking he was seducing her into a little onetime fling, a onetime unrestrained great fuck, after she *got* something on him, no doubt the terrorist in her would come out, demanding that he stay with her or sentencing him to be stalked. Wasn't that always how it had gone down before with her type?

Oh, this was stupid. He was *engaged,* for chrissakes. Why was he even thinking about this?

Gordon knew why he was thinking about this.

Ever since Alexandra had said she'd marry him, he seemed to see nothing but possible sex partners. The same thing had happened the instant Julie had said she'd marry him. *I can never have sex with another woman,* was his first thought waking up the next morning. And, actually, feeling the sexual attraction to Jessica did not really alarm him—it was when he felt a sexual attraction to someone like *Betty,* kooky Betty, his assistant, that he was alarmed, because not only was it not rational, but it came from another angle entirely.

Do I really want to spend the rest of my life with Alexandra? was the killer question, the one that flitted in and out, though he supposed that as time passed it would go away. He wrote it off as nerves, as being scared of the marriage not working. But then, sometimes, it was a simple thought like, how was he supposed to fulfill Alexandra's expectation of complete fidelity, when he could be away for weeks or months on end and she had no way or intention of leaving New York to see him? Wouldn't he have to have someone like a Betty to—

Stop it! he commanded himself. *After seven years of wanting to marry Alexandra, ten days after she finally says yes—now, all of a sudden, you're not sure if you want her?*

Well, it didn't help that Alexandra had been acting pretty strange herself since she said yes. Or could it be mere coincidence that, after ten years of a good mood, as soon as she was engaged to him she started to develop a melancholy personality? Well, not melancholy exactly. But she wasn't herself, that was sure. And he supposed it was what she said it was, that she wasn't sleeping very well and the pressure at work was getting a little tough. But then he'd think, *Oh, great, if she's like this now, imagine what's she going to be like if her ratings fail, or if . . .* And what *would* she be like five years from now, anyway, even under the best of circumstances? Still at the studio no doubt—any studio, any newsroom, anywhere USA but not with him because he'd probably be working on location somewhere . . .

Stop it! What is your problem, Strenn? You're in love with Alexandra, and she's in love with you, case closed. You'll work it out.

Gordon got up from behind his desk and walked over to what he and Betty had set up as a viewing area. They had pulled the couch out from the wall and swung it out across the office to face the TV and swung the coffee table out in front it as well. And then, on either side of the couch, he had pulled up a chair so that, no matter where Jessica chose to sit, he could distance himself.

Jessica had called from a restaurant about an hour ago to say she would be coming to watch the rehearsal but wanted to know where there was a deli or something so she could pick up some snacks. Gordon told her that Alexandra had invited them all to come down and have a drink and something to eat with the crew in Studio B after the rehearsal, but Jessica insisted she could not watch TV without eating something (which seemed pretty strange, considering she was supposedly eating lunch when she called).

"I gave her directions how to get back," he said to Betty. "It's only a couple of blocks—how could she be lost?"

"Oh, one suspects she would get lost a lot faster than she would read directions," Betty said, taking a moment to look at "General Hospital" on Channel 7 before going on to the color-bar test pattern on Channel 10, the closed-circuit station within West End. She came back to the couch, sat down and put the remote control down on the table.

Jessica, at that moment, appeared in the doorway carrying a large white shopping bag. Her hair, from the wind outside, was all over creation, and her face was bright, flushed, her eyes shining. "Well, hi," she said with a definite Southwestern flair, coming in. She pulled out a large bag of popcorn and placed it on the coffee table, followed by a six-pack of Amstel Lite beer. Then she looked over her shoulder, toward the doorway, and waved for the older man standing there to come in.

Older, as in around seventy, or at least clearly past the usual retirement age—white-haired, slight, impeccably groomed and dressed in a red plaid jacket and dapper green bow tie. However old he was, he appeared to be something of a dandy.

"This is Mr. Graham," Jessica said, crumpling up the shopping bag and making a heck of a racket. "We just met downstairs. He says he works for Alexandra."

"Hello, Mr. Graham," Gordon said, walking over to shake hands and hoping he did not look as baffled as he felt. "I'm Gordon Strenn."

"How do you do?" Mr. Graham said, enunciating every syllable.

Gordon looked at Betty, who was just sitting there, openly staring at the older guy. "And this is Betty Cannondale, Mr. Graham. Betty works with me—we're in the miniseries group."

"How do you do?" Mr. Graham said, turning to offer Betty a slight bow.

"Great, thanks," Betty said, not looking or sounding very convinced about this.

"How do you do, Betty-Cannondale-who-works-in-the-miniseries group?" Jessica said, tossing the popcorn bag at her—which she caught. "May I interest you in a beer?"

"Can't audition for a year," Betty said, getting up, "so why not? I'll get some glasses."

Gordon was standing there, sort of smiling at Mr. Graham, who was standing there, sort of smiling at him.

"I must say, Gordon," Jessica said, kicking off her shoes and gesturing to the empty couch and chairs, "when you throw a party, you sure go all out. Hey, Mr. Graham," she added, "why don't you sit down here on the couch? Get a good seat before all of Gordon's friends here squeeze us out into the hall?"

"Thank you," Mr. Graham said, walking over.

Jessica gave Gordon a slight smile and then went about pouring beers.

Mr. Graham lowered himself down into the couch. Once settled, he looked up to see Betty standing there, smiling at him, and Gordon standing there, smiling at him, and then Jessica too, glass in hand, standing there, smiling at him. "I hope I'm not intruding," Mr. Graham said. "I would not like to intrude."

"Oh, no," Gordon said quickly.

"Let me tell you something, Mr. Graham," Jessica said, holding out a glass of beer to him, "the test of any party is whether or not there's anybody there who's more interesting than yourself—and I suspect you may well be the most interesting person here."

"Thank you, Miss Wright," Mr. Graham said. "It's very kind of you to say so."

"Not at all," Jessica said, pouring more beer. "So tell us, Mr. Graham, what exactly is it that you do for Alexandra?"

"I'm afraid I am not at liberty to discuss it at the present time," Mr. Graham said.

"I knew he would be interesting," Jessica murmured, handing a glass of beer to Betty and then turning back to Mr. Graham. "Why not?"

Mr. Graham touched at his bow tie. "My work with Miss Waring is a privately contracted arrangement and at the present time is of a confidential nature."

"Oh," Betty said, eyes wide, turning to look at Gordon as she sat down on the couch, "just like you, Gordon."

"Here, Flash Gordon," Jessica said, nudging him with her elbow and handing him a glass. Then she smiled at him again, saying under her breath, "Flash Gordon and Alexandra Eyes—I bet you two are a pair to watch."

She had been drinking, Gordon realized. He could smell it. Vodka, maybe. That was why her face was so flushed. But still, there was something intoxicating in the air around Jessica not connected with booze that was making Gordon flush a little too. *God,* he thought, taking the beer and moving away from her, *I've gotta be careful around this one.* He was definitely getting the feeling that Jessica would be delighted if only he'd excuse them both and take her to the conference room for a quickie. He was definitely getting the feeling that it would be very fast and very good. He was definitely getting the feeling that he had to concentrate on something else fast because there was nothing he liked more than a quickie during the workday, which he had not had in over a year because Alexandra was never accessible that way. Crazy actresses, bosomy talk show hostesses and inaccessible anchorwomen—Gordon thought maybe he should be in another line of work. Gordon thought maybe he better get married sooner. Or maybe he should just fuck Jessica while he had the chance and was still single. *(Maybe you could stop looking at her, for starters,* he thought.)

"Is this ginger ale?" Mr. Graham said, holding his glass up to the light.

"It's light beer, Mr. Graham," Jessica said, sitting in one of the chairs.

"Beer!" Mr. Graham exclaimed with a mild intake of breath. "Why, I'm afraid I must refuse," he said, quickly handing it to Betty. "When the Devonshire was bombed before my eyes, I swore I would never drink beer again if only I got safely through the war."

"Which war?" Jessica said.

"Two," he said. "I was in the foreign press corps in London. Ed and the others—"

"Ed?" Jessica said.

"Murrow, Mr. Edward R. Murrow," Mr. Graham said. "He was in radio, you know. He worked out of Broadcasting House, used to be a regular at the Devonshire pub before—" He pointed to the TV. "Excuse me, but I believe Miss Waring's newscast is about to begin."

Mr. Graham was right, the rehearsal had begun, only the opening graphics and film and titles and theme music were not ready yet and so they ran some stock footage of American landscapes, supered titles from the character generator and played something that sounded suspiciously like music stolen from Charles Kuralt.

"Oh, my," Mr. Graham said as they cut to Alexandra in the studio.

"Wonderful eyes," Betty murmured. "She really does."

Gordon smiled, feeling his stomach flipflop. If he ever doubted he was in love with Alexandra, all it took was seeing her on the screen to remember how much he was. Oh, *God,* was she ever beautiful.

Is that you? he thought. *Are you my Alexandra? Do those eyes, that mouth—do those shoulders belong to me? If they took off your dress, would my scar still be there, or would it be gone in the magic of TV?*

He sat there marveling at her.

But then, after about fifteen minutes, he felt vaguely uneasy. There was something not quite right about her voice, her delivery, something . . . Come to think of it, Alexandra didn't look quite right either. There was something vaguely detached about her—stiffer? Or was it the camera angle? And there was something about her intensity that was, was . . . Well . . . Missing?

On the other side of the couch, sitting in the other chair, Jessica was making noises. First she sighed. Then she made a sound with her tongue off the roof of her mouth. Then she was tsk-tsk-ing. Then there was a quiet groan. Then, during the next break for commercials, she poured herself another beer, sipped it and said, "Why is she so—so . . . ?" She finished her question with a wave of her hand and took another sip of beer.

"Serious?" Betty offered.

"Hard, was what I was going to say," Jessica said.

"It's only a rehearsal," Gordon said, wishing he did not agree with Jessica. There was something hard about Alexandra that wasn't working.

"She is a newscaster," Mr. Graham announced, as if this should explain everything.

"Well, she better cast again—" Jessica said.

"It's on," Gordon said, pointing to the screen.

"—because Jackie showed me her reel," Jessica continued, "and she was never hard like this. Here, she looks like she's got a broomstick up her ass. And why do they have her keep turning away from the camera?"

Mr. Graham, frowning deeply, turned to look at Jessica. "Shhh!" he said.

Jessica frowned and got up from her chair, walked around in back of the couch, leaned over to get a handful of popcorn out of the bag by Betty and then sat down on the couch arm between Betty and Gordon. "Of course he'd like it," she said under her breath to Gordon, "he thinks we're back in London with Edward R. Murrow."

"Hey," Gordon said quietly.

"Hey, nothing," Jessica muttered, pausing to take several swallows of her beer. Lowering her glass, "I'm the one who's gonna be stuck with Snooziola City and the Narcolepsy Sandbaggers here as the lead-in to my show."

"Please, Miss Wright," Mr. Graham said with a pained expression.

"Okay, okay," she said, getting up and going back around to her chair. She sat down and ate her popcorn and drank her beer, eyes glued to the screen, and did not say anything more.

When the newscast was over they all went downstairs and were the first to arrive in Studio B, where there were three tables of catered foodstuffs and a wine-beer-soda bar. People began drifting in behind them, and then Jackson arrived with his assistants, Ethel, Randy and Claire, and then Langley and Adele, and then some of the news group started trickling in, and within forty-five minutes there was a quite lively crowd scene, with everyone, it seemed, there except Alexandra.

When she did finally make it—at almost six-thirty, after some people had already eaten, drunk and left for the weekend—Gordon met her just inside the studio door. She looked tired, troubled; but she smiled, glad to see him, and discreetly squeezed his hand once.

"You were great," he said, "considering everything that was missing or makeshift."

She was looking at him, appearing doubtful.

"What's the matter?" he asked her.

"Oh, I don't know," Alexandra sighed, looking at the door as if she longed to leave.

"Hi ya, Alexandra Eyes," Jessica said, sweeping in from nowhere, "how's tricks?"

Alexandra laughed. "You tell me," she said.

"Funny you should ask," Jessica began.

Gordon quickly started shaking his head at Jessica. *No,* was the implied message. *Don't. This isn't the time to do a critique.*

Jessica stopped talking and stared at him. "Why can't I ask her about Mr. Graham?"

Alexandra turned to Gordon. "You met Mr. Graham?"

"Jessica brought him upstairs. He watched with us."

"The rumors are running rampant, my dear," Jessica said, edging in close to Alexandra, conspiratorially close. "What sort of personal contractual arrangement could the two of you have? we poor mortal souls wonder."

Alexandra laughed again.

Jessica was cheering her up, Gordon realized. Huh. You could never tell with Alexandra—she made friends with the strangest people.

"Is he still here?" Alexandra asked, looking around.

"No, he went home," Gordon said.

"Hi," Cassy said, coming over with Kate Benedict.

"Hi," Alexandra said.

"This is for you," Kate said, holding out a glass of Perrier and lime to her.

"Thank you," Alexandra said, taking a sip of it immediately.

"So are you going to tell us about Mr. Graham or not?" Jessica said.

"Not yet," Alexandra said.

"Well," Jessica said, turning her eyes on Kate, "we can always try plying Alexandra, Jr., here with liquor to find out."

"Excuse me," a voice said. They all turned to look. It was Emma Bolton, the lovely lady who was the head receptionist for Darenbrook III. "Excuse me, Ms. Wright," she said, "but a lady keeps calling upstairs, a Mrs. Wright, who keeps insisting on leaving messages for a Sarah Wright. I keep telling her that we have a Jessica Wright but not a Sarah Wright, but she says, no, take a message for *Sarah* Wright—"

"Oh, thank you," Jessica said, reaching for the message, "that's for me."

"Sarah?" Gordon said.

"It's got to be my mother," Jessica said, unfolding the paper. "Yep, it is."

"Are you holding out on us, Jessica?" Alexandra said, starting to smile. "Do you have another life we don't know about?"

Jessica rolled her eyes, drinking some wine. "Sarah Elizabeth Hollingstown Wright," she said then, "that's me. My mother calls me all four when I'm in trouble, Sarah to annoy me, and Mrs. Gary Turner when she's really feeling mean."

"I'll write that down in my book," the receptionist promised as she walked away (laughing to herself).

Everybody watched as Jessica drained her wineglass.

"But—" Gordon finally said.

Jessica handed him her empty glass. "But what, Captain Flash?"

"Where did Jessica come from?" he asked her.

"Savitch," she said.

"Oh, no!" Kate exclaimed in horror, looking to Alexandra.

Jessica glanced at Kate, frowning slightly, and then looked to Alexandra. "Didn't you want to be Jessica Savitch?" she asked her.

Alexandra smiled, nodding. "Of course. We all did."

"Yeah," Jessica said, sticking her tongue out at Kate before continuing. "She let me interview her for my school paper once, when I was a senior in high school. Let me watch her do her newscast one weekend and everything. She was really great."

"God help me," Cassy said, wincing, "you were only in high school when Jessica Savitch was at NBC?"

"Yeah," Jessica said. "And so on the way back to Essex Fells, after seeing the newscast, I just decided it was time that I had a name that I liked. And so I told everybody to start calling me Jessica—and they did."

Alexandra roared, Cassy and Gordon laughed and Kate looked vaguely scandalized.

Jessica looked down at her glass in Gordon's hand. "Oh, brother," she sighed, taking it back from him. "I tell ya, Captain Flash, you are positively a barrel of fun as a host." And off she walked toward the bar, prompting Alexandra to pull Gordon aside.

"Gordon," she whispered, sounding surprised, "what have you guys been doing? Jessica's absolutely bombed."

"She was well on her way before she got to my office, I swear," he said, raising his hand.

Alexandra was watching Jessica make her way to the bar, frowning. Jackson and Langley had walked over to Cassy and Kate; Alexandra signaled she'd be over in a minute and then turned back to Gordon. "Do you think she has a problem?"

He laughed slightly. "I think she's got problems other than booze."

"What's that supposed to mean?"

He lofted his eyebrows, looking up at outer space.

"Gordon!"

He smiled, looking into her eyes. (It was amazing how Alexandra could pick up the slightest innuendo out of the air. It had also not escaped his notice how carefully Alexandra had been watching Jessica's flirtatiousness with him, so he might as well get it out in the open, right? Besides, such things tended to bring out the best in Alexandra's discreetly, though irrevocably, competitive nature.)

"Well, be careful, Gordie," she said.

"Me be careful?" he said, pointing to himself, wondering how he could be feeling so giddy on four beers.

"You," she said, nodding once. "And remember . . ."

"What?" he said, wishing like hell he could just take her in his arms and kiss her.

Her eyes had traveled down to his mouth; she was thinking the same thing. "Remember," she murmured, raising her eyes back up to his, "she's a friend of mine."

"A friend?" he said, laughing. "Oh, man, if that's the best you can do—"

"No, I *don't,* thank you," Cassy said very loudly, sounding angry.

They turned to look. Cassy had just turned away from Jackson, who was shrugging to Alexandra as if he didn't know what Cassy could be upset about. Langley was nervously smiling and Kate was looking a little stunned.

"What's wrong?" Alexandra said, stepping over, eyes shifting back and forth between Jackson and Cassy.

"She doesn't feel like talking about it," Jackson finally said.

"Certainly not with you," Cassy said, breaking away from the group. "Excuse me." And she walked quickly out of the studio.

"Jesus, Jack," Langley said, shaking his head.

"What did you say to her?" Alexandra asked Jackson. Her tone of voice made Gordon look at her. Yes—she was angry.

Jackson held his hands out. "All I said was that I heard her husband got a new job. That's *all* I said."

Alexandra whirled around and went after Cassy, leaving Jackson, Kate, Langley and Gordon standing there in a rather uncomfortable silence. Then Kate excused herself and walked over to another group.

"The job's in L.A.," Langley said to Gordon. "We heard about it this morning." He shrugged. "We didn't know what to make of it."

"Shit," Jackson muttered, looking upset. "I didn't mean to upset her. I didn't, Lang." He looked at Gordon and then his expression changed, as if he was seeing him for the first time. "What are you doing here, Strenn?"

"I was invited," Gordon said.

"Hi, Jackie, hi, Mr. Mitchell," Jessica said, swinging in with a new glass of wine in hand. "Hey, Flash—where's Alexandra Eyes? I gotta leave soon but I gotta talk to her first."

Gordon shrugged. "She went somewhere."

"Somewhere where? The moon? Ladies' room? Southeast corner of Toidee-toid and Toid? Huh? Answer me," she said, holding his chin in her hand. Her eyes narrowed. "God, you're good-looking. You know that?"

"Help's sure gettin' kinda familiar around here," Jackson remarked, taking a swig of his Coke.

"Try the newsroom," Gordon told Jessica, who was still holding his chin.

"Why don't you come try it with me?" she said, her mouth slowly stretching into a smile.

Langley cleared his throat.

"Good idea," Jackson declared, stepping over to push Gordon toward the door. "I think you're just the man to help Jessica find her way."

"Jack," Langley said sharply.

"Come on, Captain Flash," Jessica said, taking Gordon by the hand and leading the way as if her wineglass was a lantern. She pulled him down first one corridor and then down another, asking everybody where Alexandra Eyes was. Finally someone told them that they thought she was in her dressing room.

"Dressing room, dressing room," Jessica muttered, pulling him down the hall.

"Other way," Gordon said, and so they veered around—pausing for Jessica to take a sip of wine—and Jessica pulled him the other way down the hall.

Just as they reached Alexandra's dressing room, Jessica released his hand, saying, "What do you bet hers is nicer than mine?" and reached for the door.

"Knock first," Gordon said, but Jessica wasn't listening. She just threw open the door.

And there was Alexandra. Sitting on the bench in front of her makeup mirror, holding Cassy, gently rocking her as Cassy cried.

18

Jessica Has to Tell Alexandra Something

When the door of Alexandra's dressing room flew open, Cassy started, lurching upright, away from Alexandra, tears running down her face.

Jessica stood there, staring, until Gordon said, "Excuse us," and reached around her for the door.

"No," Jessica said softly, pushing the door back open. "What happened? Cassy, are you all right?"

Cassy turned away, embarrassed. Alexandra plucked several tissues from the box on her dresser and handed them to her, which she used.

"Come on, Jessica," Gordon said, taking her arm.

"Let go of me," Jessica said, irritated, jerking her arm back from him and spilling some wine on the floor in the process.

"I think I'll slip into the bathroom and pull myself together," Cassy murmured to Alexandra, standing up. She walked across the dressing room and into the bathroom, closing the door behind her.

Alexandra immediately turned around to look at Jessica and Gordon, the latter of whom, standing behind Jessica, threw his hands up, indicating he couldn't help what had just happened.

"So what's wrong?" Jessica whispered, walking in, eyes on the bathroom door.

"Not now, Jessica," Alexandra said.

"Oh," Jessica said, leaning against the wardrobe and sipping her wine, eyes still on the bathroom door.

Alexandra looked at Gordon. He shrugged and then said, "Anything I can do?"

Alexandra glanced back at Jessica and then shook her head, sighing a little. "No. It's all right. Why don't I see you a little later?"

He nodded and then peered around the door. "Good night, Jessica."

"Huh?" she said, turning around. "Oh, bye, Captain Flash. Thanks for the swinging soiree."

"You're welcome."

Gordon closed the door.

"I really like Cassy," Jessica said, eyes back on the bathroom door. She took another sip of wine. "Nobody died or anything, did they?"

"No," Alexandra said. "Jessica—why don't you sit down? I'm not sure those doors are as strong as they look and I'd hate to see you fall in."

Jessica shrugged, walking over and sitting down in a chair next to the dresser. "So you weren't being mean to her, were you?"

Alexandra's mouth parted in astonishment. "Jessica," she finally said.

"What?" she said, putting her glass down on the dresser. "A little bird told me you've been giving her a hard time lately."

"Who told you that?"

Jessica met her eyes. "A little bird."

"What little bird?" Alexandra said.

"A big little bird, if you must know," Jessica said.

"Who?"

"Me," Jessica said. "I heard you yelling at her last week."

"I doubt very much that you heard me yelling at Cassy—or anyone," Alexandra said.

"You're not the type who has to raise your voice to yell, Alexandra Eyes," Jessica said, picking up her glass. "You're the mysterious woman in the dark flowing clothes who slips in to murder people in Saturday afternoon movies."

"Well, thank you, Jessica, maybe we can use that in an ad for 'News America Tonight,' " Alexandra said.

The bathroom door opened and Alexandra turned around to look.

Cassy smiled. With the exception of her nose being a little red, she looked very much herself again. To Alexandra she said, "I'm fine," and then, to Jessica, she added, "I think I'm going to head home now."

"I wanted to help, not drive you away," Jessica said.

Cassy laughed a little, walking over to toss a crumpled tissue into the trash. "You're not. It's just that I'm very tired and this is not a good place for me to be in tears."

"It's the best place I know of," Alexandra said, smiling warmly up at her. "Call me later, okay? I'll be home."

Cassy nodded.

And then Alexandra gave Cassy's hand a little shake, turning to Jessica. "This woman's the absolute best, you know—the best."

"At what?"

"Everything."

"Well, she sure has some mug on her," Jessica said, sipping wine. "Every TV woman's nightmare—a producer who's better-looking than she is."

"Hardly," Cassy said.

"Look," Alexandra said, pointing to the mirror.

And for a moment the two women looked at themselves and at each other in the mirror, Alexandra sitting and Cassy standing. Then Cassy looked away, briefly touching the back of Alexandra's head. "I better go," she murmured, walking to the door. She turned. "Jessica, good night, dear—have a nice weekend."

"Thanks. You too."

To Alexandra, "I'll talk to you later."

"Okay."

Cassy closed the door behind her.

Jessica drained her glass and put it down on the dresser. "So," she said, "are you going to tell me what's going on, or am I still the outsider?"

Alexandra smiled, turning back from the door. "You haven't been here very long."

"Ah, yes," Jessica said, resting her arm on the dresser, "but we have a friend in common, Alexandra Eyes, that must count for something."

Alexandra looked at her for a long moment. And then she said, "But are you discreet, Jessica? That is the question."

Meeting her eyes directly, Jessica smiled. "I am very discreet."

"Are you?" Alexandra said quietly, eyes narrowing slightly.

"Oh, man," Jessica said, closing her eyes and letting her head fall back against the wall, "hang around with me and you'll see. I've got more secrets than Gary Moore had guests."

Alexandra considered this for a moment. "It was about Cassy's husband," she said. "Michael—who's also a friend of mine. They've separated."

"Oh," Jessica said, opening her eyes and bringing her head back down. "Yeah, well, you know, husbands can do that to you. Kill ya, I mean." And then, frowning a little, she looked down at the floor. "So —since you've been honest with me, it's time for me to be honest with you." She brought her eyes up. "There's something I gotta tell ya, Alexandra Eyes."

Alexandra looked at her, expression unreadable.

"Only it's going to be a lot harder for me, because you'll probably never speak to me again after I tell you."

Alexandra's expression remained unchanged.

"Or maybe I'll be lucky and you'll think I've had too much to drink and will forgive me tomorrow," Jessica said. "But what I'm about to say is honestly how I feel—and you should know that."

Alexandra hesitated and then shook her head slowly. "I don't . . ."

"It's about 'News America Tonight,'" Jessica said.

"Oh," Alexandra said, visibly relaxing and starting to smile. "What about it?"

Jessica frowned, as if to remind Alexandra that this was serious business at hand. "I have to tell you something," she said solemnly.

"Please do," Alexandra said, smiling.

"Alexandra," Jessica started to say.

"Yes, Jessica," Alexandra said, laughing, "what on earth is it?"

"Your newscast—"

"Yes, what about it?"

"It stinks," Jessica told her.

19

The Changing Times of Cassy Cochran ·

If Cassy started regretting that she had cried at West End last night, then she knew could save herself some time if she simply regretted her entire life, because with a life such as the one she had led, regrets tended to multiply with a horrifying velocity after she indulged in even only one. So unless she wanted to spend the weekend working her way back through all her regrets to reach the original one—that she had ever been born—she had to accept the fact that last night, after Jackson said he had heard Michael was going to be the news director at KCA in L.A., she had broken down and cried with Alexandra and told her they had separated.

She had not been able to bring herself to tell Alexandra about the separation until now—now that word was out on the street about Michael's new job—and she still wished that Alexandra did not know. Alexandra had enough pressure on her right now without having to worry about her.

Nice try, she thought to herself, cleaning off the breakfast bar in the kitchen, *but that's not it.*

No, it wasn't.

Well, what is it then?

I don't want her to know my marriage is over.

Why?

Why do you think? she yelled inside of her head, stripping off the rubber gloves she had been wearing and throwing them into the sink. She sighed, pushing the stray hairs away from her face.

"Mom?" Henry called from the back hall.

Cassy took a breath, trying to pull herself together, and said, "Yes, dear?"

"What about the computer stuff?"

"That's all mine," she said, walking down the hall to stand in the doorway of the den. "Your father never learned how to use it." She turned away then, pressing her hand to her mouth and closing her eyes, willing herself not to start crying again. Henry was going through a hard enough number as it was, though Cassy thought Michael had really outdone himself by asking Henry to pack up the rest of his stuff to ship to California. ("How the hell am I supposed to get it if you won't let me in the goddam house!" Michael had yelled over the phone. "You only *had* two months to pack, Michael!" Cassy had yelled back.)

But though Cassy, and then Michael too, told Henry he was not to pack up the stuff, he arrived home from New Haven late last night anyway, insisting he wanted to. So now Cassy had to hang around and watch this morbid enterprise because, one, Henry didn't really know what it was he was supposed to be packing since Michael never bothered with such details; two, the only other person besides Cassy who did know was her cleaning-woman-turned-part-time-housekeeper, Rosanne, who couldn't get here today until after her morning classes were over (she was working on a nursing degree)—and of course Henry couldn't wait for Rosanne to start because his girlfriend was arriving late this afternoon (which gave Cassy a good idea who might end up packing for Michael); and, three, Langley was supposed to drop by to discuss "something" sometime before noon.

The timing in her life always struck Cassy as remarkable.

She took a breath and turned back around. Henry was standing there, looking at the hundreds of videotapes in the bookcases that represented the hours and hours of TV news programs and specials and interviews that had been produced by Michael and Cassy either separately or, from their early days, together. "Sweetheart," she said gently, walking in, "he doesn't need any of those now. And if he does, I'll send them." She stood just behind Henry, resting a hand on his shoulder, an uphill effort since her nineteen-year-old-son was now a little over six-two.

Henry glanced back at her; Cassy saw that his eyes were glistening and her heart ached. Her big, beautiful blond boy, who looked so much like her father; her son, who had been so loving over the years despite . . . despite everything. Oh, God, everything that this child had seen, had heard, had overheard in the night. How had he ever grown up to be such a wonderful young man? How had he?

Henry swallowed, looking backing at the tapes. "This is harder than I thought, Mom."

"I know," Cassy whispered, closing her eyes and resting her forehead against the back of his shoulder. She took a moment to make sure she could get through it and, when she was pretty sure, said, "You mustn't ever forget that your father will always be there for you, and that I will always be here for you. You mustn't ever forget how much we both love you—and how much we loved each other when we had you. How much we love each other, even now—and always—because of you." Her throat was killing her, it was so tight. She couldn't go on. No, no way. She cleared her throat, backing away from him, giving his back a pat as she did so. "I'm sorry, sweetheart. I wish—"

"Hi! I'm here," they heard Rosanne call, followed by the sound of the front door slamming. In a few moments she appeared in the doorway, turning up the long sleeves of her shirt. She took one look at each of them and said, "Aw, come on, you guys—no one's sick and no one's dying, so let's lighten up a little, okay?"

Since Rosanne had been widowed two years ago at age twenty-six, she did have a point. After everything she had been through (which the Cochrans had at various times been a witness to) and after everything the Cochran household had been through (which Rosanne had almost always been a witness to), the fact that everyone was healthy and well, when Michael, in particular, could have been dead by now, did put a different light on things.

"Come on," Rosanne said, directing traffic with her hands, "outta here, Mrs. C. Too many cooks started bangin' spoons over each other's heads."

"Okay," Cassy said, grateful to be dismissed. She turned to Henry. "Okay?"

He nodded.

"Where are the boxes, Henry?" Rosanne asked him.

Cassy turned. "They're in the guest room."

Rosanne looked at her. "Thank you, Henry," she said. "Come on, Mrs. C," she said, going over to get hold of Cassy's arm and pull her to the door, "you've got better things to do than hang out with us college kids."

"Thanks, Rosanne," Cassy murmured on her way out. She went down the back hall and into her bedroom, the master bedroom, and closed the door. She walked over to one of the windows and looked down at Riverside Park and the Hudson, resting her hand on the window sash. After several moments she said to herself, "Well, Cassy, you're finally getting what you said you always wanted—a peaceful house." She blinked several times, looking at the water, and then added, "Course, nobody's going to be living in it. But you can't have everything, can you?"

And then she squeezed her eyes shut, tears burning, and let her head fall forward to rest against the back of her hand on the sill. *Oh, Lord, please help me get through this. It hurts, it hurts so much and I don't want it to. I'm so tired of being hurt. This feeling of loss, this ache—it feels so much like when Daddy died. And help me, God, please, not to let Henry down. Help me to not hate Michael.*

In a minute she felt a little better. Sniffing, she straightened up and checked her watch. She sighed, looking back out at the water.

It was moments like these, when she felt so lonely, for what she didn't know *(Did we ever really have a family in this house? Wasn't it always me and Henry, or Michael and Henry, or me and Michael, never the three of us? Wasn't it always?),* that she longed to call Alexandra. So much of the reason why she had not wanted to tell Alexandra about the separation had to do with her own dependencies, of knowing how easy it would be for her—working situation or no working situation—to swing her emotional needs in Alexandra's direction.

And last night, within moments, hadn't that been what happened? That Jackson had set her off and she had fled and then there had been Alexandra, taking her into her dressing room and holding her while she cried? And hadn't there been something very familiar about being on the phone with Alexandra later last night, curled up in bed, feeling grateful, warm and secure, basking in Alexandra's never ending, never failing stream of reassurances about how everything would work out for the best? And wasn't that what Cassy wanted and needed—and wasn't that exactly what had gotten her into trouble with Alexandra before? To so sorely want that comfort and gentleness—to hear Alexandra's laughter and her compliments, to see the adoration in her eyes?

Oh, please, God, Cassy thought, holding her head in her hands, *don't let me mislead Alexandra. Don't let me start encouraging "that" side of things again to make myself feel better.*

She dropped her hands, looking out the window again, out to the Hudson River. *But I am so scared of being alone,* she thought.

And then Cassy sighed, turning away from the window, and went into the bathroom to splash cold water over her face—wondering what other women did when their homes were suddenly vacant, void of purpose, empty of warmth. Surely they did not contemplate flirting with their women friends to cheer themselves up. Or maybe they did —how would she know since she had never really had any close women friends? Her family and work had taken everything she had to offer for years—and look at what trouble she had gotten into with the only friend she *had* made!

Cassy stood up, reached for a towel and patted her face dry, looking at herself in the mirror. Yes, she still had her looks. For a little while longer, anyway. But even if her looks hadn't worn out yet, Cassy was afraid that her heart might have. Men. Good grief, after twenty-two years with Michael, could there possibly be anything left inside to take on another man? *But what might you catch out there, Cassy old girl, if you tried?* she asked herself, pulling the skin back from her eye, wondering in the next moment whether she would ever have her eyes done.

"Mom?" Henry was calling through the door. "Mr. Peterson's on his way up."

Cassy went out to the bedroom door and called, "Could you let him in, please, sweetheart? Take him into the living room? I just want to pull myself together—I'll be there in a minute."

" 'kay."

Cassy let her hair down and, bending over, brushed it out. Then she put it back up on the back of her head, inserting two hairpins while walking over to stand in front of the mirror. She unzipped her blue jeans to tuck her blouse in properly, zipped them back up, and then went over to the closet to kick off her Topsiders and slip on some low blue heels. Then she went into the bathroom to put on a little blue eye shadow, a little blush, mascara, lipstick and some small gold hoop earrings.

Presentable, yes.

She went out to the living room and almost laughed when she saw Langley because it was so strange to see him dressed casually. She had seen him only in suits—perfectly pressed, quiet suits—but here he had on a flannel shirt, khaki pants and sneakers—which would be fine if they didn't look as though he'd just taken them out of the box to wear.

They settled down at the dining-room table and, while leaning on her elbow, tapping the eraser end of a pencil against her mouth, Cassy listened as Langley explained that there was going to be a reassessment of the financial structuring of DBS by the Darenbrook board this summer, and how Langley and Jackson wanted the numbers on DBS News to look as good as they possibly could.

"What on earth can I do but what I've already done for you?" Cassy asked him. "The budget, budget revisions, projections, cost analyses, rundown sheets, P and L's, it's all there for the board to look at any time."

"Coffee's ready," Rosanne announced, bringing a small tray with a small china pot, two cups and saucers, milk and sugar.

"Oh, thank you," Cassy said as she put it down. "Rosanne, I'd like you to meet my boss, Langley Peterson. Langley, this is our housekeeper, Rosanne DiSantos."

Langley, who had stood up when Rosanne came in, nodded. "Hello."

"Hi ya," Rosanne said, leaving.

"As I was saying," Cassy said, pouring coffee for him, "I don't understand what I can do for you that I haven't already."

"We'd like to cut as much debt from DBS News this year as we can."

"Debt?" Cassy said.

"Or, rather—" Langley said quickly, "increase the forecast on the return on investment."

Cassy, eyes on Langley's face, pushed his cup and saucer in front of him. "You're not thinking of moving us out of Manhattan, are you?"

"No, no," Langley said quickly, shaking his head. "West End is home free for the next nine years."

"It sure isn't free in my overhead," she observed.

"The rent in your overhead is being applied to your debt within the corporation."

"What debt? Why do you keep talking about my debt?" Cassy said. "We haven't borrowed any money. Darenbrook Communications invested money in DBS News and expects a return on it within five years—so if there's any debt, it must be somebody else's." She pushed her chair back and stood up, muttering, "As if I don't have a good idea whose," and headed into the kitchen. She came back with some Sweet'n Low, which she proceeded to stir into her coffee. "There's a story going around about DBS, you know."

Langley looked at her.

"That DBS is being awfully slow about payouts on the miniseries. Is that going to happen to us?"

Langley shook his head. "We are slow on the miniseries, but that's because of the production moving overseas. Financial transactions have to go overseas and then come back into this country—that's all," he said, lowering his eyes to his coffee. "That's why we're having the review this summer."

"Mom," Henry said, coming in. "Sorry—but Dad wanted to make sure I sent his rowing machine. Do you know where it is?"

"It's right where he left it eight years ago—in the basement," she said. "Sorry, Langley—you were saying."

Langley turned around to make sure Henry was gone before continuing. "We'd like to strengthen DBS News' financial outlook by consolidating production of 'The Jessica Wright Show' under you. You'll be named president of news and information and—"

Cassy waved her hand through the air. "Wait, wait, wait, wait a minute." She dropped her hand and looked at him. "Why are we consolidating production?"

"Because Jessica can pay a lot of your bills—"

"Let me get this straight," Cassy said. "You're going to let me drain the profits of 'The Jessica Wright Show' to make DBS News look better for a corporate review this summer?"

"Not drain—" Langley started to say. Seeing Cassy's expression, he shrugged. "Essentially, yes."

"Why?"

"Sorry—" Henry said, reappearing in the doorway.

Cassy looked over.

"Do I have to call the super or something to get into the basement?"

"Yes, sweetheart. His number's in the book."

"Okay, thanks."

Langley waited a moment to make sure Henry was gone. And then he leaned forward to say, "This is purely a preventive move—one we're taking only to make sure that DBS News is not interfered with in any way by the board."

"Why should it be interfered with?"

And so Langley explained that one of Jackson's brothers would be stepping down from the board, thus altering the balance of the vote and reducing the majority who had originally endorsed the idea of DBS News to the minority. And since DBS News had been launched much earlier than originally planned, and was actually twice the size of what had originally been approved, they were simply making sure that DBS News would be left alone.

Cassy was looking at Langley like he was crazy.

"What?" he said.

"There's got to be more to it than that," she said evenly.

"All we're doing is asking you to consolidate your position and get promoted in the process," Langley said.

"Langley," Cassy said, leaning forward in her chair, "what you're asking me to do is help you defraud the board. That's what you're asking me to do—to skew the numbers between news and entertainment."

"No, no, Cassy," Langley said quickly, reaching across the table to touch her wrist. "We want you to consolidate them as a financially attractive investment—as our initial block of in-studio programming—and do it in such a way so as to discourage anyone from thinking of trying to separate them."

"And going after the vulnerable one," she said, blinking rapidly. "Which would be DBS News."

"Really, Cassy," Langley said, "the only reason why we're asking you to do this is to clear the way for smooth sailing."

"It must be the Virginia Woolf school of sailing then," Cassy said, "because it seems like every time I turn around I catch Jackson putting rocks in my pockets."

"No, that's wrong," Langley said. "It's absolutely wrong. I know you think otherwise, but Jack is a tremendous supporter of yours."

"Oh, right!" Cassy said, slapping the table and throwing her head back to laugh.

"I'm serious, Cassy," Langley said. "Regardless of your personal differences and conflicts over Alexandra, he has no doubts about your capabilities and contribution." After a moment, "Cassy—Cassy, listen to me."

She stopped laughing and brought her head back down, wiping the trace of a tear from one eye. And then, sniffing once, her expression grew quite serious. "No, you listen to me, Langley," she said, lowering her voice and leaning forward. "I will do this, Langley—I will do whatever you tell me I have to do in order to protect my people, to protect their jobs, and to protect our collective future. And I will now work to protect Jessica and her people too. But I've got to tell you, Langley, I don't like it—and I don't like how arbitrarily you guys trade on the good faith of the people you lured to DBS. As for Alexandra—"

"Jack's going to talk to her himself about it first thing Wednesday."

"Wednesday," Cassy repeated, thinking.

"And there's something else, Cassy," Langley said. "About you, and why Jack wants to do this."

Cassy looked down at first her one side and then her other, murmuring, "Just checking for rocks."

Langley smiled. "I'm not supposed to tell you, but I will. Before the year is out, Jack is hoping to make you president of DBS. Turn the whole operation over to you."

Cassy looked up, stunned.

Langley's smile expanded. "So you see? We do have other reasons for wanting to put Jessica's show in your hands now."

"But what about you?" she finally managed to say.

"Oh, I'll be running Darenbrook Electronics. And you and I will be doing a lot of business together over the years. You know, Cassy, we had more than one reason for naming the network DBS." He paused. "It's also the nickname for the direct broadcasting system—transmitting from satellite directly into homes. And we're ready to do that now.

The day a home is equipped to receive is the day we can broadcast directly. And five years down the road I'm going to have a whole slew of interactive programming to offer DBS, Cassy." He paused, his smile expanding further. "Imagine the possibilities for the news division if DBS were the first broadcasting network to have spontaneous interaction with its viewership."

"We could take the pulse of the country at any given moment," Cassy murmured.

"But the big plan, Cassy, the real dream behind this effort—*my* dream . . ." he said, voice trailing off.

Their eyes connected.

"As Xerox was to carbon paper, DBS will be to broadcast television," he said. "It's not really a network we're building—it's a technological revolution." He waved his hand through the air. "But that's the dream. The reality is, for the moment, DBS is a struggling venture which Jack and I both believe could flourish under your direction."

After a long moment Cassy laid a hand on her chest, looked down at the table and said, "I never . . ." She looked up. "I came to DBS to be near the newsroom again."

"And you've been building the network instead," Langley said.

They were both quiet for a while, smiling, looking at one another.

Then there was a crash in the kitchen.

"What was that?" she called.

"Nothing, Mom. I'm just moving a box to the front hall."

Cassy looked at Langley. "Could I possibly interest you in taking a walk?"

It was a gorgeous day, this first Saturday in May, and they walked out of the building, across the Drive to the brick esplanade under the trees, and then took the steep concrete stairs down into Riverside Park. As they made their way down the hillside and through the glen, they talked on about the consolidation, and paused for a long while at the flats of the community garden, looking at all of the flowers. ("This park is so beautiful—I had no idea," Langley said, looking up to see how the apartment buildings on the ridge of the Drive towered over the tops of the trees in the park.) They strolled to the end of the gardens, went down some old stone stairs, walked through a tunnel underneath the West Side Highway and came out on a lovely promenade running along the edge of the river.

The Hudson was blue today. At eye level, the twelve hundred yards of water across made New Jersey seem miles away. The wind was light and sea gulls were screaming overhead, and the afternoon sun, moving down toward New Jersey, felt warm on their faces as they walked south along the promenade, hands in their jacket pockets.

After a while they stopped to lean on the wood railing and look out across the Hudson. Eyes dropping to the water lapping against the rocks below, Cassy noticed her engagement ring and wedding ring on her hand, and wondered when or if she shouldn't take them off. It felt very strange to think about this, about taking off the rings she had been wearing every day of her life for over twenty-two years. It gave her a sick, hollow feeling inside and so she looked up and took a deep breath—drawing in that funny mixture of salty sea air from the south, the harbor, and the fresh-water-and-greenery smell from the river north—and it helped make the awful feeling go away. And the sun, so warm on her face, and the breezes, playing with her hair, felt lovely.

"Can you keep a secret?" Langley asked her.

Cassy looked at him. He was looking overhead at the circling gulls, the breezes playing with his hair too. She was struck by how pale he looked, how alien he seemed to the outdoors. She wondered when was the last time he had had a vacation—and what he did when he took one. "Sure," she said.

Langley looked straight out across the water, still leaning on the railing, holding his hands together in front of him. "Ever since you people arrived at West End," he began. And then he stopped, looking down at his hands.

"Tell me," Cassy said, moving a little closer to him, sliding her elbows along the railing.

"I've been having fun," Langley said. He looked up, back out over the water. "I complain all the time, I know, but truth is—" He turned to look at her. "We weren't having much fun around there—at Darenbrook Communications. Not since Jack's wife died. It all changed then. Jack changed. Everyone changed." He looked back at the water, thinking. "And I'm beginning to think that maybe it *is* Alexandra. That she's making things come alive again—making people feel alive again. *Pro-*

voked, certainly," he added, laughing to himself. "God knows, she sure gets Jack all worked up and me worked up and you . . ."

"I love her very much," Cassy said with a smile, closing her eyes and angling her face toward the sun.

"And it's exciting these days, you know?" Langley said. "Even with all the problems, all the headaches."

Cassy opened her eyes and shielded them with her hand to get a good look at him. And then she smiled again and leaned over to nudge him. "And the best part's to come. You haven't lived until the day you walk by a TV store and see Alexandra on the set in the window. Or Jessica. And watch people watching. 'I helped make this happen,' you say to yourself. 'This is what I do for a living.' " She laughed, softly, bending to rest the side of her head on the railing a moment. "It's a little like motherhood."

"I guess," Langley said, sounding distracted. And then he looked down at Cassy. "You're very special, you know."

Cassy hesitated, blinked twice and said, "Thank you," straightening up. "I think you are too."

"No," Langley said, touching her arm, "I mean it. It's been a long time since I've known someone like you."

Cassy smiled faintly, turning to look out across the water.

After a long moment Langley said, "I haven't offended you, have I?"

"Of course not," she said gently, glancing at him. "Actually," she added a second later, turning toward him, resting one elbow on the railing, "I was thinking about Jackson's interest in Alexandra."

Langley looked a little surprised by this.

"I worry about him," Cassy said, "about his reaction down the road when he finds out about Alexandra and Gordon. It's one thing to keep it quiet from the public for now and cash in on the publicity about Jackson—but it's quite another to keep him in the dark about it if he's seriously interested in her—if he genuinely . . ." She shrugged.

"I know his interest in her is real," Langley said slowly, "but I'm not convinced anything else is. Jack can get a little star-struck sometimes."

"Don't we all," Cassy murmured, turning back to the railing and leaning on it with both arms. After thinking a moment, she looked at Langley. "Someone told me that Alexandra's a lot like Barbara—like his first wife."

"His only wife," Langley said. And then he started chuckling to himself, bowing his head to hold it in his hand for a moment. "Oh, God, no," he said, smiling still, bringing his head back up. "Alexandra's nothing like Barbara."

"Oh," Cassy said, turning back to look at the water.

"Barbara was just like you," he said.

20

Langley's Luncheon

"I'm sorry," Kate Benedict said, standing by Langley's table in the upstairs dining room of the "21" Club, "but Alexandra said she has to have some sort of an answer in writing."

Langley nodded, rereading Alexandra's note, marveling to himself how quickly their young anchorlady could move and still maintain the illusion around West End that she "didn't have a head for business." Nonsense. Alexandra looked after her business the same way she looked after the business of gathering news—she surrounded herself with excellent people whom she could trust to accurately inform her. So, instead of reporters and newswriters, Alexandra's crack attorney, agent and probably her accountant as well had helped prepare this note—and in record time. Alexandra had been told of Cassy's promotion to president of DBS news and information only this morning and already she was playing hardball in response.

Mr. Graham, who was sitting across the table at "21" from Langley, was frowning. "Miss Waring must be very upset if she sent this young lady all the way here," he said.

"Yep, she is," Kate confirmed. "Like your bow tie, Mr. Graham."

"Miss Waring is upset about my bow tie?" Mr. Graham said, forehead furrowing.

"No," Kate said, "I was just remarking on how much I like it."

"Oh. Thank you," Mr. Graham said, touching it with his hand.

Langley listened to this exchange, thinking how the day was getting stranger by the minute. He was supposed to have had lunch with Gordon Strenn and Sven Hagerstrom, a Swedish producer, but when they arrived at the restaurant there was a message that Hagerstrom had fallen ill. Gordon then begged off from lunch, saying he really could use the time to run up to FAO Schwarz to see if he could find a special building set for his son's birthday. And so Langley had been standing there, in the foyer of "21," debating whether to eat alone or not, when Alexandra's mysterious personal employee, Mr. Graham, came strolling in (just as he had for thirty-three years, the maître d' said) and Langley thought, what the heck, he'd ask the old guy to lunch. Mr. Graham had been delighted to accept.

"Here," Langley said to Kate, moving over on the banquette and patting the seat next to him. "Sit." He signaled the waiter, who had been watching Kate carefully. (Luncheon upstairs at "21" was to be a quiet, elegant and dignified affair, and so the staff was a bit wary of breathless young women dashing in who, in this case, could have been anyone from Mr. Peterson's scorned mistress to a drug-crazed daughter home from Bennington. One simply couldn't tell anymore.) "She will be joining us for lunch," Langley said.

"Oh, no, I'm sorry—I can't," Kate said quickly. "Really, I have to get back as soon as I can. I promised."

"At least have a drink then," Langley said, returning his attention to the note.

"Oh," Kate said, looking surprised.

The waiter was patiently waiting.

"Grapefruit juice—and Perrier," Kate said. When the waiter left, she turned to Langley. "Gee, Mr. Peterson, I didn't expect you to invite me to lunch. Thank you. I thought you'd yell at me."

Langley looked at her. "Have I ever yelled at you?"

"A lot," she said, but cheerfully so.

That's right, he had. But since it had always been Alexandra he really wanted to yell at, it had never occurred to him that Kate would consider his yelling about Alexandra as yelling at her. "Did Alexandra yell at you today?" he asked her, curious.

She shook her head. "No. Alexandra doesn't really yell. She gets very quiet—which in a way is worse, you know what I mean?"

He knew what she meant, though judging from how white Jackson's face had been this morning—after telling Alexandra that DBS had to expand Cassy's managerial responsibilities to include overseeing "The Jessica Wright Show"—Langley was not so sure Alexandra hadn't done some yelling in that meeting. And though Jack had promised to "take care of it" with Alexandra, the fact that he had suddenly decided to fly to Hilleanderville to talk to Cordelia (a week early) had signaled to Langley that Jackson had not taken care of anything with Alexandra, a fact that Cassy shortly thereafter confirmed.

"He gave her the impression that it was *my* idea!" Cassy had said to Langley over the phone. "And now he's gone, leaving us holding the bag."

"So Alexandra's angry?" he had asked.

"Angry? She's furious she wasn't consulted. And then I explained to her that the restructuring was only meant to strengthen the financial future of DBS News."

"And what did she say to that?" Langley asked.

"She said that was no excuse for her not being consulted, that we didn't have the right to present it to her as a *fait accompli*," Cassy said. "How Darenbrook presented it to her in their meeting—I don't even want to think about it. Anyway, I told her that the reason why she wasn't consulted was because Jackson didn't want to burden her with anything more while she was working on the newscast."

"And she said?" Langley asked.

"And she said that, since I seem to be so keen on show biz these days, maybe I ought to think about replacing her with Jessica and hiring a fire-eater along with a weatherman."

"She said that?"

"Oh, yes, Langley, she said that and a whole lot more." Cassy sighed then. "We've scared her, Langley. She's taken it completely wrong—and I should have thought of it, but I didn't."

"What do you mean? How did she take it?"

"Well, she's been squaring off with me over this format thing, she's been squaring off with you since day one, there was that horrible story about her in the *Banner* last week with more quotes from that idiot Clark Smith, and then all of a sudden the one person whose support she thought she would never have to question—Jackson—suddenly announces that DBS can't afford to let me spend all my time on her. She thinks it's all connected—she thinks Jessica is more important to DBS than she is, and she's scared. I mean, she's angry, but what's behind it is a very badly shaken young woman who desperately needs a demonstration of support—but I can't give it to her right now, not until she backs down on this damn format. And now she's more adamant than ever about it, because she's so angry."

"Well—should I make a demonstration of support in some way? Would that help?" Langley said.

"Well, somebody's got to do something," Cassy said, "because Jackson told her—get this—he told her the reason why I had to take on Jessica's show was because Jessica *needed* me. Now how the hell is that supposed to make Alexandra feel?"

Yes, Langley had to admit, it didn't look very good, did it? That Jessica arrives at a time when Alexandra is fighting with Cassy over the format of her newscast and then—bingo—all of a sudden Jackson announces that Alexandra has to share her executive producer and part of her studio crew with Jessica. But Alexandra didn't know all that they did, that this was a move to insure her professional well-being. (But then, she had no way of knowing that her professional well-being was at risk with Darenbrook Communications in the first place. How was she supposed to know that Jack stole the money to launch DBS News? How was she supposed to know that they were doing this in order to protect her, not take anything away from her?)

But, thankfully, this note Kate had brought indicated to Langley that Alexandra was not nearly as undone as Cassy had led him to believe:

Langley [it said],
Since Cassy—legally speaking—works for me, and "The Jessica Wright Show" is now under her, DBS News now handles the overseas syndication of any of Jessica's shows that fit the classification of "news," correct? Please verify immediately as my attorneys are awaiting instructions on how to proceed in response to the nine contract violations DBS incurred with this morning's announcement. Thanks.

Alexandra

Now that sounded like the Alexandra he knew, quietly blackmailing him into giving her "The Jessica Wright Show" to syndicate overseas in exchange for her "allowing" DBS to have Cassy and the studio crews work on Jessica's show too.

Langley had known the syndication-arm clauses in Alexandra's contract would one day come back to haunt him. They were fairly innocuous at first glance. Once the Federal Communications Commission recognized DBS as a network, the only programming DBS could syndicate overseas would be news, and since news tended to be so American, with so few foreign outlets, Jackson had given Alexandra everything she asked for in connection with said syndication arm, DBS News International.

But, as Langley had learned, there were certain kinds of "news" programming that did lend themselves to foreign markets. Every week down the road at CBS, for example, the legal department made up a list of rights restrictions and permission clearances for that week's edition of "60 Minutes," detailing how they did not have foreign rights on one correspondent's commentary pieces but did on their field correspondents' pieces; or that maybe a celebrity had only granted certain permissions on how his or her interview could be used, and so the celebrity interview could not be shown in X, Y or Z countries, and so on and so forth. CBS could then repackage an edition of "60 Minutes" with the pieces that were cleared for foreign markets and sell it, outright, for a flat fee, to an overseas news distribution service, which, in turn, went on to sell it in various markets around the world, from French TV to a Brazilian hotel chain.

According to Alexandra's contract, not only did she receive a piece of the action (albeit small) on anything that was sold through DBS News International, but *all* other profits had to be channeled back into DBS News—and as funds that *only* Alexandra could allocate for expenditure. What Alexandra was after, Langley knew, was those one-on-one celebrity interviews from "The Jessica Wright Show" that could be classified as news and that she could easily sell overseas—and thus funnel what would otherwise be DBS profits under Langley's control into DBS News as funds exclusively under her control.

Langley had to hand it to Alexandra, she was swift and clear in her message. DBS had to pay a price to DBS News for making them share

Cassy and their production crew with "The Jessica Wright Show," or they could expect big trouble from her for violating her contract.

Well, you really took care of her, Jack, Langley thought.

How easy business would be if there weren't people to deal with! Every single problem at DBS could be worked out if it weren't for so many overblown personalities involved.

It had only been on Saturday that Langley had had such a great time with Cassy, envisioning all of the things that they could do with DBS and Darenbrook Electronics. It had only been on Saturday that he had been thinking how everything might get straightened out for Jack with the board. He had been thinking that he and Alexandra were getting along better, and that maybe he had passed judgment on her too quickly. He had even been thinking that one day, when he was back running Darenbrook Electronics, maybe there might be something to be pursued with Cassy—outside of work, on another one of those long walks. (Her husband moving to Los Angeles couldn't be a sign of a very good marriage, could it? And she was so very, very beautiful. He had been surprised at how much he wanted to kiss her Saturday, watching her, down by the water, the sun on her hair, her eyes so blue, her mouth so . . .) But then—whammo—now Alexandra was furious at him, Jackson had fled, Cassy was upset, DBS was still improperly funded and the board still had to be dealt with.

"By the way, Mr. Graham," Kate was saying at the table, "your editing console arrived downstairs today. And Alexandra says she has an assistant coming for you tomorrow."

"Wonderful," Mr. Graham said.

Langley looked at him. "Are you in film?"

"At one time," Mr. Graham said. He looked at Kate. "I suppose it would be all right to tell him I was once in newsreels, don't you think, Miss Benedict?"

"We better hope so," Kate said.

Mr. Graham returned his attention to Langley. "I was once in news-reels—until 1963, at which time I sold my archives to ABC."

"Uh-oh," Kate said.

Langley looked at her and then followed Kate's eyes to see that Jessica Wright was making her way toward them, looking very pretty in a narrow skirt, silk blouse, and blazer with the sleeves pushed up. Her earrings, necklaces and bracelets were on the conservative side today; her hair was unusually well brushed; and she was looking surprisingly respectable and normal, although her skirt was short enough to take many an eye with her. "Hi," she said, drawing up to the end of the table.

"Hello," Langley said.

"My oh my, Mr. Graham," Jessica said, "I bet Alexandra doesn't know that it's you who's out dancing with the Kaiser. Oops," she added, turning toward Langley. "I don't really think you're the Kaiser, Mr. Mitchell—and I don't think many other people really do either, but everybody's pretty upset today about who's invading whose territory and so maybe you can understand from where these nicknames can come."

Langley was so caught up in how together and pretty Jessica looked that it took a minute for what she had said to register.

"If you could just sign that thing," Jessica said, pointing to Alexandra's note, "we could send Alexandra, Jr., here back to West End and I could join you for lunch. Sorry," she said in an aside to Kate, patting her shoulder. "I know your name is Kate. I meant it as a compliment." Then she looked back at Langley, rested her hands on the table and leaned forward to say, in a very low voice with unmistakable innuendo in it, "Or wouldn't you enjoy being with me?"

Langley would have enjoyed the moment more had Kate not audibly gasped and then giggled, and had Mr. Graham in his blue and green bow tie not been smiling at him from across the table.

"Do you understand what this note is about?" Langley asked Jessica, swallowing, trying not to look at her mouth (which at the moment had her tongue running over it).

"I know it makes no difference to me," Jessica said, "not with the contract I have."

"So Alexandra's talked to you," Langley said.

"Maybe for the last time if this doesn't get straightened out. Look, Mr. Mitchell," Jessica said, tapping one long finger on the table, "nobody knows what's going on except that Alexandra's upset and it has something to do with me—so I want you to sign that thing so everybody at West End stops looking at me like I'm Typhoid Mary or something. I want to get to work, Mr. Mitchell!" she added loudly, pounding the table in such a way as to make the silverware jump and a couple of diners as well.

Langley looked back down at Alexandra's note. He took out a pen from the inside pocket of his jacket, pulled the cap off, turned the barrel, stuck the cap on the end and sat there a moment, pen poised, thinking. And then, writing slowly and deliberately, on the bottom half of Alexandra's note, he wrote:

Alexandra,
  Of course DBS News International will handle foreign on newsworthy Jessica Wright material. And however ironic it may seem to you now, I hope one day soon I may fully explain to you how the restructuring of Cassy's responsibilities is, in fact, a sign of our deepest commitment to you, our unshakable faith in you, and of our pledge to offer strong and lasting support to DBS News as a whole.
  Until then, I hope you will trust me.

                                                              Langley

And then he dated it, folded the paper up, slipped it back in the envelope and handed it to Kate, feeling pretty good about it. If that wasn't an open declaration of support, then what was?

Kate went back to West End with the note and Jessica sat next to him in the banquette, swiftly drinking one vodka tonic down and ordering another. When that arrived, she said, "Well, Mr. Graham, it looks as though Mr. Mitchell's a nice guy after all." She leaned into Langley's side as she said this, smiling rather sweetly (he thought). "I am so relieved, you don't know," she said, eyes briefly fixing on his chest and then coming back up. "I do so hate family fights, don't you?"

Langley laughed—a little nervously—glancing over at Mr. Graham, who was looking quite perky and festive after his glass of sherry. "As a matter of fact, I do," Langley said, meaning it, looking into her eyes and wondering why he was looking into her eyes since he knew better. Idle notions about Cassy were at least sane and alluring. But the Terror of Tucson? Was he ready for this?

"This is so nice," Jessica sighed, looking around the restaurant and sipping her drink. "I haven't been here since I was a little girl, with my grandfather."

"Perhaps I knew him," Mr. Graham said.

"Harold Wright?" Jessica asked.

"Of *The Saturday Evening Post*?" Mr. Graham said.

Jessica, opening her mouth, just stared at him. Then she looked at Langley and back at Mr. Graham again.

"Oh, yes," Mr. Graham said, chuckling, "I knew old Hare-Hare. He was here quite regularly."

"Hare-Hare!" Jessica said, excited, bouncing up and down in the banquette. "That was his nickname—you really did know him!"

"When you're my age," Mr. Graham said, "you tend to know a great many people, Miss Wright."

Jessica grew more and more festive as the lunch went on, talking with Mr. Graham, telling funny stories about herself and her family, leaning into Langley every ten seconds or so as if to make sure he was awake and paying attention. She needn't have worried. He was quite awake and quite content to eat the delicious food, sip the icy-cold white wine and, by the second bottle, feel Jessica's hand periodically resting on his thigh.

Somewhere along the line the lunch had turned unreal. It had turned into a slow-motion, warm, fuzzy dream where this splendidly warm, buxom creature next to him promised all sorts of seductive, wonderful times if only this lunch could last forever, or at least last long enough to find out what her hand on his thigh might want to do next. Langley very badly wanted to stay in this dream, to wander on, following this woman who was making him laugh and smile, who was making him feel like nothing mattered but that he might just this once —just once in his life—forget his responsibilities, forget everybody else and simply be himself, this laughing self, this man who was drinking too much wine but not caring, this guy who was thrilled by this young woman beside him, by this whole luncheon, by this whole idea that people found him worth laughing with, talking to . . . flirting with.

Making love with?

Oh, wouldn't that be great?

What a wonderful lunch this was, languishing in the fantasy of simply asking Jessica to spend the afternoon with him in bed somewhere, making love and laughing and feeling as warm and fuzzy and content as they did right here, at the table, the two of them, sitting here, thighs pressing against each other, her hand rubbing his leg—

what? What? When had this started? *Don't think. For once in your fucking life, don't think, Peterson.* And so he drifted back into what it might be like to make love to Jessica, how wonderful it would be to make love with someone who would not go crazy, screaming and yelling and running around the house threatening to kill herself. And he drifted further, leaving Belinda far far far behind, continuing in the fantasy of Jessica—what those breasts must be like he could not even imagine. . . . Oh, yes, he could, imagine those breasts—certainly, if he kept on like this, staring and getting caught, he would be in her blouse, yes, certainly.

He felt her hand again on his leg and he looked at her. She was smiling—no, laughing—but then the check was there and Langley noticed that everyone else in the dining room was gone. He looked at his watch. It was almost four.

Langley reluctantly signed the check, feeling depressed. By the time they were downstairs, outside, standing under the awning on 52nd Street, his warm fuzziness had turned into a headache. Jessica shook hands with Mr. Graham, explained she had to go on to the Plaza, thanked Langley for the lunch, and then, just after Langley directed Mr. Graham to where his car and driver were waiting, she grabbed his arm, whispered in his ear, "Do you want to come with me?" and then stepped back, looking at Langley with the most innocent of expressions.

Langley was shocked. Maybe a little appalled. No—it was more like scared out of his wits. *Jesus, now? Just do it? Now? After all these years, I just go and do it now? In the afternoon? With the Terror of Tucson?* "Thank you, thank you very, very much," he heard himself say, touching her arm, "but I'm afraid I can't."

She shrugged, smiling, digging her hands into her blazer pockets, backing down the sidewalk. Then she waved to Mr. Graham. "Now don't you let this wild guy take you to Atlantic City or anything."

Mr. Graham laughed.

And Langley laughed, dazed, watching Jessica skip down the street, wondering if what had happened could have possibly really happened.

21

In Which Jackson Flees Alexandra and Flies to Hilleanderville

Jackson knew how upset he was because, for the first time in a very long time, he actually wanted to go to Hilleanderville. Alexandra had lost her temper this morning and she had lost it at him, and something had profoundly changed between them because of it.

No. What had changed was his feeling for her.

No, what had changed was that he knew his feelings for Alexandra, romantically speaking, were not as unique as he had thought.

Oh, fuck, he thought, looking out the Gulfstream window. *It couldn't have been just another obsession, could it?*

But if he really cared for Alexandra in a special way, then why did he just want her to go away and leave him alone? And why did he feel so incredibly disappointed and depressed that Alexandra seemed to be just as scared and insecure as everybody else, only she hid it better?

And why did she suddenly seem so young?

When Alexandra arrived this morning in his office, she had been her usual buoyant, lovely self, cheerfully greeting him and throwing herself down in a chair, wondering what Jackson wanted to see her about. And so Jackson had started to explain about consolidating DBS News and "The Jessica Wright Show" under Mrs. Cochran and then Alexandra had been on her feet, her face scarlet, firing questions at him so fast that after a while he didn't even know what he was saying, and then, suddenly, Alexandra had slammed both her hands down on his desk.

"I *never* thought you would betray me, *never,*" she said. "And if you feel that I've betrayed you in some way, that I've failed to pay some kind of personal debt to you—then you've *got* to put it on the table now. Because you *can't*"—she slammed his desk again—"take your personal feelings about me out on DBS News—by endangering it. Do you understand me? I won't let you do it!"

"I'm not taking anything out on anybody," he said, "and I'm not endangering DBS News—"

"But you *are!*" she screamed.

They looked at each other. Alexandra seemed as stunned by her scream as he was.

And then she whirled around and flew out of his office, slamming the door behind her.

Sitting there in the plane, Jackson felt miserable. Where there had been fun and excitement and the possibility of happiness now there was only a sea of problems. Yesterday Alexandra had been a goal; today he wanted to avoid her forever because he felt so guilty. Because he realized, perhaps truly for the first time, just how much DBS News meant to Alexandra and how devastated her life and career would be if it failed. And he realized how terrified Alexandra was that it would fail —and that she would fail.

Wasn't it strange that only yesterday he had thought she was fearless.

Wasn't it strange that it had never really bothered him before about what shaky financial ground he had built DBS News on.

But then, none of it had seemed quite real, had it? It never was during the chase. Meeting Alexandra and launching the network a year early.

And . . .

And—

Jackson held his face in his hand a moment.

And wasn't it true that, if Alexandra had slept with him in the beginning, he never would have gone to such lengths for her and DBS News? Isn't that how his obsessions had always worked before? That they lasted as long as he was happily in pursuit, and he was only happy when obsessed?

No, no, he told himself, dropping his hand, *you're going overboard as usual, you wanted Alexandra as the anchor of DBS News.*

But would he have ever gotten into this mess had the anchor been a man?

Would he have?

No, he wouldn't have. He wouldn't have launched it a year early and he wouldn't have—

Oh, what did it matter? If DBS News could work—and it had every chance of working if the board didn't interfere with it—Alexandra Waring was the one to make it fly. And he genuinely believed she could do it and that *they* could do it. And so what if Alexandra was mad at him? She'd get over it. Everybody was always mad at him, sooner or later, and they always got over it—so why did he feel so damned depressed now? What was so wrong now that wasn't wrong before?

Because you know you're not in love with Alexandra, he thought, looking out the window. *You'd like to sleep with her, but you're not in love with her and you don't even really know her. It was just another one of your obsessions and so now you don't have anything to do in your head, nothing to do but feel how goddam lonely this life is and how work is nothing but endless, unsolvable problems and disappointments and everybody complaining and now there's not a goddam thing in this world to look forward to that means a goddam thing.*

As the plane landed at Hartsfield, he felt more depressed than ever.

"Well, well, what a surprise," Cordelia said, voice booming down the great hall of the Mendolyn Street house, "looky who's here. Better let him in, Salissy, before he starts selling snake oil to the neighbors."

The maid, Salissy, stepped back from the door, indicating that Jackson was now welcome in his family's house. "Hi, Cordie," he said, striding over the black and white tiles of the hall and—though at five-eleven she was no featherweight—picking fifty-year-old Cordelia up off the floor to hug her.

When he set her back down, Cordelia looked at her brother with more than a hint of skepticism on her face. But then she smiled, giving him a warm kiss on the cheek. "I don't know what you're selling, brother," she said, "but I hope you're genuinely glad to see me because I am glad to see you. And you just missed Belinda."

"Belinda was still here?" he said, surprised, walking with Cordelia into the living room.

"Yes sir, she was. I wanted her to stay for a while longer, but she left as soon as her suitcase got here. No!" she said, making a face and swatting the air with her hand. "I will not talk about that case one more time! Just take it from me, she found it and she left." She took his hand. (The living room was enormous and so one did have to stroll a bit to get across it.) "I don't know what is going on up there in New York with Langley," Cordelia said, stopping to face her brother, "but, Jackie, you've got to talk to him. Baby B's just getting worse and worse, and she says Langley doesn't care."

"He cares," Jackson said. "Believe me, Cordie, he cares. I was in Palm Beach with them—"

"Shhh," Cordelia said, adding in a whisper, "we don't have to let everybody know our problems."

Somewhere in the house a telephone was ringing.

"I was just with them the other day," Jackson whispered. "And I couldn't put up with Belinda—I don't know how Lang does it. One minute she tells him to go away, the next minute she's screaming for him, then she packs her bags and leaves—"

"She says he won't spend any time with her," Cordelia said.

"That's not true," Jackson said. "I was sitting right there the other morning—Langley wanted to come down here with her for a few days and she told him she didn't want him to come. She told him to go back to New York."

Cordelia frowned and folded her arms. "I can't believe he's not part of the problem, Jackie. The only time he's around is when she's—well, when she's not right. And the only time she seems to be right is when he's not around—only now she never seems to be quite right. Noreen says she thinks, if this keeps up, she's going to have to be put somewhere."

"Oh, Cordie," Jackson muttered, angry, "Noreen just says that to get attention. Belinda's fine. She's just got a few problems to work out."

"Excuse me, Mrs. Paine?" Salissy said from across the living room.

"Yes, what is it, Salissy?"

"It's the airline, ma'am, they want to make sure Mrs. Peterson got her suitcase."

"That suitcase again!" Cordelia cried, clapping her hands over her ears. "I swear, if anyone brings it up again I'm gonna lose my mind!"

"Tell them she got it," Jackson told Salissy. "Right?" he said, laughing, to Cordelia, pulling her arms down.

"And hallelujah," Cordelia said. "Belinda went on and on about that accursed bag—that's all she talked about from the minute she got here. 'Where's my bag, have they found my bag, did they call about my bag?'" she mimicked, gesturing wildly with her hands. Then she folded her arms again and looked at Jackie. "Somebody walked off with one of her bags at the airport and she got absolutely hysterical."

"What was in it?" Jackson said.

"Oh, cosmetics and things. Have you ever? I don't know, Jackie, I'm beginning to think the twins are right. Belinda must have sixty million of her own and there she was, carrying on about this stupid bag. And then—I haven't even told you the rest of it, and you better be glad that I'll spare you the repetition of it because it was enough to drive any sane person crazy—Belinda called up to New York and had her maid —her *maid,* Jackie, imagine—she had her *maid* fly all the way down here to bring her more cosmetics! I said, 'Belinda, you're not even forty years old, what do you need makeup for? You've been a beautiful girl all your life.' But did she listen to me? Of course not."

Jackson did not like the sound of this. It sounded like Noreen— sending servants flying around the country for lipsticks—not Belinda.

They proceeded toward the back of the house, toward the sun room where Daddy would be, and on the way Cordelia gave him an update on the household: her husband, Kitty, was away on business (trying to put a syndicate together to buy the PTL Club); Cordie's son, Eziekiel (Freaky Zekey), was on some kind of business in Las Vegas; Little El's kids—Kirky and Bipper—and their spouses and children were supposed to come visit in June; Big El was being impossible as usual (Cordelia still did not know how all these liquor bottles kept finding their way into the house); and Cordelia herself did not know how she was, since it had been so long since anybody had bothered to ask, thank you.

"Why, Daddy, look who's here," Cordelia said, stepping into the sun room.

"Well I'll be a son of a bitch," Big El said in his wheelchair. "How are ya, Johnny Jim?"

"It's Jackson, Daddy," Cordelia said, marching over to swipe the mug out of her father's hand and smell it. "I swear, that Lucille must be running moonshine," she muttered, taking the mug with her. "Jackie, bring Daddy into the kitchen and I'll fix you some coffee and muffins. I just made some blueberry this morning."

"Hi, Daddy," Jackson said, bending to kiss his father on the cheek.

Big El was about to turn eighty and no one could figure how he could still be alive and kicking after all the drinking he had done over the years, but there he was, looking a bit like an old crocodile with a big reddish-purple nose. "I knew it was you," Big El said.

Jackson unlocked the brakes on the wheelchair and pushed his father out of the sun room, through the breezeway, through the hall, through the breakfast room and, finally, into the kitchen. This had always been Jackson's favorite room because his mother, when he was young, had made it a kind of battalion headquarters, the one room big enough and indestructible enough to accommodate all her family's yelling and fighting while she relaxed from a hard day at the office. Alice May had loved to cook and had loved this room, with its sixteen-foot ceilings and huge windows at one end, looking out at the hills. It still smelled wonderfully of old wood and good food and spices, and it had everything in the world, it seemed, hanging from the walls somewhere—copper pots, wire whisks, colanders—and had two six-burner stoves, three sinks, huge wooden counters and open shelves, and, by the windows, two large round wood tables.

Cordelia was a great cook also, although now she kept a part-time cook. The cook's name was Lucille and was the same Lucille that Cordelia now suspected of running moonshine on the premises.

Jackson parked Big El at one of the tables and sat down next to him while Cordelia set about making coffee.

"How's Barbara? Why doesn't she come to see us anymore?" Big El said.

Jackson looked to Cordelia, whose expression was sympathetic. "Now, Daddy," she said, looking at him, "you know Barbara's been dead for going on seven years." Her eyes shifted back to Jackson. "I'm sorry—that darn Lucille's been here today."

Big El looked at Cordelia and said, "I *like* Lucille. I wish Lucille lived here. Lucille loves me."

"Ha!" Cordelia said. "And the South won the war." She came over and plunked down a basket of warm muffins on the table, looked at her father and added, in a softer voice, "Unless you're thinkin' of my little friend Lucille from grade school, Daddy. She was always very sweet on you."

"I shoulda killed *that* little Lucille with rat poison," Big El growled. "Told your mother I goosed her in the pantry."

"She did not, Daddy," Cordelia said in her normal voice, moving back to the stove. "That was that girl Gitchy, from McCaysville, the girl who was supposed to wash the dishes and never did."

"Well," Big El announced, reaching for a muffin, "somebody did."

Now that that was settled, Jackson plunged in with why he had come. He wanted to invite everybody up—the board and their families, the cousins, everybody, up to New York for a weekend in July for a special tour of the DBS network facility at West End, and while Jackson would schedule fun things for the families to do around the city, the board would have a special meeting at West End, where Jackson and Langley would do a complete financial review of the network.

"I still want my audit," Cordelia said, wiping her hands on her apron and picking up her cup of coffee off the counter. (Cordie was one of those women who, unless dining in the dining room, rarely ate sitting down.)

"If the presentation doesn't answer all of your questions," Jackson said, "I promise, I'll make a motion for an audit myself."

Cordelia swallowed some coffee, eyes on Jackson, and lowered her cup. "I don't understand why you do this, Jackie Andy—how you can let Beau throw all your money away."

"He didn't throw it away—not on purpose. He's got a problem, Cordie, he couldn't help it."

"And it's not going to help things if you keep paying his debts!" Cordelia said, banging her cup down on the counter. "And I will not have Darenbrook Communications mixed up in it any longer. You know I love you, Brother, but I am warning you—if I find out you've been using the family company to pay Beau's gambling debts, you are going to be in a lot of trouble. Now I mean it, Jackson Andrew Darenbrook," she said, shaking her finger at him, "so don't you go pretending you didn't hear me."

IN WHICH JACKSON FLEES ALEXANDRA

"I hear you, Cordie," Jackson said.

Big El—who had been chewing on a muffin, staring at Jackson during all of this—stopped chewing and said, "I smell funny money, Cordie Lou."

"I have from the beginning, Daddy, that's why I wanted the audit," Cordelia said, folding her arms and looking at Jackson. "July, you said?"

"July," he said.

"July then," Cordelia said, picking up her cup. "I will wait until July."

Jackson went into town to spend the rest of the day at the *Parader* offices, and then, that night, took a drive out to the plant to watch the next morning's edition come off the presses. He met the city editor for a late steak at Coach and Six, checked into the Buckhead Ritz-Carlton, tried to sleep, but couldn't.

He kept thinking about Barbara.

About how much he missed her, about how much he needed her, still, and about how lost he felt in his life whenever he thought about her. And he thought about how he wished he did not think of her, but wondered who else he could think about when it seemed like he would never be able to fall in love again.

Obsessions, like the one with Alexandra, had their purpose.

Because thoughts of Barbara depressed him. And his family depressed him, his kids—what kids? who was he kidding? how can one have kids if they didn't want him?—depressed him, and he depressed himself. It was getting harder and harder to feel as though any of this was worth it—the business, the family—and the hope that maybe there would be something to look forward to seemed to grow fainter each year.

He could look forward to getting older. Alone. Sleeping with ditzy Miss Something-or-Others, playing big shot, trying to keep his messed-up family together.

For crying out loud, you'd think *one* member of his family would be happy, be healthy! Did all of them have to be such losers at life, bumbling around, year after year, fighting and fussing and feuding for the lack of anything better to do, grasping for money and raising tormented kids who hated them but stuck around long enough to get some of their money so they could get away from them forever?

And what exactly was it that they had done that made them deserve so many tragedies in their family? Why them, why the Darenbrooks? Why did his brother have to be murdered, why did his mother have to be struck down by a car and his wife have to have her neck broken? Why did his kids have to avoid him, hate him; his siblings hate each other? Why did Belinda have to be losing her mind, the twins and Little El be so awful? Why did Daddy have to drink and Cordie have to stay with horrible Kitty and Beau have to gamble? And why did it have to go on forever?

Jackson got up, finally, and turned on the TV. Cable of course, CNN of course, this was Atlanta, wasn't it? Sitting there, watching it, drinking two things of orange juice and one Clamato from the bar, Jackson wondered if maybe the answer lay in giving up and hoeing beets. Finally, around three, he started feeling sleepy (imagining all those acres of beets under the hot sun), and he tried bed again and this time it worked.

And then the phone rang. He sat bolt upright, his heart pounding. *Oh, no—Lydia? Kevin? Daddy? Cordie? Who? What's happened?* He took a breath, turned on the light, and then snatched up the phone. Before he even got it to his ear, he heard a voice say, "Don't be alarmed— everything's okay."

"Alexandra?" he said.

"Yes," she said.

Silence.

"What's wrong?" he said.

He heard her sigh and then, her voice sounding funny, she said, "Nothing that can't be fixed, thank God."

He let out a breath and fell back against the pillows, relieved. "Where are you?"

"Jackson," she said, "I'm wrong. I've been wrong about the format for the newscast. Cassy was right. Her format's right and mine's wrong. Even Jessica could see that mine was wrong. I think I've known it all along too, but I couldn't—" Her voice broke.

Mrs. Cochran had once taken Jackson to task about Alexandra—one of many times—and it was funny, but what she had said this one particular time came back to him now. That Alexandra was so driven that she was often unaware of her own needs; that she was young and had gaps in her experience and was very slow to accept the notion of either; and that Alexandra had an overdeveloped sense of responsibility that they had to be very careful about.

According to Mrs. Cochran (Grand Controlleress of West End, whom Jackson, until now, had not paid very much attention to in the matter of Alexandra), they had to teach Alexandra how to swing the double-edged sword of her nature without cutting her own head off in the process. They needed to support and encourage Alexandra, but to tell her no when they had to and mean it. They had to remind her to think of herself as part of a group, never as an individual, in order to wrest away some of that overdeveloped sense of responsibility from her—the same kind that had eaten alive so many news people before her. And Mrs. Cochran had said (shouted, actually, as Jackson recalled) that they had to show Alexandra that it was okay for her to make a mistake once in a while, that she did not have to be perfect, but that she *did* have to accept herself as occasionally vulnerable and always mortal, always human.

And now that Jackson's obsession with her was coming to a crumbling end, he saw no reason why he shouldn't think of Alexandra as mortal and human now too.

"Good, you were wrong," Jackson said. "I'm glad to hear it, because now everybody can relate to you as a human being. Everyone except you has made mistakes thus far, so now you can be part of the group again."

Pause. "What?"

"Listen, Alexandra," Jackson said, "it's okay. Really. It's okay. We haven't gone on the air yet, we have time to change over—absolutely no damage has been done. And you know, kid—listen to me—that by rehearsing your format you've improved the other format by making everybody reassess every single element of the newscast again and again. You know that's true."

A sigh. "I suppose." And then, "And, Jackson, this morning, when you told me about reassigning Cassy, I thought—I don't know what I thought. I guess I thought you were pulling your support from me. I thought maybe you were angry about Gordon or something—and I apologize. I really, truly apologize from the bottom of my heart. I'm so sorry for misjudging—for flying off the handle—" Her voice broke again and Jackson realized she was crying.

He sighed, thinking about how much pressure was on Alexandra. And then he sighed again, knowing that Mrs. Cochran had been right all along. His chasing Alexandra around had been an additional strain on her. What had Alexandra just said? That she had thought he had increased Mrs. Cochran's responsibilities to punish Alexandra because of her relationship with Gordon Strenn? (What *was* their relationship these days? he wondered.) "Alexandra," he said gently, "you don't ever have to worry about my support of you. Ever. I swear, honey—please don't cry."

"I'm just so sorry for screaming at you, for misunderstanding everything," she said. She sniffed. "And Langley wrote me the most wonderful note today, Jackson. You wouldn't believe it. I didn't. And then he came down here tonight to talk to me—and he explained that there were things that had to be worked out at DBS, that Cassy's promotion was meant to help DBS News, and he asked me to trust him. And he said that the three of you—you and Cassy and Langley—were looking out for me—"

Her voice broke again.

He reached over to the night table to look at his watch. It was four-fifteen in the morning. No wonder she sounded the way she did. "Alexandra, where are you?"

"In one of the editing bays," she said.

"You're still at West End?" he said, sitting up.

"I've been looking at the rehearsal tapes," she said. "Oh, God, Jackson—they're awful. I don't know how I could have—"

"Listen, Alexandra," he said, interrupting her, "I don't want you there at this time of night. Not alone."

"The guard's around somewhere," she said, "don't worry. And Tirge is on newsroom duty."

"I want you to go home, Alexandra," Jackson said. "Do you hear me?"

"Yes," she said faintly.

"Honey, listen," Jackson said, "I hired you because you are the kind of glue that makes people want to work together. And so I want you to go home and get some sleep, and then come back in tomorrow and work with your colleagues, as a *team,* Alexandra, and let everybody do their jobs too. You've been doing far too much. So tomorrow you just switch the format and get to work—and the sky's the limit, kid. You hear me?"

"I hear you," Alexandra said softly.

"Because the only question out of all this," Jackson said, "is whether you and I are going to be able to stand Mrs. Cochran after we tell her that she was right." He laughed.

"Cassy's almost always right," Alexandra sighed.

"So thank God *you* hired her, Ms. Waring," Jackson said. "Because now I need her to solve a lot of problems for us—and *you* are not a problem, Alexandra. You're the best thing going for us. I mean it."

Alexandra paused and then said, "Thank you, Jackson."

"You're welcome," he said.

Silence.

"Have you talked to Mrs. Cochran yet?" Jackson said.

"No," she said.

"Call her," Jackson said. "Call her now. You'll feel a lot better. And so will she."

"Yes," she sighed, "I will. Okay."

"And then you'll go home?"

"Promise," she said.

Pause. "And maybe you should call Gordon," he said.

Silence.

"Well, you know," Jackson added, "he's your beau and all. And this is the kinda night a beau can be kinda nice."

Pause. And then Alexandra whispered, "Thank you, Jackson. Thank you."

"Thanks for thinking enough of me to call me," Jackson said. "So, good night, sweetie pie. I'll see you tomorrow."

Jackson hung up the phone, no longer feeling depressed. In fact he felt pretty good. He had done the right thing. Said the right thing. For once. And that was a start, wasn't it? In any direction but the same old one?

22

Jessica Has Two Visitors in Her Office

Oh, *maaan*, what had she done? If Langley Peterson "just stopped in
to say hello" again, she was going to have a nervous breakdown. *God,*
what was it with this guy? Ever since she had had lunch with him and
Mr. Graham . . .

Jessica stood there, rubbing her right temple, looking down at the
piece of paper lying in her office chair.

> Jessica,
> I'll stop in around eleven.
> Langley

What was this, junior high school? What was he going to do, ask her
to the sock hop?

She sighed, picked up the paper, crumpled it up and, dropping
down into her chair, threw it in the trash. *Oh, God,* she thought,
leaning forward to lie down on her desk, *just make me stop feeling so
seasick.*

One of the great disadvantages of being scared to death of cocaine
was that, whenever Jessica went out to a "Y & T, S & S" Club (Young
& Trendy, Scratch 'n' Sniff), she always drank too much. Now how
drinking was supposed to help her stay away from cocaine when it
only hastened and increased her trips to the ladies' room where, of
course, at least half of the cocaine in the club was being consumed, she
didn't know. But she did know she had not done any cocaine last
night, nor any illegal drug, and hung over as she was this morning, was
very grateful for that.

At least if the ship went down, it would go down legal.

Alicia came in (quietly, bless her) with a stack of backup materials, a
few phone messages and a carton of chocolate milk, and set them

down on the desk. Jessica sat up, ran her hands back through her hair once, wondering if she was more likely to die of thirst or to get sick if she tried to drink anything. Ugh. Her stomach. Her mouth, her head, her eyes. Dizzy. Oh, God.

She sank back down on the desk.

And she had a lot to do. Cassy wanted at least seven shows in the can before they started the regular daily tapings on Memorial Day. So Jessica's bookers came up with those "timeless classic" panel discussion pieces that they said never dated and always rated: unfaithful spouses, rotten kids, satanic cults, prostitutes, homosexuals and overeating, and Jessica had rejected them all as too daytime. (Jessica thought her bookers were too daytime and called them shnookers.) This afternoon, actually, she would be taping a show Alicia thought of: "So What Is Normal Sex, Anyway?" which should be fun. Buses were bringing in to West End the "mixed" audience Jessica requested on this show, picking up groups from three locations: Landmark Square in Stamford, Connecticut; the Ocean County Mall in Toms River, New Jersey; and one from the Lion's Head bar in Greenwich Village. If nothing else, *they*—the audience—would be interesting.

"Jessica?" a male voice said.

Oh, no, she thought, *it's him.* Why had she ever had lunch with him? Why had she ever flirted with him? Why, oh, why had she been drinking that day when she *knew* how she got sometimes when she drank—and with the president of DBS? He who looked like Dennis the Menace's father and was married to Jackie's sister, for crying out loud?

Jessica sat up. "Hi ya, Mr. Mitchell," she said, falling back in her chair.

"May I come in for a minute?" he asked her. "Do you have a minute?"

"Sure," she said, waving him into the seat, squinting. Her eyes were killing her and the late morning sun was streaming in through the glass wall behind her. She opened her desk drawer, took out a pair of sunglasses and put them on. There, better.

"Um," Langley said, staring at her.

"It's either this or I have to draw the curtains," she told him. "So what can I do for you?"

"No, it's fine," Langley said quickly. "As long as you're comfortable. Um," he said, "I just wondered how everything was going."

This is what he had said, almost verbatim, every single workday since they had had lunch. "It's great," Jessica said, just as she had said, almost verbatim, every single workday since they had had lunch. "The production crew's great, Cassy's the best—Denny loves her, I love her, we all love her. She might even do something with those blockhead bookers. They have no imagination. Alicia's come up with more good ideas than they have."

"Then maybe Alicia should be a booker," Langley said.

"Please," Jessica said, holding her head in her hands, "let me have her for six months." She dropped her hands. "I've never had anyone like her before. Denny thinks I should marry her."

Langley laughed.

"Why is it the men with wives always laugh at that line?" she wondered out loud, partly to remind him that she knew he had a wife, but mostly because it was true. "I never met a working woman who didn't need a wife. Somebody's gotta keep the home fires burning and, God knows, it's rarely you guys." That reminded her of something. She made a note on her calender to call her divorce lawyer. Note made, she dropped the pen and sat back in her chair, noticing how solemn he looked. "What's the matter?"

"Oh, nothing," he said, eyes down.

Oh, great, now he was moping. Which was worse, anyway, married men who habitually screwed around, or the married men who dragged around with long faces and woebegone eyes, hoping for an affair without having to really have it somehow?

No, she decided, the worst was having the president of DBS who was the brother-in-law of the chairman who normally was as strait-laced as they come suddenly turn into a dopey adolescent every time they were alone. Even if she could be attracted to him (without several drinks), did he think *this,* moping, was going to turn her on?

"You have to remember," she said, "I'm a woman in the middle of the longest divorce in the history of Arizona, or so it seems. So I'm a little grouchy on the subject of spouses."

His eyes came back up. "I was wondering if you would like to have dinner with me," he said in a rush. And then he lunged to his feet, jammed his hands into his pockets and walked over to look at the pictures on her wall as if he hadn't said anything.

Oh, no, she thought, sitting up to her desk again. "Thanks," she said, "but could we wait a few weeks? I really need to get more settled with the show."

He nodded, still looking at the pictures, as though he hadn't said anything—as though Jessica was not even there, practically.

"Thank you, though," Jessica added. "It would be fun." There now, was that nice or what? He didn't have to know that the few weeks she had in mind added up to about six hundred.

He turned to look at her. And then he smiled. "It might be fun, yeah. Yeah," he repeated, nodding enthusiastically.

Oh, God, he looked so happy. What kind of life did this guy have, anyway?

He left and Jessica applied herself to the task of trying to finish reading the last of her backup material for today's show. One of the few real rules Jessica had regarding the guests on her show was that she refused to have on anyone whose book did not personally interest her, or whose movie she did not want to see herself, or whose record she did not want to hear, and so on. To her, it was the only way to draw a line between a talk show and payola, i.e., we'll give you ratings if you give this guy's junk air play. And so she really did try to read all of her guests' books and in this case her guest had written several. And this one, which was actually an anthology, Jessica had been saving for last. It was called *Pleasures: Women Write Erotica,* edited by Dr. Lonnie Barbach, and it would have been turning Jessica's morning around (at least internally) for sure if the type hadn't started jumping around on the page. And then Jessica heard someone laugh. She looked over at the door. It was Alexandra.

"Look at you," she said, coming in, laughing still. "What on earth are you doing?"

"Shhh," Jessica told her, pushing her dark glasses up higher on her nose, "I'm reading for my show, if you must know."

"Must be some book if you have to read in disguise," Alexandra said, reaching across the desk. "What is it?"

"Sex," Jessica whispered loudly.

"I think I've heard of that," Alexandra said, sitting down.

"Ha-ha," Jessica said, putting the book down and reaching for the carton of chocolate milk. "Want some?"

"As a matter of fact, I would," Alexandra said, sitting down, holding a hand just over her stomach. "I haven't been right all morning."

Jessica opened a desk drawer and found a Styrofoam cup. She poured some milk into it for Alexandra and then some into a mug (from Tucson, that said STUMBLE INN on it) for herself, pushed the Styrofoam cup toward Alexandra and said, "You don't look so hot."

"No, I know," Alexandra said, taking a sip. She closed her eyes for a moment and then opened them. "Thank you. I think this is just what I need."

Jessica lifted her sunglasses to see her better. "Night out on the town?"

"Night with Hex and Kyle, remixing the opening," she said.

To Jessica's profound relief, the guys in DBS News had been working night and day to revamp the format of "DBS News America Tonight." Not only had Alexandra loosened up and gone with Cassy's ideas, she had suggested a number of "livelier" changes regarding music and graphics, which Jessica heard were great. Alexandra had even gone so far as to thank Jessica for telling her how much she hated the old format—an act which Jessica greatly appreciated, since it seemed to put them on an equal footing with each other. At least Jessica felt on an equal footing, and Alexandra treated her that way, both privately and publicly, and that meant a lot to Jessica.

Being around Alexandra Eyes had its drawbacks, though. Alexandra had made a habit of stopping into Jessica's office for a few minutes each day ("to hide"), and while Jessica enjoyed her visits, hanging out with Miss Perfection tended to make her feel more than a little disorganized in comparison and, perhaps, a teeny tiny bit inadequate—like maybe like a total fucking mess at times. So it was sort of fun to see Alexandra looking a little bent out of shape for a change.

"Editing, were you?" Jessica said, dropping her sunglasses back down on her nose. "Silly me for thinking you might have gone out on the town. Perish the thought."

Alexandra smiled, sipping her milk again. Lowering her cup, "Just how boring do you think I am, exactly?"

"Well, I would consider promoting you on milk cartons and vitamins," Jessica admitted.

"That's pretty boring," Alexandra said.

"I don't think you're boring, Alexandra Eyes," Jessica said in earnest, pushing her dark glasses up higher on her nose, "I think you're terrifying. I think you probably believe in self-improvement." She dropped her voice. "Come on, give me a good scare—tell me you believe in self-improvement."

Alexandra's smile expanded, eyes sparkling. "It's the American way," she said, starting to laugh.

"Arrrg," Jessica said, bringing her legs up to sit cross-legged in her chair. (She was wearing a gray dress today and matching snakeskin cowgirl boots.) "I believe in urban renewal myself. One day they'll just come in here and tear me down—what can I tell you?"

Alexandra could tell her, she said—all smiles—that they had sold the Richard Barnes interview as an hour-and-a-half piece to PBS. It was for a very nominal sum, and Alexandra started to explain why, but Jessica didn't care and she instantly felt much, much, much better! In fact she jumped out of her chair and yelled, "Yaaaaa-hoo!" circling her chair twice, shaking her fists in the air. Alicia came flying in to see what was going on and Jessica asked her to please find Denny and then to call up everybody in the whole wide world and tell them that *she*— the girl excommunicated from Essex Fells Brownie Scout Pack 51— was going to be on public television.

"Whoo-hoooooooo," Jessica said, now sitting in her chair—rather, spinning around in her chair.

Alexandra was laughing.

When Jessica came to a stop (whoa, this was not one of her better ideas, her head was going around still), she held her face in her hands for a second.

"You okay?" she heard Alexandra ask.

"Oh, yeah," she said, raising her head, flicking her hair back over her shoulder.

Alexandra looked at her seriously for a moment and then started to smile, shaking her head. "I'm sorry, but those sunglasses—"

"Anything for you," Jessica said, taking them off and tossing them on the desk, "when you bring me news like that."

"There're strings attached, you know," Alexandra said.

"Cut them," Jessica suggested, taking another sip of milk.

Alexandra shook her head, smiling. Then she recrossed her legs and leaned forward. "You have to promise me you'll watch a tape of the newscast this week and tell me what you think."

Jessica put her mug down on the desk. "You want the Terror of Tucson to critique your newscast? My, oh, my, Alexandra Eyes, what would your adoring public say?"

" 'If Jessica doesn't like it, we won't either'?" Alexandra said, prompting them both to laugh. "Listen," she added, putting a fist down on Jessica's desk. "I won't go on the air with this format until I know for sure it won't put you to sleep."

"I didn't fall asleep during the rehearsal," Jessica said, putting her dark glasses back on, "I just said I hoped narcolepsy wasn't contagious. And I was, if I recall correctly, a bit tipsy at the time, and so I trust, Ms. Waring, that you have the good sense to forget the remark. But past that point," she added, "I am flattered and honored, and will be delighted to do exactly as you, my esteemed benefactress, have bidden me to do."

Alexandra was smiling at her but then, a moment later, her smile started to fade—and then faded altogether. "Jessica?" she said quietly, eyes falling to the desk.

Jessica looked at her for a moment. "Hey—what's the matter?" she said, lowering her head toward the desk in an attempt to catch her eye. When Alexandra still didn't look at her, Jessica reached for the book she had been reading when Alexandra arrived. "Here," she joked, pushing it toward her, "you can borrow it. You don't have to be embarrassed to ask."

Alexandra shook her head, smiling. "No," she said. Then she raised her eyes to look at Jessica, leaned forward to rest her arms on the desk and sighed. "I have something to say to you that is very, very difficult." She paused. "Could you take off those glasses for a minute?"

Jessica complied, instantly wishing for them back. The intensity of Alexandra's eyes was almost painful. It felt like she was trying to see inside her.

"I really like you, Jessica," Alexandra said, eyes unwavering. "I think you're extremely bright. And gifted. And it's because I do like you, and because I do respect your work, that I feel I have to say this."

Jessica wiped her forehead with the back of her hand. She was feeling a little warm suddenly. Part of it was hangover, part of it was from this sudden, tingling fear running along her back. "What is it?" she said, sort of wanting to know, sort of wanting for Alexandra to go away, sort of wanting to maybe get sick. This couldn't be good.

"I've been around—I've worked around people who drink a great deal before," Alexandra said. "And I can't get to know you, and to work with you—or work next door to you downstairs—and pretend I don't see your drinking, and pretend I don't worry about what it might do to you—what it might be doing to you now."

Jessica could feel her face flushing hot, her back teeth clenching down.

"It's none of my business, I know," Alexandra said.

"No—it's not," Jessica said sharply, diverting her eyes. "It's really not."

"I know," Alexandra said quietly. "That's why I wish I didn't like you so much. Or admire you."

Jessica blinked several times, staring at a packing case. On one hand, she was furious, on another—perversely flattered. But then the overriding feeling became a longing to jump out the window, run to the river and hop a slow freighter to New Zealand to have some time to sort this out. But then on the other side of this overriding feeling was the bewilderment from wondering why she didn't feel like killing Alexandra. And then while Jessica debated about whether or not she should explain to Alexandra just how far she had come, that drinking was *nothing* compared to what she *could* be doing, it felt like her head had detached itself and had floated outside to look back in at them through the window. That's what it felt like, that as a third person she could see herself immobilized in this chair. She could see Alexandra looking at her. She could see the two of them frozen in this moment, in her office, in sunny New York City.

Alexandra stood up and waited, saying nothing.

Finally Jessica looked up at her. "So what the fuck am I supposed to say?" she asked her. "Thanks for making me feel like I have to avoid you for the rest of my life? That now I have to worry about you judging me—Miss Teetotaler from Kansas?" She looked down at her desk, scratching the surface of it with her thumbnail. Then she slapped the same hand down and looked up at her again. "Just what the hell do you want from me?"

Alexandra's face flushed slightly. Then she leaned over, snatched a pencil out of the BUM STEER mug, muttering, "I want you to be careful," and scribbled something on the pad. "Look," she said, throwing the pencil down, ripping the paper off and thrusting it across the desk at Jessica. "Just take this and stick it somewhere so if you get into trouble you have someone besides the *National Enquirer* to call, okay?"

"I know where I'd like to stick it," Jessica growled, snapping it out of her hand. "What is it?"

"My home phone number," Alexandra said, turning and going for the door. "Lose it and I'll kill you." She whirled around, hand on the door. "Hate me?"

"Loathe you," Jessica said, starting to put her sunglasses on but changing her mind. She threw them at Alexandra instead and missed by a mile.

Alexandra laughed.

"You've got some fucking nerve, Waring," Jessica said.

"Yeah," Alexandra said, smiling, "I know. See ya later."

Jessica sat there a minute, thinking. And then she folded up Alexandra's number and put it in her wallet.

23

Alexandra Tells Gordon She Doesn't Like to Disappoint Him

Gordon was starting to mind Jackson Darenbrook. A lot. It was bad enough that DBS News seemed to be draining every ounce of energy out of Alexandra (while they were dining with Gordon's uncle she fell asleep, literally, in the banquette at La Côte Basque the other night), but now something had changed in her relationship with Jackson, too, and Gordon was not at all sure that it was unconnected to Alexandra's state of mind lately.

Always, before, they had joked about Jackson's flirtations with Alexandra. And, before, Gordon had felt free to vent his frustration about some financial irregularities in DBS that were forever messing up the production schedule for *Love Across the Atlantic.* Oh, yeah, he was allowed to joke about Jackson's flirtations still, but Alexandra did not laugh anymore because Alexandra was suddenly taking Jackson Darenbrook very seriously. And when Gordon complained to her about Hargrave Studios' interference on the miniseries, which Langley said he had to put up with for what reason no one would explain, Alexandra had, one morning, dropped her spoon in her bowl of cereal and said, "Then go and talk to Jackson about it," to which he had said, "Why? So he can try to get rid of me again?" to which she said, "Oh, Gordon, just do your job. Ignore the personalities involved and just do it."

Now who the hell could ignore a personality like Jackson Darenbrook? But Gordon had dropped the issue, like he always had to drop the issue lately, because Alexandra was so, so *funny* at home these days. She wasn't sleeping well and her appetite was off, and she was very, very quiet. He knew it had to be connected to the pace she was keeping, the stress and pressure she was under, but he also couldn't help but notice that it had started right around the time that Jackson announced he was giving Cassy "The Jessica Wright Show" to produce.

And that's why Gordon wondered about what was going on between Alexandra and Jackson. Because it appeared to Gordon that Alexandra had lost considerable power within DBS of late (Cassy's responsibilities *had* been reassigned against Alexandra's wishes, after all), and so if Jackson had undermined Alexandra in the very capacity he had promised to support her in, what sense did it make that Alexandra now seemed to respect Jackson in a way she had not before?

It was impossible for anyone to spend any time around Alexandra and not notice how she attracted powerful people to her. And it wasn't just power in the normal sense, but the power in any given situation. Whether it was a minister in a church, the head stewardess on an airplane or the chairman at The Network, whoever was in power—and it was the strangest thing—as soon as they set their eyes on Alexandra, they made their way toward her, pulled her aside and started talking to her as if she were the one intelligent listener they had been waiting for all of their lives—the only person who could *really* understand them and their work.

Part of it came, no doubt, from years of Alexandra watching her parents politick, herself developing a presence that commanded instant attention and appeal; part of it came, no doubt, from the intuitive instinct of a good reporter who knew when to shut up and listen; a *lot* of it came, no doubt, from Alexandra not only being very good-looking but looking like a very *nice* person too; but most of it came, Gordon knew, from that place inside Alexandra that had always craved power of her own, and that had developed a sixth sense about how to attain some, instantly, by association.

But Alexandra's concept of power was different from most people's. Despite her contract with DBS, despite her arguments and struggles there, Gordon knew Alexandra had very little interest in running things. In fact she hated it. The power she was after had to do with the ability to not be controlled by others. Her struggle at DBS was just another mile on the road leading to a place where she could trust everybody to run everything so she could be left alone to concentrate on how best to represent the whole of their efforts. She really wasn't the power-hungry tsarina that Langley seemed to think she was. She was—and always had been—just a very talented, very decent human being who longed to see what she could do outside the systems that had been developed by less talented, less decent human beings.

Even in her personal life, at least between the two of them, she had always been careful about maintaining a balance of power. Even when they lived together in California she had made Gordon sit down with her and figure out money so that they were contributing the same ratio of their incomes toward those expenses that had to do with their lives together. And they still did it! They both contributed the same ratio of their incomes to a "household" account that covered everything they shared, from trips to dinners to whatever. (Who else, Gordon wondered, who made almost a million and half dollars a year, knew, if asked, that his contribution to a pizza should be $6.45?)

Sexually, certainly, the balance of power, as such, had always enhanced their relationship. Because they both had such up-and-down work lives, with energy varying accordingly, the "upper hand," so to speak, sort of naturally fluctuated between them. Some of the best times making love that Gordon could remember were those nights that practically all he had done was just lie there while Alexandra made love to him. And then other nights, the reverse had been true, when he did almost everything for her. And then, happily, there had been all those wonderful nights when each of them had felt like the aggressor.

And that was part of what was bothering him lately, too. It seemed like every day that Alexandra was at DBS their sex life grew less energetic, less inspired, less a source of revitalization—for her. And while he knew, intellectually, that it was because of the demands at DBS, of the constant stress and pressure she was under, he couldn't help but wonder if Jackson Darenbrook had anything to do with it. Oh, he knew Alexandra wouldn't have an affair with Jackson, not while she was with him (she was incapable of being with two people at the same time, he absolutely knew that). But when Gordon knew how important power at DBS was to Alexandra, and that Jackson had stripped her of some of it, how could he not suspect that their professional relationship had turned personal—because personal relationships were the only kind of relationships where power was *not* important to Alexandra?

Gordon knew there was nothing going on—but he kept feeling as though something *might* be going on, or was going to be going on if he didn't watch it.

But today, this Tuesday before Memorial Day, things finally seemed to be breaking in his favor. Tomorrow he was taking the Concorde to Paris for Christopher's birthday; then he was flying to London to work Thursday and Friday; taking the Concorde back to New York on Saturday; either flying or driving out to spend two nights with Constantine Moscowitz, the director of *Love Across the Atlantic,* and their hostess and star, actress Vanessa Winslow, at her home in Amagansett; and then on Memorial Day returning to New York for the unveiling of DBS. He hadn't spent the night with Alexandra for the past four nights (because she hadn't been feeling well, or so she said), and he had been depressed about her having to go to some benefit for the Museum of Broadcasting (with Jackson, no less) on his last night in town.

But then Alexandra called after lunch to say that Jackson was stuck in Vancouver, trying to find newsprint for the Darenbrook papers, and wanted to know if he would be her official escort. For the first time in weeks Alexandra sounded delighted and excited, and so Gordon was delighted and excited too. He went home to Gramercy Park, whistling, changed into black tie, and returned to West End with a car to pick her up.

She had showered and changed in her dressing room and, when Gordon arrived, was sitting in front of the mirror—looking absolutely smashing in a black dress—laughing with Cassy while Cleo, the West End makeup and hair lady, was touching up her hair.

"Oh my, look at you," Cassy said when she saw him.

Alexandra smiled at him in the mirror. "You do look very handsome."

"And you look beautiful," he told her, leaning to kiss her.

"Ahck!" Cleo said, whacking the top of his head with her comb. "Plenty of time for that in the car. Let me at least get her hair looking like something before she leaves here."

"Cleo!" Cassy said.

"It's all right," Alexandra said. "She's doing me a personal favor as it is."

"I don't think it's necessary to hit the executives," Cassy observed.

"You'd be surprised what you have to hit to keep your self-respect in this business," Cleo said, making them laugh.

"Aren't you going?" Gordon asked Cassy, knowing that, since she was sitting there in a skirt and blouse, with a clipboard and pen in her lap, her hair slipping down, and her reading glasses perched on the end of her nose, she obviously was not.

"Oh," Cassy said, taking off her glasses, "maybe next year." She looked at Alexandra. "I'm not really anxious to see a whole lot of old friends right now. Too much to explain." Her eyes came back up to him.

That's right. Her husband. Gordon had forgotten. Still, he thought she would have wanted to go. Cassy was the kind of person who believed in things like the Museum of Broadcasting.

"She gave her tickets to Kyle," Alexandra said, looking at him in the mirror. "So he'll be at our table with his wife, Lucy. You'll like her."

"Great," Gordon said, thinking how terrific it was to see Alexandra happy, so like herself.

"I tell you, Alexandra," Cleo said, bending close to poke at a strand of hair with her comb, "you're a piece of cake compared to Jessica Wright. She came in today looking like something out of an episode of *Combat.*"

"She did?" Alexandra said, wincing slightly.

"She looked like a million on the tape," Cassy said.

"Well, I do very good work," Cleo said, backing away to survey her progress.

"And you have a lot to work with," Alexandra said. "Jessica's very attractive." Her eyes shifted to Gordon in the mirror. She smiled. "I know Gordon finds her very attractive. Don't you?"

"Certain parts," he said, grinning.

"I'm sure we don't have any idea which," Alexandra said, smile expanding.

Gordon glanced at Cassy and cleared his throat, sticking his hands in his pockets. "No, actually, I find all of Jessica very attractive."

"Pretty houses last only as long as their foundations do," Cleo told them, turning Alexandra's head to the side.

"Oh, God," Cassy said, slumping against the wall. "There goes mine."

Cleo looked over at her. "Isn't anything wrong with you," she said.

"There sure isn't," Gordon said, meaning it. He had always found Cassy enormously attractive, and it wasn't just her looks. There was something quite seductive about her that had to do with the hints, here and there, that she might be the kind of mild-mannered woman who'd have an absolutely torrid love life if only someone messed her up a little—took away her clipboard, at any rate. Took down that hair. It had crossed his mind more than once since he had met her that he wouldn't mind finding out what she was like that way. He had even thought it was a shame she wasn't just a bit younger, because she was the kind of woman he knew would be a good mother, but who still— well, just look at her—would be alluring for years. She reminded him a little of Julie, actually, except that Cassy was warm and receptive and caring. He wouldn't have minded having Cassy as Christopher's mother. Not at all. No, as a matter of fact, had Cassy been Christopher's mother, Gordon would still be married to Christopher's mother. Cassy was very much what he had hoped for in Julie.

Cassy was peering around the edge of the mirror at herself. "If I'm all right, then why do I have these cracks in my foundation?"

"Those aren't cracks," Cleo said, glancing at her and then stepping back to survey Alexandra's hair again, "that's life. And let me tell you, I've been around and I haven't seen many blondes who've weathered it as well as you have."

"I haven't seen many real blondes, period," Gordon said, winking at Cassy.

"And let's face it," Alexandra said, looking at her, "you are one of the most beautiful women any of us has seen."

"True," Cleo said, fiddling now with the back of Alexandra's hair. "In a way, it's a shame you're not out there in front of a camera, but in a way . . ." She paused, looking at Cassy. "But in a way it's great that you're not," she said, returning her attention to Alexandra's hair. "Nice to know someone with your kind of looks made it with her head, you know? Lotta very unhappy women out there. Seen a lot of them on their way down. Course," she added, frowning a little, "that's when they most need me. It's hard, sometimes—to watch, I mean." She stepped back to look at Alexandra's hair in the mirror. She smiled at Alexandra, resting her hands on her shoulders. "That's why it does my heart good to work on someone like you. This can be a nasty business to be in."

Alexandra beamed. "Thank you," she said.

"So that's it," Cleo announced, tossing the comb on the bureau. "You're done."

And so they went off to the benefit at the Waldorf, where Alexandra generated a bit of attention (which pleased her enormously, Gordon knew, since there was some very heavy traffic from network news there, particularly from CBS, whose founder, William Paley, was the chairman of the museum's board of trustees). And Alexandra was bright and outgoing and gracious right on through cocktails and dinner and three dances and right on out past the reporters and into the car, inside of which she promptly keeled over into Gordon's lap, laughing, but moaning too that she was so tired she thought she was going to die.

When they got to The Roehampton, Alexandra kicked off her shoes and collapsed on the couch. Gordon took off his jacket and tie, poured himself a brandy, came over and sat down on the couch, plunked Alexandra's feet in his lap, and sipped his brandy, smiling at her.

She took off her earrings, yawning as she did so.

With his free hand he patted her ankle and then, after a moment, started sliding his hand up her leg.

"Please don't take this wrong," she said, yawning again, "but I'd like to go straight to sleep tonight."

"Sure," he said, hand continuing up her leg. (She always said this on a work night, but it didn't mean anything except they couldn't mess around for long.)

"No, Gordie, I mean it," she said, sitting up and placing a hand over his, which was, at the moment, under her dress. "I'm sorry," she added, "I know what you expect when you come over."

"Expect?" he said. What was that supposed to mean? He felt like having sex and they *always* had sex after going out and he knew she was tired but she was *always* tired these days and it had been four nights since the last time they had slept together and tomorrow he was leaving for Paris and if he had to see Julie, then he certainly preferred to do so with a distinct memory of having made love with Alexandra in his mind, and *not* a scenario that seemed an awful lot like the ones he had always had with Julie. (Julie: "I don't want to, Gordon, stop it.")

"I've hurt your feelings," Alexandra said, pulling his hand out from under her dress and bringing it up to her mouth. "That's exactly what I didn't want to happen," she sighed, kissing his hand once and then returning it to him. "I should have sent you home," she said, getting up.

"Hey," he said, "come back and talk for a second, will you?"

"Gordon, I'm so tired," she said, turning around.

"Please come back and talk a minute," he said.

Reluctantly, she dropped back down on the couch.

"Do you think I *expect* you to make love when I come over?" he asked her.

She smiled slightly. "Uh-huh," she said, nodding. "Always have." And then her smile faded a little, and she sighed, dropping her eyes. "And it's very difficult for me to say it—that I really just can't tonight."

He doubted that. She had been this tired before plenty of times.

"It's okay," he said, putting his brandy snifter on the coffee table and reaching for her hand. "Come here."

She frowned slightly.

"Come on, come here—" he said, pulling her hand.

"Gordon—"

"What? Just come here," he said. "I just want to hold you."

"You don't just want to hold me," she said. "You never just want to hold me, you know that—it always turns into something else. Gordon, please—please just let me go to bed. I am so tired."

"Okay, okay," he said, releasing her and waving her away. "Go on, go to bed." He reached for his brandy.

"Please don't be angry," she said, standing up. "I'm not going to be able to sleep if I know you're lying there next to me, angry."

"I'm not angry, all right?" he said. He was, of course. There was something more than vaguely familiar about this scene and he hated it. "Go on," he said, softening his voice. "Really, I'm not angry. Go in and I'll be there in a minute."

She went.

He sat there, sipping his brandy, taking off his cuff links, wondering if this was some kind of rite of passage for women. Maybe this was what all women did once they were sure they had a man. But at least, with Julie, it had happened after they were married—with Alexandra, apparently, all it took was being engaged. Oh, God, if this was what their married life was going to be like, Alexandra could have it.

He threw back the rest of his brandy, got up and went into the master bedroom. She was in a nightgown *(flannel,* for God's sake—he didn't even know Alexandra *had* a flannel nightgown) and was getting ready to turn down the bed.

"I'm not sure why," he said from the doorway, "but I feel very upset."

"I'm sorry," she said, tossing the decorative pillows onto the floor. "I should have sent you home. You wouldn't have been disappointed then."

"And that's what upsetting me—your attitude," he said.

She didn't say anything but continued clearing the pillows.

"You make it sound like until now you've felt *obligated* to have sex with me," he said. And when she still didn't say anything but started turning down the bedspread, he added, "You make it sound like we have some sort of contractual arrangement. Like you have to accommodate me whether you like it or not. Like you want *contract* revisions."

She let go of the bedspread and turned around to look at him. "I have never felt obligated to do anything for you. Anything I've done is because I want to do it for you, Gordon, and I want to do it because I love you and I'm trying the best I can to give you enough so that this relationship can work."

"So you feel obligated to act like my mistress or something. Every time I come over you *have* to fuck me, right?"

"Oh, Gordon," she groaned, holding her forehead in her hand for a moment. And then dropped her arm, sighed, and sat down on the bed. "Come here," she said, patting the bed. He walked over and she took his hand, pulling him down to sit beside her. "Listen to me carefully," she said, holding his hand between both of hers. She took a moment to gather her thoughts, looking into his eyes, and then she said, quietly, "I know that sex is your way of feeling close to me—"

Oh, fuck, not this again, he thought. Out loud he said, "I can't help it if I'm not all touchy-feely, Alexandra—we've been through this."

She smiled a little. "I know you're not 'touchy-feely,' Gordie—but I *am*. And sometimes I need to be held. And somehow you and I have to try and figure out how it's going to work when we live together full time."

"We lived together full time before," he said.

"But, Gordon," she said, "it was different then—I was different then. I had more energy than I knew what to do with in those days. And I still have an enormous amount of energy, but right now I'm really going through a very difficult time. And I just don't have it—anything—to give right now. In fact," she said, sounding very close to tears, "what I'm longing for is for someone to hold me." She paused, swallowing. "And, Gordon," she said, reaching to touch his hair, "I know you don't feel comfortable being affectionate—but you've got to understand that I *do* need to be affectionate and that, when I am, it doesn't necessarily mean I want to have sex."

He sighed, closing his eyes for a moment and then reopening them.

"And what am I supposed to do when I get turned on while you're being affectionate?" he asked her.

"I'm changing the rules, I know, I'm sorry," she sighed, lowering her hand from his hair. "I don't know what to do—but we have to do something. At least right now we know you better not come over unless I know I can have sex."

"Will you stop it?" he yelled, jumping up. "You're not my fucking mistress!"

Alexandra covered her face, groaning, "Gordon, please—I just can't take this tonight." And then she took a deep breath and dropped her hands. "I didn't mean to get you over here and change the rules on you."

"Stop it!" he yelled.

"Stop what?"

"This long, elaborate explanation of why you feel obligated to fuck me every time I come over!"

"Damn it, Gordon!" she said, slamming her hand down on the bed. "Can't you hear what I'm trying to say? I just don't like to disappoint you—that's all I'm trying to explain. I feel like I'm letting you down and I hate it. I thought I could continue in a certain way and obviously I can't. My body just won't do it. And do you think I like it? Well, I don't!" She stood up. "There's not that much I can do for you, you know. You're very independent and so am I and sex has been just about the only area of your life where you've really let me in—and sex is the one thing I've been able to be consistent about and so if you think I enjoy feeling so numb I can't even feel the nose on my face, then think again—because I hate it, Gordon! I don't know what's the matter with me, but I do know you're not helping tonight!"

She was crying now, and she pushed her way past him, banged open her closet door and then banged it closed again. "I'm so tired I don't even know what I'm doing," she said, stumbling into the bathroom. She slammed the door behind her.

This was like a bad movie.

He and Alexandra did not fight. They never fought. But they were fighting now and Gordon, standing here, stunned at what had just happened, had to wonder if the only reason they did not fight was because they spent so little time together.

She was brushing her teeth. He could hear her.

He could imagine exactly what she looked like brushing her teeth because Alexandra brushed her teeth a lot. Come rain or shine, happiness or sorrow, good health or sickness, the world could depend on Alexandra Waring brushing her teeth, and tonight was no exception. A regular dentist's dream, this girl, with terrific teeth and an obsessive commitment to keeping them that way.

The door opened and there she was and he could not see those terrific teeth because Alexandra was not smiling. But at least she wasn't crying anymore.

She came over to him, slid her arms around his waist and rested her head on his shoulder. "I'm sorry, Gordie," she whispered. "I love you and I find you the most sexually attractive man on earth—and I know you know that—but I just don't have it in me to make love tonight."

Uh-oh. He was getting an erection, which was hardly making a good case for how understanding he could be, but his body wasn't used to the new rules yet. It was still following the old rules, the ones that said every time she touched him sex would follow; that when they came in through this door together it was to make love; and that whenever he got an erection she was aroused by it.

She lifted her head up to look at him. "I don't ever want to fake it with you," she said.

"You?" he said, smiling.

"Me," she said, lowering her head to his shoulder again. "It would upset you if I didn't come—and I'll be damned if I start our marriage by faking it."

Silence.

"Have you ever faked it with me before?" he asked her.

"No," she said.

"I love you," he said softly, bringing her face up with his hand.

He kissed her and there was barely a response and so he held her a little more tightly and kissed her a little more tenderly. There was a response then, from her mouth, and instantly Gordon felt his anger and hurt vanish. "There," he said, raising his lips to kiss her forehead and then hug her, "this is more like it. See? I *can* hold you."

"Thank you," she said.

"And I'm glad you told me," he whispered, kissing the side of her head.

After a minute he let her go and she crawled into bed while he undressed. He used the bathroom, turned off the light and, in his boxer shorts, slipped into bed. Alexandra had settled in on her side, away from him; he reached over her to turn off her bedside lamp and kissed her on the temple. She turned her head and they kissed briefly, and then they murmured good nights. He pulled the covers up over his shoulder, settled down in behind her, slid his arm over her waist, and she curled up slightly, bringing his hand up to hold against her chest.

Lying there in the dark, listening to her breathe, he wondered if she was at all angry with him still. "I love you," he whispered.

"And I love you," she said, drowsy, not moving.

Lying there in the dark, listening to her breathe, he suddenly became aware—acutely so—of how neatly fitted in he was against the curve of her derrière. For an understanding, no-sex bed partner, it was definitely the wrong thought to be contemplating. But he did, and the fact that it was the wrong thought to be thinking about of course led to thinking about other parts of Alexandra's anatomy, which of course led to thinking about some of the experiences he had had with those parts of Alexandra's anatomy, which of course was making him more deliciously frustrated by the second, particularly when he knew that all of Alexandra would be out of his reach for at least a week.

And then Alexandra turned over, murmuring, "You are impossible," and slid her tongue into his mouth and reached down to touch him, and in a minute he pulled up her nightgown and pulled down his shorts and he did not press his luck but entered her quickly and she came quickly, very quietly so, with a kind of sighing sound, and he came almost as quickly, relieved in a number of ways, and so it was done and soon thereafter, holding on to her, he fell asleep.

He awakened at around five and found Alexandra crying in the living room.

"I just can't sleep," she said through her tears.

And so Gordon sat down on the couch, enveloped Alexandra in his arms and simply held her, and in a few minutes she did fall asleep, leaving him sitting there, wide awake, watching the sun come up over Central Park, wondering if she had or had not faked her orgasm.

24

What Cassy Wanted

The Friday before Memorial Day, Cassy knew that if she even thought about sleep for more than thirty seconds all would be lost. She would be rendered unconscious and would quite possibly remain so forever. This was one of those times she bemoaned being forty-three because she knew that the third wind she had carried with her in her twenties and thirties was no longer there, but, on the other hand, it was also a time she rejoiced being forty-three, since experience had taught her to hire people so good she didn't feel tempted to do their jobs herself—the activity for which she had always used her third wind anyway.

But forty-three, twenty-three, a hundred and three—who ever heard of anyone producing a national network newscast and a talk show at the same time? And on a network she was *still* recruiting affiliates for? (A newspaper columnist called Cassy for her response to what the executive producer of Clark Smith's nightly newscast had said about her expanded duties at DBS: "It sure sounds like the Happy Hands at Home Network to me. You know, where after she finishes milking the cows, then she has to go in and cook breakfast for everybody." To which Cassy responded, "It's true—I am very happy here, and we all do consider DBS a wonderful home. As for the milking-the-cows-and-cooking-breakfast part, well, all I can say is that it beats having to swallow the kind of b.s. Mr. Proctor does where he works.")

But they were doing it, by God, and everything would be done and in place by Monday—only it wasn't so much "by God" with Cassy as it was "Please, God," as in, "Please, God, if I wake up in three hours and can move I will take it as a sign that this newscast is meant to be." And she would wake up and she would be able to move, on three hours' sleep, and it would seem as if the newscast with its revised format was meant to be, and that "The Jessica Wright Show" was meant to share the production overhead.

Within DBS News, however, they were all getting, as Jackson would say, "squirrelly." The hours were too long, the pace too fast, the work overwhelming. They had hired, they had revamped, they had torn apart and rebuilt. Will Rafferty and his people were walking in their sleep, still moving on from affiliate newsroom to affiliate newsroom, teaching the "DBS News Way," handing out *Standard and Practices* workbooks, working with crews and reporters. Dr. Kessler and the Nerd Brigade were running tests around the clock with the affiliates, practicing tape feeds, live reports and simultaneous transmissions. The editorial crew was selecting, debating, rewriting, revamping, editing, drilling in daily rehearsal as if it was the real thing; the studio crews were on their "regular" hours, shooting "The Jessica Wright Show" in the late afternoon (to air at ten), breaking for early dinner and coming back to rehearse "DBS News America Tonight with Alexandra Waring" with a complete run-through from nine to ten; Alexandra and the in-studio correspondents were rehearsed and rehearsed and rehearsed, and there were changes of delivery style, changes in hairstyle and wardrobe; and there were set changes and graphics changes and lighting changes and music changes and opening changes and closing changes and transition, bumper and relay changes.

Even Kyle—the most even-tempered soul Cassy had ever worked with—had broken the lamp in her office the other night, screaming at the top of his lungs that he was *fucking going to murder her if there was one more change.* And then he had burst out laughing, crying a little at the same time, and the two of them, at two o'clock in the morning, had sat there, half hysterical, half nauseous from lack of sleep, laughing and crying in her office about what they didn't even know.

Oh, and the weather! Lest anyone ever forget what Alexandra had put them through over the weather! Poor Gary Plains, meteorologist or not, had all but been fired five times before he (and they) had really heard Alexandra.

"Listen," Alexandra had said in a meeting, "I grew up on a farm. I *know* how important the weather is—but what I don't know is how you can expect anyone to believe that you can forecast the weather for three and a half million square miles in two minutes. I mean, why don't we just do a national horoscope instead?"

"The affiliates will cut in with a local weather forecast," Cassy had said, utterly sick of the subject.

"And who the heck are the weather people at independent stations?" Alexandra said. "I've worked at indies, I *know* what they hire to do the weather."

"Suggestions, please," Kyle said.

"No suggestions," Alexandra cried. "Start over!" And then she had swept all of poor Gary's papers and tapes onto the floor. "Finally—a promising beginning," she said, nodding to the empty space in front of him. "Now then, Gary." She plunked her arms on the table and smiled at him, quite friendly actually. "This is the one and only chance of your career to come up with a segment that you can be proud of—not only as a meteorologist but as a broadcast journalist. So don't listen to them," she said, gesturing to everyone else sitting around the conference-room table. "Listen to yourself, to your own scientific head and journalistic heart, and when you think of something that gets your heart pounding and your head humming, come back and we'll give it a try."

And wouldn't you know, Gary did. He came back with trial segments to watch. The first opened with him standing in front of a topographical map of the United States (showing mountain ranges, desert flats, etc.), reporting the major weather story in America that day, which in this case was an electrical storm in Arizona. It cut away to footage taken by their Phoenix affiliate, and while they watched an incredible storm of lightning moving down out of the mountains and over the city, Gary described the storm, the kind of damage it had done and how damage had been minimized. Then they cut back to him at the map, where he gave a clear and concise explanation of how and why storms like this occur (cutting away to an illustration of the elements of an electrical storm like this one), and where in the United States they tended to occur (cutting back to the map, where he pointed out other regions). Then he led to a cut-in for a local weather forecast from each affiliate, as provided to them by the regional station of the National Weather Service.

The next segment was on flooding in Mississippi, the third on fog socking-in Boston, the fourth on a blizzard in Minnesota.

"This is fantastic!" Alexandra cried, vaulting out of her seat to hug

Gary. And they all had to agree, there *was* something to this angle, of presenting the most dramatic footage of the day related to the weather ("Pictures every day! Floods! Fires! Lighting! Blizzards! Ice! Drought!" as Alexandra so eloquently put it), explaining the phenomenon and its consequences, pointing out the parts of the country where it was a part of their weather pattern, and presenting a twenty-second local forecast according to weather experts. What Gary was offering, then, was an ongoing lesson in natural science and American geography with fantastic visuals—which, to Alexandra, fit in perfectly with their concept that viewers would better understand life in the United States if they watched "DBS News America Tonight."

And so Gary Plains and the weather won the highly esteemed nine thirty-two slot in the newscast.

Their official press conference at West End went off without a hitch, and Derek had done a great job of booking interviews for Jessica, and as good a job as could be done with Alexandra, who they decided should stay off TV until after the newscast was on the air. Jessica was an unqualified publicity hit, since she gave much more entertainment than she ever did interview. ("My beauty secret for working women like me? Oh, gosh, I'd say—turn off the lights.")

It did not work out so well for Alexandra. No one, it seemed, was very interested in talking about DBS News with her; all they wanted to know about was the state of her personal life. "Tell us about your relationship with Jackson Darenbrook," they would say. "He's my boss," Alexandra would say, answer complete. And so, when that didn't pan out, the interviewers would ask about Alexandra's relationship with Clark Smith. "I have no relationship with Clark Smith," she would say, answer complete. And so, when that didn't pan out, the interviewers would get ticked off and try to rattle her with a great question like, "Why would *any*one want to watch you on DBS?" to which Alexandra would start laughing and say something like, "Because there isn't anywhere else they can see me." And once there, at that point where Alexandra felt as though she had played along far enough, she would simply seize control of the interview and tell them about DBS whether they liked it or not—and about how "DBS News America Tonight" was really a nightly inventory of America's day, of what had gone right and what had gone wrong and why; and how it was also "an inventory of the state of our relationships, with each other, as fellow Americans—which we believe is key to understanding our national identity."

And even if a lot of this fell on deaf ears, Alexandra's glossies were still knockouts (as were the color transparencies of her for the magazines) and she was still "the lady who got shot on national TV" and she still had taken the time to talk to reporters personally and DBS News was still newsworthy, and so they could still count on extensive pickup about the debut in at least picture/caption form. And they *finally* got Alexandra's fan mail back from The Network, and in time to send a special letter, photograph and release about "DBS News America Tonight" to each of the over one hundred thousand people who had written her after she had been shot.

DBS was up to seventy-three affiliates now, and their first-quarter advertisers looked good. Normally a TV network or temporary linkup had to offer at least a hundred stations to be considered a national advertising vehicle, but Rookie had offered such a bargain package for the first quarter, they had a full dance card of fairly classy sponsors. The idea was, after the first-quarter ratings results were in, and the demographic breakdowns on both programs were in, DBS would raise ad rates accordingly, and first-quarter sponsors would have first shot at buying into the second quarter. If one or the other program bombed completely—well, they did not speak of that. It was simply understood that, if DBS failed to deliver the audience they promised any time after the first quarter, then they would simply do "makegoods," running the sponsor's ad as many more times as it took to reach the audience they had guaranteed.

So they had two great programs, two great talents, good PR, a network to show them on, advertisers paying for the privilege of coming along for the ride, and Cassy's two great "What if?" fears had been dealt with: if something happened to Alexandra, they knew their political editor, John Knox Norwood, and their editor-at-large, Chester Hanacker, could coanchor to substitute (they had done a complete run-through the other night, when Alexandra went to the benefit, and it had worked fine); and if something happened to Jessica, they had seven good shows in the can as backup.

Still, however, in the privacy of her own bed—in those increasingly infrequent times she had reached it in these last days—Cassy worried about how audiences for national newscasts were in decline, about the risks of airing in prime time, about debuting in the summer, about going out early with only seventy-three affiliates, about how they would ever get the two hundred affiliates they wanted and needed, about what might happen this summer with the board of directors in July about DBS News, about the extent of financial problems within DBS, about whether she really wanted to run DBS . . .

And these thoughts would rouse Cassy out of bed and have her wandering around the halls and rooms of her apartment. Of her empty apartment, now that her husband lived three thousand miles away with a twenty-nine-year-old girl, and now that her baby was six foot two and striding the campus of Yale University, embarking on a life of his own, separate from her. And then the eight rooms of the apart-ment would turn into a hundred cavernous rooms, all of them haunted. *I once had a husband and child that I fed at this table twice a day? I slept with someone for almost twenty-three years? When I first came here to this apartment, I had to put up window guards because my son was three years old? Could I ever have been young enough to have a three-year-old son? Could that have been me who bundled him up in his snowsuit in this hall? Attached his mittens to his coat? Took him sledding with his father—the three of us on that big Flexible Flyer, little Henry between us, my legs locked around Michael's waist? Was I really there? Did Michael and I have sex in this room? Have I ever had sex? Then why can't I remember what it's like?)*

Hopefully leaving the last of her fears at the haunted house, Cassy packed up her exhaustion and hurried to West End this Friday morn-ing, May 27, anxious to see how their newspaper ads had come out. They had a very limited ad budget but had worked out a campaign of quarter-page ads to run in newspapers across the country, some run-ning today and some on Sunday. She got her first shock of the morning when she opened the C Section of her New York *Times* in the car on the way to West End and found, instead of a quarter-page ad, *a double-page spread.*

On Monday Night, May 30
Meet Some of the Nicest People in America

the headline said. And then on the left-hand page, below it, there was
a close-up of Alexandra, underneath which it said:

9 P.M. DBS NEWS AMERICA TONIGHT WITH
ALEXANDRA WARING
The Coast-to-Coast Chronicle of America's Day

Under that were entries, each with a small head shot:

With the Special DBS News Correspondents

BROOKS BAYERSON AMES Arts and Entertainment	HELEN KAI LU, M.D., Ph.D. Health and Science
PAUL LEVITZ Business and the Economy	JOHN KNOX NORWOOD Government and Politics
GARY PLAINS, Ph.D. Weather	DASH TOMLINSON Sports

and
CHESTER HANACKER
Editor-at-Large

And then, on the opposite page, there were six pictures of Jessica,
standing out in a studio audience, taken about ten seconds apart. She
looked terrific, and her pose and expression in each were dramatic, but
the expressions on the faces in the audience were a scream—ranging
from adoration to horror.

10 P.M. THE JESSICA WRIGHT SHOW
The Terror of Tucson Comes to National TV

This week:

Monday   Wonderful Moments in Sexual Intimacy
Tuesday   Paul Hogan [She tried to get him to come on Monday.]
Wednesday   What to Do When You Think You Might Get Fired
Thursday   Bette Midler [Only if Jessica listens up on Wednesday.]
Friday   Jessica's Friday Cocktail Party: Traveling Salesman, Exotic

Dancer, Unpublished Poet, Corvair Owner, Cabana Beach
Boy

And then, along the bottom of both pages, it said:

THE DBS TELEVISION NETWORK
A Darenbrook Communications Company
9—11P.M., Monday through Friday, WST, SUPER TV-8

It was a fabulous ad—only it had to have cost about a hundred
thousand more dollars than they had allocated for the *Times* today,
and Cassy couldn't believe that Derek could have canceled so many
other ads to run this *one*—and without even checking with her. Good
God, this one ad alone represented a fifth of their total newspaper
budget!

When she arrived at West End, she went charging into Derek's
office, only to have him yell, "Cassy, what the hell is going on?" And
then Cassy looked at all the newspapers around Derek's office, and her
eyes grew larger and her stomach sank further as she walked to first
one paper and then another, seeing the same double-page spread ad
. . . the New York *Daily News,* the New York *Post, Newsday,* the
Boston *Globe,* the Baltimore *Sun,* the Philadelphia *Inquirer,* the Washington *Post,* the Chicago *Sun-Times,* the Detroit *Free Press,* the Cleveland *Plain Dealer,* the Miami *Herald* . . .

"Great!" Derek said later, slamming the phone down in her office.
"They don't know where our account executive is—and this kid says
he's not sure whose ads these are!"

"Papers west of the Mississippi are starting to come in," Chi Chi
announced, bringing in another pile.

A flurry of phone calls were made ("Dear God, I can't believe this,"
Cassy said at one point, holding her hands over her eyes, dropping
down into her own lap, "we're over budget by a million already." She
dropped her hands, looking to the ceiling. "God, we don't have a
million, don't you understand?"), a flurry of phone calls were returned,
and at nine-thirty Cassy received confirmation in her office that all of
the Friday DBS ads had been canceled at one agency and a whole
other set—*this* set—had been ordered for DBS at another, the bill for

which came to *one million nine hundred and seventy-six thousand dollars and fifty-eight cents.*

The order had been placed, approved and verified for DBS billing by none other than Jackson Darenbrook.

"You've wiped out our entire advertising and promotion budget!" Cassy said, flying into his office. "Do you understand what that means? It means we have nothing, *nothing* left for anything after today!"

"And good morning to you, Mrs. Cochran," Jackson said, addressing her reflection in the mirror of his closet door. He was dressed in blue jeans, sneakers and a sweat shirt that had Jiminy Cricket on it, and he was, at the moment, adjusting a New York Mets cap to a jauntier angle on his head.

"God damn it, Jackson!" Cassy said, swatting the door with the copy of the Dallas *Morning News* in her hand.

"Tsk, tsk, tsk," Jackson said, giving his cap a final tug, "such language from such a lovely lady on such a lovely day."

The tears came up before she knew what hit her. She was so tired there was no chance of stopping them. And so she threw the *Morning News* on the floor, covered her face, slumped against the door—banging it into the wall—and moaned, "Why are you doing this to me? Why?"

Jackson's head whipped around and he was bounding across the office in an instant. He reached Cassy just as Ethel poked her head around the doorway to see what was going on. "It's okay," Jackson said, waving her away, pulling Cassy in by the arm and closing the door.

"It's not okay," Cassy said into her hands. "You're killing me. Honest to God, you are killing me." And then she felt Jackson's arms slide around her, pulling her close, one hand directing her head to his shoulder.

"They were a present," he murmured. "They were for you, for all of you. For working so hard."

"God damn right we've worked hard," she sobbed, thinking how nice his sweat shirt smelled and wondering if it was fabric softener. "Having to build the stupid network in the first place—keeping you from driving Alexandra crazy. You stick me with a talk show, tell me I have to keep double books—I don't even know—"

"I know, I know," he said, holding her. "And I promise I'll make it up to you. Reward you for all you've done."

"I don't want a reward," Cassy said, crying. "I want you to stop driving me crazy."

He laughed then, a deep, warm, gentle laugh, holding her tighter.

"Jack!" Langley said, bursting in through the door from his office. In his hand was a copy of the New York *Times*. "Derek said—"

Silence.

Cassy was thinking about how nice it would be to go to sleep right here. And then she thought maybe she should be worrying about what Langley was thinking. She imagined it must look pretty funny to him to see her standing here with her face buried in Jiminy Cricket, and to see that Jackson, who he knew drove her crazy, was holding her in his arms.

"What did you do to her?" Langley finally said, angry, hurling his newspaper down.

"Pushed her past the breaking point," Jackson said, rocking her.

"Not a chance, buster," Cassy said into Jiminy Cricket, laughing.

Jackson released her, his hands sliding up to rest on her shoulders. "I didn't mean to upset you. No," he then said, smiling, "I did mean to upset you. I wanted you to be angry and then be surprised. I'm sorry. I really only meant to give you a big present."

Cassy smiled, backing away. "It's okay," she said, wiping one eye with the back of her hand. "I'm just tired, that's all." She looked up at him. He was staring at her with a very peculiar expression. And then she realized that she was staring too, caught by his eyes.

"What the hell is going on?" Langley demanded.

"What?" Jackson said, startled. He looked at Langley and then back to Cassy, pulling a bandanna out of his back pocket and offering it to her.

"What is going on?" Langley repeated.

Cassy accepted the bandanna and dabbed at her eyes, turning to Langley. "I was a little upset about the ads," she said.

"Yeah, well," Langley said, bending to snag the *Times* up from the floor, "some of us are more than a little upset. Some of us are furious because some of us are worrying about meeting the payroll as it is." He looked at Jackson. "Do you know how much these cost?"

"Yes," Jackson said, striding back across the office to the closet, "one million nine hundred seventy-six thousand dollars and fifty-eight cents. Don't worry, Lang," he said, bending to retrieve a large brown paper bag from the bottom of the closet, "they're a present—for Alexandra, Jessica, Cassy, you, everybody." He tossed the bag down on the carpet and a little cloud of dust came out from inside it. "From me."

"Yeah, right," Langley snapped. "Paid with whose money?"

Cassy did not like the sound of this. And apparently Jackson didn't either, because he slammed the closet door so hard the mirror crashed and shattered inside. "Ethel!" Jackson bellowed. In a moment the door opened and she appeared. "Bring in my checkbook, please, and show Mr. Shithead Peterson here the entry for the last check I wrote and the balance left in that account. In my *personal* account," he added, giving Langley the finger. Then he turned around and opened the closet door again, moved some pieces of broken mirror around with his foot, and then squatted down, moved some pieces of glass with his hands, and then stood up again, holding a basket of what looked like— if Cassy wasn't mistaken—gardening trowels.

Ethel came back in and went to Langley, offering him a look into a leather-bound book. Langley traced something with his finger and then looked over at Jackson. "Not a wise thing, considering your situation," he said.

"Ten to one it's the best investment I ever made," Jackson said. He picked up the brown paper bag and moved toward the door. "Come on, you guys," he said to them, "I want an hour of your time this morning." He turned around in the doorway, waiting for them, basket in one hand, bag in the other, Mets cap jaunty, and Jiminy Cricket smiling. To Ethel, "If anybody comes looking for them, either come out to the square or they wait. Okay?"

"Okay," Ethel said, smiling, looking at her watch. "Y'all better get a move on. Not the kind of crowd you can keep waiting for long."

Cassy and Langley looked at each other and then followed Jackson out and down the stairs to the day-care center, where Jackson picked up four three-year-olds, one two-and-a-half-year-old and one teacher, Miss Thomas, and led them outside into the square. It was one of those freakishly warm May days, feeling more like late June, and the morning sun was quite bright as well as hot. Behind the wall of fir trees they could hear cars going by on the highway, but they could also hear the birds—the chickadees, sparrows, robins, starlings and cardinals that were perching in the firs, swooping the skies, and hopping, singing and flitting in the trees and shrubs of the square.

Jackson led them to the center of the square, where the walkways met and where someone had recently turned over the soil of an empty flower bed. Jackson put down his bag and basket and helped Miss Thomas spread out two large blankets on the ground, which the children were directed to sit on, while Miss Thomas, Cassy and Langley were directed to a nearby bench. And then Jackson began to lecture on —on what, Cassy wasn't exactly sure. Cherokee roses? Cherokee roses in New York City? No, no—he was talking about how he had loved helping his mother tend her Cherokee roses when he was a boy. And now he was talking about begonias, how they were going to plant some today. Tuberous begonias. Right. And then while Jackson was going on and on about begonias and England and Ireland—and while the children, growing restless, started to squirm—Alexandra came walking out into the square.

Her smile grew wider with her every step. And then, when she was just a few yards away, she suddenly threw herself forward, bending to the ground, and then flung herself upright, reaching for the sky. And then she stretched, a long, languid stretch toward the sun, and then, smiling at Cassy, she relaxed, dropping her arms.

Apparently she was very glad to be outdoors.

Alexandra gave Jackson a little wave, slipped off her shoes, walked, in her stocking feet, around the back of the bench to squat down behind Cassy and Langley. "This is wonderful," she said, smiling, lightly resting one hand on Cassy's shoulder and one on Langley's. "Almost as wonderful as the ads. They are unbelievable. I don't know how you did it, but thank you." She kissed Cassy on the cheek.

"I didn't do it," Cassy said out of the corner of her mouth, watching Jackson. "They were a present from Jackson—to all of us."

"God makes the flowers grow," Jackson was explaining to his audience.

"Eeek—ya-yi—grrr-yoyoyoy—ha-ha," his younger audience was saying, now crawling all over each other on the blankets.

"Jiminy Cricket says to listen to Uncle Jack," Jackson told them, pointing to Mr. Cricket on his sweat shirt.

"Jiji-jaaahhh—eech-eech," his younger audience said, not paying the slightest bit of attention to him.

"Shhh—children," Miss Thomas said, laughing.

"Aaah!" a child said as another stood on her hand.

"Aha! A volunteer," Jackson said, scooping up the offended child in his arms.

While Jackson got down on his hands and knees to show "Patsy" how to plant a begonia tuber, Alexandra told Cassy and Langley that, according to the latest edition of the *World Crier,* she was now three-timing Jackson.

"That you're what?" Cassy said, turning around to look at her.

Alexandra smiled. "That I'm three-timing him. They bribed one of the doormen, apparently, for a record of who visits my apartment, and so now they say I'm three-timing Jackson with Gordon and Mr. Graham."

"Mr. Graham!" Cassy said.

"Naaahhh!" Patsy cried, not liking Uncle Jack's gardening lesson a bit, smacking him on the ear so he would leave her alone and prompting Miss Thomas to rush to his assistance.

"Come, sit," Cassy said to Alexandra, patting the seat beside her.

"They of course neglected to mention that Mr. Graham is forty-one years older than I am," Alexandra said, coming around the bench to sit down. "A bit of a stretch, this romance, don't you think? Even for them?"

"I think it's disgusting," Langley said.

"Oh, I don't know," Alexandra said, "I think Mr. Graham's rather handsome myself."

"I meant invading your privacy like that," Langley said, leaning forward to look past Cassy at her. "It's disgusting. Bribing your doorman. How's a person to live?"

"Very carefully, evidently," Alexandra said, turning to watch Jackson, voice no longer sounding quite so cheerful.

Cassy turned to look at her for a moment. And then she reached down to take Alexandra's hand and give it a squeeze. "You okay?"

"I think so," Alexandra said, turning to meet her eyes.

She looked tired, Cassy thought. And she had lost some weight. Not much, but enough to make her cheekbones even more pronounced. Great for the camera but not so great, Cassy thought, for real life. Cassy let go of her hand and touched Alexandra's cheek. "We have to get you to eat. We've taken care of the newscast, but I feel like we've forgotten to take care of you."

"It's sleep," Alexandra said. "Though I slept very well last night. Ever notice that? How, when you don't sleep, you look better than when you finally do?"

Langley leaned forward again. "We have to do something about your doorman," he said. "No one should have to live that way."

Alexandra looked surprised; and then she smiled at Langley with what Cassy knew was genuine fondness. (Would miracles never cease? These two got along now?) "Thank you, Langley," Alexandra said.

Langley looked embarrassed and sat back against the bench.

They all sat back to watch Jackson, then, trying to plant the begonia tubers on his hands and knees while the children, giggling, crawled all over him, yanking at his hat and pulling on his sweat shirt.

After a bit Cassy smiled and said, "You know, I really do love it here." She took Alexandra's hand again and squeezed it. "And I love working with you. With both of you," she said, turning to look at Langley. "All of you," she added, releasing Alexandra's hand and returning her eyes to Jackson. "Whatever happens, this has been one of the most wonderful things to ever happen to me—to wake me up in this life."

There, that was as close as she could come to explaining how she felt right now. How her heart felt full and happy, but ached too, longing to bring this moment, this little patch of sunlight, back to 162 Riverside Drive to make it home again. She wanted Langley to come home with her and live in Henry's room and be awkward and adolescent and wonderful and lovable; she wanted Alexandra to glide from room to room, trailing yards of silk, ministering to Cassy's every emotional need; and most of all, right now, what Cassy wanted . . .

What Cassy wanted was to bury her face in Jiminy Cricket again and feel the strength of Jackson's arms around her.

"I feel the same way," Langley murmured, startling her.

Cassy looked at him; his eyes were fixed straight ahead on Jackson.

"Oh, no," Alexandra said suddenly, making Cassy turn to look at her. Alexandra leaned over and whispered, "How upset do you suppose Jackson would be if I told him he's planting the begonias upside down?"

"Oh, no," Cassy said, starting to laugh, bringing up a hand to cover her mouth.

"Oh, yes," Alexandra said.

"Oh, she's right," Cassy said, to Langley, laughing, sliding down in the bench.

"Well, you better go tell him, Alexandra," Langley said, laughing too, "or he'll be standing at his window every day, depressed, wondering why they didn't come up."

"Okay," Alexandra said, standing up, smoothing her dress and then walking over to the flower bed.

And so Cassy and Langley sat on the bench in the sunshine of the square, watching as Alexandra pushed up her sleeves, hiked up her dress, and got down on her hands and knees to show Jackson, Miss Thomas and the children how to plant begonias, "so they don't come up in China."

It was one of the loveliest mornings Cassy could remember.

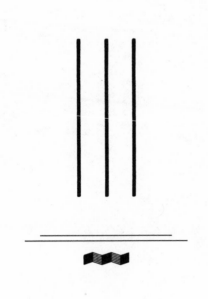

25

The Unveiling
Part I: Jackson

It was late afternoon on Monday, Memorial Day, and the West End Broadcasting Center was open for business. Downstairs, on Sub Level 2, the newsroom, the satellite room and the editing bays were in organized chaos as DBS News employees hustled, nervous, toward the deadline for their first newscast. In engineering, Dr. Kessler had the Nerd Brigade scurrying around in drill teams, while in the control room next door technicians were running equipment tests. All kinds of people were running the halls, evidently all doing very urgent things. Only Clancy Stevens, wheeling a cart loaded with flowers—some tagged for Jessica's dressing room and others for Alexandra's, and three more big bouquets simply marked DBS News—seemed to be relaxed, enjoying himself.

In the studio the partition between Studios A and B had been pulled back, and the audience seating risers for "The Jessica Wright Show" had been rolled forward and were, at the moment, being bolted into the floor, thus completing Jessica's set. The twenty-foot metal fire doors that sealed off the studio equipment rooms from Studio A were open, and a camera crane was being slowly rolled out; nearby, the fire doors to set storage and the carpentry shop were also open, through which Jessica's "living room" furniture was being carried out. Microphones were being plugged into the floor of Jessica's set; the lighting director was showing his staff the floor plan; a bit of set carpeting was being nailed down; the books in the shelves were being straightened; and Bozzy Gould was dashing around, supervising all of this, while

Denny and Cassy stood talking on the corner of the set. Across the studio, the DBS News sets sat idle, vacant.

Upstairs, in the cafeteria, the two hundred special ticket holders for "The Jessica Wright Show"—bused in from the pickup point in midtown Manhattan—were enjoying a lavish buffet luncheon, courtesy of the DBS Television Network. It was a very lively, nice crowd, with a lot of out-of-towners mixed in, and it was a hungry crowd, too, because after two hours of eating they were *still* eating, still walking over to the buffet with the same bright eyes and smiles they had had on their first trip.

Jackson Darenbrook himself, tall and tan, had been standing at the cafeteria doors to greet them as they came in. The visitors—eyeing Jackson's expensive pale gray suit, his pale blue shirt with a white collar ("Now what would you think, Bets, if *I* wore a shirt like that?" a man whispered to his wife, who said, "I'd think you'd be the same damn fool you've always been, Rudy"), his red and gray striped tie, the twinkle in his eye, the flash of his smile and the confidence in his stance—had been thrilled by Mr. Darenbrook's presence but had also felt shy. And so, after filing past Jackson, they had spread out into a kind of lost-sheep formation inside, with everybody milling around, not sure whether to sit or stand, not even really sure anymore if they were supposed to be in this room at all. It had obviously been set up for some sort of special inner circle, but were they it? Or did Mr. Darenbrook think they were somebody else?

But Jackson had made his way around the room, shaking hands, patting backs, urging people to sit down and eat, and soon they had, and soon most everybody had relaxed and started talking to him like he was anybody else. ("Hey, how ya doing? I'm in from Jersey," a guy said, shaking Jackson's hand. "So like this is great. I was lookin' for the M-10 and like I got on this bus and I knew—fast, ya know? 'cuz of the seats and stuff?—that this bus weren't like no M-10 I ever got on before. But like I figured, what the hell? and so like I'm here, just hanging out. And so what's the story on this Jessica chick? What, is she a dancer or something? She's got some kindavah show?")

One lady bodily dragged Jackson over to her table. Her name was Mrs. Judy Filanderbin and she was from Truth or Consequences, New Mexico. ("It was the only way we could get Ralph Edwards to come to our annual fiesta," Mrs. Filanderbin said, explaining how it had come to pass that the fair town of Hot Springs had renamed itself after a radio game show in 1950. Mrs. Filanderbin thought there was a possibility that the town might rename itself Jessica Wright, New Mexico, if only DBS played its cards right.)

With Mrs. Filanderbin was her very good friend, Mrs. Dertsy Baker, also of Truth or Consequences. Jackson sat down with the ladies for a while and Mrs. Filanderbin explained how she was Jessica Wright's greatest fan and how—after she had written Jessica a long, long letter once, listing all of her favorite moments on the show over the years— Jessica had called her up and invited her to Tucson to be on the show.

It had been a very tough show to do, Mrs. Filanderbin said, because Jessica had also had on two people who absolutely hated her show, and so Mrs. Filanderbin and another man who was a fan of Jessica's had to sit there and try and *talk* to these horrible people for an hour. Well, according to Mrs. Filanderbin, they did little more than scream and yell at each other, stop to run a clip from an old show, and then start yelling and screaming at each other again. And then they took phone calls and a fight broke out in the studio audience and my, oh, my—but what fun it had all been! And it had been said, Mrs. Filanderbin confided, that the ratings had been particularly high that night. . . . Not that Mrs. Filanderbin thought that her being on that show—that show for which the ratings had been so unusually high—had made that much of a difference. "But isn't Jessica just the most wonderful gal?" she asked Jackson.

"Yes, she is," Jackson said, accepting the taste of cheesecake that was offered to him by Mrs. Dertsy Baker (whose husband, Mrs. Filanderbin then proceeded to tell him, while Dertsy went up to get more cheesecake, had run off with a teaching assistant from the University of Guadalajara, where he had been sent to take an accelerated Spanish class for reasons of business—sent there, no less, by Mrs. Filanderbin's very own husband, who had not, she assured Jackson, "intended to send him for reasons of *funny* business! Shhh—she's coming back").

And then Mrs. Filanderbin told him about how she had sent a homemade coconut cake to Jessica three weeks ago, with a note saying how she hoped Jessica was well and happy way up here in New York

City. Well, the next thing she knew, Jessica's nice secretary called to say that Jessica was homesick for the Southwest and wanted Mrs. Filanderbin and a friend to fly up to New York for the weekend, as her guests, and be in the audience of her first show! For free! And so they did! And here they were! Staying at the Sheraton Centre and everything!

Jackson smiled, his eyes drifting to the door.

He liked Mrs. Filanderbin and Mrs. Baker very much, and he liked the other people who had come today to be in Jessica's studio audience too. He was very excited about DBS going on the air today, and he felt very proud as well. But his mind was still not on what was going on around him.

His mind was on Cassy Cochran.

He had spent most of his time since Friday thinking about Cassy Cochran. And it unnerved him, the suddenness with which this feeling had hit him after whatever it was had happened between them Friday morning in his office. And whatever it was that had passed between them, he knew she had felt it too, because he had seen it in her eyes. Only for a moment, but he was sure he had seen it.

And he hadn't been able to shake it. This feeling. This feeling that had started Friday morning, when he let go of her in his office and looked into her eyes, and when he had felt almost ill for second, so strong had the feeling kicked in—the surge of adrenalin, the tightness in his chest, the inexplicable thought in his head that had said, *I'm in love with you.*

The thought, at least, had quickly disappeared, but the feeling—this weird, edgy, alternating sense of elation and despair—had remained with him, rising and falling according to how much he thought about her.

He had fled West End before lunch on Friday, wanting very badly to see her again but feeling vaguely panicked about what new path of emotional self-destruction he might have started on this time. Or worse, that he was starting down an old familiar one. And so he had flown down to Bermuda Friday, to get some exercise and sun, and to get rid of this feeling by thinking it through.

But it hadn't worked. All he seemed to be able to do was wonder how he could have ever fought with Cassy about anything. And he honestly couldn't remember what it was about her that had made him so dislike her in the beginning. And when he thought about how she had looked in his office Friday morning, remembered her eyes, he wondered how he had ever even talked to her before—why he hadn't just fallen, sick with longing, into a chair, staring at how beautiful she was, knowing he could never have her because she not only was married, but because he represented everything he knew she detested.

But she did not detest him. No, not at all. That's what he had seen in her eyes Friday morning, and as soon as he had seen that something had lurched into gear—or out of gear, who knew?—and all he could think about was that she was separated and that she did not detest him. And ever since Friday, every time he had consciously tried to visualize her in his mind—while playing golf, while swimming in the Atlantic, while jogging, eating dinner, lying in his bed—he had felt as though some undefinable weight was settling onto his heart, was trying to labor his breath, cloud his vision.

Sitting here, in the cafeteria, with all the noise around him, Jackson was feeling like that now.

He wanted to see Cassy very badly—and yet he did not want to see her. Because he was scared to see her. Because he was scared of her. *Not another obsession. Not again—not at work, not anywhere.*

And then—a thought.

Could he take it if it was something other than an obsession?

And then there she was, coming in through the cafeteria doorway with Denny.

Cassy. Laughing. In a pale white/gray suit, almost the color of his own, with high heels matching exactly. Her hair was, as usual, swept up; there was an iris pinned to her lapel.

She was smiling now, looking around the room. And then her eyes found him. She was looking at him, smiling at him.

But Jackson looked away, to Denny, scarcely able to do even that. He couldn't look at Cassy. He couldn't. It was hurting him too much and he didn't know why.

26

The Unveiling
Part II: Jessica

It's only a Bloody Mary . . . , Jessica told herself.
It's still a drink and you know the rules.
But it's three o'clock. . . .
And you just got up.
I can't go to work twitching like a spider's crawling around in my dress!
But you have a show to do. No drinking before a show!
It's just an eye-opener.
An eye-opener.

Jessica remembered the first time she had seen that phrase. She had been on a trip with her parents, staying at a very expensive resort on Hilton Head Island. The Wrights had been there to improve their tennis and to knock some good sportsmanship into Jessica's twelve-year-old head so she would stop fighting with her tennis-team partner at home and start playing to win. (The Wrights were very big on winning.) Anyway, Jessica's parents had gone to a dinner dance the night before and were, that particular morning, looking very bleary-eyed and depressed until her father opened his menu and said, "Look, an eye-opener," and then her mother opened her menu and her eyes lit up too.

Jessica immediately looked inside her own menu to find out what was causing such quiet elation on their side of the table. (It didn't occur to Jessica to ask her parents, because one didn't ask questions in the Wright household. It was generally understood that one was either born with a certain set of knowledge or one should be at the library looking it up. At any rate Jessica knew better than to risk annoying her parents by asking them what would surely be interpreted as a dumb question.)

THE EYE-OPENER

Begin your country-style breakfast with your choice of an
icy Screwdriver made with freshly squeezed orange juice;
our special spicy Bloody Mary made with clam juice;
or a chilled glass of our driest champagne.

Followed by
two farm-fresh eggs, any style;
bacon, ham, sausage or chicken livers;
golden home-fried potatoes;
warm buttered toast or a freshly made muffin.

"What do you think?" Mr. Wright asked Jessica's mother.

Mrs. Wright looked at her gold watch. "I think it's four o'clock in
another part of the world," she said with a sly smile.

"We'll have the eye-openers," her father told the waiter. "Bloody
Marys, skip the eggs on mine. Just give me some whole wheat toast.
And my wife . . ."

"I'll have the toast too," Jessica's mother said.

"Very good, madame," the waiter said, writing this down. "And for
the young lady?"

"I'd like an eye-opener too," Jessica said.

Everybody looked at her.

"With a Virgin Mary," she added more quietly.

"She likes to act grown up," her father said, winking at the waiter.

"She likes to be the center of attention," her mother said, sniffing
sharply once and handing her menu to the waiter.

"And . . . ?" the waiter asked Jessica.

"Two eggs, over easy. And bacon, potatoes and a muffin, please."

Her mother turned to the waiter. "Bring her half a grapefruit and a
bowl of shredded wheat with skim milk," she told him. "And I suppose
you can bring her the bacon." She sighed, turning back to the table.
"Do you want to look like Kate Smith? Is that what you want?"

"I like Kate Smith," Jessica said, glum.

"Well, let's hope you like singing 'God Bless America' because that's
all you're going to be good for and you're going to have to wait until
she's dead to be able to do that," her mother said in one breath,
looking around to smile at people sitting at other tables. Then she

sniffed again, glancing over at Jessica, adding, "No one's going to want to marry you if you're fat, you know."

Jessica folded her arms across her chest, sinking in her chair. "I'm never getting married. I'm going to be rich and famous and have an old and faithful servant."

"If I were you," Mrs. Wright said to her husband, "I'd get her to put that in writing and hold her to it." She started looking around the room again, saying under her breath, "It takes a lot of money to marry off spoiled little girls who want to be fat when they grow up."

"Yeah, I *bet,*" Jessica said meanly, narrowing her eyes at her mother (who Jessica knew had been heavy as a child and whose family had had a bit of money).

Mrs. Wright, exasperated, let her hand fall to the table. "Where did she come from?" she asked her husband. "Well, wherever it was," she added, turning to look at Jessica, widening her eyes like Joan Crawford, "maybe we should send her back."

Jessica sat up, leaning menacingly toward her mother, widening her eyes like Joan Crawford too, and said, "Yes, maybe we should."

"Stop it," her mother said. "You look like that poor man with the thyroid problem who does your grandmother's pool."

"She'll be going away to school soon," Mr. Wright said, smiling because the waiter had arrived with their drinks.

As soon as they all got their drinks, magically, it seemed, the mood at the table lifted. In fact, between the time her parents finished the first Bloody Mary and decided to have a second (because they would be sweating it out on the courts anyway, or so Jessica heard them tell each other in the course of deciding whether or not to have another), her mother suddenly leaned over and kissed Jessica on the cheek. "When you look better, you feel better, Jessica. That's why I nag you so. I want you to grow up and make the most of your looks, that's all. You'll be happier if you do. I know."

So big deal, what was one Bloody Mary? Jessica thought, opening the lovely wood cabinet housing the bar in her hotel living room. As she made the drink she tried not to think about it.

About how she had sworn she would not do this.

After trial sips—to see how her stomach would take it—she finished the Bloody Mary quickly, knowing already that it was going to be okay.

She opened a bottle of club soda then, confident that her body could now move on to the business of relative good health, and she went into the bathroom to take her birth control pill. Jessica had suffered lapses of irresponsibility in almost every area of her life, but birth control had never been one of them. Whether it was because she was terrified of getting pregnant or because she so loved children and would never wish a mother like herself on one, she wasn't sure—but she did know that after the facts of life and sexual health had been explained to her in detail at a Planned Parenthood clinic when she was young, she had never been able to pretend that she didn't know the consequences of failing to take precautions and have regular exams.

(The irony that a trip to a Planned Parenthood clinic was the only thing protecting Jessica from the fate of so many of her classmates! One of the best boarding school educations money and clout could buy, and so many girls getting pregnant! And not just in school but later on, too. So many well-educated, fortunate young women who had supposedly had it all—except the simple knowledge that if you had intercourse without birth control you ran a good chance of getting pregnant. Who would have ever guessed that a twenty-dollar exam in a *clinic* would make Jessica Wright the one who would never have to go through the emotional indecision, pain and agony of so many of her classmates—that Jessica would go ahead and make a mess out of her life, but confine the mess only to her own?)

Oh, God, she thought, feeling a little dizzy there in the bathroom, leaning forward to splash cold water on her face, *why did I drink so much last night?*

And she had been so good for the last two weeks! She had barely had anything to drink for days. And last night, at a cocktail party for mostly media people stuck working the holiday, Jessica had had every intention of simply making an appearance, having one glass of wine and then going home to the Plaza, taking a bath and going to bed early. Well, she made her appearance (instantly depressed, since at a glance she could tell she was the most interesting person there), had her glass of wine and dutifully tried to be charming to everyone her host introduced her to.

And then she was introduced to this guy Curt, a DJ. Jessica did not like him at all, and the feeling was apparently mutual since in very short order Curt told her he thought she was full of shit and didn't know what the fuck she was talking about (very eloquent was he, this Curt of the radio airwaves) and Jessica had another glass of wine during this exchange and then, a while later, she found herself sitting at a table in the kitchen with Curt, drinking Finnish vodka, thinking, *I hate this son of a bitch—why am I talking to him? What am I doing?* At first the caterers were upset to have guests sitting in the kitchen, but when it was determined that Jessica and Curt were not moving, a nice lady named Ragna from Russia cleared off the table and—after asking them to hold their drinks—she threw a nice white linen tablecloth over it, put the Finnish vodka bottle back down on it and brought Jessica the ice she requested in a silver bowl, complete with silver tongs.

Jessica did not know what time it was that Curt suggested she come downtown with him to see his studio. Jessica had no desire to see it, but she no longer knew anything except that it was time to go somewhere because Morris the caterer was banging things; Scott, their host, had long given up on them and had gone to bed; and her friend Ragna from Russia had stopped laughing when Jessica, each time she went to the powder room, opened the broom closet door and asked Ragna if this wasn't where they should put Curt the Vampire before the sun came up.

Jessica remembered being in a cab and being aware that Curt was getting angrier and angrier about something—she couldn't understand what he was talking about. Oh. Something about some goddam fucking faggot who fucked his motherfucking career. Jessica remembered looking down at her hands, her hands she could not feel, wondering if she shouldn't be frightened. But she didn't feel frightened. She didn't feel much of anything. A little lost, maybe. She looked out the taxi window and saw a fenced-in baseball field go by and she thought, *I know where we are. That's where the Little League night games are played. The Circle K's just up on the next corner,* and then she laughed, realizing that the Circle K wasn't on the next corner but was more like two thousand five hundred miles down the block in Tucson—which she tried to tell Curt, because it was so funny, but Curt was busy slamming the back of the driver's seat, screaming about something, and Jessica thought again that maybe she should be scared. But she wasn't. She felt very safe, tucked away, untouchable somehow.

The next thing Jessica knew, a man was looking down into her face, asking her if she was all right, could he help her.

She blinked, wondering where, exactly, she was.

The man helped her to sit up, saying something about how lucky it was that he and his friend had just happened to come around the corner when they did.

"Yes," Jessica said, allowing the men to lift her to her feet. The other one picked up her bag and handed it to her.

"He didn't hurt you, did he?" the first man asked, brushing the back of her dress off.

"Who?" Jessica said, not feeling drunk, not feeling hurt, not feeling anything but confused. Wherever she was, the buildings were brick and only four stories high, and the street was cobblestone. "Where are we?" she asked them.

The men looked at each other and told her she was on Bleecker Street in Greenwich Village and then went on to describe how a man had been shaking her against the lamppost—

Jessica held up her hand, indicating she did not want to hear any more.

"Is there someone we can call?" the first man said gently.

Now that was an interesting question. It was interesting because it reminded Jessica that there were really only two people she was free to call in New York. One was Denny, who had had many such calls over the years, and the other was Alexandra—that is, if whoever had been shaking her against the lamppost had not stolen her wallet, she had Alexandra's number. But then she remembered that Denny's number at his new apartment was still on the pad by her phone at the hotel, which made her wonder if she should ask these men if this was a nice part of town to live in, because she was supposed to have moved out of the Plaza a month or so ago and needed to find an apartment. But then she remembered she was supposed to be thinking of someone for them to call, which made her think they should call her limo driver, which made her wonder what *had* happened to her driver, anyway, but then she remembered she had walked up the street to the party. But wait a minute, she was supposed to be—

Now what was she supposed to be doing?

Nope. She had lost it; she couldn't remember.

So Jessica checked to see if she had any money—and she did—and asked the men to help her find a cab—which they did—and she arrived at the Plaza just as day was breaking, and a very nice house detective saw her safely escorted to her room.

Dressed now and feeling a little better and knowing she was late, late, late, Jessica brushed her teeth and gargled extra well, grabbed her bag and was just at the door when she stopped. She turned around to look at the cabinet across the room. And then, slowly, she walked over to it. And then she opened it. Then she took two little two-ounce bottles of vodka out and put them in her bag, and then she put one of them back, and then she started to reach for it again, but then she took a bar of Tobler dark chocolate out of the cabinet instead, threw it in her bag, closed the cabinet and ran out.

In a minute she was back, looking at herself in the full-length mirror (wearing a new blue-green dress and brand-new cowgirl boots, dyed to match) and then ran over to the dressing table to pick out pieces from the box of costume jewelry. Her hands were shaking so badly she finally just opened her bag, dumped everything in and took off.

"You're to go straight into makeup," Alicia said, waiting for her in the West End carport, evidently alerted to her arrival by the guard at the gate. "Langley's wife, Belinda Darenbrook Peterson, wants to meet you and Cassy says she's a very important board member—but Denny's got to see you first. He's in makeup with the guests and has your notes."

"And hello to you too," Jessica said, walking quickly toward the cement staircase that led to the level above. "I'll be there in a minute."

"Where are you going?" Alicia wailed.

"I'll be right down," Jessica said, going up the stairs.

"Jessica," Alicia pleaded, following her, "please. Denny and Cassy said you have to—"

"Hey!" Jessica yelled, whirling around to point a finger at her. "I've been doing this show for seven years and I know exactly what I have to do and what I don't have to do and I'm telling you right now, I sure as hell don't have to take any shit from you. Got it?" She wheeled back around, dress and hair whirling after her, and marched up the stairs.

And then, a moment later, she called, "Where the hell are you, Alicia? Come on!"

Alicia followed her up the stairs.

"Okay, okay," Jessica said, seeing her expression, "I'm sorry."

"You're not the least bit sorry," Alicia told her, "so don't even bother."

"Alicia," Jessica groaned, going down a stair, grabbing her hand and pulling Alicia up the stairs with her, "I *am* sorry. I'm sorry I was ever born, I'm sorry I ever got married, I'm sorry you can't understand that my only problem in life is that I can't deal with the human race and that that has nothing to do with you because I think you're an angel." She glanced back at her, still pulling her up the stairs. "I'd die without you—how's that?"

"Better," Alicia told her.

When they reached the top of the stairs Jessica led Alicia outside and then through the little gate between Darenbrook I and III into the square. "See, this is all I wanted to do," Jessica said, looking up at the cafeteria window and waving. Someone waved back and within seconds, it seemed, there was a crowd of people pressing against the glass, waving down at her. "Hi!" Jessica called, laughing in delight, waving. "Hi!" And then she said, "Okay, let's beat it before anyone gets down here," and they made for the door into Darenbrook III.

"There you are!" a production assistant cried as they got off the elevator on Sub Level 2. "Hey—hey, everybody," he yelled, running ahead, "she's here. Jessica's here!"

"If everyone was so worried I wouldn't show," Jessica said, breezing down the hall past several people, "why the hell didn't anyone call me?"

"Because Denny said you would be here," Alicia said from behind her.

She went into makeup, got her notes from Denny, went with him down to the greenroom to say hello to the guests, and then came back to her dressing room to throw her bag down. There were several beautiful bouquets of flowers around the room and on her dressing table (just left by Alicia no doubt) was a tall glass of Coca-Cola over ice and several kinds of granola bars. Jessica ripped a bar open and ate it while reading the cards on the flowers, wondering why she never had a secret admirer, but only ones she knew and wished would go away.

Then she took the Coke and her bag into the bathroom, closed the door and locked it, sat the Coke on the sink and dug into her bag to come up with the little vodka bottle. She drank some of the Coke, set it back down and then opened the vodka. She brought it over the Coke to pour in, but caught sight of herself in the mirror and froze, staring at herself. Her expression was of someone who had been caught in the act. Caught by herself?

She sighed, closing her eyes. Then she opened them, quickly screwed the cap back on the vodka bottle, looked around, opened the linen closet, hesitated, and then stuck it inside a roll of toilet paper. Then she walked out, sipping her Coke, opening her dressing-room door to go to makeup, and found Cassy there, just about to knock.

"Hi," Cassy said softly, touching her arm. "How are you feeling?"

"Like a great show," Jessica said.

"Good, good," Cassy said, not looking very sure that she believed this. "Listen, Jessica," she whispered, looking back over her shoulder, "Belinda Darenbrook Peterson, Langley's wife, appeared out of the blue and she wants to meet you."

"She's not packing a gun, is she?" Jessica said, smirking over the rim of her glass. This was rich. After he asked her out for dinner, now Langley expected her to charm his wife?

"She's on the board, did you know that?" Cassy said. "Which doesn't mean anything, really, one way or the other—but it could be that she's here to make some kind of report to the rest of the board. And so . . ."

"Langley doesn't know why his wife's here?" Jessica asked her.

"I think he thinks she really is a fan of yours—she says she watches you in Aspen every year."

Jessica shrugged, signaling that this sounded plausible to her.

"You don't have to do it, Jessica," Cassy said, "not if you don't want to. It's just that it might be a good thing for all of us if . . ."

Jessica smiled, moving across the hall toward makeup. "Just tell me what you want me to do and I'll do it."

"Could you make her feel like DBS is the most wonderful investment in all the world?" Cassy asked her.

"Sure," Jessica said, hand on the door to makeup. "Bring her in."

"Oh, no," Cassy said, "not now. After the show."

"No, bring her in now," Jessica insisted, pulling the door open. "I don't want to think about the show until the warm-up, else I'll be bored with it. Besides, it'll make the show a lot more exciting for her if she talks to me first."

"Are you sure?" Cassy asked.

"Sure."

"Okay," Cassy said.

"Hi, Cleo," Jessica said, putting her Coke down on the counter and climbing into one of the chairs.

"Hi, sugar," Cleo said, turning around. Her mouth pressed into a line as she looked Jessica's face over.

"No editorials today, please," Jessica said.

"I won't say a word," Cleo promised, plugging the hot rollers in and then putting a bib on Jessica. "But other people might say they should be paid time and a half for working on circles like these."

"We're having company in here in a minute," Jessica said.

"I told you, I won't say a word." Then Cleo clucked her tongue, eyes on Jessica's neck. "People in television should know better," she sighed then, reaching for the jar of cosmetic she used to neutralize a number of sins before applying foundation.

Jessica quickly turned her head to the side, craning her neck to see in the mirror. . . . *But where . . . ? Oh, God—not Curt the Vampire. I couldn't have.*

Denny came in twice to tell her something, and Alicia and Bozzy Gould both came in once before Cassy brought Belinda Darenbrook Peterson in. Jessica saw the resemblance to Jackson immediately, particularly in the eyes, though her eyes didn't twinkle like his did, nor did she appear to have his energy, his sense of humor. On the other hand, she was much younger than Jackson. And she was pretty, but there was something holding her looks back that Jessica couldn't put her finger on, and then she realized that what was holding back her looks was the fact that she *looked* as though she was being held back. "Batten down the hatches," was the expression that came to mind, because there was definitely a strapped-down feeling about her, of something tight, not clenched, just tight, holding things together.

Jessica smiled at her in the mirror. "Hello, Mrs. Peterson. I'm deeply flattered that you've come to see my show." *Watch out, gang, here comes the snowball express.*

"Oh, please—call me Belinda," she said, looking a little shy.

After Cassy finished the introductions, Jessica asked Belinda some questions to get her talking and found that Belinda got better-looking and more likable as she did. (Animation, *that's* what had been missing in her face.) And even if her husband was a jerk for putting her in this position, Jessica actually found Belinda rather sweet, charming even— particularly when she told Jessica how much she loved watching her show every winter in Aspen, and how thrilled she was that she could watch her all the time now.

At this point Cassy left them and Jessica had Belinda draw up a chair. So while Cleo worked away on transforming her, Jessica and Belinda—in between Denny's various updates (how much time Jessica had, how long the warm-up would be, the state of the guests, what the audience was like)—chatted about Jessica's show, about clothes, cowgirl boots, riding, skiing, Colorado, DBS and how wonderful her brother, Jackie, was.

When Cleo was finished Jessica took Belinda with her across the hall to her dressing room, where she heaped all of the jewelry from her bag on the dressing table, handful after handful, telling Belinda how it had taken her three years to find out that junk jewelry looked fifty times better on TV than real jewelry did. Then she sat down at the dresser, opened a drawer of earrings and asked Belinda to pick what she liked best with this dress. Belinda made her selections, opting for silver.

"I like this one too," Jessica said, reaching for the necklace Belinda had chosen. She tried to put it on, but the clasp on it was delicate and her hands were shaking so badly she could barely hold the damn thing, much less get it open.

"Aren't these just the worst?" Belinda said, taking the necklace from Jessica and moving behind her. She undid the clasp, parted the neck- lace and then draped it around Jessica's neck. "You get nervous," she said, not unkindly.

"Sure," Jessica said, wishing it were true. ("No, Belinda," she imagined herself saying, "it's more like being shell-shocked.") She held her hair up as Belinda attached the necklace in the back.

"There now," Belinda said, stepping to the side.

Jessica dropped her hair and nodded, looking in the mirror. "Very good," she said. Then she reached for the earrings Belinda had chosen, put one in, and then, while she was putting in the other, heard a clicking noise and turned to see what it was.

Belinda was looking inside something that resembled a gold cigarette case. Only there weren't any cigarettes in it; there were pills in it. "I have something that will help you," Belinda said.

"Oh," Jessica said, not doubting it in the least, since she recognized some of the pills in the case—the triangular yellow ones—as Valium, which not only did wonders for hangovers but which Jessica had always found heaven in general. No smell, no mess, no telltale anything —only that blissful sensation in the head, back of the neck, shoulders . . . a kind of extra-dry martini with a twist in space travel form. The only problem was, ever since her cocaine days, something told Jessica to be scared of it. It was too easy, too good to be true. And there was no sociability attached to Valium either, and no rules like "Not until five."

"This is a very mild tranquilizer," Belinda said, picking out another kind of pill.

"What is it?" Jessica said, putting on a ring because she didn't want to take the pill from her, but knowing she wouldn't say no to it either.

"Librium," Belinda said. "I'll put it here." She placed it on the dresser, closed the pill case and returned it to her purse.

"Thank you," Jessica said, wondering what those other pills had been and if it was too late to get some of those, even though she didn't want any of them. "I appreciate it."

"You're very welcome," Belinda said. "I'm just glad a silly housewife like me can be of some use."

Jessica looked at her, surprised by the statement, but before she could think of what to say there was a soft knock on the door and Denny poked his head in to tell Jessica that the warm-up would start in ten minutes, and to tell Belinda that Langley was waiting for her. So Belinda went on to the studio with Denny, and Jessica quietly sang some scales while putting on her jewelry—eyeing the Librium all the while.

There was another knock on the door and Jessica sang, "Come i-ennn."

"Hi," Alexandra said, coming in, "I came to walk you to work. Wow, Jessica—" she said, stopping next to the dresser, "do you ever look wonderful. That dress is fabulous."

"Thank you," Jessica said, standing up so she could see it. "I call this my Mrs.-Zorro-at-Home dress. Suitable for a discussion about great moments in sexual intimacy, don't you think?"

Alexandra laughed. "But wait," she said, reaching for something on the dresser, "I think you should wear—"

"I've got to wear exactly what I've got on, because Langley's wife . . ." Jessica let her voice trail off, aware that Alexandra was staring at the Librium. Jessica picked it up. "Throw it out, will you?" she said, handing it to her.

Alexandra looked down at it in her hand and then back up at Jessica.

"Oh, come on, Alexandra Eyes," Jessica said, stamping her foot, "it's not even mine. Langley's wife gave it to me because she thought I needed to calm down."

Alexandra was still looking at her.

"I *asked* you to throw it out, didn't I?" Jessica said.

Alexandra walked to the bathroom.

"Great, just great," Jessica muttered, throwing her hands up. She looked up at the ceiling. "Now she thinks I'm a drug addict. This is all I need."

The john flushed in the bathroom and Alexandra came back out. She was smiling. "I do not," she said.

"Then why didn't you just throw it in the trash?" Jessica asked her.

"Because you're not the only one who gets tempted," Alexandra said.

Jessica's mouth fell open. "You?" she finally said.

"Sure. When you're in a line of work that demands all-nighters, pills can't help but cross your mind," Alexandra said. "And lately, with the problems I've had sleeping, anything starts looking pretty good to me around dawn." She shrugged. "So I don't keep anything around."

"You're kidding," Jessica said.

Alexandra smiled, reaching to pick a piece of lint off of Jessica's shoulder. "No, I'm not."

"Did you ever . . . ?"

Alexandra glanced at her and then walked over to the door, shaking her head. "No, thank God," she said, taking hold of the doorknob and turning around, "because I never would have gotten here if I had." She smiled. "It's not in my nature to do anything in moderation, I'm afraid."

"Yeah, tell me about it," Jessica said, looking at herself in the mirror one last time. "Okay, Alexandra Eyes," she said a second later, walking to the door, "I'm ready." Alexandra opened the door and held it for her. Jessica took a step and then stopped. She looked at Alexandra. "Thanks for telling me that," she said.

"Thanks for being someone I can talk to," Alexandra said.

Jessica smiled.

Alexandra smiled.

And then they walked down the hall to the studio.

27

The Unveiling
Part III: Gordon

"Damn it, I don't believe this," Gordon said, hitting the steering wheel. "And I can't get over to the parkway for another five miles. And why the hell is everybody on the road? This is Memorial Day—why aren't they on the beach?"

"Don't look at me," Betty, his assistant, said, turning on the radio. "But if you want to *ask* me," she added, tuning in a station, "I say let's put the top down."

They were in Alexandra's car, a 1972 navy-blue MG, sitting there, stuck, in the center lane of the Long Island Expressway. His flight had been delayed getting in Friday night, so Gordon had stayed over with Alexandra and then early the next morning, at her request, had taken her car to Amagansett to give it a sorely needed open-highway run.

While the drive out had been a breeze, Gordon doubted that this "drive" (sitting at a dead stop in three lanes of traffic) was doing very much toward cleaning out the fuel line.

Betty was in a group house this summer in Quogue, and while Gordon had known that she would be out for her first weekend, he had hardly expected to see her walk into Vanessa Winslow's house this morning for brunch. "Not everybody thinks of me as the hired help," she had whispered to him, just as Vanessa came sweeping out of the kitchen, trailing yards of silk from the outreached arms of her robe or whatever the heck it was, saying, "My dear friend, I'm so glad to see you!"

(The endless delays in Vanessa Winslow's contract payments from DBS had started this unlikely friendship between Betty and one of America's biggest—and most insecure—television stars. While Vanessa's agent and lawyers had—quite rightly—forbidden Gordon to talk to her until the monies involved were received from DBS, Betty had started calling her up to tell her how much Gordon and *everybody* at DBS revered her, and how crazy it was making all of them that their accounting department was so slow. After a while Vanessa had started calling Betty to find out what was going on, to gossip, and to hear more nice things about the work she had done in the past, all of which Betty had evidently seen. When the money had finally been paid three weeks ago [at which time Gordon had given Betty a seventy-five-hundred-dollar bonus], Gordon had been allowed to talk to Vanessa again, and while he had expected Betty to remain friendly with Vanessa, he had not expected to see her as a guest this morning.)

At brunch Betty had asked him if she could hitch a ride back to the city and, rather than dissuade her, Gordon's explanation that he wanted to stop off in Locust Valley to see his parents had only made her insist. "Oh, *please,*" she begged him, pulling on his arm. "All my life I've wanted to play Locust Valley Lockjaw. Come on, Gordon, I *swear* I'll clench my teeth the whole time. I will!" And so Betty had come with him to Locust Valley Lockjaw Land and now they were sitting, stuck in traffic.

But Betty was right—they should at least put the top down and enjoy the late afternoon sun. He reached behind their seats to unzip the back window, undid the two hooks in the front, looked around to make sure that everybody was still in this unbelievable dead stop, slipped off his shoulder harness, opened the door and climbed out to bring the top down.

For a car that was almost three hundred thousand miles old, the MG was still a beauty. This was its third black convertible top. (The first had been ruined in 1980, while Alexandra was conducting an interview at a medical research center in Portola Valley. A monkey from the lab had somehow clawed and torn it, so that when Alexandra came back outside it appeared as though the little monkey was eating her car. The second top had been lost in '87, at the hands of a politically inspired vandal in Washington, who had slashed I R A through it while Gordon and Alexandra were eating in a restaurant.) The engine had been rebuilt about a hundred thousand miles ago; the outside of the car had been meticulously color-matched, repainted and resealed twice; the underside had been recoated several times; and the black leather interior had been so well cared for in the sixteen years of its life that it seemed only to look better and smell more wonderful each year.

Alexandra swore she would never part with this car and Gordon didn't blame her. Besides, he was the only other person she had ever trusted to drive it all these years.

"There," Gordon announced, plunking back down in his seat and closing the door.

"Nice," Betty said, holding her hair back with one hand and angling her face toward the sun.

Gordon watched Betty a moment (she had closed her eyes) and thought of Alexandra at twenty-one, sitting in almost the exact same pose. He remembered it very well, her sitting like that, because they had been sitting in the MG for two hours on Route 1 that day in 1979, waiting for bulldozers to carve a new lane out of the hillside because the southbound one had slipped into the ocean. ("Even if a house does fall out of the sky every once in a while," Alexandra had sighed, "at least in Kansas the roads stay pretty much where we put them.") The wait had been worth it, though. He remembered their weekend at Big Sur, what they had done there, still.

Gordon blinked a couple of times, refocusing on the license plate on the car in front of them, thinking how strange it was to be in this car with anyone but Alexandra.

"What exactly is it that your mother has?" Betty suddenly asked him, shielding her eyes from the sun with her free hand.

He sighed, gave a little shrug and looked over across the divider at the cars passing the other way. "The vapors, I think."

"The what?"

"I was kidding," he said, looking straight ahead. The car ahead of them was moving. He pushed in the clutch, revved the engine a little, shifted into first, let out the emergency brake and let up on the clutch.

ZOOM.

Errrt.

Into neutral.

Wow. Twenty whole feet.

He yanked up the emergency brake. *Thump, thump;* his feet came down off the pedals to the floor.

"If I'm being nosy, just tell me," Betty said.

"No, it's okay," he said. He propped his elbow on the steering wheel, gently gnawing on the back of his knuckles. "She's, um," he said, dropping his hand into his lap, "reclusive at times. I don't know why, exactly, or if there's a name for it or anything—she's always been that way. As long as I can remember, anyway."

"So it wasn't that she didn't like me," Betty said.

When they arrived, Gordon's father had been out playing golf, and his mother kissed him hello, shook Betty's hand and promptly fled upstairs with the excuse that she wasn't feeling well. (God only knows what she would have done had Gordon introduced Betty as more than simply "Betty." How could he ever explain Betty having his mother's maiden name?)

"Oh, she liked you fine," Gordon said, feeling embarrassed, as he had always felt embarrassed about his mother's behavior all of his life. "She's just not very good with strangers." *Or anyone,* he thought.

"How is she with Alexandra?"

Gordon looked at her.

"You're going to marry her, aren't you?" Betty asked him.

The cars ahead were starting to move; he released the brake and put the car into gear to follow. "Yeah," he finally said. "I am. But that's not for public consumption yet."

"Okay," Betty said.

They passed an accident in the left lane and, immediately after, the traffic began to clear. Gordon reached over to open the glove compartment, groped around, found a pair of sunglasses, shook them open and put them on. Then he closed the compartment, shifted gears and shot ahead into the left lane.

"I do like her, you know," Betty said over the wind a few minutes later, holding her hair back, looking at him. There was a roaring sound and Betty looked over at the pickup truck that had drawn up beside them in the middle lane. Then she looked up and gave the young man —who was leering down at her from the cab—a little wave. "How ya doing?" she called up to him.

"All *rrrriiight,"* the guy declared, grinning and hitting his horn twice in approval.

Gordon looked up at the guy in the pickup, saluted and stepped on it, pulling ahead.

"Hey," Betty protested, hitting him on the arm, "that could have been my future husband."

"Oh, come on," Gordon said, "you can do better than that."

"Better than what? If he isn't on drugs, likes women, doesn't have a sexually transmitted disease and speaks English, he's the best bet I've had in years."

Gordon laughed.

"Yeah, you laugh. All you guys do. A hundred pretty women for every single, straight guy in this town—I guess I'd laugh too if I were you," she said. Betty leaned closer. "If I want to get married I *have* to be rich and famous or I'll never find anyone. And you wait and see, Mr. Tee-Hee-Ha-Ha, when I'm rich and famous, *believe* me, I *will* meet a guy like you and he *will* want to marry me."

He laughed again.

"It's not funny," she said, trying not to laugh herself. "I mean, what am I supposed to do? Marry the homeless?"

They could hear the truck honking hopefully behind them.

Betty looked around at the truck and then sat back in her seat again.

She turned to him. "So how *is* a girl supposed to meet a guy like you if she isn't famous?"

"Alexandra wasn't famous when I met her," Gordon said, glancing over. "She was nine. I met her in Kansas, over the holidays. Her brother was my roommate at school."

"But her father was really rich, right?" she said. "Didn't you meet her because they were rich—and famous? Her father was a senator or something, right?"

"A congressman. And no, he wasn't rich. Her mother's family had money though—but most of that went into the farm."

"So she really is from a farm," Betty said.

Gordon smiled. "She really is from a farm—can bale hay, drive a tractor, ride a horse and everything." He changed lanes before continuing. "But she hasn't had it quite as easy as you think, you know."

"That's what they all say," Betty said. "Okay. So let me guess. Her father married her mother for her money."

Huh. He had never thought of that. "No, no," he said, feeling he should give his prospective father-in-law the benefit of the doubt. He glanced over at her. "Now this is between you and me, right?"

"Sure," she said.

"Well," he said, eyes back on the road, "Lexy's grandfather, Granddad, had a drinking problem, and he sort of let the whole farm go to hell and then, when Lexy's father married Mrs. Waring, she rebuilt the place and got it running again. She still runs it."

"So what happened to the grandfather?"

"Oh, he stayed around. He was a great guy, don't get me wrong. And he didn't drink all the time. And he loved the farm, he had grown up on it—he just couldn't run it. And he was absolutely crazy about Lexy—and she was about him, particularly since she was so much younger than the rest of the kids and didn't really have anyone to play with there. And so, since the Warings lived in Washington most of the time, Granddad was more of a father to her in ways than her own was. At least, he was the one who spent the most time with her."

"Her parents left her with an alcoholic?" Betty said, incredulous.

"Well," Gordon said, "he wasn't an alcoholic exactly. He just sort of —you know, at night sometimes, or maybe he might go on a quiet bender for a day or two. Maybe on holidays too. Nothing spectacular."

"I repeat," Betty said, "her parents left her with an alcoholic?"

"Oh, no, Mrs. Waring was there—Mrs. Waring, Sr., Gran. And Granddad didn't even live in the house anyway, so it wasn't as if he sat there drinking in front of Alexandra."

"What do you mean he didn't live in the house?"

"He lived in a nice little cabin by the barn. Near the house."

"What?" Betty cried.

Gordon laughed. "I guess it does sound a little strange. It didn't at the time, though. Granddad and his wife loved each other—they just couldn't live together. Gran was very much the God-fearing disciplinarian type, so they were always arguing with each other, and she was always sniping at him about something. But in their own way they were inseparable, you know what I mean?"

Betty shook her head. "No," she said, "I don't. I'm afraid my grandparents not only lived in the same house together but slept together in the tiniest bed you ever saw. My parents are the same way."

"Well, whatever," Gordon said, pausing to wonder why he was trying to explain all this to Betty, why it bothered him that she had never seemed very high on Alexandra. "Anyway, Alexandra loved them very, very much. So when they died she had a very hard time getting over it."

"They died?" Betty said. She frowned, leaning closer. "What happened?"

Gordon sighed, lofting one eyebrow. "Gran was driving—not him— and some drunk kid hit them. Can you believe it?" He sighed. "He shot right across the highway and hit them head on."

"Oh, no," Betty said.

"Yeah," Gordon said, nodding.

Betty thought about this for a second and then said, "How old was she?"

"Alexandra?" Gordon said, glancing over.

She nodded.

"Fifteen."

"Oh, no," Betty said again, looking away.

After several minutes she turned back toward him. "I do like her, you know."

"You said that."

"Yeah, well, I do," Betty said. She paused and then said, "Will you guys get married on the farm? Could I come if you did? I always wanted to see where Auntie Em lived—see if Kansas is in black and white."

Gordon smiled, glancing over. "We're thinking maybe New York, but either way—of course you'll be invited."

Betty nodded, looking away again. Then she turned back again. "Will Christopher come?"

Oh, great, just what he needed to get depressed—to think about Christopher. "Yeah, sure," he said, although he doubted it, certainly after what had happened this week on his trip to Paris.

It had started out well enough. His flight had been on time, a car was waiting there at the airport and they drove to the Place Vendôme, where he checked into the Ritz. While the driver rewrapped Christopher's present for him in the trunk of the car (customs had really done a number on it), Gordon showered and changed, trying to dispel any anger (or at least hide it) that he felt toward Julie, since Christopher was the kind of kid who picked up vibes like that out of the air. And, after all, it *was* with Julie that Christopher lived, and it *was* that old man, Ruvais, that Christopher saw every day, and so if Christopher loved them, then . . . So as they drove over, along the magnificent Avenue Foch, along the rolling lawns and lines of trees and fairy-tale urban mansions stretching west from the Arc de Triomphe, Gordon tried to view the past through Julie's eyes, a tactic which had proved helpful in changing his attitude on previous visits.

I am pretty and talented and have a beautiful son. I am married to a man I do not love. I do not like sex. I am bored. I want to go back to work but the husband I do not love does not want me to. I meet Émile Ruvais, the director, the national treasure of France. He is class and he is genius and he is in love with me. He is much older, affectionate and not as sexually demanding as my husband. Émile says he cannot live without me. He says three wives have made him wise about marriage. He says I will be his last wife, that he can guarantee custody of my son, that he does not want more children, that I will be free to work as much as I please. He will put this all in a premarital agreement. All I have to do is write Gordon a note, open this door, carry my son out to that car and get in, and I will be free of Hollywood, free of him I do not love, and free of this house I hate.

A house in Paris, a château in Burgundy, a flat in London, an apartment in New York. Film work in Émile's movies. Everything I want.

"Papa! Papa!" Christopher had cried, coming down the steps of the house and nearly falling.

Gordon swept him up into his arms, hugging him for dear life. "What's this Papa stuff?" he growled, kissing his son's head.

"Daddy," Christopher sighed, clinging.

Gordon smiled, his throat hurting not a little. And then he held Christopher out, his feet dangling three feet off the ground. "Look at the size of this guy, will you?" he said. He was growing quickly, this son of his. And he was blond, this child of his and Julie's, with Gordon's brown eyes, but otherwise showing Julie all over—the mouth, the narrow face, the high cheekbones. And Christopher would not be very big, taking after Julie's side too. But he was a great kid, his son, a smart, lively, loving little kid, even if Julie was trying to make a sissy out of him. God, what was this outfit? Dress gray shorts and jacket and cap? What was he supposed to be, Little Lord Fauntleroy?

"Qu'est-ce qui'il y a dans la boîte?" Christopher said, pointing to the birthday present that Gordon's driver was taking out of the car.

Didn't Julie even have him speak in English anymore? "English, please, slugger," Gordon said, setting him back down on the ground.

"What's in the box?" Christopher said, pulling him over to it.

"Bon jour, Monsieur Strenn," the butler said to Gordon, coming down the steps in his uniform.

"Hi," Gordon said, offering a small hint that he didn't feel like switching over to French. Christopher was tugging on his hand with one hand and clutching the ribbon around the box with the other. "Just a second, slugger," he whispered.

"Madame est sortie," the butler said.

"Where'd she go?" Gordon asked him.

The butler smiled, bowing slightly. "Madame has gone out for the afternoon and wishes that you use her home in her absence."

"Can I open this now?" Christopher said, scrunching one eye up as he looked up at Gordon, as if this effort might somehow get a yes out of him.

"Madame thought perhaps the garden," the butler said. "Madame thought since it was such a lovely day."

"Yeah, madame," Gordon muttered, stooping to pick up Christopher's present.

"The footman will—" the butler started to say.

"Daddy's going to carry it," Christopher told him.

"Okay, Christopher," Gordon said, hefting the box, "lead the way to Madame's garden."

And so Gordon and Christopher went out into the garden and opened his present and spent all afternoon building things with his building blocks. Julie arrived home (looking wonderful, of course—but at least she was getting *older,* which he knew killed her a little every day, if she was still the Julie he knew), and she and Gordon even managed a laugh or two before he left. But then that night, after Christopher had gone to bed, Julie called Gordon at the hotel to discuss Christopher's plans for the summer. The problem, she explained, was that she and Émile were going to Yugoslavia to shoot his new movie, and so, unless Gordon wanted to take Christopher full time in London for July, the Ruvaises would be taking him with them. Gordon asked how was he supposed to take care of Christopher when he had an entire production to baby-sit, and pointed out that it was damn strange that all of a sudden Ruvais had to shoot in Yugoslavia in July when he *knew* Gordon had been planning to spend every weekend with Christopher in Paris.

"Of course I'd like Christopher with me in July," Julie said, "but I'm offering you the chance to have him with you. Don't you understand? You can have your son all month and then see him every weekend in Paris in August. I'll send the nanny and—"

"He's not going to want to be away from you," Gordon said quickly. "And I can't take care of him while I'm working."

"I'll send Mrs. Twickem, his nanny," Julie said.

"I can't have him around when I'm working," Gordon insisted.

"Why not? I do," Julie said. "I'm dying to take him to Yugoslavia with us."

"What do you mean working?" Gordon said. "You're not even in the stupid movie."

"It's not stupid, I am in it and besides, Gordon," she said, her voice growing louder, "Émile is my husband and he likes for me to be with him when he works on location."

"You never went with me anywhere," Gordon said.

"You never went anywhere after you married me," she snapped. "If you had, we'd probably still be married. So just grow up, Gordon, and at least pretend you'd like to spend some time with your son."

"What?" Gordon yelled, about to throw the phone out the window. "I *do* want to spend time with him—I want him with me."

"Well then, take him! You always say you want him and then you never do. For crying out loud, Gordon, with all your girlfriends in the last four years, you'd think you could have found one by now that even likes children."

"Alexandra loves children," Gordon said.

"Oh, Alexandra," Julie groaned. "Is she back again?"

"Yes, she is, for your information," he said. "Permanently, if you must know."

Julie's voice turned as cold as ice. "Oh, don't you start in on me about Alexandra, Gordon Strenn. I heard about her almost every goddam day we were married. We *all* know how wonderful your Alexandra is. We *all* goddam well know how great she is in bed—don't we? Don't we, Gordon? You sure as hell threw it in my face often enough!"

"Yeah, and it sure didn't help, did it?" Gordon said.

There was a long silence.

And then Julie hissed, "You listen to me, Gordon Strenn. I am sick and tired of your complaining and your tantrums about Christopher and about Émile and about me and about our life as a family when you don't make the slightest effort to help raise our son."

"That's not true—"

"It *is* true," Julie screamed. "And as long as you're screwing Alexandra, you're *never* going to participate in his life because she won't have anything to do with him."

"That's not true!"

"It *is* true! You don't love Christopher and you never loved me—"

"Julie, stop it!"

She was sobbing now. "You don't love anyone—you don't even know what it is! All you know how to do is fuck—you never knew how to love anyone—you never did—your goddam mother saw to that, didn't she!"

"I've got a token for the tunnel," Betty said.

"What?" Gordon said, startled.

Betty was holding out a large metal coin. A token. "For the tunnel. Here."

"Oh," he said, taking it from her, "thanks." He downshifted into third, changing lanes as they approached the toll for the Midtown Tunnel.

"Something I said?" Betty asked him.

"I'm sorry, what?" he said, glancing over at her.

"Ground control calling Gordon," she said, holding a fist to her mouth like a microphone, "come in, please." She leaned closer. "You okay?"

"Yeah, I'm fine," he said, downshifting to second.

"Hey, Betty," he said a few moments later, as they waited in line for the toll, "how are you about kids?"

"Adore them," she said.

"You do?" he said, taking off his sunglasses. "An aspiring rich and famous actress like you?"

Betty looked around to see if anyone was eavesdropping and then she leaned forward. "Don't tell anybody," she whispered as Gordon inched the car ahead, "but children are right up there over being rich and famous."

"Really?" he said, looking at her.

She nodded, smiling.

"I didn't know that," Gordon said, turning back to the road.

Huh. Maybe there was a way to bring Christopher to London after all.

28

The Unveiling
Part IV: Langley

Until Jessica came into the studio, Langley couldn't believe that she was responsible for putting Belinda in such a euphoric mood. He hadn't seen Belinda this happy in a long, long time. From the time they had taken their seats in the studio audience, Belinda hadn't stopped talking about how marvelous Jessica was, how Jessica absolutely had to come out for dinner this summer, and all about how Jessica's makeup and hair were done, and how Belinda had picked out Jessica's jewelry for the show. But then, when Jessica came into the studio, Langley realized that this Jessica—the good sport who had been nice to his wife (god, he had died a thousand deaths when Belinda insisted on meeting her)—was a Jessica he was not familiar with. And then he thought what an idiot he was, because of course this was the Jessica Wright that people loved, the Jessica Wright that had made Jessica such a success.

When Jessica made her entrance the audience—unprompted—started to clap and then were up on their feet, clapping and cheering. (Langley and Belinda too; the moment was like that. The moment Jessica appeared there was an inexplicable surge of energy in the studio, as if she were their victorious candidate coming in to make her acceptance speech.)

"Hi, everybody, hi!" she called, waving at everybody, hopping onto the set. (Even her guests were standing, clapping.) "Thank you, thank you," Jessica said, smiling, radiant. Then she went quickly down the line of guests, shaking their hands—while everyone continued to clap —and then she turned around, still smiling, shaking her head, clearly elated. "Oh, gosh—come on, you guys, we've got a show to do—thank you, thank you. Oh, no—look," she said, looking across the studio.

Everybody in the DBS newsroom and conference room was waving.

"Hi, you guys," Jessica called, waving back. "Remember, everybody," she said, turning back to the audience and pointing to the newsroom, "Alexandra Eyes and the Dancing DBS Newsettes over there are on just before us at nine—Channel 8 here in New York, WST." (People were taking their seats now.) "This show today," Jessica continued, "as I think you know, will be taped and broadcast tonight at ten. But we do tape it as if it is a live show—meaning that these cameras roll for one hour, no more, no less."

And then Jessica walked out to the edge of the stage and, walking back and forth across it, started explaining various things about the show. (It took a while before Langley caught on that she was not so much warming them up for the show as she was gradually calming them down, trying to draw them into a mood far different from the jubilation of moments before.)

She reminded them that the topic of discussion today was wonderful moments in sexual intimacy (some guy said, "Yeah!" and Jessica smiled, lowered her voice to its sexiest and breathed, "Exactly," making everyone laugh and prompting two catcalls to be made—one by someone in the audience and one by a member of the crew), explained the format of the show and then briefly ran through some of the technical stuff that would be going on in the studio. They were told they should ignore Lilly, the floor manager, who would be running around giving Jessica signals pertaining to cameras and time; and they should ignore Mel, the man with cue cards, who would no doubt be jumping up and down because *she* was going to do her best to ignore him. ("I mean really, look at this," Jessica said, snatching a card out of his hand and holding it up:

HI, EVERYBODY, I'M JESSICA WRIGHT
AND THIS IS THE JESSICA WRIGHT SHOW

"As you can see," Jessica said, "everybody around here's real relaxed about me going national. Notice the generous allotment of ad lib." While everybody laughed, she looked at Mel, putting one hand on her hip. "So what do you think I'm going to say? 'Hi ya, I'ma Missa Pookie Pie-ya'?")

She told them to try and ignore the cameras, particularly the one zooming around on the crane ("Hi ya, Zeph," she called, waving. Zeph, perched on high, waved back); and they could, if they wanted, look at any of the monitors to see what was going out over the air. ("But please, remember that only one of us around here is allowed to be narcissistically self-involved with how she looks over the air and if you don't know who that is, ask my producer, Denny—Denny, say hello to everybody—" "Hello," Denny said, waving from near the studio door.) Jessica asked, however, that they *not* ignore the assistant producers, who would come out into the audience during commercial breaks to hear what audience members would like to say on the air. ("They'll want to know the general thrust of your question or comments," she explained, "just to make sure you're in step with the show, that's all.")

And then, finally, she reminded them that there were no cues for laughter or applause or anything, so they should simply be themselves. "Which means," she added, stepping down off the stage and walking up one of the aisles into the audience, "that you should give our guests the same consideration that you would give your best friend. The kind of stuff we're talking about today is the kind of stuff your best friend might tell you at two in the morning, after a whole lot of partying. It's special, it's personal, and it's being shared with us today because— well, just for once, we thought we should dwell on one of the positive aspects of life, of the gifts connected with sex. Yeah . . . The gifts of sex. Remember? Like that one wonderful time you had that has kept you going back for more ever since—even though you've never been able to quite reproduce that wonderful one time? Find that magic combination again?"

Then Jessica took her seat on the set and introduced her four guests to the audience, explaining that when those cameras rolled she wanted the audience and guests to feel as though they were on the same side —that a kind of intimacy was occurring here, in the studio, between them, as they shared their life experiences with one another. She wanted them to forget about the cameras and to trust her to take care of establishing a relationship between all of them and the viewers who were locked outside, who were sitting at home and could only look in at them, through the window, so to speak.

The guests then talked a little about themselves to the audience: Karen, a sixty-three-year-old wife, mother and grandmother; Ted, a forty-two-year-old husband and father; Cindy, a twenty-four-year-old wife of four years; and Hart, a thirty-year-old newlywed. Jessica started asking some questions of her guests, and of her audience, about sex. At first everything was pretty stilted, but after a while, aware that the cameras were not on yet, everybody loosened up a little and people started laughing a little, fooling around, and Jessica then, suddenly, it seemed, was having problems trying to keep her guests from telling their "best moment of sexual intimacy" before the show started.

By the time the actual taping began (right on time, to the second, Langley noticed, as if indeed it were live), Jessica had succeeded—they all did feel like they were on the same side, audience and guests and Jessica, and like whoever might be watching through the camera was definitely an outsider. Langley thought it was like playing poker all night and then having someone come in to watch for a while, someone you had to trust wouldn't disturb things so you could get on with the game.

"Hello, everybody," Jessica said into the camera after her real cue, standing with a wireless microphone, "I'm Jessica Wright and"—she paused, smiling, clearly delighted by it all—"and hello, America," she said, very friendly. "This is *so* neat, because, as most of you know, this is the first time our show has been seen nationally. So one day we're in Tucson—hi, everybody!" she said, waving into the camera. "So one day we're in Tucson, and the next we're in New York City, appearing over the DBS television network. And do I love it," she said, laughing, stepping back.

"Can we get a camera down here?" Jessica then said, suddenly sweeping down off the stage and into the audience. This was a total surprise to everyone. "Some of my old friends, fans from out West, flew all the way here to be with us today," Jessica said. She asked them to stand up and quickly (without anything about it on the cue cards), pointed out who was who: "Mr. Roger Hacksdergen, from Portland, Oregon; Mrs. Judy Filanderbin, from Truth or Consequences, New Mexico, Ms. Ellen Sinclair from San Francisco, California; Mr. Rudy McQuire from Dallas, Texas; Mr. Bill Mecujah from San Diego, California; and Mrs. Helen Potter of Lawton, Oklahoma. And the shy woman sitting here is Mrs. Belinda Peterson, part of the time from Aspen, Colorado. And while we're at it I'd like everybody to meet Mr. Langley Peterson, the president of the DBS television network. He's my boss, guys, so everybody please say hello to him. Won't you take a bow, Langley?"

Langley, stunned, stood up slightly and nodded, as everybody in the audience, laughing, said hello.

("Smile," Belinda whispered.)

Langley smiled and quickly sat down.

"Okay, everybody," Jessica said, whirling around (her dress flying up after her) and going back up on the stage, "for those of you watching at home, we've been talking about the most exquisite moments of sexual intimacy that we've ever had." (Jessica just talked away, seemingly oblivious to staging, though after a while Langley realized she was indeed very aware of the camera placement since, with all her waltzing around, she always stopped directly in position for one of them.) "Lucky people," she murmured most provocatively, standing onstage, smiling into a camera, "you get to drop in just when we're getting to the good part." And then her voice returned to normal.

"For those of you who don't know much about television, one of the best ways to generate ratings is to promise to talk about sex. But our idea tonight was not so much to titillate you as it was to try and give you something. I don't know quite how to say it, but I'll try."

She paused for a long moment. And then, "I'd like every person in this room, and every person watching at home, to feel a little bit better and a little happier about life in general after watching this show. I'd like couples out there who haven't made love to each other in a long time—for whatever reason—to at least look at each other a little more kindly, remembering the good days that first brought you together. I'd like couples to make love to each other—*after* the show, please—this is not Johnny Carson—" (Laughter.) "I'd like people who are temporarily alone to remember that they *are* temporarily alone—and that perhaps this show might inspire you to take some action on behalf of yourself. To maybe make that phone call, write that letter, sign up for the dating service, go to the church mixer—whatever—or maybe to just recognize the fact that, as human beings, companionship is a basic necessity, and that sexuality is part of the package we're given at birth. We can't just wish it away—just as we are not meant to throw it away.

"I don't know," she said then, sighing slightly, moving across the stage to stand at one corner of it, "I'd just like for all of us to pretend tonight that we all belong in the same universe, and that there are some really wonderful things about being a part of it, about being human, about falling in love, and about how we physically express it to one another." She smiled, into the camera, blinking twice. "We'll be back," she whispered, and the monitor faded to black and then faded up to a soap commercial. Jessica lowered the microphone and went to sit with her guests. A hushed, congregational feeling had settled over the studio.

"She's wonderful, Langley," Belinda whispered, watching as an audio assistant clipped a microphone on Jessica.

Langley nodded, looking up at their national commercials running over the monitor: dishwashing liquid; a Japanese car built in America; disposable diapers ("Thirty seconds, Jessica," Lilly said); and the monitor went blank for the thirty seconds where the DBS affiliates would insert the local ads they had sold themselves in their markets.

The taping resumed, and the guests started to tell their simple, brief stories of their most exquisite sexual moments—each of which, Langley noticed, was linked with being in love with the partner. (He was relieved, thinking they would at least have some kind of leg to stand on when Cordelia saw this—though this would not help them at all if Jessica later did what she said she would do: do this exact same show except with homosexuals.)

Belinda, sitting beside him, kept sighing, quietly. But they were not unhappy sighs. No, she looked captivated, caught up in the romance of it.

He couldn't believe it when Adele announced this afternoon that Belinda's car had just been waved through the West End gate. He had invited her, of course—she was just out in Greenwich—but never dreamed she'd show up. But then, once Belinda had arrived upstairs, telling him she wanted to meet Jessica Wright, the full story came out.

Belinda had a "friend" named Patience "Pooh" Tillington Hubin whom she hated very much. They kept roughly the same rotation schedule—Greenwich, Manhattan, Aspen, Palm Beach, Europe—and Pooh had taken to sabotaging Belinda's dinner parties when she was not invited. (In January, in Aspen, Pooh had hijacked some mega singing star who was supposed to have come to dinner at Belinda's. "It is beeyawn mah comprahenchun hayow *eny*wun kin stayund that beeyutch," Belinda had said over the phone to Langley. [Belinda's accent tended to come out when she was upset.] She was so upset, in fact, she actually asked Langley if there wasn't some way he and Jackson could put Pooh's third husband out of business so as to pull the plug on all that new LBO money that Pooh was using to make her life miserable with.)

In any event, at the club this weekend, apparently Pooh had asked Belinda if she could arrange for her to attend a taping of "The Jessica

Wright Show." Pooh said she had always watched her when in Aspen and in Taos when she visited her mother, thought Jessica was just divine, a real card, and was dying to meet her. And so Belinda had come to West End posthaste to meet Jessica and to try and figure out what the heck Pooh could be up to. (Belinda felt sure that Pooh was anticipating major celebrity and would like nothing more than to be the first to trot Jessica Wright out at a charity function when Belinda and her family owned the damn network that employed her!)

So here they were, Langley and Belinda, unexpectedly spending the day together, sitting side by side, listening to a young woman talk about how her most wonderful sexual experience had been when she and her husband had had intercourse in the laundry room off the kitchen while they were supposed to have been serving dessert to their dinner guests. She was saying how special it had been—a conspiracy, urgent, quick—and how close it had made them feel. And then she described the afterglow, of sitting there, looking at one another across the table as their guests nattered on, having no idea of the wonderfully exciting thing that had just transpired in the other room.

Belinda's hand crept over to Langley's. He held it.

The show went on, and they broke for commercials, but the spell never broke. The newlywed talked of what had been his greatest moment, but how he later lost the girl, but then how he had known there was another one out there for him somewhere, and how he had found her, married her, and that his former greatest moment paled in comparison to the fourth night of his honeymoon with his wife. The married father of three talked about the night he had done what his wife asked him to do—simply hold her, in bed, without any sex—and how, when they practiced this, their sex life reawakened on other nights in ways he had never imagined. And then, finally, the older woman shared the most provocative story of them all (and it was so strange, because she was older and not very good-looking—at least not before she started talking). Her story was about how, after thirty-one years of marriage, she had finally gotten up the courage to ask her husband to do something to her differently, and how that night had ended up being the most sexually thrilling night for them both in all the years of their marriage.

During all this Jessica would periodically slip down to the audience and murmur to someone, "How does hearing this story make you feel?" to which people responded in a variety of ways: special, warm, hopeful, excited. (Yes, excited. Langley had noticed that there was definitely a rising sexual tension in the air. The young man next to him had taken off his blazer and covered his lap with it; everybody looked a little warm in the face; and Belinda was getting caught up in it too, he could tell.)

He tightened his grip on Belinda's hand, half delighted and half terrified that she might get that vacant, half-drowsy, half-seductive look that she seemed to get just before she "went off." *Oh, God,* he thought to himself, *what has happened to us that I think Belinda can only have sex when she's crazy?*

Because that's the way it's been the last couple of years, he answered himself.

When he thought back to the first decade of their marriage, of the fun they had had, it became hard to believe that Belinda was the same woman.

He had first met Belinda at a Darenbrook Communications Christmas party in Richmond. He had been twenty-five and a little drunk. He also had been with the company for less than two months, and so when this beautiful blond girl, who said she was going to VCU, asked him back to her apartment for a nightcap, he said sure, having no idea that Belinda Smith was actually Belinda Darenbrook, Jackson's baby sister. They had had lots more Christmas punch; they had gone to bed; Langley had passed out; and in the morning, when he saw the apartment he was in (it was *some* apartment), he had a feeling that Belinda Smith might not be the struggling young scholarship student, orphaned in Arkansas, that she had said she was. Then Belinda had come bounding into the bedroom and onto the bed, made love to him again, and *then* she had told him who she was.

Six weeks later, shortly after Belinda told him she thought she was pregnant, Jackson (whom he had scarcely met), came into his office, said, "Congratulations, brother," slugged him, helped him up and then took him outside to a waiting car, in which they went downtown so Langley could apply for a marriage license. It was announced that Belinda and Langley had secretly eloped the night of the Christmas party; a wedding was then held, "for the family," in Hilleanderville in

February; and the next thing they knew Langley and Belinda, man and wife, had been sitting there looking at each other in a suite at the Royal Hawaiian in Honolulu, supposedly embarking on their lives together.

That was when Belinda had apologized profusely for all the drama —and for trapping Langley into marriage. That was also when she told him that she wasn't pregnant—and that she never really had been, but that it had been the only way to make her family let her quit school and start her own life. That was also when Langley said it was okay because—if she didn't mind him saying it—when he had told her before that he thought he was sort of in love with her anyway, so he didn't mind marrying her and having her be the mother of his child, he had meant it. "Except," he had added, sitting there on the bed, "I think maybe I really do love you."

Belinda was only nineteen then, so it was hard to know what she really felt for him, but nonetheless Langley had proceeded to fall violently in love with his wife. And there had been a lot to love! Belinda was so full of life, so mischievous, so full of laughter and energy, it was near impossible not to love her. When she came bounding into a room, he felt it—in his heart. And she adored "messing up" Langley, taking his studious and controlled demeanor as a personal challenge to her powers of seduction. (She won, easily, over most anything, even—in those days—work.)

They lived in a house outside Richmond and Langley did very well at Darenbrook Communications, and as it became clearer to Langley that Belinda had somehow really fallen in love with him too ("It's time for us to have children together," she said one night, "because I love you and I think I would like to look at at least six combinations of us"), Langley became less nervous around Jackson and actually became quite friendly with him. (Which was easy, since Jackson and Belinda had been so much alike.)

Belinda had always loved her sister-in-law, Barbara, and so the two couples started seeing a lot of each other, particularly after Jack's kids were born. Langley eventually became Jackson's right hand at Darenbrook Communications as well as his best friend, but in those days, while Langley had worked hard, he had also played hard, though Belinda and Jackson and Barbara were much, much better at everything than he was: tennis, swimming, riding, trapshooting, golf, flying and soaring.

And then Barbara died and everything just seemed to fall apart. Whether it was because both Barbara and Jackson were lost to the Petersons; or whether it was Belinda's increasing despair over her apparent inability to conceive; or whether it was because Langley had to run Darenbrook Communications for the next eighteen months (while Jackson was falling apart in Hilleanderville), so that he spent precious little time with Belinda; or whether it was because Belinda started traveling by herself, then buying houses and co-ops in which to live parts of the year away from him—whatever it was (and maybe it was a combination of all these things), it or they had started the decline in their marriage and had also started the decline in Belinda's mental health.

"Make love to me, darling," Belinda whispered in his ear.

Langley started, looking around them in the studio. The show was over and Lilly was giving the all-clear signal. He turned to look at Belinda, fearing the worst—that she was about to "go off." But no, she did not look that way at all. She looked like his Belinda, *his* Belinda— the one who used to love him. The one he had been so very much in love with.

Belinda smiled, slowly. "There must be somewhere," she whispered.

Could this be real? he wondered. Could his Belinda be back?

"We'll have to hurry if you want to," she whispered, smiling still. "It would be like the old days, remember?"

Of course he remembered. How could anyone forget the days when they were in love?

Her eyes were searching his, anxious, but eager too. Funny—that old spark seemed to be there. Her eyes were twinkling like they used to, too.

"I love you," she whispered, but looking down then, looking acutely embarrassed.

Oh, God, he had hurt her feelings. She thought he didn't want her.

"Come on," Langley said, taking her hand and standing up. "This way." He led her out of the studio, down the corridor and the halls, nodding at people but making sure it was understood that he did not wish to stop and talk. He took Belinda upstairs, to the third floor, and led over the carpeted hallway to his office. He sent Belinda into his office, told Adele that he was not to be disturbed for any reason, went into his office, closed and locked the door, turned off the light, and then went over to the connecting door to Jackson's office and locked that too.

Belinda was sitting on the couch. "The curtains?" she said, smiling, tossing her purse on the coffee table.

"Can't see in with this glass," he murmured, taking off his jacket. He walked over to the couch, throwing the jacket over a chair. He sat down, taking Belinda's hand. "Honey, are you sure?"

She smiled. "You're not scared of me, are you?"

"Never," he said.

"Then why don't you touch me?" she asked him.

He felt shy, and he didn't know why. Maybe it was because it had been so long since he felt as though he were really talking to *Belinda,* face to face. He put his arms around her and pulled her close. Then he really hugged her, tight. "I love you," he whispered.

"Then show me, tough guy," she said, laughing.

Tough guy? She hadn't called him that in years.

He sat back, looking at her again.

"Oh, God, Langley," Belinda sighed, taking his face into her hands, "must the South initiate everything?" And she kissed him, the way she used to kiss him—not frantically, not harshly, but expertly in her quest to "mess him up." They could be right back in his old office in Richmond right now.

"Adele's right outside," he whispered.

"Goody," she whispered back, sliding her hand down between his legs and stroking him. "As I recall, her proximity used to enhance the experience. Remember?"

"Uh-huh," he murmured, kissing her neck.

"Oh, my, Mr. Peterson," she whispered, feeling him, "if Adele could see this, you'd give her heart failure."

"Uh-huh," he said into the base of her neck, thinking this felt so good he could die.

Belinda was undoing his belt now. As he felt her mouth on his ear, she unzipped his pants and then he could feel her hand sliding down to touch him. She stopped licking his ear to murmur, "Gorgeous, darling," and then she used both her hands to tug his pants and shorts down further. Then she took a gentle, firm hold on him and began stroking him. In a minute she sat back to look at him, her hand still stroking. "Not with your glasses," she whispered, laughing, kissing him on the nose.

He tossed them and kissed her, running his hands over her dress, over her breasts, running his hands down her, pulling up her dress, and then sliding his hand up over her stockings, up between her legs, and then stroking her, massaging her as best he could. In a minute she broke away and stood up, hiking her dress to get rid of her stockings and panties. "There," she whispered, dropping down again, kissing him. "There, honey," she murmured, lowering her head to kiss his neck. Her mouth continued down, down over his chest, and she gave his tie a playful tug as she continued on down, down, down, over his stomach, and then, holding him gently in her hand, she went down, sinking her mouth over him.

He inhaled, slowly, bringing his hands to the side of her head, trying to restrain himself from pushing down on it.

Jesus but this was good.

"Oh, honey," he sighed, feeling her work him, perfectly, down and then up, down and then up, feeling her mouth, sinking and rising, sinking and rising, her hand moving in tandem, her tongue swirling at play, down and then up, down and then up, the warmth growing hot, the sounds getting messy; down and then up, down and then up—

He gently tried to bring her head up. She wanted to do a little more, and he let her, closing his eyes, thinking there was no other feeling like this.

And then he felt her kissing him and he smiled, opening his eyes and bringing his face up to hers, kissing her lips, kissing all around her mouth, and then really kissing her, shifting around to ease Belinda back down on the couch. He broke their kiss, giving her one last quick one, and then quickly stood, just long enough to pull his pants down— making her smile, reaching out to touch him—and then he crawled down on top of her, both of them laughing, softly, but anxious too, as he tried to maneuver with the back of the couch, his tie and shirttails and her dress everywhere, but then she drew her outside leg up and out, trying to give him room, and then he managed to get himself up against her and then—in a moment—he was inside of Belinda and he was moving.

The couch was not the greatest, but she was.

It was nothing really, nothing but making love to his wife on the couch in his office while Adele typed letters outside and West End produced television shows and Belinda kept saying, in his ear, over and over, "I love you, I love you, I love you," and he thought about moving to the floor so he could do this a little better, but they squirmed a little so that Belinda was a little bit on her side, so then he could move into her better, around her and into her, around her and into her, around her and into her, the way she used to love it and, apparently, still did, because she stopped saying, "I love you," because she was coming, he knew she was, because in the old days she had always talked her head off until she came, at which time she became deadly silent, frozen, when inside her body, she used to say, everything would be going absolutely crazy, so violently, wonderfully berserk she couldn't speak. And she could not speak now, he knew, his beautiful, beautiful girl, because she was coming, he knew she was, and she was not crazy, she was just his Belinda, his-his-his-his—

Belinda he was coming inside of right now—

Just-right-in-there-oh-God-yeah. Jesus.

"Yeah," he sighed, collapsing, then swallowing, catching his breath. "Oh, Belinda," he said into the side of her neck. "Oh, baby, I love you. I love you," he said. "I always have, I always will."

"Shhh," she said, stroking his hair. "Shhh."

They lay there for a minute, and Langley became more aware of the noise on the floor. People were around. In droves they were around and getting louder by the minute. "I bet they're all coming up into the cafeteria," he whispered.

"We better get up," she said.

He pulled out of her and slid, slowly, to the floor, laughing. He got up, pulled his pants up and walked over to his jacket, pulled out his handkerchief, came back to the couch and offered it to her, which she accepted. They helped each other pull their clothes together, smooth their hair, get Langley's glasses back on, and then they sat for a moment more on the couch, holding each other. Langley kissed her once more, for a long time, thinking that he might never have loved her more.

Langley turned the lights on, while Belinda, giggling, sprayed a little cologne around. Then he called Adele on the intercom and asked her if she could go downstairs and get a copy of the story line up for "DBS News America Tonight," waited a minute, and then peeked outside to make sure she was gone. She was. So Langley and Belinda sneaked out and across the hall, where he dropped her off at the ladies' room and he went on to the men's.

He washed his hands and face, retucked his shirt in, combed his hair and retied his tie. He smiled at himself in the mirror, thinking how very, very glad he was that he hadn't cheated on Belinda. And how very, very happy it made him to think that maybe things were heading back on track now. He thought about going out to Greenwich with her tonight and how maybe they might make love by the pool. He thought maybe they should plan a trip—Europe, Paris maybe—or maybe they could go to London together when . . .

He smiled at himself in the mirror again. There were so many things they could do.

He walked out of the men's room, his step as strong and as jaunty as he felt. (God, was this the greatest feeling, making love to his wife like this, or what? Just making love to the woman he loved, having fun, like kids, just going ahead and doing it wherever they felt like because it was so good?) He knocked on the ladies' room door.

"Just a minute," she called.

He smiled, pushing in the door. "Hi," he whispered. "Can I come in?" He slipped inside and walked through the little dressing area. Belinda was standing at one of the sinks, holding a paper cup in one hand and holding out the other to him in a "stop" motion. She ducked her head slightly, swallowing, and then lowered her hand.

"I didn't want you to make me laugh," she said. "I was just taking some aspirin."

"Headache?" he said, coming over to stand behind her, sliding his arms around her waist and nuzzling her neck.

"A little one," she said, closing her purse. She turned around and kissed him on the mouth. "Do you love me, Langley?" she whispered.

"More than anything," he said, kissing her again and then releasing her. "Come on." He took her hand, leading her to the door. "I want to take you on a tour of this place." He held the door open for her. "I want everyone to see what a beautiful wife I have. I want everyone to see how lucky I am."

And so Langley and Belinda Peterson, in love, went for a tour.

29

The Unveiling
Part V: Cassy

"Why, I'd be delighted to give Mr. Brobbent a tour," Cassy said to Rookie Haskell, turning then to smile at their guest.

Mr. Rupert Brobbent, founder and president of KlapTrap Insecticides, Elrama, Pennsylvania, was just standing there, staring at her, entranced.

Oh, good, Cassy thought, *we'll get this guy to sign for life.*

"Wonderful, wonderful," Rookie said, slapping Mr. Brobbent on the back. "I see you'll be in excellent hands. No one knows more about 'DBS News America Tonight' than Cassy here, and Cassy also happens to be quite an outdoor chef herself."

Cassy looked at Rookie.

"Cooks in the backyard all summer long," Rookie said, smiling at her. "So nobody knows better than Cassy that what KlapTrap says is true."

Mr. Brobbent looked into Cassy's eyes, eyebrows rising. "Only time flies in our backyard?"

"Yes, right," Cassy said, nodding and smiling.

Mr. Brobbent was their very recent and very lucrative sponsor for the weather segment for the summer quarter, and so Cassy was quite happy to tell him most anything he wished to hear. Certainly, she would be happy to give him a tour of DBS News—particularly since she had a few other people waiting for the same thing: the station owner of their potential Little Rock affiliate, Ketton Harper; the daughter of some friends of Norbert and Noreen Darenbrook's,

Amelia Randsworth, who thought maybe she might like to be an anchorwoman (but who Kyle said was the type best beheaded to stave off revolt by the masses); and a very distinguished gentleman, about sixty or so, with immaculate silver-gray hair, dressed in a gray pinstripe suit, who arrived in the newsroom on the arm of Jackson's assistant, Claire, and was introduced simply as Greg, a friend of the family's who wished to sit quietly and watch, which he had.

Meanwhile, upstairs, the studio audience for "The Jessica Wright Show" was back in the cafeteria. The buses had been ready to take them away, but only nine people wanted to leave and one hundred and ninety-one wanted to stay and talk to Jessica. So nine people were sent back to the midtown drop-off point in radio cabs and one hundred ninety-one—plus the four guests from the show—were having wine with Jessica and, if the latest rumor was correct, Jackson had offered to roll TV sets in and call out for pizza and salad if they cared to stay and watch "DBS News America Tonight."

Nothing was going quite the way Cassy had expected today. She had thought Jessica would be fine, seeing that she had already done seven shows, but Jessica had arrived late and looking like a wreck. But then, when Cassy thought they might have to run one of the earlier tapes because Jessica was so obviously under the weather, Jessica turned around and produced not only one of her best shows but one of the most extraordinary pieces of television Cassy had seen in quite some time. (She had sat there, dumbfounded, in the control room. The topic of sex aside, Cassy decided that Jessica had missed her calling—there was an inexplicable streak of evangelical grace in this young woman.)

Instead of tired and nervous, Alexandra was the calmest and happiest Cassy had seen her in weeks. And she looked like a million—healthy, radiant—and she said she had slept like a baby last night. ("My body doesn't understand endless management and planning meetings," she laughed, "but it does understand putting on a newscast.")

Kyle, on the other hand, was a nervous wreck, his efficiency in hand but his usual calm nowhere to be found. And Langley, who Cassy thought would be fretting about everything, was spending the day drifting around West End with his wife. And then Jackson, who had

always been so eager to feel included in the process, had come nowhere near Alexandra, the newsroom or anyone connected with DBS
News today. And if Cassy hadn't gone upstairs this afternoon to see
how the luncheon was going, she wouldn't have seen him at all.

And when she had seen Jackson, it was so strange because he barely
spoke to her—he didn't even *look* at her, really—choosing instead to
focus his attention on Denny. But Cassy did not want to try and guess
why this was so. Because not only did she not have the time to think
about Jackson today, but it scared her to because it reminded her of
how much she had been thinking about him all weekend. And about
how exhausted she had been Friday night, but how she had not been
able to sleep because her heart had started to pound every time she
thought back over the events of the day—about how Jackson had held
her in his office and the feelings it had triggered inside, and about how
those feelings had increased sitting outside in the square.

It was loneliness that was triggering these thoughts, these feelings,
she felt sure. It was her defense against being too acutely aware of how
alone she was in this apartment, sleeping in this big bed, so alone that
she could be horribly ill and have no one to call out to. (Sleeping alone
and dying in her sleep were somehow, irrevocably, connected in her
mind of late.)

But was it loneliness that had brought on this surge of sexual desire?
A kind of deep-seated ache that she had not felt in years?

For *Jackson?*

Granted, he did have a wonderful body, just the kind Cassy had
always been attracted to. But it was a body that also belonged to the
type of man that drove her crazy—a man like her ex-husband-to-be,
except this one didn't even have to drink to cause trouble.

And the real killer—the thought that Cassy wished she could avoid
acknowledging but couldn't because it was true—was that her sexual
feelings were rarely, if ever, disconnected from her emotions. And
there was no denying it, standing there in Jackson's office, looking up
at him after he released her, she had looked into his eyes and thought,
My God, he's in love with me, and then there *had* been a decided
change of emotion on her part. She had felt close to him; she had felt
safe with him; she had felt inexplicably happy. He had not been a jerk;
he had not been a loudmouth. He had been an earnest, deeply caring,

deeply troubled, lonely person who was suddenly and inexplicably the most wildly attractive man she had ever met in her life.

Lying there, stretched across her bed Friday night, looking out at the night sky over the Hudson, Cassy had wondered if maybe she was losing her mind.

Jackson?

"What the hell is Jackson Darenbrook doing in my head?" she had cried to the bedroom then, flipping over and trying to hide underneath the pillows.

But Jackson Darenbrook had remained a guest in her head for the rest of the weekend anyway. In the rest of her body, too.

Cassy took Mr. Brobbent and the others through the newsroom to the conference room, closed the glass door against the noise and began a general overview of what went into their newscast. She pointed to the newsroom, explaining that news arrived at DBS in five basic ways: from their affiliate newsrooms, whose reporters and facilities operated as bureaus for DBS; from the wire services; from free-lance reporters and crews they hired as stringers; from foreign networks and news services they contracted with on special events, such as the coverage on President Reagan and the Moscow summit that they would be seeing tonight; and from (she laughed) monitoring CNN, CBS, NBC and ABC.

She also explained that it was there, in the newsroom, that all facts concerning incoming news stories were checked and rechecked by multiple sources, and that their news coverage was quite often enhanced by DBS News's access to various computer databases. For example, on one database they could type in the entries "Reagan," "Human Rights," and "Soviet," and within a minute they could have a list of every article in which those three words had appeared in seventy-five daily newspapers for the past ten years—any one of which they could call up on their computer screen to read.

Here, in the room they were standing in, the editorial staff met several times over the course of the day to discuss the breaking news, the coverage they had on it, and how the story line-up for that night should be revised. It was here that it was decided which story was more important than another, the length of time they would devote to covering it, and which way—out of the options they had—they would cover it (film report, live report from the field, the anchor report, etc.).

Cassy punched a few commands into the computer terminal sitting on the conference table and showed them the current story line-up for that night, pointing out the estimated segment times.

Then they went on to the satellite room where Cassy briefly outlined how the DBS TELENET satellite enabled DBS News to enjoy two lives. First, as a functioning news network, able to receive local news coverage from all over the country, and then able to transmit out all over the country a national newscast. And, secondly, as a clearinghouse of information, story coverage and pictures for their affiliate newsrooms.

Out in the hallway (where Langley and Belinda joined the tour), Cassy explained that every newscast was made up of many different inputs—both visual and audio—that could be used in endless combinations. What they would be seeing, then, were a number of these inputs and, in the control room, how they were put together in combinations and sequences that hopefully most effectively communicated the news.

She took them into editing (explaining that they would still hear the word "film" used all the time, though everything was on videotape), sliding open one of the soundproof glass doors that sealed each editing bay, pointed out some of the equipment used in editing stories, and explained that, once a story was finished, it was put on a video cassette and sent on to engineering.

They went into the graphics lab, to see where artists were working on visual stills by hand, and to see the "magical" paintbox. The head artist, Becky Seidelman, cued up a graphic on the paintbox screen and with the metal stylus—her "paintbrush"—demonstrated how she could dab in colors or paint over with new ones, airbrush images, or do almost any kind of alteration imaginable.

They went into engineering, an enormous place with islands of machinery and six-foot-high metal casings along the walls, holding all kinds of electronic equipment, dials and meters—all of which, Cassy said, were used to monitor the electronic information flowing both into and out of the DBS television facility. "If the newsroom is our conscious brain at DBS News," she said, "then engineering is our nerve center."

There were a number of small chambers, alcoves really, off of engineering, and Cassy stopped at one, showing them a big machine that looked sort of like a soda bottle machine with a glass door running down the side. She opened this door and pointed out how video cassettes had been inserted into it from top to bottom. These were the commercials they were to run tonight, stacked in sequence. The identical machines to the right of the commercial machine, she explained, were for cassettes of news stories, loaded in the same sequence as the rundown sheet.

She also stopped by the character generator, into which subtitles and credits were typed, on a single "page" (superimposed over an interview, for example, to identify the speaker) or on a scroll, to be rolled, such as credits were.

They went into the audio booth (where Belinda Peterson collided with Cassy and then backed away without apology), a glassed-in area that looked onto the main control room. Each of the many sliding levers on the boards they were looking at, Cassy explained, represented a channel input of sound—everything from Alexandra's microphone in the studio to the sound on a commercial—that could be switched in or out, faded in or faded out of the newscast. The audio person sat in here, listening for the director's cues, responsible for every input of sound in the newscast.

They moved on to the control room, where a very long desk ran almost its entire length, in front of which were rows of television monitors stacked to the ceiling. Cassy explained that, for each visual input source they had seen on their tour, there was a monitor in the control room to represent it. For example, she pointed out that each of the SAT monitors (marked SAT 1, SAT 2 . . .) showed the director what satellite signals were coming in that he or she could cut to (and to preview the signal, for example, to make sure the reporter was indeed standing there, ready to do his live report from the field).

Monitors marked CAM referred to cameras in the studio; GRPH stood for graphics; VTR for video sources, and so on. The most important monitor, she said, was the one marked PRGM, which stood for program—which showed what was going out over the air. Belinda

Peterson then knocked into a chair and Langley said something to her. (Belinda was making Cassy very nervous. She was acting very strangely and Cassy knew it wasn't her imagination because everybody else on the tour had half an eye on her too.)

Cassy went on to explain that the director—who sat in the middle of the long desk—was in charge of orchestrating all inputs of the newscast, everything from when to roll the opening sequence and bring up the sound to what the camera angle looked like; to cuing the talent; to cutting from one video source to another (such as camera 2 in the studio to the commercial cued up on VTR 3).

Sitting next to the director was the technical director, who operated the video switcher, a vast array of banks, buses, buttons, knobs and fader bars with which he or she carried out the director's every visual command. As the audio engineer was responsible for all sound, the technical director was responsible for all visuals, including special effects.

The assistant director, also sitting at the long desk, kept track of time and—

At this point the little tour group turned around to look at the Petersons, between whom a furious bout of whispers had broken out. Langley, looking embarrassed, murmured apologies, and then Belinda, looking pale and glassy-eyed, threw her arm out, saying (in a voice far too loud), "We're reeeal sorry. Y'all just go on and we'll be as quiet as mice back here."

Cassy led the group into the studio, where the crews had already pushed back the audience seating for "The Jessica Wright Show" and had closed off Studio B. Jessica's living-room set was dark; but here, on the other side of the studio, the work lights were on for the three connecting sets for DBS News: Alexandra's set, the in-studio correspondents' set, and the weather stand-up set.

Cassy asked them to take special note of the background of Alexandra's set—

"Take note of what?" Belinda Peterson said, too loudly again, making everyone look at her again. "Oh, stop it, Langley!" she said, shaking his hand off her arm. Langley looked as though he wanted to die. "Thank you," Belinda said, turning back to Cassy and plunking one hand on her hip. "Now what were you saying?"

Cassy repeated that she wished them to take special note of Alexandra's set because over the course of the newscast it would appear to change. Their video switcher—which they had seen in the control room—could make the color of the set absorb the image of another video signal, so that they could, for example, make Alexandra and her desk appear to be sitting in front of the newsroom—which was, as they could see, actually way over there.

"I'll do whatever I want!" Belinda said to Langley. "I own the place, don't I?"

Everyone in the studio—Cassy, the tour group, stagehands, technicians—fell silent.

Langley said something to Belinda, trying to pull her to the side. "I'm sorry," he said to Cassy, "she's not feeling very well."

"If I'm sick, then ids—isss because, because . . ." Belinda said, her voice trailing off. Belinda did not look at all well now. She brought her hand up to her face and Langley rushed to her side, and this time she did not object to his holding her.

"Bozzy," Cassy said, waving him over. "Show them the sets and then take them back to the newsroom, okay? I'll see you back there," she added to the group, walking over to Langley and Belinda.

"I'm sorr—" Belinda was mumbling, slumping against Langley. "I don't know whaddatiz."

"Let's take her to one of the dressing rooms," Cassy murmured, taking her other side.

"Id must be da flu," Belinda said, slurring badly.

Kyle appeared out of nowhere. "Cass?"

"Doctor," Cassy whispered to him.

"No," Langley said, leading them along. "It's okay. It's happened before, it'll pass."

"Lang?" Belinda said, her voice sounding weak.

"I'm right here, honey," he whispered. "Just walk with me. We're just going to go somewhere you can lie down for a little while."

"Lang?" she said again, sighing. Her eyes were closed, her head resting against Langley's shoulder and she was—

If Cassy was not mistaken—and she wasn't because she was four inches from Belinda's face—Belinda was *smiling*. If she didn't know better, she would have thought Belinda was drunk. "Is she diabetic?"

she asked Langley as they came through the studio doors into the corridor.

"No, but it's sort of like that," Langley said.

"You better get Jackson," Cassy said to Kyle.

"Yeah," he said, bounding off.

They took Belinda into one of the spare dressing rooms and laid her down on the open-back couch in it. Langley sat on the edge, holding his wife's hand, and by the time Cassy came out of the bathroom with a glass of water for her, Belinda was asleep.

"She'll be okay now," Langley whispered, gently brushing the hair back off Belinda's forehead with his hand.

"I'd feel better if we had a doctor take a look at her," Cassy whispered, putting the water down on the dressing table.

Langley looked up at her. "It's a nervous condition. She has these, uh, periods . . ."

Cassy was about to say, "Like what, schizophrenia?" but thought better of it.

"It's something like manic depression," he continued, looking back down at his wife and taking her hand. She murmured something, moving slightly, and then was still again, breathing peacefully. "But it's not. She's seen a lot of doctors, they've done blood workups and everything, but she's not manic-depressive, they say. It's not like that."

The door opened and Jackson came in. "Is she all right?" he whispered, going to her.

"Yes, she's okay," Langley said.

Jackson went down on his knees next to the couch, by Belinda's head. "Baby B, are you okay?" he whispered.

Belinda murmured something and turned over on her side, away from them, tucking her hands under her head to use as a pillow.

"She'll be fine," Langley said, looking at his watch. "She'll sleep, for about a half hour or so, and then I'll take her home."

Jackson looked up at him, bit his lower lip, patted the side of Langley's knee twice and got up. "Anything I can do?"

"Call outside and tell them to have the car ready," Langley said. "Other than that, no. I'm just going to sit here with her. She'll be fine." He turned to look at Cassy. "You won't need me tonight, will you?"

"Oh, no, of course not," she said, stepping closer and putting a hand on his shoulder. "I just wish I could do something for you. Call a doctor . . ."

"You could just go back to work," he suggested, smiling slightly. "You know—the show must go on and all that."

Cassy looked down at him—at his worried face behind those serious glasses—and, before she thought about it, leaned down and kissed him on the cheek. "If you need anything, call us here. You know to do that, don't you?"

He nodded. "Thanks." He looked to Jackson. "Just leave us, Jack. She'll be fine now."

Jackson nodded and then looked over at Cassy. He gestured to the door; she walked over to it, went outside and he followed. Closing the door behind him, Jackson turned to her. Then he sighed, fell against the wall and stayed there, looking into her eyes. "Well," he finally said in a low voice, averting his eyes then, "now you know one of our many family secrets."

"How long?" she murmured, so that no one passing by could hear.

"Hmmm?" he said, looking back at her.

"How long has she . . . ?"

He bit his lip, looking somewhere past her, thinking. "I don't know —on and off, I guess, about five years or so." He met her eyes. "It could have been earlier. I wouldn't have known—there was a period I wasn't around much."

She didn't say anything.

He sighed abruptly, looking back at the door. He blinked several times in rapid succession, swallowed and then looked at her again. "My sister Cordie says it might have started when my wife died. My wife, Barbara. She and Belinda were real close. And then I wasn't there for a while." He looked away, eyes following an intern going by. "We don't do well with death in our family. None of us." Then he took a breath, looked as though he might say something else—but didn't. He just yanked at his tie, pulling it loose as though it were strangling him.

"Come on," Cassy said, touching his arm. "Why don't you come to the newsroom with me? We'll call for his car from there."

"No," he said, stopping. "If you wouldn't mind—would you call? I think I better stick around here."

"Sure," she said, lowering her arm.

"Thanks," Jackson said.

They stood there, looking at each other.

"Okay," Cassy finally said, touching his arm again for a moment and then walking on.

"Cassy?" he called a second later.

She turned around.

"Later—" He stopped, looking around at all the people coming and going in the hall. He walked over to her. "Later—do you think I could watch the newscast from the control room with you? If I promise—"

"Of course," Cassy said quickly. She smiled. "And I would really like it if you did."

His face brightened and he ran his hand over his jaw once, backing away. "Great," he said. "I'll see you later then."

"Later," Cassy said, smiling still. And then she turned around and walked briskly down the hall, wondering if her face was as red as it felt.

30

DBS Unveiled
Part VI: Alexandra

After she had escorted Jessica to the studio for her show, Alexandra attended the editorial meeting, at which they finalized the story line-up for the newscast. It was a holiday and there was not much hard news, certainly not domestically, but they had expected that and so, as planned, each of the in-house specialty correspondents would get on tonight. When the meeting was over Alexandra went out into the newsroom with Dan, the senior news editor, and Kyle, talked with some of the producers and writers, and then she went over into the corner with her notes, sat down at a computer terminal and worked on the copy she would be reading on the major stories, and read through all the copy filed by other correspondents and writers thus far.

When she was finished she went to the satellite room to see what kind of Memorial Day footage they were getting in from the affiliates to make a closing piece for their "elder statesman" and editor-at-large, Chester Hanacker, to do. And then, at Chester's request, she joined him and Hex and a segment producer in editing to work on the piece, and when they had a good sense of it she went back to the newsroom with Chester to bang out some notes. Then Alexandra passed the notes—and Chester—on to Shelley, one of the writers. Someone handed her a copy of the newscast rundown sheet on her way out, and Alexandra took it with her into her dressing room. Later, as she scooted across the hall to makeup, Kyle intercepted her, giving her a revised rundown sheet and pointing out some changes.

A few minutes before eight Alexandra walked into the studio and took her seat on the set. A script was waiting for her there. On the connecting set, an inverted V-shaped desk for two (which they could use for in-house correspondent reports or as the setting for in-studio interviews), the government and politics correspondent, John Knox Norwood, and the sports editor, Dash Tomlinson, were sitting. On the third connecting set, sitting at a small desk, next to which was the large blank wall of the set, was Gary Plains, the meteorologist. Sitting in chairs just off the sets were Dr. Helen Kai Lu, their health and science editor; Paul Levitz, their business and economics editor; Brooks Bayerson Ames, their razzle-dazzle arts and entertainment correspondent; and, finally, their editor-at-large, Chester. They ran through sound and lighting checks. They ran through the transitions, the openings and closings. Okay. Okay. Okay. Everybody knew where to go and how. Everybody could read the TelePrompTers okay. Everybody could see the program monitors okay. Everything *is* okay, right?

At eight thirty-eight Alexandra took off her microphone, stepped down off the set and walked to the newsroom. She opened the door and stood there, smiling.

If Alexandra Waring was beautiful, then she was never more so than at that moment—when the clocks hit 8:39 P.M. on Monday, May 30, 1988—standing in the doorway in a soft blue-gray dress that matched the color of her eyes. All activity in the newsroom momentarily stopped.

"I think it's going to be wonderful," she said.

And then all newsroom activity resumed and Alexandra walked out, closing the door behind her, going back into the studio to take her place on the set.

"Ten minutes to air," Lilly, the floor manager, said, hearing the cue from the control room through her headset.

The studio work lights went out.

Alexandra sat down at her desk. Her microphone was reattached and a small beige earphone was inserted into her right ear. A glass of water was brought to her, which she took a sip of and then placed on a small shelf down under her desk. Cleo touched her up with some powder and blush, fiddled a little with her hair, and then held a mirror for her as Alexandra applied fresh lipstick. An assistant leaped onto the set, exchanging a page of her script with a new one, which Alexandra scanned before stacking her copy neatly in front of her.

"Dick says no more running around," Lilly told her. "They need another sound level."

" 'We the people of the United States, in order to form a more perfect union,' " Alexandra said, picking up her pen and twiddling it, " 'establish justice, ensure domestic tranquillity, provide for the—' "

"Okay," Lilly said, making a cutting motion under her neck.

"Yes," Alexandra then said, smiling, holding her hand up to her right ear, "I can hear you fine, Kyle. How many times do I have to tell you? It's only when you say things I don't want to hear that the earpiece doesn't work."

"Five minutes to air, five minutes to air," Lilly announced.

Cassy walked out of the darkness, stepped up into the glare of lights on the set and leaned over Alexandra's desk, smiling. "Feel good to be back at work?"

Alexandra's smile was a very happy one. "Sure does."

Cassy nodded, still smiling. "Good luck."

"Thanks," Alexandra said.

Cassy stepped down and disappeared into the darkness. Alexandra lowered her eyes to her copy, quickly flicking through the pages.

Time passed, time signals were given. Kyle flew in, said something to Dash on set 2, and then flew out again.

"Two minutes to air, two minutes to air," Lilly announced, moving over by the middle camera that was facing Alexandra. "Quiet on the set!" And then she added, in a quieter voice, "We're going to open on 2, Alexandra," pointing to the camera beside her.

Alexandra nodded, gathered her copy together, tapped it in line on the desk, and then placed it down flat in front of her. She moved her pen an inch to the side and left it there. Then she took a very slow, deep breath, drawing the air in through her nose, clasped her hands in front of her on the desk, pulled herself up tall in her chair and leaned forward slightly, closing her eyes and slowly letting out the breath. Then her eyes opened.

"One minute to air, one minute!" Lilly said, holding her index finger high in the air.

The studio was dark, the lights on the set brilliant. Alexandra's earrings sparkled, as did her eyes. She unclasped her hands, settling them on the desk on either side of her copy.

"Forty-five seconds," Lilly said. "We open on 2."

Alexandra's eyes glanced at the program monitor—on it was some sort of commercial—and looked back at camera 2, over the lens of which her copy could be seen on the TelePrompTer.

"Thirty seconds," Lilly said.

On set 3, Gary dropped his pointer and it clattered off his desk, off the set and down onto the studio floor. "Shit," he said.

Alexandra did not blink.

"Twenty seconds," Lilly said. She was facing Alexandra, standing by camera 2, pointing at it with her left hand and holding her right arm straight up in the air. "Fifteen seconds—stand by."

Through the headsets of the camera operators they could hear a lot of verbal action going on in the control room. On the monitor there was a station I.D. running for WST, the New York affiliate.

"Ten—nine—eight—" Lilly said.

Alexandra's eyes moved to the monitor and then back to the Tele-PrompTer over camera 2.

"—seven—six—five—four—three," Lilly said.

The studio was silent.

Alexandra's eyes were on camera 2.

On the monitor, unfolding in eerie silence, was the opening. The screen was black and then a blue dot appeared, growing brighter, which then started to move as a line, quickly outlining the continental

United States, Hawaii and Alaska. Seventy-three red dots appeared within them and then suddenly each red dot sent a white line streaking toward New York and when they met there was a flash of white light, clearing to show the full-color DBS NEWS AMERICA TONIGHT lettering and logo, glowing, against a backdrop of little boxes; inside of each a film was running (children playing, construction workers, white-collar commuters, farmers, bingo players, Washington tourists, truckers, and on and on). The glow of the letters grew bright and the screen flashed out in a blaze of blue light, clearing to show WITH ALEXANDRA WARING just under the montage, only for the screen to blaze white again and then fade down to the original map of the United States, outlined in blue on black, red affiliate points twinkling, white lines leading to New York.

Lilly's right hand came down to point at Alexandra just as the red light on top of camera 2 came on.

"Good evening," Alexandra said, eyes sparkling. "This is Memorial Day, May 30, 1988. For the DBS Television News Network in New York City, I'm Alexandra Waring, and this is the news in America tonight."

Outside, under the lamplight, one of the night custodians was wheeling his cleaning cart across the square when he stopped, cocking his head as if he heard something.

Yes, there was something, a roaring sound, and he looked up at Darenbrook I to see a whole bunch of people going crazy up there in the cafeteria, jumping up and down, carrying on like the devil.

"Yeeeeeeeeeeee—" Jessica was calling from on top of one of the cafeteria tables, "haaa!" as the audience from her show danced around, echoing her sentiments.

In Jackson's office, in front of the big TV, Ethel, Randy, Claire, Adele and Chi Chi were throwing popcorn in the air.

In Gordon's office, Gordon was pounding the arms of his chair, yelling, "Yeah!" while Betty and others from the miniseries group were applauding.

Out in the carport, the drivers—huddled around the TV sitting on the roof of Alexandra's limo—cheered.

Out in the guardhouse, grinning at the tiny TV sitting in front of him, the guard nodded, saying, "That's our girl, guys, that's our girl."

In the control room, Cassy was leaning against the back wall, smiling, eyes glistening; Dr. Kessler was standing next to her, looking very proud; and Jackson was sitting in the corner, smiling from ear to ear.

Alexandra was finishing the intro into the lead story. ". . . in a public clash over civil rights, where Mr. Gorbachev complained about President Reagan's—quote—sermonizing. With a special report for DBS News, we go live, now, to Moscow, where Eric Benter of the British International News Service is standing by outside the Kremlin."

"Take satellite 3," the director, Dick Gross, said. "Ready to go to a split screen with camera 2. Make sure Alexandra can hear him."

It went along beautifully. After Benter's report Alexandra was able to look at her monitor and talk with him and ask him some questions. They came back to the studio and Alexandra led over to John Knox Norwood, who "anchored" a six-minute segment of reactions and analyses of the day's events in Moscow with political and academic figures, and then they broke for a commercial.

When they came back Alexandra went into a story about the Memorial Day services in Arlington Cemetery and similar services being held around the country; a cemetery strike in San Francisco disrupting a service; a veterans' protest held at a cemetery outside Chicago; and a smattering of short items from around the country. Then Alexandra led over to Paul Levitz for the business and economy report (which, since it was a holiday in the United States, had no "breaking" news): an anticipated rise in short-term interest rates by the Federal Reserve; growing support in the U.S. for the proposed Canada-U.S. free trade pact; and a business profile of Robert Muse Bass. Alexandra promised they would return with sports after a break.

While they were in commercial Jimmy Hallerton ran into the studio with a last-minute final on a baseball game, leaped onto set 2, landed wrong, twisted his ankle and went crashing down, snapping Dash's microphone floor connection as he did so.

"Sound's out on Dash—they want you to skip ahead to the DC-9," Lilly said to Alexandra, waving the stagehands on to carry Jimmy away. "Fifteen seconds. Coming up on camera 1. Ten, nine, eight . . ."

Alexandra was reorganizing her copy. When Lilly hit three, she looked up into camera 1 and there, on the TelePrompTer, was the copy for Dash's sports report. Her eyes went back down to her script for a second and then came back up just as the red light went on. "Dash Tomlinson isn't called Dash for nothing," she said, smiling into the camera. "He just ran off with our sports report. But he promised he'd be back in a moment with the latest breaking scores and finals."

Through the headsets of the crew, laughter in the control room could be heard.

"A fast-thinking pilot of a Continental DC-9 averted a midair collision near Cleveland this afternoon," Alexandra went on to say, glancing down to read from her copy. Kyle, in the meantime, in Alexandra's earphone, was telling her to go straight into the next story when she was done reading this one. She did and, as soon as they cut away to the film report that accompanied it, Kyle told her that she was to lead back to Dash and, after his segment was done, that she was to skip the beach in Miami story and go straight to commercial—which she did. During the commercial she was then told to move the beach in Miami story to the following segment, where the DC-9 story had been, and to cut an item on recycling. (She nodded, slashing a downward arrow through the story on her script.)

When they came back Alexandra went over the top stories and then led over to Gary for the weather. Gary, in real life, was standing next to a blank wall. On the monitor, however, he appeared to be standing next to a highly detailed topological map of the United States. (He had to watch himself on an offstage monitor to do his pointing on the map.) His footage of the day: a sudden hailstorm in Vermont (with ice balls an inch big), occurring after a series of very warm days. After he explained the mechanics of cold-front heat-wave collisions, they cut away for the local forecasts, followed by a graphic that said that the weather segment had been sponsored by KlapTrap. And then the first regular commercial rolled (in which four six-foot mosquitoes attacked a family cookout), followed by three more commercials from other sponsors.

When they came back Alexandra led to some local "town meeting" kind of stories, one from their Los Angeles affiliate, one from their Omaha affiliate, one from their New Orleans affiliate, and then she led to Helen Kai Lu for her special report on health maintenance organizations, "Should You Join an HMO?" They broke for a commercial.

When they came back Alexandra led over to Brooks for a report and mini-reviews of the top-grossing movies of the holiday weekend, and then Alexandra led over to Chester for their closing piece on Memorial Day. It was long, by TV standards, almost four and a half minutes, but it was a very strong piece, genuinely moving too, as they listened to Chester give a history of America's wars and watched how twenty-four towns and cities this day had chosen to remember the Americans who had died in them.

And then, suddenly, it was the end of the newscast, and there was Alexandra, the warmth of her smile traveling forty-four thousand miles through the sky to be felt in homes across the country. "May 30, 1988," she said. "From everyone at DBS News, we wish you a very good night—and an even better tomorrow."

They closed with a shot of a single flag on a single grave. The camera then slowly drew back to show the breathtaking hillside the solitary grave was located on, with mountains steepling in the background. The frame froze, the color faded to black and white, the resulting image looking very much like an Ansel Adams photograph.

"All clear!" Lilly announced a minute later.

"All right!" Kyle announced, leaping into the studio and throwing his script in the air.

"Hi," Cassy said, poking her head around the dressing-room door. "I thought you might be hiding in here."

Alexandra smiled, wiping some of the studio makeup off with cotton pads. It was after midnight; standby for updates on the West Coast feed was over.

"What?" Cassy said to somebody out in the hall, leaning back out the door. "Oh, you're welcome, Greg," she called down the hall. "Please come again—any time—you were a pleasure." She laughed and then came inside, closing the door behind her.

Alexandra lowered the pad to her dressing table and looked at Cassy in the mirror. "You don't know who that was, do you?"

"Here," Cassy said, holding up a glass of champagne. "I lost half of it in the hall, but there's still enough to say that someone left you some. It's quite a party upstairs." She leaned past Alexandra to put it down on the dresser, and then she stood behind her, resting her hands on Alexandra's shoulders, smiling at her in the mirror. "I am so very proud of you," she said.

Alexandra smiled but then lowered her eyes, reaching for another cotton pad.

Cassy stood there a moment, but when Alexandra did not look at her again she moved over and threw herself down in the chair next to the dresser. "Oh," she said, covering her mouth to yawn, "am I ever tired." She dropped her hand in her lap. "And we've got Paul Hogan coming in to do his interview in the morning. I hope Jessica remembers."

"She will," Alexandra said.

"I hope so," Cassy said, watching her. After a moment, "So don't you even want to taste your champagne?"

Alexandra smiled, eyes moving to her. "I can tell you've had some."

"A little."

"Uh-huh," Alexandra said, eyes returning to the mirror as she finished wiping her chin. "Okay," she said then, throwing the cotton in the trash and picking up the glass. "To Cassy Cochran—I drink to your good health, to your future happiness and to your generosity of spirit, which serves us all so well." And then she leaned over and kissed Cassy softly on the cheek.

"Wow—thank you," Cassy said, looking a little embarrassed.

Alexandra sat back, took a sip of champagne, swallowed, smiled and then held the glass out to Cassy. "It doesn't work unless you drink to your own good health," she said. "No one can do it for you."

Cassy took the glass from her and brought it to her mouth.

Alexandra watched her sip. Her eyes watched Cassy's mouth, skipped up to her eyes and then she turned away, getting up and walking to the bathroom. "I think you should go find Gordon," she said over her shoulder, "and ask him about your friend Greg."

Cassy frowned, putting the champagne glass down on the dresser. "My friend Greg?"

"In the newsroom today," Alexandra said from the bathroom. She left the door slightly ajar but was standing out of Cassy's line of sight. "Greg—the guy you just said good night to."

"What about him?" Cassy said, standing up, smoothing her skirt.

In the bathroom Alexandra was leaning back against the towel rack, looking up at the ceiling. She did not look very well. "That was Lord Gregory Hargrave," she said, her voice sounding normal. "Gordon told me when he came down."

"Lord Gregory Hargrave!" Cassy gasped. "And no one recognized him?"

"I know," Alexandra said from behind the bathroom door. "So maybe you ought to find out what he was doing here."

"I knew he looked familiar," Cassy said, moving to the door. "I'll strangle Jackson—his secretary told me he was a family friend."

"You better go find Gordon now," Alexandra said, "because I'm going to want to leave soon."

"Oh, no," Cassy groaned, clapping a hand over her eyes. "We gave Lord Gregory Hargrave a slice of pizza on a paper towel for dinner?" She dropped her hand and, mimicking somebody, added, " 'Ey, Greg —ya wanna sloyce of *saw*sage?" Laughing to herself, she opened the door, shaking her head. "Alexandra—you coming?"

"I'll be up in a minute," she said. "But could you ask Kyle to stop in here for a second?"

"Sure," Cassy said, going out. "I'll see you upstairs."

When Alexandra heard the door close she brought her hands up to her face and held it for a long moment. Then she dropped her hands, closed her eyes, drew in one long breath, held it and slowly let it out. Then she opened her eyes and went over to the sink to look in the mirror.

Her eyes were wet and her nose was slightly red. She turned on the water, leaned over and scooped water over her face with her hands. The water running, still leaning over, she held her hands over her face again for a moment. Then she dropped them, sniffed, straightened up, turned off the water and reached for a towel. She held it against her face and then patted her face dry. She put the towel back in the rack.

"Alexandra?" Kyle said.

"Just a second," she called. She grabbed a tissue, blew her nose, threw the tissue out and looked at herself in the mirror again. She waved her hand, trying to dry her eyes. Then she cleared her throat, ran her hands back over her hair once and went out, flicking the light off.

Kyle was standing half in the door. "What's up?"

"I changed my mind," she said, walking out.

"About what?" he said.

Alexandra walked over to pull Kyle inside the dressing room, closed the door and then turned to face him. "The tour," she said. "I don't want to wait until fall, Kyle. I want to go on the road soon—this summer."

"Already?" he said.

"Already," she said. "Just as soon as we can put it together."

31

DBS Mail and Memorandums

Delivery by hand
*****CONFIDENTIAL*****

31 May 1988

MEMORANDUM TO: Catherine Cochran
FROM: Jackson Andrew Darenbrook
REGARDING: Lord Gregory Hargrave

Cassy,

That's okay—you can leave me notes like that all the time. What I like is how you can shout through your handwriting.

Lord Gregory Hargrave, better known as Old Hardhead, is contemplating forming a global broadcast news network in the same way we formed DBS. His visit yesterday was entirely informal, however, only to view our facilities and get a sense of our operations.

So, to answer your question: on the record, he was not here. Off the record, yes, he was; I'm hoping to offer DBS News the resources of a global network within a year. Please act surprised if and when it happens.

In the meantime, please rip up this memo and know that you and yours have done a brilliant job. I'm very proud of you and—you know what? I just decided we should have a party. More later.

Jackson

•

5-31-88

> Cassy,
> Here are the overnights from Nielsen.
> Chi Chi

•

May 31, 1988

Memorandum from Langley W. Peterson

> Jack,
> Here are the overnights. Better than we expected!

•

31 May 1988

MEMORANDUM TO: All DBS Employees
FROM: Jackson Andrew Darenbrook
REGARDING: A Party

Dear Everybody,
  I'm very, very proud of you and so I'm going to give a party in your

honor. (So you all better come or there won't be anyone there to honor yourself with.)

The idea of the moment is a dinner dance while sailing around Manhattan. You will be allowed to bring one person with you. Past that point, all I know is that it will be Saturday night, June 25, so please block it off on your calendar. (It has to be that Saturday so the miniseries folks can join us before going to England.)

Thank you, everybody, for all of your hard work. You are wonderful.

Jackson

•

6-1-88

Jackson,

Thank you for the flowers. They're beautiful. And I wasn't really angry about my friend Lord Greg—it's just that I can't stand not knowing everything. Call it my obsession with control—which, come to think of it, isn't a bad thing to have in a producer.

Thanks again. (But please don't let me feed him pizza next time.)

Cassy

•

6/3/88

Dear Belinda,

I don't suppose one often writes thank you notes for thank you notes, but in this case I think one is in order.

Thank you, thank you, thank you. I'd like to say you are too kind in your praise, but with the shape my self-esteem has been in lately, I will merely take it all and say thank you.

I hope I see you again soon.

With warm regards,
Jessica Wright

•

June 3, 1988

Mrs. Belinda Darenbrook Peterson
18 Old Woods Hill Road
Greenwich, Connecticut 06830

Dear Belinda,

Thank you for your note, though I hasten to assure you there is no reason to apologize—except, that is, for neglecting to write the one thing I wanted to read in your letter, that you would be coming to visit us all at West End again soon.

Thank you for coming on Memorial Day. Your presence meant a great deal to me and to all, especially Jessica. Television is a very demanding and often difficult—physically, mentally, emotionally—field of work, so the interest and support of someone like you go a long way toward revitalizing our energies.

Please come again soon.

With my very best wishes,
Cassy Cochran

•

June 6

Langley,

The first week's ratings. Alexandra's doing beautifully—Jessica is a hit, a *hit.*

Cassy

•

June 6, 1988
Memo to Cassy from Derek
DBS NEWS AMERICA TONIGHT reviews

Hey, lady, look here. The complete set of reviews. Raves are of course on top. It looks like a clean sweep through flyover land, with a few shots to the head and gut from the East (but then, what would the East be without shots to the head and gut?) and one or two from out West.

•

June 6, 1988
Memo to Cassy from Derek
THE JESSICA WRIGHT SHOW reviews

What more is there to say? She is a smash across the board. (Did I tell you Letterman's guy called? They want *her* as a guest.)

•

6-7-88
Cassy,
Here's my favorite review:

> Okay, shoot *me* for sacrilege, but I can't watch "DBS News America Tonight" without thinking that maybe Alexandra Waring should play Hope on "thirtysomething." One gets the sense *she* wouldn't let Hope be such a pill.
>
> Alexandra

P.S. I also liked our friendly critic in Washington's comment:

> What more appropriate time to launch the Star Wars of TV News than during the Moscow summit? There are enough technical credits on this newscast to scare the Soviets into signing anything.

•

June 8

Alexandra,
Here's my favorite:

> Executive Producer Catherine Cochran has created a hodgepodge Americana hour of long hard-news stories and short fluff, anchored by a glamorous yuppie, supplemented by a rainbow coali-

tion of specialty editors, highlighted by reporters yakking—live, mind you—in forty different dialects, drawls and accents from around the country, and packaged in graphics ranging from trendy glitz to Hallmark schmaltz. The amazing thing is, it works, and Cochran may have won herself the distinction of producing the first newscast that genuinely reflects the nature of the country that it's supposed to be about.

Your hodgepodge producer signing off, my glamorous yuppie friend—

Cassy

•

June 8

Jackson,
Thank you for the beautiful flowers, but there is no need to thank me. I meant every word I wrote Belinda. But I'll take the flowers anyway—they make me smile every time I look at them. Thank you.

Cassy

•

*****PERSONAL AND CONFIDENTIAL*****
8 June 1988

MEMORANDUM TO: Jessica Wright
FROM: Jackson Andrew Darenbrook
REGARDING: The Plaza Hotel

Jessica honey,
  I know you're making a fortune for us but, sweetie pie, the suite you're living in is a part of the guest suite for Darenbrook Communications and someday you're going to have to do one of the following:
    1) Find a place to live.
    2) Decide that you are living in the place you wish to live.
      a) Which means your name must be Eloise.

b) Which means you better audition for Ivana's Eloise Suite or you're going to personally find out the shocking truth regarding how much it costs to house mischievous young ladies in the Plaza.

Sweetie pie, please try and figure out what you're doing by July 1. I've got this crazy family of mine coming to town that month and some of them are expecting to stay in that suite.

As Cassy, I think, told you (like six weeks ago), if you'd only call this nice lady, Mrs. Heidelson, she will help you find an apartment and arrange everything.

Your pal and fan and employer,
Jackie

•

*****PERSONAL AND CONFIDENTIAL*****

6/8/88

So, Jackie,

You think you can get away with sending me an eviction notice hidden in a basket of flowers, eh? Well, just wait and see what happens to you. (I hear Ivana and Donald baby don't want the Atlantic City crowd here, so they'll be trying to evict you for sure —I mean, if this network isn't a crapshoot, what is?)

Also, did it ever occur to you that I might want to stay in the suite when your crazy family arrives because one filthy rich scoundrel like one of your brothers might be worth more than some poor, mass-murdering crack dealer pervert, which is just about all that there is left to date in this town?

Love and kisses,
Jessica, the crown jewel of your network

WEST END

•

6/9

*****PERSONAL AND CONFIDENTIAL*****
by hand

Here's a crown, Jessica. Now please find a new palace by July 1.
Love,
Jackie

•

Dear Jackie,
Thanks for the crown. I'm wearing it on the show today. As for the palace, I hear that Harry and Leona aren't entertaining much anymore.
Love,
Jessica

•

6/9/88

Langley,
Attached is our revised schedule for London. We will stay for the boat party and leave the following day, Sunday, June 26, and begin work at Hargrave Studios on the 27th.
Gordon

•

Thursday afternoon, 9 June 1988

Dear Jackson,
How can I ever thank you? For such a lovely luncheon at Café des Artistes, for such a wonderful place to work, and for, literally, changing my life.
But what I wish most of all to thank you for is your friendship. I can't tell you how much it means to me to have your support personally, as well as professionally. I'll miss sharing the tabloids with you (though I'm sure my marriage won't faze them in the

least). For myself, and for Gordon too, I thank you. And I love you.

Alexandra

•

*****CONFIDENTIAL*****

June 10, 1988

TO: Langley W. Peterson
    Derek Deltz
FROM: Cassy Cochran
RE: Alexandra Waring's Engagement to Gordon Strenn

This is to confirm that Alexandra and Gordon will announce their engagement at the boat party on Saturday, June 25.

This is also to confirm that you, Derek, may release this information to the columnists of your choice on Wednesday, June 22.

cc: Jackson Darenbrook
    Gordon Strenn
    Alexandra Waring

•

6/10/88

MEMO TO: Cassy Cochran
FROM: Deeter Page
RE: DBS AFFILIATES

Cass,

Thanks for the PR package. We're sending them out immediately.

As I said on the phone, the affiliates couldn't be more pleased with the performance of both shows. And from what I've gotten back thus far, they are uniformly crazy over the idea of Alexandra's tour this summer.

•

June 10

Please, Deeter! Stop calling "DBS News America Tonight" a show!

Cassy

•

June 10, 1988

For: Langley W. Peterson
From: Cassy Cochran
Re: DBS Across America Tour

Langley,

This is to confirm our intention to kick off the DBS Across America tour on July 4. Our tenative schedule has Alexandra anchoring the news from 40 different affiliate newsrooms in 60 days, starting in Portland, Maine, and ending in Honolulu. Will Rafferty and his team will travel with her. Dash Tomlinson may go too, we haven't decided.

It *is* a killer schedule, but Alexandra is determined (and able) to do it. Kyle and Dr. Kessler concur. Deeter says initial feedback is good from the affiliates, and Rookie says the sponsors are lining up. (It looks like United Airlines and Ford might pick up travel.)

More later—but I would consider this a done deed. We have our bases covered, everyone is in agreement, and the publicity, I think, can only help our case at the July board meeting.

Let me know if there's a problem.

•

June 14, 1988

For: Alexandra Waring
From: Celia B. Smith, Public Relations

Miss Waring,
Enclosed herewith is the copy we received from your mother. Please check it over and return to me. You will of course see the final announcement before it is released. Thank you.

The engagement of Alexandra Bonner Waring and Gordon Cannondale Strenn, the son of Mr. and Mrs. Bradden Strenn of Locust Valley, L.I., has been announced by Mr. and Mrs. Paul Allen Waring of Haven Wells, Kansas.

Miss Waring graduated cum laude from Stanford University and is Anchor and Managing Editor of "DBS News America Tonight," the nightly newscast of the DBS Television Network. Her father is a practicing attorney and served nine terms as a United States congressman. Her mother is general manager of Waring Farm and chairperson for the Great Plains Foundation for the Arts.

The future bride is the granddaughter of the late Mr. and Mrs. Thomas Alexander Waring of Haven Wells, the fifth generation of farmers on the Waring homestead, and of Mrs. Hayston Lee Bonner of Lawrence, Kansas, and the late Dr. Bonner. She is also the great-great-granddaughter of Peter S. Bonner, founder of the First Bank of Kansas-Missouri.

Mr. Strenn, who graduated from the Hill School and the UCLA Film School, is a television producer whose most recent miniseries, *This Side of Paradise,* an adaptation of the F. Scott Fitzgerald novel, won Mr. Strenn an Emmy Award. He is currently Executive Producer of DBS International Films. His father, who is retired, was the president of Cannondale Clothing.

The future bridegroom is the grandson of Mr. and Mrs. Drew Strenn of Boca Raton, Florida. He is also the grandson of the late Mr. and Mrs. Percival Scott Cannondale III of New York City.

An April wedding is planned.

WEST END

•

15 June 1988

MEMORANDUM TO: All Board Members of Darenbrook
                    Communications
FROM: Jackson Andrew Darenbrook, Chairman
REGARDING: DBS Television Network

Dear Gang,
    Enclosed please find the excellent report regarding the ratings
for the first two weeks of DBS programming. It is an excerpt from
a report to Langley, written by the president of DBS News and
Information, Catherine Cochran.
    As you know, Langley and I will be making a complete report
on the DBS Television Network at our July board meeting. Until
then, may I say that it is turning out to be a most exciting and
profitable and prestigious venture for Darenbrook Communications.

Jack

•

6/14/88

—Memo to Peterson from Cochran—DBS (cont'd)—6—

RATINGS

To fully appreciate the ratings performance of the DBS programming in the past two weeks, it is helpful to view DBS in
comparison to the major commercial broadcasting networks,
ABC, CBS and NBC, henceforth referred to as The Big Three:
    **The Big Three each has approximately 207 affiliates to our
71, a ratio of roughly 3:1.
    **CBS and NBC have been household names as broadcasting
networks for 50 years; ABC for over 25; whereas we are virtually
unknown, offering largely unknown programming, part time, over
independent stations often considered to be the "less-than" station against the Big Three affiliates in town.
    **In the A. C. Nielsen ratings system, each point represents

DBS MAIL AND MEMORANDUMS

880,000 viewers. The Big Three run their half-hour newscasts in the evening hours and, in season (end of September–May), generally tie at around a 9.5 rating. In the summer, with lower viewership, this number drops by at least a third.

**For prime-time programming, in season, a Big Three program needs at least a 12 rating to survive, an 18 to be strong, and in the 20s to be a hit. In the summer quarter, these numbers drop by a third as well.

DBS NEWS AMERICA TONIGHT
WITH ALEXANDRA WARING

If we carried the comparison through, then, in Big Three terms, a summer newscast should have a rating of about 6.3. When we apply the ratio of a 207-affiliate network to our 71-affiliate network of 3:1, the rating would be 2.1 *for an established network anchor on an established network newscast on an established network.*

***Our anticipated rating on "DBS News America Tonight with Alexandra Waring" was 1.5 and has averaged, for the past two weeks, 2.2. In other words, "NAT" is already "pulling" like Big Three news (2.2 × 3), and in prime time—where The Big Three wouldn't dare run their newscasts.

THE JESSICA WRIGHT SHOW

For *regular* prime-time programming, in the *regular* season (end of September–May), a new program would have to achieve a rating of at least 12 to survive. When we apply the ratio of The Big Three to DBS, 3:1, the necessary rating would be 4.

—Our anticipated rating on "The Jessica Wright Show" was 2.5 and has averaged, for the past two weeks, 5.3. In other words, if we apply the ratio in reverse, Jessica would be pulling a 15.9 on The Big Three, which means that, on DBS or anywhere, "The Jessica Wright Show" has made an extremely healthy start. And if we take into consideration the third lower viewership in the summer, then her reverse-ratio rating in Big Three terms would be 21:1—*an unqualified hit.*

NOTES:
—Of course, we expect our ratings to rise as the number of our affiliates increase.

—Of course, we expect our ratings to rise as word gets around.

—Of course, we're all deliriously happy here because, unlike The Big Three, we here at DBS do not carry the kind of overhead they do, and so we are well on our way to becoming an extraordinarily profitable venture.

•

17 June 1988

MEMORANDUM TO: All DBS Employees
FROM: Jackson Andrew Darenbrook
REGARDING: The Boat Party

Dear Everybody,

This is a reminder that you don't have to come but are absolutely expected to come to my boat party that is in honor of all of you.

SATURDAY, JUNE 25TH

6 P.M.—?

THE 79TH STREET BOAT BASIN,

HUDSON RIVER, MANHATTAN

DINNER AND DANCING

You are allowed to bring one person with you: spouse, friend, other half, better half, half and half, roommate, cellmate, whatever. Or come on your own, please. (I am.)

Please come because I've worked very hard to plan this. Honest. Ask Ethel, Randy and Claire—who almost quit in the process.

Jackson

32

The Boat Party

"Good Lord," Cassy said, standing at the top of the gangplank leading down to the docks of the 79th Street boat basin.

"I don't believe it," Kyle said, standing beside her, blinking.

"Better get those smiles in order," a photographer said, standing by the security guards, raising his camera to take their picture. "Mr. Darenbrook says anybody who doesn't look happy goes overboard."

Cassy and Kyle looked at each other.

Kyle was in a white dinner jacket; Cassy was in a floral Chanel number that she had decided she didn't have the courage to wear and had been about to change when Kyle arrived to pick her up. She had opened the front door and Kyle had at first smiled at her, but then his eyes had dropped and come back up and then dropped again and then come back up again—having him utterly miss the time for any polite hello—his expression one of blatant awe. "Is this you?" he had finally said, eyebrows crashing together.

So she had worn the dress.

Since Kyle's wife and children were at the McFarlands' house in Maine for the summer (Kyle flew up on weekends) and Cassy's husband would not be her husband for very much longer, they had decided to go to the party together. Kyle had a car waiting outside and they had driven down Riverside Drive to 79th Street, turning off for the parking lot overlooking the boat basin. They had then made their way down the footpaths and terraces to the basin, smiling and nodding to all of the people who had been—and were—staring and smiling at them in their finery.

Late June was a somewhat magical time for Riverside Park. And in the evening it was at its most beautiful, because the light was at its most beautiful. The sun was streaming down from the southwest, warming still those baby children snoozing in their strollers, the elderly gossiping along terrace benches and the young couples twisting around each other on blankets in the grass (ostensibly still seeking a tan at this hour). On the waterside promenade the light glinted off the bikes riding past, shone on the perspiration of joggers huffing by and flashed sexy over sunglasses everywhere. It was the light of summer seashore, as if this were a resort town and the summer people had just arrived: sea gulls cried overhead while ice cream vendors cried below; uniformed policemen smiled at kids who smiled at them; and people moved along, sunburned, a little loopy from the excesses of the day.

And then there was the boat basin. Half of it was residential, with barges and houseboats and shacks on floats, and the other half was regular marina, with cabin cruisers and sailboats—fiberglass and teak —and Boston Whalers and speedboats and rowboats. Every generation was represented in the maze of interlocking docking berths, with old faded cotton clothes denoting the bottom end of the class spectrum in the residential half, while old faded cotton clothes denoted the top end of the class spectrum in the other. There were loud, social people whose boats demanded attention—"Look at me, look at me"— and there were quiet, languid-eyed romantics, supposedly reading, but really watching others until it was time to slip down into the holds of their sailboats to make love with the incoming tide. There were people there too who everybody wished would go away—as was always the case in New York City—but who never did go away because there was no place to go to where anyone would like them anyway and so they stayed on in New York City.

Though Cassy knew the basin had probably seen everything, she bet it had been quite some time since it had seen the likes of the huge white ship that was moored out in the river tonight. It was a beautiful old ship, something from another era, the thirties perhaps, and there were two white launches cruising back and forth from it, skippered by men in white uniforms.

"Say yes, pretty lady," the photographer said to Cassy.

She looked at him. "Not on your life," she said cheerfully.

He took their picture.

"Name?" one of the guards asked them.

"Cochran and McFarland," Kyle said, peering over the guard's arm to see the guest list. "With a C."

Mr. Graham appeared from behind Cassy, with a very attractive woman on his arm. She was in her late sixties or so, with a stunning head of white hair, and was dressed sedately in black and pearls. He, on the other hand, was looking rather festive in a pink blazer, red pants, white shirt and pink and blue bow tie.

Introductions were made; the woman was a Miss Alice Moffat who, according to Mr. Graham, would be working with him for Alexandra, starting on Monday. While Mr. Graham and Miss Moffat had their picture taken, Kyle gave Mr. Graham's name to the guard as part of their party.

"Cochran, McFarland and Graham plus guest, Moffat, one, one and two," the guard said into his walkie-talkie. There was the sharp sound of static and then a voice shot back, "Cochran! McFarland! Graham plus guest, Moffat, A-okay, one-one-two all clear!"

"Right down there, ladies," another guard said, pointing down the gangplank. "Go straight out and they'll pick you up."

"Are you working with Mr. Graham for the first time?" Cassy asked Alice as they walked down a ramp in front of the men, thinking that this was a pretty good question considering she still didn't know what it was that Mr. Graham did for Alexandra.

"No," Alice said, smiling, glancing back at Mr. Graham before looking at Cassy, "we've worked together before."

"Oh, that's nice," Cassy said.

"I was his secretary for thirty-four years," Alice explained.

At the end of this dock outreach they met up with guests who had come in through another gate: Chi Chi and her husband, Richie; Hex and his wife, Debbie; Kelly Harris and her boyfriend, Steve; and with great dramatic flourish, their arts and entertainment editor, Brooks Bayerson Ames and her (fourth) husband, Dickie. The launch arrived and the attendants helped them step into it; they took their seats around the sides, the rope was cast and the launch moved away from the dock.

"Hey, Cass," Hex said, leaning to see her at the front end of the launch. "When Debbie saw you, she thought you were an actress."

"Hex," his wife complained, elbowing him.

"She did," Hex said. "She said, 'Who's that? That's somebody, isn't it?' "

"I'm going to kill him," his wife told everybody.

Hex was laughing. "She's never going to let me edit anything with you anymore. She thinks you're beautiful."

"That's it, Hex," his wife said, looking at the sky.

"But I told her," Hex said, " 'Naw, she isn't beautiful, that's just Cassy.' "

Everybody laughed.

"Thank you, Debbie," Cassy said, smiling at her. And then she settled back in her seat, looking over her shoulder at the water ahead of them.

The water was very calm this evening, the breezes light. The ship ahead was beautiful, seductive, the water lapping gently around her largesse. White lights were strung across her; they could hear the strains of orchestra music.

Cassy swallowed, eyes on the bridge. She knew that the tall figure standing there with the binoculars was Jackson; she knew his body by sight now. She had no idea what was going on between them these days, nor did she know where it was leading. She was supposed to be, if what Langley told her was true, made president of DBS by the fall, and she knew that the last thing the president of DBS should be doing was making eyes at the chairman of Darenbrook Communications. But it had been so pleasant—so *very* pleasant—these last weeks, when it seemed that, whenever she had a spare moment, there Jackson would be in her line of sight. When she was in her office, between phone calls, she'd look out and he'd be sitting out in the square, on a bench, dictating letters to Claire. Or she'd stop in the cafeteria for something to eat and the door to his office would open and out he would come. He always smiled, always waved, always stopped to talk if she indicated she had a moment.

There was a definite energy in the air between them and they were both aware of it, careful with it and clearly made happy by it. It was a delicious sensation, no doubt because it was still safe. Still innocent. It was not terribly unlike Cassy's first flirtation in junior high school, when she had first become aware of a very appealing boy being endearingly "in like" with her.

These will be the good old days, she thought. She'd look back on these last few weeks and think that times had never been better, had never been more fun. All there seemed to be was good news and more good news. Jessica's ratings were up. Alexandra's ratings were holding steady and the DBS News tour promised tremendous publicity. Ad revenues for the next quarter were high. Alexandra got an exclusive with Speaker of the House Jim Wright, when questions arose about his outside income. They had signed eleven more affiliates, bringing their total to eighty-four. ("More twinkling cities tonight," Kyle would tell graphics over the phone. "Tonight, on the opening, we need to see Rochester, Winston-Salem, Memphis, Orlando, Corpus Christi . . .")

Since the first day of the newscast, Alexandra had been caught up in the day-to-day newsgathering process and Cassy had seen less and less of her as her own responsibilities were taking her farther from the newsroom and Alexandra's were taking her farther from managerial meetings. But while Cassy did miss working as closely with Alexandra as she had been on a daily basis, she was delighted to see how well Kyle was working out in her stead. Because this—what her and Alexandra's working relationship was shaking down to—was pretty much what it would have to be if Cassy were to become president of DBS. And it seemed to be working.

It was also wonderful to see how Alexandra's commitment to Gordon was strengthening. Prior to this, Alexandra had scarcely acknowledged at West End that she even *had* a personal life, so it was a nice surprise when she announced that she wanted to tour for DBS News in July and August, anchoring the news from different affiliate newsrooms, not only to build ratings they could take into the fall with them, but because she wanted to tour while Gordon was in England. She didn't want Gordon to be away for two months, she said, and then have him come home when she was leaving for two months on the road. On top of that, Alexandra wanted to announce her engagement to Gordon before he left, and when Cassy asked her what she thought Jackson's reaction would be, Cassy was surprised and delighted (no— make that unnervingly elated) when Alexandra said she had already discussed it with Jackson and he thought it was great.

"Hey, Cass," Kyle whispered over her shoulder, "look up on the deck there. Isn't that our pal Greg again? Lord Hargrave?"

"Oh—yes," she said, "it is. You're right, that's him." But her eyes had moved toward the front of the ship again, to the bridge, and Cassy smiled slightly, wondering if it could be herself that Jackson was watching through the binoculars.

"Creeping catfish, is she the most ever-lovin' beautiful woman this side of the Mason-Dixon line or what?" Jackson said, looking out across the water through the binoculars.

Langley, who was on the ship-to-shore telephone, was not listening. He was shouting, "The Hudson River. Just tell him the Hudson River. Go north, Jessica, on the Hudson River and you can't miss us." He paused, grimacing, covering his free ear. "Everybody knows where the Hudson River is." Pause. "Oh, christ!" he said, holding the phone back as though he were about to throw it.

"What's the matter?" Jackson said, still following the launch with his binoculars. He was in a white dinner jacket, looking very dapper indeed, with a red carnation in his lapel.

"She's on Staten Island with some jerk who doesn't speak English." Langley raised the telephone to try again. "Let me talk to Ms. Wright," he shouted. "Will you just shut up and hand the phone to the señora, please?"

"Ask her if we should send the Coast Guard," Jackson said, chuckling, still watching through his binoculars.

"All right, all right," Langley was saying. "But be careful. Tell him we'll pay him very well on this end. Right. North on the Hudson River. We'll wait for you. Okay, bye. Phew," he said, handing the phone to the steward who was standing by. Langley walked over to stand next to Jackson. He was in a white dinner jacket too, though his black tie was not tied very well.

"What's up?" Jackson said, binoculars still to his eyes.

"Don't even ask," he groaned, leaning on the railing. "Steward," he said over his shoulder, "can you call down for a gin and tonic, please?" He looked back at the water. "She did a publicity appearance at South Street Seaport—"

"She is unbelievable," Jackson murmured under his breath, refocusing the binoculars. And then a second later, "Yeah? So what about Jessica's publicity appearance?"

"So she thought it would be fun to hire a boat to bring them around.

So they did, but Jessica says the driver's a Brazilian drug runner or something and Denny got left at the Seaport and *I* don't know what she was talking about!" he finished, throwing his arms in the air.

Jackson lowered his binoculars, hitting Langley on the arm. "Come on, let's meet this launch."

Within a half hour everyone from DBS had arrived: Kate Benedict and her boyfriend, Mark; Adele; Ethel and her husband; Randy and his wife; Claire and her boyfriend; Betty Cannondale and handsome friend; Dan Shelstein and his wife; Rookie Haskell and his girlfriend; Shelley Berns and her husband; Bozzy Gould and his girlfriend; Alicia Washington and her boyfriend; Jimmy Hallerton and his wife; Dr. Kessler and his wife; the Nerd Brigade and all kinds of attachments; Dick Gross and his wife; Helen Kai Lu and her husband; Paul Levitz and his wife; John Knox Norwood and his girlfriend; Gary Plains and his wife; Dash Tomlinson and his wife; Chester Hanacker and his daughter; Lilly Kertz and her husband; Zeph, Mel, Becky Seidelman, and on and on and on. . . .

And Denny arrived with his roommate Bill, and another guy named Rob, who was apparently Jessica's date. ("Why did Denny bring his roommate—ow," Langley said, getting it in the ribs from his boss and friend Jackson. "What?" Langley said. Jackson rolled his eyes and Cassy leaned over to whisper something in Langley's ear. "Oh," he said, looking around at Denny and Bill again.)

Everyone had arrived—that is, except Alexandra and Gordon and Jessica; the latter, everyone understood, was floating around somewhere with a Brazilian drug runner, and the first two, according to Kate Benedict—who was up on the radar deck of the ship with her boyfriend—were coming out in the launch now.

"They were out on Long Island today," Cassy said, standing at the railing with Langley and Jackson, sipping on a white wine spritzer that had been brought to her on a silver tray.

"She is a most attractive young woman," Lord Gregory Hargrave said from behind them. All three of them turned around. "Mrs. Cochran, I believe I owe you an apology," he said, smiling, offering his hand to her.

He was a very good-looking fellow, Lord Hargrave was, and it certainly helped his cause to know that he had not only inherited his title but that he had made it worth something again by parlaying mortgage land deeds into a media empire appraised at close to a billion pounds. He was clean shaven, with very white skin and the barest blush of red in his cheeks; his eyes were clear and pale blue; and he had the most attractive head of silver hair. And Lord Hargrave was not in a white dinner jacket; Lord Hargrave's dinner jacket was demurely black.

"I hope you will forgive me for not properly identifying myself the last time we met," he said, "but I was told that, had you known who I was, you might not have granted me permission to observe your newsroom."

Cassy smiled, shaking his hand. "You're right, I wouldn't have. It's a pleasure to see you again, Lord Hargrave."

"Greg," he said softly, leaning forward to smile at her.

"Watch it, Sir Smoothie," Jackson said, patting Lord Hargrave's shoulder with the back of his hand. Out of the corner of his mouth he added to Cassy, "Gotta watch out for these guys. Give the king a drink of water and a thousand years later they think the world still owes 'em."

"Charming fellow, he," Lord Hargrave said to Cassy, smile expanding.

"There *is* a Lady Hargrave, you know," Jackson told Cassy. "Locked up in some castle somewhere—so don't tell me I didn't warn you. Excuse me," he added, touching her arm and then slapping Lord Hargrave's back as he moved away, "but I want to meet Alexandra."

Lord Hargrave stepped in next to Cassy at the railing to watch as the launch pulled alongside the ship. "I must say," he said, "I was most impressed by your Miss Waring. She has a remarkable speaking voice for an American—that is to say, it has character but doesn't carry the hard edge we have come to associate with the American manner of speaking."

Cassy smiled, swallowing a sip of wine. Lowering her glass, she looked at him and said, "I didn't know there was an American manner of speaking."

"Exactly," Lord Hargrave said, bowing slightly. "I did not wish to offend."

THE BOAT PARTY

The party had suddenly grown quite festive. The grips and gaffers and technicians and secretaries and assistants and executives and correspondents and producers were all mixing on the aft deck; everyone was smiling and drinking and laughing and snacking; people's eyes were sparkling, faces were sunburned, clothes were festive and spirits were high. The orchestra under the awning struck up the theme music to "DBS News America Tonight" as Jackson helped Alexandra step aboard, and people started crowding over to see her.

Alexandra's smile grew wider and her eyes brighter as people made a fuss around her, over her, about her. And she was worth the fuss. Her hair was sensational; her little bit of suntan against the navy and white strapless floral dress made her eyes their drop-dead bluest, her teeth their whitest and the rest of her appear all body-brown-beautiful and long-limb extraordinaire. And just below her shoulder, amid the bare, smooth brown skin, was the mildly shocking reminder of the shooting in the form of her scar. The strange thing was, it only made Alexandra seem lovelier, her skin more beautiful, her neck longer, sleeker and the silver bar necklace around it more precious. And stranger yet, everyone seemed to want to touch it—the scar—as they came over to say hello. They would look into her eyes first and then glance down and see it. Immediately they would wince (as if Alexandra had been injured only just that second) and—after sucking in their breath between their teeth—they would make a motion to touch it, murmuring something like, "Oh, ow—how's your shoulder? Does it hurt still?"

The party began in earnest and the guests fanned out over the ship, exploring what there was to do, where there was to go. There was the orchestra, of course, and dancing and drinks out here on the aft deck; below, there was a bar, and a dining salon with a buffet set up, and also an open gaming room with billiards, darts and pinball machine; there were the port and starboard decks and bow to roam, as well as the upper deck, the bridge, and the staterooms and bathrooms below.

"Mr. Peterson," the loudspeakers on the ship said, "this is your captain speaking. We believe this may be Jessica Wright approaching on the port-side bow."

Sure enough, it was Jessica, cruising in on some sort of long, narrow speedboat, now coasting in on its wake. (Painted along the side of this speedboat, it said—in very flashy lettering, complete with bolts of lightning—"57 SHARK RIVER RAVAGER MIAMI.") The orchestra struck up the theme of "The Jessica Wright Show" and RRROOOMMM-BAAARRROOOMMM went the powerful engines of the speedboat as the squinty-eyed, viciously smiling fellow at the controls maneuvered it alongside the ship.

Holding her high heels in one hand, Jessica stepped up onto the side of the speedboat. "Believe it or not," she said, reaching up for Denny's arms, "my virtue is still intact. No thanks to Pancho Villa here."

Mr. Squinty laughed through viciously bared large white teeth.

"Up we go," Denny said, lifting her onto the ship. (There was scattered applause.)

"I'm sorry we lost you," Jessica said, giving Denny a kiss on the cheek.

"I'm not," Denny said.

"I told him you would give him some more money, Mr. Mitchell," Jessica told Langley, moving on. "Hi, Bill," she said, giving Denny's other half a kiss. "Hi, everybody. Hi, Alexandra Eyes," she said, giving her a kiss on the cheek. "My," she added, looking Alexandra over and then pulling her to stand beside her. "Okay, everybody—guess which one of us is the anchorwoman?"

Everybody roared. Jessica, in a flimsy yellow minidress, shoes in hand and her hair wind-whipped à la speedboat, was looking a little like a refugee from a disaster movie.

Jessica said she was freezing and within moments Alexandra had talked one of the stewards out of his white jacket. Jessica, with her new outfit, went inside with Alexandra to pull herself together, while Jackson announced that they were pulling up anchor.

"So you're really going to do it," Betty said, sliding in to stand next to Gordon at the bar. "I saw the ring—it's beautiful."

"Yeah," Gordon said, accepting his drink from the bartender. "Would you like something?"

"No, I'm fine, thanks," Betty said, showing him her glass.

Gordon sipped his scotch, looking at her. She really was looking great tonight. It always surprised him how attractive Betty was when he remembered to look at her. "So where's Jerry?"

"Barry," Betty corrected him. "He's waiting for me over there."

Gordon turned around to look. He was sitting at one of the tables in a corner with two plates of food from the buffet. He turned back to Betty. "He looks like a decent sort of a guy," he said.

"He is," Betty said, reaching for some peanuts in a dish on the bar. "That's why I don't seem to like him very much, I think. Why do they put this stuff out? They must hate women—all this junk food does is get us fat."

"Run that by me again?" Gordon said.

She was chewing. She swallowed. "I don't like him very much and I don't know why. The only thing I can figure is that it's because he seems to like me. I don't know," she added, shaking her head, sipping her drink.

Gordon smiled. "We'll find you a nice guy in London."

She looked at him. "Will you?" she asked him, smiling.

"Sure," he said.

"Yeah," she murmured, moving away, "I bet."

"I will," he called after her.

She only smiled, drifting across the room toward Barry.

"Having a good time?" Langley asked him, coming up to the bar.

"Huh?" Gordon said, turning around. "Oh, hi."

"Gin and tonic," Langley told the bartender. He turned, leaning his elbow on the bar. "So, what do you think?" he asked him, looking around the bar.

"I think it's great," Gordon said.

"Yeah," Langley sighed, pushing his glasses higher on his nose. "It's too bad my wife missed it." He looked at Gordon. "Where's Jessica?"

"Oh, with Alexandra somewhere, I think," Gordon said. "Jackson wanted some pictures of them—"

"No, there she is," Langley said, raising his hand.

Jessica saw them and made her way over—still in the steward's white jacket—sipping from a glass with one hand and scooping up an hors d'oeuvre off a waiter's tray with the other.

"Hi," Langley said.

"Hi," Jessica said, eating. She pushed her way between them and turned around, resting her back against the bar. Both Gordon's and Langley's eyes slipped down to her bust for a second and their eyes met on the way back up, prompting Gordon to turn away, grinning. "This is a great party, Mr. Mitchell," Jessica said, oblivious to what had just transpired.

"I'm glad you're having a good time," he said.

"So," Jessica said, looking at Gordon, "Alexandra Eyes tells me she was playing daughter-in-law today."

Gordon smiled. "Yeah. She was great. My parents really like her."

"Everybody likes Alexandra Eyes," Jessica commented, looking to Langley. "Ever notice?"

Langley nodded, accepting his drink from the bartender. "But it seems like an awful lot of America loves you, Jessica," he said, taking a big swallow of his drink.

"Thanks, Mr. Mitchell," she said. To Gordon, "He's catching on fast about how to handle us—you notice?"

It was getting very dark. The lights of Manhattan twinkled, the waters swirled dark, the lights and music of the ship were gentle, exotic. Standing at the railing next to Cassy were Kyle and Dr. Kessler and Mrs. Kessler; they were talking about what, Cassy didn't know, so lost was she in the mood of the night, in the air, in the light and shadows and sounds of the water.

"May I talk to you a minute?" Alexandra whispered in her ear.

Cassy started, turning. "Oh, hi," she said.

"Hi," Alexandra said, voice low. She turned to the others, sliding her hand into Cassy's. "Will you excuse me if I borrow her for a minute?" And then she pulled Cassy along the deck to a place on the railing where they were comparatively alone. "Okay, then," Alexandra murmured, turning toward her, releasing her hand and leaning one elbow on the railing. "It's the moment of truth—I've only got about a half hour left."

Cassy smiled. "Scared?"

Alexandra nodded, turning to the railing, looking out across the water. After a while she turned to Cassy, holding her hand up so Cassy could see the ring on it.

"It's beautiful," Cassy said, taking her hand, turning it slightly to see the diamond glitter. Then Alexandra's hand closed around hers and Cassy looked up.

They looked at each other for a long moment.

And then Cassy smiled, pulling her hand away, dropping her eyes.

"Hi," Rookie Haskell said, zooming in to lean on the railing next to Cassy.

"Go away, Rookie," Cassy said without looking at him, "and we'll come find you in a minute."

"Bye," Rookie said, sailing off.

Alexandra lowered her head to the railing, resting her forehead on her hands. "I wish I hadn't been through this before—announcing my engagement. I wish this felt new, as if I knew this was an irrevocable decision, a done deed, something I could not change."

Cassy reached over and patted her on the back. "Everybody gets scared at this point."

Alexandra was quietly laughing, head still down on the railing. Her back was beautiful in the light, her arms too. "It makes me wonder what would have happened to me had I married Tyler. Where I would be now. But then, every time I think about that, I wonder why I think I'm someone who should get married."

"Gordon's not Tyler," Cassy said quietly.

"And let's hope I'm not the Alexandra Tyler was engaged to," she sighed, straightening up.

Cassy looked at her and Alexandra laughed.

"Oh, don't worry," Alexandra said, touching her arm, "no one's asked me to run away this time." She paused and then added, very quietly, her smile disappearing, "No one's asked me to run away with her this time."

Cassy was finding it a little hard to breathe, looking into Alexandra's eyes like this. But it was important that she say something, and so she tried. "You get married because you want to get married," she said quietly. "There will always be people wanting you to run away with them, Alexandra. Always. You're the kind of person people long to have belong to them, probably because they know you never will. So if a wonderful man who loves you very much understands that, the way Gordon does, I think you think long and hard about how much your love for him counts, and the likelihood of ever finding someone like him again."

"And it's what you really think I should do," Alexandra said. "What you really want me to do."

Cassy nodded.

"Cassy—" Alexandra started to say, reaching to touch her arm.

"He can give you everything you can't get by yourself," Cassy said quickly, turning back to the railing, looking at the lights of Manhattan. "And there is so much more you can have with him—than you could have with anyone else."

Silence.

"Cassy," Alexandra said.

Cassy turned to look at her.

"Don't worry," Alexandra said. "I've always known what my options are—for the way I want to live. But I want you to know that that doesn't mean I've ever discounted what I've felt—or what I might otherwise want to do if I were anybody else but me." She paused, glancing at some people walking by.

She looked back at Cassy. "I think I just want to acknowledge something before I—" She started blinking, rapidly. "I wanted to tell you that I love you very much. And that I've never regretted what happened between us—" Her voice faltered and she tried to smile, blinking even faster.

"Oh, sweetheart—I know," Cassy said, smiling, giving her a brief hug. Then she stepped back and kissed her gently on the cheek. "I love you too," she said.

Alexandra looked at her. "Do you really think it's going to be okay?"

"Oh, yes," Cassy said, nodding. "It's going to be just fine."

"And you'll always be my friend?"

Cassy smiled. "I'll always be here for you. Always."

Alexandra sighed, smiling. "Well, you better be," she suddenly declared. "Particularly if you've got your hat in the ring to be president of DBS. You know," she added, pointing a finger at her, "for somebody I wanted as my executive producer, you sure haven't wanted to stay in the job very long."

Cassy's mouth fell open. "How do you know about that?"

"Oh, for heaven's sake," Alexandra said, throwing her arm through the air, "what kind of reporter would I be if I didn't know what was going on at my own network?"

"I'll have another, please," Jessica said to the bartender. "But make it vodka over ice this time."

"Same here," Langley said, pushing his glass across the bar.

"As you were saying," Jessica said, turning back to him, leaning against the bar.

"As I was saying," Langley said, eyeing the front of Jessica's dress, "Belinda is very difficult to live with sometimes." He brought his eyes up. "She's troubled."

"And who isn't?" Jessica asked him, frowning deeply.

"No, I mean really troubled, Jessica." He leaned closer to her. "She goes off sometimes—"

"Mr. Mitchell," Jessica said, plunking her hand down on his shoulder and pushing him back a few inches, "I hate to ruin a good story, but how would you know if your wife's difficult to live with?" She reached for her new drink. "Thanks." To him, as she raised it to her mouth, "You haven't lived with Belinda since I've known you."

"Oh," Langley said, reaching for his drink, "I forgot. You're pals with Belinda now, aren't you?"

"Oh, fuck you," Jessica said, taking a gulp of her drink. "Do you want to know what I think or not?"

Langley took a gulp of his drink, shrugging, eyes on her breasts.

Jessica waved her hand in front of his eyes. "Hey, I'm talking to you."

Langley's eyes came up.

"I think you should pay more attention to her," Jessica said. "Or don't you like her anymore?"

Langley looked at her. "I like her fine—but she's crazy."

"I don't think she's crazy at all."

"You should have been there this morning," Langley said, banging his glass down on the bar so that some of the vodka sloshed over the side.

"I think she's got what they call housewife's disease," Jessica said. "That's what they called it where I grew up."

"Belinda's no housewife," Langley said, reaching for his drink again.

"But she's a human being, isn't she?" Jessica said, slamming her drink down on the bar this time, making some of the vodka slosh over the side. "You husbands like us just fine until something goes wrong with us inside, don't you?"

"That's a stupid, shitty, fucking lousy thing to say," Langley told her. "And you don't know a goddam thing about it."

"Then why the fuck are you talking to me about it then?" Jessica asked him.

"Jessica honey," Jackson said, coming up behind her, "I've brought your beau back." He pulled Jessica's date, Rob, up alongside her and hitched Rob's arm to hers. "There now. Pay attention to him and he won't run off again."

Jessica looked at Rob. "How are you?" she asked him in close to a yell.

"Good," Rob said.

"Good," Jessica said. She looked at Langley, who was staring at her breasts again. "Fuck you!" she told him.

"What?" Langley said, startled.

"Creeping catfish, what are you guys drinkin'?" Jackson said, frowning, peering over the rim of Langley's glass.

"Relaxer," Jessica said. "We were trying to get Langley un-uptight, but we've overdone it. He's turned into a scout for Maidenform."

"Are you getting drunk, Lang?" Jackson asked him. "Because if you are—"

"I am not drunk," Langley said.

Jessica looked at Rob again. "We're date-dates, right? For some reason I can't seem to recall the terms of our relationship from the last time we went out."

"You told me I was a stupid son of a bitch," Rob told her. "Heineken, please," he told the bartender.

"Oh, well, sorry," Jessica said.

"Sorry for what?" Rob asked her. "I had a great time."

"Oh," Jessica said, forehead furrowing. A second later, squinting at him, "Refresh my memory—are you married?"

"Uh-huh," Rob said cheerfully. "My wife lives in Boston. She's an investment banker. She graduated fourth in her class from Harvard."

"Oh," Jessica said, thinking. A moment later she nudged Rob. "Hey, listen, I think he should be your date," she said, pointing to Langley. "I think you have a lot in common."

"Jessica honey," Jackson said, "could I trust you to see that Langley eats something?"

"Talk to Rob," Jessica advised him, reaching for her glass. "He's his date—yow!" she said, whirling around. "Nice action back here," she said to the man who had just fallen down on the floor behind her. "Langley, come here and do something. One of your drunken employees has just been socked a-sluggo."

"He's not drunk," somebody said. "He's telling a story."

The crush of people around the bar was growing even tighter.

"What happened to the orchestra?" Jackson said. "Why isn't anyone dancing? Rob—will you make these two eat something, please?" And he pushed off into the crowd.

"Hi, Mr. Peterson," Kate Benedict said, flushed in the face and carrying an empty glass. "Excuse me—could I just get to the bar?"

"Sure," Langley said, scrunching around her, holding his glass high in the air.

"Hi, Jessica," Kate said, standing next to her now. "Margarita, please," she told the bartender.

"Hi, Alexandra, Jr.," Jessica said.

Kate giggled, weaving slightly.

"Here," Jessica said, guiding one of Kate's hands to the bar. "Hold on. These gale winds at sea can be something."

"How you doing, Jess?" Denny said, pushing in between her and Rob.

"Hi," Jessica said. She looked past him. "Where's Bill?"

"Maybe getting a job," Denny said. "Kelly's boyfriend works for Exxon and says they have some geologists on staff in New York."

"I love working at DBS!" Kate announced, new margarita in hand.

"My, my," Jessica said to Denny, "our little Alexandra, Jr., appears to be a little crocked." Kate laughed and laughed and Jessica took the drink out of her hand before she spilled it and put it on the bar. She turned to Denny. "I think someone should find whoever it is that's supposed to be guarding this child."

"Leave her alone," Langley told Jessica, "she's just having a good time. Barkeep!" he yelled, snapping his fingers.

"Not with me she's not," Jessica said. "Alexandra, Jr.," she said to Kate, guiding her over to Denny, "listen, Denny's going to take you and your margarita off to find your beau, okay? Have fun and stay away from me, or I'll never hear the end of it from your boss lady."

"Alexandra's wonderful," Kate sighed dreamily.

"Then go find her," Jessica said, shooing Kate away.

"Hi," Gordon said, coming down the deck toward Alexandra and Cassy.

Alexandra turned. "Hi," she said, stepping back from the railing.

He slid his arm around her, pulling her close to kiss her forehead. "Some catch, huh?" he asked Cassy.

Cassy smiled. "Yes."

He looked at Alexandra. "What's the matter? Cold feet?" he asked her.

She smiled slightly, nodding.

"Me too," he said, putting his other arm around her and giving her a hug.

"Everybody happy?" Jackson asked, grabbing the microphone on the orchestra stage.

"Yeah!" said the crowd.

"Where is everybody?" Jackson then said, peering around. "I detect about fifty people are missing."

"Who?" said the crowd.

"Langley, for one," Jackson said.

"Here!" cried a voice. It belonged to Langley—somewhere. And then there he was, standing in front of the crowd, looking none too steady on his feet.

"Where's Cassy?" Jackson said.

"Behind you!" everyone said.

"Oh," he said, turning around. "Hi."

"Hi," she said.

THE BOAT PARTY

"Where's Jessica?"

"Up there!" everyone said.

"Up where?" Jackson said, looking up, shielding his eyes against the lights.

"Where stars are supposed to be," Jessica said. A spotlight was moving around up there and found her, sitting on the floor of the second level with Rob, peering down at him through the railing. "I'm up here in the sky."

"Well, come on down, Jessica honey," he said. "I want everyone onstage here with me."

While everybody gathered around and waiters passed trays of champagne and Perrier with lime in champagne glasses, Jackson did a little spiel on their success to date and introduced, one by one, Langley—who stumbled onto the stand—Cassy, Denny, and then Jessica—to great roars of applause—and then Kyle and then Alexandra—to great roars of applause—and then Gordon. There they were, all pressed together on the tiny stage, and everybody was clapping and cheering.

And then Jackson offered a toast, holding his glass of Perrier high: "To you, you who are the DBS television network. I salute your talent, your energy and your commitment, and I wish you good health and happiness and a terrific career."

"Hear, hear," Cassy said, raising her glass.

They all drank to the toast, except Langley, who tried to rest his arm on a cymbal and nearly fell into the drums, causing a mild chain reaction that resulted in Kyle's being shoved off the other side of the stage, spilling his champagne down Alexandra's back as he went.

"Yikes," Alexandra said, jumping to wide-eyed attention.

"Right," Jackson said, turning back to the microphone. "And here's to Alexandra's success on the DBS Across America tour—forty cities in sixty days!"

Not even one cheer from the crowd.

"Hey!" Jackson said. "How about a little support?"

"Not unless we get to go with her," somebody called from the back.

"Yeah," somebody else called.

"So much for the tour," Jackson said, shrugging and looking at Cassy. "Well, how about this announcement, gang?" He elbowed Gordon to stop mopping Alexandra's back with his handkerchief and look alive. "Listen up, everybody," Jackson continued, raising his glass again. "I have a very special announcement."

"Notice how I'm suddenly chopped liver," Jessica grumbled to Denny.

"Alexandra is engaged to be married—"

A series of "Ohhh"s rippled through the crowd.

"—and she's marrying none other than . . ." Jackson waited for the drumroll, but the crowd came surging forward with their congratulations, pulling him off the stage, forcing him to explain individually that, no, no, *he* wasn't the one engaged to Alexandra, Gordon was.

"We could have a great deal to talk about," Lord Hargrave said, dancing with Alexandra, "so I hope you will come over."

She smiled. "Talk to Cassy."

"Oh, I will," Lord Hargrave assured her. "Jackson tells me she may soon be representing the whole network."

Alexandra nodded, looking over Lord Hargrave's shoulder and smiling at Gordon, who was dancing with Adele. "We're certainly very interested in your global concept," she said, turning back to him.

"You should be," he said. "Particularly when your husband-to-be is doing so much work on our side of the Atlantic."

"I meant DBS News," Alexandra said.

"I meant you," Lord Hargrave said. "You can never tell when even America's horizons might not be large enough for you."

Alexandra looked at him.

He smiled, nodding slightly. "Why not?" he asked her. "Why not dream of greater glories?"

Alexandra looked at him, still, expression impossible to read.

He threw his head back, laughing, turning her on the floor with a little livelier pace. "So you do dream of greater glories. My dear, dear Alexandra—you are a most charming young woman."

This time Alexandra laughed.

"May I cut in?" Gordon asked, appearing at their side.

Lord Hargrave looked at him. "Of course," he said after a moment, turning Alexandra over to him.

"So what was that all about?" Gordon whispered, taking her in his arms, kissing her lightly on the temple and moving her around. "You've got that look on your face."

"I think Lord Hargrave may make you and me some kind of offer," she said.

"Maybe," Gordon said, looking over at him. "Boy, that would be something, wouldn't it?" he asked, looking back at her. "The two of us leaving the States?"

She shook her head—no—and pressed the side of her face to his.

"So now you know it all," Jackson said, eyes still on Cassy.

She lowered her eyes to the table, fingering the stem of her water glass. She glanced up, forehead furrowed. "So what happened to your money?"

"Beau defaulted on the payments and"—he snapped his fingers— "the bank took two-thirds and the IRS took the rest. So"—he shrugged — "except for my salary, I pretty much lost everything. But I make a great salary, and the plane and hotels and everything are part of it."

"And your children?"

"Oh, they're all set," Jackson said, bending a straw, playing with it. "I set them up years ago. Though," he sighed, "sometimes I think my kids and the whole family would be a lot better off without this kind of money. They're a pretty confused bunch—and sometimes you have to wonder if it isn't the money that's keeping them that way."

Cassy was nodding. Then she sat back in her seat, resting one hand on the edge of the table.

Jackson threw the straw down and looked at her. "I didn't expect that."

"Expect what?" she said softly.

"That you'd want to know about me. I thought you'd be firing questions at me about the miniseries and DBS News."

She shook her head. And then she shrugged. "What's there to say? I figured it had to be something like this. Not that you lost your money trying to help your brother, though." She smiled. "I knew that you had to have done something to get DBS News started a year early. When I first came, you know, Langley hated Alexandra and I always got the feeling he thought she was responsible for some terrible corporate problem."

Jackson sighed, smiling, leaning farther across the table. "Well, she was a pretty inspiring investment, I must say."

Cassy laughed. "To sell your miniseries, I should say so." She shook her head, smiling, looking at him. "Does Hargrave own all of it?"

"Two thirds now."

"So you do have some ground to stand on when you tell your family."

"A smidgen," Jackson said, smiling at her.

"And Gordon has no idea?"

Jackson shook his head, still smiling.

"Well," Cassy said, "seems like I'll have my work cut out for me."

"You still want the job?" he asked her.

"Sure," she said, smiling back. And then, a moment later, she said, "Or do you think there might be some reason why I shouldn't take it?"

His eyes were searching hers. "I don't know," he said. "You tell me."

"Uh, excuse me," Alicia, Jessica's secretary, said, appearing out of nowhere.

"Alicia," Cassy said, straightening up.

Alicia leaned over to whisper something in her ear.

"Come on," Cassy said to Jackson, quickly getting up.

Leaning back against the rail in the shadows of the bow, Jessica exhaled cigarette smoke in Langley's face. Her dress, underneath the steward's jacket, was pulled down to her waist, and her breasts were in Langley's hands. She held the cigarette to his mouth—stabbing his cheek with it twice before finding his lips—and he shook his head and buried his face in her neck, falling forward against her.

She laughed, letting her head fall back, and she brought the cigarette to her mouth up over his shoulder, smoking to the stars, while Langley, in a state of half collapse, continued to feel her breasts.

There were whispers across the deck. Figures moved away, leaving three there in the shadows. Then, in a moment, they started across the deck.

Jessica flicked her cigarette away, blowing smoke, and let her head fall forward, chin thumping down on Langley's shoulder. She squinted over Langley's shoulder and then smiled. "Hello," she said.

Jackson reached out to tap Langley on the back. "Lang—Lang," he whispered.

Langley made some incoherent sound, more determined to feel Jessica's breasts than ever.

"I need to talk to you, Lang," Jackson whispered, taking hold of his right elbow and gently tugging. "Over here, Langley, I have to talk to you over here."

"What?" Langley said, lifting his head from Jessica's neck.

"Oh, just *go,*" Jessica said, giving him a shove.

Langley tripped and nearly fell; Jackson caught him and righted him, pulling him to the other side of the deck.

Jessica stood there, jacket open, her breasts exposed, squinting, closing one eye to see.

"Jessica?" Cassy said gently, moving closer.

"Hello," Jessica said, trying to lean back on the railing, but her elbow kept missing, slipping off.

"You must be cold," Cassy said. "Let's do up your coat and take you inside to get warm." Cassy closed the steward's coat over Jessica's breasts and started to do up the buttons.

"Can I have a cigarette?" Jessica asked her.

"No," Cassy said, finished with her coat and now pushing Jessica's hair back off her face.

"Excuse me," Jessica said, eyes wandering, unfocused.

"Yes?" Cassy said.

"Can I have a cigarette?"

"Let's go see if we can find one," Cassy said quietly, taking Jessica's arm and looking back over her shoulder. "Denny?"

"I want a cigarette," Jessica said, slipping down against the railing.

In a second Denny was on the other side of Jessica, holding her up. "Come on, Jessica, stand up. That's it."

Jessica looked at him, closing one eye again to see. "Do you have a cigarette?"

"You don't smoke, Jess," he said.

"Oh," Jessica said, allowing them to lead her away.

Across the deck, Jackson was holding Langley while he threw up over the railing.

"She's fine," Denny whispered to Alexandra outside the stateroom. "She's washing up. She's not in a blackout anymore."

Alexandra sighed, shaking her head. "And I'm told my assistant is drunk in another room around here somewhere."

"Kate, right?" Denny said.

"Yes."

"She's in that one," Denny said, pointing to a door down the hall. "But she's just crying—maudlin, you know. Her boyfriend's in there with her, so I'd knock first if I were you."

"Thanks," Alexandra said, continuing on. She knocked on the door, listened, knocked and listened again. Someone said, "Come in," and she opened the door. Kate was lying face down on the bed, crying, while her boyfriend was sitting there, looking as though he felt pretty useless. "Hi," Alexandra whispered. "Why don't you let us talk for a minute, okay?"

He got up off the bed, seemingly eager to get out of there.

Alexandra closed the door behind him and then leaned back against it.

Silence.

Kate sniffed and then, cautious, raised her head to look.

"Hi," Alexandra said.

Kate sniffed again, wiping the side of her tear- and mascara-stained face with the back of her hand, sitting up. Alexandra pushed off the door, went into the bathroom and came out with some tissues. Handing them to Kate, she sat down on the edge of the bed. Kate blew her nose and then, dropping her hand, sighed. Then she sniffed again and looked at Alexandra. "I'm sorry," she said, eyes starting to fill again.

"For what?"

"I don't want you to leave," Kate wailed, falling forward to cry on Alexandra's shoulder.

Alexandra smiled slightly, patting her back. "I'll be back before you know it. It's okay, Kate, it's okay," she murmured. "Really, it is. You're overtired and—"

"And why didn't you tell me you were getting married?" Kate suddenly said, jerking away from her. "Before, I mean. Before this week." She wiped at her eyes with the tissues. "Chi Chi said she's known for months," she added. "Do you know how that makes me feel?"

"No," Alexandra said quietly. "How does it make you feel?"

The question seemed to throw Kate. She gave Alexandra a look out of the corner of her eye—like, *Oh, fuck you*—and blew her nose. Then she slammed her fist down into her lap. "It makes me feel horrible, that's how it makes me feel. Like I'm some sort of lackey for you, like you don't even like me."

"But you know that I do like you, very much," Alexandra said softly. "And that I care about you a great deal. And the reason why I didn't tell you was because I wasn't sure I was going to get married myself."

"Chi Chi says Cassy knew you were getting married months ago."

"Well, maybe Cassy did," Alexandra said, "but I didn't, and you can tell Chi Chi that from me. And I didn't think there was any point in telling you that I was engaged if I didn't think I was going to get married, all right? And in the meantime, I'll have you know—you've known more about my life with Gordon than any other human being on earth. For heaven's sake, Kate, you even know what kind of birth control I use—don't you?"

Kate nodded.

"So I'm sorry if I hurt your feelings," Alexandra said, her voice softening again. "I didn't mean to. I would never want to."

Kate had lost her despairing look and was quickly regaining her adoring one.

"And I'm going to miss you too," Alexandra said. "But you're going to have a very important job while I'm on the road. Otherwise, I'd take you with me."

"But—" Kate said, getting a pained looked again.

"But what?" Alexandra said.

"But I love you," Kate blurted out, starting to cry.

Alexandra looked pained then too, debating, it seemed, what to do next. Then she smiled and said, "I love you too, Kate—that's what close friends are all about."

Kate looked at her, sniffing.

"You are my friend, aren't you?" Alexandra asked her.

Kate nodded.

"Good," Alexandra said, getting up from the bed. "Then why don't you let Gordon and me drive you and Mark home tonight? Friends do that, you know—double-date."

Kate's face lit up. "You mean in your limo?"

"There it is," Betty said, standing next to Gordon on the bridge.

"Looks strange from here, doesn't it?"

They were talking about West End. There was the bright ribbon of the West Side Highway running past but, because of the high fir trees behind it, this close to shore all they could see of West End was the second floor, when they had hoped to see the square.

"I'm going to miss it," Betty said, moving away.

"Me too," Gordon said.

"Oh, look," Betty said, pointing over the railing to the aft deck below. "Jessica's back in action."

She was sitting in a deck chair, Alexandra standing next to her, resting a hand on Jessica's shoulder, both of them talking to Mr. Graham and Lord Hargrave.

"Never would have paired those two as friends," Betty said, shaking her head.

"Alexandra has a thing for the walking wounded," Gordon said.

"So I noticed," Betty said.

The launches glided back and forth from the ship to the dock, the wakes spreading white over the black night water. The orchestra stopped playing and voices became hushed, reverent, for under the lamps of Riverside Park, under the glow of light from buildings on the ridge above, under the light of the moon filtering down across the water, it was so eerily beautiful. Eerie because it was New York City and yet it smelled only of ocean and of cool damp earth and of lush green trees, and there was the gentle ebb of the tide, the strange echo of their voices over calm water, and a very keen sense of being alone and alive in a place where no one else seemed to be.

"This, right now," Alexandra said quietly, sitting in the launch across from Kate and Mark and Cassy and Kyle, "makes everything worth it." She looked up at Gordon beside her, and he kissed her on the mouth.

Cassy turned away, looking back over the water to the ship. She wanted to see if she could see Jackson.

But she couldn't.

And she felt awful.

33

After the Party
Part I: Rendezvous

"Psst," said a voice from behind the rock wall bordering Riverside Park.

Uh-oh, Cassy thought, pulling her shawl tighter around her shoulders and veering toward the Drive, *after all these years, I'm finally going to be a statistic.* She stood under a street light, happy to have the cars passing by, waiting to cross the four lanes to the residential side of the street where the doormen were.

When she climbed into Alexandra's limo with Kyle and Kate and Mark and Gordon and Alexandra, Cassy had been so depressed she could have screamed. She was not up for men who had wives and children they loved in their summer houses in Maine; she was not up to watching twenty-three-year-olds with their whole lives ahead of them; and she was certainly not up to watching a handsome young man nuzzling the neck of his fiancée. And so, before she did start screaming, she had asked to be let out at 79th and Riverside Drive, and they had waited there—Kyle and Kate and Mark and Gordon and Alexandra—until Cassy got a cab and was safely on her way. And then, at 81st Street, Cassy had gotten out of the cab to walk along the brick promenade edging the park, to think, to *breathe* (she couldn't breathe in that damn limo, she had felt so upset), figuring that the dog walkers would be out. And the dog walkers were out, but there wasn't one at hand at the moment, now that someone was hissing over the wall at her.

"Psst—hey," the voice whispered.

God help me, a cordial killer, she thought, willing the light to change so she could cross. And then she thought she could just toss her bag over the wall. *Right, Cassy, then he can afford to take a cab over later to return your wallet and kill you at home.*

But then, at the same moment that she saw a man waiting to cross the Drive with what she hoped could somehow be a savagely fierce beagle, she realized that she recognized the "Psst—hey" voice, that it had sounded like . . .

She whirled around to look at the rock wall. The streetlight was filtering down through the arborway of trees over the promenade, casting an intricate pattern of shadows over it. She took a step closer. "Jackson?" she whispered.

A glint of eyes appeared just over the top of the wall. "What are you doing walking out here at this time of night?" he hissed. "Have you lost your mind?"

"Oh, God," she sighed, letting her shoulders slump. "It is you. I thought you were a mugger."

"Excuse me?" the man with the beagle said, walking past her to the brick promenade that ran along the wall.

"Oh, hi," Cassy said, smiling. "I was just talking to my friend over there." She pointed to the wall. Of course, Jackson was no longer there. "Jackson," she said sharply.

Silence.

The beagle was taking a whiz against the tree; the man was looking at Cassy.

"A friend of mine is playing games behind the wall."

The man looked at the wall and then back at Cassy. "He could be dead by now," he said. "Something coulda gotten him by now."

"Jackson," Cassy said, walking over to the wall. She started to lean over it but decided against it.

"What?" came a whisper.

"Would you come out of there?"

"What's he doing behind there?" the man with the beagle said, coming over. "Is he all right?"

"I'm fine," Jackson said, finally standing up, the white of his dinner jacket and shirt luminous in the night. "I was just following this lady here. You know what she did? She got out of a limousine, caught a cab, took it two blocks, got out and walked over here to get attacked and killed. What's the matter with you, anyway?" he asked her.

"So you're okay now?" the man asked Cassy. "I can go ahead and walk Mickey-Luck?"

She nodded.

The man and his dog went on their way.

"Bye, Mickey-Luck," Jackson called softly.

Cassy watched the man and his dog stroll down the arborway, acutely aware of how hard her heart was pounding. The second she realized it was Jackson, something inside her head had clicked over into a dream world, where none of this was quite registering as real. And there was this peculiar feeling coming up over her shoulders, into her neck, this strange sensation that something was about to happen and that it was going to be very important. And then that feeling passed and she felt scared; she could feel it, the fear, a chill, right there, in her diaphragm, making her breath difficult. But mixing in with that fear was—coming fast—the adrenalin of thrill, creating something new, keenly alive, urgent, swelling her chest, making her chest feel tight. She turned back to him. "You were following me?" she managed to say.

"Yes, I was following you," he said, putting his hands on top of the wall and swinging himself on top of it. "I didn't want them to see me." He jumped down to the other side, dusting off his hands, and walked over to her. "And I wasn't sure if I wanted you to see me either." And then he took her in his arms and kissed her very hard on the mouth.

Is this happening? she thought, letting him hold her, letting him kiss her, not being able to respond yet.

He kissed the side of her mouth. He kissed the other side of her mouth. Then he hugged her to him, enveloping her in his arms. "I don't know what the right thing to do is," he whispered. "But as soon as you left, I knew that wasn't right. I knew I—" She felt him kiss the top of her head.

His arms felt wonderful. He felt wonderful. But her mind was racing back over what was wrong with this. Why she couldn't do this. "I'm not sure I can do this," she whispered.

His body tensed for a moment, and then he released her. "Oh," he said, backing away a step, sliding his hands down her arms to take her hands. He looked at her—frowning—and then he dropped one of her hands and pulled her to walk with him under the trees of the promenade. "I keep forgetting that you don't know," he said, more to himself, it seemed, than to her.

Cassy felt elated suddenly, strangely, wonderfully elated, walking along with him like this, holding his hand, feeling the breezes of summer, walking through the moving nighttime shadows.

"That I don't know what?" she asked him, thinking how nice his hand was, how large and warm it was.

"That I think I might be in love with you," he said, looking straight, walking on.

There were no cars on the Drive at this moment, and the sound of their soles over the brick inlay seemed very loud.

"I'm pretty messed up, you know," he continued after a while, still walking, still looking ahead, still holding her hand. "I'm not the sort of guy who's done real well with love. I don't seem to know how to do it very well. Love people, I mean. Something always seems to happen to them. And so I don't think I've liked it for a long time. Love, I mean. I mean I do love people—there are a lot of people I love, but I guess what I'm trying to say is that it doesn't seem to do very much good for any of us. What I mean to say is, Cassy," Jackson said, abruptly stopping and turning to her, taking her other hand, "is that there aren't any recommendations for somebody like me. I've tried and it didn't work out. And I've had an awful lot of women in the last years. So, for someone like you, I don't think you'd want someone like me, but I guess I wanted to find out if maybe there wasn't something about you that maybe could make it not be such a disaster."

Cassy didn't know what to say, so she didn't say anything.

"What I'm trying to tell you is that you scare me," he said, frowning. He paused, swallowing. "But I'm more scared of not saying anything, of not doing anything, now, while you're—before someone else—I mean, I know this isn't a good time with your divorce and all, but then someone like you—some other guy will—" He looked away, searching for whatever it was he was trying to say, and then he looked back at her, anxious.

She smiled.

He smiled, nervous, put his arms around her and kissed her again. This time Cassy slid her arms up his back to hold him too.

But then he backed away slightly, parting them, and he held her hands again, just standing there, staring down into her eyes, the wind rustling through the trees above them. Another dog owner went by; Cassy could hear the jingle of tags, though she couldn't see anything but the pain in Jackson's eyes, and all she could feel was the gentle warmth of his hands and how hard her heart was pounding because in this moment, in this very second, she did not think she had ever felt such an exquisite kind of pain as this.

She reached up to kiss him again, and he must have wanted proof that she really wanted to kiss him because he didn't lean down this time, but just looked at her, his mouth parted slightly, his eyebrows flinching. "Come here," she said, pulling on his neck. "Come down here so I can kiss you," and he did, and she, holding his face in her hands, kissed him as warmly, as tenderly as she knew how.

When she stopped, they parted, and stood there, smiling at each other.

He closed his eyes then, inhaling deeply and holding the breath, and Cassy stepped in close to him, sliding her arms around his waist, laying the side of her face against his chest. He gently rubbed her back, sighing. "I don't know what to say now," he said.

"Please don't say anything," she murmured. "Please, let's not talk at all. Not now." She pressed her forehead against his chest and held it there, wondering how it could be that she had done something to deserve this. This that she thought she had long lost. This that she had told herself would never, could never happen to her again. That in one moment she could step out of the world and into this wondrous basking of healing, where nothing existed save the divine sensation of slipping away. Just gone from the world, born into another, into a place where it felt splendid to be alive, so impossibly, exquisitely alive in ways that could only register in the ache of her heart and the longing of her body, and not get analyzed to death in her mind.

Somehow they were standing at the wall, when or how they got there she was not aware, but they were standing by the wall now, looking over it. At this place, overlooking the glen, the wall dropped fifty feet down and so they were looking down through the trees into the park, seeing how the lamps glowed along the paths below, how richly green were the trees and grass. The forest smell was delicious.

He turned to her and she to him and in that second Cassy felt something fall down through her that made her almost ill with longing. He was kissing her again, holding her, but that was not enough now, and she opened her mouth further, in a kind of plea he seemed to hear, because he pulled her in so tightly that she could feel him—God, yes, this was wonderful—against her.

Another dog was being walked past them and they smiled a bit in the midst of this deep exploration of mouths, but they did not give in to self-consciousness and continued, and when the sound of whoever faded away, Jackson's hands slid under her, lifting her up and closer into him, making a slightly groaning sound as he did so, finalizing Cassy's body's decision about what it wanted to do more than anything else in the world right now. But then she heard that awful mind of hers starting to argue—*What do you think you're doing? You can't do this! What about your work?*—and she wanted anything but that awful mind of hers to start up and so she tried to shut it down, only for it to conjure up Michael. Michael!

Cassy pulled away from his mouth—out of his mouth—inhaling sharply through a smile—oh, God, how good he felt against her—and pushed his shoulders back so she could look at him and make sure he was not Michael, not her husband, not the man she had been sleeping with for twenty-two years, but Jackson. And, thank God, it was Jackson, and it was Jackson who was now down into her neck, and she was thrilled it was Jackson, still not believing it was him, but knowing it had to be because it felt so different, was so different, and they were acting like fools—oh, yes; yes, yes; this was good—like teenagers, grappling with each other in the middle of Riverside Drive with people walking their dogs around them and cars going by and muggers probably ready to drop down out of the trees on them and, oh, God, Jackson practically had her off the ground, he was pulling her up so hard against him—

"We have to go somewhere," she gasped, breaking away from him, pulling him over to the edge of the Drive. "We've got to go," she repeated, waving her handbag at the cars. She looked back at him and saw that his face had fallen. "What? What?" she said, going back to him, holding his face. "We're going to go together. I want to go somewhere with you." She kissed one side of his mouth and then the other.

A vacant cab finally came down the Drive; they flagged it down and fell into the back seat.

"Where to?" the driver asked.

"Where?" Jackson asked her, kissing her ear.

"Where are you?" she asked him, pulling his head around so she could kiss him on the mouth.

"Here I am," he said, kissing her back.

"Gonna have to be a little more specific than that," the driver said in the front seat, flooring it to his unknown destination.

Jackson felt around in the pocket of his jacket. He withdrew from her mouth, holding up a key and looking at it. He looked at her. "Plaza? We're in New York, right?"

"I think so," she said, smiling.

"The Plaza," Jackson said, staring into her eyes.

Somewhere around the sixties he kissed her and pushed her down across the seat, both of them laughing because there was no room, no room at all for this kind of thing, and because they were crazy to carry on like this, in a cab, for heaven's sake, but oh—oh, who the hell cared so long as she could go on feeling his hands, Jackson's hands, running over her dress, over her breasts, her hips, down over her legs, up under her dress—

But damn the Central Park South lights anyway!—forcing them back into an upright position, or something that resembled one (or resembled the inside of a clothes dryer stopped in motion), and Cassy laughed at his hair and couldn't imagine what hers—oh, no, she could feel what had happened to her hair. It was down, it was all over the place, and she tried to pull herself together, trying to convince herself that she cared that she would be seen crossing the lobby of the Plaza, looking like this, feeling like this, when clearly there was only one reason she would be there at this hour with Jackson, and then suddenly there they were, at the side entrance to the hotel, and Jackson was hurling money at the driver and then they were out and the doorman smiled at her and they were going around the bronze door and they were crossing the lobby and then they were in the elevator and the doors closed and they were alone and Jackson was on top of her.

Oh, this was great, Jackson didn't even know where he was going— what floor? This floor? The next floor? But this way? What does the key say?—and as Jackson led her around, Cassy noticed how wonderfully thick the carpeting was and wondered if this was left from the old Plaza management or if this was part of the new, and then they were at a door with an ornate brass handle and Jackson fitted the key in the lock but before he turned it he turned to her. "I've never had anything," he said. "And I got tested last fall. I haven't been with anyone since."

Her mouth fell open and her mind came back on. "I—" She was overwhelmed by this. Was this what everyone had been talking about? Safe sex?

"I didn't mean to shock you," he said, looking at her.

"Oh, no," she said, kissing him. "No, it's just that I'm a little new at this." She smiled, nervous suddenly. "Um," she added, realizing that he was waiting, "let's go inside," she said, pointing to the door. He opened it and they slipped inside. She stopped him from turning on the light and slid her arms around his waist. The two of them stood there, holding each other, in the dark.

But it was not really dark. The drapes were pulled back from the windows and by the lights of Central Park and the lights of Fifth Avenue stretching north and the lights casting up from Central Park South, Cassy could make out the living room they were in quite well.

"My tubes are tied," she whispered. "I want you to know that." She swallowed, looking up at him.

He kissed her. And then he took her hand and brought it down to touch him. It was like a bolt through her, the rush of desire that came, and for a moment she could scarcely touch him for the reaction inside her. "Here," she said, breaking away from his mouth.

"What?" he whispered, sounding hoarse.

"Here," she said. "Right here."

He smiled. "You can bounce to the ceiling on the beds in—" His voice broke off and his eyes closed against the touch of her hand.

"Here," she whispered, wanting only to act and not to think anymore.

"Oh, here," he managed to get out, pressing against her hand. Then he jerked back from her, whipping off his jacket with such ferocity that she had to laugh. "Funny, huh?" he said, throwing the jacket and fumbling at his tie. He pulled the bow apart and yanked it out of his collar, tossing that too. "You think this is funny," he said as she laughed, eyes on her, tearing now at his cuff links and throwing them and then saying, "Oh, hell," taking hold of his shirt and simply tearing it apart, buttons flying. Then he lunged at her, taking hold of her dress—

"Not my Chanel!" she cried, laughing, and he laughed too, but then they were quiet, their breath picking up as he unzipped her dress and helped her out of it. She tossed it over a chair and turned to him in her slip and, as he kissed her, she undid his belt, unhooked his pants, unzipped them and eased them down over his hips. And then, gently, she brought her hands back up to ease his shorts down over his hips as well. And then, with her lower body in a lock of anticipation, she allowed herself the pleasure of sliding her hands down to feel him.

Oh, glory.

She groaned a little, he felt so wonderful.

Glory.

Oh.

This was for her, all for her; and she was gentle with her hands, reverent, and was grateful. Because he was—*Thank you, God, thank you*—so very different from Michael, and now he really was completely and only Jackson, his personality complete, right down to this physical vulnerability, to this wonderfully expressive part of him that was longing for her. For her. All of this was for her. And she couldn't stop touching him because he was so different and she wanted to know him, immediately, she wanted to know every detail of him— imagine, *Jackson,* this was Jackson in her hands, so plentiful, and so hard here, and so sleek there, and so soft here—and there, how soft he was under there—and she wanted all of him, wanted to touch all of him, make him feel how in awe she was, make him feel how splendid he felt to her and how much she wanted him, so much so that she was willing to simply go on like this and maybe give herself over entirely to the effort of giving him pleasure—

Holding her shoulders, his breath had turned ragged. And now, holding his breath, he pulled down the straps of her slip and then pulled the whole thing down over her breasts. "Oh, yeah," he sighed, taking her breasts in his hands, "oh, yeah. Oh, Cassy, you are . . . You are so beautiful," he finished, feeling her. And then his body seized up for a moment—his hands going rigid on her breasts—and she stopped her hands and simply held him. "Oh, yes," he said, voice scarcely audible, his body relaxing just a bit and hands moving over her breasts again. With each breath he made a small sound of exertion in his throat, and his hands grew stronger, massaging her breasts, pulling the rhythm of her breath to his, to that of his hands, of his sounds and sighs, and then, a moment later, to the rhythm of his gyrations in her hands.

One hand left her breast and slid down over her waist, over her hip and under her slip, feeling for her panties, finding them, tugging at them, an inch on this side, an inch on that, and then his hand slipped down inside and in between her legs. "Oh, Cass," he sighed, touching her, feeling her, "oh, Cass."

She was very wet and at first couldn't believe the sound his hand was making with her, wondering at this body of hers that kept fooling her about just how much life was in it, about just how much—

"Jackson," she gasped, on the verge of coming. "Oh, wait, please— let's—can we . . . ?" and he understood exactly what she meant because he dropped to his knees, pulling her slip all the way down to the floor and then her panties too, and then pulling her down to the floor. He kicked his shoes off, rolling to his side to kick his pants off too, and Cassy lay there, on the floor, watching him. Wanting him.

Pants off, he scooted up beside her and touched the side of her face. Then he slowly moved over and gently lowered himself down on her. She felt him pressing heavily on the inside of her thigh, and she reached down between them as he lifted himself slightly, found him, and held him for a moment.

God.

She brought her knees up slightly, shifting, guiding him to her. She brought her hand away. For a moment they hung there, on this threshold, looking into each other's eyes. He let out a breath, then, took another, held it, and, looking her straight in the eye, grasping her shoulders more firmly, he surprised her by one long, slow, continuous push inside her, spreading her to what felt like the limit—the divine limit, oh, God—and she closed her eyes, gasping in both pleasure and surprise, and when she opened them again and saw his face, his expression, she almost came on the spot.

Oh, God, it was just such a good, good fit, the two of them—it was just so teeth-clenching, lower-ache-agony good. And he lurched into his first move and it was never steady after that, and she realized that he was as close as she was already, because he was trying to be smooth in his withdrawal, smooth in his reentry, trying to give her the best of him, all of him, by drawing out very far and then pushing back into her as far as she would take him, which was just about exactly how much he had striving to get in, but there was no doubt about it, they *were* lurching, muscles straining to perform gracefully but bodies demanding—

Oh—*could there be anything, anything in the world as good as this?* she wondered.

"I can't hold it, I'm sorry," he said into her ear, holding up against her, breathing frantic.

His saying it, this declaration of Jackson needing to come, tore it right out of her. Cassy sucked her breath in, said, "Oh, God, Jack," feeling it way down there, right deeply down in there, right in where he was agonizing up against her. It all came tearing loose out of her there in the next second, rolling outward and then barreling up through her spine, pulling everything up with it, tearing her up with it, spreading, rising, rising, "Oh, God, God, Jack, Jack," she gasped, arching up against him, feeling it, feeling it, feeling him furiously resume with her, making her come, oh, God, making her come, God, how good-good-good this was, how good it was to come under him, how good it was to feel her muscles convulse around him, knowing that it was him, Jackson, that was inside of her, that it was for him she was coming so hard, and then how good, good it was, easing, letting it ride, lowering herself, easing, lying flat once more, feeling warm everywhere, all over everywhere, easing, heaven, yes, this was heaven, easing, sliding her hands down over his buttocks, easing, feeling him slow, feeling his muscles, easing, feeling the warmth seeping between them to know how it was for him now, easing, the two of them sharing it, the warmth, the wetness, easing, stopping—sighing, a final sigh—stopping, yes.

She lay there, reveling in the feel of him, in his warmth, in the certainty that Someone had to have spent aeons perfecting this fit.

Oh, but he was a wonderful man. So lovable, so kind, so bright, so very lost and so very, very wonderful.

He raised his head from her shoulder to look at her. He kissed her. And then he licked her mouth. And then he kissed her again. And then he rubbed his cheek against her mouth. And then he kissed her again. And then he said, "I want to be married to you. I do."

34

After the Party
Part II: Alexandra Has a Long Night

Back arched and straining, Alexandra let out a sharp breath and collapsed on the bed. "I'm sorry," she sighed, "I just can't." She pulled Gordon's head closer to kiss the side of his face. "I don't know what's wrong," she whispered, lifting her head to kiss his ear, "but it sure isn't you." She let her head fall back on the pillow, sighing again. "You're an angel for going on."

The candle flickered, spreading an uneven light over her face. "Are you sure?" he asked, looking down at her.

She nodded. "Oh, Gordon," she said a moment later, running her hands through his hair twice and then framing his face in her hands, "I can hear you from here. It's wonderfully pleasurable for me, all of it. It's not the same for you as it is for me. I don't have to come to . . ."

He cocked an eyebrow. "But admit it, this is something new."

She looked at him. And then she nodded.

"I think you're losing your infamous powers of concentration," he said, smiling, twisting slightly to withdraw from inside her, and then

twisting back to stay on top of her. "And there's this horrible correla-
tion between your newscast and you not being able to—"

"Don't," she whispered, pressing her hand to his mouth. "Please
don't. It won't help if I know you're keeping score."

"I'm not," he said, kissing her hand once and pushing it away with
his chin. "It's the stress, I bet." He shifted a little to bring his hand up
and pull a strand of hair out of the corner of her mouth. He hesitated
and then said, "Do you think you could bring yourself? Do you want to
try—"

The phone rang.

Alexandra reached over, blindly groping for—and finding—the receiver on the nightstand. She brought it back to her ear. "Hello?" she
said, rubbing the stubble of Gordon's beard with her free hand. And
then her body tensed and she moved her hand down to Gordon's
shoulder, frowning. "No, it's okay," she said. After a moment she
absently kissed his face and pushed his shoulder. He rolled off of her
and reached down to pull the covers up over them both. "No, I want
you to tell me," Alexandra said into the phone.

He curled up around a pillow and lay there, on his side, watching
her profile against the light. Her face was set, serious, alert. Blink.
Blink. Blink. Her lashes.

She sat up, holding the phone with both hands, letting the covers
fall to her waist. "Where are you?" she said gently. She swallowed,
regripping the phone, listening. "Jessica—Jessica," she said, "listen to
me—please." Pause. "Tell me where you are." She threw the covers
back and swung her legs over the side of the bed.

He reached over to touch the outline of her spine.

"Okay," she said, "I'll be right over." Pause. "Really. No, I'm coming.
Just sit tight until I get there." Pause. "I'm really coming, Jessica. Yes, I
am. Promise me you won't move, you won't do anything until I get
there." Pause. "Promise me." Pause. "Twenty-five minutes, tops.
Okay? Yes. Yes, I'll be there. Sit tight. I'll be there before you know it."
She hung up the phone and sat there for a moment. "Jessica's thinking
about killing herself," she then said, jumping up from the bed and
heading for the bathroom.

"What?" Gordon said, propping himself up on one elbow.

"Call downstairs for a cab, will you?" she said, leaving the bathroom door open. "She's at West End."

Gordon sat up, scooted over and turned on the light.

"Six," Alexandra said.

"Why is she calling you?" Gordon said, picking up the phone and punching 6. "Where's that guy she was with? Why didn't she call Denny?"

The john flushed; there was the sound of running water in the sink; and then she came out. "I didn't think it was a good time to ask," she said, opening a bureau drawer, pulling out some underwear and putting it on.

"Yeah, hi, this is 12D calling. Can you hail a cab for Ms. Waring, please? She'll be down in five minutes. Thanks." He hung up the phone, watching her sling on a brassiere and head for the closet. "Do you want me to come with you?"

"No—the guards are there," she said, yanking a blouse off a hanger. She put it on, turning to look at the clock. "You've got to leave in seven hours, Gordie—you better try and get some sleep."

He shrugged, falling back against the pillows. He turned his head, watching her. "Why do you suppose she called you?"

Alexandra was pulling on a pair of jeans. "I don't know," she said, zipping them up. She looked over at him. "Trusts me, I guess." She walked over to stand in front of the dresser mirror, finishing the buttons on her blouse.

"You know I like Jessica," Gordon said, "but you also know what I think about her—about this."

Alexandra didn't say anything.

"I think she called you because she knows a live one when she sees one."

Alexandra reached for the brush on her dresser and gave her hair a few vigorous strokes.

Gordon sat up. "She's calling you because she knows you'll come. I've seen it a thousand times, Lexy. You go running around after her tonight and she'll be calling you every time she's drunk and nobody else is around. She's like half the actresses I've ever worked with."

Alexandra was slipping on some Topsiders now. "Do me a favor, will you?" she said, coming back to the bed.

"What?"

She gave him a quick kiss on the mouth. "Go to sleep," she said, walking out of the bedroom.

"Sure you don't want me to come with you?" he called.

"I'll be back," she said.

As the headlights of the cab swept over the back wall of Darenbrook I, one of the security guards, flashlight in one hand, walkie-talkie in the other, came out of the square through the gate. "Hi, Miss Waring— Chuck said you were coming in," he said as she climbed out of the cab, slamming the door behind her.

"Have you seen Jessica Wright?" she said, walking quickly past him to the gate, taking her keys out of her purse as she did so. She turned around at the gate. "I said, have—"

"Yeah, yeah, I've seen her," the guard said. "I'm just trying to think of a delicate way to put it."

"What happened?" Alexandra said.

The guard shrugged, gesturing with his flashlight to the square. "She was out there, raising all kinds of hell, and we didn't know who it was—and so I went out there, and there she was, just—well, just out there with this guy—"

"Where is she now?" Alexandra said, charging on through the gate, heading for the door to Darenbrook III.

"In her office, I think," the security guard said. "Door's open, Miss Waring."

Alexandra switched her keys to her other hand and tried the door; it opened and she stepped inside the reception area of Darenbrook III. One safety light was on, making it very dark, very eerie.

"Lucas!" the security guard yelled from behind her.

"Yo!" said a deep voice, coming closer, accompanied by the sound of jangling keys.

"Where's Miss Wright?"

The guard appeared from around the corner. "Oh," he said, seeing Alexandra. "Uh, she's downstairs, on 2."

"Thank you," Alexandra said, walking on to the elevator.

"The guy in the newsroom said everything's okay," the second guard called after her.

"Maybe I should come with you," the first guard said.

"Thank you, no," Alexandra said as the elevator doors opened, "that won't be necessary." She took the elevator down to Sub Level 2. Here, too, only the safety lights were on, leaving parts of the hallways very dark. It was very quiet; the air was still; Alexandra walked quickly through the hallways of gloom to the newsroom. She rapped twice on the door and opened it.

"Jesus, Mary and Joseph!" Tirge cried, jumping up from his chair behind the night desk. He slapped his hand over his heart, "Oh, thank God. Hi. I thought you were *her* again."

"Jessica?" she said, still holding the door.

"Yeah," he said, nodding. "She's running around here somewhere."

"Where?" Alexandra said sharply.

"Down the hall somewhere." Catching her expression, he added, "Not alone. She's with one of the Nerd Brigade. He said he'd watch out for her."

Alexandra sighed, relaxing a bit. "Okay," she said, looking down the hall. She turned back to him. "Well, go back to what you were doing. I'll check in with you before I leave." She held on to her keys and tossed her purse on a chair.

She stepped back into the hall, closed the door and listened. Nothing. She started down the hall, checking doors, finding most of them locked, others dark and empty inside. She reached Jessica's dressing room and knocked. "Jessica?" No answer. She tried the knob; it was locked. She sorted through the keys on her ring and tried a key; it worked; she turned the knob and looked inside. Dark. She turned on the light. Empty, unused. She turned the light off and closed the door, continuing down the hall.

She went into engineering. Lights were on, machinery was humming, a TV monitor was on to CNN. But no one was there.

"Hello?" Alexandra said, walking through.

No answer.

She made her way through, looking around, continuing out through the back. The hallway to the control room was fully lit. As she approached the side door into the control room, through the window she could see a soft, reddish-orange light playing on the back wall inside. She tried the door. Locked. She knocked. Nothing. She listened. There was some sort of noise in there. Music? This time she pounded the door with her fist and then started looking for the key on her ring.

The door swung open suddenly and music came flooding out and Alexandra was standing face to face with a member of the Nerd Brigade, who looked scarcely older than twenty. "I didn't do anything to her, I swear," he said.

Alexandra pushed past him.

She stopped just inside the door, taking the scene in, mouth open. There, basking in the red-orange light, lying on her side across three observation chairs, was Jessica, watching the wall of monitors. Alexandra looked at the monitors. "What the . . . ?" she said, turning behind her. The door was closed, the Nerd Brigade guy was nowhere to be seen.

Alexandra turned back to the monitors. Dancing across the entire monitor bank—some forty screens—in red-orange light was a young woman in some kind of macrame bikini. Then, dancing onto the screens with her was a young guy who had nothing on except a G-string, from which hung—or bounced—a fox head, whose prominent nose was evidently made so prominent by what was hanging inside of it. The music that was blaring had a woman's voice singing something about her wanting to bang somebody's box.

Alexandra took three steps forward. "What the hell is going on?"

Bang, bang, bang, the chorus of the woman's song said.

Jessica said something that could not be understood.

The woman and man were now gyrating wildly, and the light from the monitors was doing the same thing all over the control-room walls.

Bang, bang, bang, the song was saying.

Alexandra walked over and flicked on the overhead lights.

"Arrrgh!" Jessica said, covering her face with her arm.

Across the forty screens, the fox's head was being pulled down so as to show what had been inside it.

Bang, bang, bang . . .

Alexandra went over to the console by the director's chair, scanned it with her eyes and flicked a switch.

The sound cut out.

Silence.

"Meanie," Jessica said from under her arm.

Alexandra picked up the white phone on the console and punched a few numbers.

"I was taking the pulse of American culture," Jessica said, trying to sit up now but not doing a very good job of it.

"I want somebody in here tomorrow to check this control room from top to bottom, do you understand me?" Alexandra said into the phone. She glanced at the monitors; the man and woman were dancing—spooning really—their way across the stage; Alexandra turned around. Jessica was watching the monitors through one eye. "I don't care what happened," Alexandra said, "I just want this control room in absolutely perfect order come Monday." She slammed the phone down and walked around the long desk.

" 'The Robin Byrd Show,' " Jessica said, pulling at her dress, trying to pull herself together in an abstract sort of way. "See?" She was pointing—weaving a little, but pointing—to the forty screens that were now showing an orange-red heart that said as much inside. "It's a public-accesses—*ack*cess show," Jessica explained. "I wanna have her on the show. She's great."

"I am not amused, Jessica," Alexandra said, snapping the monitors off one by one, starting at the top and working her way across.

"Shoulda watched the show then," Jessica mumbled, watching her, closing one eye again. She did not look very well. Her hair was a mess, her makeup had run down one side of her face and one of her earrings was missing. She didn't have any shoes, either.

Alexandra continued to turn off the monitors.

"You're such a fucking goody-goody," Jessica said. When there was no response to that, she added, "You make me sick."

"And you're about to make me lose my temper," Alexandra told her, moving to the bottom row of monitors.

"Oh, fuck you anyway!" Jessica said, stumbling out of her chair.

"Then don't call me in the middle of the night!" Alexandra said.

Snap, snap, snap, snap, snap went the switches on the monitors.

"Who the fuck would ever call you?" Jessica mumbled, falling over into a chair, righting herself and then continuing on toward the door.

"I hate you, I hate you—I hate all you fucking prom queens—" She knocked into another chair, cracking it into the wall.

Alexandra stopped then, rubbed her eyes for a moment, and turned around to look at her. Jessica was at the door now and Alexandra winced at the sight of claw marks on her back and someone's clumsy attempt to do the buttons of her dress back up. Alexandra closed her eyes, bringing her hand up to her mouth, murmuring, "Oh, God, help her," and opened her eyes just in time to see Jessica whack herself in the head with the door. Alexandra dropped her hand. "Oh, Jessica—wait."

"Fuck you," Jessica told her, tottering out.

"Jessica!" Alexandra ran around the desk, grabbed her keys, flew out the door and down the hall. She stopped at the doorway to engineering—no one—looked back over her shoulder and then ran back the other way, past the control room to the doors to Studio A. She pushed the bar on one of the doors and stepped inside, letting it close behind her.

The safety lights over the exits were on, and some light was coming in from the newsroom but not much. The studio was pretty dark. Empty. Huge. Alexandra took another step, listening.

And then she saw her.

Jessica was slowly making her way across the studio, toward her set. She was about halfway, there in the middle of the studio, when her form stopped and began to sway. And then, ever so slowly, her body sank to the studio floor.

Alexandra went running over. Jessica was lying on her side, curled up in fetal position, hugging her knees. Alexandra knelt down next to her, dropping the keys on the floor beside her. "Jessica?" she whispered.

"I want to die," Jessica said. "I just want to die."

"No, you don't," Alexandra said.

"I can't do this anymore," Jessica said, crying, hiding her face against her knees. "I can't stand it. I just want to die."

"No," Alexandra whispered, reaching to touch her, but hesitating.

"But I do," Jessica whimpered, curling up even tighter. "I do. I do. I want to die, but I can't even do that. I can't even kill myself."

For a long while Alexandra just sat there, hands in her lap, tears running silently down her face. And then, when Jessica stopped sobbing and started whimpering again, trembling, Alexandra murmured, "Let me hold you," and after a bit of a struggle, got Jessica to let go of her knees. "Oh, Jessica," Alexandra said, starting to cry in earnest, scooping up the top half of Jessica in her arms, "we can't let you go down like this." She held her head against her chest and began to rock her. "And we won't," she whispered, "we won't. We can't let it happen to you."

He started, and then flipped over on the bed. "How is she?"

"Better," Alexandra whispered, sitting on the edge of the bed, dressed still.

"Good," he said, pulling up the covers around him. He yawned. "You should sleep now."

"I will. As soon as she does," she said. A ray of morning light was falling between the curtains, falling right over the corner of Gordon's forehead. Alexandra reached to touch this patch of sunlight with her hand. Then she leaned over and gently kissed it. "Go to sleep," she whispered, slipping away.

She closed the door behind her and walked down the hall to the guest room. Jessica was sitting up in one of the two beds—clean and washed and dressed in a flannel nightgown—sipping on a glass of beer. She looked up when Alexandra came in and lowered the glass. "Are you sure I didn't say anything horrible to you?" she asked her.

"I'm sure," Alexandra said, coming around to sit on the inside of the bed, by the night table.

"So why the doctor?" Jessica said, holding the glass in her lap with both hands. Her expression, as she said this, looked as though she half expected Alexandra to reach out and slap her in the face.

Alexandra smiled, patting Jessica's leg through the covers. "For my peace of mind. Besides, he lives down the hall. You heard him—what are neighbors for?"

"Yeah right, Alexandra Eyes." Jessica smirked into her glass, sipping again. "We all know what kind of bill he's got in mind for you."

Alexandra laughed. "You are feeling better."

"Much," Jessica said, leaning over to put the glass down on the night table. She frowned, turning the clock toward her. "It's almost eight."

"Yes," Alexandra said.

Jessica settled back against the pillows, looking down at her hands. Then she looked up, nodding her head toward the night table. "Thanks for the beer."

"The doctor suggested it," Alexandra said.

"Yeah, I know," Jessica sighed, looking back down at her hands again.

Alexandra reached over and covered her hands with her own. "It's okay," she whispered.

Jessica shook her head. "It's not okay. I mean, what if I don't want to stop drinking?"

"Then you won't stop drinking," Alexandra said, shrugging.

"Oh, man," Jessica muttered, looking across the room. Then she brought her eyes back to Alexandra. "So isn't there ever anything wrong with you? Why do I always have to be the one who's a mess?"

Alexandra threw her head back and laughed.

And laughed.

And laughed.

Jessica was smiling, laughing a little too. "Well, thank God—the first sign that there is something."

Alexandra smiled, clearing her throat.

"Come on—you can tell me, Alexandra Eyes." Jessica leaned forward. "What is it? A stable of lovers, right?"

Alexandra laughed. "Hey, my fiancé's right down the hall, remember?"

"Who could forget? Flash Gordon marries Alexandra the Great— one for the record books. Meanwhile, back at the ranch," she said, sagging against the pillows with a sigh, "Jessica quietly drowns in despair."

"No," Alexandra said, shaking her head.

"No?" Jessica asked her.

"No," Alexandra said.

Silence.

"I'm pretty scared," Jessica admitted. She sighed, closing her eyes.

"You couldn't hold me for a minute, could you?" She opened her eyes, sniffing.

"Of course," Alexandra said, opening her arms as Jessica leaned forward.

Jessica rested the side of her face on Alexandra's shoulder, eyes closed, as Alexandra held her, lightly rubbing her back. "I have to tell you," she said after a while, "but I'm afraid I'd go crazy if I didn't drink. It's the only thing holding me together these days."

"No, Jessica, no," Alexandra said. "It's what's making your body chemistry so screwed up."

"I'm screwed up, period," Jessica said.

"Right," Alexandra said, pushing Jessica back against the pillows. Then she reached over for some tissues from the night table and handed them to her. "That's why I like you, right?" she asked her. "That's why you're my friend—because you're all screwed up, period."

Jessica, wiping her eyes, started to laugh.

"And I have nothing better in my life to do than to invest my emotional energy in screwed-up people," Alexandra continued. "As a matter of fact, the single most important responsibility of anchors everywhere is to collect screwed-up people who have absolutely nothing to contribute to them and do nothing but waste their time." She gave Jessica's shoulders a little shake. "Right? Isn't that why I care about you?"

Jessica smiled and blew her nose.

"And I'll tell you something else," Alexandra said.

Jessica lowered the tissue. "What?"

"If you didn't drink, I'd have a ton of secrets I could tell you about myself. And heaven knows," she added, rolling her eyes, "I could use somebody to tell them to these days."

Jessica turned her head slightly, narrowing her eyes at her. "Secrets —yeah, sure."

"*Yeah,*" Alexandra said, widening her eyes. "Enough to ruin me, believe me."

Jessica's eyebrows went up, expression hopeful. "Yeah?"

"Yeah," Alexandra said, nodding.

"No shit," Jessica said, looking at her. "Huh." And then she sighed, turning to toss the tissues in the wastepaper basket by the bed. "Well, it's a motive anyway." She looked at Alexandra. "It's got to be pretty good, though. If I stopped drinking and found out that your secret was that you once got a C in field hockey, I'd be pretty upset."

Alexandra laughed a little but then turned serious, saying, "Jessica," and reaching for her hand.

Jessica looked at her.

"I don't know if you want to stop drinking," Alexandra said quietly. "All I know is that I'm willing to help you in any way I can. It's your life, it's your business—and you're my friend, but that doesn't give me the right to interfere. And I wouldn't want to." She swallowed. "But being your friend does give me the right to say that your drinking's interfering with our friendship, and that it frightens me to think about how much worse things can get for you. Your health, your sanity, your dignity." She bit her lower lip, looking up at the wall for a moment. Then she looked at Jessica again. "I just don't want you to have to lose any more." She let go of her hand, dropping her eyes. "I'm sorry," she murmured, "I don't mean to lecture you."

"You're not," Jessica said. After a moment, "I just don't want to let you down. Because I've got to tell you, I'm not sure I can do it."

Alexandra looked at her. "Let me down?" she whispered. "Oh, Jessica—you really don't understand, do you?" She paused. "I haven't had a real friend in years. You're not letting me down—you're already my friend. There's only you we have to worry about—about whether or not you can see yourself through my eyes and know what a truly wonderful person you are." She smiled slightly, eyes glistening. "And know that what you have is a gift—that you have many gifts—and that the proper response to being given a gift is to say thank you and to use it—not to throw it away or belittle it. But it's hard," she added, voice growing louder. "God knows, it's hard. I don't know why it's so hard for us to be happy in this industry," she said, waving her hand through the air and dropping it, "but it is. There's something about the burning desire that we all have to get here that seems to want to kill us once we are."

Jessica sighed, nodding. "I know."

"And I am here, and you're here, and you are my friend and I want us to help each other learn how to make the most of what we've been given, and to figure out how to build ourselves lives that replenish something of what we give away to everybody every day."

Jessica's eyes were drooping slightly.

Alexandra smiled. "Enough," she said, patting Jessica's hand. "Enough for one day. We're both exhausted."

"Hard work, baby-sitting," Jessica said.

"Look you," Alexandra said, smiling, "do you think you might be able to go to sleep now?"

"Look you," Jessica said, giving her a light punch on the arm, "yeah." She leaned forward and kissed Alexandra on the cheek. "You've got strange taste in friends, Waring, but I love you anyway." Then she fell back and nestled down under the covers.

"Sleep as late as you like," Alexandra said, standing up and then leaning over to straighten the pillows a little under Jessica. "Gordon has to leave for the airport at ten-thirty. And if you get up and I'm not here, I'm just out for a run." She pulled the covers way up and then turned them down, proceeding to tuck them in around Jessica. "The bathroom's right there and you know where the kitchen is—help your-self to anything you want. And wake me if you need me," she said, tucking the last bit of covers in, "okay?"

"Okay," Jessica said.

Alexandra smiled at her. And then she leaned over and kissed her on the forehead. "Sleep well."

"Thanks," Jessica said. And then, as Alexandra reached to turn off the bedside lamp, Jessica turned her head to look at the night table. "Take that with you, all right?"

"Take what?" Alexandra said softly.

"The beer. Take it with you."

Alexandra looked at her. "You sure?"

"I'm sure," Jessica said, closing her eyes, turning on her side and pulling the covers up over her shoulder. Then she opened her eye a crack. "I've only had about two million hangovers, Alexandra Eyes, so I should know—I'll be fine. Just leave the water."

Alexandra smiled. "Okay," she said.

And so Alexandra turned off the light and left the room, carrying out the first drink that Jessica Wright had ever not wanted to finish.

35

Lovers

She stirred. He heard her, wondering if she was asleep and merely turning over, or if she was awake still, like him. He felt her lips on his back. He felt a gentle kiss.

Jackson smiled.

"I don't hate him. I just don't want to feel anything for him."

"Yeah. I know."

"Do you?"

"Yeah. To love someone and be hurt so badly that you hate them for a while, hoping it'll swing back to something in between—something you don't really feel, one way or the other."

Silence.

"Does it work?"

"No." Pause. "You know, it's okay—you can ask me."

"About . . . ?"

"Barbara. Don't you want to ask about her?"

"I don't want—"

"It's all right, really. I don't mind. Not with you. Wait—can you scoot over a little?"

"Like this?"

"Perfect. There—comfortable?"

"Mmmm. Very."

Silence.

"Good golly Miss Molly, but you're beautiful."

Silence.

"Taste good, too."

"Silly."

"Know what?"

"Hmmm?"

"She'd approve. Barbara, I mean. She would."

They took showers, dressed, went downstairs to Jackson's car and drove to Cassy's.

He loved her apartment. He said it reminded him of a New England farmhouse with a view. And nice high ceilings. A man could breathe here, he said. He looked at pictures carefully. He looked around each room carefully. He asked many questions. He kept his hands behind his back, though, careful of her family's territory.

She changed into blue jeans and made breakfast. He sat on a stool at the breakfast bar and they talked like pals.

She had to drop off a present for the baby of some friends of hers who lived down the street. She asked him if he wanted to wait in the car or come up. He said he'd like to meet her friends. If she didn't mind. She said she didn't mind at all.

They took the elevator to the top floor. Her friends' names were Amanda Miller and Howard Stewart. Howard greeted them at the door and led them back to the living room, where his wife, Amanda, was pacing back and forth, carrying their new baby daughter, Emily Tinker Stewart. Emily was screaming her head off and her mother was crying with her. A woman who was both Cassy's and Amanda's house-keeper, Rosanne, came out with a silver tea service and announced that she was renaming the baby Screaming Mimi. Then a nice old lady named Mrs. Goldblum came in with a plate of cookies. She put the plate down, sat in the rocking chair by the window and motioned for Amanda to bring the baby to her. Amanda handed Emily over to her and Mrs. Goldblum talked to Emily. "Oh, sh-sh-shhh, yes-yes-yes, my little princess-poo, I know, we have a little gas, don't we? I know, I know, my sweet, it's no fun, no fun at all, is it? Oh-oh-oh, no-no-no, I know, my little pet, my littlest lamb," and Emily, being patted and rocked and spoken to as Mrs. Goldblum's littlest lamb, was soon asleep. And so Amanda stopped crying and starting smiling, holding hands with her husband and paying attention to her guests for the first time.

They sent the car away, deciding to walk. They walked east. With his arm around her shoulders, they strolled down through Central Park, to the Plaza. To make love.

"No, I didn't mean that. There was one other person besides Michael. But I don't want to talk about it. Not now—"
"Please—shhh. Stop. I wasn't asking. Really, I wasn't."

They took a shower together and then they walked through Central Park again to the Upper West Side. They scouted Cassy's neighborhood, shopping for dinner.
They held hands at the butcher's counter.

"It's Alexandra—would you mind terribly going in the other room? It's just that I can't talk business to her while you're sitting here like this. I—"
"No, of course not. Oh, listen, maybe I could call Langley."
"In the den, sure. Use the other line."
"We can take care of all our business and then . . ."
"Mmmm. Okay, sweetheart, come on—she's going to think I left town."

"I hope you didn't mind."
"Mind? What crazy lunatic would ever mind making love with you?"
"I meant the guest room."
"No, not at all. I like being a guest—certainly this kind of guest. We never had this kind of action in our guest room back in Hilleanderville, that's for sure."
Silence.

"Oh, you are impossible."

"No. I'm in love. With the most wonderful woman in the world."

Silence.

"So are you going to marry me or what?"

"What?"

"Well, why not? What are we waiting for?"

"I think it might be wise to spend more than sixteen hours together."

"Seventeen?"

"How 'bout we just try and take it a day at a time and see where it goes."

"A day at a time and see where it goes? I want to marry you, not go on the Lewis and Clark expedition."

"I'm serious, Jack. I just can't handle much more than this—not until I have some idea . . ." A sigh. "I just don't want to think about anything right now. I just want to be here with you and let tomorrow come when it comes. Which it will."

Silence.

"Why do you go to a therapist? You said you had to go tomorrow."

"Uh-huh." Pause. "I go because . . . because sometimes I have trouble knowing what I feel. I know it sounds funny, but it's true. I always have. Since I was little. Though I didn't know it—not for years."

Pause.

"Will you talk about me?"

Laughter. "Will I ever be talking about you!"

"And will I get a chance to defend myself?"

"What?"

"Defend myself. Show myself. State my case after he—"

"She."

"After she tells you that I'm no good for you."

"She would never say anything like that."

"Can I meet her?"

"Jackson!"

"What? I just want to know if I can meet her."

"Why do you want to meet my therapist?"

"Because I want to meet somebody, know somebody who knows

about us." Pause. "I want to ask somebody for permission to court you, all right? Oh—go ahead and laugh, you. Come 'ere."

She was not at all comfortable with the idea of Jackson sleeping with her in her apartment. But she wanted to sleep with him all night. She wanted to feel him next to her all night.

And so she packed a case, left the number where her answering service could reach her in case of an emergency, and she went back with him to the Plaza. And she slept next to Jackson all night. And she felt Jackson next to her all night.

And Cassy slept better than she had in years.

36

Langley Asks What He Should Do

"Good morning," Adele said, sitting at her desk as usual on Monday morning.

"Good morning," Langley said, pausing a moment, thinking it might be possible that Adele would leap out of her chair and yell, "You disgusting jerk! You got drunk Saturday night, attacked Jessica Wright and practically threw up on the deck. Some president you are!"

But she didn't and so Langley continued on into his office.

He half wished Adele would yell at him. He felt terrible about what had happened, about his behavior at the boat party, and he didn't think he would feel better about it until somebody did yell at him.

Actually, he thought that if someone did yell at him, then he could bring himself to tell someone how close to the edge Belinda was pushing him—about how really bad things were getting and how he thought he couldn't stand it anymore. How it felt to hate someone he loved so much, and how he hated Belinda with such a fury at times that it scared him. And it wasn't her fault! he kept reminding himself, but he still felt betrayed by her, used and played with in some sort of hideous, twisted game of mental illness.

Nobody could know what it was like to have his wife show up one tenth of the time and spend the rest of her time either running away from him or going off her rocker. What kind of life was this for either of them? And yet he had kept hoping it would somehow right itself. That things would change. But, after Saturday morning, he didn't know how long he could hack it.

Belinda had called him at two Saturday morning, pleading for him to come out to Connecticut. She missed him so much, she said, she was having nightmares, she was frightened and she needed her Langley, desperately, she needed him. And so he had gotten up and driven out there, only to have Belinda come to the front door in her bathrobe, threatening to scream her head off if he didn't go away and leave her alone. Langley tried to calm her down, but then she did start screaming, waking the servants, and she got so crazy when he tried to step inside the house that the maid and chauffeur suggested he wait outside.

Wait outside!

Then the maid came out and told him Mrs. Peterson seemed to be fine now, and told him in such a way as to suggest that she thought he must have done or said something awful to so upset her. And the maid didn't dare say it to him, but Langley got the message—it would be better if he left. So he did and drove back to the city.

He got back to the apartment, undressed and went back to bed. At seven the phone rang again and it was Belinda again, pleading with him to come out to Connecticut, apparently having no memory that he had driven out there once already. When he tried to explain that, she got hysterical, saying that she would kill herself if he didn't come. Langley promised he would come, hung up and then quickly called the house back on the other line and talked to the maid, who said she wouldn't let Belinda alone for a minute. (At this point the servants at least never seemed panicky; they seemed quite used to all this.)

Then Langley called Belinda's psychiatrist in Manhattan to ask him what he should do. Belinda had been seeing this psychiatrist, Dr. Balakudian, for over six years and, while Langley had always been grateful for one strand of continuity in her parade of problems and doctors, he secretly hated Balakudian because Balakudian had a way of making Langley feel like *he* was the crazy one somehow—as though Belinda's insanity made perfect sense if only Langley's brain could comprehend it correctly.

DR. BALAKUDIAN: Well of course you should go back out to make sure she is all right.

(Dr. Balakudian had this horrible monotone and vague accent that made Langley feel like he was being hypnotized by Bela Lugosi.)

LANGLEY: Her maid is with her—

DR. BALAKUDIAN: But she called you.

LANGLEY: I know she called me! And I'm in New York City and it's going to take me a while to get out there and so should I call someone out there? The police?

DR. BALAKUDIAN: You cannot call the police on your wife.

LANGLEY: If she's going to kill herself, I sure as hell can! Then give me the number of a doctor out there I can call, Balakudian!

DR. BALAKUDIAN: I am not going to refer you to another doctor.

LANGLEY: Then come with me!

DR. BALAKUDIAN: I cannot go to Connecticut. I have a wife and children.

LANGLEY: Then tell me what to do! What's the matter with her? What the hell am I supposed to do?

DR. BALAKUDIAN: I told you, I would drive out and see her.

LANGLEY: But what do I do about her the rest of the time? She's acting crazy—surely you can't think it's normal for your patients to be threatening to kill themselves in the middle of the night—

DR. BALAKUDIAN: She is not crazy. She suffers from acute depression.

LANGLEY: You've been telling me that for years and she's getting worse! Why is she running around like a madwoman and why don't you give a fuck?

DR. BALAKUDIAN: Excuse me?

LANGLEY: What am I supposed to do, lock her up?

DR. BALAKUDIAN: I have told you, Mrs. Peterson cannot be incarcerated in any way or it will only increase her feelings of failure.

And so Langley drove back out to Greenwich, only to be told by the kitchen girl that Belinda and her maid and the chauffeur had only just left. And so Langley called up the car and the chauffeur said everything was fine, Belinda was sound asleep in the back, and that he was driving her to Baltimore to visit her brother and sister.

"The twins?" Langley yelled into his car phone, nearly veering into the guardrail on I-95. "You're not taking Belinda to see the twins. You turn that car right around and bring her into Manhattan."

There was a long silence on the other end of the phone and then the maid got on. "Mr. Peterson? I think—" And then the phone went dead. Or they disconnected the phone on the other end, because when Langley tried to call back it just rang and rang. And so he called—oh, God—Norbert Darenbrook and found out that, yes, Belinda was expected to come down today. Why, was there something wrong?

Great. Just great, Langley thought. *I don't even know what Belinda does in her life anymore. The twins! The twins! She hates the twins!* He drove back to Manhattan and the other half of the gruesome twosome, Noreen, called him at two-thirty to say that Belinda had arrived safely and to ask him what was happening to their baby sister that she was such a wreck? "We put her straight to bed," Noreen said. "The poor little thing looked like someone washed her on the rocks and put her through the ringer."

"I know, I know," Langley said, knowing that all of this was being recorded somewhere so that one day the twins could move to take Belinda's voting stock out of her hands for reasons of mental incompetence.

"She's supposed to give out scholarship awards tonight in memory of Alice May, but I don't know if she's going to be fit to go," Noreen said as her little lapdog started yapping in the phone.

"What scholarship awards?" Langley asked, knowing that Jackson couldn't know anything about this or else he never would have scheduled the boat party. Not when it had to do with the memory of his mother.

Silence. "You mean you don't know about the fund Baby B set up this year? Piccolo, quiet. Shhh! Stop it! Mommy says stop it! Journalism scholarships for girls? Langley, what *is* going on up there, anyway? Poor Belinda's breaking up like animal crackers and you and Jackie don't seem to give a damn."

He finally got to talk to Belinda, who sounded tired and out of it, but sane at any rate. "I just want to sleep, Langley," she said, sounding very far away. "I'll tell you all about it tomorrow." And she hung up on him.

And so, late Saturday afternoon, Langley said fuck it, changed his clothes and went to the boat party, determined to have a good time.

And so he had gotten drunk, molested Jessica, thrown up over the side of the ship and gone to sleep.

Appropriate behavior all the way around this weekend in the Peterson family.

And then yesterday, Sunday, Belinda had called from Baltimore sounding not only perfectly fine but in extremely high spirits. She chattered on and on about this scholarship fund she had set up. "I just wanted to do a little something on my own, Lang. Jackie and everybody have all of their things, and Mama would have been happy that, even if I didn't amount to much, I put some of her money to use to help some other young gals get somewhere."

(Hearing this made Langley feel sick at heart. There was a kind of patheticness attached—or was it pathetic? Or was it Belinda's defensiveness? That she felt compelled to hide this—ask the *twins* for their help to do it because she was scared he and Jackson would somehow take it away from her? And would they have? Would they have thought she couldn't handle it? He didn't know. But he did know that to hear her say this hurt him more than any crazy thing she had ever said to him. It made him feel awful—just awful. And on top of it, he knew how it would kill Belinda if she knew what he had done the night before—that he had been on the make, for God's sake. And with Jessica! Whom she so liked!)

Then, as the conversation continued, it became clear that Belinda had no memory of having called him Saturday morning, of having seen him in Greenwich Saturday morning, or of having called him again. And she was furious when he told her he had called Dr. Balakudian.

BELINDA: Why did you call Claude?

LANGLEY: Because I was scared, honey.

BELINDA: Scared about what, for heaven's sake?

LANGLEY: Honey, you were screaming over the phone. You were
   threatening to—

BELINDA: (starting to cry) Why are you throwing this in my face, why? You know I can't help it—how can you yell at me for something I don't even remember? How could you be so cruel? I'm having a wonderful time and you have to be so cruel to me—

But back to the problems at hand.

Langley called Adele into his office. "Sit down," he told her, gesturing to a seat. She did so and Langley stood there, hands in his pockets. "I wanted to say something about Saturday night. About how—" He paused, thinking of how to say it, and then thinking, *Asshole, be a man once in your life,* and said, "I'd like to apologize for getting so drunk Saturday night. It was very embarrassing for everyone, and I'd imagine, um, particularly for you—since you work with me." He looked at her. "I'm really sorry, Adele—that you had to see it. And I hope you'll accept my apology."

She smiled a little and nodded. "It brought back memories," she said.

"What?"

"Memories of the first year I worked for you." Then she lowered her eyes, as if afraid she had gone too far.

"No," Langley said, leaning back against his desk, "tell me."

She looked at him and smiled. "The only other time I've seen you or ever heard of you being drunk was at our very first Christmas party at Darenbrook Communications. In Richmond. In December of 1969. Remember?"

He smiled and nodded, although inside he felt sick. She was right. It probably was the last time he had gotten drunk like that. It was the night he had left the party with Belinda, having no idea she was a Darenbrook.

Jessica was not in yet, and so Adele left word that Langley wished to come down and see her for a moment when she was. And then Langley had her call Cassy's office, to tell her that he wished to see her in Jessica's office as soon as Jessica got in. That done, he knocked on Jackson's door and went in to apologize to him.

"Hi ya, Lang!" Jack said, jumping up from the easy chair in the corner of his office, where most mornings he read through forty-seven Darenbrook papers with his coffee.

Langley looked at him. He couldn't put his finger on it, but there was something different about him. . . . And then he realized what it was. Jack was elated. "What is it?" Langley asked him. "What's happened?"

"Nothing," Jackson said, tossing the paper in his hand over his shoulder. It unfolded in the air and came drifting down in sheets. And Jack stood there, beaming at Langley, hands on his hips. (He was in a new suit and tie, but he was standing like Jack La Lanne, ready to lead into exercises.) "So, how are ya?" Jackson asked him—in the same tone of voice one might use to ask, "So how does it feel to win ten million dollars in the lottery?"

"What's going on?" Langley said, looking around the office.

"Nothing," Jackson insisted, coming over to him and slapping him on the back. "I'm just in a good mood."

"Why?" Langley said.

"I don't know," Jackson declared, whirling around and then doing a little soft shoe over to the bar. "How about some coffee there, Lang?" he said, shuffling in behind it.

"Yeah, sure, thanks," Langley said, digging his hands into his pants pockets and walking over. "Listen, Jack, I came in to formally apologize for my behavior Saturday night."

"Apology accepted," Jackson said, picking up a mug, tossing it in the air and catching it in his other hand.

Langley looked at him.

"No problema," Jackson said, pouring coffee into the mug.

Langley frowned. "Excuse me, Jack, but there is a problem. And, uh, I've got to make it up to Jessica somehow."

Jack was whistling through his teeth, pouring some milk into the mug. "You make it up to her by never doing it again," he told him, looking up and handing him the mug.

Langley nodded once, accepting the mug. "Yeah, right. Thanks." He took a sip.

"And never do it again to any Darenbrook employee so long as you live," Jackson added, still smiling, but his voice sharp.

Langley looked at him and nodded.

"And if you have needs that aren't being met," Jackson said, averting his eyes and lowering his voice, "remember that there are more discreet ways of getting them taken care of." He moved away from the bar, adding, "So if that's what's happening, tell me and I'll arrange something."

And then Jackson went on to talk about other things, leaving Langley at first unsure that he had heard him correctly. Had Jackson just told him that, if he wanted to cheat on Belinda, he would arrange it? Langley was feeling vaguely sick again, the same way he had when Belinda told him about her scholarship fund.

"Lang?" Jack said, sitting in his easy chair again. "Did you hear what I said? Jessica's going to try and stop drinking, so Cassy wants us to be very careful with her the next couple of weeks—"

"Jessica's going to stop drinking?" Langley said. "Why? I mean, what . . . ?"

"Look, I don't know what Jessica's problems are," Jackson said, "but I do know that if she's at Alexandra's because she can't be alone and tells Cassy she wants to try and stop drinking, then I'm just going to take her word for it that she should try and stop drinking. Or do you want our talk show lady tearing her clothes off in public every night?"

Langley felt his face get warm.

In a few minutes Adele knocked and poked her head in to say that Jessica had come in, and so Langley went over to her office in Darenbrook III. Cassy was there when he arrived, sitting at one of the chairs in front of Jessica's desk. Jessica, looking fine, he thought, was sitting behind her desk with a bottle of Perrier in her hand. He sat down in the chair next to Cassy and stammered his way through an apology for his behavior Saturday night, saying that, as Jackson had said, the only real apology he could make would be to see that it never happened again. And then he said he would never dream of compromising Jessica—

"Wait a minute, Mr. Mitchell," Jessica said, stopping him by holding up her hand. She took a sip from the straw in the Perrier and then said, "Listen, I don't remember much about what happened—and I don't really want to know what happened." She put the bottle down on the desk. "And it was probably my fault anyway."

"No," Langley said firmly, shaking his head.

Jessica looked at Cassy then, and there was an uncomfortable silence in the room. Cassy cleared her throat and turned to Langley.

"Thank you for saying it, Langley. It's important that you did." She looked at Jessica. "And it's important that you heard it."

"But I was so smashed I—" Jessica started.

"So you accept responsibility for what you did," Cassy said quickly, "and Langley is accepting responsibility for what he did. And that's the way it should be."

Again, there was an uncomfortable silence.

"And we were very, very lucky," Cassy said. "As hard as it is, thank God you two are grown up enough to work through this so you can continue working well together. I don't have to tell you it usually doesn't happen that way."

Jessica and Langley, both reddening slightly, glanced at each other.

"Oh, God," Jessica groaned, lowering her head to her desk. "I don't want to be a grownup." She covered her head with her arms. "I want to go back to Tucson so I can blame everything on that rotten son of a bitch husband of mine and have everybody pretend to agree with me."

"I know the feeling," Langley said.

"So," Cassy said after a moment, patting the arms of her chair once and standing up, "are you guys okay?"

Jessica sat up, sighed and nodded. "Yeah."

Cassy turned to Langley.

"Yes," he said. "Thanks a lot for coming. Um, I did want to talk to Jessica briefly about something else, so if you need to go . . ."

Cassy did need to go and Langley watched her leave the room. Then he turned back to Jessica, shifting uneasily in his seat. He did not want to ask her what he was about to, and yet he knew he had to. If he didn't do it this morning—while he was feeling so awful—he knew he might never ask. And he had to. He had to. And it scared him.

"Um," he said, voice unsure, eyes on her desk, "I wanted to ask you about something you said Saturday night."

"Oh, no," she groaned, falling back down on the desk. "Don't tell me."

Langley watched her for a moment and then said, "It was about Belinda, something you said."

"Oh," Jessica said, sitting up, looking surprised. "What was it?"

Langley took a breath. "You said something about Belinda having housewife's disease—"

"Oh, that," Jessica said. "I'm sorry, that wasn't any of my business. I shouldn't have—"

"But I want to know what you meant by that," he said in a rush. "I want to know what it is."

"It's not a real disease," Jessica said, gesturing with her hand, looking a little nervous.

"But what is it? Belinda's had more goddam doctors and none of them have said anything about—I mean, I've never heard the phrase before. Any you said it right away, like you knew exactly what you were talking about."

Jessica looked at him for a long moment. Her expression was very serious. Then she dropped her eyes, still not speaking.

"Jessica—"

"I'm not sure that I want to get involved in this," she said, reaching for her Perrier. "I really don't think I knew what—"

"You knew what you were saying," Langley said firmly, leaning forward in his seat. "And I want you to tell me what you meant. I love my wife!" he blurted out. He pulled out his handkerchief and held it to his mouth for a second, falling back in his chair. Then his breathing slowed, and he lowered the handkerchief, swallowed and looked at Jessica. "Did you hear what happened when she was here?" he asked her. "When she was at West End that day? After your show?"

"I heard something," Jessica admitted.

"Something," Langley repeated to himself. He sighed. "There is something—there's something. And I know you know something, Jessica. Because the way you said it—"

"But I *don't* know, Langley," Jessica said, looking him straight in the eye. "That's just the point. I don't know. And I don't want to cause any problems in your marriage that might not even be there. It's just that I thought I might know something about your wife's mood changes."

"Mood changes!" Langley said, holding his handkerchief to his mouth again. Then he shook his head, took off his glasses, wiped his forehead and jammed his handkerchief back in his pocket. He stood up and turned away, putting his glasses back on, and then turned back to her, holding out his hand. "Just tell me what you would do, would you? Would you, please?" He dropped his hand. "If you were me, Jessica, and you were scared sick about your wife—about the person who means more to you than anyone has ever meant to you—what would you do?" He paused and then whispered, "Tell me, please— what would you do if you were me?"

Jessica blinked several times, looking at him. And then finally, quietly, she said, "I would ask the pharmacy for a complete record of the prescriptions they've filled for my family." She sighed, looking away for a moment but then bringing her eyes back to meet his. "And then I'd start looking for pharmacies I didn't know were filling prescriptions for my family."

37

The Strange New Life of Jessica Wright

Jessica remembered asking Alexandra to throw out the rest of her beer early Sunday morning, but she certainly did not remember asking to be taken to an Alcoholics Anonymous meeting. But then, Sunday night, when Alexandra put her on the phone with Cassy and Cassy said, "Jessica, sweetheart, would you like to sign into a treatment center, or would you like to try an AA meeting tomorrow and see how you like it?" she didn't know quite what to say. (Oh, yeah, she knew what she *wanted* to say—"Are you out of your fucking mind? I was *kidding*. It was a *joke*. I just said all that last night so Alexandra wouldn't throw me out in the street!") But then she heard herself tell Cassy that she would like to try an AA meeting to see what it was like.

AA? was all Jessica could think. Had her life come to this? From Essex Fells to AA? Surely national talk show hosts did not go to AA. ("Do you think AA is the right place for someone like me?" she asked Alexandra. When the question provoked the faintest hint of amusement around Alexandra's mouth—as much as to say, "Well, dolly, seems like you've got the credentials to me"—Jessica muttered, "Never mind.")

Alexandra was very keen on this idea of her not drinking for a while. And since Jessica had never dreamed of not drinking something every night and therefore had never *not* had something to drink every night (at least not willingly, not since her first night of college, except—let's see—hospital stays, temperatures over 102, and the stomach flu [unless it was the kind of "flu" that magically disappeared with two drinks]). And so the idea of really not drinking—absolutely not even one glass of wine—even for one day, *voluntarily,* was something of a revolutionary, if not radical, idea for Jessica.

(It had always baffled Jessica how people who did not drink had lives. What did they use as a bribe to get all the things done they had to during the day? What did they have to look forward to all day? And if they didn't drink at night, how and when did they turn the world off? The pressure? The work? The pace? The endless demands? And how the heck did they ever have sex?)

In any event, Jessica spent her very first night of voluntarily not drinking making chocolate chip cookies from scratch with Alexandra and watching a movie on her big television. "Waring," Jessica yelled from the front hall, looking inside the Video Access bag that had just been delivered, "you've got to be kidding—I'm not watching this!" The movie was *Days of Wine and Roses.*

But she did watch it. And cried through a lot of it. And—oh, brother, yes, it was true—she really liked it. And the cookies were great and the couch was comfortable and the afghan was nice and Alexandra was too and Jessica even drank a glass of milk, for Pete's sake, and it was all very—very *Kansas,* Jessica thought. And later, after she took a hot bath, after she put on a fresh flannel nightgown, after Alexandra tucked her in again, after Alexandra kissed her good night on the cheek, she said so.

"Very Kansas," she sighed, curling up on her side, sleepy.

Monday was a very weird day. Jessica had felt very strange when she woke up—not bad, just strange. Dreamlike. Weird. But okay. Just not "with it." Alexandra made her breakfast and it tasted very good. They had seedless purple grapes and strawberries and blueberries with plain yogurt poured over them, topped with Grape-Nuts. Jessica also had a piece of toast. And two pieces of bacon. She was very hungry. She drank a lot of fresh orange juice mixed with seltzer too. She insisted on going to work and doing her show as usual. This morning was an extremely important interview for everybody, including the DBS News international syndication group—a closed-set hour interview with Clint Eastwood at ten-thirty.

Alexandra offered to sub for her.

Jessica told her she could take a flying fuck at the moon.

And so Jessica went to work and had a very bizarre conversation with Langley, who wanted to apologize for what she couldn't remember from Saturday night, and then the conversation turned very scary when Langley asked her if she knew anything about his wife Belinda's problems. It was a very difficult moment for Jessica. She had no desire to tell on Belinda, to say anything about her carrying around enough tranquilizers to render half the set gaga, but Langley was so upset and she knew that if Belinda Peterson was in trouble with pills it could be the kiss of death for her—and certainly she was well on her way if her reputation around West End as periodically insane was in fact connected. And Langley seemed completely oblivious to the possibility. And so she led him to the possibility by telling him if she were he, she would check her prescriptions.

Guilt, talk about guilt! Jessica came close to picking up the phone and calling Belinda Peterson to warn her. And then she thought, *But what if she's going to die?* And then she thought, *But so what? If she wants to zonk out on pills, that's her business. This is America. . . . But she's a mess, everybody thinks she's crazy—well, maybe she is crazy. Oh, yeah, crazy like me, that's why I liked her so much. Call her before he does something and gets her pills! LISTEN TO YOU. If she doesn't have a problem, there won't be a problem. Stay out of it, stay out of it. Oh, God, do I feel like a drink!*

So this was the shape she was in when she went downstairs to meet Clint Eastwood. Ironically enough, her feeling too numb to set much of a pace for the interview resulted in one of the best shows she had ever done. As everybody declared afterward, her getting out of his way, letting him set his own pace, had done more to bring out Eastwood's personality than anything else she could have done. ("No offense, Jess," Denny said, "but when you have a personality like a freight train, getting it off the tracks sure has a way of bringing the sound up on everything else." Jessica looked at him. "For seven years you tell me I'm great and the second day I'm trying to stop drinking you tell me I have a personality like a freight train? I must have been drunk to hire you." "You were," Denny cheerfully reminded her. "But I hired you.")

Showing some of the tape to Alexandra in the late afternoon, Jessica shook her head and said, "While all the world thinks I was falling in love with Clint, you'll know that I was detoxing."

Detoxing. A new word in Jessica's vocabulary. Ah, yes. After the taping session, a friend of Cassy's, a handsome black guy named Sam, came to West End to take her away to an AA meeting. On the way over, Jessica—very scared but determined not to show it—told Sam that she thought she knew pretty much what AA was all about. So she really blew it when they went into a building near Lincoln Center and she peeked into a room and saw all of these good-looking young faces in it and commented to Sam that she never knew they had acting classes here and Sam told her it wasn't an acting class, it was the AA meeting.

Oh.

It was very strange. There were about forty or fifty people in the room and no one looked like Jessica thought they were supposed to look. First of all, they were all so incredibly healthy-looking and attractive. In fact, many of them were downright knockouts. Sam said that, because of the part of town they were in, this meeting did tend to have a number of actors and performers in it. At this, Jessica's eyes flew back across the room to stare at a woman across the way. "Ohmygod," she said, "then that really *is* her."

Sam smiled and tapped the cover of the book he had given her. She looked down. *Alcoholics Anonymous,* it said, and Sam was tapping his finger on the word *"Anonymous."* "Anonymity is the foundation of the program," he said.

"What?" Jessica said.

"Anonymity. The program works because we leave our identities outside the door. Yours, hers, everybody's. Okay? That's the deal here."

Oh. And then Jessica felt the tiniest bit better about the fact that no one seemed to be staring at her. (When Jessica was not stared at, Jessica tended to worry about her ratings.)

The meeting itself was nothing like she had imagined. She kept looking around at everyone, wondering if it could be true, that they all at one time couldn't stop drinking either. But that's what everybody was talking about, about their drinking, about how it had eaten into their lives, about how they had tried to control it, manage it, do anything with it except stop it because life without drinking had not been something they could ever imagine as being bearable, much less fun.

The company line around the room, it seemed to Jessica, was that until they came to AA they had not realized that alcohol had robbed them of the capacity to be happy.

Huh. She could identify with that.

Some were periodic drinkers, who only got loaded every once in a great while; some were nightly drinkers like Jessica; some were day and night drinkers; there were sneak drinkers, openly drunk drinkers, rich drinkers and poor drinkers, famous drinkers and drinkers who had not left their neighborhoods for years; straight drinkers, gay drinkers, or— according to one lady—sexually indifferent drinkers. There was a Jewish guy who wanted to know how he could be an alcoholic when everybody knew that Jews don't drink (laughter); a woman said she was Irish Catholic and that statement alone sent a fifth of the room into laughter; a WASP commuter from Connecticut said that, where he lived, it didn't matter if you rolled out of the train on your head, cracked up your car or slugged your wife in a blackout because everybody knew that alcoholics were people who didn't have jobs (roars of laughter); and a young woman holding a baby in her lap said that she prayed that her getting sober had broken the family curse, and that her son wouldn't have to grow up with what she had and her father had, and his father had. . . .

Jessica was fascinated.

And that one message kept getting across. That every single person in the room at one time had had a drinking problem they could not— and did not want to—do anything about. And that every single one of them, once they had been able to stop, did not want to go back to it because life on this side had turned out to be so incredibly different than they had imagined.

Huh.

When the meeting was over, Sam walked her back to West End and they talked. Jessica said she loved the meeting but didn't have the time to go to AA meetings. Sam asked her how many hours had she devoted to her drinking—she didn't have to include the hours spent *recovering* from her drinking, just the time she allocated each evening to drinking itself? And so Jessica said, okay, so maybe she did have an hour free each day.

But then she said she couldn't get way over to that meeting. It was inconvenient, she thought, the location of that meeting. And the time wasn't good. Sam told her that she was in luck—there were eight hundred other meetings for her in Manhattan. (Jessica swallowed. "Eight hundred?" "Uh-huh," Sam said, "in Manhattan. There's over two thousand in the New York area." Jessica looked at him. Sam was smiling. "And if you like to travel," he added, "there're about seventy-eight thousand other meetings in well over a hundred countries.")

Okay, okay.

But what if she ran into someone she knew at AA? she wanted to know. And what, Sam asked her, did she suppose that person would be doing there at an AA meeting? Wouldn't they be there for the same reason she was?

Hmmm. (There had to be a loophole here somewhere.)

Jessica said she just didn't know. She had never belonged to anything because she hated rules.

Sam laughed and said, "I'm afraid none of us are very big on rules either—that's why there aren't any in AA. There's only one requirement for membership and that's a desire to stop drinking. That's it."

Jessica gave up and promised she would meet Sam at that same meeting the next day.

"He's such a wonderful guy," Jessica said that night, lying in bed, all tucked in, Alexandra sitting on the edge of it, listening to her. (Jessica waited for Alexandra to get home from the studio before going to bed. She kind of liked this Kansas Care she was getting. "If it felt safe and cozy as a child," Alexandra's motto was, "then chances are it will feel the same as an adult. And maybe that's what poor little Jessica needs to feel right now—safe and cozy." Poor little Jessica? No one had ever called her poor little anything. A monster, maybe, *lunatic, screwball, tramp* . . . But poor little Jessica? It made her envision a shivering little match girl, huddled in the street, in the snow—which, come to think of it, was exactly what she had felt like for much of her life.)

"But I'm scared to ask him what he does for a living," Jessica continued.

"Why?" Alexandra said.

"I think I'm scared he's going to turn out to be someone looking for a job or something. He looks like he could be in TV."

"I don't think a friend of Cassy's would be going to AA to find a job," Alexandra said, laughing softly.

"No. But do you know what I mean, Alexandra Eyes? Why is he being so nice?"

"You mean is he going to make a pass at you."

"No, I don't get that feeling at all. I would have picked that up. I figure it's got to be something about a job." Jessica propped herself up on her elbows. "You're in the same racket, sort of. When was the last time anyone did anything for you who didn't want you to help them with their career, or give them money, or wanted you to sleep with them, you know? When was the last time anyone genuinely gave you anything, just because they wanted to give you something?"

"I know what you mean," Alexandra said. "It's very hard sometimes." And then she frowned slightly. "Do you think I'm after something from you? Having you here?"

Jessica didn't know why, but she blushed. "No." But after a moment she smiled and added, "Though I must admit, it has crossed my mind that if I died you wouldn't have much to syndicate overseas."

"Oh, you are a most charming girl," Alexandra said, pushing her back down on the bed and standing up.

"Well then, you tell me," Jessica said, sitting all the way up as Alexandra headed for the door. "Why are you being so nice to me?"

Alexandra turned around. "You haven't heard a thing I've said to you in the last few days."

"I don't think my brain's working all that well," Jessica admitted, hitting her head in such a way as to convince Alexandra that all cogs and wheels inside were definitely amiss, askew or otherwise severely aslip.

"Because you are my friend," Alexandra said quietly, smiling, standing there with her arms folded. She was still in her on-air clothes, still in her studio makeup, still looking very much the part of Miss DBS News America. She tilted her head to the side. "You called me Saturday night. You didn't want me to boost your career, you didn't want money, you weren't drawn to me by my fame, you didn't want to sleep with me—you called because you wanted my understanding." She paused, letting her head fall to the side. "Jessica, do you have any idea how long it's been since I've had a real friend stay with me?" She moved over to the door and, holding it, turned back again. "I guess what's in it for Sam to be a friend to you right now is pretty much the same. You need something he can give—and he needs someone to need what he has to give. Just like I need you to need me this way. Just like I need what you have to give me in other ways."

Whoa.

Alexandra Eyes could get like that sometimes. Heavy. You know. But Jessica liked it.

When Jessica met Sam at the meeting the following day, Tuesday, she asked him a little about himself. Well, one thing was for sure, he was not looking for a job. He was a corporate vice-president of Electronika International. And he was married to a vice-president of Gardiner & Grayson Publishers, a woman named Harriet, with whom he was "shamelessly in love." He had a daughter who would be a senior at Columbia in the fall (who was, as a matter of fact, an intern this summer over at the "Donahue" show) and a daughter still in grade school.

That afternoon Jessica did a show on how women's relationships with their fathers influenced their relationships with men for the rest of their lives. They had on this great Harvard psychiatrist, Dr. William Appleton, who was terrific with all the messed-up women and fathers they had in the studio audience. But he was best with the messed-up woman named Jessica Wright, who inexplicably started crying in the middle of the show when they were talking about how fathers who ignore their daughters tend to make them terribly insecure in their future relationships with men. Dr. Appleton somehow turned the horribly embarrassing moment (Denny said later they had almost shut the taping down) into one of those magical moments in television when viewers are genuinely helped by seeing someone they "know" admit that she had some of the problems they were talking about. ("But will you come back on Mother's Day?" Jessica asked Dr. Appleton at the end of the show.)

After the show, as was her custom, she read up for the next day's show and then later that night, at Alexandra's, she made brownies. When Alexandra got home from the studio around eleven-thirty, Jessica was thrilled when Alexandra asked for her opinion about certain parts of her tour itinerary. (What was thrilling, actually, was realizing that Alexandra was getting scared about the tour. Big bad Alexandra, Miss Perfect, sitting there at the kitchen table, smiling a little sheepishly, the silent question being, "Will you reassure me that I can do this, please?") "My thoughts?" Jessica said. "Waring, not only can you have my thoughts, you can have one of my brownies. It's very Kansas, you know. Here."

On Wednesday Jessica went by herself to the meeting because Sam was in Washington on business, and then she got through a wild show about how famous women having babies out of wedlock were or were not influencing teenage girls. (Was the studio ever rocking and rolling on this one.) That night Jessica picked up some more of her things from the Plaza and, on an impulse, took out her meeting book, looked at it, and—just for the heck of it—stopped in at an East Side meeting. It was no big deal, Jessica told herself, but when Alexandra came home that night the first thing out of her mouth was, "I went to a meeting by myself—one I've never been to. On the East Side. And I stayed for the whole thing." And after seeing the look on Alexandra's face, for some strange reason Jessica felt prouder of herself than she had in years.

On Thursday the guests for the serial killers show were late for the special morning taping ("Good God, call the cops," Jessica said) and so the taping ran late and Jessica could not make the afternoon meeting. So she "caught" a meeting on her way home to Alexandra's that night. Later on Alexandra asked for her help on what she should do in the Southwest leg of her tour, and the two of them got all excited when Jessica screamed, "We'll bring my show to Tucson! We'll meet you there! And you'll be my guest on the show!" And they called up Cassy in the middle of the night—Jessica in the kitchen, Alexandra in the bedroom—going on and on, chattering like magpies at her, until Cassy promised that, yes, Jessica could do a show from Tucson and have Alexandra as her guest, and it was only when she got off the phone that Jessica realized just how crazy she had gotten this week because she heard herself say, "And I really can go because there're AA meetings in Tucson."

Alexandra, standing in the doorway of the kitchen, let her mouth fall open.

"Oh, hell," Jessica said, "stop gawking, Alexandra Eyes. It beats turning into Blanche Dubois every night."

Friday was an okay day too. Jessica read up for her show, got to the meeting okay, and a closed-set interview with Kim Basinger went very well. She stayed on at West End (taking a nap, having a snack and hanging out in the newsroom) until eleven, when Alexandra threw a little catered farewell dinner for the crew because, come Sunday, she'd be out on the road for two months on the DBS Across America tour.

Saturday morning Alexandra announced that it was final. Jessica had to stay in her apartment for the next two months because she needed someone to look after her plants. Jessica had not fully responded to this idea—they were sitting at breakfast—when the doorbell rang and Jessica saw all of her stuff from the Plaza being carried in.

In the afternoon Jessica lay down on Alexandra's bed and watched her pack. They talked about—no, Jessica did all the talking. For about four straight hours she talked, about her life, about what a mess it had been, about anything and everything, and all the while Alexandra kept packing, organizing, looking over every once in a while, smiling, laughing, murmuring sympathy, whatever was appropriate.

That night, after they ate dinner, Alexandra went with Jessica to an "open" AA meeting, where friends and family of AAs were welcome to sit and listen, to see what AA was like. At one point in the meeting some guy asked if there were any newcomers. Jessica's heart started pounding and before she thought about it too much she raised her hand—for the first time that week. The guy smiled and pointed to her.

Jessica cleared her throat and said, "My name's Jessica, and I'm an alcoholic." Her face was burning. "And I have, uh, six days," and everybody clapped and Jessica looked down at her lap, feeling so embarrassed she didn't know what else to do. Then the clapping stopped and the guy called on someone across the room, and so Jessica raised her head. And then she heard someone sniff and she looked over at Alexandra and saw that she was crying. Smiling, laughing a little, but crying.

Alexandra was crying for her.

And so Jessica cried a little too. For herself.

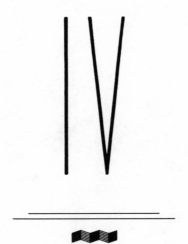

38

Alexandra Across America

Alexandra, the DBS sports editor, Dash Tomlinson, and a gofer, Marc Ogakani, flew up to Portland, Maine together Sunday evening and met Will Rafferty and his field team, technical engineer Oscar Podanski and technical assistant Pete "Parky" Wilson, at the hotel. The group from New York was not greeted with good news. WMN had only signed as a DBS affiliate the week before and tonight was the first Will had ever seen of it—and was the last he wished to ever see of it.

"How bad is it?" Alexandra asked, riding over to the station with him that night to take a look.

"Remember the time we went down into that Metrorail tunnel to see the cave-in?"

"Yes," Alexandra said.

"It looks sort of like that," Will said.

Alexandra said she couldn't quite understand how WMN could be as bad as Will said it was. Only a year ago it had been part of Burton Rydale's chain of indies, and Mason Communications, who bought them when Rydale retired, was a very good company. And even though Mason Communications was a subsidiary of General Merchants & Wire, and so had been included in the leveraged buyout of General Merchants & Wire two months ago by Orvatz, Slatterly, a Wall Street investment bank—

"That explains it, then," Will said, interrupting her. "What happened to the staff and the equipment—they've stripped the place."

Alexandra looked at him, horrified. Over the next eight weeks, every weekday morning they were to arrive in a new city and that affiliate station was supposed to have lined up a local story for her (and one for Dash) to do, which in some way captured a sense of their community. Then Alexandra was supposed to anchor the news from that affiliate that night and run her local story as well as Dash's, and then move on and do the same at the next station the next day. The idea of kicking off their tour at a dysfunctional TV station was not an appealing one. And yet, they both knew, all of their promotion had promised a kickoff from Maine, and WMN had been the only available indie *in* Maine to sign.

"Wait until you see," Will told her. "There're *out*lines—on the walls —where equipment used to be. They've sold all the good stuff and replaced it with junk."

It was true. The station had been stripped of everything valuable and this included the employees. Usually, even the tiniest TV station with the most modest equipment imaginable had some devoted worker or workers who would do almost anything for the pleasure and satisfaction of producing a newscast and community affairs programming in their studio. Like newspaper and magazine and book publishers, the success of the enterprise depended on a seemingly irrational devotion to painstaking hands-on production work within a maelstrom of financial and technological schemes. While putting movie cassettes into a machine or receiving a network feed could be fast and easy and money-making with complete idiots as staff, in-studio production was more often than not complicated and demanding and required an investment of money and brains and talented people to do it "the old-fashioned way." However, it was that old-fashioned way within the streamlined high-tech bucks and bang that, in the long run, with local news, more often than not made enormous amounts of money.

But the new owners of WMN were evidently uninterested in even maintaining the station, much less investing in it. Evidently they were looting the place and dumping it. Evidently the term "investment banker" needed a little revision in America.

In any event, putting cassettes of movies in the machine seemed to be the most demanding production work left at WMN. As for their news department, they were down to doing one half-hour newscast that could scarcely be called local news—or even television news, for that matter. It was like an old rip-and-read show, where the advertising manager ripped the AP reports off the machine, put on a tie and sat in front of a camera and read it.

"You don't do any public affairs programming, not even on Sunday?" Alexandra asked the station manager.

"Nope," he said.

"Then how do you expect to hold onto your license? You're a broadcast station. Remember the American people? The ones who grant you your license and whom the FCC says you have to service with public affairs programming?" Alexandra said.

"We don't have to do diddily as long as Reagan's in office and you know it," the station manager said, lighting a cigarette. "At the other station I managed?" he asked her, tossing his match into a metal ashtray. "We didn't even *do* the news. Nobody cares anymore."

Alexandra, face scarlet, left his office without comment.

Back at the Sheraton Tara, in the living room of Alexandra's suite, Will called Kyle with a list of their complaints about WMN and all they would need to even make it on the air by the following night. Something had to be done about the WMN set and fast, Will said, otherwise they could look forward to Alexandra looking like she was reporting from prison. The one minicam the station owned was not working properly. ("They do have a sixty-pound pack that shoots sixteen-millimeter film, Kyle," Alexandra said over Will's shoulder into the phone. "Maybe you were planning for us to reshoot *Birth of a Nation* while we're here.") The station had not prepared any local stories for Alexandra and Dash to cover tomorrow; there was no computer system or fax machine to send tomorrow night's script over; there was no TelePrompTer in the studio; and there was not even a decent typewriter to use.

And then Alexandra grabbed the phone from Will and told Kyle to call back by midnight with some solutions or the whole thing was off, she was taking everybody on to their Boston affiliate. And then she called somebody in Washington, D.C., named AJ and dictated a seventeen-point complaint about WMN that she wanted filed with the FCC as soon as she left Portland.

"You can't file a complaint against one of your own affiliates," Will said, laughing, listening to her on the phone.

"Hang on a sec," she said, covering the phone. "Why not? Being a reporter disqualifies me from being an American citizen?"

"Alexandra," Will said.

She thought a minute and then spoke back into the phone, telling whoever AJ was that AJ was to draft the complaint but to leave everybody's name out of it except WMN and Orvatz, Slatterly, and to send it—stamped URGENT, but blind, without a return address—to the Portland newspapers, both Maine senators, both congressional representatives and the governor. And AJ was to make sure that everybody who received the blind complaint knew everybody else who had been sent a copy, but nobody was to know who had sent it. It was just a hint of things someone might want to look into to score a story or to score in an election. Then AJ was to call the FCC in two weeks and find out if there had been any inquiries or complaints about WMN in Portland and report back to her.

"Nobody cares anymore," Alexandra muttered, hanging up. "I'll show that smarmy little—"

By eleven o'clock that night a van had left West End, heading for Portland, carrying pieces of set, TelePrompTer screens, a lap-top computer, a fax machine, a portable editing console and a minicam.

Near midnight Kyle called back to say that a reporter from the Portland *Press Herald* was willing to take Alexandra and Dash along to cover the Fourth of July whaling-boat races if they were interested. ("Yes," Alexandra told Will. "Dash can do the teams and race, I'll cover the crowd and history of Portland.") And, Kyle assured them, they were triple-checking the stations down the itinerary to make sure nothing like WMN would happen again on the tour.

In the morning Alexandra "sat in" by phone on the editorial meeting at West End and then headed out to cover the whaling-boat race with the *Press Herald* reporter, Dash and Marc. Since it was unclear if there really was anyone at WMN who could operate a minicam properly— who, even if there was, had the holiday off, as apparently most everybody at WMN did—and since it was going to take all of Will's and Oscar's and Parky's efforts to get the studio in working condition by tonight, Alexandra ended up shooting almost all of the footage of the day herself, teaching Marc enough to shoot the footage that she herself needed to appear in.

When they got back—sunburned and salty—Alexandra sat in the DBS van with Dash and edited their piece. It was nothing to win awards, but it was colorful and interesting and did do something to capture the dichotomy of Portland, the cottage industry yuppies and the historic port of call, still receiving oil, but not the whale kind. Will liked the piece but agreed with them that it needed some music or something. So they called New York, cued up the tape in the control room and Dr. Kessler and the Nerd Brigade zapped it back to Kelly in the West End satellite room. Kyle called ten minutes later to coordinate voice-over narration from Alexandra and Dash in the WMN control room to Hex in the editing bay at West End, and a half hour later the Nerd Brigade transmitted the finished three-minute piece so they could see it at WMN, complete with original sound, voice-over narration and music on the sound track. It was now a good piece, they decided.

The working script from West End did not get faxed to WMN until an hour and a half before air time. By now a new crisis had evolved in the studio: almost every light over the set had shorted out in rehearsal. Will and Oscar managed to rewire the system for it to hold, but they had lost the fill lights—most of which had not been working to begin with—and there were of course no replacements to be had. So now they were stuck trying to use all key lights against backlights—lights so strong and harsh that, without fill or mood lights to diffuse them, they could flash the faces of Alexandra and Dash right out of the screen.

And so, when Alexandra wished to rewrite the copy on three of the stories in the script faxed from West End, she had to work on the lap–top computer on the set (her hair in rollers, no less) while Will and Oscar, up on ladders, moved lights—filtered them, screened them, bounced their light off all kinds of angles—testing them over and over in a kind of freaky light show around her, and Dick Gross yelled through Will's headset that everything looked like hell (and demanded to know what idiot was operating camera 1 up there who thought "to frame Alexandra" meant to cut off the corner of her head). But Alexandra typed away, pausing to read aloud every once in a while—as one of the DBS van drivers, filling in as an audio man, tried out various microphones on her to see which ones worked—and she handed off her revised copy to Marc to be faxed back to West End and to be photocopied (yes, they had a photocopier here) and be inserted into the final scripts for everyone at WMN.

Her portable makeup mirror and kit were set up in the all-purpose control room, and after changing her clothes Alexandra sat down and quickly went through the cosmetic routine she had done for herself until coming to West End. "Stand back," she warned everybody, shaking a can of hair spray, "Time to bomb my hair."

At West End, Dick called for mini-rehearsal and Alexandra hurried out to the set. Although things seemed to be working pretty well (cues were being given and heard back and forth from West End to WMN well; the TelePrompTer screens over the cameras were hooked up to West End, where Alexandra's usual operator was doing her usual smooth job; Parky, acting as stage manager, was quite good at it; the studio monitors were working and in position), unfortunately, according to Parky, Dick said Alexandra and Dash "looked like two faceless ghouls" back at West End, prompting Alexandra to jump out of her chair and cry, "Will!"

"Don't worry, don't worry!" Will assured her, running out of the control room. "Come into the control room—both of you. I've got Cleo on the phone and she's going to tell you what to do."

And so Alexandra and Dash went into the control room and Alexandra sat down in front of the makeup mirror and followed Cleo's instructions while Dash held the phone to her ear. "Heaven help me," Alexandra said a while later, "I'm starting to look like an aging madam. Am I supposed to look like an aging madam? Cleo? Am I supposed to look like an aging madam in normal light?"

"I think she's laughing," Dash said, holding the receiver to his ear.

And then it was Dash's turn—who recoiled from Alexandra's lipstick brush as if it was a cobra—but Alexandra managed to coax him into complying with Cleo's instructions by reminding him that it was the only way he was going to have a face on camera. But when she was finished and Dash looked at himself and groaned, "Aw, geez, I look like that guy on 'Batman,' the guy Cesar Romero played," Alexandra couldn't help laughing and then Dash started laughing, but then Parky called the ten-minute cue and they raced back into the studio and onto the set, put on their microphones and waited for the verdict.

"Passable," Parky said, relaying the message received through his headset from Dick back in the West End control room. "Okay, Alexandra," Parky continued, "we're in business. We're going to open on camera 2. Program will be on that monitor—keep an eye out. If anything goes wrong, Dick says to remember that Chester's waiting to back you up in New York."

"You mean if my face melts off," Alexandra said, flicking through the pages of her script a final time to make sure they were in order. "Shut up, Tomlinson," she growled out of the corner of her mouth at Dash, who was laughing again.

Time passed, last-minute checks were made, Alexandra was waiting, calm, hands on either side of her copy, looking straight ahead at camera 2. The countdown took place; Alexandra leaned forward slightly, toward camera 2; the "DBS News America Tonight" opening unfurled on the monitors, with a special banner added, reading, ACROSS AMERICA TOUR; the red light on camera 2 came on and Parky gave the cue.

"Good evening, everyone, and happy Independence Day," Alexandra said, as if everything in the whole wide world was just as it should be. "July 4, 1988. Reporting for the DBS television news network from Portland, Maine, I'm Alexandra Waring and this is the news in America tonight."

"Well," Cassy said back at West End, watching the monitor in the satellite room with Langley and Dr. Kessler, "it doesn't look too bad."

"Vut do you mean?" Dr. Kessler said. "She looks like she's in Sib*ee*-riah."

Cassy grimaced and abruptly turned away.

"It's okay, Cassy," Langley said, touching her back. "Really, it doesn't look that bad."

When she turned back around, they realized she was laughing and was trying very hard not to—but when she looked at the monitor again it was all over. "Oh, she looks so awful," she managed to get out, doubling over with laughter, shielding her eyes from the sight. "She'll never forgive us, never."

"*Vut* is dat?" Dr. Kessler said.

Cassy straightened up, wiping her eyes. Then she leaned closer to the monitor. "Good Lord, what *is* that?"

"A moose," Kelly called out from the console. "The WMN logo."

"Well, no more mooses!" Cassy said, cracking up again and hobbling toward engineering. At the door, she looked back. Langley had his glasses off and was wiping his eyes with his handkerchief, he was laughing so hard, and Dr. Kessler was lying over the top of a machine, sides heaving, his hand banging the top of his head.

With the exception of Alexandra and Dash looking so dreadful (prompting a number of phone calls and letters to DBS, i.e., "For a million and a half a year, she could at least brush her hair"), the newscast actually went very well. The transitions from Portland to New York were smooth. And when Alexandra led over to Gary Plains for the weather, and he smiled and waved, saying, "Thanks, Alexandra. It's great to see you, even if you are way up in Maine," it gave viewers a sense of the distance, but also a taste of the real friendship and camaraderie that had developed among the DBS crew over the months. And there was another special feeling viewers got—or so many wrote to her—a feeling that, via satellite, Alexandra was as close to her colleagues in New York as she was to them in their homes, that there was a very strange sense of, as one viewer put it, "neighborhood." ("The town meeting," Alexandra would later say in an interview, "that's what we'd like. To bring this tremendous country of ours together for an hour each night with a sense of community.")

After striking the set, the DBS gang gladly said good-bye forever to WMN, the van started back to West End, and Alexandra, Dash, Marc, Will, Oscar and Parky went back to crash at the hotel. They were up at six the next morning, in a plane by seven forty-five and at their Boston affiliate by ten.

The Boston affiliate was paradise and they had a wonderful day.

"Hey," Cassy said that night, watching the Boston rehearsal in the West End control room, "you know, I actually like their set better than ours here."

"I like that Alexandra looks like Alexandra," Dick called back over his shoulder.

"I like the story they lined up for her," Kyle said. "Wait till you see it." (And it was a great one. It was called "College Town, America" and was about the population and demographic shifts of Boston at various times of the year. Dash did a story on Red Sox fever, that affliction which strikes all Bostonians in the spring and lasts through the summer into fall.)

The next morning they flew into Philadelphia and were equally pleased with their affiliate there and the newscast that night was very good again. They were getting the hang of this traveling road show. Thursday morning they arrived in Washington D.C., where Alexandra did a very funny piece on D.C. as a summer ghost town, giving viewers a tour of all the hot spots around the city where the powerful and the mighty normally hung out. Friday was at their small but very talented affiliate in Columbia, South Carolina, where Alexandra and Dash both did pieces connected with the university, and after the newscast everybody flew home for the weekend except Alexandra, who flew ahead to Atlanta to work on a special Democratic convention piece for their Tuesday night newscast from there.

Alexandra also went out to Hilleanderville to meet Cordelia Darenbrook Paine and Jackson's father ("Just call me Big El, gorgeous gal"), a meeting which, according to Jackson, was a huge success and for which he thanked her profusely.

Monday reunited the DBS team in Miami; Tuesday they were in Atlanta; Wednesday found them in Nashville; Thursday in Louisville; and Friday in Cleveland. They were five for five that week, good newscasts all. Again, Friday night, everyone flew back to New York for the weekend except Alexandra, who stayed on at the Bond Court to catch up on her sleep and take up the station owner's offer of some tennis in Shaker Heights Sunday afternoon.

Come Monday morning, Alexandra, Will, Marc, Oscar and Parky met at one of their biggest and best affiliates, WXA in Detroit. When Alexandra arrived at nine o'clock everyone from the station manager on down was lined up at the door to greet her. The news director showed her into an office that was hers for the day; the producer offered her *four* stories to choose from; the sports editor offered Dash *six*. WXA was one of the best-organized and inspired TV stations that any of the West End crowd had ever seen, and Will, Oscar, Marc and Parky had virtually nothing to do all day.

Alexandra opted for a story on the special summer programs for inner city kids and had a ball with the producer and the WXA mobile unit. On their way back to the studio, going north on Route 375, a stretch limo went flying past them at what had to be ninety miles an hour. And then, when not one but two police cars went flying past them to chase the limo, Alexandra did not even have to say it—the news van had already joined the chase, and the cameraman sat in the passenger side window, with Alexandra holding his legs, to film it. The chase was short, ending in the first-time arrest of an underaged boy. The film of the chase was so funny in places, though (shooting back into the van through the windshield, showing the news team looking like mobsters in a getaway car and Alexandra holding onto the camera-man's legs), they used some of it to do a little thirty-second piece at the expense of themselves on how ninety-nine percent of all news leads don't lead to the scoop all reporters hope for.

The newscast was wonderful that night. The hard news broke well that day, with a little natural disaster, a little man-made disaster, some hot political fighting, rounded out by a little good news here and there around the country, and the usual update on the ongoing mess in the Middle East. Everything flowed, transitions were terrific. The visuals were arresting, the film first rate, the writing tight, the mix of segments fulfilling, knowledgeable. The smiles around the studio at the close of the newscast were real; the talent displayed over the hour had been real.

It was the best they had ever done and everybody knew it.

"Boffo, gang!" Will said, leaping into the studio from the WXA control room. "They're dancing in the aisles back in New York!"

But the really big news of July 18, 1988, missed the live feed of "DBS News America Tonight" by minutes, and Chester Hanacker, pale beneath his makeup, had the honor of being the first DBS News anchor to interrupt programming-in-progress to scoop everybody on a major news story.

The news was that at 10:04:22 P.M., in the studio of WXA in De-troit, another crazy with a handgun almost killed Alexandra Waring.

39

Cassy Flies to Detroit

"Oh thank God, thank God," Cassy said, rushing past Will into Alexandra's bedroom at the Pontchartrain Hotel.

She was curled up on the corner of the bed, talking on the phone, still in the dress from her newscast. She looked up and saw Cassy and her expression was one of relief. "Cassy just walked in," she said into the phone, "hang on a minute," and dropped it to receive Cassy's embrace.

"Thank God, thank God," Cassy repeated, hugging her for dear life, "thank God you're all right." She held her for a full minute more and then sat back, holding Alexandra's arms, to look at her. "How do you feel, sweetheart?" she said gently, releasing one of her arms to brush the hair back off Alexandra's face.

"Very glad to see you," Alexandra said. "Very glad to see everybody." Her eyes skipped to somewhere behind Cassy. "Jackson, hi—it's okay, I'm quite alive, you can come in."

"Creeping crickets, kid," he said, coming in from the living room, "you've gotta cut out this Calamity Jane stuff. My heart can't take it." He leaned over the bed to give her a brief hug, kissing her on the side of the face once too.

Alexandra looked back to Cassy, touching her hand. "Thanks for coming." She looked up at Jackson. "Both of you." Then she looked around for the phone, found it and picked it up, explaining to Cassy and Jackson, "This is Jessica. What?" she said into the phone. "Jessica who is hysterical," Alexandra told them, laughing. "You're not hysterical, Jessica, everything's fine." She looked at Cassy. "Why don't you go out in the living room and have a drink or something—let me get off here and then I have to call Gordon, and then I'll be out, okay?"

"Okay," Cassy said, kissing Alexandra softly on the cheek.

"No," Alexandra said as they left the room, "you can't have a drink,

Jessica, I was talking to Cassy. You can eat some of the Godiva chocolates in the freezer, though, if you want. Oh—you found them already."

Jackson went downstairs to check in, and Will went to the bar to pour Cassy a glass of white wine and a scotch for himself. The TV set was on, the sound low. Cassy threw herself down on the couch, listening to Will as he told her the story. It was almost identical to what the station manager of WXA had told them over the phone while she and Jackson were flying here on the Darenbrook plane.

The newscast had ended, the lights had come on and Will had been dancing around the studio with glee. Dash had been signing an autograph for a summer intern. Alexandra had taken off her microphone and was just stepping down off the set to shake hands with the floor manager when someone yelled, "Who are you? You're not allowed in here," and everyone turned to look.

The man was young, white, in his twenties. He looked fairly well kept but a little strange nonetheless, since he was wearing a tweed jacket with leather elbows and corduroy pants in the middle of July. He had loafers on without socks—why that stuck out in Will's mind he didn't know. Anyway, the guy had been staring at Alexandra, holding a folded newspaper under one arm, slowly walking across the studio toward her, ignoring the assistant producer who was talking to him.

"Hey! Outta here, buddy!" the stage manager had barked, pointing to the exit. "You gotta wait outside like everybody else. George, escort this gentleman outta here."

A hefty stagehand reached out to take the guy's arm and he jerked away, pulling a pistol out of the newspaper. He pointed the gun at the stagehand—sending him diving—and then swung his arm in a slow arc across the studio (making everyone in its path dive for cover) and stopped when he had Alexandra in his sights. Alexandra, eyes on the gunman, was slowly backing her way toward the desk on the set. The gunman tracked her with the gun, holding it out with both hands, smiling this bizarre smile.

Dash yelled, "Watch out!" and the gunman looked over at him but pulled the trigger with the gun still pointing in Alexandra's direction. (Will thought the shot was accidental—not that it mattered much, since the bullet only missed Alexandra by three feet.) She dove behind the desk; Will hit the guy from behind and then Dash from the side, cracking the gunman's head into the base of camera 2. Alexandra yelled to find out if everybody was all right and, when they said yes, then she started yelling for somebody to get behind a camera and get the scene on tape.

The Detroit police were there in seconds, it seemed, an ambulance right behind them; and now the gunman was in the hospital with a concussion; Dash was in his room, sound asleep after the sedative a doctor had given him; and Marc, Oscar and Parky were all fine, playing poker down in Oscar's room.

Will nodded in the direction of the bedroom. "She hasn't cried or anything yet. Me neither." He shrugged, smiling, sipping his scotch. Lowering his glass, "I don't know, maybe the two of us are getting used to this."

"Good Lord," Cassy sighed, "I hope not."

"She went downstairs about an hour ago and gave a statement, you know," Will said, pointing to the TV. There Alexandra was on the screen, talking to reporters. "She said that since we had a film exclusive for tomorrow's newscast we might as well let everybody advertise it for us." He laughed at Cassy's expression and then shrugged. "You know how she gets, Cassy—I couldn't stop her."

"*No,* Gordon, I'm serious!" they heard Alexandra say. The door to the bedroom was ajar. "I absolutely forbid it. No—no! Even if you don't have work to do, *I* do and I can't give in to this thing. Not now." Silence. "I told you, I'm fine! Wait—wait a minute. Hold on."

Silence.

The bedroom door closed.

Cassy cleared her throat and took a sip of her wine.

"He used to work in commodities," Will said.

"What?" Cassy said, looking at him.

"John, the dingdong with the gun. He's from Chicago—at least a couple years ago he was. They haven't told us anything else."

Cassy sighed again and turned to look out the window. The suite overlooked the Detroit River. The night lights of Windsor across it, in Canada, were quite beautiful.

"And I should warn you, Cass," Will said, yawning then and covering his mouth. "Oh—excuse me," he said, dropping his hand. "But I'm not so sure Alexandra's going back to New York."

"Of course she's coming back," Cassy said. "All of you are."

"You better talk to her about it then," Will said, putting his drink down and getting up. Somebody was knocking on the door.

It was Jackson. "The bodyguards are here," he said, pointing back over his shoulder with his thumb.

"Half the Detroit police department's here," Will reminded him, closing the door.

"Yeah, well," Jackson said, walking over to Cassy, "from now on that young lady has a bodyguard every minute she's working for us— around the clock, if she wants it."

"But don't scare her, Jack," Cassy said, sipping her wine.

"I'm not going to scare her," Jackson said, throwing himself down in a chair. "But I'm not going to let any son of a bitch near her again, either. Those days are over."

The bedroom door opened and Alexandra leaned against the doorway. She was smiling but looked exhausted. Her color was not terrific either. "I think it's time for all good little girls and boys to go to sleep," she said, rubbing her eye. "Tomorrow morning's going to come awfully early."

"It's been tomorrow morning for a while," Will said, looking at his watch.

"I think Cassy should stay with you," Jackson told Alexandra.

Alexandra looked to her.

Cassy nodded. "Me too. Okay?"

"Sure. Thanks," Alexandra said, walking in. She went over behind Will's chair and leaned over it, slid her arms around his neck and gave him a big kiss on the cheek. "Good night, Superman. Thanks for saving my life."

Will smiled, reaching back to rub her head. "Any time, Waring, any time."

"You need anything?" Jackson asked Cassy.

She smiled. "No, thanks." And then she got up, leaning toward him on the way up to whisper, "But I'll miss you."

He stood up too, smiling at her. "Me too," he mouthed. Then he turned around, jingling the change in his pocket. "Will, you all set with a room?"

"Yep," Will said. He was holding hands with Alexandra, walking to the door.

"Everybody meets here at ten o'clock, okay?" Alexandra said, opening the door.

"Agreed," Jackson said. He gave Alexandra a hug, lifting her off the floor and then setting her back down. "We love ya, kiddo." He turned to Cassy, giving her a salute. "Good night."

"Good night," Cassy said, sitting back down on the couch.

"Good night, you guys," Alexandra said, but then she stepped outside so the uniformed policeman and -woman could introduce her to her bodyguards. Afterward, stepping back into the suite, she closed the door, locked it and then slumped back against it with a groan. "Armed guards. Me. In America. Unbelievable."

Cassy looked at her for a long moment and then said, "You think you might be able to cry?"

Alexandra, still slumped against the door, nodded.

"Come here," Cassy said, holding out her arm. Alexandra walked over to the couch and sat down. Cassy reached over for her and in a moment Alexandra had collapsed in her arms. "Just let it come," Cassy said, rubbing her back.

"If it will," Alexandra said, closing her eyes. "It's so strange, because I don't feel scared, I just feel . . ." Her eyes opened. "Just the other night Jessica and I were talking about how it almost physically hurts when someone doesn't like us."

Cassy frowned.

"She has the same thing I've always had," Alexandra said. "And she said it was one of the reasons why she drank so much—that drinking was the only thing that seemed to turn it off, so that she didn't care." She swallowed, closing her eyes again. "And a perfect stranger pointing a gun at me—even when I think he wants to kill me—doesn't hurt as much as when someone disapproves of me. Now is that crazy, or what?"

Cassy just sighed, continuing to rub her back.

"A stranger pointing a gun at me just doesn't register," Alexandra said. "There's just this dull shock, a delayed reaction—like, *Uh-oh, this is going to be too horrible to even think about and so I'm deciding this isn't really happening.* It feels like when I was little and spilled cranberry sauce all over Gran's linen tablecloth in the middle of Thanksgiving dinner."

Cassy smiled, stroking Alexandra's hair.

"You know how you sat there—as a child? Looking at what you just did? How it felt like years going by before anyone saw it and said anything? And how you couldn't say anything first, but could only sit there, watching it seep into the tablecloth that meant so much to Gran? The horror of what has just happened, is happening—that it's so horrible it can't register, so it turns into a dream?" She swallowed. "Realizing someone wants to shoot me feels just like that."

She sighed, then, and Cassy felt her body go limp.

"He wanted to make my heart stop beating," Alexandra whispered. She paused and then added, "And that's what it is, isn't it, when someone wants you to die? You'd think he'd stop and think about that. Visualize it. About how my heart would stop beating, how it would look, beating for the last time. And then be still. And then how everything else inside of me would slow to a stop. Forever. Oh, God, Cassy," she said, hiding her face against Cassy, clinging to her. "I don't want to die," she whispered, starting to cry, "not yet."

And then she really began to cry, and Cassy held her tight, rocking her, murmuring, "It's all right, it's all right—everything's going to be all right."

"Please don't leave," Alexandra said, crying.

"No, sweetheart," Cassy murmured, kissing the top of her head, "I'm not leaving. Shhh, shhh, shhh, shhh . . . Everything's going to be all right. . . ."

After a minute or two Alexandra stopped crying. She swallowed. "Cassy?"

"Yes?"

Alexandra sniffed. "Would you mind staying with me tonight?"

Cassy opened her eyes. And then she blinked. "You mean sleep in the bedroom?"

Against her shoulder, she felt Alexandra nod. "I feel so . . ." Alexandra started to say, and then she started to cry again.

Alexandra cried for just a little while longer and then was so exhausted she could scarcely keep her eyes open. They went into the bedroom and Alexandra gave Cassy a nightgown. While Alexandra was in the bathroom, Cassy turned down the king-sized bed, fluffed up the pillows, set the alarm, turned off all the lights except one by the bed, changed into the nightgown and hung up her clothes. When Alexandra emerged, Cassy went in to use the bathroom, washed her face and hands, brushed her teeth with the extra toothbrush Alexandra left out for her and brushed out her hair.

When she came out Alexandra was lying on her back in bed, one arm over her face against the light.

"Are you all right?" Cassy said.

"Just tired," Alexandra said, not moving.

Cassy went around to the other side of the bed, climbed in and reached over to turn off the light, murmuring good night as she settled in under the covers.

It was very still, quiet. Dark.

"I hate my scar," Alexandra said.

Cassy opened her eyes. And then she blinked. "What?"

"My scar," Alexandra said. "I hate it. I can't even look at myself in the mirror anymore. If I could cut my shoulder off tonight I would."

Cassy thought about this for a moment and then turned over on her side, toward Alexandra. "I've got just the person for you to see. We'll make an appointment for you as soon as we get back."

"What kind of person?" Alexandra said a moment later.

"A doctor," Cassy said. "A surgeon—a plastic surgeon."

Silence.

Cassy laughed softly, scrunching her pillow into a more comfortable position. "So aren't you going to ask me why I know a plastic surgeon?"

"I was being polite," Alexandra said, sounding more like herself.

"You know Chet at WST," Cassy said.

"Sports, sure."

"Right," Cassy said. "Well, remember when that hockey player got his tendons and a nerve in his wrist slashed?"

"A couple of weeks ago," Alexandra said.

"Right," Cassy said, yawning and pulling the covers up over her shoulder. "Well, the surgeon who operated on him has a specialty in microsurgery—you know, hands—but she's also a plastic surgeon. And so Chet—get this—asks me to go see this doctor, pretending I want a *face* lift. And then once inside, you see, I was supposed to try and get the inside scoop on the player's recovery."

Alexandra was now laughing.

Cassy sat up. "So I said, 'Thanks a lot, Chet! A whole face lift? Forget it! I won't go unless it's just to get my eyes done.' "

"You mean you went?" Alexandra said, turning over.

"Uh-huh," Cassy said. "Oh—but she was wonderful, Alexandra. You'd love her. She's—"

"And did you get it?" Alexandra said.

"What, a face lift?" Cassy said.

"The scoop on the player."

Cassy leaned over and whispered, "I forgot completely about it— can you believe it?" She sat back, laughing. "Never even crossed my mind after I got in there."

"You're kidding."

"Oh, I'm not," Cassy said, "ask Chet. I don't know—I just had so many questions about so many things I've always wondered about. Because I *have* thought about it, you know—getting my eyes done. And then I started asking her about face lifts and—" She laughed a little, embarrassed. "Oh, Alexandra, you'd have to meet her to understand—she's just the most extraordinary doctor. She seems to know more about how people feel about themselves than—I don't know, I think I'd rather see her every week instead of my therapist."

"So what about your eyes?" Alexandra said, sounding a bit dubious.

"Oh," Cassy said, sighing, "we agreed I'd come back and see her in a couple of years."

"You mean she didn't think you should do it?"

Cassy gave Alexandra's shoulder a little shove. "Why, you think I should?"

"No," Alexandra said, yawning, "it's just that I've never heard of a plastic surgeon who didn't think someone needed surgery."

"That's why I want you to go see her," Cassy said, yawning too, sliding back down under the covers. "She's wonderful. And I told her about your scar and she said she does that kind of work all the time."

"I'll go see her," Alexandra promised, yawning again, rolling over on her other side, away from Cassy. She sighed, quietly. "Good night."

"Good night," Cassy said.

Silence.

Cassy sat up. And then she reached over to touch Alexandra's back. "Sweetheart," she said, "you're shivering. Are you cold?"

"At this point," Alexandra said, "I'm so tired I wouldn't even know."

"Well, here, wait—" Cassy said. She moved over and slid down in behind Alexandra, putting one arm under her pillow and the other around Alexandra's waist. "Better?" she said gently.

"Reassuring," Alexandra said, closing her eyes, "thank you."

"You're safe, absolutely safe," Cassy whispered.

"I know," Alexandra murmured, taking Cassy's hand in her own then and holding it to her chest.

In a minute, breath fading, her body still, Alexandra was asleep.

In a while Cassy fell asleep too.

When Cassy awakened in the morning it was to find Alexandra sitting over her, smiling.

"Good morning," Alexandra said.

For a moment Cassy forgot where she was, what year she was in. And then she thought of Michael and then she remembered that Michael was no longer an issue; and then she remembered Jackson and remembered that, no, their affair was not a dream, she awakened with him almost every morning now; and then she thought, *Alexandra?* but remembered that she had stayed the night with her because someone had tried to shoot her again and she had been frightened.

"Good morning," Cassy said, sitting up on her elbows, looking for the travel alarm that was no longer there. "What time is it?"

"Ten to nine," Alexandra said.

Cassy looked around the room; everything was packed up. She looked back at Alexandra. She was dressed in a skirt, blouse and heels, earrings and bracelets, ready to go.

"I'm not going back to New York with you," Alexandra said.

Cassy looked at her.

"I don't want to argue, I don't want to talk about it either," Alexandra said, getting up and walking to the window. "Just take my word for it"—she was opening the drapes now, letting the light in—"I need to stay out on the road and get my head straight."

Cassy sat up. "Get your head straight about what?"

After a moment, looking out the window, hands in her skirt pockets, Alexandra said, "I want to marry Gordon." And then she paused, squinting at the horizon. "I want to be married. I want to belong somewhere. Like other people do. A home, I guess—I guess that's what I mean." She shook her head, slowly, and then sighed. "I'm so tired of feeling like a special case all the time."

"That's not something that marriage fixes," Cassy said.

"No, I suppose not," Alexandra said, still looking out the window. Silence.

"Strange things happen when you almost die," Alexandra said then. "And it scares me that all I have to do is think that maybe I won't be alive tomorrow and then everything that was so important suddenly isn't so important." She paused, swallowing. "Like getting married to Gordon." She paused again. "I get scared because I think I might know what I really want."

"And what's that?" Cassy said.

For a moment Alexandra did not react. And then she laughed to herself, letting her head fall back so that she was looking up at the ceiling. "Oh, God," she said. And then, laughing again, she lowered her head and turned around to look at Cassy. "That's what I love about you."

"What?"

"That you are the brightest, most capable person I've ever met— and yet," Alexandra said, "you can be so incredibly dumb sometimes." She took a step forward. "I used to think it was an act—but I've come to recognize that if Cassy Cochran doesn't want to see anything wrong with someone she cares about, then, by God, she doesn't see anything wrong."

"That's not the nicest thing you've ever said to me," Cassy said.

"No, it's not," Alexandra said, coming over to the bed, "but people who get shot at get to have one self-indulgent morning—don't they?" She sat down on the edge of the bed. "Listen, Cassy, I need some distance from New York. I need some time away from everybody—to think things through, sort stuff out in my head. Now—while Gordon's away. I need to work, move around, get some perspective. And I won't be able to do that if I go back with you."

Cassy sighed, brushing a piece of hair back off Alexandra's forehead. "I still think you should come home for a few days. We can start up the tour again—next week, maybe."

Alexandra was shaking her head.

"Look, Alexandra, you can't—"

"What I need is to get right back in the saddle," Alexandra said, getting up and going into the dressing room. In a moment she came back out again, slinging a large bag over her shoulder. "I left some clean underwear for you in the bathroom."

"Jackson's going to go berserk," Cassy said.

"But not for an hour," Alexandra said, walking over to the bed. "And what's one more fight between you two? And I have every confidence you'll handle the situation beautifully." She leaned over and kissed Cassy on the cheek. Looking at her, "Thanks for staying with me last night."

"You're welcome."

"I love you," Alexandra said.

"I love you too," Cassy said. "But wait, Alexandra—"

"I'm fine," Alexandra said, halfway to the door, "really." She opened it and then turned around. "You're taking Dash and Jackson home and I'm taking everybody else to Indianapolis, bodyguards too. Okay?" She looked at her watch. "I gotta run—they'll be waiting for me downstairs."

"I still don't think—" Cassy started to say.

"You should let me go, Cassy," Alexandra told her. In a moment she added, "Really. I wouldn't say it if it wasn't true. You should let me go."

They looked at each other for a long moment. And then Cassy sighed. And then she nodded. "Okay," she said. "But please be careful."

"To the Crossroads of America," Alexandra said, closing the door behind her.

40

Jackson Can't Believe It

Jackson was furious. The only thing that kept him from going after Alexandra and physically dragging her back to New York was the fact that the bodyguards he had hired for her had been taken along and that Cassy kept insisting, over and over again, that Alexandra knew what she was doing and that they should leave her alone.

"If what she's doing is so right," Jackson said for the fifth time, "then why did they sneak out of the hotel? She told me we were meeting at ten."

"Because she knew you'd try to stop her," Cassy said for the fifth time.

They were flying home in the Gulfstream. Dash was sitting across from them, facing them in one of the six seats in the main cabin area. He was trying to read a copy of *Sports Illustrated,* the pages of which were turning faster and faster as Jackson and Cassy started in again.

"She should come home where we can protect her," Jackson said, slamming his armrest.

"Give it up, will you?" Cassy said.

"I won't, damn it!" he said. "Not until you tell me why you let her go."

"I will say this one more time, Jackson. One," she said, striking her index finger against the palm of her other hand, "she refused to come home. Two, I can't make her come home, thanks to her contract. Three, she's a newswoman—not a politician, not a movie star. If she can't go out and cover the news, then she's no longer a newswoman. Four, she's been through this before and knows she has to get back in the saddle again."

"She *doesn't* know," Jackson said, "she's a kid."

"Five, she knows that if she goes on with the tour the ratings for DBS News will—"

"Oh, great!" Jackson said, hurling his newspaper across the cabin. "So we just sit around and wait to see which new kook's gonna blow her head off next to raise her ratings?"

Cassy stared at him. "How dare you say such a thing to me," she finally said, fumbling with her seat belt, getting it undone and standing up.

"I still don't understand why you let her go," Jackson said.

"I don't know!" Cassy said, throwing her hand out. "All right? I don't know why I let Alexandra go. I'm just *dumb*, I guess. So if you want her to come back to New York, *you* do something—*you* go and get her." She whirled around and walked away.

"Where are you going?" he demanded.

"Anywhere," she said. "Out the window maybe." She walked to the head of the cabin, all of fourteen feet away, and threw herself down in one of the seats facing forward.

Jackson sighed, rubbing his eyes. Then he dropped his hand and looked across the way at Dash. His eyes were glued to the magazine.

Jackson undid his seat belt, got up and went around to the curtain into the tail section where the steward was. "You got that Dodgers tape somewhere?" he asked. The steward came up with a video cassette and Jackson took it back out into the cabin and over to the bar where the TV screen was. "Wanna see yesterday's Dodgers game?" he said.

"Sure," Dash said.

Jackson opened a drawer, took out some earphones and tossed them to him. "Just stick in that plug there on the side." He turned on the unit, slid in the cassette, pushed a button and the Dodgers came onto the screen. He looked in another drawer, took out a remote control and tossed this to Dash too. "Okay?"

Dash nodded, giving him the OK sign.

Jackson walked up and stood next to Cassy's seat. When she looked up his heart gave way, and his anger did too. She was crying. And it was very hard to be angry with the woman he was falling hopelessly in love with when she was crying. Particularly when he was making her cry.

"I have to leave," she said, pressing the bridge of her nose with her hand. "I can't do this job properly anymore. Dexter wants me to come back to buy some stations for them and I think I should go."

Jackson sank down, kneeling by her seat, resting his arms on the armrest. He looked back down the cabin at Dash. He was busy with the Dodgers. He looked back at Cassy, reaching to take her hand.

"Don't," she said, pulling it away.

"Dash is watching a video," he said.

"Just don't, please," she said, turning to the window.

Jackson sighed, taking out his handkerchief and pressing it into her hand. "I'm sorry," he said. "It's just that I'm worried about Alexandra."

"And I'm not?" she said. She wiped her eyes with his handkerchief, dropping her hand in her lap.

"Look, darling—"

She covered her face with her hands for a moment. And then she dropped them, sitting up in her chair, looking at him. "I can't work like this, Jack. I can't work with you—having you call me darling."

"I won't, I'm sorry," he said.

"And it's not just you. It's Alexandra too." She sighed, looking straight ahead. "We're too close. I know too much about her—I keep trying to make decisions for her that I have no business making." She looked at him. "And our relationship. Do you know how it feels for me to hide it from Alexandra? And how Langley—Jessica—" She cut herself off, wiping her eyes again. "How am I supposed to be worthy of their trust, to do my job while I'm carrying on like this with you?"

"But you're not carrying on," Jackson said.

"Damn right I'm not," she said, blowing her nose. "That's just the problem," she added. "And I hate it." She made a fist around the handkerchief and then hit her thigh with it. "I can't stand not operating aboveboard. I can't stand secrets—all this, this . . ."

"I know, I know," Jackson said, reaching into her lap for her hand and getting it this time.

Cassy sighed, closing her eyes, tightening her grip on his hand. "Oh, Jack," she said, opening her eyes and turning to look at him. "What have I done?"

"You haven't done anything," he told her. "You're just having a—an affair, that's all."

She looked at him. "No, that's not all," she said.

He swallowed. "No?"

She hesitated. And then she whispered, "I've fallen so in love with you—and it terrifies me, Jack. Because I don't know how I can go back if I have to. Back to before."

Jackson blinked several times. "Did you just say that you love me?"

She nodded.

He searched her eyes. After a moment, he said, "Could you say it again? Would you? Please?"

"I love you," Cassy said. "I love you very, very much, Jackson."

"Oh," he said. And then he closed his eyes and let his head fall forward, not caring if Dash saw his head in her lap or not.

He couldn't believe it. He couldn't believe that she had said it.

She loved him. Cassy said she loved him.

41

The Complicated Feelings
of Gordon Strenn

Gordon strode down the second-floor hallway of Darenbrook III, ignored Chi Chi's protests and went straight into Cassy's office, slamming the door behind him. He went over to her desk and stood there, waiting for her to get off the phone.

Cassy, giving him only a cursory glance, made a few more notes on the legal pad in front of her and then hung up.

"Where the hell is she?" Gordon demanded.

"Indianapolis," Cassy said, slipping off her reading glasses and placing them on the desk in front of her.

"And you let her go?"

"Yes, I did," Cassy said evenly.

He was so angry he could not speak. He looked around her office—grabbed the coffee mug on her desk and turned to hurl it at the door. It smashed into pieces. "God damn it!" he yelled, turning back and slamming his hands down on her desk. "What's the matter with you? Don't you know there's something wrong with her?"

There was a knock on the door and then it opened. It was Derek, with Chi Chi and Kate standing anxiously behind him. "Everything okay in here?" he said.

"Yes, thanks," Cassy said calmly, standing up and walking around the desk. "You can close the door," she told them. When they did, she took Gordon by the arm and led him over to the couch. "If I'd known you were coming home," she said, sitting first and pulling him down beside her, "I would have told you to fly on to Indianapolis."

"Oh, yeah?" he said, yanking his tie, loosening it. "Try again. She doesn't want to see me. She made it very clear, believe me." He dropped forward, resting his elbows on his knees, clasping his hands down between them. "So I thought I'd come back and meet her at home anyway, and what do I find? Alexandra? No. I find all of Jessica's junk all over our apartment." He looked at her. "I walk in—oh christ, why bother?" he said, jumping up. "I don't know what's going on anymore." He walked toward the glass wall. "Our apartment—listen to me!" he said, throwing his arm through the air. He turned toward Cassy, holding his hand out. *"We* don't even have an apartment. She has hers and I have mine." He leaned forward, pointing at her. "And what do you bet that won't change after we get married?" He wheeled around to the window, jamming his hands into his pockets.

Cassy sat there, watching him. "You asked me if I didn't know something was wrong with Alexandra," she said. "What did you mean by that?"

After a long moment he said, "I meant that everything's been going to hell between us ever since she got here. To this fucking place," he added, giving the glass a kick. "She's pretty hard to live with, you know. She's not like everybody thinks. Not at home."

"For instance . . . ?" Cassy said.

He sighed, shifting his weight to both feet, and looked straight out over the square. "For instance," he said, "she stopped talking. Then she stopped sleeping. Then she started crying in the middle of the night—and every time I ask what's wrong she's says, 'Nothing.' " He paused and then said, turning around, "And after years of great sex, ever since she came here to work, that's gone to hell too."

Cassy looked down, folding her hands in her lap. "I don't mean to pry, Gordon."

"Oh, it's okay. Believe me, I welcome the chance for someone to explain it to me." He paused, watching Cassy, and then said, "Oh, she's been dutiful, Cassy—God forbid anyone should tell Alexandra she hasn't performed her duties. But that's what she's been doing—performing—I know, Cassy, believe me, I know."

"Stress can do all those things, Gordon," Cassy said.

"So can falling in love with someone else," Gordon said.

"What?" Cassy said.

"I didn't figure it out until this morning—when she called me in London," he said.

Cassy looked confused.

"I knew it, you know," he said, walking back toward the window. "In the beginning, somewhere, I knew there was more to it than what she said. I could tell by the way he acted. Even when he congratulated me —I knew something was up at the boat party. I felt it in her and I saw it in him."

"What?" Cassy said. "Who?"

"Darenbrook," he said. "And I bet he's still out there with her. As soon as she told me he flew out there, I knew—"

"No, Gordon," Cassy said sharply, "he's not still out there. He came back with me this morning."

The sound of her voice made him turn around.

Cassy stood up. "And not only are you wrong about Jackson, but I think you're being horribly unfair to Alexandra. For your information, the job that that young woman's trying to do right now would be enough to kill the sex drive in five people. And I thought you understood that, Gordon—I thought you understood what the first months of stress and pressure can do—"

"I understand stress and pressure," Gordon said, "and that's not what—"

"Alexandra is not having an affair with Jackson!" Cassy said.

"I didn't say she was," he said. "I said she's falling in love with him. Alexandra's incapable of sleeping with two people—I know that, but—"

"Gordon Strenn, you listen to me!" Cassy said, stamping her foot.

He looked at her.

"I swear to God as I'm standing here that only this morning Alexandra told me how much she wants to marry you. Do you hear me?

Alexandra is not cheating on you. She is not in love with Jackson. Yes, she has problems—we all do. And guess what? You take on an extraordinary job, you develop extraordinary problems. And Alexandra's got some. But she loves you, Gordon," Cassy said, walking over and touching his arm. "You know she loves you."

His eyes had fallen to the floor.

"Don't you?" Cassy said.

He nodded, sighing.

"I know, sweetheart," Cassy said, rubbing his arm. "It's very hard on you. But give her some time. And give you two some time. It's all been happening so fast, coming at you from all directions—you two need some time together." She picked up his hand and gave it a little shake. "And you need to trust her."

Gordon raised his head to look at her. "I guess I should go back to London," he said.

"I think you should do whatever you need to do," she told him. "If you need to see Alexandra, go see her."

Gordon looked at her a moment. "Or trust her," he said. He sighed. "Leave her alone and trust her."

Was trusting Alexandra even an issue really? Wasn't it really projecting his own guilt on her? That, when she called him this morning to tell him that she almost died, he had been on his way to eat breakfast with a woman he was thinking about having an affair with? Wasn't that really what had happened today? That it had been his own guilt and fear that had put him on the Concorde to New York?

Did he really think Alexandra was falling in love with Jackson?

No.

But she *was* acting strange and she *had* been acting strange.

But did that give him license to sleep with someone else while he was in London?

No.

But yes—at least he had thought so yesterday, when one of the married producers from Canada working at Hargrave Studios for the summer suggested they give it a try. With all the horrible stuff floating around these days, she had no desire to sleep with anyone on the circuit, or so she said, and she had no desire to break up her marriage. And so if Gordon was clean and had been otherwise monogamous to his fiancée ("And it isn't as if you're married yet, eh?" she said with such a lovely sly smile), then why didn't they meet twice a week for an hour or so? No strings attached?

He had been about to leave for the Grosvenor House to discuss the matter further.

But it wasn't as if Alexandra had made much of an effort to even try and work out some rendezvous weekends for them while she was on tour. (He wondered what she expected him to do, knowing him the way she did. Or did she *want* him to find someone else and just leave her alone while she worked, trusting that he wouldn't bring anything home with him or anyone or any clues about how he had satisfied himself for nine weeks?)

It was not as if he had not tried to lead a pristine life in London. To date, he had. When he and Betty first arrived on the twenty-sixth of June at the May Fair Hotel on Stratton Street, a block over from Piccadilly, it was Gordon who had been unsure about the suitability of Christopher staying there. It was a very luxurious hotel, but it catered to the La La Land crowd and it was from La La Land that Julie had fled with Christopher in the first place. And Gordon got the feeling that an English nanny named Mrs. Twickem might not think hanging out with crazy Constantine Moscowitz, their director, and a bunch of actors was the best environment for her little charge.

According to Betty, Constantine wanted the May Fair because they had the screening facilities to run dailies each night, and Vanessa Winslow wanted it because she heard Madonna stayed there, and Hargrave Studios wanted it because they had gone to considerable trouble to arrange for the top American cast and crew to stay there as the director and famous actress wished.

Gordon had been assigned to something called the Monte Carlo Suite on the seventh floor, a gorgeously (or ridiculously, depending on one's affinity to French-harem-New Hollywood decor) appointed suite with a split-level dining room and living room, the latter of which had a domed ceiling, a chandelier with a mass of crystal rodlike things hanging down, and opened out onto a terrace. It had nice furniture, but this strange carpeting with red and blue swirls (not terribly unlike something from the sixties), and all of these big pillows were on the floor. The dining room was all mirrors, or so it appeared, had a glass table and another one of those crystal chandeliers. ("There's not much point being in London if you live in something like this, is there?" Gordon whispered to Betty, who had come in for a tour with the porter before going on to her room.)

"So did Madonna stay here? Is that true?" Betty asked the porter after he showed them the Jacuzzi.

"Oh, yes," the porter said with an air of confidentiality. "It was quite an event, that, Miss Madonna."

"So where did she stay?" Betty said.

The porter looked up at the ceiling. "The penthouse." He looked back at Betty. "Twelve rooms. We opened the entire floor for her. And it has a separate entrance, you see, which Miss Madonna needed as she is quite popular here. And there is a very nice piano up there too, you see."

"Oh, I'm sure that's why she stayed here—for the piano," Gordon said, patting the head of one of the two tremendous gold greyhounds that were sitting at attention on either side of the sitting room, at the top of the steps. "But you're so skinny," he whispered to the dog, running his fingers over its ribs. "Christopher will cry because he'll think you're starving."

"Where's Vanessa Winslow staying?" Betty asked the porter.

"Oh, Miss Winslow, yes," the porter said, clapping his hands once. "We do so enjoy her television program here."

"Right, right," Gordon said, squinting up at the chandelier.

"She'll be in the Penthouse Suite, I believe. Not the entire floor, mind you, not like Miss Madonna, but still, the nicest suite in the hotel —in all of London, I'm sure."

"I'm sure," Gordon said, patting a gold heron statuette on the head.

"Oh, she'll be happy then," Betty said. "So long as Madonna stayed there."

"It's quite fit for a movie queen," the porter assured her.

"A movie queen," Gordon said, laughing.

"The only kind of queen you have over in America," the porter said, winking to Betty.

"Ooo," Betty scolded him, shaking a finger, "cheeky, cheeky. We may be ugly Americans, but we do so love our movie queens. Besides," she added, sweeping up the stairs to the sitting room and waltzing around by herself, "she may not be the only movie queen in the hotel."

"Sick her, sick her," Gordon told the gold greyhounds out of the corner of his mouth.

"And you're an actress too, miss? I thought so," the porter said, hands clasped behind him, rocking back on his heels once. "You're quite pretty, miss. If you'll excuse me for saying so."

"Excuse you?" Betty said, stopping her dancing. She looked at Gordon. "I think I ought to marry him." She looked at the porter. "If I brought you back to Valley Stream, I could tell them you were fourth in line to the throne and they'd never know."

In any event, it was Gordon who decided, the next morning, that they were moving to the quiet, Old World grandeur of the Dorchester on Park Lane. It was right across the way from Hyde Park and it was not that far away from the Ruvaises' London flat, so Mrs. Twickem was very familiar with the area. It was also close enough so that Gordon could walk over to the May Fair after dinner each night and see the dailies and check on everybody, but was far enough away to keep the inevitable soap opera away from Christopher. And the private offices of Lord Gregory Hargrave, where he had been offered the use of a small office and telephone during his stay, was just over on South Audley Street, literally not a minute's walk away.

They picked up Christopher and Mrs. Twickem (a lovely woman in her sixties, who was much better natured than she at first appeared to be) at the airport on Friday, and Gordon received an unexpected reward for his choice of hotels on the ride back.

"Did you hear that, Christopher dear?" Mrs. Twickem said. "Your father has chosen the Dorchester Hotel for us. Do you remember what your mother told you about the Dorchester Hotel? What is so special about it? About who was there during the war?"

Christopher nodded, nuzzling the side of his father's arm with his head.

"Can you tell your father?" Mrs. Twickem asked him.

("He's so cute," Betty was sighing, sitting in the seat opposite them in the car.)

Christopher nodded, taking a breath and sitting up. "Grandfather was there," he said. "With the gen'rall."

Gordon looked at Mrs. Twickem in amazement. He himself had forgotten all about it—how his own father, when he was in the Army during World War II, had worked out of the Dorchester when General Eisenhower used it as his headquarters.

"Has concreek," Christopher added, twisting his father's finger.

Gordon looked to Mrs. Twickem.

She laughed. "Concrete. When we are here, in London, every time we pass by the Dorchester, Mrs. Ruvais tells Christopher the story about his grandfather being there during the war. And she always explains to him that the Dorchester was chosen for the general's headquarters because it had reinforced concrete walls."

"Grandfather was a tennent," Christopher told Betty.

"A lieutenant?" she exclaimed. "Why, I bet he was a very brave man."

Christopher nodded with an expression of some seriousness.

"Julie liked him," Gordon said to Betty. "My dad. They got along."

"Dad," Christopher repeated, giggling, trying to stick his foot in his father's hand.

The four of them had had a ball thus far. Mrs. Twickem and Christopher, for propriety's sake, had a suite to themselves next to Gordon's, and Betty had a double room to herself down the hall. The way it had worked out was that Christopher would come in and breakfast with his father in the morning, and then Gordon and Betty would go off to work while Mrs. Twickem took Christopher to a little summer school play group. Sometimes they got back early enough to take Christopher out somewhere special, but usually they got back in time for an early dinner with him, a walk (run) in Hyde Park, roughhousing in Daddy's room, a bath as supervised by Mrs. Twickem, and then jammies and a story from Daddy and sometimes from Betty too.

They had gone on two weekend jaunts thus far, giving Mrs. Twickem the time off and giving Betty what Gordon freely admitted was the majority of the responsibility, but she said—and it was clear that it was true—that she loved doing it. They were great pals, these two, Christopher and Betty, and it was unclear if it was a personality mix or the fact that Betty seemed to have the mind of a four-year-old.

THE COMPLICATED FEELINGS OF GORDON STRENN

At any rate Gordon was spending almost every day and night with Betty. She was a pleasure to work with, as always (she was so funny—she had Lord Hargrave practically on the floor the other day with the history of her love life to date and the current dating scene in New York City), but what was so much fun about her all the time was how excited she was about everything. She took nothing for granted in London—all of it seemed fascinating, wondrous to her, a source of multiple and sometimes inexplicable joys.

She was just plain happy over here and it was contagious.

And it *was* a happy time, this mix of hard work in a strange country and the strange work of trying to be a father to his son. At night, after Christopher was in bed, Gordon and Betty would usually walk over to the May Fair to see the dailies, check on people, hear the gossip, and then walk the streets, stopping for a beer or for coffee and dessert. They certainly talked a lot, about work, about Christopher, about whatever had happened that day. And as the days went by, they had so much to talk about, they never got to it all.

It worried Gordon a little—for Betty, he worried—that maybe all of this might just be a little too romantic, all of this time they were spending together. In London. And so much of the time they were acting like parents, like married people, and certainly as dear friends—which they were now, no doubt about that—and as colleagues in a way they had never been before. She shouldn't be his assistant anymore, he knew that. He could make her a producer tomorrow for the level of work she was doing. But she didn't seem any more eager for changes while they were here than he was.

But he had started getting pretty itchy for a release. Somewhere safely out of range of his domestic setup, somewhere safely away from the prying eyes of the cast and crew, somewhere safely out of everyone's eyes save his own. And that's why this Canadian producer had appealed to him so. To take this edge off—find a release, a safe one—so that he need never do something stupid, like sleep with Betty.

Now why did he think of that?

Because he knew he could have her. In five minutes he could. If he wanted. He knew it.

Gordon thought poor Betty might be a little in love with him.

Flying back to London that same night of the day he had flown to

New York to be with Alexandra, it made him feel angry and hurt to think about the fact that all the things he was doing in London that was giving him so much pleasure—with Christopher and Betty and even Mrs. Twickem—were things that he and Alexandra had never done, and would probably never do. And Gordon wondered what kind of a father would he be—or could he be—to Christopher after he married Alexandra. And then he wondered if he would ever have another child, and then he wondered how it was that he had never really pinned down Alexandra about her intentions in that regard. Alexandra loved children, he knew, but would she ever have time for them?

Would she ever have time for him?

He knew he loved Alexandra. Oh, God, he had loved her for so many years, there was no doubting that. And he felt it—yes, he knew he loved her because of how much it hurt sometimes. And when she called him this morning and told him what had happened, he had at first panicked, but then felt guilty, but then felt elated when he realized that she needed him. And despite their fight over the phone, about her insistence that he not come, he had never doubted that she would be glad to see him once he got there. And in the back of his mind, flying home, he had imagined that this trip would be just like the last time she nearly died. That the phone call had come just in time, just before he was going to betray her, and that he would race back to New York and find her at home and he would stay with her, holding her, reassuring her, protecting her, feeding her, making sure that she would be all right again.

Making sure she knew how much he loved her.

Making sure she experienced what it could be like between them. As partners. That he really could take care of her if she let him. That they could spend hours together, not doing anything in particular, having no goals for once, and yet never being bored.

He wanted it to be like those weeks in Washington.

But Alexandra had not been there.

Alexandra hadn't been there in a lot of ways recently.

Or ever, maybe. He just didn't know anymore.

And so Gordon completed his one-day whirlwind six-thousand-mile trip and was back at the Dorchester by ten o'clock. Betty had left a note for him with the porter, saying that she and some of the DBS gang were over at Shepherd's Tavern on Hertford Street and suggested he come over. So he did, wondering, as he walked along Curzon Street under the streetlights, listening to the sound of his footsteps echo off the buildings, how he could explain to Betty what had happened without making his trip sound like the complete and utter waste of time and money it had been.

When he arrived at the tavern, the DBS gang had pretty much taken over the place, a big crowd of talking and laughing and chatting Americans, hurrying their drinking as closing time approached. Gordon said hellos, nodded several times, making his way through the crowd to the bar to get a mug of ale, and then pushing his way through to the tables, looking for Betty.

("What kind of city *is* this?" the director's assistant said. "The streets are clean, cab drivers know where they're going, bars close at eleven and nobody carries a gun. It's got no character." "And don't you wonder what they're like in bed?" a production secretary giggled. "Pardon me," she mimicked, "but would it be possible for you to move your leg? Would that be too much trouble? Oh, marvelous, thank you, that's quite good, thank you, thank you very much indeed." "I was in Hyde Park today," a unit manager said, "sitting in a chair. And this gal's coming over to me—in jeans with the knees torn out? So I think, *finally,* a homeless person asking for money—but she says, 'Good afternoon, your ticket, please, sir.'" "So I said," an actor said, "'Listen, ducky, Green Park bean park, back home we can play whatever we want in our parks and I'm telling you, we're playing croquet.' And so we set up some wickets and then I knocked one of her balls up the hill and under the fence and it rolled out onto Piccadilly and the next thing I know, a whole battalion of big—and I mean *big*—guys are riding up through the park toward us. So I thought, *Oh great, the whole fucking Army's after me!*" "So they asked us if we had reservations," the locations manager said, "and I said no, and so they said they were sorry but they couldn't seat us for tea because they were booked. But then I said, 'Excuse me, but we're visiting from New York and Lord Gregory Hargrave suggested we come over for tea—and it was the Ritz he recommended especially.' Well, let me tell you, the Palm Court was ours in a minute. We're going to try it at Brown's tomorrow and see what happens." "He can't get the hang of the cars being on the other side," the art director said, "and so at intersections he sort of—well—careens into the side of them and then falls over backward on the traffic islands. It's too bad in a way, because if we were back home, the cars would just run him over and finish him off—which is what anyone who's ever had to work with the son of a bitch wishes would happen.")

He spotted Betty. She smiled and waved, pushed some guy out of the seat next to her and waved Gordon down into it. "Hi," she said, smiling, clearly delighted to see him. "When the front office said you were coming back, I figured you might want to get out and stretch your legs."

"You mean get drunk?" he said, sampling his ale.

"No," she told him. Then she said, "Well? Aren't you going to tell me how she is? If she's all right?"

"Yeah," he said, putting his mug down on the table. "She's fine. She's going on with the tour. So I decided to come back." He looked at his watch, saying to himself, "It's still today, right?"

"And?" Betty said.

"Hmmm?" he said, looking at her. She was wearing new earrings.

"And?" she repeated.

He shrugged, picking up his mug and taking another sip. Swallowing, "And they say she's going to break all kinds of rating records tonight."

"Good for her," Betty said, picking up her glass. "That will make her very happy."

Gordon looked at her. "Hey."

"Okay, okay," Betty said. "So we'll toast to me, okay?" She raised her glass. "Here's to me being very happy that you're back tonight." And then she leaned over and gave him a quick kiss on the mouth. And then she sat back and sipped whatever she was drinking, smiling at him.

"You're drunk," he said.

"Not at all," she said. "Just happy."

42

Alexandra Across America—Again

The newscast from Indianapolis Tuesday night, the night following Alexandra's near shooting in Detroit, went on the record books at the Association of Independent TV Stations in Washington, D.C., as the highest-rated "collaborative network" program in American history. Up against summer reruns, "DBS News America Tonight with Alexandra Waring," with an exclusive eyewitness account by the near victim herself and footage from the WXA studio, scored a 17.4 Nielsen rating —and on an affiliate system of less than half the size of the Big Three. And at that time of the year the some fifteen million viewers were enough to push "News America Tonight" to number twelve in the national ratings for the week.

A shocker for the industry.

"How do you think I feel?" Alexandra was quoted as saying after the overnights had been announced. "I'm thrilled people are watching us, I'm very grateful to be alive—and I'm horrified by the whole thing.

"I'm sorry," Alexandra said to Derek Wednesday night over a speakerphone in an office at WMI in St. Louis, "but I couldn't help it. It *is* horrifying. I mean, Derek, am I going to have to get shot at every six months to get people to watch the news?"

On the other end of the phone, Derek was laughing. On her end, Alexandra was hunched over her portable makeup mirror, just finishing her makeup for the newscast.

"Listen, sweetie," Derek said, "you're all set with the new schedule, right? I'm sorry we had to switch things around—"

"Minneapolis tomorrow, Chicago on Friday," Alexandra said, tossing her mascara into the bag. "Will's got the schedule."

"Right," Derek confirmed. "And it really is worth it. 'Morning, Chicago' is the biggest thing in town and I think you'll have fun on it. Then you've got two newspaper interviews, plus *Chicago* magazine—"

"Derek, I gotta go," Alexandra said, checking her watch and standing up. "Let's talk tomorrow, okay?"

"Wait a minute," Derek said. "Alexandra?"

"Make it fast," she said, hand on the speaker switch.

"Listen, I wanted you to hear it from me first—before you saw it."

"Saw what?"

"You're not going to be the cover story after all for—"

"Not even when I got shot at again?" she said, straightening up and laughing. "Well, give them ten points anyway for wanting to do a story on me a month ago. Don't worry about it, Derek," she said, reaching for the switch again. "I don't much want to be in a magazine that wants pictures of me sitting on my bed in my apartment watching TV news anyway."

"Oh, no, you're still in next week's issue," Derek told her. "But, sweetie, listen—the cover . . ." Derek sighed. "They're going with John Darly on the cover, with the line, 'America's Affluence Goes Haywire—Preppie Assassin John Darly.' And then there's a little picture of you up in the corner."

Silence. Alexandra slowly sat back down.

"I'm sorry, Alexandra," Derek said. "Cassy and Langley and Jackson —we all called over there today when we heard, but they're not going to change it." A moment later, "Sweetie, are you all right?"

"I'm fine," she said, swallowing. And then she gave her head a quick shake, blinking a couple of times, sat forward on the desk and said, "But listen to me, Derek—carefully. John Darly is not a PR piece. John Darly is news. The guy tried to shoot me. That's news. So if you guys ever try to interfere with the way someone else covers the news, I will personally come back to New York and break your legs—do you understand me? And I want you to tell the mighty triad that—and that they, of all people, should know better."

Derek laughed.

"I'm not laughing, Derek," she told him, switching off the speaker phone.

"Good morning, this must be Minneapolis," Alexandra said into the phone.

ALEXANDRA ACROSS AMERICA—AGAIN

"Hi, sweetheart!" Cassy said. "How are you?"

"Fine. I just got your message as I walked in," Alexandra said, holding it—on top of several other messages—in front of her. She was standing by a desk in the corner of the newsroom of their Minneapolis affiliate, WLS. "Boy, it sure makes my day—my year—and my life, I think," she said, laughing. "It's wonderful news. Tell Langley and Jackson I'm ecstatic. I can't believe it, can you? We'll have real international desks now, right? I mean, like London, Paris, Milan—"

"Well, not for a couple months yet," Cassy said. "But soon. And Langley's going to the board meeting this weekend to see if we can expand to seven days a week. Speed the whole schedule up by a year."

"Oh, wow," Alexandra sighed, sinking down on the edge of a desk. "I can't believe it, can you?"

"Just wait," Cassy said, "you haven't even heard the best yet. Are you sitting down?"

"Yes," Alexandra said, squinting slightly.

"Come Monday morning," Cassy said, "DBS will have one hundred thirty-three affiliate stations across America."

Alexandra dropped the phone and screamed. For joy.

"No, I'm right in the middle of the Mississippi River," Alexandra said, sitting in a chintz-covered wingback chair, looking out the window at the night sky. "It's lovely, really lovely."

"What's it called?" Jessica asked her.

"The Nicollet Island Inn," Alexandra said. "Will's room looks over at downtown Minneapolis—I look straight out over the river. I wish I could stay another night, it's so lovely—but Chicago calls."

"What time do you have to get up?"

"Six," she said, sighing.

"Why don't you just come home for a week?" Jessica said. "You need some rest. You looked tired tonight."

"I'll catch up on sleep this weekend," Alexandra said. "At home. Kansas-home, I mean."

Silence.

"I'm looking at Central Park," Jessica told her. She laughed then. "Oh, you should have seen me this afternoon, Waring. It seemed like such a great idea to take everybody roller-skating after the show. It was beautiful out, Wollman rink was practically empty, and we just got the word on my ratings—By the way," she added, her voice dropping, "did I ever thank you? Didn't I always say the surefire lead-in to a talk show was an hour-long boring newscast? Haven't I always said that?"

Alexandra laughed, sliding off her shoes and bringing her legs up into the chair with her. "So how was the skating?"

"Oh, brother," Jessica groaned. "I thought, what could be so hard about skating? You know, I only did it my whole childhood and then it was a big thing in Tucson. Well, forget it! You would have thought I'd never done it before. I looked like Grandma Moses walking across a wet kitchen floor."

Alexandra roared.

"Oh, it was awful," Jessica said. "I tell ya, Alexandra Eyes, it's terrible being somebody who *used* to know how to do everything. I always hear these guys in AA talking about how they stopped doing stuff when their drinking increased, and I always think, *Not me!* But then, whenever I stop and think about it, I realize I haven't done *any*thing except work, talk, drink and fuck for years—and I haven't even done the last two with people I like in a long time."

"Now, now," Alexandra said, "I'm sure that's not true."

"Oh, it's true," Jessica assured her. "Skating, skiing, tennis, golf, sailing, even bike riding—I don't even know how to ride a bike anymore. Talk about the youngest has-been."

"But now you can start again," Alexandra said gently, smiling.

Pause. "I guess I can, can't I?"

"Sure. My bike's in the basement," Alexandra said. "Ask the doorman and he'll get them to bring it up for you whenever you want. And listen, on the refrigerator is the number of my tennis club. Why don't you ask Cassy if she'd like to take a couple lessons with you? She keeps saying how she'd like to start again. And the club's right—"

"Forget it," Jessica told her. "Cassy's up to her kazoo in work with the new affiliates. Besides, it's you she'd want to play with. She misses you a lot, you know."

"I miss all of you," Alexandra said.

"And I gotta ask you something, Waring," Jessica said. "How is it everybody thinks you're their best friend? Cassy, Kyle, little Alexandra,

Jr.—all of those guys have been moping around ever since you left. And they all talk about you and they all look at me, like, 'Scat, you're a mess, get out of here—you're no substitute for our best friend.' "

"That's not true," Alexandra told her. "They're all just nervous about the board meeting this weekend. Oh, hey, before I forget—Jackson's sister, Cordelia, she called me this morning to see how I was."

"The guiding light of the family, I hear, the Divine Miss Cordie Lou," Jessica said. "I told Jackson if he insists on me serving corn bread to his kooky family—and did you hear that? We're having a *cookout* in the square Saturday night? A kooky cookout?"

"Yes, I heard."

"And that Jackson and Langley want *me* to kiss up to his family? How you got out of this, Waring—"

"I didn't get out of it," she said. "I went to the Darenbrooks' house, didn't I?"

"And now Cordelia thinks you're her best friend too, right?" Jessica asked her.

"Listen," Alexandra said, "let me give you a word of advice about Saturday, okay?"

"I mean, why else would she call you?" Jessica continued. "But then, why not? Everybody likes Alexandra Eyes. Everybody calls you—even Cordelia Paine, who hates everybody in secular TV. Alexandra, are you a mere mortal or what?"

"Would you listen for one second, *please?*"

A sigh. "Okay. What is it?"

"Wear something jazzy, but don't show a lot of your—your—"

"My bust?" Jessica asked her.

"Yes, your bust," Alexandra said. "I'd wear that black dress of yours, the one with the gray. It's very pretty and you look wonderful, and it's still sexy in a way but doesn't . . ."

"Strut my stuff?" Jessica asked her.

Alexandra laughed softly. "Exactly. Because I'll tell you, Cordelia Paine is one tough cookie—and she's not real high on some of the topics on your show, although she did seem encouraged when I told her you changed your cocktail party shows to a coffee hour. She's not as different from you and me as you'd think. She's very bright, has lots of energy, is a mover and a shaker—"

"That's what we are?" Jessica said. "And here all these years I thought I was a hopeless wretch."

"Only she's very, very conservative," Alexandra continued. "But if you keep that in mind you'll do fine with her."

"Jackie says she's so right-wing her plane only flies in circles," Jessica said.

"Jessica?" Alexandra said.

"Yes?"

"Just pay a lot of attention to her, okay? She's a very important member of the board. And be yourself—but please, don't drop any four-letter words."

"I'm much better about that," Jessica told her.

"Right," Alexandra said. "Didn't you just tell me you haven't fucked for years with anyone you liked?"

"Made love with," Jessica said. "That's what I said."

"Okay, so you understand me," Alexandra said.

"Operation Beguile Cordie Lou," Jessica said. "Got it."

Alexandra sat up in bed and turned on the light.

2:06 A.M., the clock said.

She reached for the phone, listened for a dial tone, pushed a button for a long-distance line and then punched in a number. She sighed, closing her eyes, bringing the phone to her ear.

Her eyes opened. "Is this the answering service?"

She frowned slightly. "Um . . ." She looked at the clock again. "I guess she doesn't want to be disturbed."

"Well . . . I was going to leave a message for Cassy Cochran, but I changed my mind. Thanks. Bye."

She reached over and hung up the phone. She turned off the light and lay back down on the bed, looking up at the ceiling. After a while she sighed, murmuring, "Oh, God, what am I doing?" rolled over on her side and curled up around a pillow.

ALEXANDRA ACROSS AMERICA—AGAIN

MORNING, CHICAGO   Transcript p. 12

7-22-88   Guest: Alexandra Waring   Host: Martin Hailer

HAILER:

Before you leave, Alexandra, I'd like to ask you your opinion about the recent biography of anchorwoman Jessica Savitch. Have you read it?

WARING:

Yes. I found it very painful.

HAILER:

And the allegations of drug use? Bisexuality? How do you feel about that?

WARING:

About the allegations?

HAILER:

Yes.

WARING:

Um . . . I feel—I feel sick at heart, really. Because Jessica Savitch will always be a hero to me and hearing these kind of things—well—hurts. Because, you see, she was the one I watched, the one who made me think, gosh, maybe I could anchor the news someday. . . . No—no doubt about it, watching Jessica Savitch anchor the news changed my life. And so to hear these things about her is painful—because my admiration for her runs very deep.

HAILER:

Pardon my astonishment, but you, who pride yourself on being a journalist, openly admire a woman who people say merely cashed in on her looks—

WARING:

Did you ever see her in person?

HAILER:

No.

WARING:

I didn't think so.

HAILER:

Um—well, as I was saying, people said she cashed in on her looks—

WARING:

I really don't understand how you feel free to make a statement like that. You make it sound as though she just fell out of the sky into NBC, that she didn't do any work to get there. She did not just bounce in from a Miss America pageant. This was a woman from very modest means who worked her way up from scratch. There was no head start for her in this life. She started way back there, worked her way up to here, and then—granted—she got lucky and was thrown to the top—if you can call it lucky, considering what happened to her.

HAILER:

But how can you admire somebody who was underqualified, supposedly a monster to people she worked with, who was taking drugs, had innumerable affairs, some with—

WARING:

Because she was there! Don't you understand? Jessica Savitch was there for me. She was there anchoring the news for NBC on Saturday night—and I wanted to be just like her. I don't do drugs, I've never done drugs in my life, and I would never wish for anyone to feel compelled to experiment with them or even try them once. And yet Jessica Savitch was my idol—and it is because of her that I'm here today. And thousands and thousands of other women my age raised their sights in life because of her too—because of seeing Jessica Savitch on television, seeing that the world was possible for women in a different way than ever before.

HAILER:

Yes, but—

WARING:

So how do you explain that? How do you explain it that a person with so many problems could be such an unfailing role model to me and thousands and thousands of women like me? Jessica Savitch never let *me* down, me the viewer.

HAILER:

But she went on the air once—

WARING:

And stumbled over some of the words in one of the "News Updates." Yes, I know.

HAILER:

And?

WARING:

And so imagine what you'd be saying about her if she had stormed off the set and forced the network to go to black for six minutes!

HAILER:

But they say she was on drugs.

WARING:

Yes, that's what they say—that there was a reason for her behavior. What's not clear is the reason why it was allowed to go on. She was certainly not the first newsperson to have a problem. But she may have been the first news*woman* to, and that probably had a lot to do with it. The flip side, the nice side, is that it need never happen again.

HAILER:

Do you think Dan Rather should have been fired when he walked off the set and CBS went black?

WARING:

No, I don't. I think people who anchor the news are human beings and are vulnerable to the traits of being human too. I think people who anchor the news are allowed to make one mistake—and not repeat it. And let me be perfectly clear on this, Dan Rather is one of the finest journalists the world has today, and I used that incident only to point out that women and men tend to be judged differently in the first place in this industry. Had it been a woman who had walked off, I'm sure she would have been fired—demoted, certainly.

HAILER:

And you think that Jessica Savitch—

WARING:

I think I'm tired of hearing people tear Savitch apart as if she made no contribution to anyone or anything. She was one of the few to come down out of the ivory tower to meet with young people, for example. She traveled all over the country to talk with us, teach us—she answered our letters, wrote a book. I mean, do you understand the significance of her relationship with viewers? That, regardless of what anyone says, regardless of anything she might have done, Jessica Savitch changed young women's lives across America for the better? Whether you like it or not?

HAILER:

Yes, but the point is, a woman who was a role model—

WARING: .

Is *dead.*

HAILER:

Yes, well, of course, she's dead—

WARING:

And that's not paying a high enough price for you?

HAILER:

I didn't—

WARING:

And you know, something else—I still hear people trashing her autobiography. But you know what? That book, *Anchorwoman,* contains the single most important insight about public life in America.

HAILER:

Which is?

WARING:

Jessica Savitch wrote, and I quote, "We don't just shoot our heroes; we often destroy them by setting up unrealistic expectations."

"Kyle says the publisher wants to send you flowers," Will yelled to Alexandra across the Chicago affiliate newsroom, covering the phone with his hand. "Every copy of that Savitch biography was sold out in Chicago by lunchtime."

Alexandra groaned, hiding her head under the papers in her hand.

"And he asks that you try and refrain from making any further editorials on the state of network television news."

"Yeah yeah," Alexandra said, swatting the air with her papers.

"Psst," a woman said, standing nearby at the editor's desk.

Alexandra looked over.

"I'm glad you said what you did," she said. "I'm here because of Jessica Savitch too."

The Friday night DBS newscast from Chicago went very well. At the end of it, as a conclusion to this rather wild week of the tour, Alexandra looked straight into the camera (her eyes spectacular), and said, "Reporting from WCO in Chicago for the DBS television news network, I'm Alexandra Waring," adding, under her breath, with a mischievous smile, "who is very happy to be here, believe me," and then finished with, in her regular voice, "Good night, everybody. Have a wonderful weekend—we'll see you Monday in Kansas City."

At one-thirty in the morning, Central Standard Time, a set of car lights swung over the side of a gray clapboard-and-stone house. A dog started to bark. The car lights turned off, the engine stopped. The car door opened and closed. It was dark.

There was the sound of a low whistle and the dog stopped barking. It was still.

The silhouette of a person moved along the side of the house and stopped at the steps of a small porch. Shoes were taken off and left there. A pair of stockings next. A blazer.

The figure moved on, floating across the backyard, through the split-rail fence, down through a field, through another fence, disappearing into a row of corn. There was the sound of movement, of the rustling of cornstalks, but it was a quiet sound, hushed with the night. The moon came out from behind a cloud and the field turned blue-gray, bright, under the light. The rustle, the movement of corn, continued down the row. At the far end of the field the figure emerged, slipped through another fence and ran alongside it to a grove of trees. The figure walked through the trees, hesitated for a moment, turned, and then continued on, picking up the pace, moving out of the grove and up onto a grassy rise to another fence. The figure climbed up and over to sit on the top rail.

"Hi Gran, hi Granddad, I'm home," Alexandra said to the sky.

43

Alexandra's Visit with Her Parents

Saturday morning Mrs. Waring said she was sorry but Alexandra couldn't sleep in because April was going to be here before they knew it and Alexandra had to start in on the wedding books. And if Alexandra wanted a wedding dress made by the same seamstress who had made her grandmother's wedding dress she was going to have to hurry because Mrs. Huddlesmith was ninety-four and, while she wished Mrs. Huddlesmith only good health and happiness, one never knew how long people that age would be around, did one?

As her mother sent the shades and windows flying up, flooding the corner bedroom with light and fresh air, Alexandra—from under the covers of the four-poster bed—murmured something about nearly being shot that week. Mrs. Waring said mothers couldn't relate to guns and shootings nearly as well as they could relate to weddings, and she was sure that when Alexandra was in her old age she would much rather think back on how lovely her wedding had been than on how much nicer it would have been had she gotten out of bed that morning instead of giving in to those twisted, tormented, sick creatures of God who were determined to spread fear through the world.

Alexandra said only her mother could make sleeping in sound like letting the whole world down.

"And about this nonsense of having the wedding in New York, young lady," Mrs. Waring said, coming to stand next to the bed, hands on her hips, her own blue-gray eyes flashing.

Alexandra groaned, squirming further down under the covers.

"Your father had to drive into Topeka this morning and left instructions that, if the wedding hasn't moved backed to Kansas by the time he comes home, he's only going to have four children. Lexy darling," Mrs. Waring said, easing herself down on the bed, "you must think of your father—how it would look for him to have his very own daughter be married out of state."

"But I don't want a political caucus for a wedding," came the muffled reply from under the covers.

Mrs. Waring gave a well-placed spank to the body beneath the covers. "No, you want a New York wedding so we can all be written up in a police report instead of the social section after we all get murdered in the streets."

Alexandra threw the covers back and sat up. "I thought you just said we couldn't give in to twisted, tormented, sick creatures of God."

"That doesn't include drug dealers," her mother told her, standing up.

"You've got them in Kansas City now, you know," Alexandra said. "Two gangs, crack."

"I'm not asking you to get married in Kansas City," her mother said. "I'm asking you to get married in Haven Wells."

There were several reasons why Alexandra had to be married in Kansas, according to Mrs. Waring, and she made sure Alexandra heard them all. Even when Alexandra jumped out of bed, threw on a pair of gym shorts, a T-shirt and running shoes, went downstairs, down the front porch and literally ran away from her mother—jogging—Mrs.

Waring slipped behind the wheel of the Land Rover in the driveway and followed her down the dirt access road to the fields.

Besides the fact that her father might run for office again in 1990, her mother told her (as Alexandra jogged and Mrs. Waring drove right alongside her) that, after this awful year of drought and Bob Dole not getting the party nomination for President, the state of Kansas needed her wedding to cheer everybody up. And if Alexandra's grandparents were alive, it would kill them if Alexandra didn't get married in Haven Wells.

"Not fair, Mom," Alexandra said, jogging along, perspiring in the morning sun.

"But it's true," Mrs. Waring said, easing the clutch a little to rev the motor and accentuate her point. (Vroommm.) (Despite Mrs. Waring's otherwise thoroughly lady-like demeanor and appearance, she was quite at home in four-wheel drive.)

"Granddad never thought I'd get married in the first place," Alexandra said. "He always said that."

"Well, your granddad had a rather cockeyed view of life to begin with, you know that, Lexy."

And Alexandra knew it would break Dr. Bates's heart if he didn't perform the ceremony. He had baptized her when she was a baby, given her a Bible at ten, accepted her into the church at fourteen and had those wonderful talks with Alexandra after her grandparents died. ("And before you even suggest it," Mrs. Waring said, "I'm quite positive Dr. Bates hates to travel. I don't think he's left town in forty years.") And Alexandra's brothers and sister hated New York. Mrs. Waring hated New York. Her father hated New York. All of their family and friends hated New York, and so how was Alexandra going to feel when she came down the aisle and saw how much everybody hated being there? ("Mother!" Alexandra said, laughing, breaking stride.)

And, last but not least, Mrs. Waring said she wouldn't mind rubbing Alexandra's marriage to Gordon in Tyler Mandell's face a little.

"Mom," Alexandra said, "I was the one who broke off the engagement. Tyler didn't do anything—I keep telling you that."

Mrs. Waring made a gesture, indicating that she believed this to be utter malarkey, and let her hand drop back down on the wheel. "We all know he was not what he appeared to be," she said, addressing the horizon.

Puffing now, Alexandra said, "He's very happily married—with a baby and everything—so I don't know why—you say that," and then she turned down another dirt road, losing her mother.

Mrs. Waring stopped the Land Rover, threw it in reverse, backed up, put it in first and went down the road after her daughter.

When Mrs. Waring caught up with her Alexandra stopped running and bent over for a minute, hands on her hips, catching her breath. "Mom," she said then, straightening up, breathing heavily, perspiration running down her face, "I'll be honest with you. One of the reasons why I—"

Her mother was frowning, looking down at something.

"What?" Alexandra said.

"Pull up your shirt," her mother said.

"What?" Alexandra said, wiping her forehead with the back of her wrist and looking down. "Why?"

"I want to see your stomach."

Alexandra pulled her T-shirt up so her mother could see her stomach.

"Lexy," Mrs. Waring said, raising her eyes, "how much weight have you lost?"

"Oh," Alexandra said, pulling her shirt down.

"Darling," Mrs. Waring said, voice softening, "you're not getting some kind of eating problem, are you?"

"No," Alexandra said, walking over. She leaned on the Land Rover door, looking face to face with her mother. "Really, Mom, I'm not. It just comes off, the weight, when I'm not sleeping well."

"And why aren't you sleeping well?" her mother asked her. She reached out and pushed a strand of moist hair back off her daughter's face. "Hmmm? Is it too much for you? The work?"

Alexandra shook her head, averting her eyes.

"Then what is it?" Mrs. Waring asked her.

After a moment Alexandra looked at her mother. "I'm not sure if I love Gordon the way I should."

Her mother smiled slightly. "Of course you do," she told her.

"Even if I'm not *in* love with him?"

"But you do love him," her mother said.

"Yes, I do," Alexandra said. She sighed, looking over at the field and then back at her again. "But more as a friend, I think."

Her mother really smiled then and patted her hand. "Then you have nothing to worry about. You'll probably have the best marriage of the lot."

Mrs. Waring shared her thoughts on the subject of love and marriage with her daughter for the rest of the day—as they covered the county on wedding-related errands (showrooms, books, catalogs, magazines and leaflets for Alexandra to look through to give her mother *some* idea of what she was thinking about in terms of wedding dresses, bridesmaid dresses, tuxedos, photographers, flowers, wedding cakes, orchestras, dance floors, caterers . . .)

Mrs. Waring said it was perfectly natural for Alexandra to feel unsure about the marriage because, the older one got, the more fears one got about everything and certainly marriage was one of them. That was why it was so much easier to get married when younger—like she had and Alexandra's sister had. But Alexandra had been on her own for so long—and she had always been like that, since she was a little girl—and so, at thirty ("Good heavens," Mrs. Waring said, "when you stop and think that at thirty I was having my fourth child"), of course Alexandra was going to be much more nervous and doubtful about getting married than most.

And regardless of what Alexandra may have heard, marriage was no institution for star-crossed lovers. Marriage was a partnership, and the love that counted in a marriage was exactly the kind Alexandra had for Gordon—because that was the only love that endured everything. Oh, yes, romance came and went—and it did come back, Alexandra should know that and expect that, romance came in cycles and she was just in an "out" cycle right now. ("You, my baby," Mrs. Waring said, patting Alexandra's knee, "are the product of a renewed romantic cycle in our marriage.")

Alexandra did not say very much over the course of the day. She just let her mother drive her around the county in the station wagon, smiled at the people to whom she was introduced and nodded, yes, or shook her head, no, when asked her opinion about whatever wedding thing her mother was trying to make up her mind about.

That evening, when Mr. Waring came home and Alexandra's sister, Elizabeth, and her husband and four children arrived, and then her eldest brother, Paul, Jr., and his wife and the two youngest of their three children arrived, everybody was in such high spirits, no one noticed how little Alexandra had to say. Mr. Waring and Paul and Elizabeth's husband happily argued economic policies and discussed Mr. Waring's possible reelection bid in the next congressional race, and after talk sped past DBS and the shooting and landed on The Wedding, Mrs. Waring, Elizabeth and Alexandra's sister-in-law were into a subject from which they would never return. When Elizabeth went upstairs to find the train of her wedding dress to prove to Mrs. Waring that Mrs. Huddlesmith was wrong, Alexandra should wear a very long one, Alexandra slipped outside to lead her youngest nephew, age four, around by the barn on a pony.

Sunday morning Alexandra went to church with her parents, and Dr. Bates was so glad to see her that he said so in the middle of the service. Afterward, on the steps of the church, he said a little bird had told him they might be having "a little do here in April," and Alexandra smiled, kissed him on the cheek, told him that her mother would keep him posted and walked away. "We understood, of course," he called after her, "why you transferred your church membership to New York, but your home will always be here, with us, in our hearts, Alexandra."

"Where are you and Lisa having dinner?" Mrs. Waring asked Alexandra on the way home, from the front seat of the station wagon.

"The Bristol," Alexandra said from the back seat.

"That's the one with the Victorian architecture you took me to once, isn't it?" Mrs. Waring asked.

"Yes," Alexandra said.

"Lisa who?" Mr. Waring asked, turning south onto Route 59.

"Connors," Mrs. Waring told him. "You remember Lisa. Alexandra's having dinner with her in the city tonight."

"Oh, that crook Connors' daughter," Mr. Waring said.

"Lisa's not a bit like her father," Mrs. Waring said. "Is she, Alexandra?"

"No," Alexandra said, looking out the window.

"You used to love Lisa," Mrs. Waring told Mr. Waring. "Or don't you remember?" She looked out her window, smiling slightly. "We remember, don't we, Alexandra? How your father used to get around Lisa?" She chuckled softly, shaking her head.

"Lisa was a very beautiful girl as I remember," Mr. Waring said gruffly. "Very nice, very interesting."

"We still have that painting of hers in the cellar, Alexandra," Mrs. Waring said. "You don't suppose she'll be driving out to see us, do you?"

"I doubt it," Alexandra said.

"Good," Mrs. Waring said, "then I won't have to find somewhere to hang it." Pause. "Why don't you take it back to New York with you? You used to like it."

"Where's Lisa living these days, Alexandra?" Mr. Waring said.

"Denver, mostly," Alexandra said.

"I'm glad you're seeing her," Mrs. Waring said. "Because remember how she said she'd never get married? And then—boom—she got married, to a nice young man—what was his name?"

"Matt," Alexandra said.

"That's right," Mrs. Waring said, nodding her head. "And what does he do?"

"He's some sort of a consultant," Alexandra said.

"About what?" Mr. Waring said. "You have to be consulted about something specific to be a consultant."

"About resorts, I think," Alexandra said.

"A consultant about resorts?" Mr. Waring said.

"Well, you know," Mrs. Waring said, "they do move in those kind of circles. Resorts and developments and the like. The Connors do."

"Connors is a crook," Mr. Waring said. "That's what circle he moves in. Lisa's husband work for her father, Alexandra?"

"Indirectly," she said.

"She's not getting divorced, is she, Alexandra?" Mrs. Waring asked, turning around to look at her. "That's not why she's coming to see you, is it?"

"Now why would you say that?" Alexandra said.

"Because that girl was always upset about something," Mrs. Waring said, turning back around in her seat. "And she always ran to you when she was." She looked out her window. "I used to tell your father that she walked and talked a good game but was too dependent on you —that I didn't think it was very good for either one of you."

"I don't ever remember you saying that," Mr. Waring told his wife. "And I don't ever remember Lisa being upset."

"I do," Mrs. Waring said. "Oh, look, Paul," she added, tapping her fingernail against the window, "see what they've done there? They took down the wood fence and put up a metal one. Awful."

Everybody looked at the fence.

"Hideous," Mr. Waring said, shaking his head, looking back at the road.

"Alexandra . . ." Mrs. Waring said, turning around to look at her again. "You're not going to forget what we were discussing yesterday, are you? If Lisa's having problems, you're not going to listen to her, are you?"

"What were you discussing yesterday?" Mr. Waring asked his wife.

"Oh, we were just talking about Gordon and the wedding," Mrs. Waring said, turning back around in her seat.

"What about Gordon and the wedding?" Mr. Waring said quickly, glancing over at his wife.

"Alexandra's just a little nervous, that's all," Mrs. Waring said. "Nothing to worry about."

"This isn't going to be another Tyler Mandell, is it, Alexandra?" Mr. Waring said to her in the rearview mirror. "We're not going to have to go through that again, are we?"

"Oh, don't be silly," Mrs. Waring said.

"Lexy?" Mr. Waring asked.

"Leave her alone, Paul," Mrs. Waring said. "She knows it's time."

"I know it's time for what?" Alexandra said.

"To get married," Mrs. Waring said.

"Daddy always said she'd be the tough one to marry off," Mr. Waring said, looking over at his wife. "Remember?"

"How could I forget?" Mrs. Waring said, sighing, looking out her window. "He told her that so many times, look what happened."

Mr. Waring looked in the rearview mirror. "What's the matter, Alexandra?"

"You make me feel like . . ." Alexandra said, voice trailing off.

"Like what?" Mrs. Waring said, following a tree with her head as it went by.

"Like I'm some sort of social pariah who needs to redeem herself before it's too late," Alexandra said.

Mr. Waring laughed.

"You're not a social pariah," Mrs. Waring said, "don't be silly."

"Thank you," Alexandra said.

"You sound just like your brother when you're being sarcastic," Mrs. Waring told her.

"What is it, Alexandra, what's the matter?" Mr. Waring said, squinting into the rearview mirror. "Why are you looking like that?"

"Why, what is she looking like?" Mrs. Waring said, turning around to look at her.

"Some parents would be happy to have me as a daughter the way I am," Alexandra told them.

"We're very happy with the way you are," Mrs. Waring said. "We couldn't be prouder. Could we, Paul?"

"No one's prouder of you than we are, Alexandra," Mr. Waring said.

"Then why do I always get the feeling that you won't be happy until I get married and have children?"

"We never expected you to get married and have children like Elizabeth and the boys did, not right away—did we, Paul? You've always been different, Alexandra. Elizabeth would sooner hang herself than live the way you do."

"We knew it would take time," Mr. Waring said. "Didn't Daddy always say—"

"It's never going to be enough, is it?" Alexandra said.

"What?" Mr. Waring said. "What did she say?" he asked his wife.

"She said, 'It's never going to be enough, is it?'" Mrs. Waring said.

"What isn't going to be enough?" Mr. Waring asked Alexandra in the rearview mirror.

"My life. Me. If I don't get married and have children, then deep down inside you'll always think of me as a failure, won't you? No matter what I do."

"Alexandra Bonner Waring!" Mrs. Waring said, turning around to look at her. "You are the strangest child who says the strangest things." Then she turned back around in her seat and looked out the window.

"Of course you'll get married and have children—if you'd just stop analyzing everything. If you'd just stop thinking so much and do it, Alexandra, everything would work out exactly the way it's supposed to. I've told you that."

"Now why didn't I think of that?" Alexandra said, turning to her window. "Just stop *thinking*, Alexandra," she told herself. And then she laughed, letting her forehead fall forward to bang against the glass.

In the front seat, Mr. and Mrs. Waring exchanged looks with each other.

44

The Reunion

Jackson remembered something about everybody in his family staying in the same hotel, but no one except Beau seemed to be suffering from the same delusion. Cordelia usually stayed at the Plaza on her trips to New York, but then Kitty Paine got a last-minute chance to foil a buyout of the PTL by a businessman "not of owah perswayshun" and wasn't coming to the reunion after all, and so Cordelia decided to join Big El at Belinda's.

Cordelia's son, Ezekiel, alias Freaky Zekey, was staying at the Marriott in Times Square because he wanted to be "somewhere near a little action, if you catch my drift." Little El had some sort of Hilton towel collection going and so he and his wife were staying there, while their son, Kirky, and his wife had taken rooms at the Ritz Carlton and their daughter, Bipper, and her husband—flying in from Paris—were staying uptown at the Westbury.

The twins, Norbert and Noreen, and their respective spouses were staying at the Pierre. Norbert's son, Knightsbridge Collier, alias "K.C.," had his reservation adamantly refused at the Carlyle and was, with his two women friends, staying at the Parker Meridien. Norbert's daughter, Jane, was not coming (explaining that the next time she would expose her husband to her father and Aunt Noreen would be to point out their graves). And Noreen's only child, Poor Luanne—as everyone called her (presumably because of her unfortunate looks)— was in the Algonquin, where, her mother said, she hoped Poor Luanne would trip over a half-decent poet looking to marry money.

Jackson's son, Kevin, was mountain climbing in Tibet and would not be coming. Jackson's daughter, Lydia—after saying she was coming and then not coming six different times—finally decided, on Friday night, that she was not coming, no explanation given.

Ethel, Randy and Claire kept a running chart in the computer of these hotel arrangements, plus an intricate tracking system of what Darenbrook wished to participate in which of the following organized Saturday activities: shopping, museum tours, horseback riding in Central Park, carriage ride in midtown, helicopter ride around the city, roller-skating at Wollman rink, Mets game at Shea, tea at the Stanhope, hot dogs and roller coaster at Coney Island. Saturday evening, of course, everyone was to come to West End for cocktails, a tour of the facilities and a big cookout in the square, and then Sunday was the board meeting.

Saturday morning Jackson picked up Beau and Tiger at the Darenbrook suite in the Plaza and took them downstairs to the Edwardian Room for breakfast. A few minutes later Cassy left Jackson's suite and came downstairs, where she was introduced as the future president of DBS who had just run over from West End to meet the brother she had heard so many wonderful things about. (At this, Beau looked at Jackson, as much as to say, "You must have forgotten the part about my gambling away sixty million dollars of your money on the stock market last year.") And, as everyone did, Cassy said she couldn't get over the resemblance between the brothers.

Cassy could only stay for a cup of coffee, but it was clear that she and Beau liked one another on sight. When she left the table and the men sat back down, Beau turned to his brother and said, "Don't let her get away—marry her, Jack."

"What?" Jackson said. "What are you talking about?"

"Cassy," Beau said, his own Darenbrook blue eyes twinkling, pointing in the direction of the door. "The woman you're in love with." He turned to Tiger. "At first she reminded me a little of Barbara."

"Me, too, at first," Tiger said. "But she's not like Barbara—she just carries herself the same way."

"But she certainly has the same effect on Jackie," Beau said. He turned to grin at his brother. "It's great to see you in love again, Jack. It's been a long time."

"You mean you can just tell?" Jackson asked, trying to look concerned, but secretly elated.

"Like chicken feathers on a fox," Beau told him.

After swearing his brother and Tiger to secrecy, Jackson told them a bit more about Cassy and their situation, to which Beau responded with the advice that he give Cassy all the time she needed to sort things out in her life and career, instead of doing the Darenbrook-like thing of demanding instant gratification and screwing everything up.

And so, while they were on the subject of screwing up, they moved on to Jackson's presentation to the board tomorrow, about how his personal intervention had saved the magazine group from being compromised in any way by Beau's stock option debts. And then Beau shared with Jackson what he was going to tell the board: that for the first time in his life he had honestly taken steps to get help for his gambling problem. For ten months now he had been going twice a week to group therapy (a kind of private Gamblers Anonymous meeting for leading L.A. businessmen) and was going to one-on-one therapy twice a week as well. On top of that, he said, Tiger had only moved back with him four months ago, and promised to walk if he so much as bought a lottery ticket. ("You left Beau?" Jackson said in astonishment, having no idea of this. Tiger nodded. "I couldn't take it anymore. I couldn't listen to his excuses and promises and have it happen all over again.")

Jackson said he thought this sounded good, and that he would then read the company comptroller's report summarizing the excellent performance and financial return on the magazine group, *Field Day* in particular. All of this, they agreed, made Beau's chances of being forgiven by the board for using *Field Day* as collateral on his personal debts pretty good—to keep him out of court, at any rate.

After breakfast Jackson rode up Fifth Avenue to Belinda and Langley's to see how everybody up there was doing. He called Cassy at West End on the way. "Hi," he said on the car phone.

"Hi," she said, "I'm just listening to Kyle and Denny's presentations for tonight."

"I just wanted to tell you that my brother knows I'm in love with you. He said he knew it the second you walked in and he saw my face."

"Oh," she said.

"But he won't tell anybody," Jackson assured her.

"Oh, I'm sure of that. Actually, I think it's great you have someone to talk to about it. Don't you?"

"Uh-huh," he said. "Listen, I want to ask you something."

"What?"

"Would you ever consider moving? To a new place, I mean? Here, in New York?"

"This isn't a good time," she said.

"But just tell me," he said. "Would you? You wouldn't, would you? It's too soon—"

"And way too complicated," she said, "even if it wasn't impossibly too soon for me to know what I'm doing. Wait—hang on. No, don't go —" he heard her say. "I'll just be a second." She came back on. "Hello?"

"So you won't be moving for a while?" he said.

She paused. "How can you expect me—"

"I don't, I don't," he said quickly, smiling to himself. "I just wanted to make sure you're not moving anywhere for the next year or so. That's all."

She laughed, sounding confused. "No, I'm not, silly."

"Silly loves you, you know," he said, his smile expanding.

"Thank you," she said. "I feel exactly the same way this morning. I really do. And I really appreciate your calling to tell me."

"Hi-ya, hi-ya, hi-ya, hi-ya, guys!" Jackson said, skipping around the Petersons' dining-room table, where Belinda and Langley and Cordelia and Big El were eating breakfast.

"It was irritating when you were six, Jackie Andy," Cordelia said, "and it isn't any less so now."

"Duck," Jackson said, touching Belinda on the shoulder as he went past her; "Duck," he said, patting his father's shoulder as he went by; "Duck," patting Langley on the back as he went by; "Goose!" he said, reaching in through the chair to goose Cordelia.

"Ahhh!" Cordelia said, jumping in her chair. "Jackson Andrew Darenbrook!" She turned around, trying to swat her brother as he pulled a chair up to the table to sit between her and Langley.

"It's good for the circulation, Cordie Lou," Big El said, laughing in his wheelchair across the table from her. "That's what Lucille says."

"Lucille?" Cordelia said, turning to stare at her father. "And what, I'm afraid to ask, does Lucille know about pinching derrières?"

"From the way she swings her backside," Belinda said from her end of the table, "I imagine quite a lot. More eggs, Daddy?" She directed the woman who had just come in from the kitchen to take the chafing dish over to her father. "Jackie, have you eaten?"

"I'm fine, Baby B," he told her, crossing his arms and settling them on the table. "I just ate with Beau and Tiger."

Cordelia clucked her tongue. "Tiger," she sighed, shaking her head and buttering her toast. "Whenever I think that I thought that that boy was helping little Beau at school with his football—"

"Little Beau was twenty-two," Jackson reminded his sister.

"And he did help him with his passin'," Big El said. "Remember that game, Jackie Andy? Your brother never threw a touchdown pass like that twice in his life till Tiger came around."

"And Tiger painted the house, remember?" Belinda said to her sister. "You used to like Tiger then."

"That was before I knew what was going on up there on the third floor," Cordelia said, sniffing sharply, reaching for the jam.

"Heh-heee!" Belinda said, leaning forward over the table. "Remember the night, Jackie, we told Cordie Lou that it was the ghosts of wounded Confederate soldiers groaning up there? Remember?"

Jackson laughed and Cordelia dropped her knife on her plate. "Enough!" she said.

Belinda and Daddy kept laughing, while Jackson looked over at his brother-in-law. "Well, hi, Langley," he said.

Langley was watching Belinda at the other end of the table, over the top of his coffee cup. He lowered it, swallowing, eyes still on her.

"Langley," Cordelia said, "Jackie's speaking to you."

Langley looked over. "What?"

"What's the matter, Lang?" Jackson said.

"Oh, don't even bother, Jackie," Belinda said. "We think he's undergoing a personality change—he's been acting strange for days."

"How would you know? You haven't been here," Langley said.

"See what I mean?" Belinda said.

"If you didn't want us to stay with you, Langley," Cordelia said, swallowing a bit of toast, "then you shouldn't have told us to come."

Langley seemed to wake up a little then. "Don't be foolish, Cordelia," he said, pushing his glasses up his nose. "We love having you."

Big El laughed in his coffee.

"Stop it, Daddy," Belinda scolded her father. "It's true. We love having you stay with us. You haven't stayed with us since Barbara died." Belinda's eyes quickly went to her brother, looking as though she wished she hadn't said that. Cordelia stopped chewing and looked at Jackson too.

Jackson looked at both of them. "What?" he asked Belinda. "Daddy and Cordie haven't stayed with you since Barbara died—so what?"

Cordelia looked past Jackson to Langley.

"Cordie," Jackson said.

Cordelia looked at him.

"It's okay," Jackson said gently. He smiled. "Really. It's okay. Barbara died—we all know that. You can say that."

"Jackie, I—" Belinda started to say.

"No, Baby B, it's fine," Jackson said. He looked around the table. "It's time we talked about her out in the open, don't you think? Beau and I did this morning. It was fine. Really."

Cordelia looked to Langley again, whom Jackson caught shrugging. Jackson shrugged back at him, smiling, and then turned to Belinda. "Hey, B? Do you know any good real estate brokers?"

Everybody around the table started exchanging looks.

"Sure," Belinda finally said.

"What for, Jackie Andy?" Big El said. "You thinkin' of buying a place?"

"Yeah, Daddy, I am," he said. To Belinda, "I need somebody who really knows the ins and outs of the West Side. Somebody who knows the buildings."

"Hey, that's great, Jack," Langley said.

"But Jackie," Belinda said, "I'm sorry, but I don't think I know any-one who would know anything about the West Side."

"Why not?" Big El wanted to know.

"Because it's not the East Side," Belinda explained.

"That's okay," Jackson said. "I just thought I'd ask." He winked at Cordelia. "So, what are you guys doing today?"

"That big ol' yellow house over on Rose Hill Road's going to come up for sale soon, Jackie," Cordelia told her brother, smiling sweetly. "You used to like that ol' house when you were a boy."

"I used to like the girl who was in it, Cordie Lou," he told her. "Thanks, sweetie pie, but Hilleanderville's a bit of a commute." He looked at Belinda. "So what's up?"

"Cordie wants to do some shopping and then she and the twins are going to the museum," Belinda said. "Daddy's going to West End with Langley."

"And what about you?" Langley said. "What are you going to do?"

"Oh, I'm going to do some errands." She looked at Cordelia. "If you can believe it, sister, I haven't been in the city in near a month. But summer in New York is for fools and unfortunates, that's what I al-ways say—"

"What kind of errands?" Langley asked Belinda.

Belinda looked down the table at him, frowning slightly. "What do you mean, what kind of errands?"

"I mean, what kind of errands?" Langley said. "What is it that you have to get that can't wait until Monday?"

Belinda looked at him. "Is there something you would like me to do, Langley?" She blinked. *"Dear?"*

"Are you going to the pharmacy?" Langley said.

"I might," she said.

"Which one?" he asked her.

"Why, what is it that you want?" she said.

Langley leaned forward. "It's not what I want—it's what you want, Belinda. What is it that you have to get that's so important?"

Belinda looked at Cordelia. "You've been here since I got home. Have I done anything to deserve to be spoken to like this?"

"I'm sure I wouldn't know," Cordelia said quickly, sipping her cof-fee.

"I just want to know why it's so important you do errands today," Langley said. "Why everybody else are doing things together and you want to go off by yourself and do errands at the pharmacy."

"I'm sure you wouldn't be interested," Belinda said, sounding very annoyed now.

"I'm interested," he told her.

Belinda hesitated and then said, "And what is it you wish me to do instead, Langley?"

"You could come to West End with your father and me," he said.

"Go to the office with you and Daddy," Belinda said. "Thank you very much," she said, patting her mouth with her napkin, pushing back her chair and standing up, "but I have no desire to sit by myself in a chair in your office listening to the two of you talk about God knows what that I couldn't understand and would bore me to death if I did."

"I don't want you spending the day alone," Langley said.

"Pardon me? Come again, mister?" Belinda said, squinting down the table at him, swinging her weight to one side and plunking her hand down on her hip. "And just how many years has it been since you've given a god damn about what I do? How many years has it been since you've cared about how much time I spend alone? *Huh?*"

"I've always cared and you know it, Belinda," Langley said. "But you made it your business not to be around to feel it."

Jackson and Cordelia were looking down the table during this exchange; Big El was looking back and forth between Belinda and Langley, following it like a tennis match.

"Well, I apologize," Belinda said, "but y'all will have to excuse me because I have no intention of staying here and arguing with this man." She moved away, whirling around in the archway to the hall to add, "My husband left for work one morning and I haven't seen head or tail of him since—not for years! So tell that stranger down at the end of the table to mind his own business and leave me alone!"

"Belinda," Langley said, jumping up.

She was gone.

"Excuse me," Langley said, throwing his napkin down on the table and going after her.

"Oh, lordie," Cordelia sighed when they heard them arguing down the hall. "Somehow I knew this was not going to be a good idea. If something happens to her this weekend I'll never forgive myself."

"I've never seen 'em fight before," Big El said. "What's going on?"

"I don't know," Jackson said.

"You have no right to interfere in my life—none!" they heard Belinda shriek. "You just stay out of it!" A door slammed.

"If I find out it's been him driving poor Baby B nuts all these years, I'll kill the son of a bitch," Big El said, as they heard the Petersons yelling at each other somewhere in the back of the apartment.

"Daddy," Jackson said, "that's Langley we're talking about."

"Yeah, well, he better straighten up and fly right or his big chance may just pass him by," Big El said, looking at Cordelia.

Jackson looked at Cordelia. "Chance for what?"

"Oh, Daddy's just talking," Cordelia said, reaching for her coffee.

Jackson was surprised at how low key, uneventful and pleasant the evening at West End was turning out to be—considering that Langley and Belinda were not talking to each other (as nor were many other combinations of his relatives). And Langley refused to discuss the matter with Jackson, saying that it was a private matter between him and Belinda. And so Jackson left it alone, particularly since Belinda seemed fine this evening—in fact, in very good spirits.

They were *all* in amazingly good spirits, actually, thanks in large part to the whiz-bang tour of DBS Cassy had planned. The big hit—which had turned the evening into an instant success—was her idea to have the members of the board "sit in" for the regular DBS News on-air talent in a mini mock newscast. Cordelia "sat in" for Alexandra as the anchor; Noreen covered arts and entertainment; Norbert, politics; Little El, business; Belinda, health and education; Beau, sports; Jackson, the weather; and Big El did a special family reunion commentary. They shot it on tape as each read his or her part off the TelePrompTer (with some coaching by the regular on-air staff, and Jessica pinch-hitting for Alexandra as a coach for Cordelia); and then shot everyone else at the reunion on tape too in the context of a made-up story, all of which was then edited into a "newscast," a copy of which each guest would take home as a souvenir.

And Jackson didn't know what had gotten into Jessica, but she was absolutely wonderful with his family. Even Cordelia, who thought Jessica's show was "half disgrace and half an outrage—but interesting, I must admit," said she thought Jessica was enchanting. And she was.

And if Jackson had ever doubted that Jessica had had a drinking problem, then he never would again after tonight, because the change in her, physically and emotionally, had never been so evident. She had very little makeup on and was in a very conservative outfit, but she had never been so pretty and eye-catching. She was *radiant*—there was no other way to describe it. Her skin was aglow, her eyes bright, her whole face looked thinner, different, younger. And while she had been very nervous in the beginning, when his family first arrived—drinking fruit juice like it was going out of style—she soon settled in as hostess (fairy princess hostess?), her laughter ringing free and easy through the complex. That hard, cynical edge was nowhere to be found, though she was as sarcastic and funny as ever.

("Oh, I lost my accent years ago," Belinda had said, stepping into the elevator with Jessica to ride down with Jackson, Cordelia, Big El and Little El to the studio.

("Say e-c-o-n-o-m-i-c-s," Jessica had said.

(*"Eeek*anomics," Belinda said.

("And the capital of Vietnam, H-a-n-o-i?" Jessica said.

(*"Han*oy," Belinda said, starting to smile.

("And the city in Connecticut, N-e-w H-a-v-e-n?"

(*"New* Haven," Belinda said, as everyone in the elevator started to laugh.

("And I don't suppose Reno is in the state of Ne-vah-dah, is it?" Jessica said.

("Ne*vaaa*da," Belinda said, laughing with everyone else.

("Oh, you're right," Jessica said, slinging her arm through Belinda's and escorting her off the elevator, "you've lost your accent completely. No one would know you're from the South. Not in a million years.")

"I can't get over Jessica," Jackson said, watching her down in the square. He was standing with Cassy and Langley on the roof of Darenbrook III, just under one of the satellite dishes, where they had come up for a breather.

"It is wonderful to watch, isn't it?" Cassy said. "It's like seeing a whole new person come alive."

The three of them stood there a minute, watching. The walkways below were lined with torches, the river breezes making them cast an exotic, flickering light over the square. Tables for dining were set up along Darenbrook I and III, and the grills and tables of food and drink were set up along the line of fir trees at the end. Jackson's family, the on-air staff of DBS News and most of the DBS production staff were fanned out everywhere over the square, and some were milling around inside Darenbrook III, in empty offices on the first floor given over to the occasion. But all three sets of eyes on the roof were on the table where Jessica was eating dinner with Cordelia, Big El and Belinda.

"Alexandra asked me to keep an eye on her," Langley said. "She thought Jessica might feel more at ease if she knew I was around and willing to run interference for her in case any of our relatives picked on her." He laughed. "I'll have to tell her that Jessica ran interference for us."

"When did you talk to Alexandra?" Cassy asked him.

"Today," Langley said. "She called this afternoon."

Cassy frowned. "How come everybody seems to be talking to Alexandra these days but me?"

"Doesn't like you anymore, I guess," Jackson said, smiling.

"She was in some phone booth in Kansas," Langley said. "She said she was hiding from her mother, who couldn't decide what kind of wedding cake to have and was making her taste all of them."

They laughed.

"Oh, good," Cassy said, smiling back down on the square, "I'm glad she's getting things squared away for her wedding. Take her mind off other things this weekend."

Jackson shook his head, smiling. "Our little Alexandra. Getting married."

Langley looked at him. "Our little Alexandra?" He pushed off the wall, heading for the stairway door. "Boy, have things changed around here," he said over his shoulder. "Must be something in the water."

Cassy laughed, bowing her head.

"Must be," Jackson said.

————

After spending all day with his family, something very peculiar happened to Jackson at eleven o'clock that night.

He was standing by one of the grills, listening to Poor Luanne and Kirky reminisce about visiting Richmond—about how their aunt Barbara would lock up the TV and make them run around the house ten times before she would feed them—when he looked across the square and saw Cordelia talking to Cassy. The two women were standing face to face, in the torchlight, talking away, and Cassy said something that made Cordelia laugh. And then Cassy touched Cordelia's arm, saying something further, which made Cordelia laugh harder, and when Jackson saw this he felt something fall down inside of him, something that made him feel very scared suddenly, anxious. Afraid.

Poor Luanne touched Jackson's arm, asking him if he was all right, while Kirky took the glass out of his hand and looked back over his shoulder to see what his uncle was looking at. Turning around, he said, "Jesus, Uncle Jack, you're not having a heart attack or something, are you?"

"No," Jackson managed to say, trying to focus on Kirky but finding it very hard. "I'm fine," he said, looking back at Cassy. "You kids have fun." And then he started across the square.

He was having a hard time negotiating the walkway because he felt so strange. It was as if his ballast was suddenly gone and he was starting to float off somewhere. As if he was floating—no, no, now it was more like something was pulling him *down,* down somewhere inside of himself, some sickly, dark, horrible place he remembered, or he thought he remembered, or remembered well enough to feel terrified of going there.

Cordelia and Cassy were looking at him now and he went right up to them and asked Cordie to excuse them, grabbed Cassy's arm and rudely pulled her off through the people toward Darenbrook I. They barely got inside the door—barely got the door closed behind them—before Jackson threw his arms around Cassy and dropped his head down on her shoulder—and started to sob.

Jackson sobbed and sobbed, his great shoulders heaving, standing there in the lobby, clinging to Cassy, and he couldn't stop sobbing and for the life of him he didn't know why.

All he knew was that he could not live without her.

45

Alexandra's Dinner with Lisa Connors
Part I

"I'm just so grateful to you for flying in tonight," Alexandra said, touching the bridge of her nose. She brought her hand back down to the table. "I needed to talk to somebody and"—she shrugged—"I'm just glad to see you. Really. Thank you. I, um, have a lot on my mind. I needed to see a friend. Needed to talk to somebody."

Alexandra lowered her eyes to the table then and left them there for a long while. Then she cleared her throat and reached for her water glass, raising her eyes across the table again. "The stress has been something," she admitted, pausing to sip her water, "but we're in great shape now." She lowered her glass to the table. "This board meeting that's going on tonight is—um, well—never mind." She paused, dropping her eyes again. "Anyway, I thought I would have heard from Cassy by now about what happened. But I did leave the number here for her so she could call." She raised her eyes again, tentatively smiling at her friend across the table. "I'm sorry," she said, "you didn't come all this way to hear about board meetings."

No response.

Alexandra cleared her throat again. Her face was a little red. "Lisa?" she said, raising her eyebrows. "Are you there?"

Lisa was smiling, resting her chin in her hand, gazing at her from across the table. "Oh, I'm here, Alexandra," she said in a low voice, "am I ever here."

"Good," Alexandra said, swallowing and looking around. "We wouldn't want you to be bored."

"Bored? Looking at you?" Lisa said.

Alexandra made a little sound in her throat, eyes widening slightly.

Lisa's smile expanded. "What's the matter, Alexandra? You used to like it when I watched you."

"Uh-oh," Alexandra said, looking at her water glass. She picked it up. "She lied to us," she told it. "She's not going to behave at all. Not at all."

Lisa fell back in her chair laughing—a low, throaty, pleasant laugh carrying about a thousand innuendos.

Lisa Connors was thirty-seven, a blond, deeply tanned woman with very white teeth. She was wearing a white sleeveless dress as well. She was not the kind of woman who needed an Alexandra Waring around to draw attention. They were sitting in the back room of the Bristol Bar and Grill, with its Victorian architecture, modern art and leaded glass Tiffany dome overhead. And while Alexandra was tucked away discreetly around to the right of the stairs, Lisa, on the other side of the table, was in plain view and—judging by the reaction of the other diners—wasn't considered a plain view at all. But Lisa Connors seemed quite accustomed to this kind of attention; in fact, she seemed unaware of it. Her attention was focused entirely on Alexandra.

"It's just that you should have warned me," Lisa said, picking up her wineglass and bringing it up to near her mouth, adding, "I'd forgotten what you're like. In person." Eyes on Alexandra, she took a sip of wine, swallowed and then put the glass down. She sighed, smiling. "Poor Matt. It could take me weeks to get over this. I'll be impossible." Then she turned to look at the man and woman sitting at a nearby table and then turned back to Alexandra, shaking her head. "But honestly, Alexandra—bodyguards?"

"I told you," Alexandra said, "I have to have them on the tour and tonight I'm back on tour."

"But you must be awfully scared of me," Lisa said, smiling, picking up her wineglass again and sitting back in her chair. "He must be fifteen feet tall, that guy."

"I'm not scared of you in the least," Alexandra told her.

Lisa was rubbing the rim of the wineglass against her lower lip. After watching Alexandra watch her do it for a while, she stopped, lowered the glass and smiled. "That's how I knew, you know." She leaned forward, holding her wineglass in her hands on the table in front of her. "When you told me that night—when we first knew each other—that you were a little afraid of me and didn't know why." Eyes still on Alexandra, she took a sip of wine and swallowed. "That's when I knew it was going to happen. Between us. I knew it as soon as you said that."

Alexandra lowered her eyes to the table, her face flushing scarlet.

"Why don't you want to tell me?" Lisa said.

"Because it's none of your business what Gordon and I do in bed," Alexandra told her, sounding exasperated, finally getting a piece of fish into her mouth.

"But if you don't like sex with him—"

Alexandra struggled to swallow before speaking. "That's not what I said—that's not it, Lisa." She dropped her fork. "Just forget it—I just can't talk about this." She sighed, shaking her head. Then she looked at Lisa. "I don't mean to bite your head off. It's just that our sex life is fine—*would* be fine if my head were fine. Which it isn't. The problem is not him. He's a very wonderful person. And he's a very sexy man." She paused, picking up her fork and dangling it for a moment. "And sometime," she said, looking at her plate, "in the course of this dinner, I'm going to work myself up to what I wanted to talk about—what I need to talk about."

"Why don't you just tell me?" Lisa said.

"Because I can't," Alexandra said. "I need time to work up to it."

"Take all the time you need," Lisa said, resuming eating her salad.

After a couple of minutes, eating her fish, Alexandra looked across the table. "Oh, Lisa," she said, "please, do anything but be quiet. Now I've gotten you depressed."

"Who, me?" she said, swallowing. "I'm not depressed. I'm behaving."

"Well then, don't behave," Alexandra said. "I can't stand this. Do something—say something."

"Anything?" Lisa said, eyes taking on a very different light.

Alexandra looked at her for a moment, shaking her head, smiling. "Oh, Lisa," she said, sighing a little, picking up her fork.

Lisa leaned forward. "Admit it, Waring," she whispered, "you love being flirted with, you always did."

Alexandra leaned over her plate to whisper back, "I told you— you're supposed to try and help me with a problem, not try and start a new one by making eyes at me."

"Oh, right," Lisa said, slapping the table with her hand. "Listen to her." She leaned over the table and whispered, "You, the woman who *invented* orgasm by eye contact. Why do you think people watch you on TV anyway?"

"Lisa!" Alexandra said, dropping her fork.

"And what does Jessica call you? Alexandra Eyes?" Lisa turned to the wall. "Oh, but she's already told us all about *that,* hasn't she?"

"She's just staying in my apartment until she gets her head together," Alexandra said. "I told you. While I'm on tour."

"And since when does anyone stay with you who isn't sleeping with you?" Lisa asked her.

"Since Jessica and I became friends," Alexandra said.

"Could this be true?" Lisa asked the wall.

"It's true," Alexandra said. A moment later, "Look, I was surprised too. I don't make friends easily."

"A word of advice," Lisa said, pointing a finger at her. "Don't ever tell your ten million friends that you don't make friends easily, or else they might catch on that they don't even know you."

They looked at each other for a moment, smiling.

"I was attracted to Jessica," Lisa said then.

"I thought so," Alexandra said. "The way she described meeting you —I thought your inspired interest in her seemed vaguely familiar."

Lisa laughed. "But let me tell you, Alexandra, either that girl was deaf, dumb and blind, or she was the best actress I ever saw—because she did *not* get it."

"I thought you said you hadn't—"

"Oh, I haven't," Lisa said quickly. "But that doesn't mean I haven't thought about it." She shrugged. "And I don't know, since she was married too, I thought . . ." She rolled her eyes, gesturing with her hand. "I don't know what I thought. But I was pretty upset around then." She looked at Alexandra. "It was after I found out about Matt's little friend."

Alexandra nodded and then said, "Do you love him?"

Lisa sighed, thinking a moment. "I'd love him more if I could get pregnant," she said.

"If you hadn't slept with me," Lisa said over coffee, "then you never would have known about that side of yourself. Is that what you're trying to tell me?"

"I would have known," Alexandra said, "but I never would have acted on it. And had I never acted on it—"

"You would have married that jerk," Lisa said, shuddering.

"He was not a jerk," Alexandra said. She smiled. "Why does everybody always say such awful things about poor Tyler?"

"Because he *was* awful!" Lisa cried. "You were the only one who liked him, Alexandra."

"That's not true," Alexandra said, laughing.

"It *is* true," Lisa insisted. She paused and then leaned forward. "And if he wasn't so wrong for you, then why were you so terribly lonely when I met you?"

Alexandra lowered her eyes, stirring her coffee.

"And you were so terribly lonely when I met you," Lisa said softly. "I saw it right away, in your eyes, the night I met you." She paused, smiling. "Do you remember?"

Alexandra nodded, putting her spoon down on her saucer.

"And remember how much we liked each other—right away?" Lisa said, eyes growing brighter. "Oh, Alexandra," she murmured, shaking her head, "do you remember how exciting it was? And it was! Remember how I kept calling you, running around after you? At the station? At all those parties? God, was that fun!"

Alexandra was smiling now, touching the bridge of her nose with her hand, shaking her head. She dropped her hand, looking at Lisa. "And Tyler couldn't figure out what was going on." She laughed. "And neither could I—for a while. Every time we went out, you just appeared out of nowhere. And then at the governor's ball—" She snapped her fingers, laughing. "That red dress—I thought, *What is this, a Bette Davis movie? What is this woman doing?*"

They both laughed.

"I wanted you to notice me," Lisa said.

"And then you showed up at the ceremony when Tyler got that thing from the Chamber of Commerce," Alexandra said, laughing. "Oh, brother," she said, covering her face, laughing, "when I think of it now."

"I know," Lisa said.

Alexandra dropped her hands suddenly. "And I can remember Tyler saying to me, 'Doesn't she live in Denver? What's she doing here? Doesn't she ever go home?' And I kept saying, 'I don't know! I don't know!'"

They both cracked up.

And then Lisa sat forward, looking across the table into Alexandra's eyes. "But you did know. By then, you knew."

Alexandra was still smiling, but her forehead had furrowed slightly. "Yes," she finally said, "I did. But I never thought I'd ever actually . . ." She sighed, her eyes drifting down to Lisa's mouth for a moment. Then she looked away.

"Do you remember what you said that night?" Lisa asked her.

Alexandra looked at her. She nodded. Then she smiled again. "I said I was so tired of being good I couldn't stand it."

"And I said," Lisa said, "'So don't be!' And you drank your glass of champagne straight down, I remember. And then you had another, and another—"

"And another," Alexandra joined her in saying.

"And then you asked me to please take you somewhere," Lisa said. Her eyes widened in delight. "'Anywhere!' you said."

"Oh, no," Alexandra said, wincing, covering her face with her hand, laughing. "And we even stole Tyler's car, didn't we?"

"Oh, but was it great," Lisa said, watching her. She waited for Alexandra to lower her hand before continuing. "For once you didn't care about that damn job of yours, about Tyler, your family—anything. You just wanted . . ." She let her voice trail off.

Alexandra was nodding, looking down at the table now. In a moment she said, "And I'll never forget sitting on that couch with you. Just sitting there, not doing anything, not even talking."

"Hmmm," Lisa said, nodding. After a moment, "And do you remember what I said?"

Alexandra nodded.

Lisa smiled and whispered, " 'I'm scared to do what I want to do.' "

Alexandra looked up. Her eyes looked a little sad.

"And you said," Lisa said quietly, dropping her voice to a whisper again, " 'You can do whatever you want.' " She paused, running her tongue over her lower lip once. "The six sexiest words I've ever heard in my life."

Alexandra swallowed. "And you did, too," she managed to say. "Do what you wanted. As I recall."

"And you were wonderful, Alexandra," Lisa murmured. "You were the most wonderful lover I ever had."

"Yes, well," Alexandra said, dropping her eyes and abruptly picking up her coffee cup, "those days are over." She took a sip and glanced over at Lisa. "Of being a good lover, I mean." She put the cup down. "I seem to be losing the capacity."

Lisa hesitated and then said, "But you know why."

Alexandra didn't say anything.

"You do, Alexandra," Lisa said. "Because the same thing happened with me. As soon as you knew it wasn't going to work for you and you knew—" She stopped herself and looked down at the table. "I don't think I want to reminisce about that part." After a minute she looked up. "Anyway, my friend, remember who you're talking to. This is someone who knows you. So maybe you should just tell me the truth about what's going on."

Alexandra looked at her for a long moment. And then she looked down, playing with her spoon. She started to speak and then stopped. Twice.

"It's okay," Lisa said.

Alexandra closed her eyes then, fighting tears. She covered her face with her hand.

"There's somebody else, isn't there?" Lisa said softly.

Alexandra nodded.

Lisa watched her for a moment. "And you've fallen in love."

Again Alexandra nodded. Her hand was shaking.

"It's okay," Lisa said, reaching across the table to touch the top of her head.

Alexandra lowered her hand to the table, eyes full of tears. "But it's not okay, Lisa," she said. "Because it's a woman." She shut her eyes and dropped her face into her hand again. "And I'm so in love with her I don't know what to do."

46

Alexandra's Dinner with Lisa Connors
Part II

"Look, Alexandra," Lisa was saying, waving the waiter away again, "whoever this woman is, you have to be honest with her. You have to lay your cards on the table and say, 'Hey, I may be crazy, but this is how I feel, I've only got one life to life, and I have to try and see if somehow this can work.' And then, whatever happens, at least you'll know, one way or the other, and then you can get on with your life."

Alexandra sighed. "But I know she thinks—"

"You're not psychic, Alexandra," Lisa said. "I know you think you are, but you're not—and you're going to have to sit down with this woman and find out exactly how she feels."

"But if—"

"And if it doesn't work out," Lisa said, interrupting her, "then you go ahead and get married with a clear conscience."

"With a clear conscience?" Alexandra said, verging on tears.

"She'll be the one that got away, that's all," Lisa said. "Listen, Alexandra, how many women do you think marry their first choice anyway? Man or woman, what difference does it make? You fall in love with whoever you fall in love with."

"But Lisa—"

"But Lisa nothing," she said. "You can't just let her slip away without saying a word, Alexandra. You didn't know she was going to get divorced—you didn't know that she was going to become available. And now you've got the chance to find out if it could work."

"Oh, but I don't know, I just don't know," Alexandra said, shaking her head. "This is so crazy. Because, Lisa, you don't know all of it—the circumstances—and you really don't understand the kind of responsibility I have, the kind of commitment I've made, and to how many people I've made that commitment—"

"Excuse me," the manager said.

"Oh, just double the bill and leave us alone!" Lisa said.

The manager looked at her, blinked a couple of times and then turned to Alexandra. "Excuse me, Ms. Waring, but the call from New York you were expecting just came in."

Alexandra jumped up from the table and followed the manager back to his office, where he showed her the telephone and left, closing the door behind him.

"Hello?" she said.

"Alexandra?"

"Hi, Cassy," she said. "Boy, is it great to hear the sound of your voice. How did it go?"

"Sweetheart, listen," Cassy said, "I've got some rather shocking news—but don't worry, everything's fine in terms of DBS News. The board's behind us a hundred percent, and behind you a thousand percent."

"What about Jessica?" Alexandra said quickly.

"Oh, she's fine too," Cassy said. "They're fully behind her."

"Great," Alexandra said, "but what's the other?"

"Okay, here it is, officially," Cassy said. "Jackson's been voted out as chairman of Darenbrook Communications and Langley's been voted in, effective immediately. I'm president of DBS, and it is unclear whether Jackson will have any executive role at Darenbrook Communications in the future."

"My God," Alexandra murmured, "what happened?"

"A family quarrel, to say the least," Cassy said. "I've got to go in to see Langley now, but I wanted to tell you something else before Jackson gets ahold of you."

"What?" Alexandra said.

"And please understand the position I'm in," Cassy said, sounding tired and upset, "and why it's impossible for me to advise you about what comes next—about what you should or should not do."

"What comes—"

"Just listen to me for a second," Cassy said. "Because it's very important to me that you understand what my immediate responsibilities are and in whose interests I have to act, regardless of where my personal loyalties lie. Do you understand?"

"Of course," Alexandra said. "You have to protect DBS. Cassy, I've got a good idea of what you're worried about and—"

"Just listen to me, please, Alexandra. It's been a long day and night here and I'm—"

"I'm sorry, go ahead," Alexandra said.

"Okay." Cassy sighed. "As soon as the board fired Jackson, that automatically activated some clauses in your contract."

"Yes, I know," Alexandra said.

"And Jackson's so furious with his family right now," Cassy continued, "that he's bound and determined to see that you exercise one of them."

"To buy out my contract," Alexandra guessed.

"To buy out all of DBS News," Cassy said.

47

Jackson Decides to Kick Up a Fuss

It seemed funny now that he had never considered the possibility that his father and brothers and sister might someday vote him out as chairman of Darenbrook Communications. It frankly never entered his head that there was anyone to replace him—Langley, yes, of course, but Langley was *not* a Darenbrook; he was only married to one—and the board's unwritten rule had always been that, so long as Jackson made them money and kept a prestigious empire going, they would forgive him for anything.

But not this time.

Beau made out okay at the meeting. The family listened thoughtfully to what he had to say (that is, Daddy, Cordelia and Belinda did) about the help he was getting for his gambling problem, and the family listened thoughtfully (that is, Little El and the twins did) to the comptroller's report about the ongoing fortune Beau had made for them with *Field Day,* and the issue of pressing charges against Beau for illegally using the magazine group as loan collateral was dropped. And after a lengthy discussion (during which Beau promised Cordelia that he would have a serious talk with her son, Zekey, who everyone knew had a gambling problem too—ever since he moved to Atlantic City), it was decided that the board would formally forgive Beau, hence all mention of the matter would be stricken from the company record, but that if he were ever to start gambling again he would be dismissed from the magazine group immediately.

It was at this point in the meeting that Cordelia started staring at Jackson. She was waiting, he knew, for his end of the explanation of how he could have personally intervened between Beau's debts and a lien on the magazines to the tune of sixty million dollars, and then launch a new news network for another eighty million without using company assets as collateral on loans. But she had to wait through the whole presentation on DBS, all the wonderful news and numbers on "The Jessica Wright Show" and "DBS News America Tonight with Alexandra Waring," before she got her answer.

The answer being, Jackson had pretty much sold the miniseries to Lord Gregory Hargrave and rerouted the money into DBS News, along with a few other stray funds from around the corporation.

Cordelia did not say anything during the presentation. She sat there, watching him, for the almost two hours it took to present the whole five-year plan for the network, at the conclusion of which the twins, Little El, Belinda and Beau actually started clapping. (And why not? They were looking at a virtual gold mine down the road.)

And then Cordelia stood up and cried, "You lied to me!" And then she banged both of her fists down on the table, saying it over and over again, "You lied, you lied, you lied!"

"Cordie, I didn't lie—you asked me if we used the magazines as collateral—" Jackson started to say, a little unnerved by Cordelia's outburst.

"You swore to me you didn't use our company to pay for Beau's gambling debts—you swore to me!"

"I didn't!" Jackson said. "I just rearranged the financing in the net-work to launch DBS News and it's a good thing I did. It's going to make tons more money for us—we shouldn't be in the dramatic programming business. We need to stick to news and information, keep in line with the rest of our companies."

"But that isn't a decision to make by yourself!" Big El said, banging the table with his hand. "This company is not your personal possession, boy. You're sittin' in that seat—"

"Because nobody else in this family does anything except Beau!" Jackson said. "And you just forgave him. Why don't you forgive me? I was wrong, I admit it—but I'm going to make you a ton of money and win you a lot of acclaim to make it up to you."

"He's got a point," Norbert said.

"But arrogance is not an illness!" Cordelia said, pounding the table again. She was starting to cry. "We can give Beau another chance because he's trying to get some help. Well, you've got to do the same, Jackie—only there's no therapy group for arrogance, for high-handedness—for contempt for one's own family!"

"Cut it out, Cordie," Jackson said. "I've never been—"

"But you *are* contemptuous," Cordelia said, taking the handkerchief from Big El that he held out to her. "You've always been contemptuous of us. And this company is not yours, Jackie—it's *ours*. The whole family's. And we all know you're better suited for business than we are —and every single one of us has been grateful for all you've done. But, God almighty, Jackie!" she said, hitting the table again. "The company's assets are not yours to buy and sell as you please. Johnny Jim never would have done something like this. Daddy never would do something like this. And your mama, Alice May, would be the first to throw you out on your ear for such—"

"I think you're being unfair," Beau said.

"We've heard enough out of you, boy," Big El shot across the table, pointing at Beau. "Your ass is still on the line around here."

"Well, mine isn't," Belinda said, "and I think poor Jackie—"

"Oh, great," Norbert said loudly, interrupting her. "First we hear from the fruit, now we have to listen to the fruitcake."

Both Jackson and Langley were out of their chairs in a second. Jackson reached him first, because Beau caught Langley's arm on the way and held him.

"You stupid fucking son of a bitch," Jackson said, pulling Norbert backward in his chair by his tie, "take that back before I stuff your head up your goddam ass."

"Jackie!" Cordelia said, jumping out of her seat.

"Bully!" Noreen said, hitting Jackson on the back with her fist.

"Take it back, Norbert," Jackson said, pulling him farther back by his tie. Norbert's face was turning purple.

"I didn't mean it," Norbert said.

Jackson released him immediately. "I didn't think so," he said quietly, walking back around to his end of the table. "Come on, Lang," he said, patting him on the arm on his way.

Belinda had started to cry, and Langley changed places with Beau so he could put his arm around his wife.

Although Jackson realized that Cordelia and Big El must have planned this, in the event Jackson had been lying about how he had handled Beau's debts and his own, with Belinda crying in Langley's arms, Cordelia crying by herself at the end of the table, Norbert enraged at being nearly strangled, Noreen hating Jackson for attacking Norbert, Big El livid that an outsider ("A ferriner!") owned a controlling interest in a Darenbrook Communications project, when Little El made the motion that Jackson step down as chairman and Langley be named in his place, it felt like spontaneous mutiny.

No one had been more surprised by this motion than Langley and Belinda—the former's mouth dropped open, and the latter was shocked right out of her tears. "My Langley?" she said, looking at him.

"You can't elect a chairman from outside the Darenbrook family unless you amend the bylaws," Jackson told them.

And so Cordelia and Daddy and Norbert and Noreen and Little El carried through a vote to amend the bylaws so they could put Little El's motion back on the floor.

"Seconded," Norbert said in response to Little El's motion.

"Okay," Jackson said, "all those in favor of Jackson Darenbrook stepping down as chairman of the board and electing Langley Peterson as the new chairman of the board say aye."

"Aye," Cordelia, Daddy, Norbert, Noreen and Little El said.

"All those opposed—" Jackson said.

"Nay," Belinda, Beau and Jackson said.

"Did you get that?" Jackson asked Ethel, who was sitting in the corner, weeping, taking notes.

She nodded, holding the handkerchief Jackson had given her over her mouth and nose as she tallied the vote. "Fifty-nine percent of the voting stock, aye, forty-one percent, nay," she managed to say through the handkerchief and her sobs and sniffles.

"The motion is carried then," Jackson said. He turned to Langley. "Mr. Peterson, will you accept the job of chairman of the board of Darenbrook Communications?"

Langley just looked at him.

Jackson nodded.

Langley swallowed. "Yes, yes, I will," he said.

"Terrific, he has accepted," Jackson said to Ethel. Then he stood up, smiled at Cordelia and said, "Fuck you, Cordelia," his smile vanishing, pointing at Big El, Norbert, Noreen and Little El in succession, "and you, and you, and you, and you—fuck all of you," and he walked out.

Belinda jumped up from her chair. "If you think you are coming to *mah* house," she yelled down the table at Cordelia and her father, "then you are sadly mistaken. You can sleep in the streets for all I care!"

"Belinda, don't be such an idiot," Norbert said. "Your husband's chairman now."

"I know!" she wailed, running out of the room.

Jackson had the essentials of the deals done within three hours.

As soon as he walked out of that boardroom he had known exactly what he wanted to do. If his family was so upset about how he had launched DBS News, then he thought the least he could do was demonstrate to them how easily he could take it away from them. They didn't *have* to make money or receive honors from his ideas and work. He'd buy DBS News with Belinda and Old Hardhead through Alexandra's contract and take the foreign syndication of "The Jessica Wright Show" with it. He'd unhinge the whole goddam network and threaten to move it out of West End, abandoning the facilities, if they did not sell him "The Jessica Wright Show." He'd also undo the Darenbrook Communications deal to buy the San Diego *Star* and put the financing together himself. He'd intervene on the proposed site for a new printing plant in Mississippi and steal that deal too. He'd build his own goddam company and let his family be damned!

Vote him out, would they?

Fine. Let them stagnate with one idea between them for the next million years.

Good old Alexandra! Jackson just smiled and smiled reading her contract in his office. ("Out, out," he had said to Cassy, hustling her next door to Langley's office, "you work for the enemy—shoo!") To protect herself against a less supportive management, Alexandra had insisted on a contract rider that said, in the event that Jackson ever left Darenbrook Communications (which at the time had been extremely unlikely, unless he died—in which case Jackson asked Langley what the hell would he care), Alexandra had the option to buy her contract back and leave DBS or, within thirty days, exercise an option to *buy* DBS News at a price arrived at by a specific formula. The only hitch was ("Damn," Jackson said, reading the next part of the contract rider, "Langley must have added this,") that if Alexandra did buy DBS News, then DBS News had to continue to lease Darenbrook Communications facilities for one hundred years or until such time as Darenbrook Communications wished to cancel said lease.

No matter. So they kept DBS News here and rubbed their noses in it on a daily basis.

Hardhead said he wished to meet with Alexandra first, to hear straight from the source what kind of DBS News she envisioned, but this was a mere formality. Afterwards Jackson could publicize the fact that he would be going partners with him. Belinda also said she had thirty million Jackson could have (but he'd only take ten and let her underwrite twenty in loans).

He made two more calls and lined up partners for his newspaper and printing plant. He knocked on Langley's door and poked his head in to announce this news—Cassy was in there with him—said he hoped they were having as much fun as he was, and closed the door.

By the time he got ahold of Alexandra in Kansas City, in his own head he had already bought DBS News. Alexandra, while clearly intrigued with the proposal, was not as raring to go as he had thought she would be. When he explained to her that things would go on as before, except now DBS News employees would own a piece of the company for which they worked, including a combined voting share block of forty-nine percent, she started to come around. And then when he said that he and Lord Hargrave and Belinda would hold combined voting shares of forty-nine percent, and that Alexandra, in addition to all of her personal interests as an employee of the company, would retain a two percent voting block as the "owner" of DBS News—therefore maintaining the capacity to swing the vote in case of a disagreement between employees and backers—she agreed to fly to London on Tuesday to meet with Lord Hargrave.

By the time Jackson went home to the Plaza a little after one in the morning he was whistling.

He was sitting on the couch in the living room, in his robe, playing with numbers, when Cassy dragged in at two. She stood there, just inside the door, looking exhausted. Her pale blue suit was crumpled; her hair was slipping down everywhere; there were circles under her eyes; and she was frowning. She dropped her briefcase on the floor.

"Hi," he said. "I wasn't sure you'd come."

She sighed, taking a couple of steps in. "What are you doing to poor Alexandra?" she asked him. "You can't be serious about this."

"What do you mean, poor Alexandra?" he said. "Poor Alexandra's going to own her own network."

Cassy couldn't find whatever words she was looking for. She threw her hand out finally, saying, "Jack—we haven't even finished figuring out what the network is. Alexandra's still trying to figure out the job she has. You can't just step in and rip the operation apart."

"I'm not ripping the operation apart," he said. "It's no different from a newspaper. I'm just backing the editor-in-chief to buy it, that's all."

"But that's not what you're doing," she said. "What you're doing is dragging Alexandra into the middle of a fight with your family. You're taking advantage of her sense of obligation to you, Jackson, and I don't think that's fair."

"I'm not taking advantage of her," he said. "I'm going to make her and her people some money, instead of making it for those jerks in my family. She knows that—look, Cassy," he said, tossing the legal pad he had been writing on down on the coffee table, "she wouldn't have had the clause in her contract in the first place if she wasn't interested in the idea."

"She's going to London out of personal loyalty to you and you know it," Cassy told him. "You can't do this, Jackson, and not do damage. You can't try and fix something that's not broken." She stamped her foot. "For God's sake, you guys made me design the division to be inseparable from the network!"

"Come on," Jackson said quietly, holding his arms out to her, "come here. Sit down here and we'll talk about it."

"No, Jack," she said, turning to walk over to a chair, "I can't do it like that." She threw herself down in the chair.

"Then don't come here," he told her, smiling, "and don't hear what I have to say." (He loved to see her energy; he loved seeing her energy come surging back through her, even if it was with anger.)

She rolled her eyes. "What do you have to say?"

"That maybe I know everything you're saying and that maybe I just feel like kicking up a little fuss because I got canned tonight—by my own family."

She raised an eyebrow. "And?"

"And so maybe I think you should go to London this week too and, after we make her an offer, you make a counteroffer to Alexandra on behalf of DBS to keep DBS News. And while you're there, finalize an international tie-in agreement with Hargrave. Then you call back home and tell dumbo Darenbrook Communications that, if they want to keep Alexandra and DBS News, then they're going to have to in-crease their budget, expand the newscasts to seven days a week and have international affiliation immediately."

Cassy was starting to smile.

"And if I was a real stickler I'd tell you to tell dumbo DC that Alexandra won't keep DBS News with them unless I'm voted back in —but I'm not doing that," Jackson said, making a face at her. "Because I'm a grownup and can find my own means of employment."

"Really?" she said.

"Really," he said. He really did wish for Cassy to stay in love with him, and so he saw no reason to tell her that he had just made all this up on the spot. That, until she said it, he hadn't realized that what she said was true—that he had intended to take advantage of Alexandra's personal loyalty. She had no fight with Darenbrook Communications, and buying DBS News would only pit herself against the corporation she would be forced to deal with on a daily basis for the next hundred years. Well, so, now he had a different purpose in mind—

One he actually liked a whole lot better. He'd make a show of power to the board—that he *could* take DBS News if he wanted—and he'd let Alexandra win some concessions out of them for DBS News in the process. That was fair. Heck, that was fun! (It sure was a lot more fun poking holes in a corporation than it was trying to plug up the leaks.)

"You cause such a ruckus," Cassy said, smiling. "You're just one big fuss, aren't you?"

"Part of my charm," he said, getting up and walking over to her. Cassy slid her arms around his waist and rested the side of her face against his stomach. He cradled her head in his arms, leaning over to kiss it once, and then straightened up.

"I'd like to let Alexandra stay the week in London then," she said. "Open and close from the BINS studio. She'll have to do it at two in the morning over there—but at least she could see Gordon and they could have the weekend together."

"Sounds good to me," he said.

After a long moment she said, "I love you, Jack." She looked up at him. "And I'm very sorry about what happened to you today."

He smiled, touching her nose.

"Darling?" she said, standing up.

"What?" he said, taking hold of her hands and bringing them up to his mouth to kiss.

"When I see her in London," she said, "I want to tell Alexandra about us."

He looked at her. "Fine with me."

She smiled. "Okay. . . . Jack?" she said a moment later, touching his cheek.

His eyebrows went up.

"Someday I'm going to ask you to remember tonight. And I'm going to want you to remember that I wanted to tell you something then, but I couldn't without breaking a personal trust to someone else."

He looked confused.

"All I want you to know is that I love you and that I want you to know everything about me." She kissed him, gently. "It's late," she said, taking his hand and leading him to the bedroom.

While she took a bath, Jackson stretched out on his back across the king-size bed, hands behind his head, smiling at the ceiling, listening to the water sounds. When the sounds stopped he picked up the phone, pushed the button for the second extension and dialed the number of the first. The phone in the bathroom rang and rang.

"Jack?" Cassy called.

He got up from the bed, picked up his telephone and moved the cord from around the table so he could carry it with him across the room.

Cassy finally picked up the phone in the bathroom. "Hello?"

"Well, hi," he said. "Whatcha doing?"

"If you must know," she said, "I'm toweling myself dry."

"Can I help?" he said, moving through the dressing room.

"I'm almost done."

"Cassy?" he said, standing in the doorway of the bathroom.

She was holding the phone between her chin and shoulder and was wrapping a towel around herself. "Yes?" she said, just as she looked up and saw him standing there.

"Ignore that man in the doorway," Jackson whispered into his phone.

"Why?" she whispered into her phone.

"Because he's going to ask you to marry him again and the bum doesn't even have a job."

She smiled. "Tell the bum to take off his robe—I like his looks," she said, hanging up the phone. And then she went over to help him, conveniently losing her towel on the way.

48

Alexandra Goes to London

Immediately following her newscast from KSCT in Kansas City on Monday night, Alexandra and Will raced out of the studio and to the airport and just made a 9:45 P.M. (Central Time) flight to New York. Arriving at Kennedy at 1:36 A.M. (Eastern Daylight Time), they dashed through the terminals with Alexandra's dress bag and their carry-on bags to make a 2 A.M. flight to London. Five minutes after takeoff, Alexandra was sound asleep in her seat in first class, head against the window. She slept through all offers of food and drink; she slept through Will putting a pillow under her head; she slept through the stewardess throwing a blanket over her; she slept through the movie; and she even slept through the lady who kept coming up to loudly ask if Alexandra wasn't awake yet so she could get her autograph.

Will finally drifted off to sleep, and as they began their descent into Heathrow he awakened to find Alexandra sitting there, smiling at him, eating dried fruit and nuts out of a plastic bag. "Wait until I tell Sissy we spent the night together again," she said, winking and holding out the bag.

"Seat belts—I can't!" They heard a woman saying from somewhere behind them. "But if she gets off the plane I'll never catch her! I had to chase Ed Bradley halfway across Paris last year and still didn't get his autograph!"

The stewardess came up and got Alexandra's autograph for the woman.

They got in at 7:40 A.M., New York time—or 6:40 A.M., Kansas City time—which meant that it was 12:40 P.M. Tuesday afternoon in London. After getting through immigration, they found the driver Lord Hargrave had sent to meet them, who led them outside to a Silver Spur Rolls-Royce.

"Buy the company, buy the company," Will urged Alexandra, climbing in after her. "We like this."

"Oh, my," Alexandra sighed, looking at the inside of the car.

"Alexandra Waring," Will said, holding his hands up in front of him, reading it off an imaginary marquee, "Media Mogul. I *like* it."

She winced, hitting him in the arm.

The car took them into London, where Lord Hargrave had made arrangements for them to stay at the Ritz. As they turned off Piccadilly onto Duke Street, nearing the hotel, Alexandra suddenly said, "What has happened to all of us? What am I *doing* here?" She looked at Will. "I'm from Haven Wells, *Kansas,* for heaven sakes."

"Marcellus, New York," Will said, holding up his hand.

"And I'm a reporter—right?"

"You're a star, baby," Will said, elbowing her.

She groaned, sinking in her seat. "You know how sometimes it takes awhile for reality to sink in? Well," she sighed, looking out the window, "I think it just did." She looked at Will. "I'm supposed to be part of the fourth estate, not a plaything of the landed gentry."

"You can always give your money to me," he said, shrugging, as they turned onto Arlington Street. "Oh, wow," he said then, leaning forward, "look at this." Sitting at the head of the taxi line, in front of the west entrance into the Ritz, was a green and black brougham, drawn by two beautiful black horses.

"Miss Glitz from America has arrived," Alexandra said under her breath as the car stopped and her door was opened.

Will snapped his fingers. "That's it," he said. "That's the story we do while we're here—the treatment of British anchors as opposed to American."

"Yes," Alexandra said, jumping out of the car. "Yes! The American anchor and the English presenter, news anchor versus news reader, celebrity versus authority. Oh, Will, we've got to get to Sue Lawley, she's leaving the BBC—and Alastair Burnet at ITN, we have to get to him." She was walking backward up the stairs while talking to Will—confusing the doorman a bit as to what this young lady was doing—and stopped altogether when Will pulled a pad and pen out of his jacket pocket to write this down. "Oh—thank you very much!" Alexandra called, waving to the driver.

ALEXANDRA GOES TO LONDON

"Who else?" Will said. "I'll get BINS working on it today—I don't know any of these English guys."

"At the BBC, Martyn Lewis. And then over at ITN, I told you, Burnet—that's Sir Alastair Burnet—and let's try one of the new ones." She winked. "One of *my* contemporaries." She pointed to his pad. "Fiona Armstrong—she's the one I keep hearing about. Hargrave's going to try to hire her, I hear."

There were messages waiting for them at the desk. After they signed in and were shown up to the third floor, they parted ways to meet later that night at the BINS studio. Alexandra was shown into 321, a lovely, elegant suite overlooking Green Park. The architecture was turn of the century, and both the living room and bedroom had pale yellow walls, high ceilings, intricate wood moldings and touches of gold leaf decoration. In the living room there were two sets of triple windows—practically floor to ceiling—and in the bedroom there was one set of windows, and all had gold drapes hanging to the floor. The living room was furnished in a Louis XVI style; at the end of the room was a marble fireplace, elaborate mantel and gorgeous mirror above. In the bedroom there were two full brass beds pushed together and a dressing table and mirror in front of the window. There was a small crystal and brass chandelier in each room, as well as brass lighting fixtures in the wall.

There were also two flower arrangements in the living room. Alexandra opened the card to the first. It was a plain card, with a small coat of arms engraved on the corner.

Welcome to London

it said.

The second was a florist's card.

Dorchester is expecting you and/or your things any time tomorrow. I should be back by seven, hoping to find you. Dinner? I promise to get you to the studio on time. Call me in Rye Harbor.

Love, G

Alexandra called downstairs for tea and sandwiches. When the tray arrived she settled onto one of the two small sofas in her living room to eat while returning telephone calls. Yes, she was here, she told Lord Hargrave's office, and would be there at four. Yes, she was here, she told BINS, and would be there tonight. Then she returned Chi Chi's call from West End, who said they couldn't get Cassy into the Ritz but that she should be at the Connaught on Carlos Place by six or so. Then Chi Chi transferred her to Kate so she could check in with her. Then she called the number in Rye Harbor for Gordon, where he was shooting on location this week, and left a message for him that she had arrived, her plans were a little up in the air at the moment, but yes, she would see him tomorrow night for dinner. And then she called her apartment to return Jessica's call. Jessica just wanted to say hello and wondered if Alexandra happened to have the number of a plant doctor.

"Oh, no," Alexandra said. "Plant *doctor?* We're that far gone?"

"Just kidding, just kidding," Jessica said. "We're having a great time here—aren't we, guys? We're just sitting here eating breakfast. Here, Greenie, have some grapefruit. Hey, Waring—Lisa called me last night."

"I told you we were having dinner," Alexandra said.

"Yeah, you did—but you didn't say anything about being down in the dumps. I know you're busy taking over the company or whatever it is you're doing over there—by the way, you're supposed to go into food companies, or don't you pay attention to your own newscast? And you'd be much better off in food. You're perfect for a cake mix box—Kansas Home Cooking with the Divine Miss W."

Alexandra was laughing.

"*Any*way," Jessica continued, "Lisa seems to be a little concerned about you. She wouldn't tell me what it was about, only that you weren't very happy. And that she thought you needed someone to talk to."

Silence. Alexandra was looking into her cup of tea.

"Oh, great," Jessica said, "now I've shut you up completely. Listen, Alexandra, this is not an interrogation. I'm not mad at you for telling Lisa things you don't tell me—I'm not even mad that, after pretending that you scarcely know her, she turns out to be one of your closest friends." She was laughing. "I'm beginning to understand the enormous entertainment factor in being friends with you. Half the fun is trying to figure out who the person is I might be friends with." She paused. "You still there?"

Alexandra swallowed, clearing her throat. "Yes."

" 'Yes,' she says," Jessica said. "Look, I'm not trying to be nosy. I don't want you to tell me anything you don't want to—especially since, as you said once, it's not good to tell people who drink too much too much, is it? And I know I haven't been sober for very long—"

"Oh, Jessica," Alexandra said quickly, "that's not it. Really, it's not. I trust you very much. Really." She paused. "It's just me. Lisa's known me a long time. Um, she . . ." She sighed. "I don't know." She laughed to herself. "That's exactly it—I don't know. That's my problem, Jessica—I just don't know a lot of things anymore that I thought I did. About myself."

"Are you okay?"

"Actually, this crazy trip over here is probably a very good thing for me. It's just crazy enough to inspire me to find out some things while I'm here."

"Like what?" Jessica said.

"Like what I'm doing in this life." Alexandra hesitated, then went on. "One of the reasons why I don't like to talk about my problems is because, as soon as I hear myself talking, I can't pretend there aren't any problems anymore. And if I tell someone else, then I feel compelled to do something, because I can't *not* do something when other people expect me to do something. And I just don't have the time to drop everything and try and sort out some of this stuff that's been so confused for so many years."

"But you don't have to do it all in one day," Jessica said. "Waring, listen to me, you're allowed to be human too, you know. You're allowed to have a life to work on."

"But this isn't about someone being sick, or not being able to pay the rent, Jessica," Alexandra said. "It's just feelings—and feelings aren't real things."

"What?" Jessica said. "Feelings are real things—and they're very important—"

"Not in my line of work they're not," Alexandra said.

"Yeah, but your work is not your life," Jessica said.

"But it is," Alexandra said.

Jessica sighed. "Yeah, I guess. Right now, anyway."

"So is it any wonder I don't *want* to talk about it?" Alexandra said.

Pause. "It?" Jessica said.

Alexandra sighed, pressing the bridge of her nose for a moment. Dropping her hand, "Yes. It. Something in particular." She paused. "And the reason why I can't talk about it is because I'm scared to, Jessica. I'm scared of what you'd think—of me. And I'm scared what it would do to our friendship. Because I've been so grateful to have a friend my age at DBS—a friend, period—and I just couldn't take it right now if you were to—"

"I *am* your friend!" Jessica said. "It's a done deed, Waring. You can't just undo it. Do you hear me? No matter what, I'm on your side. Got it?"

Alexandra sighed. "I know I'm not making any sense—"

"You're making perfect sense," Jessica said. "Because it's something I recognize very well. It's called fear, which in some circles is better known as Fuck Everything And Run—a method of coping with emotional pain that I know very well, believe me. And maybe I got drunk doing it and maybe you look very productive doing it—but either way, haven't you noticed how often you and I keep meeting around the quicksand?"

"I know," Alexandra said.

"But I feel sorry for you, Waring," Jessica said. "Because at least my drinking dragged me down, whereas with you—you're so goddam perfect and driven to be perfect, and so goddam strong and otherwise unself-destructive, it's gonna take hurricanes and earthquakes and centuries to wear you down to where you have to start talking to people."

"I think that's changing," Alexandra said. "I think that's why I saw Lisa. And I think it probably has to do with the shooting."

"What do you mean?"

"Oh," Alexandra said, sighing, "the first time I got shot, it sent me running in one direction—the safest direction, I guess. Because I was scared, Jessica. Nobody knows how scared I was after that happened." She paused. "But then this time—I don't know, I seem to be reeling in another direction." She cleared her throat. "And definitely not the safest direction. But maybe the one that's right—I just don't know."

Pause. "It's Gordon, isn't it?" Jessica said.

ALEXANDRA GOES TO LONDON

Alexandra sighed. "It's me. My life, my work, what I want, where I'm going, what makes me happy."

"Oh," Jessica said, "just the whole thing then."

Silence.

"Should I be worrying about you?" Jessica said.

"No," Alexandra said.

"You do know that I'd do anything for you, don't you?" Jessica said. "And I guess that's really all I wanted to say. That I'm here if you need me. And that—oh, brother, Alexandra Eyes, I mean, come on—you never let me do anything for you."

"Thanks," Alexandra said.

"Now is Cassy going to be over there or what?"

"Uh-huh. She'll be here tonight."

"So I don't have to worry about you, right?" Jessica said. "You'll talk to her if you need someone—right?"

Alexandra was rolling her eyes. "Right," she said.

Promptly at four Alexandra rang the bell of Lord Hargrave's offices on South Audley Street. The offices were contained in a four-story Victorian house of red-orange brick, gray stonework, white window sash and black wrought-iron railing. The front entranceway extended out in a porch from which a large wrought-iron lantern was suspended. Alexandra was standing just past the lantern, in the recess of an enormous mahogany door. There was a single brass knob in the middle of the door and a brass mail slot to the left of it, on which was engraved:

Hargrave World Communications, Ltd.

The door was opened by a pleasant young woman who introduced herself as Antonia. She led Alexandra right upstairs. There were the sounds of telephones ringing in the house, of typewriters clacking away, but thus far there had been no sign of where these sounds might be coming from. It simply appeared to be a gracious old home of gorgeous woodwork, sedate carpets, and paintings and furniture older than the hills. Alexandra looked up the stairs; the gallery of portraits and pictures on the stair wall continued upward for another two flights. On the second landing Antonia led her down the hall, knocked softly on a set of mahogany parlor doors and slid them slightly apart. "Alexandra Waring, Lord Hargrave," she said softly. And then she nodded and stepped back, sliding the one door back for Alexandra to pass through.

She stepped into a very large, wonderful room that was part library, part office. At the far end of it were tremendous windows in a bay, looking out over South Audley Street and down Stanhope Gate, and then the room widened slightly, with bookcases from ceiling to floor, and a few leather chairs, lamps and tables. There was a very large Persian rug, dark wood floors gleaming at the edges of it.

But this end of the room was a square sort of office, with a heavy carpet down, and there was Lord Hargrave's ornate and obviously very old desk that had papers piled in mahogany boxes all over the place. There were a few shelves along the walls, holding books and things—a brass sextant, a crystal globe—and there were several old paintings. There were a large leather couch, coffee table and chairs, and back to the side of the doors was a huge wardrobe, whose doors were opened at the moment, displaying a four-foot television screen inside.

"My dear, hello, how very wonderful it is to see you," Lord Hargrave said, coming around his desk and holding out his hand to her.

As Alexandra took a step forward, one of the floorboards beneath the carpeting creaked.

"Hello, Lord Hargrave," she said, taking his hand.

He smiled, bowed slightly and kissed it, making her smile. "One of the few pleasures of growing older in England," he said, winking as he straightened up. "Certainly the weather is not. Here, my dear, do please sit down. I cannot tell you how very glad I was to hear you were coming," he continued, walking over to the double doors and sliding them open. "Ah! Miss Dillon, wonderful—I was just coming to look for you." He stepped back as a woman rolled in a tea cart. "I hope you don't mind if Miss Dillon does the honors, Alexandra. I'm afraid I'm quite particular when it comes to my tea."

"No, of course not," Alexandra said, sitting on the edge of her chair, legs together to the side, hands folded in her lap. "This is a wonderful treat."

As Miss Dillon poured tea, Lord Hargrave talked a little about milk subsidies (his family estate was used primarily as dairy land now); asked Alexandra's opinion of how the American subsidy program had gone so wrong ("You are, are you not, my dear, from a farming background?"); and answered Alexandra's question about the building they were in.

"Oh, my, no," Lord Hargrave said. "Our home was in Regent's Park. This was the home of my grandfather's mistress, Mrs. Rivers. That's her portrait over there. Interesting woman, really. Of course, it was not public knowledge, the relationship Mrs. Rivers maintained with my grandfather—though perhaps some people were aware of it. One never knows, does one?" He chuckled. "There was a Mr. Rivers, or so she always maintained, though most people found it a trifle odd that anyone could be posted to India without leave for fifty-seven years."

And then, finally, he eased into the subject of the purchase of DBS News, during which time he rose out of his chair and began to walk back and forth, discussing the structure of the new company if they were to buy it. Alexandra listened to him, sipping her tea, nodding and murmuring assent as he went along. And then Lord Hargrave abruptly stopped in his tracks and turned to her, tilting his head to the side. "You're not very keen on buying DBS News, are you? Jackson was, initially. But I could tell yesterday he was cooling on the idea and now here, with you, the idea seems to be positively freezing."

Alexandra had to laugh a little.

"Well, no matter," Lord Hargrave said with a wave of his hand, moving to sit down again, "I was only trying to do my friend Jackson a favor. And I suppose I still am—you are going to use our offer to your advantage, I hope."

"They're sending Cassy over tonight," Alexandra told him. "To represent Darenbrook Communications."

"Oh, good," he said, clapping his hands. "The whole show. What fun—I'd love to see what you get out of them." He leaned forward. "Cassy's in on it too, I suppose. I imagine she's much fonder of all of you than she is of the board."

Alexandra laughed. "You probably know more than I do about what's going on right now. All I know is that Jackson asked me to come here and listen to your offer."

"But you knew he wasn't really going to buy it, didn't you?" Lord Hargrave asked her. "No offense, my dear, but DBS News isn't worth very much without the related companies—the cross-resource aspect, you understand."

"Not worth much to you," Alexandra said, correcting him.

He smiled. "You are very loyal, aren't you?"

"I know what it's worth," Alexandra said.

"No, I meant to Jackson. You're very loyal to him."

"I owe him a great deal," she said. "And that's why I'm here. Otherwise I don't think it's a good idea for me or any DBS News employee to vie for ownership of the institution we work for."

"Really," Lord Hargrave said. "You don't believe that liberating journalists from corporate types in management is a good thing?"

She blinked several times, leaning forward to put her cup and saucer down on the tray. Then she sat back and looked at him. "I don't believe in journalists as their own profit-oriented business managers, no. The temptations on many levels in such an arrangement are too much. And speaking for myself, I think I have a long enough road back to being a first-class reporter again as it is. I've had to do things—and involve myself in things—in this past year on a business level that I hope I never have to do to such an extent again."

She shrugged. "But I was hired to launch a new news network on commercial television, and so I've had to involve myself in commercial things. And lately I feel the detriment, as a journalist. Too much time being concerned with management, policy—even too much time spent in planning meetings—starts to affect my outlook. Many times, in the past few months, I've felt as though I'm somewhere way out there"— she held out her right hand—"while the world is way over here—" She held out her left hand. "And we're just *looking* at each other, *admiring* each other, but not interacting the way we should be.

"But you know," she added suddenly, leaning forward, "one of the most wonderful things about my tour across America is that it makes me know—with every cell in my body—that we're on the right track. And sometimes . . ." She stopped herself.

"Sometimes," Lord Hargrave said, nodding once.

"Sometimes I think that the reason why I keep getting shot at is because Somebody doesn't want me wasting any more time trying to become a celebrity," she said, laughing. "Like—here's the shortcut kid, now, right now, *now,* this very day, it's time to put your all into introducing the United States *to* the United States in the context of its very complicated self. And to an extent we've started to do that. Our affiliate reporters, rough as some of them may be—but only for now, because we're training them and they're getting better every day—our affiliate reporters don't talk like TV people. They talk like reporters who live in a certain part of the country, a part they know like the back of their hands and want to introduce to viewers."

Lord Hargrave was smiling.

"We are so diverse in the States," she went on, "I really believe that our way is the only way to properly educate people about the country we live in, so they can really understand national news. Understand the basic areas where we hang together as a country, and the reasons behind our constant conflicts. And a big part of my job—whether I like it or not—is to provide, along with my fellow New York editors, that kind of culturally bland glamor stuff that people seem to need if they're to watch network news. I'm the lure DBS uses to hook them, so we can drag them into the process of understanding the news until they learn enough so it becomes easy and second nature—like local news is for them. If viewers can't read, fine. If they're relatively uneducated and frightened of the world outside their town or city or block or front door, *fine.* All I've got to do is strut my stuff past their window and hope they invite me inside—and if they do . . ." She laughed. "It's all over. Our guys take over. Open the door and in marches America, accents and all!"

Lord Hargrave laughed.

"Because, you see," she said, shifting in her seat, gesturing with her hand, "if we teach a little something about different pockets of America each night—in our stories, in the way our reporters talk and walk and see the community around them—over the weeks and months viewers just start to *know* things. They get educated. And it's not from remembering specifics from our newscast, it's from the whole DBS News process. Ours is really an endeavor to use broadcast commercial television to revitalize viewers' curiosity, their capacity to learn, and to break down that resistance that comes with not knowing how to read properly, for example—"

"None of which has much to do with running shareholders' meetings in the newsroom," Lord Hargrave said.

Alexandra smiled, shaking her head. "No. It doesn't."

Lord Hargrave reached for a biscuit, took a small bite and slowly chewed it, watching her carefully. "I know quite a bit about you. Are you aware of that?"

Alexandra shrugged.

"Does that mean yes or no?" Lord Hargrave asked her.

"I know you've made some inquiries about me," she said.

"And I've been told you are quite trustworthy," he said.

"Yes," she said. "I am."

"So you would keep a confidence, if I were to ask you to."

"A personal one, yes," she said. She smiled. "I can't promise anything if it has to do with the fate of the world, though."

"If I were to make you a proposition, Alexandra," Lord Hargrave said, "and you chose not to accept it—could you maintain a confidence about that?"

"You mean, don't tell Jackson."

Lord Hargrave nodded. "No one need be upset if nothing were to come of it."

Alexandra smiled, shaking her head. "This is why I would never make it in business. You guys play games with rules I have never understood."

He smiled. "Someday you must ask Jackson about how it happened that I hired Dr. Kessler and he showed up for work at Darenbrook Communications," he said. "We've played many games over the years, Jackson and I, but we've remained good friends. And we've made good money too." He paused. "But this is not a game for you, Alexandra. This is what's known as the opportunity of a lifetime."

Alexandra waited.

Lord Hargrave pressed his index finger against his mouth, looking at her. Then he lowered his hand and said, "I would like you to do for me what you are doing at DBS, only I wish you to do it internationally. English language, of course, but we'll do four translations to start— French, German, Spanish and Japanese."

Alexandra sat there, her expression unreadable.

Lord Hargrave smiled. "That's right, my dear. I would like you to anchor my global newscast."

49

Alexandra and Cassy Have a Talk

Alexandra called the Connaught at six o'clock from Lord Hargrave's offices and found that, yes, indeed, Catherine Cochran had checked in.

"Hi," Alexandra said.

"Hi," Cassy said. "You don't suppose I could sneak to a play sometime between dinner and the studio, do you? Diana Rigg is in something somewhere."

"Ah, yes," Alexandra said, "something somewhere. I hear it's supposed to be very you-know."

"You're sounding uncharacteristically jokey, my dear," Cassy said, "which makes me suspect it's going to cost Darenbrook Communications plenty to keep DBS News."

"Enough to be interesting," Alexandra cheerfully assured her.

Instead of just meeting for dinner, Cassy asked Alexandra if she wouldn't mind going for a walk first, to get out and wander around and get some exercise. Alexandra thought it was a wonderful idea and went back to the Ritz to change into her "airport" shoes. She met Cassy downstairs and the women set out from the front door of the Ritz, heading west on Piccadilly, along Green Park. They debated about cutting down through the park to Buckingham Palace but decided to wander on into Belgravia instead and promptly got lost. The fact that they had neglected to bring a map seemed to be a source of delight for them both. "You, Alexandra?" Cassy said. "You who still carries a map of New York City?"

"That's just for emergencies, subway and bus routes," she said. "I always carry one for whatever city I'm in, like any good reporter should. But I decided to leave my map in my work bag tonight, figuring that *you,* certainly, would bring one." She stopped, gesturing to the intersection they had reached: Pont Street, Chesham Place, Belgrave Mews, Lowndes Place. "Which way?" Cassy pointed in the direction of Pont Street and so they walked that way, and Alexandra sighed, smiling, slinging her arm through Cassy's, pressing her shoulder into hers. "I frankly love the idea of not knowing where I'm going—for an hour or two. Know what I mean?"

Cassy smiled, walking along. "Yes." She looked at her. "And it must be a relief not to be recognized."

"You mean it's nice that everyone's looking at you again," Alexandra said, laughing.

"No one's looking at me," Cassy said. "No one looks at a forty-three-year-old woman walking with a thirty-year-old who looks like you."

"Well, they're looking at this forty-three-year-old," Alexandra told her. "Look at that man there. What is it about blondes, anyway?"

"Good evening," the man said pleasantly, walking past. He had only glanced at Alexandra and had said it to Cassy.

"See?" Alexandra said, giving her a slight shove, making them weave on the sidewalk.

They had fun. It was a warm, gray-sky summer evening, and it was London, so everything seemed astonishingly attractive and neat and tidy, if not slightly magical. For a while they talked about what new concessions Cassy thought she could get out of the board for DBS News, but that conversation somehow slipped away to Cassy's son, Henry, and Cassy adjusting to the idea that he now had a life of his own, quite separate from hers.

They knew they were in Knightsbridge, then, because they stumbled upon Harrods. They decided to continue down Brompton Road, only to discover at the Victoria and Albert Museum that they were somehow not on Brompton Road anymore but on Cromwell Road. "Now where did it go?" Cassy said, turning around, scratching her head.

"Exhibition Road!" Alexandra suddenly said. "Oh, I want this— come on, I want to see something. But wait—" she said a second later, yanking Cassy back to a stop. "Which way is north? Oh, this way, I think," she said, turning them around and charging onward, pulling

Cassy along. And so they walked up Exhibition Road between the Natural History Museum and the Victoria and Albert Museum.

"I take it we're in Kensington," Cassy said later, standing on the traffic island in the middle of Kensington Gore Road that Alexandra had dragged her onto. The light had changed and traffic was flying past them on both sides.

"Okay," Alexandra said, taking hold of her arm with one hand, "now look at that and tell me what you see."

Cassy looked, "I see Kensington Gardens and Hyde Park," she said. And indeed, they were looking at an entrance leading into the magnificent acres of green.

"No," Alexandra said, "I meant the gate. What do you think of it?" Then she frowned, looking up and down the road. "I think this is the one. This is Exhibition Road, right?"

"Right," Cassy said.

In comparison with others in this part of London, the very tall, black wrought-iron gate in front of them seemed a bit plain—though it was quite stately and elegant all the same, as black wrought-iron English anythings tend to be. There were two inner carriageways, through which one lane of traffic was entering the park and the other leaving it; and there were two outer walkways for pedestrians. Flanking the carriageways on high were four lanterns.

"Do you think it's lovely, strong and expedient?" Alexandra said.

"What?" Cassy said, laughing, looking at her as if she were crazy.

"Do you think it's lovely, strong and expedient?" Alexandra repeated, laughing too. Her eyes were bright, happy.

"Okay—sure," Cassy said, looking back at the gate. "But why?"

"Lord Hargrave says I'm like that gate."

"What?"

"He did. He said I was like the Alexandra Gate—lovely, strong and expedient. That's what he said."

Cassy looked at the gate and then back at Alexandra. "Looks like the No-Trucks-Unless-Authorized Gate to me," she said, referring to the sign on it.

"No, come on—that must be it," Alexandra said as the light changed, pulling Cassy across the road. "He told me where it was."

They walked through the gate and looked around on the other side. And, sure enough, there was a sign:

ALEXANDRA
GATE

"Huh," Alexandra said, standing there looking at it. "So that's me. That's what I'm like. Interesting." She looked at Cassy, closing one eye. "Expedient?"

Cassy was looking around. "I think the concept of traffic running through you may be appropriate. Where exactly are we, anyway?"

Alexandra turned, pointing east. "I think that's the Hilton over there."

Cassy looked. There were four tennis courts, and then there were people playing soccer, and there were acres and acres of grass and trees and way, way, way off in the distance there were some buildings marking the east end of the park. "So what does the Hilton mean?"

"It means the Ritz is straight down there somewhere," Alexandra said. "But let's walk in the park some."

"The park?" Cassy said, looking at her.

"The park," Alexandra said. "But you'd rather go see Diana Rigg in something-somewhere, right?" She looked at her watch. "And I want to take a nap before going to the studio, so maybe—"

"No, no, let's walk some," Cassy said. "We need to talk some more about DBS. And I need to talk to you too—about something else."

Alexandra looked at her. "About . . . ?"

"Me," Cassy said.

"Great," Alexandra said, gesturing to the park. "There's a restaurant in here somewhere. We can get something to eat."

They looked at a posted directory of the park and then followed Exhibition Road in to a rather unusual-looking complex overlooking the Serpentine. One half was a kind of concrete and glass space-age dwelling housing a restaurant; and next door was a one-floor glass structure that looked a little like a carnival fun house with its multicolored lights. The sign said this latter building was the Pergola Café, a family restaurant.

They chose the presumably nonfamily restaurant and were immediately glad they did, for inside it was very quiet and had a wonderful panoramic view. The maître d' seated them at a small booth for two by the window, and they were very happy with it. They looked out over a grassy backyard, dotted with white wild flowers, the outer edge of which was beautifully landscaped with leafy trees and flowering bushes. And then there was a steep embankment, dropping down to the waters of the Serpentine. To the left was a stone bridge across the water; to the right, in the distance, there were boaters rowing in to shore.

It was lovely and cool, the evening drawing quickly toward night.

The only surprise Cassy had about the concessions Alexandra wanted from Darenbrook Communications for DBS News, as she sat there making some notes—increased funding, moving up the schedule of expansion, overseas news liaisons, etc.—concerned Alexandra's mysterious employees Mr. Graham and Miss Moffat, whom she had been paying out of her own pocket. Alexandra wanted them on the DBS News payroll, heading their own division called Research and Development, where they would recycle the DBS newscasts for subsidiary rights income, both domestically and internationally, and she wanted—

"But Mr. Graham is seventy years old, Alexandra!" Cassy said.

"Seventy-one," Alexandra said.

"And Miss Moffat is like—like—"

"Sixty-eight," Alexandra said.

Cassy looked at her.

"And their one hundred and thirty-eight years of experience are going to make us some money—to say nothing of producing some very prestigious projects," Alexandra said.

"Like what?" Cassy said.

"Like packaging Gary's weather segments as a natural phenomena video for junior high and high school science classes," Alexandra said. "He's already got a deal with *Scholastic* lined up."

Cassy looked at her.

"And Sony's interested in a series of videos depicting contemporary America on a regional basis. You know, edit together a year of stories pertaining to specific areas. They're interested in using it in their orientation program for employees they send here to work—and Mr.

Graham says there are fifty-six other international corporations that want to talk to us about it too."

Cassy's mouth was open.

"And then he has this whole airline deal cooking," Alexandra said. "We'll produce a weekly summary newscast—out of our regular ones —an hour long, and they're going to use it on their international flights coming into the States, to catch people up on what's going on in America. And so then he thought, well, why can't we use the same hour video for schools and libraries? So then he started talking to a friend of his at—"

"I don't believe this," Cassy said. "Mr. Graham?"

"Oh, he's wonderful, Cassy—and the stories he has to tell! He was in newsreels and he has that kind of mind—you know, waste not, want not. His whole mind is oriented toward using every little scrap of good footage for as many things as he can. He's been doing a lot of those war series for cable, using the old newsreel footage. And some video series. And Miss Moffat is sort of his sounding board, but she also makes a lot of the calls—people are quite disarmed by her. And all they're going to need is one young, smart producer and a couple of good secretaries. We can use our same editing staff. Actually, Hex has been helping them on the sly already. But I want them on the payroll. And I want to pay them well, Cassy. And I want them to have titles and I want to announce it in the press and really make a big deal out of it."

"Why?"

Alexandra looked at her. "Because I think they're wonderful and deserve to have a fuss made over them." And then she added, "And DBS News is not staying at Darenbrook Communications unless you approve it. Now. And I know you can approve it because I was going to ask you to anyway before all this stuff started—and if you said no, I was going to do it anyway out of my syndication money from Jessica's show."

Cassy threw up her hands and Alexandra laughed. "Langley was wrong," Cassy said, laughing too, bringing her hands down to the table, "you are a tsarina."

They smiled at each other, gazing at each other across the table.

ALEXANDRA AND CASSY HAVE A TALK

"Okay," Cassy said then, making a note on her pad. "Consider Research and Development approved."

They ate supper, talking over various other aspects of DBS News, but then that business was done and Alexandra asked Cassy what she thought was going to happen to Jackson. What he would do, and if there was anything she should or could do for him.

Cassy stopped eating then, sighing, looking out the window.

"What's the matter?" Alexandra said.

Cassy looked at her for a long moment. "You and I have to talk." She paused. "There's something I have to tell you before we talk any further." She dropped her eyes to the table. "Something I have to discuss with you."

Alexandra put her fork down and patted her mouth with her napkin. "Go ahead," she said quietly.

"It may be that it will be . . ." Cassy began, stopping and frowning at how it sounded.

"It may be that it will be," Alexandra said, smiling, encouraging her to continue.

Cassy sighed and plunged ahead. "That it would be best if I leave DBS. Maybe at the end of the year."

Alexandra looked at her.

Cassy glanced down at the table. "I . . ." She looked up. "Just tell me how that would affect you. My not working with you anymore. You brought me to DBS, Alexandra—to look after your interests. And I have to know what it would do to you if I left."

Alexandra thought a moment, looking out the window. "Well," she said, turning back to Cassy, "it's not as if you and I will be working very closely anymore anyway—not with you being network president." She paused, looking at her. "But it's not a matter of me needing you anymore—it's a matter of everyone and everything at DBS needing you. And so my feeling is, whatever it is that makes you think you want to leave"—she swallowed—"I think is something that could somehow be worked out."

Cassy nodded, biting her lip and looking out the window.

Alexandra was watching her. "I can't believe you could work anywhere else. I can't believe you'd give up DBS."

Cassy shrugged, still looking out the window. "Dexter Halloway wants me to come back. He wants me to buy some more stations for Rogers, Dale—build a chain." She looked at Alexandra. "While prices are down."

When Alexandra didn't say anything, Cassy looked down at her water glass, pushing it around, and continued, "With so many takeovers of the consumer goods companies, as you know, the first thing to get slashed is their ad budgets. In '86, stations were going for fifteen times their cash flow. Now," she shrugged, "some are lucky if they can get ten. And it's going to be worse next year—and it'll be a good time to buy."

Alexandra looked at her for a moment and then said, "Forget it!" making Cassy jump. "Just forget it, Cassy," she said, batting the idea out of the air with her hand. "No way. Whatever it is that you're afraid of—don't be. You're staying at DBS and that's it. We'll work it out."

"But it's not that simple," Cassy told her. "Because it's for personal reasons. And I think you might feel entirely different when I tell you what they are."

Alexandra looked at her, face turning a little red.

Cassy dropped her eyes. "And everything's at sixes and sevens right now. It's not the best time to be trying to make decisions. Not for any of us."

Alexandra was smiling slightly now. After a moment she said, gently, "Maybe you should just tell me what your personal reasons are, Cassy."

Cassy looked out the window. "I didn't realize how difficult this would be."

"It's just me, Cassy," Alexandra said softly. "You can tell me anything. We can work out anything. I know we can. But you have to tell me first." She paused. "I need for you to tell me."

Cassy hesitated and then took a sip of water. Finally she looked back at Alexandra. "I've fallen in love with Jackson."

Alexandra's expression did not change.

"I know," Cassy said, dropping her eyes. "I'm not the type to be sleeping around the office, but . . ." She smiled, shaking her head to herself. "I don't know." She looked up. "It all started the night of the boat party."

The color was draining from Alexandra's face.

ALEXANDRA AND CASSY HAVE A TALK

"Actually, it started before," Cassy said, picking up her fork and playing with it on her plate. "And then we—we slept together." She dropped her fork, her face blushing scarlet, her eyes down on her plate. "I know it seems ridiculous at my age—to carry on the way I have been—with Michael scarcely out of the house—but . . ." She swallowed, timidly looking up at Alexandra. "I don't know. I think he really might be in love with me too."

"Of course he is," Alexandra said, voice faint.

"I'm sorry, what?" Cassy said, leaning forward, anxious.

Alexandra cleared her throat. "I said, he is. I'm sure he's very much in love with you. He'd be a fool not to be. So don't worry about that, Cassy." She reached over the table to touch Cassy's hand. "I'm very happy for you," she said. "You so badly deserve someone wonderful—a very wonderful man. And you've found him." Her voice faltered and she cleared her throat again. "There are few people I love more, respect more, than Jackson. He's right for you." She looked down, adding, "Perfect for you."

Cassy's eyes were full of tears. "Oh, thank you for saying that," she said, taking her hand in both of hers. "Sweetheart, thank you. I've been so scared about what you would think—about whether I'm some sort of fool in a middle-age crisis."

Alexandra withdrew her hand, shaking her head. "You're no fool," she said.

They left the restaurant soon after that, Alexandra pleading a headache and a need to rest before going to the studio. A cab was called for and Cassy dropped Alexandra off at the Ritz. Alexandra hugged her, assured her one more time that Jackson was the right person and how Cassy should not worry about things, how it would all work out, and then she went into the hotel, picked up messages and her key, and went up to her suite.

She dropped her things on the table in the living room and went into the bedroom, turning on a light. Then she turned the light off and just stood there awhile, in the doorway, the light from the living room coming in from behind her. She slipped off her shoes. She walked over to stand by the dresser and look out the window. Then she turned around, walked toward the bed, but then stopped a few feet away, simply standing there, looking at it. And then, very slowly, she brought her hands up to cover her face. There was a high-pitched sound from inside her throat and then she took a step forward, leaning over, blindly reaching for the bed. She found the edge of it and sank to her knees beside it, putting her arm on it and burying her face in her arm. And then she slid off the bed, covering her face with her hands, curling all the way down to her knees.

"Oh, God," Alexandra whispered, crying, "oh, God—help me, please. I cannot bear this—I can't, I can't, I can't."

The studios of the British International News Service—a subsidiary of Hargrave World Communications, Ltd.—were located right there in the West End of London on the corner of Great Titchfield and Riding House streets. The ITN studios (Independent Television News) were right around the corner on Wells Street, and ABC (the American Broadcasting Company)—which had a "friendly news liaison" with ITN—had offices just up on Carburton Street. CNN (the Cable News Network), who had a "cable-friendly news liaison" with ITN, had an outpost in the neighborhood too, just a bit east on Newman Street.

Alexandra arrived at the BINS studio promptly at eleven. Will was there with a crew waiting for her. Cassy arrived shortly thereafter and went off with the production executive while Alexandra and the crew ran studio tests with West End.

After the tests were finished, Alexandra went into the newsroom, where she talked on the phone first with Kyle and then with Dan, the news editor, and then with Dick Gross, the director. Then she sat down at a computer terminal, which one of the BINS news assistants called in to a tie line with the West End computer, and within moments she was scrolling through the working newscast script. She got Kyle on the phone and he, on the computer too at his end, watched as she flagged and queried some places in the copy. In about forty minutes they were through and then Alexandra wrote her opening, including the headlines of the day, a midway intro, and a closing, and sent it off to West End. Dan's and Kyle's approval flashed back minutes later, and then seconds later the news assistant was catching the final script as it came out of the printer.

ALEXANDRA AND CASSY HAVE A TALK

It was 1:15 A.M. Alexandra went into makeup where a nice man named Luddy went to work on her. She emerged at one thirty-four, was handed her script by Will as she came into the studio and took her seat behind the desk on the BINS set. Her mike was clipped on, her earpiece connected. They had mini-rehearsal with West End. Alexandra told the TelePrompTer operator he was good.

At 9:00:15, after the opening, Alexandra appeared on television across America with the greeting, "Hello and good evening from London, England, where I am currently on special assignment. . . ." She proceeded to offer the day's headlines and then turned the newscast over to Chester Hanacker and John Knox Norwood at West End as coanchors. (Her being in London prompted an ad-lib remark or two from some of her colleagues, i.e., "The dollar fell against the pound today," Paul Levitz said in the finance segment, "and we've been assured that Alexandra had nothing to do with it.") Alexandra appeared briefly to do a lead into the second half hour, and then at the end of the newscast Chester led back to her in London for the close.

At DBS, some said they got goose bumps watching the close, seeing Alexandra sitting so very far away—blue eyes blazing, smile so familiar —saying, "From the West End of London to the West End of New York, to the western end of the world in Hawaii—this has been the DBS television news network, wishing you a very good night and an even better tomorrow."

They called it a wrap, congratulated each other and struck the set. Cassy took a cab to her hotel and Alexandra and Will shared one back to the Ritz. Alexandra gave him a kiss on the cheek good night in the hall and went into her suite. She sat down in the living room, pulled out her address book and placed a long-distance call to New York. It was 3:46 A.M., 10:46 P.M. in New York.

"Hello, John? It's Alexandra calling. I'm sorry to call so late, but I think you'll understand why I thought it worth while to risk waking you." She smiled, nodding. "Thank you. Anyway, John, I'd like you to call Lord Hargrave tomorrow. He's made me a separate offer—" She nodded. "Separate from DBS. To launch his global newscast. From London. He'll attach an offer to Gordon as well." She listened. "Right. I just want you to listen to what he has to say and then call me back and tell me what you think."

She talked with him for another fifteen minutes, hung up the phone, and then sat there for a moment, looking at it. Then she sighed —running a hand through her hair—and got up and walked into the bedroom.

And then she fell apart.

50

Langley Has It Out with Belinda

It was over. Whatever it was that had been holding him back from "telling" on Belinda—shame, guilt, protectiveness—it was gone now. It was over.

At least that's what Langley hoped as he watched Alexandra open "DBS News America Tonight" from London. He was sitting in the den of his apartment with Cordelia, who was doing some kind of needle-point, and with Big El, who was eating a dish of vanilla ice cream. (Big El, five days away from Hilleanderville and his sneak drinking with Lucille, was spending less and less time in his wheelchair. His favorite activity had come to be walking to the kitchen after dinner to bother pretty little Carmen for things to eat, and to say things like, "I'm sure this ice cream could not be sweeter than you, Miss Carmen.")

The knowledge that it was time for him do something about Belinda's pill taking made Langley's chest feel a little tight. He was scared. Christ, he had been scared for years already, hadn't he? Only then he had thought it was hopeless. He had thought Belinda was just going crazy and there was nothing he could do about it.

Strange how much scarier it was to think that there might be something that could be done.

Strange.

Strange.

But then, it was very strange to find that all of Belinda's drugs were coming from doctors, extremely expensive doctors who were supposed to be the best in their fields, and that, of the four doctors he had talked to, all of them were violently appalled at the suggestion that they might have prescribed something for Mrs. Peterson that she didn't need. When Langley explained that Belinda apparently had other prescriptions from other doctors, that what this doctor was prescribing for her was also being prescribed for her by another, it was explained to him that it was not that doctor's business what another doctor did, any more than it was his job to do anything more than treat Mrs. Peterson for the ailment for which she had come to see him. Three of the doctors were treating Belinda for anxiety, stress and sleeplessness, and one was treating her for an aching back.

They weren't being unkind, Langley realized. Behind their indignation he imagined they were scared too. The implication of maintaining a drug habit for Belinda Darenbrook Peterson was scandalous, but the idea of confronting Belinda Darenbrook Peterson with the possibility that she might have a drug problem was impossible. If she took it the wrong way, a woman like Belinda Darenbrook Peterson could damage their practices severely with a single word to her friends. The problem, if she were indeed abusing prescriptions, the doctors said, lay with her. And they strongly recommended psychiatric help.

Yeah, right.

The real problem, in terms of the doctors, Langley knew, was with Dr. Balakudian. Belinda's dependence on him over the years was not just emotional but clearly and without question tied to drugs too. Balakudian's response to Langley's visit, telling Balakudian what he had learned thus far, pleading with him to help, was to assure Langley that he would. That he was shocked and troubled to hear that Belinda was acquiring tranquilizers from other doctors, in addition to those he was prescribing for her himself—for anxiety, stress, depression and sleeplessness—and that he would take care of things, not to worry. But Langley was also to understand that Balakudian was the only person whom Belinda truly trusted, and he had to be careful not to panic her into fleeing his care.

Langley and Belinda had a hell of a fight after she talked to Balakudian, and she insisted (and actually made a very convincing argument) that any pills she took were absolutely necessary. But as she continued to talk, Langley realized that Balakudian had not told her everything that he had told Balakudian—that Belinda thought Langley had only gone to see Balakudian about the drugs *he* was prescribing for her, and that she didn't even know Langley knew there were other doctors and other prescriptions.

In any case, what Belinda did know made her angry enough to tell Langley he could go to hell and that, if he had a problem about her, then fine, he should divorce her, "But everybody knows you won't," she said, "because everybody knows you married Darenbrook Communications till death do you part and, as long as you want it, you have to be married to me!" And then she had fled to Greenwich, not to return until the family reunion, at which time she seemed to be fine—which gave Langley this weird sensation that he might have made the whole thing up in his head. Could it be that Belinda was right, that it was the pills that prevented her from going crazy? But if that were true, why did she have so many secret prescriptions and why were there stashes of pills all over their bedroom and her dressing room?

In the meantime, between Belinda's trip to Greenwich and her return for the reunion, Langley had discovered that Dr. Balakudian had no intention of returning his phone calls or of seeing him. As some woman said who finally did return his call, "Dr. Balakudian is Mrs. Peterson's doctor and must honor the trust between doctor and patient."

Son of a bitch! was all Langley could think, feeling betrayed and abandoned. Balakudian with his degrees and smoothie European accent and two hundred dollars an hour fees—how the hell had Langley let Belinda fall in so deep with this guy? Six years this had been going on! And Langley knew—he *knew*—that Belinda's problems, periodically "going off," had started right around the time she had started seeing Balakudian, when she had started staying in the New York apartment more and more, and returning to Richmond less and less, after Barbara died.

Sunday night, after the board fired Jackson and voted Langley in as chairman, Belinda had fled to Greenwich and Langley had let her go. He asked Cordelia and Big El to stay on for a few days, to help sort things out in the wake of Jackson's dismissal, but the truth was, he wanted Cordelia to stay because he wanted to tell Cordelia everything and ask her what she thought he should do. Or maybe he was hoping Cordelia would take matters into her own hands. He didn't know. It wasn't as if he didn't want to do something himself, it was that there wasn't anything definable and clear about what it was he was supposed to do. If there were, he would do it. But there wasn't, and there was this mess at Darenbrook Communications, and if Belinda refused to even acknowledge that she had a problem, what was he supposed to do? He had talked to her doctors, discussed the problem with her psychiatrist, talked to Belinda about it—what more could he do when his wife had sixty-three million dollars and was quite free to go anywhere she wanted and go to as many doctors as she wanted and, hell, could buy a whole goddam drug company if she wanted?

And then Belinda had come swaggering in tonight while they were eating dinner, parading around the dining-room table, growling at Langley that she could have died out there in Greenwich and he wouldn't have cared—that he cared more about brown-nosing Cordie and her father because he was the big shot of the whole shooting match now, wasn't he? Then she had disappeared into their bedroom, slamming and locking the door.

And so Langley was sitting in the den watching the news with Cordelia and Big El, pulling his thoughts together in preparation for telling Cordelia what was going on.

Gary Plains, the weatherman, was now on the television screen, saying, "Well, folks, we know Alexandra will be home in America as soon as she can be—particularly since the biggest rain clouds in the western hemisphere are moving toward London as we speak."

"This guy's sort of a jerk, don't you think?" Big El said to Cordelia. "Reminds me of ol' Murky Dirk Bablachek, who used to run the Triple H Five and Dime—always goin' on and on about the weather."

"I believe that's his job, Daddy," Cordelia said, looking up and winking at Langley.

Big El grunted. In a moment he turned to Langley. "I don't want us spendin' an arm and a leg on this," he said.

"No, we won't," Langley assured him. "Cassy's pretty sure Alexandra's demands will be reasonable."

"I like Cassy," Cordelia said. After a moment she added, "And Alexandra still doesn't seem the type to me who would go in for blackmail." She broke a piece of thread with her teeth and then sighed, shaking her head. "Jackie just uses anybody to get his way. I suppose we should count ourselves lucky that Alexandra has any say in it all. Jackie'd just pull the whole place apart in a tantrum otherwise."

"I don't think so," Langley said.

Cordelia sighed again. "And these stories in the press are terrible. Make us all sound like lunatics." She looked up. "Did you see that piece in *USA Today* this morning?"

"Yeah," Langley said.

Cordelia clucked her tongue, resuming her needlepoint. "You'd think we were the ones who tried to shoot the girl."

"Good for ratings," Big El said. "Isn't that right, Lang?"

"Sad but true," Langley said.

"Well," Cordelia said, "I for one would like to get out of vaudeville and back into news." She paused and then added, "Course, Jessica's doing nicely and she's not part of the news division. And she seems very grateful to be with Darenbrook Communications, Jackie or no Jackie."

Langley started to say, "Well, she doesn't have any choice," but refrained from doing so.

"I don't know why," Cordelia said, holding her work closer to the light for a moment and then bringing it back into her lap, "but I like that girl. She can be positively blasphemous, but she has a good heart." Pause. "She did tell me she had some Sunday school as a girl."

"Whatcheeyall doin', talkin' about bizness?" Belinda said, waltzing into the den in a very revealing negligee. She twirled, drawing a piece of the negligee nearly under Cordelia's nose with her hand. "Still trying to seduce my husband with power and prestige, Cordelia?"

Cordelia frowned at what her sister was wearing. "Go put on a robe, Belinda," she said, returning her attention to her needlepoint.

"But Langley likes it," Belinda said, moving toward him. "Don't you, Langley?"

"You heard your sister," Big El said, eyes on the TV. "Put on a robe or go to bed."

Langley was feeling the icy fear creeping down his neck that he always felt when he sensed Belinda was about to go off. It didn't matter that he didn't think she was crazy anymore. It didn't matter if he thought it was pills. It still made him feel sick and scared inside, panicked.

"What do you say, Langley?" Belinda asked him, standing in front of him, bringing her hands up to hold her breasts. Her eyes looked terrible, glassy. And there was this unpleasant sound in her mouth as she spoke, as if she were terribly thirsty and her tongue was sticking to the roof of her mouth. Belinda smiled a ghastly smile and dropped her breasts, turning to her sister. "Langley has a big dick, you know," she said.

"Belinda!" Cordelia gasped.

Big El lurched around in his chair. "I don't care if you are crazier than a bedbug, Belinda Cecile, I'm going to wash your mouth out with soap."

Belinda only laughed, weaving out into the hall. Langley jumped up to follow her, just in time to see her back into a table, knocking over a vase of silk flowers. He caught the vase before it rolled off. "Come on, Belinda," he said, grabbing her arm and pulling her down the hall. She was laughing; she fell down. He bent over to pick her up, she grabbed at his crotch; he slapped her hand away and pulled her up; she tried to unzip his pants.

"You know you want me," she said, throwing herself against him.

"Belinda, *stop it,"* he said, pushing her away, and yet holding her enough to guide her down the hall.

Cordelia and Big El looked at each other in the den when they heard Belinda start to scream. Cordelia got up and went down the hall —and was soon back. "I'm going to call Jackie Andy," she said, dialing the phone with a shaky hand.

"What's happening?" Big El said.

"I don't know, Daddy," Cordelia said, bringing the phone to her ear and holding herself with the other. "Langley's saying something about pills." She closed her eyes. "I just don't know, Daddy." Her eyes opened. "Mr. Jackson Darenbrook's suite, please."

In their bedroom, Langley was sitting on the side of the bed, holding Belinda's wrists, making her sit up against the pillows. Belinda was screaming obscenities at him and he was yelling back at her that it was over, this couldn't go on, they were going to do something about the pills or the marriage was over—did she hear him? Did she hear him?

"I hate you!" she screamed, her head falling forward then as she started to sob.

By the time Jackson arrived Cordelia was crying and Langley was crying and Belinda was crying and nobody was making any sense. They were in the bedroom, and when Belinda tried to get up to go to the bathroom Langley practically got hysterical, yelling that they couldn't let her go in there by herself because she would take more pills. "We can't leave her alone—she'll do it!" he said as Belinda got one of her arms free and was hitting him, trying to get away.

And then Jackson yelled as loud as he possibly could, "Shut up! Everybody shut up!"

Silence.

They were all looking at him, stunned, with their tear-stained faces: Cordelia on the bed, Belinda and Langley at the door to the bathroom, and now Big El in the doorway of the hall.

"Okay," Jackson said quietly, holding his hands out. "Belinda and Langley, go in and use the bathroom. And then come out and sit down."

Langley and Belinda looked at each other. Langley let go of her, dug in his back pocket for a handkerchief and handed it to her. She pressed it to her mouth and walked into the bathroom, Langley following her. The door closed.

"She's taking some kind of pills, Langley said," Cordelia whispered. "He said something about him thinking that that's what's wrong with Baby B."

"Oh, God," Jackson sighed, covering his face with his hands a moment. Then he dropped them, looking over at Big El and then back at Cordelia. "It's okay," he whispered, steadying the air with his hands, "it's okay. It's gonna be okay."

In a few minutes Belinda came out with Langley, her face washed, and with a robe on. She looked at Cordelia, at her father, at Jackson, and then edged closer to Langley.

"We're scaring her," Langley said quietly, putting his arm around her. "Belinda honey," he said, kissing the side of her head and giving her a squeeze. "I don't want to scare you. I don't want to hurt you." He sighed, tears springing up behind his glasses again. "I love you, honey."

She turned in toward him, hiding her face in his shoulder. After a minute he led her over to Jackson and handed her over to him. And then Langley left the room, came back in and tossed down a big red book with several pieces of paper in it. It was a copy of *The Physicians' Drug Manual*. And then he walked over to the bookcase in the corner, took down a stack of books, reached inside and pulled out a small silver box and tossed it on the bed. And then he went to another shelf and extracted a vial of pills, and another from yet another place in the shelves. He went into the bathroom and then came out with a towel, which he dropped on the bed and opened to reveal some vials from the medicine cabinet. And then he went into the dressing room and came back with a jewelry box, opened it and poured a pile of pills on the bed. And then he went to Belinda's bedside table, opened the drawers and pulled out two more vials and tossed them on the bed. And then he picked up Belinda's pocketbook from the chair, opened it, reached in, took out a gold case and threw it on the bed. Cordelia picked this up and opened it. It was full of pills. Different colors, some capsules, some not, some round, some triangular.

And then Langley stood there, looking at his wife, who was clinging to Jackson—and who had, during all this, alternated between watching Langley and hiding her face in Jackson's shoulder—and said, "I'm not going to try to find all of them, Belinda. I can't keep them from you. I can only ask that you not take any more tonight so we can talk about what we're going to do. You and me."

Jackson then sat down in a chair and held Belinda in his lap—who simply cried on his shoulder—as Langley told and showed Cordelia, Jackson and Big El all that he knew. That Belinda had several overlapping prescriptions for Valium and Librium and Ativan from doctors here in New York, but that he knew she had sources he did not know about, because she had lots of loose pills, stockpiled without vials, which he had looked up and found in the book: Xanax, Dalmane, Restoril and Halcion.

When Langley was through, they were all silent, looking at Belinda, who did not even have the energy to cry anymore but was simply cowering in Jackson's arms. After a long while she finally said, hiding part of her face behind Jackson's upper arm, "I have to have Valium and Librium to sleep, to calm my nerves. I only take other pills sometimes." She looked like a child, an ill and frightened child in her father's lap. "I have to take them, Langley. The Valium and Librium.

The others I don't, I admit it. But you have to believe me, if I don't have my medication, I'll go crazy. Forever, I'll go crazy."

After several moments of silence Langley sorted through the pills, looking at the vials, tossed four of them to the side and then wrapped the rest of the pills up in the towel and handed it Cordelia. "Why don't you take these and you guys go on to bed or whatever you want to do? Belinda and I need to be alone."

After murmured expressions of concern, Cordelia and Big El both went over to kiss Belinda and then left the room. Belinda climbed out of Jackson's lap so he could stand up, and she held his hand while Jackson told them that he would stay over. And then he too left the room.

Jackson and Cordelia and Big El sat up, talking, and in a couple of hours, a little after two, heard Langley and Belinda in the kitchen, and Jackson went in to check on them. They were making hot chocolate, he reported back to Cordelia and Big El, shrugging and holding his hands up to indicate he wasn't sure what was going on either. Big El went to bed then, the emergency apparently over, and after Langley and Belinda went back into their bedroom Cordelia and Jackson moved into the kitchen to make themselves waffles from scratch.

Sitting there, at three-thirty in the morning, Jackson told his sister that he was in love with Cassy Cochran. Cordelia looked at him, her fork—with a piece of waffle on it, dripping syrup—stopped in midair. "Tell me about it," she finally said, her voice very gentle. And so he did. The whole thing. About his feelings and Cassy's feelings and about her divorce and her son and where she lived and being at the Plaza and everything. And then he talked about Barbara and about how he still missed her and how he loved her and how messed up the kids were and how he felt responsible, and he talked and he talked and talked and ended up telling his sister everything—everything—in a way he had not done since Barbara had died.

But this time he didn't have to have a nervous breakdown to do it.

Jackson and Cordelia were even laughing—a little gaga with fatigue at this point—when Langley came into the kitchen at eight-thirty and told them, while making a tray of breakfast for Belinda and himself, that the Petersons had decided to go to California. To Palm Springs.

"What?" Jackson finally said.

"Two of Belinda's friends went to the Betty Ford Center," Langley said, pouring orange juice. "One of them had a prescription drug problem too. Belinda isn't sure she wants to do it and I promised her I wouldn't make her." He opened the refrigerator door and put the orange juice back and turned around to look at them. "But she agreed to go out to Palm Springs if I would go. Just be in the vicinity and see how she felt about it. Look into it. It's just down in Rancho Mirage— and Belinda has friends in Palm Springs and we can play golf and things."

"Golf," Cordelia repeated, blinking.

"And I told her she could take her pills with her," Langley said, moving back to work on the tray. "The Valium and the Librium. She took some to sleep before, I watched her. She told me the exact amount it would take for her to sleep for five hours and she took it and it was exactly five hours." Langley looked at them over his shoulder. "I don't know what you think about that, about my letting her take pills out there with us, but I can't pretend I know anything about this." He turned all the way around. "But, from what she says and what I've read in that book, she's addicted—and I'm no doctor, and some of those pills were apparently prescribed for good reason."

"I think being near the Betty Ford Center is a good idea," Jackson said. "I think they could probably talk to her or something. She could go see someone, just to talk about it maybe."

"That's what I think," Langley said, leaning back against the counter. He pushed his glasses farther up his nose, turning his attention to Cordelia. "Cordie, I'm sorry, I hate to leave you in the lurch, but I'm resigning. This morning. Now, actually." He turned around, fussing with something on the tray. "I don't know how long I'll be away. Or what we'll be doing." He picked up the tray and turned around. "We can't go on like this—Belinda and I." He hesitated, looking as though he were in pain. "It's not just Belinda. I can't—and don't want, the whole shebang anyway. It's too much."

"You don't worry about a thing," Cordelia told him. "You just go on with Belinda and sort things out. We'll be fine." Then she looked over at Jackson, who was grinning at her, batting his eyelashes provocatively. "Oh, you," she said, rolling her eyes and dismissing him with a wave of her hand. "Ol' Mr. Snake Oil's a-comin' to call." She looked up at the ceiling. "Good Lord, preserve us from the bill of goods he'll be tryin' to sell to us now."

51

Gordon and Alexandra Plan Their Future

What a week. They were shooting now in a castle near Rye Harbor and Vanessa Winslow was sick with strep throat; Constantine was alternating between raging and crying and so Gordon feared he was back on cocaine; and while giving an afternoon cricket lesson, the company caterer accidentally whacked one of their supporting leads in the mouth and broke his front teeth. Meanwhile, every time the phone rang on Monday and Tuesday it seemed to be about some new bizarre turn of events at Darenbrook Communications: Jackson was fired, Langley was chairman and Cassy was president of DBS; hello, seventy-five percent of the miniseries had secretly been sold to Hargrave Studios; hello, Alexandra was going to *buy* DBS News—hello, Alexandra was *not* going to buy DBS News—hello, Alexandra *might* buy DBS News; hello, Alexandra was coming to London and so was Cassy.

Come Wednesday morning, while Alexandra was telling him the latest news over the phone—that Lord Hargrave had made her an offer to launch a global newscast—Hargrave called on the other line to make him a very generous offer to develop and run a whole new international special-series television division for him.

"That's good timing," Alexandra said, back on the other line, "because I think what Cassy wants to see you about is how you'd feel if DBS sold the rest of its interest in the miniseries to Hargrave Studios."

"She tell you that?" he asked her.

"No," Alexandra said, "but the notes from the board meeting said they discussed getting out of feature production."

Gordon laughed. "And how the hell do you know what's in the notes from the board meeting? Ethel's not one of your spies."

"No," Alexandra said, "but everybody in the copy center is."

Driving up to London that day, Gordon felt in good spirits. He thought the idea of him and Alexandra living in London was wonderful. Get out of New York and start over, the two of them, in a city strange to them both—and be so near to Christopher! It would be a whole new ball game with his son—a game that would be no game at all, really, but merely an extension of what Gordon had begun to build with him in recent weeks.

He loved that little boy. And Gordon felt he was really getting to know him, and that Christopher was getting a distinct knowledge of what his real father was like, and how deep and genuine his love for him was. And it was so strange, because he and Julie were getting along—albeit over the phone—but he knew it was because, well, like she said, "Fatherhood suits you, Gordon. It brings out in you all that is very right, and is very good." (Though, admittedly, his thought in response to this had been, *Then why didn't you stay with me in California, you bitch?*)

But what frankly surprised him was how easily—no, not easily— *coldly* Alexandra seemed to be contemplating leaving DBS. In fact she sounded almost angry on the subject. It was an extraordinary opportunity that Hargrave was offering her, and it had been a very rough tenure for Alexandra at DBS, but it was very out of character for Alexandra to say—in response to his question about what it would do to her emotionally to leave DBS—"It will make me feel guilty, like it always makes me feel guilty to leave anywhere. But they'll get the global newscast at a bargain, if they want it, so I'll hardly be leaving them high and dry. And at least in England I won't get shot every six months—and we can have some privacy. I think I'm really sick of there being no boundaries at home—the tabloids, the fans, even at West End, everybody's into my business and I hate it! I'm *sick* of it."

But she was exhausted and, as she said, was in no shape to make a final decision until she had thoroughly discussed it with him. ("So absolutely no hints to Cassy that I have an offer, okay?" Alexandra said. "We want her just to go home today—so we can think this through together.") She had not gotten to sleep, she told him, until near six, and Will had scheduled four interviews for her to do at the BBC and ITN, the first of which was at one. After she finished the interviews, they agreed, she would go back to the Ritz and take a nap and then would meet him at the Groucho Club for dinner at eight. He'd drop her off at the studio; she'd come back to the Dorchester after her newscast; tomorrow she'd have her things brought over to the Dorchester; after her newscast early Saturday morning they'd drive out to an inn in Kent and stay the weekend; and then Alexandra would fly back to the States Sunday evening.

The only damper on things was how guilty Gordon felt about Betty. After all of the time they had spent together, to suddenly leave her with Christopher so he could be with Alexandra seemed slightly awful. And yet Betty had insisted she'd rather be with Mrs. Twickem and Christopher than anything else.

The real reason why he felt so guilty, the real problem, Gordon knew, was that Betty was in love with him and he had no right to keep ignoring it. But thank God he had not slept with her! At least he had not done that. (And now that Alexandra was here in England, he thanked God he had not slept with anyone else, either.) He enjoyed Betty's company enormously and she was just terrific with Christopher, but while he knew she was having the time of her life, that she was learning so much on this project and was making a very good amount of money, he knew in his heart that he should hire a new assistant, promote Betty to an assistant producer and, back in London, ship her over to the May Fair and out of his daily life. This wasn't good for her; it wasn't fair of him to continue this arrangement—this happy domestic play in which they were engaged—when she could only get hurt in the end.

Gordon met Cassy in the restaurant of the Connaught Hotel and had a friendly, cheerful late luncheon, during which he assured her that it made no difference to him if DBS sold their remaining interest in *Love Across the Atlantic* to Hargrave Studios or not. And then they gossiped about what was going on back at West End, and then worked their way to the subject of Alexandra. Gordon said he wanted to apologize again for his behavior in New York and to say that Cassy had been right and he had been wrong—that he and Alexandra were going to be just fine, and it had just been the strain and stress and long hours and travel that had been getting both of them down. And then he told her about their weekend plans ("Sleep, sex and maybe Sissinghurst Cas-

GORDON AND ALEXANDRA PLAN THEIR FUTURE

tle," he said, laughing), which she said she thought sounded wonderful.

Cassy had a little time to kill before leaving for the airport, and Gordon had time too, so he walked her over to some shops she had passed on her way back from Lord Hargrave's this morning. He helped her pick out presents for her son, Henry (bookends), Chi Chi (a small blue perfume bottle covered in silver latticework) and for some unidentified friend (a tweed cap).

Then he had a short and very pleasant meeting with Lord Hargrave and went on to the Dorchester to make some phone calls and do some work. At seven-thirty he took a cab over to Dean Street, to the Groucho Club, a private club that catered to a mostly publishing and TV crowd, and in which Gordon had always maintained an out-of-town membership. It was a nice place to hang out, particularly since there always seemed to be someone there he knew and liked enormously. (As opposed to hotels and restaurants, where there always seemed to be someone he knew and wished to avoid—which he supposed was the purpose of a private club in the first place, and certainly the reason why London had so many of them.)

He waited for Alexandra in the front room, where the bar was, and sure enough, just after Alexandra came in, someone he knew and liked enormously was going out. He introduced Alexandra to Marianne Velmans, a book publisher he had met through a mutual friend, and who, having a terrific young son of her own, had been invaluable in suggesting things he could do with Christopher in London over the summer. Marianne had just come downstairs from a book publishing party in the Soho Room and introduced to them a charming woman named Susan Watt, the editor-in-chief of a competing house, who had, Marianne told Gordon, no less than four sons of her own—so if Gordon was looking for a true expert on the subject of raising wonderful boys, then he was to look no further. And so when Gordon said that it looked as though he would be spending a great deal of time in London over the next few years, maybe even live there (he winked at Alexandra), Susan told him a little a bit about the kind of educational advantages London had to offer, in between her introductions to the people who kept stopping by to say hello to her (Mary Loring, Barbara Boote, Nick Webb, hello, hello, hello).

It wasn't until Marianne and Susan said good night and he and Alexandra were seated at a table in the back dining room that Gordon saw how unwell Alexandra looked. To anyone else she would look fine —she was, after all, an expert at pulling her appearance together—but to Gordon, who knew her body very well, she did not. Her eyes seemed a little puffy; under the makeup he knew there were circles; and she was very thin—thinner than he had ever seen her.

Of course, she had nearly been shot and killed recently, to say nothing of being on the road for weeks, to say nothing of having very little sleep for several nights running, to say nothing of a lot of corporate chaos and, now, a time of personal decision with enormous ramifications.

He was touched by her efforts to be cheerful through dinner, but he realized that this morning's enthusiasm for moving to Hargrave World Communications had turned into something a little more scary to her. Not that she admitted this. In fact she talked about where she would like for them to get a flat in the city, and where she hoped they might look for a house in the country, as if her decision were already final. They discussed Lord Hargrave's offer to him, and his offer to her, and about how excited and supportive Alexandra's agent, John Mohrbacher, was about the whole idea. And then, over coffee, she really caught him by surprise.

Alexandra reached over to hold his hand and said, "If I do this, if I sign for ten years, then I'll be settled here, and we could have a child. Maybe two children. What do you think?"

He was so stunned, for a moment he didn't say anything. But then he did. "I love you," he said, and leaned over to kiss her, not caring who watched. But, inside, he felt scared and wasn't sure why.

"You do want children, don't you?" she asked him, looking into his eyes. "You've always wanted children, haven't you?"

"Have you?" he asked her.

She nodded.

He smiled. "Me too. And I hope they look like you. Are like you."

She nodded, her eyes tearing a little.

He should be happy, he knew that. And he was—in a way.

So why, while driving Alexandra to the BINS studio, he felt this sick pit of anxiety in his stomach he wasn't sure. He kissed her for a long time before letting her out of the car, but as he watched her go into the building he realized he was terrified of the whole thing—of London, of getting married, of Alexandra! There was something—was it him? Or was it her? But there was something, something wrong. Something scary about this whole thing. Or maybe Alexandra was being scary. There was something so . . . reckless about her, about how she was handling this—more like a drunken sailor on leave than like the cool, levelheaded Alexandra who normally wished to examine options for*ever* before opting for one.

He went back to the Dorchester and reminded the desk that there would be two staying in his suite now, went upstairs, drank two scotches in rapid succession and went to bed, setting his alarm for four so he would be awake when Alexandra came home from the studio. He slept, the alarm went off and he was awake when she let herself in.

"Hi," he said, sitting up in bed, naked under the covers, praying that sex might make things feel right again—make this awful anxiety in the air go away.

"Hi," she said softly, coming over to the bed. She bent over and kissed him, lightly, lingering for a moment though, and then she sat down on the edge of the bed, putting her work bag down on the floor.

"How'd it go?" he asked her, reaching for her hand.

"Good, good," she said, nodding, "it was fine. Dr. Kessler did something to match the studio commands with the broadcast signal, so they were coordinated on our end. It made it easier."

"That's great," he said, not knowing what she was talking about because he was not listening. She did not look good. She looked utterly beaten and drained, and was just sitting there now, her hand limp in his, looking down at the floor. "Why don't you take a hot bath to relax?" he said. "I'll bring you a glass of wine."

She nodded, murmuring, "That would be nice," but then, a moment later, she was holding her face in her hands.

"What is it, Lexy?" he said, trying to put his arms around her. Her whole body was shaking. "Are you sick?"

She backed away slightly, raising her head to look at him. "No, it's not that."

But she did look sick. He had never seen her like this.

"I can't marry you, Gordon," she said then.

For one crazy instant he wondered if Alexandra had cancer or something. He didn't know why he had that thought, but he did and chased it away. "Why?" he heard himself say then, wondering if the subject of this conversation was going to register, or if he was going to continue to feel as weirdly detached from it as he did now.

"Because," she said, sighing, looking down into her lap. "Because I—" She sucked in her breath suddenly, covering her mouth, and then started to cry, holding her face in her hands.

He reached over and pulled her to him, to hold her. "Lexy, what is it? What's wrong?"

"I can't tell you, I can't tell you," she said, holding on to him.

"Yes, you can. What is it? What's the matter?"

"I just can't go through with it," she said. "Not when I'm not sure it can work. I should at least think it will work. I should at least think so, Gordon."

He held her, stroking her hair. "You're exhausted, Alexandra—"

"Because it's not just you anymore," she said suddenly, pulling back to look at him, wiping her eyes with the back of her wrist. "It's Christopher too. Even if we didn't have children—and I know you want children—but even if we didn't have children, you already have Christopher and you can't go into another marriage that you're not sure's going to work—"

"Christopher?" he said. "Christopher lives with Julie."

"Christopher is your son," Alexandra said. "And you want to be a part of his life—"

"But not with you, is that it?" he said. "You mean if we lived in New York and I never saw Christopher, everything would be fine? Is that what you're telling me?"

"No," she said, looking miserable. "I mean if you want to be a real part of your son's life you can't afford another marriage like your first one—you can't repeat the same mistake."

"Mistake?" he said.

"It's true," she said. "But it's not you, Gordon—it's me. I'm the one who's so mixed up—I'm the one who's unstable—unstable for you. And I don't think I'm good for you—I know I wouldn't be a good wife for you. I couldn't be there for you the way you'd want me to be."

He was looking at her. "There's somebody else."

"No," she said, shaking her head.

Silence.

"I don't believe you," he told her.

Her eyes were searching his. "Can you believe me," she whispered, tears flooding back into her eyes, "if I told you it's because I know I'll make you unhappy—even more unhappy than you already are?"

"I haven't been—" He stopped, dropping his eyes. It was true. He had been unhappy. And the reasons why would very likely continue.

Alexandra screwed her eyes shut, tears spilling down. "We tried, Gordon." She opened her eyes, swallowing. "You've had one woman use you already. I don't think Julie meant to do it—but she did. She was confused about her life and she used you to give direction to it— by marrying you, and then by leaving you. And I'm scared I'd do the exact same thing." She lowered her eyes, sighing. "But, unlike Julie, I know how confused I am in my life right now. And there's no excuse for me to go ahead—not with someone I genuinely care about, genu- inely love—when I know, I *know,* Gordon, that there's no reason to think I'd be good for you."

She paused, raising her head to look at him. "Not when you've changed so much—not when you finally have an idea of what you want, what you've always really wanted." She touched his cheek, clos- ing her eyes, a tear spilling down. "And it's not something I can give you." She opened her eyes, swallowed, sniffed and tried to smile. "And you do know—you finally really do know, don't you, Gordie? Don't you?" And then she threw her arms around him, hugging him, crying.

They sat there like that for a few minutes, with Alexandra crying and Gordon sitting there, numb, holding her, looking at the wall. And then she sat up, kissed him on the cheek, grabbed her bag and walked to the door. She paused and he looked over. "I'm sorry," she whis- pered. "I love you, Gordie, and I'm sorry to hurt you. And to hurt me."

And then she was gone.

He heard this. He heard this. He heard this last part and it was starting to register. Alexandra was leaving him.

He wasn't going to marry Alexandra.

He wasn't going to marry Alexandra.

He wasn't going to be talking to Lexy anymore.

David's kid sister.

The blue-eyed girl from Kansas.

Alexandra.

Gordon closed his eyes and opened his mouth, wide. And he let it hit.

52

Jessica Is a Very Good Friend

Friday morning, at a quarter to nine, Jessica was doing sit-ups in the bedroom, watching Joan Lunden, when she thought she heard something out in the living room. "Mrs. Roberts?" she called on her way down.

Mrs. Roberts was Alexandra's housekeeper, who still came by a couple days a week to check on things. Mrs. Roberts was very nice but was always saying things to Jessica like, "Alexandra likes her things neat and tidy. Isn't it interesting how different the two of you are."

"It's me," said a voice.

Jessica stopped her sit-ups and looked around at the door. It was Alexandra.

The last time Jessica had talked to Alexandra had been on Wednesday, at which time Alexandra had stunned her with the news that she and Gordon were probably going to take jobs with Lord Hargrave in London. Now normally, in the old days, Jessica would have reacted to the news—that of a coworker quitting—in one of three ways.

For example, there had been the time Maria, the coffee cart lady at Group K Productions, had announced she had a new job at Hughes Aircraft. Jessica's first option as a reaction: drink herself into some greater catastrophe.

(It was very helpful, this if-somebody-is-scaring-me-I'll-just-do-my-self-in-and-take-my-mind-off-it philosophy, because people never understood why the absence of someone like Maria the Coffee Cart Lady was so devastating to Jessica. However, they always did understand Jessica sobbing about having done something awful while drunk. They just didn't understand that Jessica's best relationships were with people she didn't know well enough to drag into the ongoing mess of her life.)

Her second option: get everybody as upset as she was.

("The sky is falling, the sky is falling!" was always the main message Jessica would try to get across, and Maria the Coffee Cart Lady leaving would be no exception as Jessica would take to the halls, spreading the word. And if she did not see the right spark of panic in people's eyes after she told them the news, then Jessica would simply keep adding irrelevant details until she hit some kind of a nerve. ["Oh, Jessica—I know he always stares at women, but you don't think he might have done something to poor Maria, do you? And you think he was the last person to see her before she quit? *Now that I think of it, I once heard him offer to fix the wheel on her wagon.*"] And as soon as pandemonium broke out, then Jessica would feel enormously better.)

And the third option: amputation. Cut the limb on the spot. If it's going, it's going now.

("Maria's leaving." "Oh, that's too bad—Maria who?" Maria would be *dead,* gone forever, within minutes. And if somehow Maria managed to track Jessica down to say good-bye, Jessica would say, "Goodbye, good luck to you," thinking about how much she hated Maria for the countless imaginary reasons from the list she always used against anyone who left. Disloyal—not one of us—probably a liar and a cheat. . . .)

In the case of Maria the Coffee Cart Lady leaving Group K, Jessica's response had actually been all three. But Alexandra was not Maria the Coffee Cart Lady. Alexandra was the first close friend Jessica had had in years outside of Denny, and the thought of having made such a friend only to lose her so quickly was—or at least felt—heartbreaking.

And drinking was no longer an option, and so Jessica had hung up the phone after her conversation with Alexandra, having only the other two options to choose from. But there had been no point in running around crying, "The sky is falling, the sky is falling!" because, once word got out that Alexandra Waring was leaving DBS, the sky really was going to fall in, and on a whole lot of people. And the last option, amputation—to cut Alexandra dead—while appealing in many regards, just didn't seem possible. She owed Alexandra far too much; she loved Alexandra too much too.

And so Jessica hadn't reacted at all the way she used to react to such news. She had merely picked up the phone, called Alexandra back and urged her to take the time to really think things through. And then Jessica had wrestled with herself for the rest of the day about whether or not to confide the information to anyone at DBS, but Langley wasn't in, Cassy was on her way back from London and Jackson had his sister and father with him, and so she didn't. Besides, as she had kept reminding herself, it was not her news to share.

Finally, late that night, Jessica had called Lisa Connors. And she had a very, very long talk with Lisa Connors about Alexandra. And Jessica had been surprised—no, shocked—by what she finally got Lisa to tell her. And as Lisa told her more about what she thought might be the problem with Alexandra, why she might want to leave DBS, Jessica had started to cry, silently, thanking God that Alexandra had never told her any of this because, if she had, Jessica didn't think she would have gotten as close to her as she had, and certainly wouldn't have stayed with Alexandra in her apartment—and certainly then, never would have stopped drinking either.

So it had worked out for the best.

But it just seemed so unbelievable.

"Is she in her early forties, very attractive, blond?" Lisa had said.

"Yeah," Jessica had said.

"Very bright, warm, funny?"

"Yeah," Jessica had said.

"And she's getting divorced?"

"Yeah," Jessica had said weakly.

"Then that's her," Lisa said. "That's who it must be."

But then, after a while, it didn't seem so unbelievable.

Sitting here, looking at Alexandra standing in the doorway, how very terrible she looked, it seemed more than believable, and for the first time in her life Jessica had no idea what to say.

Alexandra apparently didn't either, because she mumbled something about a glass of water and left.

Feeling a little numb, Jessica turned back around and watched Joan Lunden wrap her interview, thinking that she had to get up and do something, say something. That at least she had to go in and talk to Alexandra. At least she had to act like she hadn't seen her in weeks and was glad to see her. At least she should ask her what she was doing home and how long she would be here. At least she should offer to leave. At least she should pretend like she was a living, breathing human being and not a shell-shocked snoop who had forced her way into her friend's private business and now didn't know what to do with what she had found out. And so Jessica got up, put on her robe (she was in a T-shirt commemorating the 30th Anniversary of The Book Mark in Tucson) and went down the hall.

Alexandra was sitting there with her head down on the kitchen table.

Jessica stood in the doorway a moment, watching her. And then she walked over and gently placed her hand on Alexandra's back. "I'm glad you came home."

Silence.

"You okay?" Jessica asked her.

After a long moment, without moving, Alexandra said, "You know, don't you? Lisa told you."

Jessica hesitated and then said, "Yes. I made her. I was worried about you."

Pause. "And did you figure out who it was?"

"Yes," Jessica said. A moment later, "It's no big deal."

In a moment she felt Alexandra's back move under her hand. She was laughing—sort of. "It's no big deal," Alexandra repeated. Then she sighed, her back stopping. "I've failed, you know," she said, head still down on the table. "I can't get it right no matter what I do—no matter who it is." Then suddenly she threw herself back up in her chair, looking up at Jessica. "Cassy doesn't even know, you know. She doesn't even know!" The last was said in anger, tears rising. Alexandra turned back to the table, hitting it with her hand, looking away. "God, it's pathetic. I'm pathetic."

"No," Jessica said quietly, sitting down, "that's one thing you're not."

Alexandra turned toward her, eyes miserable. "She and Jackson have been having an affair—for weeks." She smiled, tears spilling down her face. "She's in love with him." She shrugged. "Isn't that great? Isn't that how it's supposed to be? If I really cared about her, wouldn't I feel happy for her—happy she has what she wants, happy that the whole wide world will be so damn happy for her? Oh, God," she added, plunking her elbow on the table and holding her face in her hand.

Jessica watched her. "If I were you, I'd hate her. I'd hate him too."

Alexandra laughed, still crying, still holding her face in her hand. "I think I hate everybody."

"I don't blame you," Jessica said.

"Jessica," she said a moment later, her face still in her hand, "I have worked so hard—so very hard all my life—" She paused, catching her breath. "So why is it I can't make my life work? I never did, I never could. And now I'm beginning to think I'm never going to have anything, anything with anyone else, ever."

"Well," Jessica said, shrugging, "with a hundred percent of the population to choose from, I think your chances are better than most myself."

Alexandra dropped her hand to the table and looked at her. "Well that's looking on the bright side, isn't it?"

"The bright side is," Jessica told her, "the world isn't over yet, Waring. And maybe there's something a whole lot better in store for you." She leaned forward. "Ever think of that, Alexandra Eyes—Miss Smarty Pants? That maybe it would have been an absolute disaster?"

"Try either one of them," Alexandra said, reaching for a paper napkin.

After a moment Jessica said, "So the wedding's off?"

Alexandra nodded, wiping her eyes and then blowing her nose.

"You're not doing something foolish, like trying to punish yourself, are you?" Jessica asked her. "You wouldn't be the first person to marry her second choice."

She sighed, looking at Jessica. "I was ready to walk out on him before I even married him."

Jessica started to laugh. She couldn't help it.

"I'm glad you think this is so funny," Alexandra said, smiling a little, wiping her eyes again.

"I don't," Jessica said. "It's just that you're so—so *sneaky*, I can't get over it. You have all these different lives going." She plunked her arms on the table. "You are so *interesting,* Alexandra, I have to tell you that. I really find it quite wonderful to have such a complicated friend."

Alexandra rolled her eyes, lowering her hand to the table. "But what am I going to do?"

"You're going to get some sleep and go to work tonight and postpone all major decisions until you get your head straight." Jessica smiled. "I don't want to be unkind, Alexandra Eyes, but I think maybe you're really sort of a mess."

Jessica swung into West End at eleven o'clock and went straight up to Cassy's office. "Knock, knock," she said, walking in.

Cassy held one finger up, talking into the phone. Then, listening into it, she waved Jessica down into a chair, talked for a minute more and then got off. "Hi, how are you?"

"Okay," Jessica said. "But my friend Alexandra's not so hot. I just came from home. She's sleeping and coming in this afternoon."

Cassy nodded, frowning, taking her glasses off and tossing them down on the desk. "I heard."

"Did you hear about her and Gordon?"

Cassy nodded.

"See, that's what I had to talk to you about," Jessica said. "I can see by your expression what Alexandra means."

"By my expression?" Cassy said.

"About how much you wanted her to marry Gordon and how upset you'd be that it didn't work out."

Cassy winced. "That's not true, Jessica."

"But that's how she feels," Jessica said. "You know how she is. And I think she feels—irrationally, mind you—that she's let you down and DBS down by not making it work."

"That is completely wrong," Cassy said, enunciating every word.

"Still," Jessica said, "that's how she feels."

"Then I'll talk to her," Cassy said.

"Well," Jessica said, sighing, "that brings me to something else." She looked at Cassy, closing one eye. "Now how do I say this tactfully?"

Cassy gestured with her hand, indicating that she didn't know.

"Look," Jessica said, sitting forward, "I'm very discreet—so please don't freak when I tell you that I know about you and Jackson."

Cassy's face began to rapidly gain color.

"Cassy—excuse me," Chi Chi said at the door. "I'm sorry, but Mr. Hadley's finally here."

"Not yet," Cassy told her, holding her hand up. "I'll be out in a minute." She returned her attention to Jessica. "Okay," she said, "so you know about me and Jackson."

"Right," Jessica said. "And I just wanted to remind you—not that you don't already know it—about how difficult it can be for someone who's just broken up with somebody else to be around couples who're in love." She paused. "Particularly when it's your best friend. Somehow it makes it worse. Do you know what I mean?"

"Yes," Cassy said.

"And so I was hoping that maybe you might make yourself scarce this afternoon," Jessica said. "It's just that she's really down on herself, Cassy, and until she gets some proper sleep there's not going to be any way of convincing her that you're not deeply disappointed in her."

Cassy studied her carefully for several moments. And then she said, very softly, "Is there anything I should know, Jessica?"

"No," Jessica said, shaking her head. "Really. There isn't."

Cassy nodded slightly. And then she smiled, gently, eyes looking a little sad. "You're a very good friend," she said.

"I'm a very good friend," Jessica said.

53

West End

She stood there for several seconds before anyone noticed her.

"Alexandra!" Shelley Berns cried, prompting everyone in the newsroom to stop working and look.

"Hi, you guys," she said, smiling.

"Alexandra!" Kyle said, running over and picking her up and swinging her around, making her laugh. "Live and in person, she's home!"

He set her down and she said, "Yes, I'm home," stretching up to kiss him on the cheek. Then she turned to kiss Dan Shelstein hello, and Shelley, and Jimmy Hallerton, and then Gary Plains, and then Helen Kai Lu came in, Dick Gross and Dash and Chester and Paul Levitz and Herb, and Bozzy Gould came running in from the studio with Lilly Kertz, and word was traveling fast because Clancy Stevens came in and Hex came in and Kelly Harris and Dr. Kessler and then the whole Nerd Brigade came piling in through the door, and then Cleo came in and said—because Alexandra was crying now and her mascara was running—"I'm glad to see you still need me," and Brooks Bayerson Ames and John Knox Norwood appeared, and Becky and Marc Ogakani and Oscar and Parky came in and then Kate Benedict was yelling, "Well, who works for her anyway? Aren't I allowed to say hello?" and Alexandra gave her a hug too, and then stepped back and felt someone touching her arm, and it was Will, asking her if she had gotten any sleep.

She really burst into tears then, and buried her face in Will's shoulder, and he held her, while everyone excitedly chattered away about how hard the schedule had been on Alexandra, how it was time for her to be home, how much they missed her, and oh, Alexandra—pat, pat, pat went the hands on her back, and "Oh, there, there," went the consoling voices, in between bursts of laughter and cross-conversations. And Alexandra pulled herself together, using the tissues Kate held out to her, trying to listen as everybody talked to her at once— smiling, laughing, sniffing and saying, "Uh-huh, uh-huh, uh-huh"— while the phones were ringing like mad around them.

"Well, well, look at what the cat dragged in," Jessica said, standing in the doorway to the studio, hand on her hip, dressed in red and in full makeup.

"Hi, Alexandra," Denny said, coming over to kiss her hello.

"Hi, Alexandra," Alicia said, coming over too.

"Not that I don't love you," Jessica said, waltzing in, "but I have a show to do and my crew seems to have walked off the job."

"We're on our way," Dick said. "Come on, guys—Bozzy, Lil, let's get everybody back in the studio."

"Hey, so listen," Jessica said, tapping her finger on Alexandra's shoulder, "why don't you let Cleo fix you up and then come out into the studio?" She smiled at her. "It's coffee party day, so you can talk to the crew and boost my ratings at the same time. Whaddayasay?"

"Oh, no," Alexandra said, shaking her head. "I can't. I've got to go upstairs and see Jackson."

"He's gone until Monday," Jessica said. "He had to go to California." •

"Well, I have to see Cassy," Alexandra said.

"She had to go with Jackson," Kyle said. "Langley's out there and they're having some sort of meeting."

"They'll be back Monday," Kate said.

"So relax," Jessica said. "Enjoy yourself."

Alexandra looked at her.

"Come on, Waring," Jessica said, tugging on her hand, "all the grownups are gone." Then her eyes widened and she whispered, loudly, so all could hear, "Open house at Jessica's."

"Miss Waring—hello!" Mr. Graham said, coming in the door behind Alice Moffat. "They told me you were here, and here you are!"

"Mr. Graham," Alexandra said, kissing him on the cheek and holding his hand. "Hi, Miss Moffat," she said, smiling at her.

"Hey, Mr. Graham," Jessica said, nudging him, "will you come on my show today? It's coffee party day and Alexandra says she won't come on unless you will."

"Oh, well," Mr. Graham said, releasing Alexandra's hand and touching his bow tie, "if Miss Waring would like me to. Though I'm afraid I have not made an appearance on a television program since 'Book Beat.' "

"You wrote a book?" Kyle asked him.

"No," Mr. Graham said.

"Perfect credentials for today's show," Jessica said. She turned to Kate. "Have you written a book?"

"No," Kate said.

"Good, then we have another guest, Denny. Alexandra, Jr.'s coming on the show too," Jessica said, patting her on the arm, making her way through the crowd. "What about you, Kyle?"

"What about me?" Kyle said.

"Got another guest over here, Denny," Jessica said. "Kyle hasn't written a book either."

"I haven't written a book," Dash said, raising his hand.

"Okay—you're on," Jessica said.

"Oh, no," Helen Kai Lu said, disappointed, "I have. I've written lots of books."

"That's okay," Jessica said, "we'll rearrange your name a little— nobody'll recognize you. Denny," she called, snapping her fingers, "over here. Lu Kai Helen here's gonna be on the show."

"Cleo," Denny said. "Can you make these guys up now? Fast?"

"Cleo's coming on the show too," Jessica said.

"I am?" Cleo said. She turned to Alicia. "Is she serious?"

"Oh, yes," Alicia assured her.

"Bozzy," Jessica directed, "get out the hand-held camera. I think we're going to come in here and visit everybody while they're working."

"Oh, no," Denny said, bringing his hands up to hold his head, "here she goes."

"You can come film me!" Hex called to Jessica, waving as he went out the door.

"Me too," Shelley called, following Hex. "Satellite room. You'll make my mom very happy."

"And I coot appeayah on your show, I tink," Dr. Kessler said to Jessica, holding a finger in the air.

"I tink so too, Doc," Jessica said, turning to call, "Organize this, Denny—we don't have much time. And don't look so smug, Mr. Director," she said, poking Dick in the stomach. "Because we're coming to visit you in the control room. So comb your hair for a change. Graphics, graphics!" she yelled.

"Here," Becky said.

"We need a banner to super over the opening," Jessica told her.

"That says . . . ?" Becky asked her, grabbing a pen and piece of paper.

" 'The DBS Across the Studio Floor Tour,' " Jessica said, "with Alexandra Waring and DBS News."

Everybody howled.

"She's serious, everybody!" Denny announced, clapping his hands.

"So let's look alive! If you have anything in your work area to hide, better hide it now."

"Kate," Alexandra said, pulling her to the side. "Listen, I need to fax a note to Lord Hargrave. Can we do that? Do we have time before the show?"

"Sure," Kate said. "It'll take two seconds." She opened the drawer in the desk where they were standing and took out a piece of paper.

Alexandra glanced over at the clocks. "It's after nine over there. Can we fax it somewhere and have it delivered to him wherever he is this weekend?"

"I'll send it through the BINS newsroom," she said, handing Alexandra a pen. "They'll know where he is."

"Good," Alexandra said, leaning over to write. "Oh," she added, looking up at her, "and make sure Chi Chi and everyone up there comes down to be on this crazy show if they want. And Ethel, Randy and Claire, and Adele too, don't forget them. And make sure to tell Emma, the receptionist. She's got more pizazz than all of us."

Kate laughed. "Okay."

"But I need some sort of job title," Jessica was saying to Mr. Graham. "I can't just say you were on 'Book Beat' in 1965."

Alexandra looked over. "Vice-President, Research and Development, DBS News," she said.

Mr. Graham's mouth parted, and then a smile started to form. "Did we—?"

"Yes," Alexandra said, eyes sparkling. "It's all approved. Cassy gave the okay in London."

"Oh, Mr. Graham!" Miss Moffat said.

"And you're assistant vice-president, Miss Moffat," Alexandra said.

"Oh, Mr. Graham!" Miss Moffat said.

" 'Book Beat' my ass," Jessica said, taking Mr. Graham and Miss Moffat by the arm and leading them away. "Come on, you two— there's a couple of former lives I think we should discuss before we go on the air."

"Excuse me," Will yelled across the newsroom.

People turned.

"KTS in Dallas is on the line. They want to know what the story is —if we're coming Monday or what."

Alexandra was writing.

"Alexandra?" Kyle said, turning to her.

She looked up. "Monday? Sure, I'll be there."

"Oscar—Parky, Marc?" Kyle said, looking at each of them.

"We'll be there," Oscar said, the other two murmuring their assents as well.

"What about you, Will?" Kyle called across the newsroom. "Can you recharge your batteries by Sunday night?"

"I can even find Alexandra's bodyguards we ditched in Kansas City," Will said.

"Okay, then," Kyle said, holding his hands up, "the tour's back on, starting Monday."

"Denny!" Jessica said from the door into the studio. "We have a crisis—DBS News Research and Development doesn't drink coffee. They only drink tea."

Alexandra finished her note. It said:

Dear Lord Hargrave,
I'm afraid my sentimental American heart caught up with me this
morning and I decided I had no choice but to return home. I can't tell
you how much your generous offer of hospitality meant to me—and
will mean to me always. I can, however, quite readily tell you how
honored I felt, and that I will never, ever forget your many
kindnesses.

With deepest gratitude and admiration,
Alexandra Waring

"That's really nice," Kate said, reading over her shoulder.

Alexandra smiled, straightened up and handed it to her. "Glad you like it," she said.

54
_____

Conclusion

On Sunday night, as the Darenbrook Communications plane was landing at La Guardia Airport, Alexandra's plane to Dallas was taxiing to
another runway for takeoff.

She went back out on the DBS Across America tour, to ever increasing acclaim, and Alexandra's suggestion that the tour be extended
another month, through September, was approved. By the time she
returned to West End in October she had anchored the news from
sixty-three cities in eighty-eight days, consolidated her ratings for the
fall, and ensured her place as one of the most widely admired women
in the United States.

But many would say, back at West End, that Alexandra had changed
since starting the tour, although no one seemed very sure about what
that change had been. She was as warm and energetic and dynamic as
ever, but still, people sensed that something was missing from her old
self. The something had to do with her eyes taking on that special
sparkle only when she was on camera now. Some said it was the
shootings that had done it, others said it was her breakup with Gordon
Strenn. It was difficult to say since Alexandra never spoke of the
shootings, was seen to resume dating, quickly, and never gave the
slightest indication that any part of her life was anything less than
absolutely terrific.

In Palm Springs, California, under a doctor's supervision, Belinda
Darenbrook Peterson began a graduated withdrawal from Valium and
Librium, and in September entered the Betty Ford Center in Rancho
Mirage. Langley joined a counseling program for the families of people
with addiction problems and also began individual therapy, suspecting
—rightfully—that he needed to focus on some of his own problems
and not just on Belinda's.

The resulting changes in the Petersons were rather startling. And while it was tremendously exciting for them to know that these changes—like *wanting* to change, wanting to work on themselves, wanting to recommit to each other and work on their marriage— would ensure that things need never go back to the way they had been, it was a little unsettling to find, for example, that their "new" selves argued with each other as their "old" selves never had.

"Sometimes I feel like I don't even know you anymore!" Langley said to Belinda one night, after they had returned to New York and Belinda said over her dead body would she attend Pooh Tillington Hubin's dinner party—the party Langley had just said he would love to take to her to. "Well, thank God you don't feel like you know me anymore," Belinda said, "because the woman you used to know who liked Pooh's dinner parties was on drugs! And what are you on, that all of a sudden after eighteen years you *want* to go to a dinner party?" "Well, things are different now," Langley said. "Well Pooh's no different," Belinda said, "she's awful."

And then the Petersons started laughing, something else they seemed to be doing a lot of recently—as well as going for walks, holding hands, arguing, making up, arguing, laughing and talking, talking, talking. And arguing. And getting to know each other again. They sold the house in Greenwich and bought a lovely place just outside Litchfield, Connecticut, as a weekend retreat.

The board of directors of Darenbrook Communications approved a reorganization and restructuring of the corporation and Langley rejoined Darenbrook Communications as Co-Chairman, Electronics & Broadcasting Divisions, setting off a string of promotions down the DBS line.

Cassy Cochran had of course already been named president of DBS, and the network was doing very well under her. By the time the Big Three networks recovered from the 1988 writers' strike and premiered their fall seasons in November, "DBS News America Tonight with Alexandra Waring" and "The Jessica Wright Show" had won a following they would never lose. DBS had also won itself 178 affiliates.

Kyle McFarland was promoted to Executive Producer of "DBS News America Tonight," Will Rafferty to Senior Producer, and Kate Benedict to Alexandra's special assistant in the newsroom. New anchors and crew were hired as the newscast expanded to seven nights a week; a newsmagazine was in the works, and a regional documentary series on America was about to go into production.

Mr. Graham and Miss Moffat were making very good money for DBS News, and rumors of romance between them hadn't hurt their careers.

Under the reorganization, Alexandra gladly relinquished her administrative involvement to concentrate on raising the journalistic standards of the network. Every Thursday night just after her newscast she headed for the airport, flying out to a different affiliate each week, where she worked the following day and anchored the Friday night newscast. Her personal attention seemed to work wonders in the affiliate newsrooms and the results did not go unnoticed. When industry prize time rolled around, DBS News won a special citation "for depicting the rich diversity of character, culture and way of life within the United States, and promoting greater understanding of the nation as a single entity bound by the Constitution."

One of the more surprising outcomes of the reorganization was the blossoming friendship between Alexandra and Langley Peterson. She frequently dropped into his office for a breather and a chat, and while some might have viewed it as politicking on Alexandra's part, Langley knew that it was not.

"I think," Alexandra said one afternoon, "it may have something to do with the fact that you seem to be the only person in America who respects my privacy."

He laughed, but Alexandra didn't. And Langley's heart went out to her because he knew what a rough time she had been going through. The tabloids were having a heyday at her expense, splashing across their pages pictures of Gordon Strenn and Betty Cannondale, using the fact that they were dating as proof that Gordon had been cheating on Alexandra while filming *Love Across the Atlantic* and that had been the reason behind their breakup. A lot of people at West End, Langley knew, thought the story was true—even Adele, who claimed that any fool could have seen that Betty had been in love with her boss since the day she arrived.

Langley was glad they'd sold the miniseries to Hargrave Studios as quickly as they had.

"I do mind my own business," Langley said to Alexandra, "but there is just one thing I'd like to say to you—and then I promise I'll never bring it up again."

Her eyebrows went up in question.

"Someone special will come along, Alexandra," Langley told her. "You're young, and you have time. And while you're going through this, know that it's just something you have to go through to get to what's coming—who's coming." He smiled. "I mean, just look at Jack. He never thought he'd fall in love again and look at what happened to him."

Denny Ladler was promoted to executive producer on "The Jessica Wright Show," and while DBS hired a producer to replace him, Alicia Washington was promoted to associate producer and was widely assumed to be on her way into the producing slot herself. Alicia managed to trick a guy fresh out of Sarah Lawrence into taking the job as Jessica's secretary, and Jessica herself hired a special new assistant to help on the show. The special assistant's name was Belinda Darenbrook Peterson.

Jessica Wright didn't ever want to drink again and went regularly to AA meetings to prove it to herself. "Better safe than sorry" had never been her motto, but in this one area of her life she refused to play around—the stakes were just too high. Jessica's life had become inexplicably precious to her, and she was still not even sure why.

She looked much more her age, having lost that intense, pained "older" look she always used to have, and the mysterious bloat that came and went in her face regardless of what her weight was. Her skin glowed, her hair gained a whole new sheen, and her energy level was higher than ever—only more consistent because those awful sinking spells of depression she had suffered for years had simply faded away.

She felt wonderful. And still couldn't quite believe it.

Jessica even found her own apartment. Granted, she only moved three blocks down from Alexandra on Central Park West into The Beresford, and granted, she hadn't really gotten around to furnishing it, but it was her own apartment. She also played tennis, swam at a health club, and every Friday morning skated at Wollman Rink in Central Park. And twice a month she and Alexandra got together on Sunday night to "play Kansas," which meant they made popcorn or baked something and then settled down with afghans in Alexandra's living room and watched movies like *Stella Dallas* and cried.

Alexandra was Jessica's best friend in the whole wide world.

Speaking of whom, when Jessica finally got around to finalizing her divorce, Alexandra promptly fixed her up with someone she thought Jessica would like. "What?" Jessica shrieked in her dressing room at West End, minutes before her Mystery Date was to arrive. "A *doctor?* You think I'm that bad, Waring, that I require full-time medical attention?" But Tim turned out to be very different from what Jessica had imagined. (Or was it that *she* had turned out to be so very different from what she had imagined? The whole world had changed when she wasn't looking, so Jessica wasn't very sure about these things anymore. Could it be that she actually *liked* a nice man who liked her? An available, interested, solid, steady, warm and wonderful guy who wasn't the least bit self-destructive?)

("Fascinating," Jessica said, "how love and romance without alcohol adds up to love and romance.")

But while her own life had changed so much for the better, Jessica couldn't help but worry a little about Alexandra. But not professionally, because Alexandra was so wildly popular with the public that Jessica couldn't help but be (only on bad days, mind you) a little jealous. Restaurants were always calling up newspapers to tell them what Alexandra ate in their establishments (and they reported it); designers were always calling DBS to see if Alexandra would like to preview their collections; and the major magazines were forever hounding Alexandra for interviews—and when she gave them, she invariably landed the cover. Alexandra's inquiries from young people were so numerous, DBS printed a sixteen-page booklet she wrote called "So You Want to Be in TV News" which DBS sent out by the hundreds each week.

Physically speaking, Alexandra had never looked better. She was eating well and sleeping well, exercising religiously, and as a present to herself bought a small farm in Somerset County, New Jersey, where she tried to get to on weekends. But the externals of Alexandra's life were not what worried Jessica—the externals of Alexandra's life had always looked great.

"I think you need to talk about it," Jessica said one Sunday night after their movie was over.

CONCLUSION

"I don't want to talk about it, Jessica," Alexandra said, getting up out of her chair, picking up the popcorn bowl and walking out of the room.

Jessica, wrapped in an afghan on the couch, got up to follow Alexandra down the hall to the kitchen, afghan trailing behind her. "You can't just pretend it never happened."

"Yes I can," Alexandra said, walking over to the kitchen sink.

"But you shouldn't," Jessica said.

Alexandra banged the popcorn bowl down on the counter and turned around to look at her—as if the next thing to be banged down on the counter might be Jessica's head. She put one hand on her hip and raised the other, started to say something but then stopped. Then she dropped her hand and sighed. "Look, Jessica," she said, "it's all over and done with—life goes on." Then she turned around and started washing out the bowl.

Jessica sighed and, after several moments, still wrapped in the afghan, she walked over to the table, pulled out a chair and dropped down into it. To Alexandra's back she said, "And I don't think this new attitude about your love life is very healthy."

"What attitude is that?" Alexandra said without turning around.

"This, from-here-on-in-it's-only-applause-and-genetic-engineering-for-me attitude," Jessica said. "I mean, Alexandra, who *are* these guys you go out with? Tim thinks you're ordering them out of a Brooks Brothers catalog."

Alexandra turned off the water and turned around to look at her.

"Alexandra," Jessica said, making a terrible face, "they're all in *finance.*"

Alexandra had to laugh a little then. Then she sighed, smiling, walked over to the table, pulled out a chair and sat down. "Look, Jessica," she said, "all I know is, if I don't talk about it, then it can never be used against me. I have no desire to get more hurt than I have been already."

"But I don't want to see you shut down, Alexandra Eyes," Jessica said softly.

"I'm not shutting down," Alexandra said.

After a moment, Jessica said, "Are you going to see Gordon?"

"I don't know," Alexandra said, eyes dropping to the table.

Silence.

"You're allowed to change your mind, you know," Jessica said.

Alexandra's eyes stayed focused on the table for a long while. And then she said, eyes still down, "If I could have told him the truth, about Cassy, we might have had a chance." She paused. "But when I couldn't tell him, I knew what was wrong between us had nothing to do with Cassy." She raised her eyes. "Gordon knew it was mistake too —he didn't say it, but I knew he felt it too." Her eyes started to glisten as she smiled at Jessica. "We both have a much better idea of what we need, and neither one of us comes very close to the fitting the bill." She laughed, one tear dropping to her cheek. "But like the best disaster-marriages in the making, we did at least look good, didn't we?"

"But Alexandra—"

"No, no—that's it, Jessica," Alexandra said, jumping up from the chair, waving her hand. "I'm not talking about any of this anymore. It's over. I mean it—I'm going to have to ask you to leave if you don't just drop it."

Meanwhile, back at West End, under the reorganization of Darenbrook Communications, Jackson Darenbrook was named Co-Chairman, Newspaper, Magazine, Textbook and Printing Divisions. He was not in charge of Cassy Cochran at all (which was obvious, he always said, because if he were she would be married to him by now), and while he missed his day-to-day participation in DBS, he welcomed the chance to focus his attention on revitalizing that part of the company which his parents built and which he had been raised to care for.

As for Cordelia Darenbrook Paine, she was surprised and delighted by Jackson's motion that she be named Managing Director of Company Relations. And that didn't mean she was just supposed to continue trying to make the relations get along for the sake of the company. It meant that Cordelia would become a very willing and eager apprentice to the corporation and would take on a more prominent role at their southern facilities.

Jackson had become a very happy man. As his relationship with Cassy grew more secure each week, so did his familial relationships. And at Cassy's suggestion he sat down for an hour and wrote a letter to his daughter, Lydia, every other Sunday, telling her his latest news, and a letter to his son, Kevin, every other Sunday, telling him his latest news. But Jackson did not expect answers. He just did it. Faithfully.

CONCLUSION

He realized that he had been absent from his children's lives for too long, but that over time he might yet earn a place in their lives with consistency—something he hadn't had in his own life for years. Until now.

When the reorganization of Darenbrook Communications was complete, Jackson's relationship with Cassy became public with a very funny and true story that Susan Mulcahy broke in *Newsday.* It seemed that Cassy was a member of her building's tenant board and she had to attend a meeting to review the application of a man wishing to buy the three-bedroom apartment next door to her—for twice the going price —only to discover that the applicant's name was Jackson Darenbrook. And so Cassy sat there, listening as the board members said that regardless of the fact Darenbrook could obviously afford to pay his maintenance fees on time, did they want a known womanizer in their building whose exploits seemed to be a regular feature of the tabloids?

When it looked as though his application was going to be rejected out of hand, Cassy spoke up, confessing that the only woman Mr. Darenbrook had been womanizing with for months had been her, that he wished to marry her, and that while, no, she was not quite ready to marry again, she did think it very likely they would down the road. And so, after Cassy (with a faint smile and scarlet face) vouched for him as a character reference, his initial application was approved for interview. Jackson then came in and charmed the lot of them, and he was allowed to buy the Irvings' apartment.

(This was all very big news in the neighborhood. First Michael Cochran ran off to California and married a woman twenty years younger than himself, and now Cassy, their quiet, calm and lovely former block association president, had taken up with Jackson Darenbrook. What next? Henry and Cyndi Lauper?)

And so, with their relationship public, it was promptly and forevermore implied in the industry that Cassy Cochran had slept her way into the job of president of the DBS television network. But since, as Cassy pointed out, everybody had always accused her—and practically every other attractive woman—of sleeping her way into every managerial job she had held in the industry anyway, she didn't much care. She did care, however, very much about what her son Henry thought. And Henry thought Jackson was a pretty good guy and went next door sometimes to hang out when he was in New York, and sometimes stayed the weekend with his mother and Jackson in the house they bought together in upstate Connecticut, not far from—surprise, surprise—the Petersons.

When Alexandra returned to West End after her tour, it became apparent to Cassy that while Alexandra wasn't avoiding her, she certainly wasn't going out of her way to see her either. And since, after the miniseries was sold, Cassy's office was moved up to the third floor of Darenbrook III, that was exactly what Alexandra had to do in order to see her—go out of her way. And she didn't.

Finally, while having a breakfast meeting with Alexandra one morning at Sarabeth's Kitchen, Cassy sighed, dropped her fork, put her hand on the table and said, "I can't stand this, Alexandra. And *don't* tell me that nothing's wrong. Something major's happened between us, and I'm not even sure what it is." She paused. "I want to know, Alexandra—and I want the truth."

Alexandra's eyes were on her plate. After a long moment, she put her fork down, raised her napkin to her mouth, looked around, lowered the napkin, turned to Cassy and said, "I wanted to marry you more than I wanted to marry Gordon."

Cassy blinked.

"I realized it in Detroit," Alexandra said. "I think," she added, her gaze drifting down to the table, "had you not split up with Michael, it wouldn't have happened. Anyway," she said with a little shake of her head, bringing her eyes up, "I guess I'm not taking it very well that I don't seem to be able to have anybody." She let her glance fall again. "I don't know, maybe it's the price I have to pay for other things." She raised her eyes, catching Cassy's expression. "Don't even think of it," she said quickly, raising her hand as if to stop Cassy's thoughts. "My reasons for wanting you at DBS haven't changed. We need you there —and I need you there—more than ever. Besides," she added, dropping her eyes yet again, "I'm tired of living on a flat earth where I seem to force everybody I care about over the edge." She looked at Cassy. "I don't want you to disappear again. I really don't. But I need some time."

Silence.

"I'm just so sorry," Cassy finally managed to say. "I really didn't know."

Silence.

Alexandra was looking at the front door of the restaurant.

"London must have been awful for you," Cassy said.

Alexandra shrugged, her eyes following some people coming in.

Cassy thought a moment and then said, "And you really don't think you and Gordon—"

Alexandra shook her head.

Cassy nodded. And then, after a moment, she said, "It—even if I— it couldn't have worked anyway. You know that. Us, I mean."

Alexandra start to laugh to herself, bringing her eyes back to Cassy. "You mean, did it escape my notice that we would have been a little out of step with the universe of *TV Guide*? No, Cassy, it didn't." She leaned forward to add, "And not to downgrade a compliment or any-thing, but I'm not sure I was really prepared to destroy my career, alienate my family, lose all of my friends, and turn my back on the opportunity of having children just for the pleasure of your company."

Cassy winced.

"Sorry," Alexandra said, falling back in her seat. "That just came out."

"You have every right to be angry."

"But I'm not angry, not really," Alexandra said. "I'm just hurt. And feeling a little humiliated, I think." She paused, looking around before continuing. "And I get scared, I think," she sighed, "that if I wait to find a man I care about as much as I cared about you, I might end up spending my life alone. And I don't want that, Cassy," she said, her eyes starting to glisten. "But I just don't think I could get married on anything less. I don't think I could use someone like that, no matter how much I want children, a family of my own—a family that's con-nected to my family back home. Because I *do* want those things, Cassy . . ."

"I know you do," Cassy said.

"But nothing I do or feel seems to add up to anything," Alexandra finished. She lowered her eyes to the table. "I don't know, maybe when time starts running out on me I'll be able to get on with it. Maybe when children shift to the priority I won't care so much."

"You'll always care as much, Alexandra," Cassy said. "More so if children are the priority." She hesitated and then reached across the table to touch Alexandra's hand. "And you'll find someone. But it won't be until you get your house in order, inside—by yourself—until you learn how to trust people, make a life for yourself where there's room for you to be who you are. I understand how your relationships with people at work, with the public, and with your family out in Kansas have to be—but that doesn't mean you can get away with not having close friends. People you can talk to honestly, about whatever it is that's bothering you. You can't put it all on marriage, Alexandra. And to be perfectly honest with you, I think that's what you wanted to try to do with me—to take all your needs and put them on one person. And when it didn't work with Gordon, I was next in line."

Alexandra was staring at her.

"I'm sorry," Cassy said gently, withdrawing her hand, "but I had to say that."

Alexandra was still staring at her.

"It's not meant to discount your feelings in any way," Cassy said, "but it is meant to explain to you why even if the world were different, and I were different, I never could have entered into that kind of relationship with you." She swallowed. "Because you'd leave me, Alexandra. Eventually, you'd finally get your house in order and then you'd leave. Gordon and I aren't any different in that regard. You don't want to be alone, Alexandra, but you just haven't done the work in your personal life to make a lifelong commitment."

Alexandra's face was now scarlet. She cleared her throat, reached for her water glass, took a sip and put it down.

Cassy waited.

Alexandra cleared her throat again, looked around the room and then back at Cassy. "I take it back—I'm filing for divorce. I think you're horrible."

Cassy smiled slightly, her eyes looking sad.

"But you can tell me that part again," Alexandra told her, looking down at her water glass, "about how I won't be alone forever."

Cassy's smile expanded a little. "You won't be alone forever, Alexandra. Believe me, you won't." She watched Alexandra move her glass

CONCLUSION

around on the table for a while. Then she said, "You have a wonderful friend in Jessica, you know."

Looking down at her glass, Alexandra nodded. "I know. She's great."

After a moment, "Does she know about me?" Cassy asked.

Still looking down at her glass, Alexandra nodded.

"Good," Cassy said. "And you're talking to her about it?"

Alexandra hesitated—and then she shook her head.

"What about Gordon? Are you able to talk to her about that?" Cassy said.

Eyes still down, Alexandra shook her head again.

Cassy leaned forward. Very gently she said, "You've got to get started, Alexandra. You've got to start getting your house in order."

Not long after her breakfast with Cassy, Gordon came to Alexandra's apartment to see her. They talked for a long time, they cried for a while, and then, holding hands, she walked him to the front door. They kissed. And then he left.

The Saturday that Gordon and Betty Cannondale were married, Alexandra spent the day at the farm wallpapering her kitchen.

Jessica was there to help. And Jessica was there to listen.

ABOUT THE AUTHOR

Laura Van Wormer grew up in Darien, Connecticut, although most of her family is from the South. She attended the University of Arizona in Tucson and graduated from S. I. Newhouse School of Public Communications at Syracuse University, where she majored in Television and Radio. She is a former media book editor and writer and is the author of *Riverside Drive,* the novel in which the character Alexandra Waring first appears. She lives on the Upper West Side of Manhattan.